ZANE GREY COMBO

Great way to get the books you want for a lower overall price! Excellent reading.

ZANE GREY COMBO 3

THE RUSTLERS OF PECOS COUNTY

THE LAST OF THE PLAINSMEN

TO THE LAST MAN

ZANE GREY

CreateSpace
2013

Zane Grey Combo #3

The Rustlers of Pecos County was originally published in 1914
The Last of the Plainsmen was originally published in 1908
To the Last Man was originally published in 1922

The Third Omnibus Edition

This CreateSpace edition prepared in 2013

ISBN-13: 978-1492117674
ISBN-10: 1492117676

THE RUSTLERS OF PECOS COUNTY

Chapter 1

VAUGHN STEELE AND RUSS SITTELL

In the morning, after breakfasting early, I took a turn up and down the main street of Sanderson, made observations and got information likely to serve me at some future day, and then I returned to the hotel ready for what might happen.

The stage-coach was there and already full of passengers. This stage did not go to Linrock, but I had found that another one left for that point three days a week.

Several cowboy broncos stood hitched to a railing and a little farther down were two buckboards, with horses that took my eye. These probably were the teams Colonel Sampson had spoken of to George Wright.

As I strolled up, both men came out of the hotel. Wright saw me, and making an almost imperceptible sign to Sampson, he walked toward me.

"You're the cowboy Russ?" he asked.

I nodded and looked him over. By day he made as striking a figure as I had noted by night, but the light was not generous to his dark face.

"Here's your pay," he said, handing me some bills. "Miss Sampson won't need you out at the ranch any more."

"What do you mean? This is the first I've heard about that."

"Sorry, kid. That's it," he said abruptly. "She just gave me the money—told me to pay you off. You needn't bother to speak with her about it."

He might as well have said, just as politely, that my seeing her, even to say good-by, was undesirable.

As my luck would have it, the girls appeared at the moment, and I went directly up to them, to be greeted in a manner I was glad George Wright could not help but see.

In Miss Sampson's smile and "Good morning, Russ," there was not the slightest discoverable sign that I was not to serve her indefinitely.

It was as I had expected—she knew nothing of Wright's discharging me in her name.

"Miss Sampson," I said, in dismay, "what have I done? Why did you let me go?"

She looked astonished.

"Russ, I don't understand you."

"Why did you discharge me?" I went on, trying to look heart-broken. "I haven't had a chance yet. I wanted so much to work for you—Miss Sally, what have I done? Why did she discharge me?"

"I did not," declared Miss Sampson, her dark eyes lighting.

"But look here—here's my pay," I went on, exhibiting the money. "Mr. Wright just came to me—said you sent this money—that you wouldn't need me out at the ranch."

It was Miss Sally then who uttered a little exclamation. Miss Sampson seemed scarcely to have believed what she had heard.

"My cousin Mr. Wright said that?"

I nodded vehemently.

At this juncture Wright strode before me, practically thrusting me aside.

"Come girls, let's walk a little before we start," he said gaily. "I'll show you Sanderson."

"Wait, please," Miss Sampson replied, looking directly at him. "Cousin George, I think there's a mistake—perhaps a misunderstanding. Here's the cowboy I've engaged—Mr. Russ. He declares you gave him money—told him I discharged him."

"Yes, cousin, I did," he replied, his voice rising a little. There was a tinge of red in his cheek. "We—you don't need him out at the ranch. We've any numbers of boys. I just told him that—let him down easy—didn't want to bother you."

Certain it was that George Wright had made a poor reckoning. First she showed utter amaze, then distinct disappointment, and then she lifted her head with a kind of haughty grace. She would have addressed him then, had not Colonel Sampson come up.

"Papa, did you instruct Cousin George to discharge Russ?" she asked.

"I sure didn't," declared the colonel, with a laugh. "George took that upon his own hands."

"Indeed! I'd like my cousin to understand that I'm my own mistress. I've been accustomed to attending to my own affairs and shall continue doing so. Russ, I'm sorry you've been treated this way. Please, in future, take your orders from me."

"Then I'm to go to Linrock with you?" I asked.

"Assuredly. Ride with Sally and me to-day, please."

She turned away with Sally, and they walked toward the first buckboard.

Colonel Sampson found a grim enjoyment in Wright's discomfiture.

"Diane's like her mother was, George," he said. "You've made a bad start with her."

Here Wright showed manifestation of the Sampson temper, and I took him to be a dangerous man, with unbridled passions.

"Russ, here's my own talk to you," he said, hard and dark, leaning toward me. "Don't go to Linrock."

"Say, Mr. Wright," I blustered for all the world like a young and frightened cowboy, "If you threaten me I'll have you put in jail!"

Both men seemed to have received a slight shock. Wright hardly knew what to make of my boyish speech. "Are you going to Linrock?" he asked thickly.

I eyed him with an entirely different glance from my other fearful one.

"I should smile," was my reply, as caustic as the most reckless cowboy's, and I saw him shake.

Colonel Sampson laid a restraining hand upon Wright. Then they both regarded me with undisguised interest. I sauntered away.

"George, your temper'll do for you some day," I heard the colonel say. "You'll get in bad with the wrong man some time. Hello, here are Joe and Brick!"

Mention of these fellows engaged my attention once more.

I saw two cowboys, one evidently getting his name from his brick-red hair. They were the roistering type, hard drinkers, devil-may-care fellows, packing guns and wearing bold fronts—a kind that the Rangers always called four-flushes.

However, as the Rangers' standard of nerve was high, there was room left for cowboys like these to be dangerous to ordinary men.

The little one was Joe, and directly Wright spoke to him he turned to look at me, and his thin mouth slanted down as he looked. Brick eyed me, too, and I saw that he was heavy, not a hard-riding cowboy.

Here right at the start were three enemies for me—Wright and his cowboys. But it did not matter; under any circumstances there would have been friction between such men and me.

I believed there might have been friction right then had not Miss Sampson called for me.

"Get our baggage, Russ," she said.

I hurried to comply, and when I had fetched it out Wright and the cowboys had mounted their horses, Colonel Sampson was in the one buckboard with two men I had not before observed, and the girls were in the other.

The driver of this one was a tall, lanky, tow-headed youth, growing like a Texas weed. We had not any too much room in the buckboard, but that fact was not going to spoil the ride for me.

We followed the leaders through the main street, out into the open, on to a wide, hard-packed road, showing years of travel. It headed northwest.

To our left rose the range of low, bleak mountains I had noted yesterday, and to our right sloped the mesquite-patched sweep of ridge and flat.

The driver pushed his team to a fast trot, which gait surely covered ground rapidly. We were close behind Colonel Sampson, who, from his vehement gestures, must have been engaged in very earnest colloquy with his companions.

The girls behind me, now that they were nearing the end of the journey, manifested less interest in the ride, and were speculating upon Linrock, and what it would be like. Occasionally I asked the driver a question, and sometimes the girls did likewise; but, to my disappointment, the ride seemed not to be the same as that of yesterday.

Every half mile or so we passed a ranch house, and as we traveled on these ranches grew further apart, until, twelve or fifteen miles out of Sanderson, they were so widely separated that each appeared alone on the wild range.

We came to a stream that ran north and I was surprised to see a goodly volume of water. It evidently flowed down from the mountain far to the west.

Tufts of grass were well scattered over the sandy ground, but it was high and thick, and considering the immense area in sight, there was grazing for a million head of stock.

We made three stops in the forenoon, one at a likely place to water the horses, the second at a chuckwagon belonging to cowboys who were riding after stock, and the third at a small cluster of adobe and stone houses, constituting a hamlet the driver called Sampson, named after the Colonel. From that point on to Linrock there were only a few ranches, each one controlling great acreage.

Early in the afternoon from a ridgetop we sighted Linrock, a green path in the mass of gray. For the barrens of Texas it was indeed a fair sight.

But I was more concerned with its remoteness from civilization than its beauty. At that time in the early 'seventies, when the vast western third of Texas was a wilderness, the pioneer had done wonders to settle there and establish places like Linrock.

As we rolled swiftly along, the whole sweeping range was dotted with cattle, and farther on, within a few miles of town, there were droves of horses that brought enthusiastic praise from Miss Sampson and her cousin.

"Plenty of room here for the long rides," I said, waving a hand at the gray-green expanse. "Your horses won't suffer on this range."

She was delighted, and her cousin for once seemed speechless.

"That's the ranch," said the driver, pointing with his whip.

It needed only a glance for me to see that Colonel Sampson's ranch was on a scale fitting the country.

The house was situated on the only elevation around Linrock, and it was not high, nor more than a few minutes' walk from the edge of town.

It was a low, flat-roofed structure, made of red adobe bricks and covered what appeared to be fully an acre of ground. All was green about it except where the fenced corrals and numerous barns or sheds showed gray and red.

Wright and the cowboys disappeared ahead of us in the cottonwood trees. Colonel Sampson got out of the buckboard and waited for us. His face wore the best expression I had seen upon it yet. There was warmth and love, and something that approached sorrow or regret.

His daughter was agitated, too. I got out and offered my seat, which Colonel Sampson took.

It was scarcely a time for me to be required, or even noticed at all, and I took advantage of it and turned toward the town.

Ten minutes of leisurely walking brought me to the shady outskirts of Linrock and I entered the town with mingled feelings of curiosity, eagerness, and expectation.

The street I walked down was not a main one. There were small, red houses among oaks and cottonwoods.

I went clear through to the other side, probably more than half a mile. I crossed a number of intersecting streets, met children, nice-looking women, and more than one dusty-booted man.

Half-way back this street I turned at right angles and walked up several blocks till I came to a tree-bordered plaza. On the far side opened a broad street which for all its horses and people had a sleepy look.

I walked on, alert, trying to take in everything, wondering if I would meet Steele, wondering how I would know him if we did meet. But I believed I could have picked that Ranger out of a thousand strangers, though I had never seen him.

Presently the residences gave place to buildings fronting right upon the stone sidewalk. I passed a grain store, a hardware store, a grocery store, then several unoccupied buildings and a vacant corner.

The next block, aside from the rough fronts of the crude structures, would have done credit to a small town even in eastern Texas. Here was evidence of business consistent with any prosperous community of two thousand inhabitants.

The next block, on both sides of the street, was a solid row of saloons, resorts, hotels. Saddled horses stood hitched all along the sidewalk in two long lines, with a buckboard and team here and there breaking the continuity. This block was busy and noisy.

From all outside appearances, Linrock was no different from other frontier towns, and my expectations were scarcely realized.

As the afternoon was waning I retraced my steps and returned to the ranch. The driver boy, whom I had heard called Dick, was looking for me, evidently at Miss Sampson's order, and he led me up to the house.

It was even bigger than I had conceived from a distance, and so old that the adobe bricks were worn smooth by rain and wind. I had a glimpse in at several doors as we passed by.

There was comfort here that spoke eloquently of many a freighter's trip from Del Rio. For the sake of the young ladies, I was glad to see things little short of luxurious for that part of the country.

At the far end of the house Dick conducted me to a little room, very satisfactory indeed to me. I asked about bunk-houses for the cowboys, and he said they were full to overflowing.

"Colonel Sampson has a big outfit, eh?"

"Reckon he has," replied Dick. "Don' know how many cowboys. They're always comin' an' goin'. I ain't acquainted with half of them."

"Much movement of stock these days?"

"Stock's always movin'," he replied with a queer look.

"Rustlers?"

But he did not follow up that look with the affirmative I expected.

"Lively place, I hear—Linrock is?"

"Ain't so lively as Sanderson, but it's bigger."

"Yes, I heard it was. Fellow down there was talking about two cowboys who were arrested."

"Sure. I heerd all about thet. Joe Bean an' Brick Higgins—they belong heah, but they ain't heah much."

I did not want Dick to think me overinquisitive, so I turned the talk into other channels. It appeared that Miss Sampson had not left any instructions for me, so I was glad to go with Dick to supper, which we had in the kitchen.

Dick informed me that the cowboys prepared their own meals down at the bunks; and as I had been given a room at the ranch-house he supposed I would get my meals there, too.

After supper I walked all over the grounds, had a look at the horses in the corrals, and came to the conclusion that it would be strange if Miss Sampson did not love her new home, and if her cousin did not enjoy her sojourn there. From a distance I saw the girls approaching with Wright, and not wishing to meet them I sheered off.

When the sun had set I went down to the town with the intention of finding Steele.

This task, considering I dared not make inquiries and must approach him secretly, might turn out to be anything but easy.

While it was still light, I strolled up and down the main street. When darkness set in I went into a hotel, bought cigars, sat around and watched, without any clue.

Then I went into the next place. This was of a rough crude exterior, but the inside was comparatively pretentious, and ablaze with lights.

It was full of men, coming and going—a dusty-booted crowd that smelled of horses and smoke.

I sat down for a while, with wide eyes and open ears. Then I hunted up a saloon, where most of the guests had been or were going. I found a great square room lighted by six huge lamps, a bar at one side, and all the floor space taken up by tables and chairs.

This must have been the gambling resort mentioned in the Ranger's letter to Captain Neal and the one rumored to be owned by the mayor of Linrock. This was the only gambling place of any size in southern Texas in which I had noted the absence of Mexicans. There was some card playing going on at this moment.

I stayed in there for a while, and knew that strangers were too common in Linrock to be conspicuous. But I saw no man whom I could have taken for Steele.

Then I went out.

It had often been a boast of mine that I could not spend an hour in a strange town, or walk a block along a dark street, without having something happen out of the ordinary.

Mine was an experiencing nature. Some people called this luck. But it was my private opinion that things gravitated my way because I looked and listened for them.

However, upon the occasion of my first day and evening in Linrock it appeared, despite my vigilance and inquisitiveness, that here was to be an exception.

This thought came to me just before I reached the last lighted place in the block, a little dingy restaurant, out of which at the moment, a tall, dark form passed. It disappeared in the gloom. I saw a man sitting on the low steps, and another standing in the door.

"That was the fellow the whole town's talkin' about—the Ranger," said one man.

Like a shot I halted in the shadow, where I had not been seen.

"Sho! Ain't boardin' heah, is he?" said the other.

"Yes."

"Reckon he'll hurt your business, Jim."

The fellow called Jim emitted a mirthless laugh. "Wal, he's been *all* my business these days. An' he's offered to rent that old 'dobe of mine just out of town. You know, where I lived before movin' in heah. He's goin' to look at it to-morrow."

"Lord! does he expect to *stay*?"

"Say so. An' if he ain't a stayer I never seen none. Nice, quiet, easy chap, but he just looks deep."

"Aw, Jim, he can't hang out heah. He's after some feller, that's all."

"I don't know his game. But he says he was heah for a while. An' he impressed me some. Just now he says: 'Where does Sampson live?' I asked him if he was goin' to make a call on our mayor, an' he says yes. Then I told him how to go out to the ranch. He went out, headed that way."

"The hell he did!"

I gathered from this fellow's exclamation that he was divided between amaze and mirth. Then he got up from the steps and went into the restaurant and was followed by the man called Jim. Before the door was closed he made another remark, but it was unintelligible to me.

As I passed on I decided I would scrape acquaintance with this restaurant keeper.

The thing of most moment was that I had gotten track of Steele. I hurried ahead. While I had been listening back there moments had elapsed and evidently he had walked swiftly.

I came to the plaza, crossed it, and then did not know which direction to take. Concluding that it did not matter I hurried on in an endeavor to reach the ranch before Steele. Although I was not sure, I believed I had succeeded.

The moon shone brightly. I heard a banjo in the distance and a cowboy sing. There was not a person in sight in the wide courts or on the porch. I did not have a well-defined idea about the inside of the house.

Peeping in at the first lighted window I saw a large room. Miss Sampson and Sally were there alone. Evidently this was a parlor or a sitting room, and it had clean white walls, a blanketed floor, an open fireplace with a cheery blazing log, and a large table upon which were lamp, books, papers. Backing away I saw that this corner room had a door opening on the porch and two other windows.

I listened, hoping to hear Steele's footsteps coming up the road. But I heard only Sally's laugh and her cousin's mellow voice.

Then I saw lighted windows down at the other end of the front part of the house. I walked down. A door stood open and through it I saw a room identical with that at the other corner; and here were Colonel Sampson, Wright, and several other men, all smoking and talking.

It might have been interesting to tarry there within ear-shot, but I wanted to get back to the road to intercept Steele. Scarcely had I retraced my steps and seated myself on the porch steps when a very tall dark figure loomed up in the moonlit road.

Steele! I wanted to yell like a boy. He came on slowly, looking all around, halted some twenty paces distant, surveyed the house, then evidently espying me, came on again.

My first feeling was, What a giant! But his face was hidden in the shadow of a sombrero.

I had intended, of course, upon first sight to blurt out my identity. Yet I did not. He affected me strangely, or perhaps it was my emotion at the thought that we Rangers, with so much in common and at stake, had come together.

"Is Sampson at home?" he asked abruptly.

I said, "Yes."

"Ask him if he'll see Vaughn Steele, Ranger."

"Wait here," I replied. I did not want to take up any time then explaining my presence there.

Deliberately and noisily I strode down the porch and entered the room with the smoking men.

I went in farther than was necessary for me to state my errand. But I wanted to see Sampson's face, to see into his eyes.

As I entered, the talking ceased. I saw no face except his and that seemed blank.

"Vaughn Steele, Ranger—come to see you, sir." I announced.

Did Sampson start—did his eyes show a fleeting glint—did his face almost imperceptibly blanch? I could not have sworn to either. But there was a change, maybe from surprise.

The first sure effect of my announcement came in a quick exclamation from Wright, a sibilant intake of breath, that did not seem to denote surprise so much as certainty. Wright might have emitted a curse with less force.

Sampson moved his hand significantly and the action was a voiceless command for silence as well as an assertion that he would attend to this matter. I read him clearly so far. He had authority, and again I felt his power.

"Steele to see me. Did he state his business?"

"No, sir." I replied.

"Russ, say I'm not at home," said Sampson presently, bending over to relight his pipe.

I went out. Someone slammed the door behind me.

As I strode back across the porch my mind worked swiftly; the machinery had been idle for a while and was now started.

"Mr. Steele," I said, "Colonel Sampson says he's not at home. Tell your business to his daughter."

Without waiting to see the effect of my taking so much upon myself, I knocked upon the parlor door. Miss Sampson opened it. She wore white. Looking at her, I thought it would be strange if Steele's well-known indifference to women did not suffer an eclipse.

"Miss Sampson, here is Vaughn Steele to see you," I said.

"Won't you come in?" she said graciously.

Steele had to bend his head to enter the door. I went in with him, an intrusion, perhaps, that in the interest of the moment she appeared not to notice.

Steele seemed to fill the room with his giant form. His face was fine, stern, clear cut, with blue or gray eyes, strangely penetrating. He was coatless, vestless. He wore a gray flannel shirt, corduroys, a big gun swinging low, and top boots reaching to his knees.

He was the most stalwart son of Texas I had seen in many a day, but neither his great stature nor his striking face accounted for something I felt—a something spiritual, vital, compelling, that drew me.

"Mr. Steele, I'm pleased to meet you," said Miss Sampson. "This is my cousin, Sally Langdon. We just arrived—I to make this my home, she to visit me."

Steele smiled as he bowed to Sally. He was easy, with a kind of rude grace, and showed no sign of embarrassment or that beautiful girls were unusual to him.

"Mr. Steele, we've heard of you in Austin," said Sally with her eyes misbehaving.

I hoped I would not have to be jealous of Steele. But this girl was a little minx if not altogether a flirt.

"I did not expect to be received by ladies," replied Steele. "I called upon Mr. Sampson. He would not see me. I was to tell my business to his daughter. I'm glad to know you, Miss Sampson and your cousin, but sorry you've come to Linrock now."

"Why?" queried both girls in unison.

"Because it's—oh, pretty rough—no place for girls to walk and ride."

"Ah! I see. And your business has to do with rough places," said Miss Sampson. "Strange that papa would not see you. Stranger that he should want me to hear your business. Either he's joking or wants to impress me.

"Papa tried to persuade me not to come. He tried to frighten me with tales of this—this roughness out here. He knows I'm in earnest, how I'd like to help somehow, do some little good. Pray tell me this business."

"I wished to get your father's cooperation in my work."

"Your work? You mean your Ranger duty—the arresting of rough characters?"

"That, yes. But that's only a detail. Linrock is bad internally. My job is to make it good."

"A splendid and worthy task," replied Miss Sampson warmly. "I wish you success. But, Mr. Steele, aren't you exaggerating Linrock's wickedness?"

"No," he answered forcibly.

"Indeed! And papa refused to see you—presumably refused to cooperate with you?" she asked thoughtfully.

"I take it that way."

"Mr. Steele, pray tell me what is the matter with Linrock and just what the work is you're called upon to do?" she asked seriously. "I heard papa say that he was the law in Linrock. Perhaps he resents interference. I know he'll not tolerate any opposition to his will. Please tell me. I may be able to influence him."

I listened to Steele's deep voice as he talked about Linrock. What he said was old to me, and I gave heed only to its effect.

Miss Sampson's expression, which at first had been earnest and grave, turned into one of incredulous amaze. She, and Sally too, watched Steele's face in fascinated attention.

When it came to telling what he wanted to do, the Ranger warmed to his subject; he talked beautifully, convincingly, with a certain strange, persuasive power that betrayed how he worked his way; and his fine face, losing its stern, hard lines, seemed to glow and give forth a spirit austere, yet noble, almost gentle, assuredly something vastly different from what might have been expected in the expression of a gun-fighting Ranger. I sensed that Miss Sampson felt this just as I did.

"Papa said you were a hounder of outlaws—a man who'd rather kill than save!" she exclaimed.

The old stern cast returned to Steele's face. It was as if he had suddenly remembered himself.

"My name is infamous, I am sorry to say," he replied.

"You have killed men?" she asked, her dark eyes dilating.

Had any one ever dared ask Steele that before? His face became a mask. It told truth to me, but she could not see, and he did not answer.

"Oh, you are above that. Don't—don't kill any one here!"

"Miss Sampson, I hope I won't." His voice seemed to check her. I had been right in my estimate of her character—young, untried, but all pride, fire, passion. She was white then, and certainly beautiful.

Steele watched her, could scarcely have failed to see the white gleam of her beauty, and all that evidence of a quick and noble heart.

"Pardon me, please, Mr. Steele," she said, recovering her composure. "I am—just a little overexcited. I didn't mean to be inquisitive. Thank you for your confidence. I've enjoyed your call, though your news did distress me. You may rely upon me to talk to papa."

That appeared to be a dismissal, and, bowing to her and Sally, the Ranger went out. I followed, not having spoken.

At the end of the porch I caught up with Steele and walked out into the moonlight beside him.

Just why I did not now reveal my identity I could not say, for certainly I was bursting with the desire to surprise him, to earn his approval. He loomed dark above me, appearing not to be aware of my presence. What a cold, strange proposition this Ranger was!

Still, remembering the earnestness of his talk to Miss Sampson, I could not think him cold. But I must have thought him so to any attraction of those charming girls.

Suddenly, as we passed under the shade of cottonwoods, he clamped a big hand down on my shoulder.

"My God, Russ, isn't she lovely!" he ejaculated.

In spite of my being dumbfounded I had to hug him. He knew me!

"Thought you didn't swear!" I gasped.

Ridiculously those were my first words to Vaughn Steele.

"My boy, I saw you parading up and down the street looking for me," he said. "I intended to help you find me to-morrow."

We gripped hands, and that strong feel and clasp meant much.

"Yes, she's lovely, Steele," I said. "But did you look at the cousin, the little girl with the eyes?"

Then we laughed and loosed hands.

"Come on, let's get out somewhere. I've a million things to tell you."

We went away out into the open where some stones gleamed white in the moonlight, and there, sitting in the sand, our backs against a rest, and with all quiet about us, we settled down for a long conference.

I began with Neal's urgent message to me, then told of my going to the capitol—what I had overheard when Governor Smith was in the adjutant's office; of my interview with them; of the spying on Colonel Sampson; Neal's directions, advice, and command; the ride toward San Antonio; my being engaged as cowboy by Miss Sampson; of the further ride on to Sanderson and the incident there; and finally how I had approached Sampson and then had thought it well to get his daughter into the scheme of things.

It was a long talk, even for me, and my voice sounded husky.

"I told Neal I'd be lucky to get you," said Steele, after a silence.

That was the only comment on my actions, the only praise, but the quiet way he spoke it made me feel like a boy undeserving of so much.

"Here, I forgot the money Neal sent," I went on, glad to be rid of the huge roll of bills.

The Ranger showed surprise. Besides, he was very glad.

"The Captain loves the service," said Steele. "He alone knows the worth of the Rangers. And the work he's given his life to—the *good* that *service* really does—all depends on you and me, Russ!"

I assented, gloomily enough. Then I waited while he pondered.

The moon soared clear; there was a cool wind rustling the greasewood; a dog bayed a barking coyote; lights twinkled down in the town.

I looked back up at the dark hill and thought of Sally Langdon. Getting here to Linrock, meeting Steele had not changed my feelings toward her, only somehow they had removed me far off in thought, out of possible touch, it seemed.

"Well, son, listen," began Steele. His calling me that was a joke, yet I did not feel it. "You've made a better start than I could have figured. Neal said you were lucky. Perhaps. But you've got brains.

"Now, here's your cue for the present. Work for Miss Sampson. Do your best for her as long as you last. I don't suppose you'll last long. You have got to get in with this gang in town. Be a flash cowboy. You don't need to get drunk, but you're to pretend it.

"Gamble. Be a good fellow. Hang round the barrooms. I don't care how you play the part, so long as you make friends, learn the ropes. We can meet out here at nights to talk and plan.

"You're to take sides with those who're against me. I'll furnish you with the money. You'd better appear to be a winning gambler, even if you're not. How's this plan strike you?"

"Great—except for one thing," I replied. "I hate to lie to Miss Sampson. She's true blue, Steele."

"Son, you haven't got soft on her?"

"Not a bit. Maybe I'm soft on the little cousin. But I just like Miss Sampson—think she's fine—could look up to her. And I hate to be different from what she thinks."

"I understand, Russ," he replied in his deep voice that had such quality to influence a man. "It's no decent job. You'll be ashamed before her. So would I. But here's our work, the hardest ever cut out for Rangers. Think what depends upon it. And—"

"There's something wrong with Miss Sampson's father," I interrupted.

"Something strange if not wrong. No man in this community is beyond us, Russ, or above suspicion. You've a great opportunity. I needn't say use your eyes and ears as never before."

"I hope Sampson turns out to be on the square," I replied. "He might be a lax mayor, too good-natured to uphold law in a wild country. And his Southern pride would fire at interference. I don't like him, but for his daughter's sake I hope we're wrong."

Steele's eyes, deep and gleaming in the moonlight, searched my face.

"Son, sure you're not in love with her—you'll not fall in love with her?"

"No. I am positive. Why?"

"Because in either case I'd likely have need of a new man in your place," he said.

"Steele, you know something about Sampson—something more!" I exclaimed swiftly.

"No more than you. When I meet him face to face I may know more. Russ, when a fellow has been years at this game he has a sixth sense. Mine seldom fails me. I never yet faced the criminal who didn't somehow betray fear—not so much fear of me, but fear of himself—his life, his deeds. That's conscience, or if not, just realization of fate."

Had that been the thing I imagined I had seen in Sampson's face?

"I'm sorry Diane Sampson came out here," I said impulsively.

Steele did not say he shared that feeling. He was looking out upon the moon-blanched level.

Some subtle thing in his face made me divine that he was thinking of the beautiful girl to whom he might bring disgrace and unhappiness.

Chapter 2

A KISS AND AN ARREST

A month had passed, a swift-flying time full of new life. Wonderful it was for me to think I was still in Diane Sampson's employ.

It was the early morning hour of a day in May. The sun had not yet grown hot. Dew like diamond drops sparkled on the leaves and grass. The gentle breeze was clear, sweet, with the song of larks upon it.

And the range, a sea of gray-green growing greener, swept away westward in rolling ridges and hollows, like waves to meet the dark, low hills that notched the horizon line of blue.

I was sitting on the top bar of the corral fence and before me stood three saddled horses that would have gladdened any eye. I was waiting to take the young ladies on their usual morning ride.

Once upon a time, in what seemed the distant past to this eventful month, I had flattered myself there had been occasions for thought, but scornfully I soliloquized that in those days I had no cue for thought such as I had now.

This was one of the moments when my real self seemed to stand off and skeptically regard the fictitious cowboy.

This gentleman of the range wore a huge sombrero with an ornamented silver band, a silken scarf of red, a black velvet shirt, much affected by the Indians, an embroidered buckskin vest, corduroys, and fringed chaps with silver buttons, a big blue gun swinging low, high heeled boots, and long spurs with silver rowels.

A flash cowboy! Steele vowed I was a born actor.

But I never divulged the fact that had it not been for my infatuation for Sally, I never could have carried on that part, not to save the Ranger service, or the whole State of Texas.

The hardest part had not been the establishing of a reputation. The scorn of cowboys, the ridicule of gamblers, the badinage of the young bucks of the settlement—these I had soon made dangerous procedures for any one. I was quick with tongue and fist and gun.

There had been fights and respect was quickly earned, though the constant advent of strangers in Linrock always had me in hot water.

Moreover, instead of being difficult, it was fun to spend all the time I could in the hotels and resorts, shamming a weakness for drink, gambling, lounging, making friends among the rough set, when all the time I was a cool, keen registering machine.

The hard thing was the lie I lived in the eyes of Diane Sampson and Sally Langdon.

I had indeed won the sincere regard of my employer. Her father, her cousin George, and new-made friends in town had come to her with tales of my reckless doings, and had urged my dismissal.

But she kept me and all the time pleaded like a sister to have me mend my vicious ways. She believed what she was told about me, but had faith in me despite that.

As for Sally, I had fallen hopelessly in love with her. By turns Sally was indifferent to me, cold, friendly like a comrade, and dangerously sweet.

Somehow she saw through me, knew I was not just what I pretended to be. But she never breathed her conviction. She championed me. I wanted to tell her the truth about myself because I believed the doubt of me alone stood in the way of my winning her.

Still that might have been my vanity. She had never said she cared for me although she had looked it.

This tangle of my personal life, however, had not in the least affected my loyalty and duty to Vaughn Steele. Day by day I had grown more attached to him, keener in the interest of our work.

It had been a busy month—a month of foundation building. My vigilance and my stealthy efforts had not been rewarded by anything calculated to strengthen our suspicions of Sampson. But then he had been absent from the home very often, and was difficult to watch when he was there.

George Wright came and went, too, presumably upon stock business. I could not yet see that he was anything but an honest rancher, deeply involved with Sampson and other men in stock deals; nevertheless, as a man he had earned my contempt.

He was a hard drinker, cruel to horses, a gambler not above stacking the cards, a quick-tempered, passionate Southerner.

He had fallen in love with Diane Sampson, was like her shadow when at home. He hated me; he treated me as if I were the scum of the earth; if he had to address me for something, which was seldom, he did it harshly, like ordering a dog. Whenever I saw his sinister, handsome face, with its dark eyes always half shut, my hand itched for my gun, and I would go my way with something thick and hot inside my breast.

In my talks with Steele we spent time studying George Wright's character and actions. He was Sampson's partner, and at the head of a small group of Linrock ranchers who were rich in cattle and property, if not in money.

Steele and I had seen fit to wait before we made any thorough investigation into their business methods. Ours was a waiting game, anyway.

Right at the start Linrock had apparently arisen in resentment at the presence of Vaughn Steele. But it was my opinion that there were men in Linrock secretly glad of the Ranger's presence.

What he intended to do was food for great speculation. His fame, of course, had preceded him. A company of militia could not have had the effect upon the wild element of Linrock that Steele's presence had.

A thousand stories went from lip to lip, most of which were false. He was lightning swift on the draw. It was death to face him. He had killed thirty men—wildest rumor of all.

He had the gun skill of Buck Duane, the craft of Cheseldine, the deviltry of King Fisher, the most notorious of Texas desperadoes. His nerve, his lack of fear—those made him stand out alone even among a horde of bold men.

At first there had not only been great conjecture among the vicious element, with which I had begun to affiliate myself, but also a very decided checking of all kinds of action calculated to be conspicuous to a keen eyed Ranger.

Steele did not hide, but during these opening days of his stay in Linrock he was not often seen in town. At the tables, at the bars and lounging places remarks went the rounds:

"Who's thet Ranger after? What'll he do fust off? Is he waitin' fer somebody? Who's goin' to draw on him fust—an' go to hell? Jest about how soon will he be found somewhere full of lead?"

Those whom it was my interest to cultivate grew more curious, more speculative and impatient as time went by. When it leaked out somewhere that Steele was openly cultivating the honest stay-at-home citizens, to array them in time against the other element, then Linrock showed its wolf teeth hinted of in the letters to Captain Neal.

Several times Steele was shot at in the dark and once slightly injured. Rumor had it that Jack Blome, the gunman of those parts, was coming in to meet Steele. Part of Linrock awakened and another part, much smaller, became quieter, more secluded.

Strangers upon whom we could get no line mysteriously came and went. The drinking, gambling, fighting in the resorts seemed to gather renewed life. Abundance of money floated in circulation.

And rumors, vague and unfounded, crept in from Sanderson and other points, rumors of a gang of rustlers off here, a hold-up of the stage off here, robbery of a rancher at this distant point, and murder done at another.

This was Texas and New Mexico life in these frontier days but, strangely neither Steele nor I had yet been able to associate any rumor or act with a possible gang of rustlers in Linrock.

Nevertheless we had not been discouraged. After three weeks of waiting we had become alive to activity around us, and though it was unseen, we believed we would soon be on its track.

My task was the busier and the easier. Steele had to have a care for his life. I never failed to caution him of this.

My long reflection on the month's happenings and possibilities was brought to an end by the disappearance of Miss Sampson and Sally.

My employer looked worried. Sally was in a regular cowgirl riding costume, in which her trim, shapely figure showed at its best, and her face was saucy, sparkling, daring.

"Good morning, Russ," said Miss Sampson and she gazed searchingly at me. I had dropped off the fence, sombrero in hand. I knew I was in for a lecture, and I put on a brazen, innocent air.

"Did you break your promise to me?" she asked reproachfully.

"Which one?" I asked. It was Sally's bright eyes upon me, rather than Miss Sampson's reproach, that bothered me.

"About getting drunk again," she said.

"I didn't break *that* one."

"My cousin George saw you in the Hope So gambling place last night, drunk, staggering, mixing with that riffraff, on the verge of a brawl."

"Miss Sampson, with all due respect to Mr. Wright, I want to say that he has a strange wish to lower me in the eyes of you ladies," I protested with a fine show of spirit.

"Russ, *were* you drunk?" she demanded.

"No. I should think you needn't ask me that. Didn't you ever see a man the morning after a carouse?"

Evidently she had. And there I knew I stood, fresh, clean-shaven, clear-eyed as the morning.

Sally's saucy face grew thoughtful, too. The only thing she had ever asked of me was not to drink. The habit had gone hard with the Sampson family.

"Russ, you look just as—as nice as I'd want you to," Miss Sampson replied. "I don't know what to think. They tell me things. You deny. Whom shall I believe? George swore he saw you."

"Miss Sampson, did I ever lie to you?"

"Not to my knowledge."

Then I looked at her, and she understood what I meant.

"George has lied to me. That day at Sanderson. And since, too, I fear. Do you say he lies?"

"Miss Sampson, I would not call your cousin a liar."

Here Sally edged closer, with the bridle rein of her horse over her arm.

"Russ, cousin George isn't the only one who saw you. Burt Waters told me the same," said Sally nervously. I believed she hoped I was telling the truth.

"Waters! So he runs me down behind my back. All right, I won't say a word about him. But do you believe I was drunk when I say no?"

"I'm afraid I do, Russ," she replied in reluctance. Was she testing me?

"See here, Miss Sampson," I burst out. "Why don't you discharge me? Please let me go. I'm not claiming much for myself, but you don't believe even that. I'm pretty bad. I never denied the scraps, the gambling—all that. But I did do as Miss Sally asked me—I did keep my promise to you. Now, discharge me. Then I'll be free to call on Mr. Burt Waters."

Miss Sampson looked alarmed and Sally turned pale, to my extreme joy.

Those girls believed I was a desperate devil of a cowboy, who had been held back from spilling blood solely through their kind relation to me.

"Oh, no!" exclaimed Sally. "Diane, don't let him go!"

"Russ, pray don't get angry," replied Miss Sampson and she put a soft hand on me that thrilled me, while it made me feel like a villain. "I won't discharge you. I need you. Sally needs you. After all, it's none of my business what you do away from here. But I hoped I would be so happy to—to reclaim you from—Didn't you ever have a sister, Russ?"

I kept silent for fear that I would perjure myself anew. Yet the situation was delicious, and suddenly I conceived a wild idea.

"Miss Sampson," I began haltingly, but with brave front, "I've been wild in the past. But I've been tolerably straight here, trying to please you. Lately I have been going to the bad again. Not drunk, but leaning that way. Lord knows what I'll do soon if—if my trouble isn't cured."

"Russ! What trouble?"

"You know what's the matter with me," I went on hurriedly. "Anybody could see that."

Sally turned a flaming scarlet. Miss Sampson made it easier for me by reason of her quick glance of divination.

"I've fallen in love with Miss Sally. I'm crazy about her. Here I've got to see these fellows flirting with her. And it's killing me. I've—"

"If you are crazy about me, you don't have to tell!" cried Sally, red and white by turns.

"I want to stop your flirting one way or another. I've been in earnest. I wasn't flirting. I begged you to—to..."

"You never did," interrupted Sally furiously. That hint had been a spark.

"I couldn't have dreamed it," I protested, in a passion to be earnest, yet tingling with the fun of it. "That day when I—didn't I ask..."

"If my memory serves me correctly, you didn't ask anything," she replied, with anger and scorn now struggling with mirth.

"But, Sally, I meant to. You understood me? Say you didn't believe I could take that liberty without honorable intentions."

That was too much for Sally. She jumped at her horse, made the quickest kind of a mount, and was off like a flash.

"Stop me if you can," she called back over her shoulder, her face alight and saucy.

"Russ, go after her," said Miss Sampson. "In that mood she'll ride to Sanderson. My dear fellow, don't stare so. I understand many things now. Sally is a flirt. She would drive any man mad. Russ, I've grown in a short time to like you. If you'll be a man—give up drinking and gambling—maybe you'll have a chance with her. Hurry now—go after her."

I mounted and spurred my horse after Sally's. She was down on the level now, out in the open, and giving her mount his head. Even had I wanted to overhaul her at once the matter would have been difficult, well nigh impossible under five miles.

Sally had as fast a horse as there was on the range; she made no weight in the saddle, and she could ride. From time to time she looked back over her shoulder.

I gained enough to make her think I was trying to catch her. Sally loved a horse; she loved a race; she loved to win.

My good fortune had given me more than one ride alone with Sally. Miss Sampson enjoyed riding, too; but she was not a madcap, and when she accompanied us there was never any race.

When Sally got out alone with me she made me ride to keep her from disappearing somewhere on the horizon. This morning I wanted her to enjoy to the fullest her utter freedom and to feel that for once I could not catch her.

Perhaps my declaration to Miss Sampson had liberated my strongest emotions.

However that might be, the fact was that no ride before had ever been like this one—no sky so blue, no scene so open, free, and enchanting as that beautiful gray-green range, no wind so sweet. The breeze that rushed at me might have been laden with the perfume of Sally Langdon's hair.

I sailed along on what seemed a strange ride. Grazing horses pranced and whistled as I went by; jack-rabbits bounded away to hide in the longer clumps of grass; a prowling wolf trotted from his covert near a herd of cattle.

Far to the west rose the low, dark lines of bleak mountains. They were always mysterious to me, as if holding a secret I needed to know.

It was a strange ride because in the back of my head worked a haunting consciousness of the deadly nature of my business there on the frontier, a business in such contrast with this dreaming and dallying, this longing for what surely was futile.

Any moment I might be stripped of my disguise. Any moment I might have to be the Ranger.

Sally kept the lead across the wide plain, and mounted to the top of a ridge, where tired out, and satisfied with her victory, she awaited me. I was in no hurry to reach the summit of the long, slow-sloping ridge, and I let my horse walk.

Just how would Sally Langdon meet me now, after my regretted exhibition before her cousin? There was no use to conjecture, but I was not hopeful.

When I got there to find her in her sweetest mood, with some little difference never before noted—a touch of shyness—I concealed my surprise.

"Russ, I gave you a run that time," she said. "Ten miles and you never caught me!"

"But look at the start you had. I've had my troubles beating you with an even break."

Sally was susceptible to flattery in regard to her riding, a fact that I made subtle use of.

"But in a long race I was afraid you'd beat me. Russ, I've learned to ride out here. Back home I never had room to ride a horse. Just look. Miles and miles of level, of green. Little hills with black bunches of trees. Not a soul in sight. Even the town hidden in the green. All wild and lonely. Isn't it glorious, Russ?"

"Lately it's been getting to me," I replied soberly.

We both gazed out over the sea of gray-green, at the undulating waves of ground in the distance. On these rides with her I had learned to appreciate the beauty of the lonely reaches of plain.

But when I could look at her I seldom wasted time on scenery. Looking at her now I tried to get again that impression of a difference in her. It eluded me.

Just now with the rose in her brown cheeks, her hair flying, her eyes with grave instead of mocking light, she seemed only prettier than usual. I got down ostensibly to tighten the saddle girths on her horse. But I lingered over the task.

Presently, when she looked down at me, I received that subtle impression of change, and read it as her soft mood of dangerous sweetness that came so seldom, mingled with something deeper, more of character and womanliness than I had ever sensed in her.

"Russ, it wasn't nice to tell Diane that," she said.

"Nice! It was—oh, I'd like to swear!" I ejaculated. "But now I understand my miserable feeling. I was jealous, Sally, I'm sorry. I apologize."

She had drawn off her gloves, and one little hand, brown, shapely, rested upon her knee very near to me. I took it in mine. She let it stay, though she looked away from me, the color rich in her cheeks.

"I can forgive that," she murmured. "But the lie. Jealousy doesn't excuse a lie."

"You mean—what I intimated to your cousin," I said, trying to make her look at me. "That was the devil in me. Only it's true."

"How can it be true when you never asked—said a word—you hinted of?" she queried. "Diane believed what you said. I know she thinks me horrid."

"No she doesn't. As for what I said, or meant to say, which is the same thing, how'd you take my actions? I hope not the same as you take Wright's or the other fellow's."

Sally was silent, a little pale now, and I saw that I did not need to say any more about the other fellows. The change, the difference was now marked. It drove me to give in wholly to this earnest and passionate side of myself.

"Sally, I do love you. I don't know how you took my actions. Anyway, now I'll make them plain. I was beside myself with love and jealousy. Will you marry me?"

She did not answer. But the old willful Sally was not in evidence. Watching her face I gave her a slow and gentle pull, one she could easily resist if she cared to, and she slipped from her saddle into my arms.

Then there was one wildly sweet moment in which I had the blissful certainty that she kissed me of her own accord. She was abashed, yet yielding; she let herself go, yet seemed not utterly unstrung. Perhaps I was rough, held her too hard, for she cried out a little.

"Russ! Let me go. Help me—back."

I righted her in the saddle, although not entirely releasing her.

"But, Sally, you haven't told me anything," I remonstrated tenderly. "Do you love me?"

"I think so," she whispered.

"Sally, will you marry me?"

She disengaged herself then, sat erect and faced away from me, with her breast heaving.

"No, Russ," she presently said, once more calm.

"But Sally—if you love me—" I burst out, and then stopped, stilled by something in her face.

"I can't help—loving you, Russ," she said. "But to promise to marry you, that's different. Why, Russ, I know nothing about you, not even your last name. You're not a—a steady fellow. You drink, gamble, fight. You'll kill somebody yet. Then I'll *not* love you. Besides, I've always felt you're not just what you seemed. I can't trust you. There's something wrong about you."

I knew my face darkened, and perhaps hope and happiness died in it. Swiftly she placed a kind hand on my shoulder.

"Now, I've hurt you. Oh, I'm sorry. Your asking me makes such a difference. *They* are not in earnest. But, Russ, I had to tell you why I couldn't be engaged to you."

"I'm not good enough for you. I'd no right to ask you to marry me," I replied abjectly.

"Russ, don't think me proud," she faltered. "I wouldn't care who you were if I could only—only respect you. Some things about you are splendid, you're such a man, that's why I cared. But you gamble. You drink—and I *hate* that. You're dangerous they say, and I'd be, I *am* in constant dread you'll kill somebody. Remember, Russ, I'm no Texan."

This regret of Sally's, this faltering distress at giving me pain, was such sweet assurance that she did love me, better than she knew, that I was divided between extremes of emotion.

"Will you wait? Will you trust me a little? Will you give me a chance? After all, maybe I'm not so bad as I seem."

"Oh, if you weren't! Russ, are you asking me to trust you?"

"I beg you to—dearest. Trust me and wait."

"Wait? What for? Are you really on the square, Russ? Or are you what George calls you—a drunken cowboy, a gambler, sharp with the cards, a gun-fighter?"

My face grew cold as I felt the blood leave it. At that moment mention of George Wright fixed once for all my hate of him.

Bitter indeed was it that I dared not give him the lie. But what could I do? The character Wright gave me was scarcely worse than what I had chosen to represent. I had to acknowledge the justice of his claim, but nevertheless I hated him.

"Sally, I ask you to trust me in spite of my reputation."

"You ask me a great deal," she replied.

"Yes, it's too much. Let it be then only this—you'll wait. And while you wait, promise not to flirt with Wright and Waters."

"Russ, I'll not let George or any of them so much as dare touch me," she declared in girlish earnestness, her voice rising. "I'll promise if you'll promise me not to go into those saloons any more."

One word would have brought her into my arms for good and all. The better side of Sally Langdon showed then in her appeal. That appeal was as strong as the drawing power of her little face, all eloquent with its light, and eyes dark with tears, and lips wanting to smile.

My response should have been instant. How I yearned to give it and win the reward I imagined I saw on her tremulous lips! But I was bound. The grim, dark nature of my enterprise there in Linrock returned to stultify my eagerness, dispel my illusion, shatter my dream.

For one instant it flashed through my mind to tell Sally who I was, what my errand was, after the truth. But the secret was not mine to tell. And I kept my pledges.

The hopeful glow left Sally's face. Her disappointment seemed keen. Then a little scorn of certainty was the bitterest of all for me to bear.

"That's too much to promise all at once," I protested lamely, and I knew I would have done better to keep silence.

"Russ, a promise like that is nothing—if a man loves a girl," she retorted. "Don't make any more love to me, please, unless you want me to laugh at you. And don't feel such terrible trouble if you happen to see me flirting occasionally."

She ended with a little mocking laugh. That was the perverse side of her, the cat using her claws. I tried not to be angry, but failed.

"All right. I'll take my medicine," I replied bitterly. "I'll certainly never make love to you again. And I'll stand it if I happen to see Waters kiss you, or any other decent fellow. But look out how you let that damned backbiter Wright fool around you!"

I spoke to her as I had never spoken before, in quick, fierce meaning, with eyes holding hers.

She paled. But even my scarce-veiled hint did not chill her anger. Tossing her head she wheeled and rode away.

I followed at a little distance, and thus we traveled the ten miles back to the ranch. When we reached the corrals she dismounted and, turning her horse over to Dick, she went off toward the house without so much as a nod or good-by to me.

I went down to town for once in a mood to live up to what had been heretofore only a sham character.

But turning a corner into the main street I instantly forgot myself at the sight of a crowd congregated before the town hall. There was a babel of voices and an air of excitement that I immediately associated with Sampson, who as mayor of Linrock, once in a month of moons held court in this hall.

It took slipping and elbowing to get through the crowd. Once inside the door I saw that the crowd was mostly outside, and evidently not so desirous as I was to enter.

The first man I saw was Steele looming up; the next was Sampson chewing his mustache— the third, Wright, whose dark and sinister face told much. Something was up in Linrock. Steele had opened the hall.

There were other men in the hall, a dozen or more, and all seemed shouting excitedly in unison with the crowd outside. I did not try to hear what was said. I edged closer in, among the men to the front.

Sampson sat at a table up on a platform. Near him sat a thick-set grizzled man, with deep eyes; and this was Hanford Owens, county judge.

To the right stood a tall, angular, yellow-faced fellow with a drooping, sandy mustache. Conspicuous on his vest was a huge silver shield. This was Gorsech, one of Sampson's sheriffs.

There were four other men whom I knew, several whose faces were familiar, and half a dozen strangers, all dusty horsemen.

Steele stood apart from them, a little to one side, so that he faced them all. His hair was disheveled, and his shirt open at the neck. He looked cool and hard.

When I caught his eye I realized in an instant that the long deferred action, the beginning of our real fight was at hand.

Sampson pounded hard on the table to be heard. Mayor or not, he was unable at once to quell the excitement.

Gradually, however, it subsided and from the last few utterances before quiet was restored I gathered that Steele had intruded upon some kind of a meeting in the hall.

"Steele, what'd you break in here for?" demanded Sampson.

"Isn't this court? Aren't you the mayor of Linrock?" interrogated Steele. His voice was so clear and loud, almost piercing, that I saw at once that he wanted all those outside to hear.

"Yes," replied Sampson. Like flint he seemed, yet I felt his intense interest.

I had no doubt then that Steele intended to make him stand out before this crowd as the real mayor of Linrock or as a man whose office was a sham.

"I've arrested a criminal," said Steele. "Bud Snell. I charge him with assault on Jim Hoden and attempted robbery—if not murder. Snell had a shady past here, as the court will know if it keeps a record."

Then I saw Snell hunching down on a bench, a nerveless and shaken man if there ever was one. He had been a hanger-on round the gambling dens, the kind of sneak I never turned my back to.

Jim Hoden, the restaurant keeper, was present also, and on second glance I saw that he was pale. There was blood on his face. I knew Jim, liked him, had tried to make a friend of him.

I was not dead to the stinging interrogation in the concluding sentence of Steele's speech. Then I felt sure I had correctly judged Steele's motive. I began to warm to the situation.

"What's this I hear about you, Bud? Get up and speak for yourself," said Sampson, gruffly.

Snell got up, not without a furtive glance at Steele, and he had shuffled forward a few steps toward the mayor. He had an evil front, but not the boldness even of a rustler.

"It ain't so, Sampson," he began loudly. "I went in Hoden's place fer grub. Some feller I never seen before come in from the hall an' hit him an' wrastled him on the floor. Then this big Ranger grabbed me an' fetched me here. I didn't do nothin'. This Ranger's hankerin' to arrest somebody. Thet's my hunch, Sampson."

"What have you to say about this, Hoden?" sharply queried Sampson. "I call to your mind the fact that you once testified falsely in court, and got punished for it."

Why did my sharpened and experienced wits interpret a hint of threat or menace in Sampson's reminder? Hoden rose from the bench and with an unsteady hand reached down to support himself.

He was no longer young, and he seemed broken in health and spirit. He had been hurt somewhat about the head.

"I haven't much to say," he replied. "The Ranger dragged me here. I told him I didn't take my troubles to court. Besides, I can't swear it was Snell who hit me."

Sampson said something in an undertone to Judge Owens, and that worthy nodded his great, bushy head.

"Bud, you're discharged," said Sampson bluntly. "Now, the rest of you clear out of here."

He absolutely ignored the Ranger. That was his rebuff to Steele's advances, his slap in the face to an interfering Ranger Service.

If Sampson was crooked he certainly had magnificent nerve. I almost decided he was above suspicion. But his nonchalance, his air of finality, his authoritative assurance—these to my keen and practiced eyes were in significant contrast to a certain tenseness of line about his mouth and a slow paling of his olive skin.

He had crossed the path of Vaughn Steele; he had blocked the way of this Texas Ranger. If he had intelligence and remembered Steele's fame, which surely he had, then he had some appreciation of what he had undertaken.

In that momentary lull my scrutiny of Sampson gathered an impression of the man's intense curiosity.

Then Bud Snell, with a cough that broke the silence, shuffled a couple of steps toward the door.

"Hold on!" called Steele.

It was a bugle-call. It halted Snell as if it had been a bullet. He seemed to shrink.

"Sampson, I *saw* Snell attack Hoden," said Steele, his voice still ringing. "What has the court to say to that?"

The moment for open rupture between Ranger Service and Sampson's idea of law was at hand. Sampson showed not the slightest hesitation.

"The court has to say this: West of the Pecos we'll not aid or abet or accept any Ranger Service. Steele, we don't want you out here. Linrock doesn't need you."

"That's a lie, Sampson," retorted Steele. "I've a pocket full of letters from Linrock citizens, all begging for Ranger Service."

Sampson turned white. The veins corded at his temples. He appeared about to burst into rage. He was at a loss for a quick reply.

Steele shook a long arm at the mayor.

"I need your help. You refuse. Now, I'll work alone. This man Snell goes to Del Rio in irons."

George Wright rushed up to the table. The blood showed black and thick in his face; his utterance was incoherent, his uncontrollable outbreak of temper seemed out of all proportion to any cause he should reasonably have had for anger.

Sampson shoved him back with a curse and warning glare.

"Where's your warrant to arrest Snell?" shouted Sampson. "I won't give you one. You can't take him without a warrant."

"I don't need warrants to make arrests. Sampson, you're ignorant of the power of Texas Rangers."

"You'll take Snell without papers?" bellowed Sampson.

"He goes to Del Rio to jail," answered Steele.

"He won't. You'll pull none of your damned Ranger stunts out here. I'll block you, Steele."

That passionate reply of Sampson's appeared to be the signal Steele had been waiting for.

He had helped on the crisis. I believed I saw how he wanted to force Sampson's hand and show the town his stand.

Steele backed clear of everybody and like two swift flashes of light his guns leaped forth. He was transformed. My wish was fulfilled.

Here was Steele, the Ranger, in one of his lone lion stands. Not exactly alone either, for my hands itched for my guns!

"Men! I call on you all!" cried Steele, piercingly. "I call on you to witness the arrest of a criminal opposed by Sampson, mayor of Linrock. It will be recorded in the report sent to the Adjutant General at Austin. Sampson, I warn you—don't follow up your threat."

Sampson sat white with working jaw.

"Snell, come here," ordered Steele.

The man went as if drawn and appeared to slink out of line with the guns. Steele's cold gray glance held every eye in the hall.

"Take the handcuffs out of my pocket. This side. Go over to Gorsech with them. Gorsech, snap those irons on Snell's wrists. Now, Snell, back here to the right of me."

It was no wonder to me to see how instantly Steele was obeyed. He might have seen more danger in that moment than was manifest to me; on the other hand he might have wanted to drive home hard what he meant.

It was a critical moment for those who opposed him. There was death in the balance.

This Ranger, whose last resort was gun-play, had instantly taken the initiative, and his nerve chilled even me. Perhaps though, he read this crowd differently from me and saw that intimidation was his cue. I forgot I was not a spectator, but an ally.

"Sampson, you've shown your hand," said Steele, in the deep voice that carried so far and held those who heard. "Any honest citizen of Linrock can now see what's plain—yours is a damn poor hand!

"You're going to hear me call a spade a spade. Your office is a farce. In the two years you've been mayor you've never arrested one rustler. Strange, when Linrock's a nest for rustlers! You've never sent a prisoner to Del Rio, let alone to Austin. You have no jail.

"There have been nine murders since you took office, innumerable street fights and hold-ups. *Not one arrest!* But you have ordered arrests for trivial offenses, and have punished these out of all proportion.

"There have been law-suits in your court—suits over water rights, cattle deals, property lines. Strange how in these law-suits, you or Wright or other men close to you were always involved! Stranger how it seems the law was stretched to favor your interests!"

Steele paused in his cold, ringing speech. In the silence, both outside and inside the hall, could be heard the deep breathing of agitated men.

I would have liked to search for possible satisfaction on the faces of any present, but I was concerned only with Sampson. I did not need to fear that any man might draw on Steele.

Never had I seen a crowd so sold, so stiff, so held! Sampson was indeed a study. Yet did he betray anything but rage at this interloper?

"Sampson, here's plain talk for you and Linrock to digest," went on Steele. "I don't accuse you and your court of dishonesty. I say—*strange*! Law here has been a farce. The motive behind all this laxity isn't plain to me—yet. But I call your hand!"

Chapter 3

SOUNDING THE TIMBER

When Steele left the hall, pushing Snell before him, making a lane through the crowd, it was not any longer possible to watch everybody.

Yet now he seemed to ignore the men behind him. Any friend of Snell's among the vicious element might have pulled a gun. I wondered if Steele knew how I watched those men at his back—how fatal it would have been for any of them to make a significant move.

No—I decided that Steele trusted to the effect his boldness had created. It was this power to cow ordinary men that explained so many of his feats; just the same it was his keenness to read desperate men, his nerve to confront them, that made him great.

The crowd followed Steele and his captive down the middle of the main street and watched him secure a team and buckboard and drive off on the road to Sanderson.

Only then did that crowd appear to realize what had happened. Then my long-looked-for opportunity arrived. In the expression of silent men I found something which I had sought; from the hurried departure of others homeward I gathered import; on the husky, whispering lips of yet others I read words I needed to hear.

The other part of that crowd—to my surprise, the smaller part—was the roaring, threatening, complaining one.

Thus I segregated Linrock that was lawless from Linrock that wanted law, but for some reason not yet clear the latter did not dare to voice their choice.

How could Steele and I win them openly to our cause? If that could be done long before the year was up Linrock would be free of violence and Captain Neal's Ranger Service saved to the State.

I went from place to place, corner to corner, bar to bar, watching, listening, recording; and not until long after sunset did I go out to the ranch.

The excitement had preceded me and speculation was rife. Hurrying through my supper, to get away from questions and to go on with my spying, I went out to the front of the house.

The evening was warm; the doors were open; and in the twilight the only lamps that had been lit were in Sampson's big sitting room at the far end of the house. Neither Sampson nor Wright had come home to supper.

I would have given much to hear their talk right then, and certainly intended to try to hear it when they did come home.

When the buckboard drove up and they alighted I was well hidden in the bushes, so well screened that I could get but a fleeting glimpse of Sampson as he went in.

For all I could see, he appeared to be a calm and quiet man, intense beneath the surface, with an air of dignity under insult. My chance to observe Wright was lost.

They went into the house without speaking, and closed the door.

At the other end of the porch, close under a window, was an offset between step and wall, and there in the shadow I hid. If Sampson or Wright visited the girls that evening I wanted to hear what was said about Steele.

It seemed to me that it might be a good clue for me—the circumstance whether or not Diane Sampson was told the truth. So I waited there in the darkness with patience born of many hours of like duty.

Presently the small lamp was lit—I could tell the difference in light when the big one was burning—and I heard the swish of skirts.

"Something's happened, surely, Sally," I heard Miss Sampson say anxiously. "Papa just met me in the hall and didn't speak. He seemed pale, worried."

"Cousin George looked like a thundercloud," said Sally. "For once, he didn't try to kiss me. Something's happened. Well, Diane, this has been a bad day for me, too."

Plainly I heard Sally's sigh, and the little pathetic sound brought me vividly out of my sordid business of suspicion and speculation. So she was sorry.

"Bad for you, too?" replied Diane in amused surprise. "Oh, I see—I forgot. You and Russ had it out."

"Out? We fought like the very old deuce. I'll never speak to him again."

"So your little—affair with Russ is all over?"

"Yes." Here she sighed again.

"Well, Sally, it began swiftly and it's just as well short," said Diane earnestly. "We know nothing at all of Russ."

"Diane, after to-day I respect him in—in spite of things—even though he seems no good. I—I cared a lot, too."

"My dear, your loves are like the summer flowers. I thought maybe your flirting with Russ might amount to something. Yet he seems so different now from what he was at first. It's only occasionally I get the impression I had of him after that night he saved me from violence. He's strange. Perhaps it all comes of his infatuation for you. He is in love with you. I'm afraid of what may come of it."

"Diane, he'll do something dreadful to George, mark my words," whispered Sally. "He swore he would if George fooled around me any more."

"Oh, dear. Sally, what can we do? These are wild men. George makes life miserable for me. And he teases you unmer..."

"I don't call it teasing. George wants to spoon," declared Sally emphatically. "He'd run after any woman."

"A fine compliment to me, Cousin Sally," laughed Diane.

"I don't agree," replied Sally stubbornly. "It's so. He's spoony. And when he's been drinking and tries to kiss me, I hate him."

"Sally, you look as if you'd rather like Russ to do something dreadful to George," said Diane with a laugh that this time was only half mirth.

"Half of me would and half of me would not," returned Sally. "But all of me would if I weren't afraid of Russ. I've got a feeling—I don't know what—something will happen between George and Russ some day."

There were quick steps on the hall floor, steps I thought I recognized.

"Hello, girls!" sounded out Wright's voice, minus its usual gaiety. Then ensued a pause that made me bring to mind a picture of Wright's glum face.

"George, what's the matter?" asked Diane presently. "I never saw papa as he is to-night, nor you so—so worried. Tell me, what has happened?"

"Well, Diane, we had a jar to-day," replied Wright, with a blunt, expressive laugh.

"Jar?" echoed both the girls curiously.

"Jar? We had to submit to a damnable outrage," added Wright passionately, as if the sound of his voice augmented his feeling. "Listen, girls. I'll tell you all about it."

He coughed, clearing his throat in a way that betrayed he had been drinking.

I sunk deeper in the shadow of my covert, and stiffening my muscles for a protracted spell of rigidity, prepared to listen with all acuteness and intensity.

Just one word from this Wright, inadvertently uttered in a moment of passion, might be the word Steele needed for his clue.

"It happened at the town hall," began Wright rapidly. "Your father and Judge Owens and I were there in consultation with three ranchers from out of town. First we were disturbed by gunshots from somewhere, but not close at hand. Then we heard the loud voices outside.

"A crowd was coming down street. It stopped before the hall. Men came running in, yelling. We thought there was a fire. Then that Ranger, Steele, stalked in, dragging a fellow by the name of Snell. We couldn't tell what was wanted because of the uproar. Finally your father restored order.

"Steele had arrested Snell for alleged assault on a restaurant keeper named Hoden. It developed that Hoden didn't accuse anybody, didn't know who attacked him. Snell, being obviously innocent, was discharged. Then this—this gun fighting Ranger pulled his guns on the court and halted the proceedings."

When Wright paused I plainly heard his intake of breath. Far indeed was he from calm.

"Steele held everybody in that hall in fear of death, and he began shouting his insults. Law was a farce in Linrock. The court was a farce. There was no law. Your father's office as mayor should be impeached. He made arrests only for petty offenses. He was afraid of the rustlers, highwaymen, murderers. He was afraid or—he just let them alone. He used his office to cheat ranchers and cattlemen in law-suits.

"All of this Steele yelled for everyone to hear. A damnable outrage! Your father, Diane, insulted in his own court by a rowdy Ranger! Not only insulted, but threatened with death—two big guns thrust almost in his face!"

"Oh! How horrible!" cried Diane, in mingled distress and anger.

"Steele's a Ranger. The Ranger Service wants to rule western Texas," went on Wright. "These Rangers are all a low set, many of them worse than the outlaws they hunt. Some of them were outlaws and gun fighters before they became Rangers.

"This Steele is one of the worst of the lot. He's keen, intelligent, smooth, and that makes him more to be feared. For he is to be feared. He wanted to kill. He meant to kill. If your father had made the least move Steele would have shot him. He's a cold-nerved devil—the born gunman. My God, any instant I expected to see your father fall dead at my feet!"

"Oh, George! The—the unspeakable ruffian!" cried Diane, passionately.

"You see, Diane, this fellow Steele has failed here in Linrock. He's been here weeks and done nothing. He must have got desperate. He's infamous and he loves his name. He seeks notoriety.

He made that play with Snell just for a chance to rant against your father. He tried to inflame all Linrock against him. That about law-suits was the worst! Damn him! He'll make us enemies."

"What do you care for the insinuations of such a man?" said Diane Sampson, her voice now deep and rich with feeling. "After a moment's thought no one will be influenced by them. Do not worry, George, tell papa not to worry. Surely after all these years he can't be injured in reputation by—by an adventurer."

"Yes, he can be injured," replied George quickly. "The frontier is a queer place. There are many bitter men here, men who have failed at ranching. And your father has been wonderfully successful. Steele has dropped some poison, and it'll spread."

Then followed a silence, during which, evidently, the worried Wright bestrode the floor.

"Cousin George, what became of Steele and his prisoner?" suddenly asked Sally.

How like her it was, with her inquisitive bent of mind and shifting points of view, to ask a question the answering of which would be gall and wormwood to Wright!

It amused while it thrilled me. Sally might be a flirt, but she was no fool.

"What became of them? Ha! Steele bluffed the whole town—at least all of it who had heard the mayor's order to discharge Snell," growled Wright. "He took Snell—rode off for Del Rio to jail him."

"George!" exclaimed Diane. "Then, after all, this Ranger was able to arrest Snell, the innocent man father discharged, and take him to jail?"

"Exactly. That's the toughest part...." Wright ended abruptly, and then broke out fiercely: "But, by God, he'll never come back!"

Wright's slow pacing quickened and he strode from the parlor, leaving behind him a silence eloquent of the effect of his sinister prediction.

"Sally, what did he mean?" asked Diane in a low voice.

"Steele will be killed," replied Sally, just as low-voiced.

"Killed! That magnificent fellow! Ah, I forgot. Sally, my wits are sadly mixed. I ought to be glad if somebody kills my father's defamer. But, oh, I can't be!

"This bloody frontier makes me sick. Papa doesn't want me to stay for good. And no wonder. Shall I go back? I hate to show a white feather.

"Do you know, Sally, I was—a little taken with this Texas Ranger. Miserably, I confess. He seemed so like in spirit to the grand stature of him. How can so splendid a man be so bloody, base at heart? It's hideous. How little we know of men! I had my dream about Vaughn Steele. I confess because it shames me—because I hate myself!"

Next morning I awakened with a feeling that I was more like my old self. In the experience of activity of body and mind, with a prospect that this was merely the forerunner of great events, I came round to my own again.

Sally was not forgotten; she had just become a sorrow. So perhaps my downfall as a lover was a precursor of better results as an officer.

I held in abeyance my last conclusion regarding Sampson and Wright, and only awaited Steele's return to have fixed in mind what these men were.

Wright's remark about Steele not returning did not worry me. I had heard many such dark sayings in reference to Rangers.

Rangers had a trick of coming back. I did not see any man or men on the present horizon of Linrock equal to the killing of Steele.

As Miss Sampson and Sally had no inclination to ride, I had even more freedom. I went down to the town and burst, cheerily whistling, into Jim Hoden's place.

Jim always made me welcome there, as much for my society as for the money I spent, and I never neglected being free with both. I bought a handful of cigars and shoved some of them in his pocket.

"How's tricks, Jim?" I asked cheerily.

"Reckon I'm feelin' as well as could be expected," replied Jim. His head was circled by a bandage that did not conceal the lump where he had been struck. Jim looked a little pale, but he was bright enough.

"That was a hell of a biff Snell gave you, the skunk," I remarked with the same cheery assurance.

"Russ, I ain't accusin' Snell," remonstrated Jim with eyes that made me thoughtful.

"Sure, I know you're too good a sport to send a fellow up. But Snell deserved what he got. I saw his face when he made his talk to Sampson's court. Snell lied. And I'll tell you what, Jim, if it'd been me instead of that Ranger, Bud Snell would have got settled."

Jim appeared to be agitated by my forcible intimation of friendship.

"Jim, that's between ourselves," I went on. "I'm no fool. And much as I blab when I'm hunky, it's all air. Maybe you've noticed that about me. In some parts of Texas it's policy to be close-mouthed. Policy and healthy. Between ourselves, as friends, I want you to know I lean some on Steele's side of the fence."

As I lighted a cigar I saw, out of the corner of my eye, how Hoden gave a quick start. I expected some kind of a startling idea to flash into his mind.

Presently I turned and frankly met his gaze. I had startled him out of his habitual set taciturnity, but even as I looked the light that might have been amaze and joy faded out of his face, leaving it the same old mask.

Still I had seen enough. Like a bloodhound, I had a scent. "Thet's funny, Russ, seein' as you drift with the gang Steele's bound to fight," remarked Hoden.

"Sure. I'm a sport. If I can't gamble with gentlemen I'll gamble with rustlers."

Again he gave a slight start, and this time he hid his eyes.

"Wal, Russ, I've heard you was slick," he said.

"You tumble, Jim. I'm a little better on the draw."

"On the draw? With cards, an' gun, too, eh?"

"Now, Jim, that last follows natural. I haven't had much chance to show how good I am on the draw with a gun. But that'll come soon."

"Reckon thet talk's a little air," said Hoden with his dry laugh. "Same as you leanin' a little on the Ranger's side of the fence."

"But, Jim, wasn't he game? What'd you think of that stand? Bluffed the whole gang! The way he called Sampson—why, it was great! The justice of that call doesn't bother me. It was Steele's nerve that got me. That'd warm any man's blood."

There was a little red in Hoden's pale cheeks and I saw him swallow hard. I had struck deep again.

"Say, don't you work for Sampson?" he queried.

"Me? I *guess* not. I'm Miss Sampson's man. He and Wright have tried to fire me many a time."

"Thet so?" he said curiously. "What for?"

"Too many silver trimmings on me, Jim. And I pack my gun low down."

"Wal, them two don't go much together out here," replied Hoden. "But I ain't seen thet anyone has shot off the trimmin's."

"Maybe it'll commence, Jim, as soon as I stop buying drinks. Talking about work—who'd you say Snell worked for?"

"I didn't say."

"Well, say so now, can't you? Jim, you're powerful peevish to-day. It's the bump on your head. Who does Snell work for?"

"When he works at all, which sure ain't often, he rides for Sampson."

"Humph! Seems to me, Jim, that Sampson's the whole circus round Linrock. I was some sore the other day to find I was losing good money at Sampson's faro game. Sure if I'd won I wouldn't have been sorry, eh? But I was surprised to hear some scully say Sampson owned the Hope So dive."

"I've heard he owned considerable property hereabouts," replied Jim constrainedly.

"Humph again! Why, Jim, you *know* it, only like every other scully you meet in this town, you're afraid to open your mug about Sampson. Get me straight, Jim Hoden. I don't care a damn for Colonel Mayor Sampson. And for cause I'd throw a gun on him just as quick as on any rustler in Pecos."

"Talk's cheap, my boy," replied Hoden, making light of my bluster, but the red was deep in his face.

"Sure, I know that," I said, calming down. "My temper gets up, Jim. Then it's not well known that Sampson owns the Hope So?"

"Reckon it's known in Pecos, all right. But Sampson's name isn't connected with the Hope So. Blandy runs the place."

"That Blandy—I've got no use for him. His faro game's crooked, or I'm locoed bronc. Not that we don't have lots of crooked faro dealers. A fellow can stand for them. But Blandy's mean, back handed, never looks you in the eyes. That Hope So place ought to be run by a good fellow like you, Hoden."

"Thanks, Russ," replied he, and I imagined his voice a little husky. "Didn't you ever hear *I* used to run it?"

"No. Did you?" I said quickly.

"I reckon. I built the place, made additions twice, owned it for eleven years."

"Well, I'll be doggoned!"

It was indeed my turn to be surprised, and with the surprise came glimmering.

"I'm sorry you're not there now, Jim. Did you sell out?"

"No. Just lost the place."

Hoden was bursting for relief now—to talk—to tell. Sympathy had made him soft. I did not need to ask another question.

"It was two years ago—two years last March," he went on. "I was in a big cattle deal with Sampson. We got the stock, an' my share, eighteen hundred head, was rustled off. I owed Sampson. He pressed me. It come to a lawsuit, an' I—was ruined."

It hurt me to look at Hoden. He was white, and tears rolled down his cheeks.

I saw the bitterness, the defeat, the agony of the man. He had failed to meet his obligation; nevertheless he had been swindled.

All that he suppressed, all that would have been passion had the man's spirit not been broken, lay bare for me to see. I had now the secret of his bitterness.

But the reason he did not openly accuse Sampson, the secret of his reticence and fear—these I thought best to try to learn at some later time, after I had consulted with Steele.

"Hard luck! Jim, it certainly was tough," I said. "But you're a good loser. And the wheel turns!

"Now, Jim, here's what I come particular to see you for. I need your advice. I've got a little money. Between you and me, as friends, I've been adding some to that roll all the time. But before I lose it I want to invest some. Buy some stock or buy an interest in some rancher's herd.

"What I want you to steer me on is a good, square rancher. Or maybe a couple of ranchers if there happen to be two honest ones in Pecos. Eh? No deals with ranchers who ride in the dark with rustlers! I've a hunch Linrock's full of them.

"Now, Jim, you've been here for years. So you must know a couple of men above suspicion."

"Thank God I do, Russ," he replied feelingly. "Frank Morton an' Si Zimmer, my friends an' neighbors all my prosperous days. An' friends still. You can gamble on Frank and Si. But Russ, if you want advice from me, don't invest money in stock now."

"Why?"

"Because any new feller buyin' stock in Pecos these days will be rustled quicker'n he can say Jack Robinson. The pioneers, the new cattlemen—these are easy pickin'. But the new fellers have to learn the ropes. They don't know anythin' or anybody. An' the old ranchers are wise an' sore. They'd fight if they...."

"What?" I put in as he paused. "If they knew who was rustling the stock?"

"Nope."

"If they had the nerve?"

"Not thet so much."

"What then? What'd make them fight?"

"A leader!"

I went out of Hoden's with that word ringing in my ears. A leader! In my mind's eye I saw a horde of dark faced, dusty-booted cattlemen riding grim and armed behind Vaughn Steele.

More thoughtful than usual, I walked on, passing some of my old haunts, and was about to turn in front of a feed and grain store when a hearty slap on my back disturbed my reflection.

"Howdy thar, cowboy," boomed a big voice.

It was Morton, the rancher whom Jim had mentioned, and whose acquaintance I had made. He was a man of great bulk, with a ruddy, merry face.

"Hello, Morton. Let's have a drink," I replied.

"Gotta rustle home," he said. "Young feller, I've a ranch to work."

"Sell it to me, Morton."

He laughed and said he wished he could. His buckboard stood at the rail, the horses stamping impatiently.

"Cards must be runnin' lucky," he went on, with another hearty laugh.

"Can't kick on the luck. But I'm afraid it will change. Morton, my friend Hoden gave me a hunch you'd be a good man to tie to. Now, I've a little money, and before I lose it I'd like to invest it in stock."

He smiled broadly, but for all his doubt of me he took definite interest.

"I'm not drunk, and I'm on the square," I said bluntly. "You've taken me for a no-good cow puncher without any brains. Wake up, Morton. If you never size up your neighbors any better than you have me—well, you won't get any richer."

It was sheer enjoyment for me to make my remarks to these men, pregnant with meaning. Morton showed his pleasure, his interest, but his faith held aloof.

"I've got some money. I had some. Then the cards have run lucky. Will you let me in on some kind of deal? Will you start me up as a stockman, with a little herd all my own?"

"Russ, this's durn strange, comin' from Sampson's cowboy," he said.

"I'm not in his outfit. My job's with Miss Sampson. She's fine, but the old man? Nit! He's been after me for weeks. I won't last long. That's one reason why I want to start up for myself."

"Hoden sent you to me, did he? Poor ol' Jim. Wal, Russ, to come out flat-footed, you'd be foolish to buy cattle now. I don't want to take your money an' see you lose out. Better go back across the Pecos where the rustlers ain't so strong. I haven't had more'n twenty-five-hundred head of stock for ten years. The rustlers let me hang on to a breedin' herd. Kind of them, ain't it?"

"Sort of kind. All I hear is rustlers." I replied with impatience. "You see, I haven't ever lived long in a rustler-run county. Who heads the gang anyway?"

Frank Morton looked at me with a curiously-amused smile.

"I hear lots about Jack Blome and Snecker. Everybody calls them out and out bad. Do they head this mysterious gang?"

"Russ, I opine Blome an' Snecker parade themselves off boss rustlers same as gun throwers. But thet's the love such men have for bein' thought hell. That's brains headin' the rustler gang hereabouts."

"Maybe Blome and Snecker are blinds. Savvy what I mean, Morton? Maybe there's more in the parade than just the fame of it."

Morton snapped his big jaw as if to shut in impulsive words.

"Look here, Morton. I'm not so young in years even if I am young west of the Pecos. I can figure ahead. It stands to reason, no matter how damn strong these rustlers are, how hidden their work, however involved with supposedly honest men—they can't last."

"They come with the pioneers an' they'll last as long as thar's a single steer left," he declared.

"Well, if you take that view of circumstances I just figure you as one of the rustlers!"

Morton looked as if he were about to brain me with the butt of his whip. His anger flashed by then as unworthy of him, and, something striking him as funny, he boomed out a laugh.

"It's not so funny," I went on. "If you're going to pretend a yellow streak, what else will I think?"

"Pretend?" he repeated.

"Sure. You can't fool me, Morton. I know men of nerve. And here in Pecos they're not any different from those in other places. I say if you show anything like a lack of sand it's all bluff.

"By nature you've got nerve. There are a lot of men round Linrock who're afraid of their shadows, afraid to be out after dark, afraid to open their mouths. But you're not one.

"So, I say, if you claim these rustlers will last, you're pretending lack of nerve just to help the popular idea along. For they can't last.

"Morton, I don't want to be a hard-riding cowboy all my days. Do you think I'd let fear of a gang of rustlers stop me from going in business with a rancher? Nit! What you need out here in Pecos is some new blood—a few youngsters like me to get you old guys started. Savvy what I mean?"

"Wal, I reckon I do," he replied, looking as if a storm had blown over him.

I gauged the hold the rustler gang had on Linrock by the difficult job it was to stir this really courageous old cattleman. He had grown up with the evil. To him it must have been a necessary one, the same as dry seasons and cyclones.

"Russ, I'll look you up the next time I come to town," he said soberly.

We parted, and I, more than content with the meeting, retraced my steps down street to the Hope So saloon.

Here I entered, bent on tasks as sincere as the ones just finished, but displeasing, because I had to mix with a low, profane set, to cultivate them, to drink occasionally despite my deftness at emptying glasses on the floor, to gamble with them and strangers, always playing the part of a flush and flashy cowboy, half drunk, ready to laugh or fight.

On the night of the fifth day after Steele's departure, I went, as was my habit, to the rendezvous we maintained at the pile of rocks out in the open.

The night was clear, bright starlight, without any moon, and for this latter fact safer to be abroad. Often from my covert I had seen dark figures skulking in and out of Linrock.

It would have been interesting to hold up these mysterious travelers; so far, however, this had not been our game. I had enough to keep my own tracks hidden, and my own comings and goings.

I liked to be out in the night, with the darkness close down to the earth, and the feeling of a limitless open all around. Not only did I listen for Steele's soft step, but for any sound—the yelp of coyote or mourn of wolf, the creak of wind in the dead brush, the distant clatter of hoofs, a woman's singing voice faint from the town.

This time, just when I was about to give up for that evening, Steele came looming like a black giant long before I heard his soft step. It was good to feel his grip, even if it hurt, because after five days I had begun to worry.

"Well, old boy, how's tricks?" he asked easily.

"Well, old man, did you land that son of a gun in jail?"

"You bet I did. And he'll stay there for a while. Del Rio rather liked the idea, Russ. All right there. I side-stepped Sanderson on the way back. But over here at the little village—Sampson they call it—I was held up. Couldn't help it, because there wasn't any road around."

"Held up?" I queried.

"That's it, the buckboard was held up. I got into the brush in time to save my bacon. They began to shoot too soon."

"Did you get any of them?"

"Didn't stay to see," he chuckled. "Had to hoof it to Linrock, and it's a good long walk."

"Been to your 'dobe yet to-night?"

"I slipped in at the back. Russ, it bothered me some to make sure no one was laying for me in the dark."

"You'll have to get a safer place. Why not take to the open every night?"

"Russ, that's well enough on a trail. But I need grub, and I've got to have a few comforts. I'll risk the 'dobe yet a little."

Then I narrated all that I had seen and done and heard during his absence, holding back one thing. What I did tell him sobered him at once, brought the quiet, somber mood, the thoughtful air.

"So that's all. Well, it's enough."

"All pertaining to our job, Vaughn," I replied. "The rest is sentiment, perhaps. I had a pretty bad case of moons over the little Langdon girl. But we quarreled. And it's ended now. Just as well, too, because if she'd...."

"Russ, did you honestly care for her? The real thing, I mean?"

"I—I'm afraid so. I'm sort of hurt inside. But, hell! There's one thing sure, a love affair might have hindered me, made me soft. I'm glad it's over."

He said no more, but his big hand pressing on my knee told me of his sympathy, another indication that there was nothing wanting in this Ranger.

"The other thing concerns you," I went on, somehow reluctant now to tell this. "You remember how I heard Wright making you out vile to Miss Sampson? Swore you'd never come back? Well, after he had gone, when Sally said he'd meant you'd be killed, Miss Sampson felt bad about it. She said she ought to be glad if someone killed you, but she couldn't be. She called you a bloody ruffian, yet she didn't want you shot.

"She said some things about the difference between your hideous character and your splendid stature. Called you a magnificent fellow—that was it. Well, then she choked up and confessed something to Sally in shame and disgrace."

"Shame—disgrace?" echoed Steele, greatly interested. "What?"

"She confessed she had been taken with you—had her little dream about you. And she hated herself for it."

Never, I thought, would I forget Vaughn Steele's eyes. It did not matter that it was dark; I saw the fixed gleam, then the leaping, shadowy light.

"Did she say that?" His voice was not quite steady. "Wonderful! Even if it only lasted a minute! She might—we might—If it wasn't for this hellish job! Russ, has it dawned on you yet, what I've got to do to Diane Sampson?"

"Yes," I replied. "Vaughn, you haven't gone sweet on her?"

What else could I make of that terrible thing in his eyes? He did not reply to that at all. I thought my arm would break in his clutch.

"You said you knew what I've got to do to Diane Sampson," he repeated hoarsely.

"Yes, you've got to ruin her happiness, if not her life."

"Why? Speak out, Russ. All this comes like a blow. There for a little I hoped you had worked out things differently from me. No hope. Ruin her life! Why?"

I could explain this strange agitation in Steele in no other way except that realization had brought keen suffering as incomprehensible as it was painful. I could not tell if it came from suddenly divined love for Diane Sampson equally with a poignant conviction that his fate was to wreck her. But I did see that he needed to speak out the brutal truth.

"Steele, old man, you'll ruin Diane Sampson, because, as arrest looks improbable to me, you'll have to kill her father."

"My God! Why, why? Say it!"

"Because Sampson is the leader of the Linrock gang of rustlers."

That night before we parted we had gone rather deeply into the plan of action for the immediate future.

First I gave Steele my earnest counsel and then as stiff an argument as I knew how to put up, all anent the absolute necessity of his eternal vigilance. If he got shot in a fair encounter with his enemies—well, that was a Ranger's risk and no disgrace. But to be massacred in bed, knifed, in the dark, shot in the back, ambushed in any manner—not one of these miserable ends must be the last record of Vaughn Steele.

He promised me in a way that made me wonder if he would ever sleep again or turn his back on anyone—made me wonder too, at the menace in his voice. Steele seemed likely to be torn two ways, and already there was a hint of future desperation.

It was agreed that I make cautious advances to Hoden and Morton, and when I could satisfy myself of their trustworthiness reveal my identity to them. Through this I was to cultivate Zimmer, and then other ranchers whom we should decide could be let into the secret.

It was not only imperative that we learn through them clues by which we might eventually fix guilt on the rustler gang, but also just as imperative that we develop a band of deputies to help us when the fight began.

Steele, now that he was back in Linrock, would have the center of the stage, with all eyes upon him. We agreed, moreover, that the bolder the front now the better the chance of ultimate success. The more nerve he showed the less danger of being ambushed, the less peril in facing vicious men.

But we needed a jail. Prisoners had to be corraled after arrest, or the work would be useless, almost a farce, and there was no possibility of repeating trips to Del Rio.

We could not use an adobe house for a jail, because that could be easily cut out of or torn down.

Finally I remembered an old stone house near the end of the main street; it had one window and one door, and had been long in disuse. Steele would rent it, hire men to guard and feed his prisoners; and if these prisoners bribed or fought their way to freedom, that would not injure the great principle for which he stood.

Both Steele and I simultaneously, from different angles of reasoning, had arrived at a conviction of Sampson's guilt. It was not so strong as realization; rather a divination.

Long experience in detecting, in feeling the hidden guilt of men, had sharpened our senses for that particular thing. Steele acknowledged a few mistakes in his day; but I, allowing for the same strength of conviction, had never made a single mistake.

But conviction was one thing and proof vastly another. Furthermore, when proof was secured, then came the crowning task—that of taking desperate men in a wild country they dominated.

Verily, Steele and I had our work cut out for us. However, we were prepared to go at it with infinite patience and implacable resolve. Steele and I differed only in the driving incentive; of course, outside of that one binding vow to save the Ranger Service.

He had a strange passion, almost an obsession, to represent the law of Texas, and by so doing render something of safety and happiness to the honest pioneers.

Beside Steele I knew I shrunk to a shadow. I was not exactly a heathen, and certainly I wanted to help harassed people, especially women and children; but mainly with me it was the zest, the thrill, the hazard, the matching of wits—in a word, the adventure of the game.

Next morning I rode with the young ladies. In the light of Sally's persistently flagrant advances, to which I was apparently blind, I saw that my hard-won victory over self was likely to be short-lived.

That possibility made me outwardly like ice. I was an attentive, careful, reliable, and respectful attendant, seeing to the safety of my charges; but the one-time gay and debonair cowboy was a thing of the past.

Sally, womanlike, had been a little—a very little—repentant; she had showed it, my indifference had piqued her; she had made advances and then my coldness had roused her spirit. She was the kind of girl to value most what she had lost, and to throw consequences to the winds in winning it back.

When I divined this I saw my revenge. To be sure, when I thought of it I had no reason to want revenge. She had been most gracious to me.

But there was the catty thing she had said about being kissed again by her admirers. Then, in all seriousness, sentiment aside, I dared not make up with her.

So the cold and indifferent part I played was imperative.

We halted out on the ridge and dismounted for the usual little rest. Mine I took in the shade of a scrubby mesquite. The girls strolled away out of sight. It was a drowsy day, and I nearly fell asleep.

Something aroused me—a patter of footsteps or a rustle of skirts. Then a soft thud behind me gave me at once a start and a thrill. First I saw Sally's little brown hands on my shoulders. Then her head, with hair all shiny and flying and fragrant, came round over my shoulder, softly smoothing my cheek, until her sweet, saucy, heated face was right under my eyes.

"Russ, don't you love me any more?" she whispered.

Chapter 4

STEELE BREAKS UP THE PARTY

That night, I saw Steele at our meeting place, and we compared notes and pondered details of our problem.

Steele had rented the stone house to be used as a jail. While the blacksmith was putting up a door and window calculated to withstand many onslaughts, all the idlers and strangers in town went to see the sight. Manifestly it was an occasion for Linrock. When Steele let it be known that he wanted to hire a jailer and a guard this caustically humorous element offered itself *en masse*. The men made a joke out of it.

When Steele and I were about to separate I remembered a party that was to be given by Miss Sampson, and I told him about it. He shook his head sadly, almost doubtfully.

Was it possible that Sampson could be a deep eyed, cunning scoundrel, the true leader of the cattle rustlers, yet keep that beautiful and innocent girl out on the frontier and let her give parties to sons and daughters of a community he had robbed? To any but remorseless Rangers the idea was incredible.

Thursday evening came in spite of what the girls must have regarded as an interminably dragging day.

It was easy to differentiate their attitudes toward this party. Sally wanted to look beautiful, to excell all the young ladies who were to attend, to attach to her train all the young men, and have them fighting to dance with her. Miss Sampson had an earnest desire to open her father's house to the people of Linrock, to show that a daughter had come into his long cheerless home, to make the evening one of pleasure and entertainment.

I happened to be present in the parlor, was carrying in some flowers for final decoration, when Miss Sampson learned that her father had just ridden off with three horsemen whom Dick, who brought the news, had not recognized.

In her keen disappointment she scarcely heard Dick's concluding remark about the hurry of the colonel. My sharp ears, however, took this in and it was thought-provoking. Sampson was known to ride off at all hours, yet this incident seemed unusual.

At eight o'clock the house and porch and patio were ablaze with lights. Every lantern and lamp on the place, together with all that could be bought and borrowed, had been brought into requisition.

The cowboys arrived first, all dressed in their best, clean shaven, red faced, bright eyed, eager for the fun to commence. Then the young people from town, and a good sprinkling of older people, came in a steady stream.

Miss Sampson received them graciously, excused her father's absence, and bade them be at home.

The music, or the discordance that went by that name, was furnished by two cowboys with banjos and an antediluvian gentleman with a fiddle. Nevertheless, it was music that could be danced to, and there was no lack of enthusiasm.

I went from porch to parlor and thence to patio, watching and amused. The lights and the decorations of flowers, the bright dresses and the flashy scarfs of the cowboys furnished a gay enough scene to a man of lonesome and stern life like mine. During the dance there was a steady, continuous shuffling tramp of boots, and during the interval following a steady, low hum of merry talk and laughter.

My wandering from place to place, apart from my usual careful observation, was an unobtrusive but, to me, a sneaking pursuit of Sally Langdon.

She had on a white dress I had never seen with a low neck and short sleeves, and she looked so sweet, so dainty, so altogether desirable, that I groaned a hundred times in my jealousy. Because, manifestly, Sally did not intend to run any risk of my not seeing her in her glory, no matter where my eyes looked.

A couple of times in promenading I passed her on the arm of some proud cowboy or gallant young buck from town, and on these occasions she favored her escort with a languishing glance that probably did as much damage to him as to me.

Presently she caught me red-handed in my careless, sauntering pursuit of her, and then, whether by intent or from indifference, she apparently deigned me no more notice. But, quick to feel a difference in her, I marked that from that moment her gaiety gradually merged into coquettishness, and soon into flirtation.

Then, just to see how far she would go, perhaps desperately hoping she would make me hate her, I followed her shamelessly from patio to parlor, porch to court, even to the waltz.

To her credit, she always weakened when some young fellow got her in a corner and tried to push the flirting to extremes. Young Waters was the only one lucky enough to kiss her, and there was more of strength in his conquest of her than any decent fellow could be proud of.

When George Wright sought Sally out there was added to my jealousy a real anxiety. I had brushed against Wright more than once that evening. He was not drunk, yet under the influence of liquor.

Sally, however, evidently did not discover that, because, knowing her abhorrence of drink, I believed she would not have walked out with him had she known. Anyway, I followed them, close in the shadow.

Wright was unusually gay. I saw him put his arm around her without remonstrance. When the music recommenced they went back to the house. Wright danced with Sally, not ungracefully for a man who rode a horse as much as he. After the dance he waved aside Sally's many partners, not so gaily as would have been consistent with good feeling, and led her away. I followed. They ended up that walk at the extreme corner of the patio, where, under gaily colored lights, a little arbor had been made among the flowers and vines.

Sally seemed to have lost something of her vivacity. They had not been out of my sight for a moment before Sally cried out. It was a cry of impatience or remonstrance, rather than alarm, but I decided that it would serve me an excuse.

I dashed back, leaped to the door of the arbor, my hand on my gun.

Wright was holding Sally. When he heard me he let her go. Then she uttered a cry that was one of alarm. Her face blanched; her eyes grew strained. One hand went to her breast. She thought I meant to kill Wright.

"Excuse me," I burst out frankly, turning to Wright. I never saw a hyena, but he looked like one. "I heard a squeal. Thought a girl was hurt, or something. Miss Sampson gave me orders to watch out for accidents, fire, anything. So excuse me, Wright."

As I stepped back, to my amazement, Sally, excusing herself to the scowling Wright, hurriedly joined me.

"Oh, it's our dance, Russ!"

She took my arm and we walked through the patio.

"I'm afraid of him, Russ," she whispered. "You frightened me worse though. You didn't mean to—to—"

"I made a bluff. Saw he'd been drinking, so I kept near you."

"You return good for evil," she replied, squeezing my arm. "Russ, let me tell you—whenever anything frightens me since we got here I think of you. If you're only near I feel safe."

We paused at the door leading into the big parlor. Couples were passing. Here I could scarcely distinguish the last words she said. She stood before me, eyes downcast, face flushed, as sweet and pretty a lass as man could want to see, and with her hand she twisted round and round a silver button on my buckskin vest.

"Dance with me, the rest of this," she said. "George shooed away my partner. I'm glad for the chance. Dance with me, Russ—not gallantly or dutifully because I ask you, but because you *want* to. Else not at all."

There was a limit to my endurance. There would hardly be another evening like this, at least, for me, in that country. I capitulated with what grace I could express.

We went into the parlor, and as we joined the dancers, despite all that confusion I heard her whisper: "I've been a little beast to you."

That dance seemingly lasted only a moment—a moment while she was all airy grace, radiant, and alluring, floating close to me, with our hands clasped. Then it appeared the music had ceased, the couples were finding seats, and Sally and I were accosted by Miss Sampson.

She said we made a graceful couple in the dance. And Sally said she did not have to reach up a mile to me—I was not so awfully tall.

And I, tongue-tied for once, said nothing.

Wright had returned and was now standing, cigarette between lips, in the door leading out to the patio. At the same moment that I heard a heavy tramp of boots, from the porch side I saw Wright's face change remarkably, expressing amaze, consternation, then fear.

I wheeled in time to see Vaughn Steele bend his head to enter the door on that side. The dancers fell back.

At sight of him I was again the Ranger, his ally. Steele was pale, yet heated. He panted. He wore no hat. He had his coat turned up and with left hand he held the lapels together.

In a quick ensuing silence Miss Sampson rose, white as her dress. The young women present stared in astonishment and their partners showed excitement.

"Miss Sampson, I came to search your house!" panted Steele, courteously, yet with authority.

I disengaged myself from Sally, who was clinging to my hands, and I stepped forward out of the corner. Steele had been running. Why did he hold his coat like that? I sensed action, and the cold thrill animated me.

Miss Sampson's astonishment was succeeded by anger difficult to control.

"In the absence of my father I am mistress here. I will not permit you to search my house."

"Then I regret to say I must do so without your permission," he said sternly.

"Do not dare!" she flashed. She stood erect, her bosom swelling, her eyes magnificently black with passion. "How dare you intrude here? Have you not insulted us enough? To search my house to-night—to break up my party—oh, it's worse than outrage! Why on earth do you want to search here? Ah, for the same reason you dragged a poor innocent man into my father's court! Sir, I forbid you to take another step into this house."

Steele's face was bloodless now, and I wondered if it had to do with her scathing scorn or something that he hid with his hand closing his coat that way.

"Miss Sampson, I don't need warrants to search houses," he said. "But this time I'll respect your command. It would be too bad to spoil your party. Let me add, perhaps you do me a little wrong. God knows I hope so. I was shot by a rustler. He fled. I chased him here. He has taken refuge here—in your father's house. He's hidden somewhere."

Steele spread wide his coat lapels. He wore a light shirt, the color of which in places was white. The rest was all a bloody mass from which dark red drops fell to the floor.

"Oh!" cried Miss Sampson.

Scorn and passion vanished in the horror, the pity, of a woman who imagined she saw a man mortally wounded. It was a hard sight for a woman's eyes, that crimson, heaving breast.

"Surely I didn't see that," went on Steele, closing his coat. "You used unforgettable words, Miss Sampson. From you they hurt. For I stand alone. My fight is to make Linrock safer, cleaner, a better home for women and children. Some day you will remember what you said."

How splendid he looked, how strong against odds. How simple a dignity fitted his words. Why, a woman far blinder than Diane Sampson could have seen that here stood a man.

Steele bowed, turned on his heel, and strode out to vanish in the dark.

Then while she stood bewildered, still shocked, I elected to do some rapid thinking.

How seriously was Steele injured? An instant's thought was enough to tell me that if he had sustained any more than a flesh wound he would not have chased his assailant, not with so much at stake in the future.

Then I concerned myself with a cold grip of desire to get near the rustler who had wounded Steele. As I started forward, however, Miss Sampson defeated me. Sally once more clung to my hands, and directly we were surrounded by an excited circle.

It took a moment or two to calm them.

"Then there's a rustler—here—hiding?" repeated Miss Sampson.

"Miss Sampson, I'll find him. I'll rout him out," I said.

"Yes, yes, find him, Russ, but don't use violence," she replied. "Send him away—no, give him over to—"

"Nothing of the kind," interrupted George Wright, loud-voiced. "Cousin, go on with your dance. I'll take a couple of cowboys. I'll find this—this rustler, if there's one here. But I think it's only another bluff of Steele's."

This from Wright angered me deeply, and I strode right for the door.

"Where are you going?" he demanded.

"I've Miss Sampson's orders. She wants me to find this hidden man. She trusts me not to allow any violence."

"Didn't I say I'd see to that?" he snarled.

"Wright, I don't care what you say," I retorted. "But I'm thinking you might not want me to find this rustler."

Wright turned black in the face. Verily, if he had worn a gun he would have pulled it on me. As it was, Miss Sampson's interference probably prevented more words, if no worse.

"Don't quarrel," she said. "George, you go with Russ. Please hurry. I'll be nervous till the rustler's found or you're sure there's not one."

We started with several cowboys to ransack the house. We went through the rooms, searching, calling out, flashing our lanterns in dark places.

It struck me forcibly that Wright did all the calling. He hurried, too, tried to keep in the lead. I wondered if he knew his voice would be recognized by the hiding man.

Be that as it might, it was I who peered into a dark corner, and then with a cocked gun leveled I said: "Come out!"

He came forth into the flare of lanterns, a tall, slim, dark-faced youth, wearing dark sombrero, blouse and trousers. I collared him before any of the others could move, and I held the gun close enough to make him shrink.

But he did not impress me as being frightened just then; nevertheless, he had a clammy face, the pallid look of a man who had just gotten over a shock. He peered into my face, then into that of the cowboy next to me, then into Wright's and if ever in my life I beheld relief I saw it then.

That was all I needed to know, but I meant to find out more if I could.

"Who're you?" I asked quietly.

He gazed rather arrogantly down at me. It always irritated me to be looked down at that way.

"Say, don't be gay with me or you'll get it good," I yelled, prodding him in the side with the cocked gun. "Who are you? Quick!"

"Bo Snecker," he said.

"Any relation to Bill Snecker?"

"His son."

"What'd you hide here for?"

He appeared to grow sullen.

"Reckoned I'd be as safe in Sampson's as anywheres."

"Ahuh! You're taking a long chance," I replied, and he never knew, or any of the others, just how long a chance that was.

Sight of Steele's bloody breast remained with me, and I had something sinister to combat. This was no time for me to reveal myself or to show unusual feeling or interest for Steele.

As Steele had abandoned his search, I had nothing to do now but let the others decide what disposition was to be made of Snecker.

"Wright, what'll you do with him?" I queried, as if uncertain, now the capture was made. I let Snecker go and sheathed my weapon.

That seemed a signal for him to come to life. I guessed he had not much fancied the wide and somewhat variable sweep of that cocked gun.

"I'll see to that," replied Wright gruffly, and he pushed Snecker in front of him into the hall. I followed them out into the court at the back of the house.

As I had very little further curiosity I did not wait to see where they went, but hurried back to relieve Miss Sampson and Sally.

I found them as I had left them—Sally quiet, pale, Miss Sampson nervous and distressed. I soon calmed their fears of any further trouble or possible disturbance. Miss Sampson then became curious and wanted to know who the rustler was.

"How strange he should come here," she said several times.

"Probably he'd run this way or thought he had a better chance to hide where there was dancing and confusion," I replied glibly.

I wondered how much longer I would find myself keen to shunt her mind from any channel leading to suspicion.

"Would papa have arrested him?" she asked.

"Colonel Sampson might have made it hot for him," I replied frankly, feeling that if what I said had a double meaning it still was no lie.

"Oh, I forgot—the Ranger!" she exclaimed suddenly. "That awful sight—the whole front of him bloody! Russ, how could he stand up under such a wound? Do you think it'll kill him?"

"That's hard to say. A man like Steele can stand a lot."

"Russ, please go find him! See how it is with him!" she said, almost pleadingly.

I started, glad of the chance and hurried down toward the town.

There was a light in the little adobe house where he lived, and proceeding cautiously, so as to be sure no one saw me, I went close and whistled low in a way he would recognize. Then he opened the door and I went in.

"Hello, son!" he said. "You needn't have worried. Sling a blanket over that window so no one can see in."

He had his shirt off and had been in the act of bandaging a wound that the bullet had cut in his shoulder.

"Let me tie that up," I said, taking the strips of linen. "Ahuh! Shot you from behind, didn't he?"

"How else, you locoed lady-charmer? It's a wonder I didn't have to tell you that."

"Tell me about it."

Steele related a circumstance differing little from other attempts at his life, and concluded by saying that Snecker was a good runner if he was not a good shot.

I finished the bandaging and stood off, admiring Steele's magnificent shoulders. I noted, too, on the fine white skin more than one scar made by bullets. I got an impression that his strength and vitality were like his spirit—unconquerable!

"So you knew it was Bill Snecker's son?" I asked when I had told him about finding the rustler.

"Sure. Jim Hoden pointed him out to me yesterday. Both the Sneckers are in town. From now on we're going to be busy, Russ."

"It can't come too soon for me," I replied. "Shall I chuck my job? Come out from behind these cowboy togs?"

"Not yet. We need proof, Russ. We've got to be able to prove things. Hang on at the ranch yet awhile."

"This Bo Snecker was scared stiff till he recognized Wright. Isn't that proof?"

"No, that's nothing. We've got to catch Sampson and Wright red-handed."

"I don't like the idea of you trailing along alone," I protested. "Remember what Neal told me. I'm to kick. It's time for me to hang round with a couple of guns. You'll never use one."

"The hell I won't," he retorted, with a dark glance of passion. I was surprised that my remark had angered him. "You fellows are all wrong. I know *when* to throw a gun. You ought to remember that Rangers have a bad name for wanting to shoot. And I'm afraid it's deserved."

"Did you shoot at Snecker?" I queried.

"I could have got him in the back. But that wouldn't do. I shot three times at his legs—tried to let him down. I'd have made him tell everything he knew, but he ran. He was too fast for me."

"Shooting at his legs! No wonder he ran. He savvied your game all right. It's funny, Vaughn, how these rustlers and gunmen don't mind being killed. But to cripple them, rope them, jail them—that's hell to them! Well, I'm to go on, up at the ranch, falling further in love with that sweet kid instead of coming out straight to face things with you?"

Steele had to laugh, yet he was more thoughtful of my insistence.

"Russ, you think you have patience, but you don't know what patience is. I won't be hurried on this job. But I'll tell you what: I'll hang under cover most of the time when you're not close to me. See? That can be managed. I'll watch for you when you come in town. We'll go in the same places. And in case I get busy you can stand by and trail along after me. That satisfy you?"

"Fine!" I said, both delighted and relieved. "Well, I'll have to rustle back now to tell Miss Sampson you're all right."

Steele had about finished pulling on a clean shirt, exercising care not to disarrange the bandages; and he stopped short to turn squarely and look at me with hungry eyes.

"Russ, did she—show sympathy?"

"She was all broken up about it. Thought you were going to die."

"Did she send you?"

"Sure. And she said hurry," I replied.

I was not a little gleeful over the apparent possibility of Steele being in the same boat with me.

"Do you think she would have cared if—if I had been shot up bad?"

The great giant of a Ranger asked this like a boy, hesitatingly, with color in his face.

"Care! Vaughn, you're as thickheaded as you say I'm locoed. Diane Sampson has fallen in love with you! That's all. Love at first sight! She doesn't realize it. But I know."

There he stood as if another bullet had struck him, this time straight through the heart. Perhaps one had—and I repented a little of my overconfident declaration.

Still, I would not go back on it. I believed it.

"Russ, for God's sake! What a terrible thing to say!" he ejaculated hoarsely.

"No. It's not terrible to *say* it—only the fact is terrible," I went on. I may be wrong. But I swear I'm right. When you opened your coat, showed that bloody breast—well, I'll never forget her eyes.

"She had been furious. She showed passion—hate. Then all in a second something wonderful, beautiful broke through. Pity, fear, agonized thought of your death! If that's not love, if—if she did not betray love, then I never saw it. She thinks she hates you. But she loves you."

"Get out of here," he ordered thickly.

I went, not forgetting to peep out at the door and to listen a moment, then I hurried into the open, up toward the ranch.

The stars were very big and bright, so calm, so cold, that it somehow hurt me to look at them. Not like men's lives, surely!

What had fate done to Vaughn Steele and to me? I had a moment of bitterness, an emotion rare with me.

Most Rangers put love behind them when they entered the Service and seldom found it after that. But love had certainly met me on the way, and I now had confirmation of my fear that Vaughn was hard hit.

Then the wildness, the adventurer in me stirred to the wonder of it all. It was in me to exult even in the face of fate. Steele and I, while balancing our lives on the hair-trigger of a gun, had certainly fallen into a tangled web of circumstances not calculated in the role of Rangers.

I went back to the ranch with regret, remorse, sorrow knocking at my heart, but notwithstanding that, tingling alive to the devilish excitement of the game.

I knew not what it was that prompted me to sow the same seed in Diane Sampson's breast that I had sown in Steele's; probably it was just a propensity for sheer mischief, probably a certainty of the truth and a strange foreshadowing of a coming event.

If Diane Sampson loved, through her this event might be less tragic. Somehow love might save us all.

That was the shadowy portent flitting in the dark maze of my mind.

At the ranch dancing had been resumed. There might never have been any interruption of the gaiety. I found Miss Sampson on the lookout for me and she searched my face with eyes that silenced my one last qualm of conscience.

"Let's go out in the patio," I suggested. "I don't want any one to hear what I say."

Outside in the starlight she looked white and very beautiful. I felt her tremble. Perhaps my gravity presaged the worst. So it did in one way—poor Vaughn!

"I went down to Steele's 'dobe, the little place where he lives." I began, weighing my words. "He let me in—was surprised. He had been shot high in the shoulder, not a dangerous wound. I bandaged it for him. He was grateful—said he had no friends."

"Poor fellow! Oh, I'm glad it—it isn't bad," said Miss Sampson. Something glistened in her eyes.

"He looked strange, sort of forlorn. I think your words—what you said hurt him more than the bullet. I'm sure of that, Miss Sampson."

"Oh, I saw that myself! I was furious. But I—I meant what I said."

"You wronged Steele. I happen to know. I know his record along the Rio Grande. It's scarcely my place, Miss Sampson, to tell you what you'll find out for yourself, sooner or later."

"What shall I find out?" she demanded.

"I've said enough."

"No. You mean my father and cousin George are misinformed or wrong about Steele? I've feared it this last hour. It was his look. That pierced me. Oh, I'd hate to be unjust. You say I wronged him, Russ? Then you take sides with him against my father?"

"Yes," I replied very low.

She was keenly hurt and seemed, despite an effort, to shrink from me.

"It's only natural you should fight for your father," I went on. "Perhaps you don't understand. He has ruled here for long. He's been—well, let's say, easy with the evil-doers. But times are changing. He opposed the Ranger idea, which is also natural, I suppose. Still, he's wrong about Steele, terribly wrong, and it means trouble."

"Oh, I don't know what to believe!"

"It might be well for you to think things out for yourself."

"Russ, I feel as though I couldn't. I can't make head or tail of life out here. My father seems so strange. Though, of course, I've only seen him twice a year since I was a little girl. He has two sides to him. When I come upon that strange side, the one I never knew, he's like a man I never saw.

"I want to be a good and loving daughter. I want to help him fight his battles. But he doesn't—he doesn't *satisfy* me. He's grown impatient and wants me to go back to Louisiana. That gives me a feeling of mystery. Oh, it's *all* mystery!"

"True, you're right," I replied, my heart aching for her. "It's all mystery—and trouble for you, too. Perhaps you'd do well to go home."

"Russ, you suggest I leave here—leave my father?" she asked.

"I advise it. You struck a—a rather troublesome time. Later you might return if—"

"Never. I came to stay, and I'll stay," she declared, and there her temper spoke.

"Miss Sampson," I began again, after taking a long, deep breath, "I ought to tell you one thing more about Steele."

"Well, go on."

"Doesn't he strike you now as being the farthest removed from a ranting, brutal Ranger?"

"I confess he was at least a gentleman."

"Rangers don't allow anything to interfere with the discharge of their duty. He was courteous after you defamed him. He respected your wish. He did not break up the dance.

"This may not strike you particularly. But let me explain that Steele was chasing an outlaw who had shot him. Under ordinary circumstances he would have searched your house. He would have been like a lion. He would have torn the place down around our ears to get that rustler.

"But his action was so different from what I had expected, it amazed me. Just now, when I was with him, I learned, I guessed, what stayed his hand. I believe you ought to know."

"Know what?" she asked. How starry and magnetic her eyes! A woman's divining intuition made them wonderful with swift-varying emotion.

They drew me on to the fatal plunge. What was I doing to her—to Vaughn? Something bound my throat, making speech difficult.

"He's fallen in love with you," I hurried on in a husky voice. "Love at first sight! Terrible! Hopeless! I saw it—felt it. I can't explain how I know, but I do know.

"That's what stayed his hand here. And that's why I'm on his side. He's alone. He has a terrible task here without any handicaps. Every man is against him. If he fails, you might be the force that weakened him. So you ought to be kinder in your thought of him. Wait before you judge him further.

"If he isn't killed, time will prove him noble instead of vile. If he is killed, which is more than likely, you'll feel the happier for a generous doubt in favor of the man who loved you."

Like one stricken blind, she stood an instant; then, with her hands at her breast, she walked straight across the patio into the dark, open door of her room.

Chapter 5

CLEANING OUT LINROCK

Not much sleep visited me that night. In the morning, the young ladies not stirring and no prospects of duty for me, I rode down to town.

Sight of the wide street, lined by its hitching posts and saddled horses, the square buildings with their ugly signs, unfinished yet old, the lounging, dust-gray men at every corner—these awoke in me a significance that had gone into oblivion overnight.

That last talk with Miss Sampson had unnerved me, wrought strangely upon me. And afterward, waking and dozing, I had dreamed, lived in a warm, golden place where there were music and flowers and Sally's spritelike form leading me on after two tall, beautiful lovers, Diane and Vaughn, walking hand in hand.

Fine employment of mind for a Ranger whose single glance down a quiet street pictured it with darkgarbed men in grim action, guns spouting red, horses plunging!

In front of Hoden's restaurant I dismounted and threw my bridle. Jim was unmistakably glad to see me.

"Where've you been? Morton was in an' powerful set on seein' you. I steered him from goin' up to Sampson's. What kind of a game was you givin' Frank?"

"Jim, I just wanted to see if he was a safe rancher to make a stock deal for me."

"He says you told him he didn't have no yellow streak an' that he was a rustler. Frank can't git over them two hunches. When he sees you he's goin' to swear he's no rustler, but he *has* got a yellow streak, unless..."

This little, broken-down Texan had eyes like flint striking fire.

"Unless?" I queried sharply.

Jim breathed a deep breath and looked around the room before his gaze fixed again on mine.

"Wal," he replied, speaking low, "Me and Frank allows you've picked the right men. It was me that sent them letters to the Ranger captain at Austin. Now who in hell are you?"

It was my turn to draw a deep breath.

I had taken six weeks to strike fire from a Texan whom I instinctively felt had been prey to the power that shadowed Linrock. There was no one in the room except us, no one passing, nor near.

Reaching into the inside pocket of my buckskin vest, I turned the lining out. A star-shaped, bright, silver object flashed as I shoved it, pocket and all, under Jim's hard eyes.

He could not help but read; United States Deputy Marshall.

"By golly," he whispered, cracking the table with his fist. "Russ, you sure rung true to me. But never as a cowboy!"

"Jim, the woods is full of us!"

Heavy footsteps sounded on the walk. Presently Steele's bulk darkened the door.

"Hello," I greeted. "Steele, shake hands with Jim Hoden."

"Hello," replied Steele slowly. "Say, I reckon I know Hoden."

"Nit. Not this one. He's the old Hoden. He used to own the Hope So saloon. It was on the square when he ran it. Maybe he'll get it back pretty soon. Hope so!"

I laughed at my execrable pun. Steele leaned against the counter, his gray glance studying the man I had so oddly introduced.

Hoden in one flash associated the Ranger with me—a relation he had not dreamed of. Then, whether from shock or hope or fear I know not, he appeared about to faint.

"Hoden, do you know who's boss of this secret gang of rustlers hereabouts?" asked Steele bluntly.

It was characteristic of him to come sharp to the point. His voice, something deep, easy, cool about him, seemed to steady Hoden.

"No," replied Hoden.

"Does anybody know?" went on Steele.

"Wal, I reckon there's not one honest native of Pecos who *knows*."

"But you have your suspicions?"

"We have."

"You can keep your suspicions to yourself. But you can give me your idea about this crowd that hangs round the saloons, the regulars."

"Jest a bad lot," replied Hoden, with the quick assurance of knowledge. "Most of them have been here years. Others have drifted in. Some of them work odd times. They rustle a few steer, steal, rob, anythin' for a little money to drink an' gamble. Jest a bad lot!

"But the strangers as are always comin' an' goin'—strangers that never git acquainted—some of them are likely to be *the* rustlers. Bill an' Bo Snecker are in town now. Bill's a known cattle-thief. Bo's no good, the makin' of a gun-fighter. He heads thet way.

"They might be rustlers. But the boy, he's hardly careful enough for this gang. Then there's Jack Blome. He comes to town often. He lives up in the hills. He always has three or four strangers with him. Blome's the fancy gun fighter. He shot a gambler here last fall. Then he was in a fight in Sanderson lately. Got two cowboys then.

"Blome's killed a dozen Pecos men. He's a rustler, too, but I reckon he's not the brains of thet secret outfit, if he's in it at all."

Steele appeared pleased with Hoden's idea. Probably it coincided with the one he had arrived at himself.

"Now, I'm puzzled over this," said Steele. "Why do men, apparently honest men, seem to be so close-mouthed here? Is that a fact or only my impression?"

"It's sure a fact," replied Hoden darkly. "Men have lost cattle an' property in Linrock—lost them honestly or otherwise, as hasn't been proved. An' in some cases when they talked—hinted a little—they was found dead. Apparently held up an' robbed. But dead. Dead men don't talk. Thet's why we're close-mouthed."

Steele's face wore a dark, somber sternness.

Rustling cattle was not intolerable. Western Texas had gone on prospering, growing in spite of the horde of rustlers ranging its vast stretches; but this cold, secret, murderous hold on a little struggling community was something too strange, too terrible for men to stand long.

It had waited for a leader like Steele, and now it could not last. Hoden's revived spirit showed that.

The ranger was about to speak again when the clatter of hoofs interrupted him. Horses halted out in front.

A motion of Steele's hand caused me to dive through a curtained door back of Hoden's counter. I turned to peep out and was in time to see George Wright enter with the red-headed cowboy called Brick.

That was the first time I had ever seen Wright come into Hoden's. He called for tobacco.

If his visit surprised Jim he did not show any evidence. But Wright showed astonishment as he saw the Ranger, and then a dark glint flitted from the eyes that shifted from Steele to Hoden and back again.

Steele leaned easily against the counter, and he said good morning pleasantly. Wright deigned no reply, although he bent a curious and hard scrutiny upon Steele. In fact, Wright evinced nothing that would lead one to think he had any respect for Steele as a man or as a Ranger.

"Steele, that was the second break of yours last night," he said finally. "If you come fooling round the ranch again there'll be hell!"

It seemed strange that a man who had lived west of the Pecos for ten years could not see in Steele something which forbade that kind of talk.

It certainly was not nerve Wright showed; men of courage were seldom intolerant; and with the matchless nerve that characterized Steele or the great gunmen of the day there went a cool, unobtrusive manner, a speech brief, almost gentle, certainly courteous. Wright was a hot-headed Louisianian of French extraction; a man evidently who had never been crossed in anything, and who was strong, brutal, passionate, which qualities, in the face of a situation like this, made him simply a fool!

The way Steele looked at Wright was joy to me. I hated this smooth, dark-skinned Southerner. But, of course, an ordinary affront like Wright's only earned silence from Steele.

"I'm thinking you used your Ranger bluff just to get near Diane Sampson," Wright sneered. "Mind you, if you come up there again there'll be hell!"

"You're damn right there'll be hell!" retorted Steele, a kind of high ring in his voice. I saw thick, dark red creep into his face.

Had Wright's incomprehensible mention of Diane Sampson been an instinct of love—of jealousy? Verily, it had pierced into the depths of the Ranger, probably as no other thrust could have.

"Diane Sampson wouldn't stoop to know a dirty blood-tracker like you," said Wright hotly. His was not a deliberate intention to rouse Steele; the man was simply rancorous. "I'll call you right, you cheap bluffer! You four-flush! You damned interfering conceited Ranger!"

Long before Wright ended his tirade Steele's face had lost the tinge of color, so foreign to it in moments like this; and the cool shade, the steady eyes like ice on fire, the ruthless lips had warned me, if they had not Wright.

"Wright, I'll not take offense, because you seem to be championing your beautiful cousin," replied Steele in slow speech, biting. "But let me return your compliment. You're a fine Southerner! Why, you're only a cheap four-flush—damned bull-headed—*rustler*"

Steele hissed the last word. Then for him—for me—for Hoden—there was the truth in Wright's working passion-blackened face.

Wright jerked, moved, meant to draw. But how slow! Steele lunged forward. His long arm swept up.

And Wright staggered backward, knocking table and chairs, to fall hard, in a half-sitting posture, against the wall.

"Don't draw!" warned Steele.

"Wright, get away from your gun!" yelled the cowboy Brick.

But Wright was crazed by fury. He tugged at his hip, his face corded with purple welts, malignant, murderous, while he got to his feet.

I was about to leap through the door when Steele shot. Wright's gun went ringing to the floor.

Like a beast in pain Wright screamed. Frantically he waved a limp arm, flinging blood over the white table-cloths. Steele had crippled him.

"Here, you cowboy," ordered Steele; "take him out, quick!"

Brick saw the need of expediency, if Wright did not realize it, and he pulled the raving man out of the place. He hurried Wright down the street, leaving the horses behind.

Steele calmly sheathed his gun.

"Well, I guess that opens the ball," he said as I came out.

Hoden seemed fascinated by the spots of blood on the table-cloths. It was horrible to see him rubbing his hands there like a ghoul!

"I tell you what, fellows," said Steele, "we've just had a few pleasant moments with the man who has made it healthy to keep close-mouthed in Linrock."

Hoden lifted his shaking hands.

"What'd you wing him for?" he wailed. "He was drawin' on you. Shootin' arms off men like him won't do out here."

I was inclined to agree with Hoden.

"That bull-headed fool will roar and butt himself with all his gang right into our hands. He's just the man I've needed to meet. Besides, shooting him would have been murder for me!"

"Murder!" exclaimed Hoden.

"He was a fool, and slow at that. Under such circumstances could I kill him when I didn't have to?"

"Sure it'd been the trick." declared Jim positively. "I'm not allowin' for whether he's really a rustler or not. It just won't do, because these fellers out here ain't goin' to be afraid of you."

"See here, Hoden. If a man's going to be afraid of me at all, that trick will make him more afraid of me. I know it. It works out. When Wright cools down he'll remember, he'll begin to think, he'll realize that I could more easily have killed him than risk a snapshot at his arm. I'll bet you he goes pale to the gills next time he even sees me."

"That may be true, Steele. But if Wright's the man you think he is he'll begin that secret underground bizness. It's been tolerable healthy these last six months. You can gamble on this. If thet secret work does commence you'll have more reason to suspect Wright. I won't feel very safe from now on.

"I heard you call him rustler. He knows thet. Why, Wright won't sleep at night now. He an' Sampson have always been after me."

"Hoden, what are your eyes for?" demanded Steele. "Watch out. And now here. See your friend Morton. Tell him this game grows hot. Together you approach four or five men you know well and can absolutely trust.

"Hello, there's somebody coming. You meet Russ and me to-night, out in the open a quarter of a mile, straight from the end of this street. You'll find a pile of stones. Meet us there to-night at ten o'clock."

The next few days, for the several hours each day that I was in town, I had Steele in sight all the time or knew that he was safe under cover.

Nothing happened. His presence in the saloons or any place where men congregated was marked by a certain uneasy watchfulness on the part of almost everybody, and some amusement on the part of a few.

It was natural to suppose that the lawless element would rise up in a mass and slay Steele on sight. But this sort of thing never happened. It was not so much that these enemies of the law awaited his next move, but just a slowness peculiar to the frontier.

The ranger was in their midst. He was interesting, if formidable. He would have been welcomed at card tables, at the bars, to play and drink with the men who knew they were under suspicion.

There was a rude kind of good humor even in their open hostility.

Besides, one Ranger, or a company of Rangers could not have held the undivided attention of these men from their games and drinks and quarrels except by some decided move. Excitement, greed, appetite were rife in them.

I marked, however, a striking exception to the usual run of strangers I had been in the habit of seeing. The Sneckers had gone or were under cover. Again I caught a vague rumor of the coming of Jack Blome, yet he never seemed to arrive.

Moreover, the goings-on among the habitues of the resorts and the cowboys who came in to drink and gamble were unusually mild in comparison with former conduct.

This lull, however, did not deceive Steele and me. It could not last. The wonder was that it had lasted so long.

There was, of course, no post office in Linrock. A stage arrived twice a week from Sanderson, if it did not get held up on the way, and the driver usually had letters, which he turned over to the elderly keeper of a little store.

This man's name was Jones, and everybody liked him. On the evenings the stage arrived there was always a crowd at his store, which fact was a source of no little revenue to him.

One night, so we ascertained, after the crowd had dispersed, two thugs entered his store, beat the old man and robbed him. He made no complaint; however, when Steele called him he rather reluctantly gave not only descriptions of his assailants, but their names.

Steele straightaway went in search of the men and came across them in Lerett's place. I was around when it happened.

Steele strode up to a table which was surrounded by seven or eight men and he tapped Sim Bass on the shoulder.

"Get up, I want you," he said.

Bass looked up only to see who had accosted him.

"The hell you say!" he replied impudently.

Steele's big hand shifted to the fellow's collar. One jerk, seemingly no effort at all, sent Bass sliding, chair and all, to crash into the bar and fall in a heap. He lay there, wondering what had struck him.

"Miller, I want you. Get up," said Steele.

Miller complied with alacrity. A sharp kick put more life and understanding into Bass.

Then Steele searched these men right before the eyes of their comrades, took what money and weapons they had, and marched them out, followed by a crowd that gathered more and more to it as they went down the street. Steele took his prisoners into Jones' store, had them identified; returned the money they had stolen, and then, pushing the two through the gaping crowd, he marched them down to his stone jail and locked them up.

Obviously the serious side of this incident was entirely lost upon the highly entertained audience. Many and loud were the coarse jokes cracked at the expense of Bass and Miller and after the rude door had closed upon them similar remarks were addressed to Steele's jailer and guard, who in truth, were just as disreputable looking as their prisoners.

Then the crowd returned to their pastimes, leaving their erstwhile comrades to taste the sweets of prison life.

When I got a chance I asked Steele if he could rely on his hired hands, and with a twinkle in his eye which surprised me as much as his reply, he said Miller and Bass would have flown the coop before morning.

He was right. When I reached the lower end of town next morning, the same old crowd, enlarged by other curious men and youths, had come to pay their respects to the new institution.

Jailer and guard were on hand, loud in their proclamations and explanations. Naturally they had fallen asleep, as all other hard working citizens had, and while they slept the prisoners made a hole somewhere and escaped.

Steele examined the hole, and then engaged a stripling of a youth to see if he could crawl through. The youngster essayed the job, stuck in the middle, and was with difficulty extricated.

Whereupon the crowd evinced its delight.

Steele, without more ado, shoved his jailer and guard inside his jail, deliberately closed, barred and chained the iron bolted door, and put the key in his pocket. Then he remained there all day without giving heed to his prisoners' threats.

Toward evening, having gone without drink infinitely longer than was customary, they made appeals, to which Steele was deaf.

He left the jail, however, just before dark, and when we met he told me to be on hand to help him watch that night. We went around the outskirts of town, carrying two heavy double-barreled shotguns Steele had gotten somewhere and taking up a position behind bushes in the lot adjoining the jail; we awaited developments.

Steele was not above paying back these fellows.

All the early part of the evening, gangs of half a dozen men or more came down the street and had their last treat at the expense of the jail guard and jailer. These prisoners yelled for drink—not water but drink, and the more they yelled the more merriment was loosed upon the night air.

About ten o'clock the last gang left, to the despair of the hungry and thirsty prisoners.

Steele and I had hugely enjoyed the fun, and thought the best part of the joke for us was yet to come. The moon had arisen, and though somewhat hazed by clouds, had lightened the night. We were hidden about sixty paces from the jail, a little above it, and we had a fine command of the door.

About eleven o'clock, when all was still, we heard soft steps back of the jail, and soon two dark forms stole round in front. They laid down something that gave forth a metallic clink, like a crowbar. We heard whisperings and then, low, coarse laughs.

Then the rescuers, who undoubtedly were Miller and Bass, set to work to open the door. Softly they worked at first, but as that door had been put there to stay, and they were not fond of hard work, they began to swear and make noises.

Steele whispered to me to wait until the door had been opened, and then when all four presented a good target, to fire both barrels. We could easily have slipped down and captured the rescuers, but that was not Steele's game.

A trick met by a trick; cunning matching craft would be the surest of all ways to command respect.

Four times the workers had to rest, and once they were so enraged at the insistence of the prisoners, who wanted to delay proceedings to send one of them after a bottle, that they swore they would go away and cut the job altogether.

But they were prevailed upon to stay and attack the stout door once more. Finally it yielded, with enough noise to have awakened sleepers a block distant, and forth into the moonlight came rescuers and rescued with low, satisfied grunts of laughter.

Just then Steele and I each discharged both barrels, and the reports blended as one in a tremendous boom.

That little compact bunch disintegrated like quicksilver. Two stumbled over; the others leaped out, and all yelled in pain and terror. Then the fallen ones scrambled up and began to hobble and limp and jerk along after their comrades.

Before the four of them got out of sight they had ceased their yells, but were moving slowly, hanging on to one another in a way that satisfied us they would be lame for many a day.

Next morning at breakfast Dick regaled me with an elaborate story about how the Ranger had turned the tables on the jokers. Evidently in a night the whole town knew it.

Probably a desperate stand of Steele's even to the extreme of killing men, could not have educated these crude natives so quickly into the realization that the Ranger was not to be fooled with.

That morning I went for a ride with the girls, and both had heard something and wanted to know everything. I had become a news-carrier, and Miss Sampson never thought of questioning me in regard to my fund of information.

She showed more than curiosity. The account I gave of the jail affair amused her and made Sally laugh heartily.

Diane questioned me also about a rumor that had come to her concerning George Wright.

He had wounded himself with a gun, it seemed, and though not seriously injured, was not able to go about. He had not been up to the ranch for days.

"I asked papa about him," said, Diane, "and papa laughed like—well, like a regular hyena. I was dumbfounded. Papa's so queer. He looked thunder-clouds at me.

"When I insisted, for I wanted to know, he ripped out: 'Yes, the damn fool got himself shot, and I'm sorry it's not worse.'

"Now, Russ, what do you make of my dad? Cheerful and kind, isn't he?"

I laughed with Sally, but I disclaimed any knowledge of George's accident. I hated the thought of Wright, let alone anything concerning the fatal certainty that sooner or later these cousins of his were to suffer through him.

Sally did not make these rides easy for me, for she was sweeter than anything that has a name. Since the evening of the dance I had tried to avoid her. Either she was sincerely sorry for her tantrum or she was bent upon utterly destroying my peace.

I took good care we were never alone, for in that case, if she ever got into my arms again I would find the ground slipping from under me.

Despite, however, the wear and constant strain of resisting Sally, I enjoyed the ride. There was a charm about being with these girls.

Then perhaps Miss Sampson's growing unconscious curiosity in regard to Steele was no little satisfaction to me.

I pretended a reluctance to speak of the Ranger, but when I did it was to drop a subtle word or briefly tell of an action that suggested such.

I never again hinted the thing that had been such a shock to her. What was in her mind I could not guess; her curiosity, perhaps the greater part, was due to a generous nature not entirely satisfied with itself. She probably had not abandoned her father's estimate of the Ranger but absolute assurance that this was just did not abide with her. For the rest she was like any other girl, a worshipper of the lion in a man, a weaver of romance, ignorant of her own heart.

Not the least talked of and speculated upon of all the details of the jail incident was the part played by Storekeeper Jones, who had informed upon his assailants. Steele and I both awaited results of this significant fact.

When would the town wake up, not only to a little nerve, but to the usefulness of a Ranger?

Three days afterward Steele told me a woman accosted him on the street. She seemed a poor, hardworking person, plain spoken and honest.

Her husband did not drink enough to complain of, but he liked to gamble and he had been fleeced by a crooked game in Jack Martin's saloon. Other wives could make the same complaints. It was God's blessing for such women that Ranger Steele had come to Linrock.

Of course, he could not get back the lost money, but would it be possible to close Martin's place, or at least break up the crooked game?

Steele had asked this woman, whose name was Price, how much her husband had lost, and, being told, he assured her that if he found evidence of cheating, not only would he get back the money, but also he would shut up Martin's place.

Steele instructed me to go that night to the saloon in question and get in the game. I complied, and, in order not to be overcarefully sized up by the dealer, I pretended to be well under the influence of liquor.

By nine o'clock, when Steele strolled in, I had the game well studied, and a more flagrantly crooked one I had never sat in. It was barefaced robbery.

Steele and I had agreed upon a sign from me, because he was not so adept in the intricacies of gambling as I was. I was not in a hurry, however, for there was a little frecklefaced cattleman in the game, and he had been losing, too. He had sold a bunch of stock that day and had considerable money, which evidently he was to be deprived of before he got started for Del Rio.

Steele stood at our backs, and I could feel his presence. He thrilled me. He had some kind of effect on the others, especially the dealer, who was honest enough while the Ranger looked on.

When, however, Steele shifted his attention to other tables and players our dealer reverted to his crooked work. I was about to make a disturbance, when the little cattleman, leaning over, fire in his eye and gun in hand, made it for me.

Evidently he was a keener and nervier gambler than he had been taken for. There might have been gun-play right then if Steele had not interfered.

"Hold on!" he yelled, leaping for our table. "Put up your gun!"

"Who are you?" demanded the cattleman, never moving. "Better keep out of this."

"I'm Steele. Put up your gun."

"You're thet Ranger, hey?" replied the other. "All right! But just a minute. I want this dealer to sit quiet. I've been robbed. And I want my money back."

Certainly the dealer and everyone else round the table sat quiet while the cattleman coolly held his gun leveled.

"Crooked game?" asked Steele, bending over the table. "Show me."

It did not take the aggrieved gambler more than a moment to prove his assertion. Steele, however, desired corroboration from others beside the cattleman, and one by one he questioned them.

To my surprise, one of the players admitted his conviction that the game was not straight.

"What do you say?" demanded Steele of me.

"Worse'n a hold-up, Mr. Ranger," I burst out. "Let me show you."

Deftly I made the dealer's guilt plain to all, and then I seconded the cattleman's angry claim for lost money. The players from other tables gathered round, curious, muttering.

And just then Martin strolled in. His appearance was not prepossessing.

"What's this holler?" he asked, and halted as he saw the cattleman's gun still in line with the dealer.

"Martin, you know what it's for," replied Steele. "Take your dealer and dig—unless you want to see me clean out your place."

Sullen and fierce, Martin stood looking from Steele to the cattleman and then the dealer. Some men in the crowd muttered, and that was a signal for Steele to shove the circle apart and get out, back to the wall.

The cattleman rose slowly in the center, pulling another gun, and he certainly looked business to me.

"Wal, Ranger, I reckon I'll hang round an' see you ain't bothered none," he said. "Friend," he went on, indicating me with a slight wave of one extended gun, "jest rustle the money in sight. We'll square up after the show."

I reached out and swept the considerable sum toward me, and, pocketing it, I too rose, ready for what might come.

"You-all give me elbow room!" yelled Steele at Martin and his cowed contingent.

Steele looked around, evidently for some kind of implement, and, espying a heavy ax in a corner, he grasped it, and, sweeping it to and fro as if it had been a buggy-whip, he advanced on the faro layout. The crowd fell back, edging toward the door.

One crashing blow wrecked the dealer's box and table, sending them splintering among the tumbled chairs. Then the giant Ranger began to spread further ruin about him.

Martin's place was rough and bare, of the most primitive order, and like a thousand other dens of its kind, consisted of a large room with adobe walls, a rude bar of boards, piles of kegs in a corner, a stove, and a few tables with chairs.

Steele required only one blow for each article he struck, and he demolished it. He stove in the head of each keg.

When the dark liquor gurgled out, Martin cursed, and the crowd followed suit. That was a loss!

The little cattleman, holding the men covered, backed them out of the room, Martin needing a plain, stern word to put him out entirely. I went out, too, for I did not want to miss any moves on the part of that gang.

Close behind me came the cattleman, the kind of cool, nervy Texan I liked. He had Martin well judged, too, for there was no evidence of any bold resistance.

But there were shouts and loud acclamations; and these, with the crashing blows of Steele's ax, brought a curious and growing addition to the crowd.

Soon sodden thuds from inside the saloon and red dust pouring out the door told that Steele was attacking the walls of Martin's place. Those adobe bricks when old and crumbly were easily demolished.

Steele made short work of the back wall, and then he smashed out half of the front of the building. That seemed to satisfy him.

When he stepped out of the dust he was wet with sweat, dirty, and disheveled, hot with his exertion—a man whose great stature and muscular development expressed a wonderful physical strength and energy. And his somber face, with the big gray eyes, like open furnaces, expressed a passion equal to his strength.

Perhaps only then did wild and lawless Linrock grasp the real significance of this Ranger.

Steele threw the ax at Martin's feet.

"Martin, don't reopen here," he said curtly. "Don't start another place in Linrock. If you do— jail at Austin for years."

Martin, livid and scowling, yet seemingly dazed with what had occurred, slunk away, accompanied by his cronies. Steele took the money I had appropriated, returned to me what I had lost, did likewise with the cattleman, and then, taking out the sum named by Mrs. Price, he divided the balance with the other players who had been in the game.

Then he stalked off through the crowd as if he knew that men who slunk from facing him would not have nerve enough to attack him even from behind.

"Wal, damn me!" ejaculated the little cattleman in mingled admiration and satisfaction. "So thet's that Texas Ranger, Steele, hey? Never seen him before. All Texas, thet Ranger!"

I lingered downtown as much to enjoy the sensation as to gain the different points of view.

No doubt about the sensation! In one hour every male resident of Linrock and almost every female had viewed the wreck of Martin's place. A fire could not have created half the excitement.

And in that excitement both men and women gave vent to speech they might not have voiced at a calmer moment. The women, at least, were not afraid to talk, and I made mental note of the things they said.

"Did he do it all alone?"

"Thank God a *man's* come to Linrock."

"Good for Molly Price!"

"Oh, it'll make bad times for Linrock."

It almost seemed that all the women were glad, and this was in itself a vindication of the Ranger's idea of law.

The men, however—Blandy, proprietor of the Hope So, and others of his ilk, together with the whole brood of idle gaming loungers, and in fact even storekeepers, ranchers, cowboys—all shook their heads sullenly or doubtfully.

Striking indeed now was the absence of any joking. Steele had showed his hand, and, as one gambler said: "It's a hard hand to call."

The truth was, this Ranger Service was hateful to the free-and-easy Texan who lived by anything except hard and honest work, and it was damnably hateful to the lawless class. Steele's authority, now obvious to all, was unlimited; it could go as far as he had power to carry it.

From present indications that power might be considerable. The work of native sheriffs and constables in western Texas had been a farce, an utter failure. If an honest native of a community undertook to be a sheriff he became immediately a target for rowdy cowboys and other vicious elements.

Many a town south and west of San Antonio owed its peace and prosperity to Rangers, and only to them. They had killed or driven out the criminals. They interpreted the law for themselves, and it was only such an attitude toward law—the stern, uncompromising, implacable extermination of the lawless—that was going to do for all Texas what it had done for part.

Steele was the driving wedge that had begun to split Linrock—split the honest from dominance by the dishonest. To be sure, Steele might be killed at any moment, and that contingency was voiced in the growl of one sullen man who said: "Wot the hell are we up against? Ain't somebody goin' to plug this Ranger?"

It was then that the thing for which Steele stood, the Ranger Service—to help, to save, to defend, to punish, with such somber menace of death as seemed embodied in his cold attitude toward resistance—took hold of Linrock and sunk deep into both black and honest hearts.

It was what was behind Steele that seemed to make him more than an officer—a man.

I could feel how he began to loom up, the embodiment of a powerful force—the Ranger Service—the fame of which, long known to this lawless Pecos gang, but scouted as a vague and distant thing, now became an actuality, a Ranger in the flesh, whose surprising attributes included both the law and the enforcement of it.

When I reached the ranch the excitement had preceded me. Miss Sampson and Sally, both talking at once, acquainted me with the fact that they had been in a store on the main street a block or more from Martin's place.

They had seen the crowd, heard the uproar; and, as they had been hurriedly started toward home by their attendant Dick, they had encountered Steele stalking by.

"He looked grand!" exclaimed Sally.

Then I told the girls the whole story in detail.

"Russ, is it true, just as you tell it?" inquired Diane earnestly.

"Absolutely. I know Mrs. Price went to Steele with her trouble. I was in Martin's place when he entered. Also I was playing in the crooked game. And I saw him wreck Martin's place. Also, I heard him forbid Martin to start another place in Linrock."

"Then he does do splendid things," she said softly, as if affirming to herself.

I walked on then, having gotten a glimpse of Colonel Sampson in the background. Before I reached the corrals Sally came running after me, quite flushed and excited.

"Russ, my uncle wants to see you," she said. "He's in a bad temper. Don't lose yours, please."

She actually took my hand. What a child she was, in all ways except that fatal propensity to flirt. Her statement startled me out of any further thought of her. Why did Sampson want to see me? He never noticed me. I dreaded facing him—not from fear, but because I must see more and more of the signs of guilt in Diane's father.

He awaited me on the porch. As usual, he wore riding garb, but evidently he had not been out so far this day. He looked worn. There was a furtive shadow in his eyes. The haughty, imperious temper, despite Sally's conviction, seemed to be in abeyance.

"Russ, what's this I hear about Martin's saloon being cleaned out?" he asked. "Dick can't give particulars."

Briefly and concisely I told the colonel exactly what had happened. He chewed his cigar, then spat it out with an unintelligible exclamation.

"Martin's no worse than others," he said. "Blandy leans to crooked faro. I've tried to stop that, anyway. If Steele can, more power to him!"

Sampson turned on his heel then and left me with a queer feeling of surprise and pity.

He had surprised me before, but he had never roused the least sympathy. It was probably that Sampson was indeed powerless, no matter what his position.

I had known men before who had become involved in crime, yet were too manly to sanction a crookedness they could not help.

Miss Sampson had been standing in her door. I could tell she had heard; she looked agitated. I knew she had been talking to her father.

"Russ, he hates the Ranger," she said. "That's what I fear. It'll bring trouble on us. Besides, like everybody here, he's biased. He can't see anything good in Steele. Yet he says: 'More power to him!' I'm mystified, and, oh, I'm between two fires!"

Steele's next noteworthy achievement was as new to me as it was strange to Linrock. I heard a good deal about it from my acquaintances, some little from Steele, and the concluding incident I saw and heard myself.

Andy Vey was a broken-down rustler whose activity had ceased and who spent his time hanging on at the places frequented by younger and better men of his kind. As he was a parasite, he was often thrown out of the dens.

Moreover, it was an open secret that he had been a rustler, and the men with whom he associated had not yet, to most of Linrock, become known as such.

One night Vey had been badly beaten in some back room of a saloon and carried out into a vacant lot and left there. He lay there all that night and all the next day. Probably he would have died there had not Steele happened along.

The Ranger gathered up the crippled rustler, took him home, attended to his wounds, nursed him, and in fact spent days in the little adobe house with him.

During this time I saw Steele twice, at night out in our rendezvous. He had little to communicate, but was eager to hear when I had seen Jim Hoden, Morton, Wright, Sampson, and all I could tell about them, and the significance of things in town.

Andy Vey recovered, and it was my good fortune to be in the Hope So when he came in and addressed a crowd of gamesters there.

"Fellers," he said, "I'm biddin' good-by to them as was once my friends. I'm leavin' Linrock. An' I'm askin' some of you to take thet good-by an' a partin' word to them as did me dirt.

"I ain't a-goin' to say if I'd crossed the trail of this Ranger years ago thet I'd of turned round an' gone straight. But mebbe I would—mebbe. There's a hell of a lot a man doesn't know till too late. I'm old now, ready fer the bone pile, an' it doesn't matter. But I've got a head on me yet, an' I want to give a hunch to thet gang who done me. An' that hunch wants to go around an' up to the big guns of Pecos.

"This Texas Star Ranger was the feller who took me in. I'd of died like a poisoned coyote but fer him. An' he talked to me. He gave me money to git out of Pecos. Mebbe everybody'll think he helped me because he wanted me to squeal. To squeal who's who round these rustler diggin's. Wal, he never asked me. Mebbe he seen I wasn't a squealer. But I'm thinkin' he wouldn't ask a feller thet nohow.

"An' here's my hunch. Steele has spotted the outfit. Thet ain't so much, mebbe. But I've been with him, an' I'm old figgerin' men. Jest as sure as God made little apples he's a goin' to put thet outfit through—or he's a-goin' to kill them!"

Chapter 6

ENTER JACK BLOME

Strange that the narrating of this incident made Diane Sampson unhappy.

When I told her she exhibited one flash of gladness, such as any woman might have shown for a noble deed and then she became thoughtful, almost gloomy, sad. I could not understand her complex emotions. Perhaps she contrasted Steele with her father; perhaps she wanted to believe in Steele and dared not; perhaps she had all at once seen the Ranger in his true light, and to her undoing.

She bade me take Sally for a ride and sought her room. I had my misgivings when I saw Sally come out in that trim cowgirl suit and look at me as if to say this day would be my Waterloo.

But she rode hard and long ahead of me before she put any machinations into effect. The first one found me with a respectful demeanor but an internal conflict.

"Russ, tighten my cinch," she said when I caught up with her.

Dismounting, I drew the cinch up another hole and fastened it.

"My boot's unlaced, too," she added, slipping a shapely foot out of the stirrup.

To be sure, it was very much unlaced. I had to take off my gloves to lace it up, and I did it heroically, with bent head and outward calm, when all the time I was mad to snatch the girl out of the saddle and hold her tight or run off with her or do some other fool thing.

"Russ, I believe Diane's in love with Steele," she said soberly, with the sweet confidence she sometimes manifested in me.

"Small wonder. It's in the air," I replied.

She regarded me doubtfully.

"It was," she retorted demurely.

"The fickleness of women is no new thing to me. I didn't expect Waters to last long."

"Certainly not when there are nicer fellows around. One, anyway, when he cares."

A little brown hand slid out of its glove and dropped to my shoulder.

"Make up. You've been hateful lately. Make up with me."

It was not so much what she said as the sweet tone of her voice and the nearness of her that made a tumult within me. I felt the blood tingle to my face.

"Why should I make up with you?" I queried in self defense. "You are only flirting. You won't—you can't ever be anything to me, really."

Sally bent over me and I had not the nerve to look up.

"Never mind things—really," she replied. "The future's far off. Let it alone. We're together. I—I like you, Russ. And I've got to be—to be loved. There. I never confessed that to any other man. You've been hateful when we might have had such fun. The rides in the sun, in the open with the wind in our faces. The walks at night in the moonlight. Russ, haven't you missed something?"

The sweetness and seductiveness of her, the little luring devil of her, irresistible as they were, were no more irresistible than the naturalness, the truth of her.

I trembled even before I looked up into her flushed face and arch eyes; and after that I knew if I could not frighten her out of this daring mood I would have to yield despite my conviction that she only trifled. As my manhood, as well as duty to Steele, forced me to be unyielding, all that was left seemed to be to frighten her.

The instant this was decided a wave of emotion—love, regret, bitterness, anger—surged over me, making me shake. I felt the skin on my face tighten and chill. I grasped her with strength that might have need to hold a plunging, unruly horse. I hurt her. I held her as in a vise.

And the action, the feel of her, her suddenly uttered cry wrought against all pretense, hurt me as my brutality hurt her, and then I spoke what was hard, passionate truth.

"Girl, you're playing with fire!" I cried out hoarsely. "I love you—love you as I'd want my sister loved. I asked you to marry me. That was proof, if it was foolish. Even if you were on the square, which you're not, we couldn't ever be anything to each other. Understand? There's a reason, besides your being above me. I can't stand it. Stop playing with me or I'll—I'll..."

Whatever I meant to say was not spoken, for Sally turned deathly white, probably from my grasp and my looks as well as my threat.

I let go of her, and stepping back to my horse choked down my emotion.

"Russ!" she faltered, and there was womanliness and regret trembling with the fear in her voice. "I—I am on the square."

That had touched the real heart of the girl.

"If you are, then play the game square," I replied darkly.

"I will, Russ, I promise. I'll never tease or coax you again. If I do, then I'll deserve what you—what I get. But, Russ, don't think me a—a four-flush."

All the long ride home we did not exchange another word. The traveling gait of Sally's horse was a lope, that of mine a trot; and therefore, to my relief, she was always out in front.

As we neared the ranch, however, Sally slowed down until I caught up with her; and side by side we rode the remainder of the way. At the corrals, while I unsaddled, she lingered.

"Russ, you didn't tell me if you agreed with me about Diane," she said finally.

"Maybe you're right. I hope she's fallen in love with Steele. Lord knows I hope so," I blurted out.

I bit my tongue. There was no use in trying to be as shrewd with women as I was with men. I made no reply.

"Misery loves company. Maybe that's why," she added. "You told me Steele lost his head over Diane at first sight. Well, we all have company. Good night, Russ."

That night I told Steele about the singular effect the story of his treatment of Vey had upon Miss Sampson. He could not conceal his feelings. I read him like an open book.

If she was unhappy because he did something really good, then she was unhappy because she was realizing she had wronged him.

Steele never asked questions, but the hungry look in his eyes was enough to make even a truthful fellow exaggerate things.

I told him how Diane was dressed, how her face changed with each emotion, how her eyes burned and softened and shadowed, how her voice had been deep and full when she admitted her father hated him, how much she must have meant when she said she was between two fires. I divined how he felt and I tried to satisfy in some little measure his craving for news of her.

When I had exhausted my fund and stretched my imagination I was rewarded by being told that I was a regular old woman for gossip.

Much taken back by this remarkable statement I could but gape at my comrade. Irritation had followed shortly upon his curiosity and pleasure, and then the old sane mind reasserted itself, the old stern look, a little sad now, replaced the glow, the strange eagerness of youth on his face.

"Son, I beg your pardon," he said, with his hand on my shoulder. "We're Rangers, but we can't help being human. To speak right out, it seems two sweet and lovable girls have come, unfortunately for us all, across the dark trail we're on. Let us find what solace we can in the hope that somehow, God only knows how, in doing our duty as Rangers we may yet be doing right by these two innocent girls. I ask you, as my friend, please do not speak again to me of—Miss Sampson."

I left him and went up the quiet trail with the thick shadows all around me and the cold stars overhead; and I was sober in thought, sick at heart for him as much as for myself, and I tortured my mind in fruitless conjecture as to what the end of this strange and fateful adventure would be.

I discovered that less and less the old wild spirit abided with me and I become conscious of a dull, deep-seated ache in my breast, a pang in the bone.

From that day there was a change in Diane Sampson. She became feverishly active. She wanted to ride, to see for herself what was going on in Linrock, to learn of that wild Pecos county life at first hand.

She made such demands on my time now that I scarcely ever found an hour to be with or near Steele until after dark. However, as he was playing a waiting game on the rustlers, keeping out of the resorts for the present, I had not great cause for worry. Hoden was slowly gathering men together, a band of trustworthy ones, and until this organization was complete and ready, Steele thought better to go slow.

It was of little use for me to remonstrate with Miss Sampson when she refused to obey a distracted and angry father. I began to feel sorry for Sampson. He was an unscrupulous man, but he loved this daughter who belonged to another and better and past side of his life.

I heard him appeal to her to go back to Louisiana; to let him take her home, giving as urgent reason the probability of trouble for him. She could not help, could only handicap him.

She agreed to go, provided he sold his property, took the best of his horses and went with her back to the old home to live there the rest of their lives. He replied with considerable feeling that he wished he could go, but it was impossible. Then that settled the matter for her, she averred.

Failing to persuade her to leave Linrock, he told her to keep to the ranch. Naturally, in spite of his anger, Miss Sampson refused to obey; and she frankly told him that it was the free, unfettered life of the country, the riding here and there that appealed so much to her.

Sampson came to me a little later and his worn face showed traces of internal storm.

"Russ, for a while there I wanted to get rid of you," he said. "I've changed. Diane always was a spoiled kid. Now she's a woman. Something's fired her blood. Maybe it's this damned wild country. Anyway, she's got the bit between her teeth. She'll run till she's run herself out.

"Now, it seems the safety of Diane, and Sally, too, has fallen into your hands. The girls won't have one of my cowboys near them. Lately they've got shy of George, too. Between you and me I want to tell you that conditions here in Pecos are worse than they've seemed since you-all reached the ranch. But bad work will break out again—it's coming soon.

"I can't stop it. The town will be full of the hardest gang in western Texas. My daughter and Sally would not be safe if left alone to go anywhere. With you, perhaps, they'll be safe. Can I rely on you?"

"Yes, Sampson, you sure can," I replied. "I'm on pretty good terms with most everybody in town. I think I can say none of the tough set who hang out down there would ever made any move while I'm with the girls. But I'll be pretty careful to avoid them, and particularly strange fellows who may come riding in.

"And if any of them do meet us and start trouble, I'm going for my gun, that's all. There won't be any talk."

"Good! I'll back you," Sampson replied. "Understand, Russ, I didn't want you here, but I always had you sized up as a pretty hard nut, a man not to be trifled with. You've got a bad name. Diane insists the name's not deserved. She'd trust you with herself under any circumstances. And the kid, Sally, she'd be fond of you if it wasn't for the drink. Have you been drunk a good deal? Straight now, between you and me."

"Not once," I replied.

"George's a liar then. He's had it in for you since that day at Sanderson. Look out you two don't clash. He's got a temper, and when he's drinking he's a devil. Keep out of his way."

"I've stood a good deal from Wright, and guess I can stand more."

"All right, Russ," he continued, as if relieved. "Chuck the drink and cards for a while and keep an eye on the girls. When my affairs straighten out maybe I'll make you a proposition."

Sampson left me material for thought. Perhaps it was not only the presence of a Ranger in town that gave him concern, nor the wilfulness of his daughter. There must be internal strife in the rustler gang with which we had associated him.

Perhaps a menace of publicity, rather than risk, was the cause of the wearing strain on him. I began to get a closer insight into Sampson, and in the absence of any conclusive evidence of his personal baseness I felt pity for him.

In the beginning he had opposed me just because I did not happen to be a cowboy he had selected. This latest interview with me, amounting in some instances to confidence, proved absolutely that he had not the slightest suspicion that I was otherwise than the cowboy I pretended to be.

Another interesting deduction was that he appeared to be out of patience with Wright. In fact, I imagined I sensed something of fear and distrust in this spoken attitude toward his relative. Not improbably here was the internal strife between Sampson and Wright, and there flashed into my mind, absolutely without reason, an idea that the clash was over Diane Sampson.

I scouted this intuitive idea as absurd; but, just the same, it refused to be dismissed.

As I turned my back on the coarse and exciting life in the saloons and gambling hells, and spent all my time except when sleeping, out in the windy open under blue sky and starry heaven, my spirit had an uplift.

I was glad to be free of that job. It was bad enough to have to go into these dens to arrest men, let alone living with them, almost being one.

Diane Sampson noted a change in me, attributed it to the absence of the influence of drink, and she was glad. Sally made no attempt to conceal her happiness; and to my dismay, she utterly failed to keep her promise not to tease or tempt me further.

She was adorable, distracting.

We rode every day and almost all day. We took our dinner and went clear to the foothills to return as the sun set. We visited outlying ranches, water-holes, old adobe houses famous in one way or another as scenes of past fights of rustlers and ranchers.

We rode to the little village of Sampson, and half-way to Sanderson, and all over the country.

There was no satisfying Miss Sampson with rides, new places, new faces, new adventures. And every time we rode out she insisted on first riding through Linrock; and every time we rode home she insisted on going back that way.

We visited all the stores, the blacksmith, the wagon shop, the feed and grain houses— everywhere that she could find excuse for visiting. I had to point out to her all the infamous dens in town, and all the lawless and lounging men we met.

She insisted upon being shown the inside of the Hope So, to the extreme confusion of that bewildered resort.

I pretended to be blind to this restless curiosity. Sally understood the cause, too, and it divided her between a sweet gravity and a naughty humor.

The last, however, she never evinced in sight or hearing of Diane.

It seemed that we were indeed fated to cross the path of Vaughn Steele. We saw him working round his adobe house; then we saw him on horseback. Once we met him face to face in a store.

He gazed steadily into Diane Sampson's eyes and went his way without any sign of recognition. There was red in her face when he passed and white when he had gone.

That day she rode as I had never seen her, risking her life, unmindful of her horse.

Another day we met Steele down in the valley, where, inquiry discovered to us, he had gone to the home of an old cattleman who lived alone and was ill.

Last and perhaps most significant of all these meetings was the one when we were walking tired horses home through the main street of Linrock and came upon Steele just in time to see him in action.

It happened at a corner where the usual slouchy, shirt-sleeved loungers were congregated. They were in high glee over the predicament of one ruffian who had purchased or been given a poor, emaciated little burro that was on its last legs. The burro evidently did not want to go with its new owner, who pulled on a halter and then viciously swung the end of the rope to make welts on the worn and scarred back.

If there was one thing that Diane Sampson could not bear it was to see an animal in pain. She passionately loved horses, and hated the sight of a spur or whip.

When we saw the man beating the little burro she cried out to me:

"Make the brute stop!"

I might have made a move had I not on the instant seen Steele heaving into sight round the corner.

Just then the fellow, whom I now recognized to be a despicable character named Andrews, began to bestow heavy and brutal kicks upon the body of the little burro. These kicks sounded deep, hollow, almost like the boom of a drum.

The burro uttered the strangest sound I ever heard issue from any beast and it dropped in its tracks with jerking legs that told any horseman what had happened. Steele saw the last swings of

Andrews' heavy boot. He yelled. It was a sharp yell that would have made anyone start. But it came too late, for the burro had dropped.

Steele knocked over several of the jeering men to get to Andrews. He kicked the fellow's feet from under him, sending him hard to the ground.

Then Steele picked up the end of the halter and began to swing it powerfully. Resounding smacks mingled with hoarse bellows of fury and pain. Andrews flopped here and there, trying to arise, but every time the heavy knotted halter beat him down.

Presently Steele stopped. Andrews rose right in front of the Ranger, and there, like the madman he was, he went for his gun.

But it scarcely leaped from its holster when Steele's swift hand intercepted it. Steele clutched Andrews' arm.

Then came a wrench, a cracking of bones, a scream of agony.

The gun dropped into the dust; and in a moment of wrestling fury Andrews, broken, beaten down, just able to moan, lay beside it.

Steele, so cool and dark for a man who had acted with such passionate swiftness, faced the others as if to dare them to move. They neither moved nor spoke, and then he strode away.

Miss Sampson did not speak a word while we were riding the rest of the way home, but she was strangely white of face and dark of eye. Sally could not speak fast enough to say all she felt.

And I, of course, had my measure of feelings. One of them was that as sure as the sun rose and set it was written that Diane Sampson was to love Vaughn Steele.

I could not read her mind, but I had a mind of my own.

How could any woman, seeing this maligned and menaced Ranger, whose life was in danger every moment he spent on the streets, in the light of his action on behalf of a poor little beast, help but wonder and brood over the magnificent height he might reach if he had love—passion—a woman for his inspiration?

It was the day after this incident that, as Sally, Diane, and I were riding homeward on the road from Sampson, I caught sight of a group of dark horses and riders swiftly catching up with us.

We were on the main road, in plain sight of town and passing by ranches; nevertheless, I did not like the looks of the horsemen and grew uneasy. Still, I scarcely thought it needful to race our horses just to reach town a little ahead of these strangers.

Accordingly, they soon caught up with us.

They were five in number, all dark-faced except one, dark-clad and superbly mounted on dark bays and blacks. They had no pack animals and, for that matter, carried no packs at all.

Four of them, at a swinging canter, passed us, and the fifth pulled his horse to suit our pace and fell in between Sally and me.

"Good day," he said pleasantly to me. "Don't mind my ridin' in with you-all, I hope?"

Considering his pleasant approach, I could not but be civil.

He was a singularly handsome fellow, at a quick glance, under forty years, with curly, blond hair, almost gold, a skin very fair for that country, and the keenest, clearest, boldest blue eyes I had ever seen in a man.

"You're Russ, I reckon," he said. "Some of my men have seen you ridin' round with Sampson's girls. I'm Jack Blome."

He did not speak that name with any flaunt or flourish. He merely stated it.

Blome, the rustler! I grew tight all over.

Still, manifestly there was nothing for me to do but return his pleasantry. I really felt less uneasiness after he had made himself known to me. And without any awkwardness, I introduced him to the girls.

He took off his sombrero and made gallant bows to both.

Miss Sampson had heard of him and his record, and she could not help a paleness, a shrinking, which, however, he did not appear to notice. Sally had been dying to meet a real rustler, and here he was, a very prince of rascals.

But I gathered that she would require a little time before she could be natural. Blome seemed to have more of an eye for Sally than for Diane. "Do you like Pecos?" he asked Sally.

"Out here? Oh, yes, indeed!" she replied.

"Like ridin'?"

"I love horses."

Like almost every man who made Sally's acquaintance, he hit upon the subject best calculated to make her interesting to free-riding, outdoor Western men.

That he loved a thoroughbred horse himself was plain. He spoke naturally to Sally with interest, just as I had upon first meeting her, and he might not have been Jack Blome, for all the indication he gave of the fact in his talk.

But the look of the man was different. He was a desperado, one of the dashing, reckless kind—more famous along the Pecos and Rio Grande than more really desperate men. His attire proclaimed a vanity seldom seen in any Westerner except of that unusual brand, yet it was neither gaudy or showy.

One had to be close to Blome to see the silk, the velvet, the gold, the fine leather. When I envied a man's spurs then they were indeed worth coveting.

Blome had a short rifle and a gun in saddle-sheaths. My sharp eye, running over him, caught a row of notches on the bone handle of the big Colt he packed.

It was then that the marshal, the Ranger in me, went hot under the collar. The custom that desperadoes and gun-fighters had of cutting a notch on their guns for every man killed was one of which the mere mention made my gorge rise.

At the edge of town Blome doffed his sombrero again, said "*Adios*," and rode on ahead of us. And it was then I was hard put to it to keep track of the queries, exclamations, and other wild talk of two very much excited young ladies. I wanted to think; I *needed* to think.

"Wasn't he lovely? Oh, I could adore him!" rapturously uttered Miss Sally Langdon several times, to my ultimate disgust.

Also, after Blome had ridden out of sight, Miss Sampson lost the evident effect of his sinister presence, and she joined Miss Langdon in paying the rustler compliments, too. Perhaps my irritation was an indication of the quick and subtle shifting of my mind to harsher thought.

"Jack Blome!" I broke in upon their adulations. "Rustler and gunman. Did you see the notches on his gun? Every notch for a man he's killed! For weeks reports have come to Linrock that soon as he could get round to it he'd ride down and rid the community of that bothersome fellow, that Texas Ranger! He's come to kill Vaughn Steele!"

Chapter 7

DIANE AND VAUGHN

Then as gloom descended on me with my uttered thought, my heart smote me at Sally's broken: "Oh, Russ! No! No!" Diane Sampson bent dark, shocked eyes upon the hill and ranch in front of her; but they were sightless, they looked into space and eternity, and in them I read the truth suddenly and cruelly revealed to her—she loved Steele!

I found it impossible to leave Miss Sampson with the impression I had given. My own mood fitted a kind of ruthless pleasure in seeing her suffer through love as I had intimation I was to suffer.

But now, when my strange desire that she should love Steele had its fulfilment, and my fiendish subtleties to that end had been crowned with success, I was confounded in pity and the enormity of my crime. For it had been a crime to make, or help to make, this noble and beautiful woman love a Ranger, the enemy of her father, and surely the author of her coming misery. I felt shocked at my work. I tried to hang an excuse on my old motive that through her love we might all be saved. When it was too late, however, I found that this motive was wrong and perhaps without warrant.

We rode home in silence. Miss Sampson, contrary to her usual custom of riding to the corrals or the porch, dismounted at a path leading in among the trees and flowers. "I want to rest, to think before I go in," she said.

Sally accompanied me to the corrals. As our horses stopped at the gate I turned to find confirmation of my fears in Sally's wet eyes.

"Russ," she said, "it's worse than we thought."

"Worse? I should say so," I replied.

"It'll about kill her. She never cared that way for any man. When the Sampson women love, they love."

"Well, you're lucky to be a Langdon," I retorted bitterly.

"I'm Sampson enough to be unhappy," she flashed back at me, "and I'm Langdon enough to have some sense. You haven't any sense or kindness, either. Why'd you want to blurt out that Jack Blome was here to kill Steele?"

"I'm ashamed, Sally," I returned, with hanging head. "I've been a brute. I've wanted her to love Steele. I thought I had a reason, but now it seems silly. Just now I wanted to see how much she did care.

"Sally, the other day you said misery loved company. That's the trouble. I'm sore—bitter. I'm like a sick coyote that snaps at everything. I've wanted you to go into the very depths of despair. But I couldn't send you. So I took out my spite on poor Miss Sampson. It was a damn unmanly thing for me to do."

"Oh, it's not so bad as all that. But you might have been less abrupt. Russ, you seem to take an—an awful tragic view of your—your own case."

"Tragic? Hah!" I cried like the villain in the play. "What other way could I look at it? I tell you I love you so I can't sleep or do anything."

"That's not tragic. When you've no chance, *then* that's tragic."

Sally, as swiftly as she had blushed, could change into that deadly sweet mood. She did both now. She seemed warm, softened, agitated. How could this be anything but sincere? I felt myself slipping; so I laughed harshly.

"Chance! I've no chance on earth."

"Try!" she whispered.

But I caught myself in time. Then the shock of bitter renunciation made it easy for me to simulate anger.

"You promised not to—not to—" I began, choking. My voice was hoarse and it broke, matters surely far removed from pretense.

I had seen Sally Langdon in varying degrees of emotion, but never as she appeared now. She was pale and she trembled a little. If it was not fright, then I could not tell what it was. But there were contrition and earnestness about her, too.

"Russ, I know. I promised not to—to tease—to tempt you anymore," she faltered. "I've broken it. I'm ashamed. I haven't played the game square. But I couldn't—I can't help myself. I've got sense enough not to engage myself to you, but I can't keep from loving you. I can't let you alone. There—if you want it on the square! What's more, I'll go on as I have done unless you keep away from me. I don't care what I deserve—what you do—I will—I will!"

She had begun falteringly and she ended passionately.

Somehow I kept my head, even though my heart pounded like a hammer and the blood drummed in my ears. It was the thought of Steele that saved me. But I felt cold at the narrow margin. I had reached a point, I feared, where a kiss, one touch from this bewildering creature of fire and change and sweetness would make me put her before Steele and my duty.

"Sally, if you dare break your promise again, you'll wish you never had been born," I said with all the fierceness at my command.

"I wish that now. And you can't bluff me, Mr. Gambler. I may have no hand to play, but you can't make me lay it down," she replied.

Something told me Sally Langdon was finding herself; that presently I could not frighten her, and then—then I would be doomed.

"Why, if I got drunk, I might do anything," I said cool and hard now. "Cut off your beautiful chestnut hair for bracelets for my arms."

Sally laughed, but she was still white. She was indeed finding herself. "If you ever get drunk again you can't kiss me any more. And if you don't—you can."

I felt myself shake and, with all of the iron will I could assert, I hid from her the sweetness of this thing that was my weakness and her strength.

"I might lasso you from my horse, drag you through the cactus," I added with the implacability of an Apache.

"Russ!" she cried. Something in this last ridiculous threat had found a vital mark. "After all, maybe those awful stories Joe Harper told about you were true."

"They sure were," I declared with great relief. "And now to forget ourselves. I'm more than sorry I distressed Miss Sampson; more than sorry because what I said wasn't on the square. Blome, no doubt, has come to Linrock after Steele. His intention is to kill him. I said that—let

Miss Sampson think it all meant fatality to the Ranger. But, Sally, I don't believe that Blome can kill Steele any more than—than you can."

"Why?" she asked; and she seemed eager, glad.

"Because he's not man enough. That's all, without details. You need not worry; and I wish you'd go tell Miss Sampson—"

"Go yourself," interrupted Sally. "I think she's afraid of my eyes. But she won't fear you'd guess her secret.

"Go to her, Russ. Find some excuse to tell her. Say you thought it over, believed she'd be distressed about what might never happen. Go—and afterward pray for your sins, you queer, good-natured, love-meddling cowboy-devil, you!"

For once I had no retort ready for Sally. I hurried off as quickly as I could walk in chaps and spurs.

I found Miss Sampson sitting on a bench in the shade of a tree. Her pallor and quiet composure told of the conquering and passing of the storm. Always she had a smile for me, and now it smote me, for I in a sense, had betrayed her.

"Miss Sampson," I began, awkwardly yet swiftly, "I—I got to thinking it over, and the idea struck me, maybe you felt bad about this gun-fighter Blome coming down here to kill Steele. At first I imagined you felt sick just because there might be blood spilled. Then I thought you've showed interest in Steele—naturally his kind of Ranger work is bound to appeal to women—you might be sorry it couldn't go on, you might care."

"Russ, don't beat about the bush," she said interrupting my floundering. "You know I care."

How wonderful her eyes were then—great dark, sad gulfs with the soul of a woman at the bottom! Almost I loved her myself; I did love her truth, the woman in her that scorned any subterfuge.

Instantly she inspired me to command over myself. "Listen," I said. "Jack Blome has come here to meet Steele. There will be a fight. But Blome can't kill Steele."

"How is that? Why can't he? You said this Blome was a killer of men. You spoke of notches on his gun. I've heard my father and my cousin, too, speak of Blome's record. He must be a terrible ruffian. If his intent is evil, why will he fail in it?"

"Because, Miss Sampson, when it comes to the last word, Steele will be on the lookout and Blome won't be quick enough on the draw to kill him. That's all."

"Quick enough on the draw? I understand, but I want to know more."

"I doubt if there's a man on the frontier to-day quick enough to kill Steele in an even break. That means a fair fight. This Blome is conceited. He'll make the meeting fair enough. It'll come off about like this, Miss Sampson.

"Blome will send out his bluff—he'll begin to blow—to look for Steele. But Steele will avoid him as long as possible—perhaps altogether, though that's improbable. If they do meet, then Blome must force the issue. It's interesting to figure on that. Steele affects men strangely. It's all very well for this Blome to rant about himself and to hunt Steele up. But the test'll come when he faces the Ranger. He never saw Steele. He doesn't know what he's up against. He knows Steele's reputation, but I don't mean that. I mean Steele in the flesh, his nerve, the something that's in his eyes.

"Now, when it comes to handling a gun the man doesn't breathe who has anything on Steele. There was an outlaw, Duane, who might have killed Steele, had they ever met. I'll tell you Duane's story some day. A girl saved him, made a Ranger of him, then got him to go far away from Texas."

"That was wise. Indeed, I'd like to hear the story," she replied. "Then, after all, Russ, in this dreadful part of Texas life, when man faces man, it's all in the quickness of hand?"

"Absolutely. It's the draw. And Steele's a wonder. See here. Look at this."

I stepped back and drew my gun.

"I didn't see how you did that," she said curiously. "Try it again."

I complied, and still she was not quick enough of eye to see my draw. Then I did it slowly, explaining to her the action of hand and then of finger. She seemed fascinated, as a woman might have been by the striking power of a rattlesnake.

"So men's lives depend on that! How horrible for me to be interested—to ask about it—to watch you! But I'm out here on the frontier now, caught somehow in its wildness, and I feel a relief, a gladness to know Vaughn Steele has the skill you claim. Thank you, Russ."

She seemed about to dismiss me then, for she rose and half turned away. Then she hesitated. She had one hand at her breast, the other on the bench. "Have you been with him—talked to him lately?" she asked, and a faint rose tint came into her cheeks. But her eyes were steady, dark, and deep, and peered through and far beyond me.

"Yes, I've met him a few times, around places."

"Did he ever speak of—of me?"

"Once or twice, and then as if he couldn't help it."

"What did he say?"

"Well, the last time he seemed hungry to hear something about you. He didn't exactly ask, but, all the same, he was begging. So I told him."

"What?"

"Oh, how you were dressed, how you looked, what you said, what you did—all about you. Don't be offended with me, Miss Sampson. It was real charity. I talk too much. It's my weakness. Please don't be offended."

She never heard my apology or my entreaty. There was a kind of glory in her eyes. Looking at her, I found a dimness hazing my sight, and when I rubbed it away it came back.

"Then—what did he say?" This was whispered, almost shyly, and I could scarcely believe the proud Miss Sampson stood before me.

"Why, he flew into a fury, called me an—" Hastily I caught myself. "Well, he said if I wanted to talk to him any more not to speak of you. He was sure unreasonable."

"Russ—you think—you told me once—he—you think he still—" She was not facing me at all now. She had her head bent. Both hands were at her breast, and I saw it heave. Her cheek was white as a flower, her neck darkly, richly red with mounting blood.

I understood. And I pitied her and hated myself and marveled at this thing, love. It made another woman out of Diane Sampson. I could scarcely comprehend that she was asking me, almost beseechingly, for further assurance of Steele's love. I knew nothing of women, but this seemed strange. Then a thought sent the blood chilling back to my heart. Had Diane Sampson guessed the guilt of her father? Was it more for his sake than for her own that she hoped—for surely she hoped—that Steele loved her?

Here was more mystery, more food for reflection. Only a powerful motive or a self-leveling love could have made a woman of Diane Sampson's pride ask such a question. Whatever her reason, I determined to assure her, once and forever, what I knew to be true. Accordingly, I told her in unforgettable words, with my own regard for her and love for Sally filling my voice with emotion, how I could see that Steele loved her, how madly he was destined to love her, how terribly hard that was going to make his work in Linrock.

There was a stillness about her then, a light on her face, which brought to my mind thought of Sally when I had asked her to marry me.

"Russ, I beg you—bring us together," said Miss Sampson. "Bring about a meeting. You are my friend." Then she went swiftly away through the flowers, leaving me there, thrilled to my soul at her betrayal of herself, ready to die in her service, yet cursing the fatal day Vaughn Steele had chosen me for his comrade in this tragic game.

That evening in the girls' sitting-room, where they invited me, I was led into a discourse upon the gun-fighters, outlaws, desperadoes, and bad men of the frontier. Miss Sampson and Sally had been, before their arrival in Texas, as ignorant of such characters as any girls in the North or East. They were now peculiarly interested, fascinated, and at the same time repelled.

Miss Sampson must have placed the Rangers in one of those classes, somewhat as Governor Smith had, and her father, too. Sally thought she was in love with a cowboy whom she had been led to believe had as bad a record as any. They were certainly a most persuasive and appreciative audience. So as it was in regard to horses, if I knew any subject well, it was this one of dangerous and bad men. Texas, and the whole developing Southwest, was full of such characters. It was a very difficult thing to distinguish between fighters who were bad men and fighters who were good men. However, it was no difficult thing for one of my calling to tell the difference between a real bad man and the imitation "four-flush."

Then I told the girls the story of Buck Duane, famous outlaw and Ranger. And I narrated the histories of Murrell, most terrible of blood-spillers ever known to Texas; of Hardin, whose long career of crime ended in the main street in Huntsville when he faced Buck Duane; of Sandobal, the Mexican terror; of Cheseldine, Bland, Alloway, and other outlaws of the Rio Grande; of King Fisher and Thompson and Sterrett, all still living and still busy adding notches to their guns.

I ended my little talk by telling the story of Amos Clark, a criminal of a higher type than most bad men, yet infinitely more dangerous because of that. He was a Southerner of good family. After the war he went to Dimmick County and there developed and prospered with the country. He became the most influential citizen of his town and the richest in that section. He held offices. He was energetic in his opposition to rustlers and outlaws. He was held in high esteem by his countrymen. But this Amos Clark was the leader of a band of rustlers, highwaymen, and murderers.

Captain Neal and some of his Rangers ferreted out Clark's relation to this lawless gang, and in the end caught him red-handed. He was arrested and eventually hanged. His case was unusual, and it furnished an example of what was possible in that wild country. Clark had a son who was honest and a wife whom he dearly loved, both of whom had been utterly ignorant of the other and wicked side of life. I told this last story deliberately, yet with some misgivings. I wanted to see—I convinced myself it was needful for me to see—if Miss Sampson had any suspicion of her father. To look into her face then was no easy task. But when I did I experienced a shock, though not exactly the kind I had prepared myself for.

She knew something; maybe she knew actually more than Steele or I; still, if it were a crime, she had a marvelous control over her true feelings.

Jack Blome and his men had been in Linrock for several days; old Snecker and his son Bo had reappeared, and other hard-looking customers, new to me if not to Linrock. These helped to create a charged and waiting atmosphere. The saloons did unusual business and were never closed. Respectable citizens of the town were awakened in the early dawn by rowdies carousing in the streets.

Steele kept pretty closely under cover. He did not entertain the opinion, nor did I, that the first time he walked down the street he would be a target for Blome and his gang. Things seldom happened that way, and when they did happen so it was more accident than design. Blome was setting the stage for his little drama.

Meanwhile Steele was not idle. He told me he had met Jim Hoden, Morton and Zimmer, and that these men had approached others of like character; a secret club had been formed and all the members were ready for action. Steele also told me that he had spent hours at night watching the house where George Wright stayed when he was not up at Sampson's. Wright had almost recovered from the injury to his arm, but he still remained most of the time indoors. At night he was visited, or at least his house was, by strange men who were swift, stealthy, mysterious—all men who formerly would not have been friends or neighbors.

Steele had not been able to recognize any of these night visitors, and he did not think the time was ripe for a bold holding up of one of them.

Jim Hoden had forcibly declared and stated that some deviltry was afoot, something vastly different from Blome's open intention of meeting the Ranger.

Hoden was right. Not twenty-four hours after his last talk with Steele, in which he advised quick action, he was found behind the little room of his restaurant, with a bullet hole in his breast, dead. No one could be found who had heard a shot.

It had been deliberate murder, for behind the bar had been left a piece of paper rudely scrawled with a pencil:

"All friends of Ranger Steele look for the same."

Later that day I met Steele at Hoden's and was with him when he looked at the body and the written message which spoke so tersely of the enmity toward him. We left there together, and I hoped Steele would let me stay with him from that moment.

"Russ, it's all in the dark," he said. "I feel Wright's hand in this."

I agreed. "I remember his face at Hoden's that day you winged him. Because Jim swore you were wrong not to kill instead of wing him. You were wrong."

"No, Russ, I never let feeling run wild with my head. We can't prove a thing on Wright."

"Come on; let's hunt him up. I'll bet I can accuse him and make him show his hand. Come on!"

That Steele found me hard to resist was all the satisfaction I got for the anger and desire to avenge Jim Hoden that consumed me.

"Son, you'll have your belly full of trouble soon enough," replied Steele. "Hold yourself in. Wait. Try to keep your eye on Sampson at night. See if anyone visits him. Spy on him. I'll watch Wright."

"Don't you think you'd do well to keep out of town, especially when you sleep?"

"Sure. I've got blankets out in the brush, and I go there every night late and leave before daylight. But I keep a light burning in the 'dobe house and make it look as if I were there."

"Good. That worried me. Now, what's this murder of Jim Hoden going to do to Morton, Zimmer, and their crowd?"

"Russ, they've all got blood in their eyes. This'll make them see red. I've only to say the word and we'll have all the backing we need."

"Have you run into Blome?"

"Once. I was across the street. He came out of the Hope So with some of his gang. They lined up and watched me. But I went right on."

"He's here looking for trouble, Steele."

"Yes; and he'd have found it before this if I just knew his relation to Sampson and Wright."

"Do you think Blome a dangerous man to meet?"

"Hardly. He's a genuine bad man, but for all that he's not much to be feared. If he were quietly keeping away from trouble, then that'd be different. Blome will probably die in his boots, thinking he's the worst man and the quickest one on the draw in the West."

That was conclusive enough for me. The little shadow of worry that had haunted me in spite of my confidence vanished entirely.

"Russ, for the present help me do something for Jim Hoden's family," went on Steele. "His wife's in bad shape. She's not a strong woman. There are a lot of kids, and you know Jim Hoden was poor. She told me her neighbors would keep shy of her now. They'd be afraid. Oh, it's tough! But we can put Jim away decently and help his family."

Several days after this talk with Steele I took Miss Sampson and Sally out to see Jim Hoden's wife and children. I knew Steele would be there that afternoon, but I did not mention this fact to Miss Sampson. We rode down to the little adobe house which belonged to Mrs. Hoden's people, and where Steele and I had moved her and the children after Jim Hoden's funeral. The house was small, but comfortable, and the yard green and shady.

If this poor wife and mother had not been utterly forsaken by neighbors and friends it certainly appeared so, for to my knowledge no one besides Steele and me visited her. Miss Sampson had packed a big basket full of good things to eat, and I carried this in front of me on the pommel as we rode. We hitched our horses to the fence and went round to the back of the house. There was a little porch with a stone flooring, and here several children were playing. The door stood open. At my knock Mrs. Hoden bade me come in. Evidently Steele was not there, so I went in with the girls.

"Mrs. Hoden, I've brought Miss Sampson and her cousin to see you," I said cheerfully.

The little room was not very light, there being only one window and the door; but Mrs. Hoden could be seen plainly enough as she lay, hollow-cheeked and haggard, on a bed. Once she had evidently been a woman of some comeliness. The ravages of trouble and grief were there to read in her worn face; it had not, however, any of the hard and bitter lines that had characterized her husband's.

I wondered, considering that Sampson had ruined Hoden, how Mrs. Hoden was going to regard the daughter of an enemy.

"So you're Roger Sampson's girl?" queried the woman, with her bright black eyes fixed on her visitor.

"Yes," replied Miss Sampson, simply. "This is my cousin, Sally Langdon. We've come to nurse you, take care of the children, help you in any way you'll let us."

There was a long silence.

"Well, you look a little like Sampson," finally said Mrs. Hoden, "but you're not at all like him. You must take after your mother. Miss Sampson, I don't know if I can—if I *ought* to accept anything from you. Your father ruined my husband."

"Yes, I know," replied the girl sadly. "That's all the more reason you should let me help you. Pray don't refuse. It will—mean so much to me."

If this poor, stricken woman had any resentment it speedily melted in the warmth and sweetness of Miss Sampson's manner. My idea was that the impression of Diane Sampson's beauty was always swiftly succeeded by that of her generosity and nobility. At any rate, she had started well with Mrs. Hoden, and no sooner had she begun to talk to the children than both they and the mother were won.

The opening of that big basket was an event. Poor, starved little beggars! I went out on the porch to get away from them. My feelings seemed too easily aroused. Hard indeed would it have gone with Jim Hoden's slayer if I could have laid my eyes on him then. However, Miss Sampson and Sally, after the nature of tender and practical girls, did not appear to take the sad situation to heart. The havoc had already been wrought in that household. The needs now were cheerfulness, kindness, help, action, and these the girls furnished with a spirit that did me good.

"Mrs. Hoden, who dressed this baby?" presently asked Miss Sampson. I peeped in to see a dilapidated youngster on her knees. That sight, if any other was needed, completed my full and splendid estimate of Diane Sampson.

"Mr. Steele," replied Mrs. Hoden.

"Mr. Steele!" exclaimed Miss Sampson.

"Yes; he's taken care of us all since—since—" Mrs. Hoden choked.

"Oh, so you've had no help but his," replied Miss Sampson hastily. "No women? Too bad! I'll send someone, Mrs. Hoden, and I'll come myself."

"It'll be good of you," went on the older woman. "You see, Jim had few friends—that is, right in town. And they've been afraid to help us—afraid they'd get what poor Jim—"

"That's awful!" burst out Miss Sampson passionately. "A brave lot of friends! Mrs. Hoden, don't you worry any more. We'll take care of you. Here, Sally help me. Whatever is the matter with baby's dress?" Manifestly Miss Sampson had some difficulty in subduing her emotion.

"Why, it's on hind side before," declared Sally. "I guess Mr. Steele hasn't dressed many babies."

"He did the best he could," said Mrs. Hoden. "Lord only knows what would have become of us! He brought your cowboy, Russ, who's been very good too."

"Mr. Steele, then is—is something more than a Ranger?" queried Miss Sampson, with a little break in her voice.

"He's more than I can tell," replied Mrs. Hoden. "He buried Jim. He paid our debts. He fetched us here. He bought food for us. He cooked for us and fed us. He washed and dressed the baby. He sat with me the first two nights after Jim's death, when I thought I'd die myself.

"He's so kind, so gentle, so patient. He has kept me up just by being near. Sometimes I'd wake from a doze an', seeing him there, I'd know how false were all these tales Jim heard about him and believed at first. Why, he plays with the children just—just like any good man might. When he has the baby up I just can't believe he's a bloody gunman, as they say.

"He's good, but he isn't happy. He has such sad eyes. He looks far off sometimes when the children climb round him. They love him. I think he must have loved some woman. His life is sad. Nobody need tell me—he sees the good in things. Once he said somebody had to be a Ranger. Well, I say, thank God for a Ranger like him!"

After that there was a long silence in the little room, broken only by the cooing of the baby. I did not dare to peep in at Miss Sampson then.

Somehow I expected Steele to arrive at that moment, and his step did not surprise me. He came round the corner as he always turned any corner, quick, alert, with his hand down. If I had been an enemy waiting there with a gun I would have needed to hurry. Steele was instinctively and habitually on the defense.

"Hello, son! How are Mrs. Hoden and the youngster to-day?" he asked.

"Hello yourself! Why, they're doing fine! I brought the girls down—"

Then in the semishadow of the room, across Mrs. Hoden's bed, Diane Sampson and Steele faced each other.

That was a moment! Having seen her face then I would not have missed sight of it for anything I could name; never so long as memory remained with me would I forget. She did not speak. Sally, however, bowed and spoke to the Ranger. Steele, after the first start, showed no unusual feeling. He greeted both girls pleasantly.

"Russ, that was thoughtful of you," he said. "It was womankind needed here. I could do so little—Mrs. Hoden, you look better to-day. I'm glad. And here's baby, all clean and white. Baby, what a time I had trying to puzzle out the way your clothes went on! Well, Mrs. Hoden, didn't I tell you friends would come? So will the brighter side."

"Yes; I've more faith than I had," replied Mrs. Hoden. "Roger Sampson's daughter has come to me. There for a while after Jim's death I thought I'd sink. We have nothing. How could I ever take care of my little ones? But I'm gaining courage."

"Mrs. Hoden, do not distress yourself any more," said Miss Sampson. "I shall see you are well cared for. I promise you."

"Miss Sampson, that's fine!" exclaimed Steele, with a ring in his voice. "It's what I'd have hoped—expected of you..."

It must have been sweet praise to her, for the whiteness of her face burned in a beautiful blush.

"And it's good of you, too, Miss Langdon, to come," added Steele. "Let me thank you both. I'm glad I have you girls as allies in part of my lonely task here. More than glad, for the sake of this good woman and the little ones. But both of you be careful. Don't stir without Russ. There's risk. And now I'll be going. Good-by. Mrs. Hoden, I'll drop in again to-night. Good-by!"

Steele backed to the door, and I slipped out before him.

"Mr. Steele—wait!" called Miss Sampson as he stepped out. He uttered a little sound like a hiss or a gasp or an intake of breath, I did not know what; and then the incomprehensible fellow bestowed a kick upon me that I thought about broke my leg. But I understood and gamely endured the pain. Then we were looking at Diane Sampson. She was white and wonderful. She stepped out of the door, close to Steele. She did not see me; she cared nothing for my presence. All the world would not have mattered to her then.

"I have wronged you!" she said impulsively.

Looking on, I seemed to see or feel some slow, mighty force gathering in Steele to meet this ordeal. Then he appeared as always—yet, to me, how different!

"Miss Sampson, how can you say that?" he returned.

"I believed what my father and George Wright said about you—that bloody, despicable record! Now I do *not* believe. I see—I wronged you."

"You make me very glad when you tell me this. It was hard to have you think so ill of me. But, Miss Sampson, please don't speak of wronging me. I am a Ranger, and much said of me is true. My duty is hard on others—sometimes on those who are innocent, alas! But God knows that duty is hard, too, on me."

"I did wrong you. In thought—in word. I ordered you from my home as if you were indeed what they called you. But I was deceived. I see my error. If you entered my home again I would think it an honor. I—"

"Please—please don't, Miss Sampson," interrupted poor Steele. I could see the gray beneath his bronze and something that was like gold deep in his eyes.

"But, sir, my conscience flays me," she went on. There was no other sound like her voice. If I was all distraught with emotion, what must Steele have been? "I make amends. Will you take my hand? Will you forgive me?" She gave it royally, while the other was there pressing at her breast.

Steele took the proffered hand and held it, and did not release it. What else could he have done? But he could not speak. Then it seemed to dawn upon Steele there was more behind this white, sweet, noble intensity of her than just making amends for a fancied or real wrong. For myself, I thought the man did not live on earth who could have resisted her then. And there was resistance; I felt it; she must have felt it. It was poor Steele's hard fate to fight the charm and eloquence and sweetness of this woman when, for some reason unknown to him, and only guessed at by me, she was burning with all the fire and passion of her soul.

"Mr. Steele, I honor you for your goodness to this unfortunate woman," she said, and now her speech came swiftly. "When she was all alone and helpless you were her friend. It was the deed of a man. But Mrs. Hoden isn't the only unfortunate woman in the world. I, too, am unfortunate. Ah, how I may soon need a friend!

"Vaughn Steele, the man whom I need most to be my friend—want most to lean upon—is the one whose duty is to stab me to the heart, to ruin me. You! Will you be my friend? If you knew Diane Sampson you would know she would never ask you to be false to your duty. Be true to us both! I'm so alone—no one but Sally loves me. I'll need a friend soon—soon.

"Oh, I know—I know what you'll find out sooner or later. I know *now*! I want to help you. Let us save life, if not honor. Must I stand alone—all alone? Will you—will you be—"

Her voice failed. She was swaying toward Steele. I expected to see his arms spread wide and enfold her in their embrace.

"Diane Sampson, I love you!" whispered Steele hoarsely, white now to his lips. "I must be true to my duty. But if I can't be true to you, then by God, I want no more of life!" He kissed her hand and rushed away.

She stood a moment as if blindly watching the place where he had vanished, and then as a sister might have turned to a brother, she reached for me.

Chapter 8

THE EAVESDROPPER

We silently rode home in the gathering dusk. Miss Sampson dismounted at the porch, but Sally went on with me to the corrals. I felt heavy and somber, as if a catastrophe was near at hand.

"Help me down," said Sally. Her voice was low and tremulous.

"Sally, did you hear what Miss Sampson said to Steele?" I asked.

"A little, here and there. I heard Steele tell her he loved her. Isn't this a terrible mix?"

"It sure is. Did you hear—do you understand why she appealed to Steele, asked him to be her friend?"

"Did she? No, I didn't hear that. I heard her say she had wronged him. Then I tried not to hear any more. Tell me."

"No Sally; it's not my secret. I wish I could do something—help them somehow. Yes, it's sure a terrible mix. I don't care so much about myself."

"Nor me," Sally retorted.

"You! Oh, you're only a shallow spoiled child! You'd cease to love anything the moment you won it. And I—well, I'm no good, you say. But their love! My God, what a tragedy! You've no idea, Sally. They've hardly spoken to each other, yet are ready to be overwhelmed."

Sally sat so still and silent that I thought I had angered or offended her. But I did not care much, one way or another. Her coquettish fancy for me and my own trouble had sunk into insignificance. I did not look up at her, though she was so close I could feel her little, restless foot touching me. The horses in the corrals were trooping up to the bars. Dusk had about given place to night, although in the west a broad flare of golden sky showed bright behind dark mountains.

"So I say you're no good?" asked Sally after a long silence. Then her voice and the way her hand stole to my shoulder should have been warning for me. But it was not, or I did not care.

"Yes, you said that, didn't you?" I replied absently.

"I can change my mind, can't I? Maybe you're only wild and reckless when you drink. Mrs. Hoden said such nice things about you. They made me feel so good."

I had no reply for that and still did not look up at her. I heard her swing herself around in the saddle. "Lift me down," she said.

Perhaps at any other time I would have remarked that this request was rather unusual, considering the fact that she was very light and sure of action, extremely proud of it, and likely to be insulted by an offer of assistance. But my spirit was dead. I reached for her hands, but they eluded mine, slipped up my arms as she came sliding out of the saddle, and then her face was very close to mine. "Russ!" she whispered. It was torment, wistfulness, uncertainty, and yet tenderness all in one little whisper. It caught me off guard or indifferent to consequences. So I kissed her, without passion, with all regret and sadness. She uttered a little cry that might have been mingled exultation and remorse for her victory and her broken faith. Certainly the instant I kissed her she remembered the latter. She trembled against me, and leaving unsaid something she had meant to say, she slipped out of my arms and ran. She assuredly was frightened, and I thought it just as well that she was.

Presently she disappeared in the darkness and then the swift little clinks of her spurs ceased. I laughed somewhat ruefully and hoped she would be satisfied. Then I put away the horses and went in for my supper.

After supper I noisily bustled around my room, and soon stole out for my usual evening's spying. The night was dark, without starlight, and the stiff wind rustled the leaves and tore through the vines on the old house. The fact that I had seen and heard so little during my constant vigilance did not make me careless or the task monotonous. I had so much to think about that sometimes I sat in one place for hours and never knew where the time went.

This night, the very first thing, I heard Wright's well-known footsteps, and I saw Sampson's door open, flashing a broad bar of light into the darkness. Wright crossed the threshold, the door closed, and all was dark again outside. Not a ray of light escaped from the window. This was the first visit of Wright for a considerable stretch of time. Little doubt there was that his talk with Sampson would be interesting to me.

I tiptoed to the door and listened, but I could hear only a murmur of voices. Besides, that position was too risky. I went round the corner of the house. Some time before I had made a discovery that I imagined would be valuable to me. This side of the big adobe house was of much older construction than the back and larger part. There was a narrow passage about a foot wide between the old and new walls, and this ran from the outside through to the patio. I had discovered the entrance by accident, as it was concealed by vines and shrubbery. I crawled in there, upon an opportune occasion, with the intention of boring a small hole through the adobe bricks. But it was not necessary to do that, for the wall was cracked; and in one place I could see into Sampson's room. This passage now afforded me my opportunity, and I decided to avail myself of it in spite of the very great danger. Crawling on my hands and knees very stealthily, I got under the shrubbery to the entrance of the passage. In the blackness a faint streak of light showed the location of the crack in the wall.

I had to slip in sidewise. It was a tight squeeze, but I entered without the slightest sound. If my position were to be betrayed it would not be from noise. As I progressed the passage grew a very little wider in that direction, and this fact gave rise to the thought that in case of a necessary and hurried exit I would do best by working toward the patio. It seemed a good deal of time was consumed in reaching my vantage-point. When I did get there the crack was a foot over my head. If I had only been tall like Steele! There was nothing to do but find toe-holes in the crumbling walls, and by bracing knees on one side, back against the other, hold myself up to the crack.

Once with my eye there I did not care what risk I ran. Sampson appeared disturbed; he sat stroking his mustache; his brow was clouded. Wright's face seemed darker, more sullen, yet lighted by some indomitable resolve.

"We'll settle both deals to-night," Wright was saying. "That's what I came for. That's why I've asked Snecker and Blome to be here."

"But suppose I don't choose to talk here?" protested Sampson impatiently. "I never before made my house a place to—"

"We've waited long enough. This place's as good as any. You've lost your nerve since that Ranger hit the town. First, now, will you give Diane to me?"

"George, you talk like a spoiled boy. Give Diane to you! Why, she's a woman and I'm finding out that she's got a mind of her own. I told you I was willing for her to marry you. I tried to persuade her. But Diane hasn't any use for you now. She liked you at first; but now she doesn't. So what can I do?"

"You can make her marry me," replied Wright.

"Make that girl do what she doesn't want to? It couldn't be done, even if I tried. And I don't believe I'll try. I haven't the highest opinion of you as a prospective son-in-law, George. But if Diane loved you I would consent. We'd all go away together before this damned miserable business is out. Then she'd never know. And maybe you might be more like you used to be before the West ruined you. But as matters stand you fight your own game with her; and I'll tell you now, you'll lose."

"What'd you want to let her come out here for?" demanded Wright hotly. "It was a dead mistake. I've lost my head over her. I'll have her or die. Don't you think if she was my wife I'd soon pull myself together? Since she came we've none of us been right. And the gang has put up a holler. No, Sampson, we've got to settle things to-night."

"Well, we can settle what Diane's concerned in right now," replied Sampson, rising. "Come on; we'll go ask her. See where you stand."

They went out, leaving the door open. I dropped down to rest myself and to wait. I would have liked to hear Miss Sampson's answer to him. But I could guess what it would be. Wright appeared to be all I had thought of him, and I believed I was going to find out presently that he was worse. Just then I wanted Steele as never before. Still, he was too big to worm his way into this place.

The men seemed to be absent a good while, though that feeling might have been occasioned by my interest and anxiety. Finally I heard heavy steps. Wright came in alone. He was leaden-faced, humiliated. Then something abject in him gave place to rage. He strode the room; he cursed.

Sampson returned, now appreciably calmer. I could not but decide that he felt relief at the evident rejection of Wright's proposal. "Don't fume about it, George," he said. "You see I can't help it. We're pretty wild out here, but I can't rope my daughter and give her to you as I would an unruly steer."

"Sampson, I can *make* her marry me," declared Wright thickly.

"How?"

"You know the hold I got on you—the deal that made you boss of this rustler gang?"

"It isn't likely I'd forget," replied Sampson grimly.

"I can go to Diane—tell her that—make her believe I'd tell it broadcast, tell this Ranger Steele, unless she'd marry me!" Wright spoke breathlessly, with haggard face and shadowed eyes. He had no shame. He was simply in the grip of passion. Sampson gazed with dark, controlled fury at his relative. In that look I saw a strong, unscrupulous man fallen into evil ways, but still a man. It betrayed Wright to be the wild and passionate weakling.

I seemed to see also how, during all the years of association, this strong man had upheld the weak one. But that time had gone forever, both in intent on Sampson's part and in possibility.

Wright, like the great majority of evil and unrestrained men on the border, had reached a point where influence was futile. Reason had degenerated. He saw only himself.

"But, George, Diane's the one person on earth who must never know I'm a rustler, a thief, a red-handed ruler of the worst gang on the border," replied Sampson impressively.

George bowed his head at that, as if the significance had just occurred to him. But he was not long at a loss. "She's going to find it out sooner or later. I tell you she knows now there's something wrong out here. She's got eyes. And that meddling cowboy of hers is smarter than you give him credit for. They're always together. You'll regret the day Russ ever straddled a horse on this ranch. Mark what I say."

"Diane's changed, I know; but she hasn't any idea yet that her daddy's a boss rustler. Diane's concerned about what she calls my duty as mayor. Also I think she's not satisfied with my explanations in regard to certain property."

Wright halted in his restless walk and leaned against the stone mantelpiece. He squared himself as if this was his last stand. He looked desperate, but on the moment showed an absence of his usual nervous excitement. "Sampson, that may well be true," he said. "No doubt all you say is true. But it doesn't help me. I want the girl. If I don't get her I reckon we'll all go to hell!" He might have meant anything, probably meant the worst. He certainly had something more in mind.

Sampson gave a slight start, barely perceptible like the twitch of an awakening tiger. He sat there, head down, stroking his mustache. Almost I saw his thought. I had long experience in reading men under stress of such emotion. I had no means to vindicate my judgment, but my conviction was that Sampson right then and there decided that the thing to do was to kill Wright. For my part, I wondered that he had not come to such a conclusion before. Not improbably the advent of his daughter had put Sampson in conflict with himself.

Suddenly he threw off a somber cast of countenance and began to talk. He talked swiftly, persuasively, yet I imagined he was talking to smooth Wright's passion for the moment. Wright no more caught the fateful significance of a line crossed, a limit reached, a decree decided, than if he had not been present. He was obsessed with himself.

How, I wondered, had a man of his mind ever lived so long and gone so far among the exacting conditions of Pecos County? The answer was perhaps, that Sampson had guided him, upheld him, protected him. The coming of Diane Sampson had been the entering wedge of dissension.

"You're too impatient," concluded Sampson. "You'll ruin any chance of happiness if you rush Diane. She might be won. If you told her who I am she'd hate you forever. She might marry you to save me, but she'd hate you.

"That isn't the way. Wait. Play for time. Be different with her. Cut out your drinking. She despises that. Let's plan to sell out here, stock, ranch, property, and leave the country. Then you'd have a show with her."

"I told you we've got to stick," growled Wright. "The gang won't stand for our going. It can't be done unless you want to sacrifice everything."

"You mean double-cross the men? Go without their knowing? Leave them here to face whatever comes?"

"I mean just that."

"I'm bad enough, but not that bad," returned Sampson. "If I can't get the gang to let me off I'll stay and face the music. All the same, Wright, did it ever strike you that most of our deals the last few years have been yours?"

"Yes. If I hadn't rung them in, there wouldn't have been any. You've had cold feet, Owens says, especially since this Ranger Steele has been here."

"Well, call it cold feet if you like. But I call it sense. We reached our limit long ago. We began by rustling a few cattle at a time when rustling was laughed at. But as our greed grew so did our boldness. Then came the gang, the regular trips, and one thing and another till, before we knew it—before *I* knew it, we had shady deals, hold-ups, and murders on our record. Then we had to go on. Too late to turn back!"

"I reckon we've all said that. None of the gang wants to quit. They all think, and I think, we can't be touched. We may be blamed, but nothing can be proved. We're too strong."

"There's where you're dead wrong," rejoined Sampson, emphatically. "I imagined that once, not long ago. I was bull-headed. Who would ever connect Roger Sampson with a rustler gang? I've changed my mind. I've begun to think. I've reasoned out things. We're crooked and we can't last. It's the nature of life, even in wild Pecos, for conditions to grow better. The wise deal for us would be to divide equally and leave the country, all of us."

"But you and I have all the stock—all the gain," protested Wright.

"I'll split mine."

"I won't—that settles that," added Wright instantly.

Sampson spread wide his hands as if it was useless to try to convince this man. Talking had not increased his calmness, and he now showed more than impatience. A dull glint gleamed deep in his eyes. "Your stock and property will last a long time—do you lots of good when Steele—"

"Bah!" hoarsely croaked Wright. The Ranger's name was a match applied to powder. "Haven't I told you he'd be dead soon same as Hoden is?"

"Yes, you mentioned the supposition," replied Sampson sarcastically. "I inquired, too just how that very desired event was to be brought about."

"Blome's here to kill Steele."

"Bah!" retorted Sampson in turn. "Blome can't kill this Ranger. He can't face him with a ghost of a show—he'll never get a chance at Steele's back. The man don't live on this border who's quick and smart enough to kill Steele."

"I'd like to know why?" demanded Wright sullenly.

"You ought to know. You've seen the Ranger pull a gun."

"Who told you?" queried Wright, his face working.

"Oh, I guessed it, if that'll do you."

"If Jack doesn't kill this damned Ranger I will," replied Wright, pounding the table.

Sampson laughed contemptuously. "George, don't make so much noise. And don't be a fool. You've been on the border for ten years. You've packed a gun and you've used it. You've been with Blome and Snecker when they killed their men. You've been present at many fights. But you never saw a man like Steele. You haven't got sense enough to see him right if you had a chance. Neither has Blome. The only way to get rid of Steele is for the gang to draw on him, all at once. And even then he's going to drop some of them."

"Sampson, you say that like a man who wouldn't care much if Steele did drop some of them," declared Wright, and now he was sarcastic.

"To tell you the truth I wouldn't," returned the other bluntly. "I'm pretty sick of this mess."

Wright cursed in amaze. His emotions were out of all proportion to his intelligence. He was not at all quick-witted. I had never seen a vainer or more arrogant man. "Sampson, I don't like your talk," he said.

"If you don't like the way I talk you know what you can do," replied Sampson quickly. He stood up then, cool and quiet, with flash of eyes and set of lips that told me he was dangerous.

"Well, after all, that's neither here nor there," went on Wright, unconsciously cowed by the other. "The thing is, do I get the girl?"

"Not by any means, except her consent."

"You'll not make her marry me?"

"No. No," replied Sampson, his voice still cold, low-pitched.

"All right. Then I'll make her."

Evidently Sampson understood the man before him so well that he wasted no more words. I knew what Wright never dreamed of, and that was that Sampson had a gun somewhere within reach and meant to use it.

Then heavy footsteps sounded outside, tramping upon the porch. I might have been mistaken, but I believed those footsteps saved Wright's life.

"There they are," said Wright, and he opened the door. Five masked men entered. About two of them I could not recognize anything familiar. I thought one had old Snecker's burly shoulders and another Bo Snecker's stripling shape. I did recognize Blome in spite of his mask, because his fair skin and hair, his garb and air of distinction made plain his identity. They all wore coats, hiding any weapons. The big man with burly shoulders shook hands with Sampson and the others stood back.

The atmosphere of that room had changed. Wright might have been a nonentity for all he counted. Sampson was another man—a stranger to me. If he had entertained a hope of freeing himself from his band, of getting away to a safer country, he abandoned it at the very sight of these men. There was power here and he was bound.

The big man spoke in low, hoarse whispers, and at this all the others gathered round him, close to the table. There were evidently some signs of membership not plain to me. Then all the heads were bent over the table. Low voices spoke, queried, answered, argued. By straining my ears I caught a word here and there. They were planning. I did not attempt to get at the meaning of the few words and phrases I distinguished, but held them in mind so to piece all together afterward. Before the plotters finished conferring I had an involuntary flashed knowledge of much and my whirling, excited mind made reception difficult.

When these rustlers finished whispering I was in a cold sweat. Steele was to be killed as soon as possible by Blome, or by the gang going to Steele's house at night. Morton had been seen with the Ranger. He was to meet the same fate as Hoden, dealt by Bo Snecker, who evidently worked in the dark like a ferret. Any other person known to be communing with Steele, or interested in him, or suspected of either, was to be silenced. Then the town was to suffer a short deadly spell of violence, directed anywhere, for the purpose of intimidating those people who had begun to be restless under the influence of the Ranger. After that, big herds of stock were to be rustled off the ranches to the north and driven to El Paso.

Then the big man, who evidently was the leader of the present convention, got up to depart. He went as swiftly as he had come, and was followed by the slender fellow. As far as it was possible for me to be sure, I identified these two as Snecker and his son. The others, however, remained. Blome removed his mask, which action was duplicated by the two rustlers who had stayed with him. They were both young, bronzed, hard of countenance, not unlike cowboys. Evidently this was now a social call on Sampson. He set out cigars and liquors for his guests, and a general conversation ensued, differing little from what might have been indulged in by neighborly ranchers. There was not a word spoken that would have caused suspicion.

Blome was genial, gay, and he talked the most. Wright alone seemed uncommunicative and unsociable. He smoked fiercely and drank continually. All at once he straightened up as if listening. "What's that?" he called suddenly.

The talking and laughter ceased. My own strained ears were pervaded by a slight rustling sound.

"Must be a rat," replied Sampson in relief. Strange how any sudden or unknown thing weighed upon him.

The rustling became a rattle.

"Sounds like a rattlesnake to me," said Blome.

Sampson got up from the table and peered round the room. Just at that instant I felt an almost inappreciable movement of the adobe wall which supported me. I could scarcely credit my senses. But the rattle inside Sampson's room was mingling with little dull thuds of falling dirt. The adobe wall, merely dried mud was crumbling. I distinctly felt a tremor pass through it. Then the blood gushed with sickening coldness back to my heart and seemingly clogged it.

"What in the hell!" exclaimed Sampson.

"I smell dust," said Blome sharply.

That was the signal for me to drop down from my perch, yet despite my care I made a noise.

"Did you hear a step?" queried Sampson.

Then a section of the wall fell inward with a crash. I began to squeeze my body through the narrow passage toward the patio.

"Hear him!" yelled Wright. "This side."

"No, he's going that way," yelled someone else. The tramp of heavy boots lent me the strength and speed of desperation. I was not shirking a fight, but to be cornered like a trapped coyote was another matter. I almost tore my clothes off in that passage. The dust nearly stifled me.

When I burst into the patio it was not one single instant too soon. But one deep gash of breath revived me, and I was up, gun in hand, running for the outlet into the court. Thumping footsteps turned me back. While there was a chance to get away I did not want to meet odds in a fight. I thought I heard some one running into the patio from the other end. I stole along, and coming to a door, without any idea of where it might lead, I softly pushed it open a little way and slipped in.

Chapter 9

IN FLAGRANTE DELICTO

A low cry greeted me. The room was light. I saw Sally Langdon sitting on her bed in her dressing gown. Shaking my gun at her with a fierce warning gesture to be silent, I turned to close the door. It was a heavy door, without bolt or bar, and when I had shut it I felt safe only for the moment. Then I gazed around the room. There was one window with blind closely drawn. I listened and seemed to hear footsteps retreating, dying away. Then I turned to Sally. She had slipped off the bed to her knees and was holding out trembling hands as if both to supplicate mercy and to ward me off. She was as white as the pillow on her bed. She was terribly frightened. Again with warning hand commanding silence I stepped softly forward, meaning to reassure her.

"Russ! Russ!" she whispered wildly, and I thought she was going to faint. When I got close and looked into her eyes I understood the strange dark expression in them. She was terrified because she believed I meant to kill her, or do worse, probably worse. She had believed many a hard story about me and had cared for me in spite of them. I remembered, then, that she had broken her promise, she had tempted me, led me to kiss her, made a fool out of me. I remembered, also how I had threatened her. This intrusion of mine was the wild cowboy's vengeance.

I verily believed she thought I was drunk. I must have looked pretty hard and fierce, bursting into her room with that big gun in hand. My first action then was to lay the gun on her bureau.

"You poor kid!" I whispered, taking her hands and trying to raise her. But she stayed on her knees and clung to me.

"Russ! It was vile of me," she whispered. "I know it. I deserve anything—anything! But I am only a kid. Russ, I didn't break my word—I didn't make you kiss me just for, vanity's sake. I swear I didn't. I wanted you to. For I care, Russ, I can't help it. Please forgive me. Please let me off this time. Don't—don't—"

"Will you shut up!" I interrupted, half beside myself. And I used force in another way than speech. I shook her and sat her on the bed. "You little fool, I didn't come in here to kill you or do some other awful thing, as you think. For God's sake, Sally, what do you take me for?"

"Russ, you swore you'd do something terrible if I tempted you anymore," she faltered. The way she searched my face with doubtful, fearful eyes hurt me.

"Listen," and with the word I seemed to be pervaded by peace. "I didn't know this was your room. I came in here to get away—to save my life. I was pursued. I was spying on Sampson and his men. They heard me, but did not see me. They don't know who was listening. They're after me now. I'm Special United States Deputy Marshal Sittell—Russell Archibald Sittell. I'm a Ranger. I'm here as secret aid to Steele."

Sally's eyes changed from blank gulfs to dilating, shadowing, quickening windows of thought. "Russ-ell Archi-bald Sittell," she echoed. "Ranger! Secret aid to Steele!"

"Yes."

"Then you're no cowboy?"

"No."

"Only a make-believe one?"

"Yes."

"And the drinking, the gambling, the association with those low men—that was all put on?"

"Part of the game, Sally. I'm not a drinking man. And I sure hate those places I had to go in, and all that pertains to them."

"Oh, so *that's* it! I knew there was something. How glad—how glad I am!" Then Sally threw her arms around my neck, and without reserve or restraint began to kiss me and love me. It must have been a moment of sheer gladness to feel that I was not disreputable, a moment when something deep and womanly in her was vindicated. Assuredly she was entirely different from what she had ever been before.

There was a little space of time, a sweet confusion of senses, when I could not but meet her half-way in tenderness. Quite as suddenly, then she began to cry. I whispered in her ear, cautioning her to be careful, that my life was at stake; and after that she cried silently, with one of her arms round my neck, her head on my breast, and her hand clasping mine. So I held her for what seemed a long time. Indistinct voices came to me and footsteps seemingly a long way off. I heard the wind in the rose-bush outside. Some one walked down the stony court. Then a shrill neigh of a horse pierced the silence. A rider was mounting out there for some reason. With my life at stake I grasped all the sweetness of that situation. Sally stirred in my arms, raised a red, tear-stained yet happy face, and tried to smile. "It isn't any time to cry," she whispered. "But I had to. You can't understand what it made me feel to learn you're no drunkard, no desperado, but a *man*—a man like that Ranger!" Very sweetly and seriously she kissed me again. "Russ, if I didn't honestly and truly love you before, I do now."

Then she stood up and faced me with the fire and intelligence of a woman in her eyes. "Tell me now. You were spying on my uncle?"

Briefly I told her what had happened before I entered her room, not omitting a terse word as to the character of the men I had watched.

"My God! So it's Uncle Roger! I knew something was very wrong here—with him, with the place, the people. And right off I hated George Wright. Russ, does Diane know?"

"She knows something. I haven't any idea how much."

"This explains her appeal to Steele. Oh, it'll kill her! You don't know how proud, how good Diane is. Oh, it'll kill her!"

"Sally, she's no baby. She's got sand, that girl—"

The sound of soft steps somewhere near distracted my attention, reminded me of my peril, and now, what counted more with me, made clear the probability of being discovered in Sally's room. "I'll have to get out of here," I whispered.

"Wait," she replied, detaining me. "Didn't you say they were hunting for you?"

"They sure are," I returned grimly.

"Oh! Then you mustn't go. They might shoot you before you got away. Stay. If we hear them you can hide under my bed. I'll turn out the light. I'll meet them at the door. You can trust me. Stay, Russ. Wait till all quiets down, if we have to wait till morning. Then you can slip out."

"Sally, I oughtn't to stay. I don't want to—I won't," I replied perplexed and stubborn.

"But you must. It's the only safe way. They won't come here."

"Suppose they should? It's an even chance Sampson'll search every room and corner in this old house. If they found me here I couldn't start a fight. You might be hurt. Then—the fact of my being here—" I did not finish what I meant, but instead made a step toward the door.

Sally was on me like a little whirlwind, white of face and dark of eye, with a resoluteness I could not have deemed her capable of. She was as strong and supple as a panther, too. But she need not have been either resolute or strong, for the clasp of her arms, the feel of her warm breast as she pressed me back were enough to make me weak as water. My knees buckled as I touched the chair, and I was glad to sit down. My face was wet with perspiration and a kind of cold ripple shot over me. I imagined I was losing my nerve then. Proof beyond doubt that Sally loved me was so sweet, so overwhelming a thing, that I could not resist, even to save her disgrace.

"Russ, the fact of your being here is the very thing to save you—if they come," Sally whispered softly. "What do I care what they think?" She put her arms round my neck. I gave up then and held her as if she indeed were my only hope. A noise, a stealthy sound, a step, froze that embrace into stone.

"Up yet, Sally?" came Sampson's clear voice, too strained, too eager to be natural.

"No. I'm in bed, reading. Good night, Uncle," instantly replied Sally, so calmly and naturally that I marveled at the difference between man and woman. Perhaps that was the difference between love and hate.

"Are you alone?" went on Sampson's penetrating voice, colder now.

"Yes," replied Sally.

The door swung inward with a swift scrape and jar. Sampson half entered, haggard, flaming-eyed. His leveled gun did not have to move an inch to cover me. Behind him I saw Wright and indistinctly, another man.

"Well!" gasped Sampson. He showed amazement. "Hands up, Russ!"

I put up my hands quickly, but all the time I was calculating what chance I had to leap for my gun or dash out the light. I was trapped. And fury, like the hot teeth of a wolf, bit into me. That leveled gun, the menace in Sampson's puzzled eyes, Wright's dark and hateful face, these loosened the spirit of fight in me. If Sally had not been there I would have made some desperate move.

Sampson barred Wright from entering, which action showed control as well as distrust.

"You lied!" said Sampson to Sally. He was hard as flint, yet doubtful and curious, too.

"Certainly I lied," snapped Sally in reply. She was cool, almost flippant. I awakened to the knowledge that she was to be reckoned with in this situation. Suddenly she stepped squarely between Sampson and me.

"Move aside," ordered Sampson sternly.

"I won't! What do I care for your old gun? You shan't shoot Russ or do anything else to him. It's my fault he's here in my room. I coaxed him to come."

"You little hussy!" exclaimed Sampson, and he lowered the gun.

If I ever before had occasion to glory in Sally I had it then. She betrayed not the slightest fear. She looked as if she could fight like a little tigress. She was white, composed, defiant.

"How long has Russ been in here?" demanded Sampson.

"All evening. I left Diane at eight o'clock. Russ came right after that."

"But you'd undressed for bed!" ejaculated the angry and perplexed uncle.

"Yes." That simple answer was so noncommittal, so above subterfuge, so innocent, and yet so confounding in its provocation of thought that Sampson just stared his astonishment. But I started as if I had been struck.

"See here Sampson—" I began, passionately.

Like a flash Sally whirled into my arms and one hand crossed my lips. "It's my fault. I will take the blame," she cried, and now the agony of fear in her voice quieted me. I realized I would be wise to be silent. "Uncle," began Sally, turning her head, yet still clinging to me, "I've tormented Russ into loving me. I've flirted with him—teased him—tempted him. We love each other now. We're engaged. Please—please don't—" She began to falter and I felt her weight sag a little against me.

"Well, let go of him," said Sampson. "I won't hurt him. Sally, how long has this affair been going on?"

"For weeks—I don't know how long."

"Does Diane know?"

"She knows we love each other, but not that we met—did this—" Light swift steps, the rustle of silk interrupted Sampson, and made my heart sink like lead.

"Is that you, George?" came Miss Sampson's deep voice, nervous, hurried. "What's all this commotion? I hear—"

"Diane, go on back," ordered Sampson.

Just then Miss Sampson's beautiful agitated face appeared beside Wright. He failed to prevent her from seeing all of us.

"Papa! Sally!" she exclaimed, in consternation. Then she swept into the room. "What has happened?"

Sampson, like the devil he was, laughed when it was too late. He had good impulses, but they never interfered with his sardonic humor. He paced the little room, shrugging his shoulders, offering no explanation. Sally appeared about ready to collapse and I could not have told Sally's lie to Miss Sampson to save my life.

"Diane, your father and I broke in on a little Romeo and Juliet scene," said George Wright with a leer. Then Miss Sampson's dark gaze swept from George to her father, then to Sally's attire and her shamed face, and finally to me. What effect the magnificent wrath and outraged trust in her eyes had upon me!

"Russ, do they dare insinuate you came to Sally's room?" For myself I could keep silent, but for Sally I began to feel a hot clamoring outburst swelling in my throat.

"Sally confessed it, Diane," replied Wright.

"Sally!" A shrinking, shuddering disbelief filled Miss Sampson's voice.

"Diane, I told you I loved him—didn't I?" replied Sally. She managed to hold up her head with a ghost of her former defiant spirit.

"Miss Sampson, it's a—" I burst out.

Then Sally fainted. It was I who caught her. Miss Sampson hurried to her side with a little cry of distress.

"Russ, your hand's called," said Sampson. "Of course you'll swear the moon's green cheese. And I like you the better for it. But we know now, and you can save your breath. If Sally hadn't stuck up so gamely for you I'd have shot you. But at that I wasn't looking for you. Now clear out of here." I picked up my gun from the bureau and dropped it in its sheath. For the life of me I could not leave without another look at Miss Sampson. The scorn in her eyes did not wholly hide the sadness. She who needed friends was experiencing the bitterness of misplaced trust. That came out in the scorn, but the sadness—I knew what hurt her most was her sorrow.

I dropped my head and stalked out.

Chapter 10

A SLAP IN THE FACE

When I got out into the dark, where my hot face cooled in the wind, my relief equaled my other feelings. Sampson had told me to clear out, and although I did not take that as a dismissal I considered I would be wise to leave the ranch at once. Daylight might disclose my footprints between the walls, but even if it did not, my work there was finished. So I went to my room and packed my few belongings.

The night was dark, windy, stormy, yet there was no rain. I hoped as soon as I got clear of the ranch to lose something of the pain I felt. But long after I had tramped out into the open there was a lump in my throat and an ache in my breast. And all my thought centered round Sally.

What a game and loyal little girl she had turned out to be! I was absolutely at a loss concerning what the future held in store for us. I seemed to have a vague but clinging hope that, after the trouble was over, there might be—there *must* be—something more between us.

Steele was not at our rendezvous among the rocks. The hour was too late. Among the few dim lights flickering on the outskirts of town I picked out the one of his little adobe house but I knew almost to a certainty that he was not there. So I turned my way into the darkness, not with any great hope of finding Steele out there, but with the intention of seeking a covert for myself until morning.

There was no trail and the night was so black that I could see only the lighter sandy patches of ground. I stumbled over the little clumps of brush, fell into washes, and pricked myself on cactus. By and by mesquites and rocks began to make progress still harder for me. I wandered around, at last getting on higher ground and here in spite of the darkness, felt some sense of familiarity with things. I was probably near Steele's hiding place.

I went on till rocks and brush barred further progress, and then I ventured to whistle. But no answer came. Whereupon I spread my blanket in as sheltered a place as I could find and lay down. The coyotes were on noisy duty, the wind moaned and rushed through the mesquites. But despite these sounds and worry about Steele, and the never-absent haunting thought of Sally, I went to sleep.

A little rain had fallen during the night, as I discovered upon waking; still it was not enough to cause me any discomfort. The morning was bright and beautiful, yet somehow I hated it. I had work to do that did not go well with that golden wave of grass and brush on the windy open.

I climbed to the highest rock of that ridge and looked about. It was a wild spot, some three miles from town. Presently I recognized landmarks given to me by Steele and knew I was near his place. I whistled, then halloed, but got no reply. Then by working back and forth across the ridge I found what appeared to be a faint trail. This I followed, lost and found again, and eventually, still higher up on another ridge, with a commanding outlook, I found Steele's hiding place. He had not been there for perhaps forty-eight hours. I wondered where he had slept.

Under a shelving rock I found a pack of food, carefully protected by a heavy slab. There was also a canteen full of water. I lost no time getting myself some breakfast, and then, hiding my own pack, I set off at a rapid walk for town.

But I had scarcely gone a quarter of a mile, had, in fact, just reached a level, when sight of two horsemen halted me and made me take to cover. They appeared to be cowboys hunting for a horse or a steer. Under the circumstances, however, I was suspicious, and I watched them closely, and followed them a mile or so round the base of the ridges, until I had thoroughly satisfied myself they were not tracking Steele. They were a long time working out of sight, which further retarded my venturing forth into the open.

Finally I did get started. Then about half-way to town more horsemen in the flat caused me to lie low for a while, and make a wide detour to avoid being seen.

Somewhat to my anxiety it was afternoon before I arrived in town. For my life I could not have told why I knew something had happened since my last visit, but I certainly felt it; and was proportionately curious and anxious.

The first person I saw whom I recognized was Dick, and he handed me a note from Sally. She seemed to take it for granted that I had been wise to leave the ranch. Miss Sampson had softened somewhat when she learned Sally and I were engaged, and she had forgiven my deceit. Sally asked me to come that night after eight, down among the trees and shrubbery, to a secluded spot we knew. It was a brief note and all to the point. But there was something in it that affected me strangely. I had imagined the engagement an invention for the moment. But after danger to me was past Sally would not have carried on a pretense, not even to win back Miss Sampson's respect. The fact was, Sally meant that engagement. If I did the right thing now I would not lose her.

But what was the right thing?

I was sorely perplexed and deeply touched. Never had I a harder task than that of the hour— to put her out of my mind. I went boldly to Steele's house. He was not there. There was nothing by which I could tell when he had been there. The lamp might have been turned out or might have burned out. The oil was low. I saw a good many tracks round in the sandy walks. I did not recognize Steele's.

As I hurried away I detected more than one of Steele's nearest neighbors peering at me from windows and doors. Then I went to Mrs. Hoden's. She was up and about and cheerful. The children were playing, manifestly well cared for and content. Mrs. Hoden had not seen Steele since I had. Miss Samson had sent her servant. There was a very decided change in the atmosphere of Mrs. Hoden's home, and I saw that for her the worst was past, and she was bravely, hopefully facing the future.

From there, I hurried to the main street of Linrock and to that section where violence brooded, ready at any chance moment to lift its hydra head. For that time of day the street seemed unusually quiet. Few pedestrians were abroad and few loungers. There was a row of saddled horses on each side of the street, the full extent of the block.

I went into the big barroom of the Hope So. I had never seen the place so full, nor had it ever seemed so quiet. The whole long bar was lined by shirt-sleeved men, with hats slouched back and vests flapping wide. Those who were not drinking were talking low. Half a dozen tables held as many groups of dusty, motley men, some silent, others speaking and gesticulating, all earnest.

At first glance I did not see any one in whom I had especial interest. The principal actors of my drama did not appear to be present. However, there were rough characters more in evidence than at any other time I had visited the saloon. Voices were too low for me to catch, but I followed the direction of some of the significant gestures. Then I saw that these half dozen tables were rather closely grouped and drawn back from the center of the big room. Next my quick sight took in a smashed table and chairs, some broken bottles on the floor, and then a dark sinister splotch of blood.

I had no time to make inquiries, for my roving eye caught Frank Morton in the doorway, and evidently he wanted to attract my attention. He turned away and I followed. When I got outside, he was leaning against the hitching-rail. One look at this big rancher was enough for me to see that he had been told my part in Steele's game, and that he himself had roused to the Texas fighting temper. He had a clouded brow. He looked somber and thick. He seemed slow, heavy, guarded.

"Howdy, Russ," he said. "We've been wantin' you."

"There's ten of us in town, all scattered round, ready. It's goin' to start to-day."

"Where's Steele?" was my first query.

"Saw him less'n hour ago. He's somewhere close. He may show up any time."

"Is he all right?"

"Wai, he was pretty fit a little while back," replied Morton significantly.

"What's come off? Tell me all."

"Wai, the ball opened last night, I reckon. Jack Blome came swaggerin' in here askin' for Steele. We all knew what he was in town for. But last night he came out with it. Every man in the saloons, every man on the streets heard Blome's loud an' longin' call for the Ranger. Blome's pals took it up and they all enjoyed themselves some."

"Drinking hard?" I queried.

"Nope—they didn't hit it up very hard. But they laid foundations." Of course, Steele was not to be seen last night. This morning Blome and his gang were out pretty early. But they traveled alone. Blome just strolled up and down by himself. I watched him walk up this street on one side and then down the other, just a matter of thirty-one times. I counted them. For all I could see maybe Blome did not take a drink. But his gang, especially Bo Snecker, sure looked on the red liquor.

"By eleven o'clock everybody in town knew what was coming off. There was no work or business, except in the saloons. Zimmer and I were together, and the rest of our crowd in pairs at different places. I reckon it was about noon when Blome got tired parading up and down. He went in the Hope So, and the crowd followed. Zimmer stayed outside so to give Steele a hunch in case he came along. I went in to see the show.

"Wai, it was some curious to me, and I've lived all my life in Texas. But I never before saw a gunman on the job, so to say. Blome's a handsome fellow, an' he seemed different from what I expected. Sure, I thought he'd yell an' prance round like a drunken fool. But he was cool an' quiet enough. The bio win' an' drinkin' was done by his pals. But after a little while it got to me that Blome gloried in this situation. I've seen a man dead-set to kill another, all dark, sullen, restless. But Blome wasn't that way. He didn't seem at all like a bloody devil. He was vain, cocksure. He was revelin' in the effect he made. I had him figured all right.

"Blome sat on the edge of a table an' he faced the door. Of course, there was a pard outside, ready to pop in an' tell him if Steele was comin'. But Steele didn't come in that way. He wasn't on the street just before that time, because Zimmer told me afterward. Steele must have been in the

Hope So somewhere. Any way, just like he dropped from the clouds he came through the door near the bar. Blome didn't see him come. But most of the gang did, an' I want to tell you that big room went pretty quiet.

"'Hello Blome, I hear you're lookin' for me,' called out Steele.

"I don't know if he spoke ordinary or not, but his voice drew me up same as it did the rest, an' damn me! Blome seemed to turn to stone. He didn't start or jump. He turned gray. An' I could see that he was tryin' to think in a moment when thinkin' was hard. Then Blome turned his head. Sure he expected to look into a six-shooter. But Steele was standin' back there in his shirt sleeves, his hands on his hips, and he looked more man than any one I ever saw. It's easy to remember the look of him, but how he made me feel, that isn't easy.

"Blome was at a disadvantage. He was half sittin' on a table, an' Steele was behind an' to the left of him. For Blome to make a move then would have been a fool trick. He saw that. So did everybody. The crowd slid back without noise, but Bo Snecker an' a rustler named March stuck near Blome. I figured this Bo Snecker as dangerous as Blome, an' results proved I was right.

"Steele didn't choose to keep his advantage, so far as position in regard to Blome went. He just walked round in front of the rustler. But this put all the crowd in front of Steele, an' perhaps he had an eye for that.

"'I hear you've been looking for me,' repeated the Ranger.

"Blome never moved a muscle but he seemed to come to life. It struck me that Steele's presence had made an impression on Blome which was new to the rustler.

"'Yes, I have,' replied Blome.

"'Well, here I am. What do you want?'

"When everybody knew what Blome wanted and had intended, this question of Steele's seemed strange on one hand. An' yet on the other, now that the Ranger stood there, it struck me as natural enough.

"'If you heard I was lookin' for you, you sure heard what for,' replied Blome.

"'Blome, my experience with such men as you is that you all brag one thing behind my back an' you mean different when I show up. I've called you now. What do you mean?'

"'I reckon you know what Jack Blome means.'

"'Jack Blome! That name means nothin' to me. Blome, you've been braggin' around that you'd meet me—kill me! You thought you meant it, didn't you?'

"'Yes—I did mean it.'

"'All right. Go ahead!'

"The barroom became perfectly still, except for the slow breaths I heard. There wasn't any movement anywhere. That queer gray came to Blome's face again. He might again have been stone. I thought, an' I'll gamble every one else watchin' thought, Blome would draw an' get killed in the act. But he never moved. Steele had cowed him. If Blome had been heated by drink, or mad, or anythin' but what he was just then, maybe he might have throwed a gun. But he didn't. I've heard of really brave men gettin' panicked like that, an' after seein' Steele I didn't wonder at Blome.

"'You see, Blome, you don't want to meet me, for all your talk,' went on the Ranger. 'You thought you did, but that was before you faced the man you intended to kill. Blome, you're one of these dandy, cock-of-the-walk four-flushers. I'll tell you how I know. Because I've met the real gun-fighters, an' there never was one of them yet who bragged or talked. Now don't you go round blowin' any more.'

"Then Steele deliberately stepped forward an' slapped Blome on one side of his face an' again on the other.

"'Keep out of my way after this or I'm liable to spoil some of your dandy looks.'

"Blome got up an' walked straight out of the place. I had my eyes on him, kept me from seein' Steele. But on hearin' somethin', I don't know what, I turned back an' there Steele had got a long arm on Bo Snecker, who was tryin' to throw a gun.

"But he wasn't quick enough. The gun banged in the air an' then it went spinnin' away, while Snecker dropped in a heap on the floor. The table was overturned, an' March, the other rustler, who was on that side, got up, pullin' his gun. But somebody in the crowd killed him before he could get goin'. I didn't see who fired that shot, an' neither did anybody else. But the crowd broke an' run. Steele dragged Bo Snecker down to jail an' locked him up."

Morton concluded his narrative, and then evidently somewhat dry of tongue, he produced knife and tobacco and cut himself a huge quid. "That's all, so far, to-day, Russ, but I reckon you'll agree with me on the main issue—Steele's game's opened."

I had felt the rush of excitement, the old exultation at the prospect of danger, but this time there was something lacking in them. The wildness of the boy that had persisted in me was gone.

"Yes, Steele has opened it and I'm ready to boost the game along. Wait till I see him! But Morton, you say someone you don't know played a hand in here and killed March."

"I sure do. It wasn't any of our men. Zimmer was outside. The others were at different places."

"The fact is, then, Steele has more friends than we know, perhaps more than he knows himself."

"Right. An' it's got the gang in the air. There'll be hell to-night."

"Steele hardly expects to keep Snecker in jail, does he?"

"I can't say. Probably not. I wish Steele had put both Blome and Snecker out of the way. We'd have less to fight."

"Maybe. I'm for the elimination method myself. But Steele doesn't follow out the gun method. He will use one only when he's driven. It's hard to make him draw. You know, after all, these desperate men aren't afraid of guns or fights. Yet they are afraid of Steele. Perhaps it's his nerve, the way he faces them, the things he says, the fact that he has mysterious allies."

"Russ, we're all with him, an' I'll gamble that the honest citizens of Linrock will flock to him in another day. I can see signs of that. There were twenty or more men on Hoden's list, but Steele didn't want so many."

"We don't need any more. Morton, can you give me any idea where Steele is?"

"Not the slightest."

"All right. I'll hunt for him. If you see him tell him to hole up, and then you come after me. Tell him I've got our men spotted."

"Russ, if you Ranger fellows ain't wonders!" exclaimed Morton, with shining eyes.

Steele did not show himself in town again that day. Here his cunning was manifest. By four o'clock that afternoon Blome was drunk and he and his rustlers went roaring up and down the street. There was some shooting, but I did not see or hear that any one got hurt. The lawless element, both native to Linrock and the visitors, followed in Blome's tracks from saloon to saloon. How often had I seen this sort of procession, though not on so large a scale, in many towns of wild Texas!

The two great and dangerous things in Linrock at the hour were whisky and guns. Under such conditions the rustlers were capable of any mad act of folly.

Morton and his men sent word flying around town that a fight was imminent and all citizens should be prepared to defend their homes against possible violence. But despite his warning I saw many respectable citizens abroad whose quiet, unobtrusive manner and watchful eyes and hard faces told me that when trouble began they wanted to be there. Verily Ranger Steele had built his house of service upon a rock. It did not seem too much to say that the next few days, perhaps hours, would see a great change in the character and a proportionate decrease in number of the inhabitants of this corner of Pecos County.

Morton and I were in the crowd that watched Blome, Snecker, and a dozen other rustlers march down to Steele's jail. They had crowbars and they had cans of giant powder, which they had appropriated from a hardware store. If Steele had a jailer he was not in evidence. The door was wrenched off and Bo Snecker, evidently not wholly recovered, brought forth to his cheering comrades. Then some of the rustlers began to urge back the pressing circle, and the word given out acted as a spur to haste. The jail was to be blown up.

The crowd split and some men ran one way, some another. Morton and I were among those who hurried over the vacant ground to a little ridge that marked the edge of the open country. From this vantage point we heard several rustlers yell in warning, then they fled for their lives.

It developed that they might have spared themselves such headlong flight. The explosion appeared to be long in coming. At length we saw the lifting of the roof in a cloud of red dust, and then heard an exceedingly heavy but low detonation. When the pall of dust drifted away all that was left of Steele's jail was a part of the stone walls. The building that stood nearest, being constructed of adobe, had been badly damaged.

However, this wreck of the jail did not seem to satisfy Blome and his followers, for amid wild yells and huzzahs they set to work with crowbars and soon laid low every stone. Then with young Snecker in the fore they set off up town; and if this was not a gang in fit mood for any evil or any ridiculous celebration I greatly missed my guess.

It was a remarkable fact, however, and one that convinced me of deviltry afoot, that the crowd broke up, dispersed, and actually disappeared off the streets of Linrock. The impression given was that they were satisfied. But this impression did not remain with me. Morton was scarcely deceived either. I told him that I would almost certainly see Steele early in the evening and that we would be out of harm's way. He told me that we could trust him and his men to keep sharp watch on the night doings of Blome's gang. Then we parted.

It was almost dark. By the time I had gotten something to eat and drink at the Hope So, the hour for my meeting with Sally was about due. On the way out I did not pass a lighted house until I got to the end of the street; and then strange to say, that one was Steele's. I walked down past the place, and though I was positive he would not be there I whistled low. I halted and waited. He had two lights lit, one in the kitchen, and one in the big room. The blinds were drawn. I saw a long, dark shadow cross one window and then, a little later, cross the other. This would have deceived me had I not remembered Steele's device for casting the shadow. He had expected to have his house attacked at night, presumably while he was at home; but he had felt that it was not necessary for him to stay there to make sure. Lawless men of this class were sometimes exceedingly simple and gullible.

Then I bent my steps across the open, avoiding road and path, to the foot of the hill upon which Sampson's house stood. It was dark enough under the trees. I could hardly find my way to the secluded nook and bench where I had been directed to come. I wondered if Sally would be able to find it. Trust that girl! She might have a few qualms and come shaking a little, but she would be there on the minute.

I had hardly seated myself to wait when my keen ears detected something, then slight rustlings, then soft steps, and a dark form emerged from the blackness into the little starlit glade. Sally came swiftly towards me and right into my arms. That was sure a sweet moment. Through the excitement and dark boding thoughts of the day, I had forgotten that she would do just this thing. And now I anticipated tears, clingings, fears. But I was agreeably surprised.

"Russ, are you all right?" she whispered.

"Just at this moment I am," I replied.

Sally gave me another little hug, and then, disengaging herself from my arms, she sat down beside me.

"I can only stay a minute. Oh, it's safe enough. But I told Diane I was to meet you and she's waiting to hear if Steele is—is—"

"Steele's safe so far," I interrupted.

"There were men coming and going all day. Uncle Roger never appeared at meals. He didn't eat, Diane said. George tramped up and down, smoking, biting his nails, listening for these messengers. When they'd leave he'd go in for another drink. We heard him roar some one had been shot and we feared it might be Steele."

"No," I replied, steadily.

"Did Steele shoot anybody?"

"No. A rustler named March tried to draw on Steele, and someone in the crowd killed March."

"Someone? Russ, was it you?"

"It sure wasn't. I didn't happen to be there."

"Ah! Then Steele has other men like you around him. I might have guessed that."

"Sally, Steele makes men his friends. It's because he's on the side of justice."

"Diane will be glad to hear that. She doesn't think only of Steele's life. I believe she has a secret pride in his work. And I've an idea what she fears most is some kind of a clash between Steele and her father."

"I shouldn't wonder. Sally, what does Diane know about her father?"

"Oh, she's in the dark. She got hold of papers that made her ask him questions. And his answers made her suspicious. She realizes he's not what he has pretended to be all these years. But she never dreams her father is a rustler chief. When she finds that out—" Sally broke off and I finished the sentence in thought.

"Listen, Sally," I said, suddenly. "I've an idea that Steele's house will be attacked by the gang to-night, and destroyed, same as the jail was this afternoon. These rustlers are crazy. They'll expect to kill him while he's there. But he won't be there. If you and Diane hear shooting and yelling to-night don't be frightened. Steele and I will be safe."

"Oh, I hope so. Russ, I must hurry back. But, first, can't you arrange a meeting between Diane and Steele? It's her wish. She begged me to. She must see him."

"I'll try," I promised, knowing that promise would be hard to keep.

"We could ride out from the ranch somewhere. You remember we used to rest on the high ridge where there was a shady place—such a beautiful outlook? It was there I—I—"

"My dear, you needn't bring up painful memories. I remember where."

Sally laughed softly. She could laugh in the face of the gloomiest prospects. "Well, to-morrow morning, or the next, or any morning soon, you tie your red scarf on the dead branch of that high mesquite. I'll look every morning with the glass. If I see the scarf, Diane and I will ride out."

"That's fine. Sally, you have ideas in your pretty little head. And once I thought it held nothing but—" She put a hand on my mouth. "I must go now," she said and rose. She stood close to me and put her arms around my neck. "One thing more, Russ. It—it was dif—difficult telling Diane we—we were engaged. I lied to Uncle. But what else could I have told Diane? I—I—Oh—was it—" She faltered.

"Sally, you lied to Sampson to save me. But you must have accepted me before you could have told Diane the truth."

"Oh, Russ, I had—in my heart! But it has been some time since you asked me—and—and—"

"You imagined my offer might have been withdrawn. Well, it stands."

She slipped closer to me then, with that soft sinuousness of a woman, and I believed she might have kissed me had I not held back, toying with my happiness.

"Sally, do you love me?"

"Ever so much. Since the very first."

"I'm a marshal, a Ranger like Steele, a hunter of criminals. It's a hard life. There's spilling of blood. And any time I—I might—All the same, Sally—will you be my wife?"

"Oh, Russ! Yes. But let me tell you when your duty's done here that I will have a word to say about your future. It'll be news to you to learn I'm an orphan. And I'm not a poor one. I own a plantation in Louisiana. I'll make a planter out of you. There!"

"Sally! You're rich?" I exclaimed.

"I'm afraid I am. But nobody can ever say you married me for my money."

"Well, no, not if you tell of my abject courtship when I thought you a poor relation on a visit. My God! Sally, if I only could see this Ranger job through safely and to success!"

"You will," she said softly.

Then I took a ring from my little finger and slipped it on hers. "That was my sister's. She's dead now. No other girl ever wore it. Let it be your engagement ring. Sally, I pray I may somehow get through this awful Ranger deal to make you happy, to become worthy of you!"

"Russ, I fear only one thing," she whispered.

"And what's that?"

"There will be fighting. And you—oh, I saw into your eyes the other night when you stood with your hands up. You would kill anybody, Russ. It's awful! But don't think me a baby. I can conceive what your work is, what a man you must be. I can love you and stick to you, too. But if you killed a blood relative of mine I would have to give you up. I'm a Southerner, Russ, and blood is thick. I scorn my uncle and I hate my cousin George. And I love you. But don't you kill one of my family, I—Oh, I beg of you go as far as you dare to avoid that!"

I could find no voice to answer her, and for a long moment we were locked in an embrace, breast to breast and lips to lips, an embrace of sweet pain.

Then she broke away, called a low, hurried good-by, and stole like a shadow into the darkness.

An hour later I lay in the open starlight among the stones and brush, out where Steele and I always met. He lay there with me, but while I looked up at the stars he had his face covered with his hands. For I had given him my proofs of the guilt of Diane Sampson's father.

Steele had made one comment: "I wish to God I'd sent for some fool who'd have bungled the job!"

This was a compliment to me, but it showed what a sad pass Steele had come to. My regret was that I had no sympathy to offer him. I failed him there. I had trouble of my own. The feel of Sally's clinging arms around my neck, the warm, sweet touch of her lips remained on mine. What Steele was enduring I did not know, but I felt that it was agony.

Meanwhile time passed. The blue, velvety sky darkened as the stars grew brighter. The wind grew stronger and colder. I heard sand blowing against the stones like the rustle of silk. Otherwise it was a singularly quiet night. I wondered where the coyotes were and longed for their chorus. By and by a prairie wolf sent in his lonely lament from the distant ridges. That mourn was worse than the silence. It made the cold shudders creep up and down my back. It was just the cry that seemed to be the one to express my own trouble. No one hearing that long-drawn, quivering wail could ever disassociate it from tragedy. By and by it ceased, and then I wished it would come again. Steele lay like the stone beside him. Was he ever going to speak? Among the vagaries of my mood was a petulant desire to have him sympathize with me.

I had just looked at my watch, making out in the starlight that the hour was eleven, when the report of a gun broke the silence.

I jumped up to peer over the stone. Steele lumbered up beside me, and I heard him draw his breath hard.

Chapter 11

THE FIGHT IN THE HOPE SO

I could plainly see the lights of his adobe house, but of course, nothing else was visible. There were no other lighted houses near. Several flashes gleamed, faded swiftly, to be followed by reports, and then the unmistakable jingle of glass.

"I guess the fools have opened up, Steele," I said. His response was an angry grunt. It was just as well, I concluded, that things had begun to stir. Steele needed to be roused.

Suddenly a single sharp yell pealed out. Following it came a huge flare of light, a sheet of flame in which a great cloud of smoke or dust shot up. Then, with accompanying darkness, burst a low, deep, thunderous boom. The lights of the house went out, then came a crash. Points of light flashed in a half-circle and the reports of guns blended with the yells of furious men, and all these were swallowed up in the roar of a mob.

Another and a heavier explosion momentarily lightened the darkness and then rent the air. It was succeeded by a continuous volley and a steady sound that, though composed of yells, screams, cheers, was not anything but a hideous roar of hate. It kept up long after there could have been any possibility of life under the ruins of that house. It was more than hate of Steele. All that was wild and lawless and violent hurled this deed at the Ranger Service.

Such events had happened before in Texas and other states; but, strangely, they never happened more than once in one locality. They were expressions, perhaps, that could never come but once.

I watched Steele through all that hideous din, that manifestation of insane rage at his life and joy at his death, and when silence once more reigned and he turned his white face to mine, I had a sensation of dread. And dread was something particularly foreign to my nature.

"So Blome and the Sneckers think they've done for me," he muttered.

"Pleasant surprise for them to-morrow, eh, old man?" I queried.

"To-morrow? Look, Russ, what's left of my old 'dobe house is on fire. The ruins can't be searched soon. And I was particular to fix things so it'd look like I was home. I just wanted to give them a chance. It's incomprehensible how easy men like them can be duped. Whisky-soaked! Yes, they'll be surprised!"

He lingered a while, watching the smoldering fire and the dim columns of smoke curling up against the dark blue. "Russ, do you suppose they heard up at the ranch and think I'm—"

"They heard, of course," I replied. "But the girls know you're safe with me."

"Safe? I—I almost wish to God I was there under that heap of ruins, where the rustlers think they've left me."

"Well, Steele, old fellow, come on. We need some sleep." With Steele in the lead, we stalked away into the open.

Two days later, about the middle of the forenoon, I sat upon a great flat rock in the shade of a bushy mesquite, and, besides enjoying the vast, clear sweep of gold and gray plain below, I was otherwise pleasantly engaged. Sally sat as close to me as she could get, holding to my arm as if she never intended to let go. On the other side Miss Sampson leaned against me, and she was white and breathless, partly from the quick ride out from the ranch, partly from agitation. She had grown thinner, and there were dark shadows under her eyes, yet she seemed only more beautiful. The red scarf with which I had signaled the girls waved from a branch of the mesquite. At the foot of the ridge their horses were halted in a shady spot.

"Take off your sombrero," I said to Sally. "You look hot. Besides, you're prettier with your hair flying." As she made no move, I took it off for her. Then I made bold to perform the same office for Miss Sampson. She faintly smiled her thanks. Assuredly she had forgotten all her resentment. There were little beads of perspiration upon her white brow. What a beautiful mass of black-brown hair, with strands of red or gold! Pretty soon she would be bending that exquisite head and face over poor Steele, and I, who had schemed this meeting, did not care what he might do to me.

Pretty soon, also, there was likely to be an interview that would shake us all to our depths, and naturally, I was somber at heart. But though my outward mood of good humor may have been pretense, it certainly was a pleasure to be with the girls again way out in the open. Both girls were quiet, and this made my task harder, and perhaps in my anxiety to ward off questions and appear happy for their own sakes I made an ass of myself with my silly talk and familiarity. Had ever a Ranger such a job as mine?

"Diane, did Sally show you her engagement ring?" I went on, bound to talk.

Miss Sampson either did not notice my use of her first name or she did not object. She seemed so friendly, so helplessly wistful. "Yes. It's very pretty. An antique. I've seen a few of them," she replied.

"I hope you'll let Sally marry me soon."

"*Let* her? Sally Langdon? You haven't become acquainted with your fiancee. But when—"

"Oh, next week, just as soon—"

"Russ!" cried Sally, blushing furiously.

"What's the matter?" I queried innocently.

"You're a little previous."

"Well, Sally, I don't presume to split hairs over dates. But, you see, you've become extremely more desirable—in the light of certain revelations. Diane, wasn't Sally the deceitful thing? An heiress all the time! And I'm to be a planter and smoke fine cigars and drink mint juleps! No, there won't be any juleps."

"Russ, you're talking nonsense," reproved Sally. "Surely it's no time to be funny."

"All right," I replied with resignation. It was no task to discard that hollow mask of humor. A silence ensued, and I waited for it to be broken.

"Is Steele badly hurt?" asked Miss Sampson presently.

"No. Not what he or I'd call hurt at all. He's got a scalp wound, where a bullet bounced off his skull. It's only a scratch. Then he's got another in the shoulder; but it's not bad, either."

"Where is he now?"

"Look across on the other ridge. See the big white stone? There, down under the trees, is our camp. He's there."

"When may—I see him?" There was a catch in her low voice.

"He's asleep now. After what happened yesterday he was exhausted, and the pain in his head kept him awake till late. Let him sleep a while yet. Then you can see him."

"Did he know we were coming?"

"He hadn't the slightest idea. He'll be overjoyed to see you. He can't help that. But he'll about fall upon me with harmful intent."

"Why?"

"Well, I know he's afraid to see you."

"Why?"

"Because it only makes his duty harder."

"Ah!" she breathed.

It seemed to me that my intelligence confirmed a hope of hers and gave her relief. I felt something terrible in the balance for Steele. And I was glad to be able to throw them together. The catastrophe must fall, and now the sooner it fell the better. But I experienced a tightening of my lips and a tugging at my heart-strings.

"Sally, what do you and Diane know about the goings-on in town yesterday?" I asked.

"Not much. George was like an insane man. I was afraid to go near him. Uncle wore a sardonic smile. I heard him curse George—oh, terribly! I believe he hates George. Same as day before yesterday, there were men riding in and out. But Diane and I heard only a little, and conflicting statements at that. We knew there was fighting. Dick and the servants, the cowboys, all brought rumors. Steele was killed at least ten times and came to life just as many.

"I can't recall, don't want to recall, all we heard. But this morning when I saw the red scarf flying in the wind—well, Russ, I was so glad I could not see through the glass any more. We knew then Steele was all right or you wouldn't have put up the signal."

"Reckon few people in Linrock realize just what *did* come off," I replied with a grim chuckle.

"Russ, I want you to tell me," said Miss Sampson earnestly.

"What?" I queried sharply.

"About yesterday—what Steele did—what happened."

"Miss Sampson, I could tell you in a few short statements of fact or I could take two hours in the telling. Which do you prefer?"

"I prefer the long telling. I want to know all about him."

"But why, Miss Sampson? Consider. This is hardly a story for a sensitive woman's ears."

"I am no coward," she replied, turning eyes to me that flashed like dark fire.

"But why?" I persisted. I wanted a good reason for calling up all the details of the most strenuous and terrible day in my border experience. She was silent a moment. I saw her gaze turn to the spot where Steele lay asleep, and it was a pity he could not see her eyes then. "Frankly, I don't want to tell you," I added, and I surely would have been glad to get out of the job.

"I want to hear—because I glory in his work," she replied deliberately.

I gathered as much from the expression of her face as from the deep ring of her voice, the clear content of her statement. She loved the Ranger, but that was not all of her reason.

"His work?" I echoed. "Do you want him to succeed in it?"

"With all my heart," she said, with a white glow on her face.

"My God!" I ejaculated. I just could not help it. I felt Sally's small fingers clutching my arm like sharp pincers. I bit my lips to keep them shut. What if Steele had heard her say that? Poor, noble, justice-loving, blind girl! She knew even less than I hoped. I forced my thought to the question immediately at hand. She gloried in the Ranger's work. She wanted with all her heart to see him succeed in it. She had a woman's pride in his manliness. Perhaps, with a woman's complex, incomprehensible motive, she wanted Steele to be shown to her in all the power that made him hated and feared by lawless men. She had finally accepted the wild life of this border as something terrible and inevitable, but passing. Steele was one of the strange and great and misunderstood men who were making that wild life pass.

For the first time I realized that Miss Sampson, through sharpened eyes of love, saw Steele as he really was—a wonderful and necessary violence. Her intelligence and sympathy had enabled her to see through defamation and the false records following a Ranger; she had had no choice but to love him; and then a woman's glory in a work that freed men, saved women, and made children happy effaced forever the horror of a few dark deeds of blood.

"Miss Sampson, I must tell you first," I began, and hesitated—"that I'm not a cowboy. My wild stunts, my drinking and gaming—these were all pretense."

"Indeed! I am very glad to hear it. And was Sally in your confidence?"

"Only lately. I am a United States deputy marshal in the service of Steele."

She gave a slight start, but did not raise her head.

"I have deceived you. But, all the same, I've been your friend. I ask you to respect my secret a little while. I'm telling you because otherwise my relation to Steele yesterday would not be plain. Now, if you and Sally will use this blanket, make yourselves more comfortable seats, I'll begin my story."

Miss Sampson allowed me to arrange a place for her where she could rest at ease, but Sally returned to my side and stayed there. She was an enigma to-day—pale, brooding, silent—and she never looked at me except when my face was half averted.

"Well," I began, "night before last Steele and I lay hidden among the rocks near the edge of town, and we listened to and watched the destruction of Steele's house. It had served his purpose to leave lights burning, to have shadows blow across the window-blinds, and to have a dummy in his bed. Also, he arranged guns to go off inside the house at the least jar. Steele wanted evidence against his enemies. It was not the pleasantest kind of thing to wait there listening to that drunken mob. There must have been a hundred men. The disturbance and the intent worked strangely upon Steele. It made him different. In the dark I couldn't tell how he looked, but I felt a mood coming in him that fairly made me dread the next day.

"About midnight we started for our camp here. Steele got in some sleep, but I couldn't. I was cold and hot by turns, eager and backward, furious and thoughtful. You see, the deal was such a complicated one, and to-morrow certainly was nearing the climax. By morning I was sick, distraught, gloomy, and uncertain. I had breakfast ready when Steele awoke. I hated to look at him, but when I did it was like being revived.

"He said: 'Russ, you'll trail alongside me to-day and through the rest of this mess.'

"That gave me another shock. I want to explain to you girls that this was the first time in my life I was backward at the prospects of a fight. The shock was the jump of my pulse. My nerve came back. To line up with Steele against Blome and his gang—that would be great!

"'All right, old man,' I replied. 'We're going after them, then?'

"He only nodded.

"After breakfast I watched him clean and oil and reload his guns. I didn't need to ask him if he expected to use them. I didn't need to urge upon him Captain Neal's command.

"'Russ,' said Steele, 'we'll go in together. But before we get to town I'll leave you and circle and come in at the back of the Hope So. You hurry on ahead, post Morton and his men, get the lay of the gang, if possible, and then be at the Hope So when I come in.'

"I didn't ask him if I had a free hand with my gun. I intended to have that. We left camp and hurried toward town. It was near noon when we separated.

"I came down the road, apparently from Sampson's ranch. There was a crowd around the ruins of Steele's house. It was one heap of crumbled 'dobe bricks and burned logs, still hot and smoking. No attempt had been made to dig into the ruins. The curious crowd was certain that Steele lay buried under all that stuff. One feature of that night assault made me ponder. Daylight discovered the bodies of three dead men, rustlers, who had been killed, the report went out, by random shots. Other participants in the affair had been wounded. I believed Morton and his men, under cover of the darkness and in the melee, had sent in some shots not calculated upon the program.

"From there I hurried to town. Just as I had expected, Morton and Zimmer were lounging in front of the Hope So. They had company, disreputable and otherwise. As yet Morton's crowd had not come under suspicion. He was wild for news of Steele, and when I gave it, and outlined the plan, he became as cool and dark and grim as any man of my kind could have wished. He sent Zimmer to get the others of their clique. Then he acquainted me with a few facts, although he was noncommittal in regard to my suspicion as to the strange killing of the three rustlers.

"Blome, Bo Snecker, Hilliard, and Pickens, the ringleaders, had painted the town in celebration of Steele's death. They all got gloriously drunk except old man Snecker. He had cold feet, they said. They were too happy to do any more shooting or mind what the old rustler cautioned. It was two o'clock before they went to bed.

"This morning, after eleven, one by one they appeared with their followers. The excitement had died down. Ranger Steele was out of the way and Linrock was once more wide open, free and easy. Blome alone seemed sullen and spiritless, unresponsive to his comrades and their admirers. And now, at the time of my arrival, the whole gang, with the exception of old Snecker, were assembled in the Hope So.

"'Zimmer will be clever enough to drift his outfit along one or two at a time?' I asked Morton, and he reassured me. Then we went into the saloon.

"There were perhaps sixty or seventy men in the place, more than half of whom were in open accord with Blome's gang. Of the rest there were many of doubtful repute, and a few that might have been neutral, yet all the time were secretly burning to help any cause against these rustlers. At all events, I gathered that impression from the shadowed faces, the tense bodies, the too-evident indication of anything but careless presence there. The windows were open. The light was clear. Few men smoked, but all had a drink before them. There was the ordinary subdued hum of conversation. I surveyed the scene, picked out my position so as to be close to Steele when he entered, and sauntered round to it. Morton aimlessly leaned against a post.

"Presently Zimmer came in with a man and they advanced to the bar. Other men entered as others went out. Blome, Bo Snecker, Hilliard, and Pickens had a table full in the light of the open windows. I recognized the faces of the two last-named, but I had not, until Morton informed me, known who they were. Pickens was little, scrubby, dusty, sandy, mottled, and he resembled a rattlesnake. Hilliard was big, gaunt, bronzed, with huge mustache and hollow, fierce eyes. I never had seen a grave-robber, but I imagined one would be like Hilliard. Bo Snecker was a sleek, slim, slender, hard-looking boy, marked dangerous, because he was too young and too wild to have caution or fear. Blome, the last of the bunch, showed the effects of a bad night.

"You girls remember how handsome he was, but he didn't look it now. His face was swollen, dark, red, and as it had been bright, now it was dull. Indeed, he looked sullen, shamed, sore. He was sober now. Thought was written on his clouded brow. He was awakening now to the truth that the day before had branded him a coward and sent him out to bolster up courage with drink. His vanity had begun to bleed. He knew, if his faithful comrades had not awakened to it yet, that his prestige had been ruined. For a gunman, he had suffered the last degradation. He had been bidden to draw and he had failed of the nerve.

"He breathed heavily; his eyes were not clear; his hands were shaky. Almost I pitied this rustler who very soon must face an incredibly swift and mercilessly fatal Ranger. Face him, too, suddenly, as if the grave had opened to give up its dead.

"Friends and comrades of this center group passed to and fro, and there was much lazy, merry, though not loud, talk. The whole crowd was still half-asleep. It certainly was an auspicious hour for Steele to confront them, since that duty was imperative. No man knew the stunning paralyzing effect of surprise better than Steele. I, of course, must take my cue from him, or the sudden development of events.

"But Jack Blome did not enter into my calculations. I gave him, at most, about a minute to live after Steele entered the place. I meant to keep sharp eyes all around. I knew, once with a gun out, Steele could kill Blome's comrades at the table as quick as lightning, if he chose. I rather thought my game was to watch his outside partners. This was right, and as it turned out, enabled me to save Steele's life.

"Moments passed and still the Ranger did not come. I began to get nervous. Had he been stopped? I scouted the idea. Who could have stopped him, then? Probably the time seemed longer than it really was. Morton showed the strain, also. Other men looked drawn, haggard, waiting as if expecting a thunderbolt. Once in my roving gaze I caught Blandy's glinty eye on me. I didn't like the gleam. I said to myself I'd watch him if I had to do it out of the back of my head. Blandy, by the way, is—was—I should say, the Hope So bartender." I stopped to clear my throat and get my breath.

"Was," whispered Sally. She quivered with excitement. Miss Sampson bent eyes upon me that would have stirred a stone man.

"Yes, he was once," I replied ambiguously, but mayhap my grimness betrayed the truth. "Don't hurry me, Sally. I guarantee you'll be sick enough presently.

"Well, I kept my eyes shifty. And I reckon I'll never forget that room. Likely I saw what wasn't really there. In the excitement, the suspense, I must have made shadows into real substance. Anyway, there was the half-circle of bearded, swarthy men around Blome's table. There were the four rustlers—Blome brooding, perhaps vaguely, spiritually, listening to a knock; there was Bo Snecker, reckless youth, fondling a flower he had, putting the stem in his glass, then to his lips, and lastly into the buttonhole of Blome's vest; there was Hilliard, big, gloomy, maybe with his cavernous eyes seeing the hell where I expected he'd soon be; and last, the little dusty, scaly Pickens, who looked about to leap and sting some one.

"In the lull of the general conversation I heard Pickens say: 'Jack, drink up an' come out of it. Every man has an off day. You've gambled long enough to know every feller gits called. An' as Steele has cashed, what the hell do you care?'

"Hilliard nodded his ghoul's head and blinked his dead eyes. Bo Snecker laughed. It wasn't any different laugh from any other boy's. I remembered then that he killed Hoden. I began to sweat fire. Would Steele ever come?

"'Jim, the ole man hed cold feet an' he's give 'em to Jack,' said Bo. 'It ain't nothin' to lose your nerve once. Didn't I run like a scared jack-rabbit from Steele? Watch me if he comes to life, as the ole man hinted!'

"'About mebbe Steele wasn't in the 'dobe at all. Aw, thet's a joke! I seen him in bed. I seen his shadder. I heard his shots comin' from the room. Jack, you seen an' heerd same as me.'

"'Sure. I know the Ranger's cashed,' replied Blome. 'It's not that. I'm sore, boys.'

"'Deader 'n a door-nail in hell!' replied Pickens, louder, as he lifted his glass. 'Here's to Lone Star Steele's ghost! An' if I seen it this minnit I'd ask it to waltz with me!'

"The back door swung violently, and Steele, huge as a giant, plunged through and leaped square in front of that table.

"Some one of them let out a strange, harsh cry. It wasn't Blome or Snecker—probably Pickens. He dropped the glass he had lifted. The cry had stilled the room, so the breaking of the glass was plainly heard. For a space that must have been short, yet seemed long, everybody stood tight. Steele with both hands out and down, leaned a little, in a way I had never seen him do. It was the position of a greyhound, but that was merely the body of him. Steele's nerve, his spirit, his meaning was there, like lightning about to strike. Blome maintained a ghastly, stricken silence.

"Then the instant was plain when he realized this was no ghost of Steele, but the Ranger in the flesh. Blome's whole frame rippled as thought jerked him out of his trance. His comrades sat stone-still. Then Hilliard and Pickens dived without rising from the table. Their haste broke the spell.

"I wish I could tell it as quick as it happened. But Bo Snecker, turning white as a sheet, stuck to Blome. All the others failed him, as he had guessed they would fail. Low curses and exclamations were uttered by men sliding and pressing back, but the principals were mute. I was thinking hard, yet I had no time to get to Steele's side. I, like the rest, was held fast. But I kept my eyes sweeping around, then back again to that center pair.

"Blome slowly rose. I think he did it instinctively. Because if he had expected his first movement to start the action he never would have moved. Snecker sat partly on the rail of his chair, with both feet square on the floor, and he never twitched a muscle. There was a striking difference in the looks of these two rustlers. Snecker had burning holes for eyes in his white face. At the last he was staunch, defiant, game to the core. He didn't think. But Blome faced death and knew it. It was infinitely more than the facing of foes, the taking of stock, preliminary to the even break. Blome's attitude was that of a trapped wolf about to start into savage action; nevertheless, equally it was the pitifully weak stand of a ruffian against ruthless and powerful law.

"The border of Pecos County could have had no greater lesson than this—Blome face-to-face with the Ranger. That part of the border present saw its most noted exponent of lawlessness a coward, almost powerless to go for his gun, fatally sure of his own doom.

"But that moment, seeming so long, really so short, had to end. Blome made a spasmodic upheaval of shoulder and arm. Snecker a second later flashed into movement.

"Steele blurred in my sight. His action couldn't be followed. But I saw his gun, waving up, flame red once—twice—and the reports almost boomed together.

"Blome bent forward, arm down, doubled up, and fell over the table and slid to the floor.

"But Snecker's gun cracked with Steele's last shot. I heard the bullet strike Steele. It made me sick as if it had hit me. But Steele never budged. Snecker leaped up, screaming, his gun sputtering to the floor. His left hand swept to his right arm, which had been shattered by Steele's bullet.

"Blood streamed everywhere. His screams were curses, and then ended, testifying to a rage hardly human. Then, leaping, he went down on his knees after the gun.

"Don't pick it up," called Steele; his command would have checked anyone save an insane man. For an instant it even held Snecker. On his knees, right arm hanging limp, left extended, and face ghastly with agony and fiendish fury, he was certainly an appalling sight.

"'Bo, you're courtin' death,' called a hard voice from the crowd.

"'Snecker, wait. Don't make me kill you!' cried Steele swiftly. 'You're still a boy. Surrender! You'll outlive your sentence many years. I promise clemency. Hold, you fool!'

"But Snecker was not to be denied the last game move. He scrabbled for his gun. Just then something, a breathtaking intuition—I'll never know what—made me turn my head. I saw the bartender deliberately aim a huge gun at Steele. If he had not been so slow, I would have been too late. I whirled and shot. Talk about nick of time! Blandy pulled trigger just as my bullet smashed into his head.

"He dropped dead behind the bar and his gun dropped in front. But he had hit Steele.

"The Ranger staggered, almost fell. I thought he was done, and, yelling, I sped to him.

"But he righted himself. Then I wheeled again. Someone in the crowd killed Bo Snecker as he wobbled up with his gun. That was the signal for a wild run for outdoors, for cover. I heard the crack of guns and whistle of lead. I shoved Steele back of the bar, falling over Blandy as I did so.

"When I got up Steele was leaning over the bar with a gun in each hand. There was a hot fight then for a minute or so, but I didn't fire a shot. Morton and his crowd were busy. Men ran everywhere, shooting, ducking, cursing. The room got blue with smoke till you couldn't see, and then the fight changed to the street.

"Steele and I ran out. There was shooting everywhere. Morton's crowd appeared to be in pursuit of rustlers in all directions. I ran with Steele, and did not observe his condition until suddenly he fell right down in the street. Then he looked so white and so bloody I thought he'd stopped another bullet and—"

Here Miss Sampson's agitation made it necessary for me to halt my story, and I hoped she had heard enough. But she was not sick, as Sally appeared to me; she simply had been overcome by emotion. And presently, with a blaze in her eyes that showed how her soul was aflame with righteous wrath at these rustlers and ruffians, and how, whether she knew it or not, the woman in her loved a fight, she bade me go on. So I persevered, and, with poor little Sally sagging against me, I went on with the details of that fight.

I told how Steele rebounded from his weakness and could no more have been stopped than an avalanche. For all I saw, he did not use his guns again. Here, there, everywhere, as Morton and his squad cornered a rustler, Steele would go in, ordering surrender, promising protection. He seemed to have no thoughts of bullets. I could not hold him back, and it was hard to keep pace with him. How many times he was shot at I had no idea, but it was many. He dragged forth this and that rustler, and turned them all over to Morton to be guarded. More than once he protected a craven rustler from the summary dealing Morton wanted to see in order.

I told Miss Sampson particularly how Steele appeared to me, what his effect was on these men, how toward the end of the fight rustlers were appealing to him to save them from these new-born vigilantes. I believed I drew a picture of the Ranger that would live forever in her heart of hearts. If she were a hero-worshiper she would have her fill.

One thing that was strange to me—leaving fight, action, blood, peril out of the story—the singular exultation, for want of some better term, that I experienced in recalling Steele's look, his wonderful cold, resistless, inexplicable presence, his unquenchable spirit which was at once deadly and merciful. Other men would have killed where he saved. I recalled this magnificent spiritual something about him, remembered it strongest in the ring of his voice as he appealed to Bo Snecker not to force him to kill. Then I told how we left a dozen prisoners under guard and went back to the Hope So to find Blome where he had fallen. Steele's bullet had cut one of the petals of the rose Snecker had playfully put in the rustler's buttonhole. Bright and fatal target for an eye like Steele's! Bo Snecker lay clutching his gun, his face set rigidly in that last fierce expression of his savage nature. There were five other dead men on the floor, and, significant of the work of Steele's unknown allies, Hilliard and Pickens were among them.

"Steele and I made for camp then," I concluded. "We didn't speak a word on the way out. When we reached camp all Steele said was for me to go off and leave him alone. He looked sick. I went off, only not very far. I knew what was wrong with him, and it wasn't bullet-wounds. I was near when he had his spell and fought it out.

"Strange how spilling blood affects some men! It never bothered me much. I hope I'm human, too. I certainly felt an awful joy when I sent that bullet into Blandy's bloated head in time. And I'll always feel that way about it. But Steele's different."

Chapter 12

TORN TWO WAYS

Steele lay in a shady little glade, partly walled by the masses of upreared rocks that we used as a lookout point. He was asleep, yet far from comfortable. The bandage I had put around his head had been made from strips of soiled towel, and, having collected sundry bloody spots, it was an unsightly affair. There was a blotch of dried blood down one side of Steele's face. His shirt bore more dark stains, and in one place was pasted fast to his shoulder where a bandage marked the location of his other wound. A number of green flies were crawling over him and buzzing around his head. He looked helpless, despite his giant size; and certainly a great deal worse off than I had intimated, and, in fact, than he really was.

Miss Sampson gasped when she saw him and both her hands flew to her breast.

"Girls, don't make any noise," I whispered. "I'd rather he didn't wake suddenly to find you here. Go round behind the rocks there. I'll wake him, and call you presently."

They complied with my wish, and I stepped down to Steele and gave him a little shake. He awoke instantly.

"Hello!" I said, "Want a drink?"

"Water or champagne?" he inquired.

I stared at him. "I've some champagne behind the rocks," I added.

"Water, you locoed son of a gun!"

He looked about as thirsty as a desert coyote; also, he looked flighty. I was reaching for the canteen when I happened to think what pleasure it would be to Miss Sampson to minister to him, and I drew back. "Wait a little." Then with an effort I plunged. "Vaughn, listen. Miss Sampson and Sally are here."

I thought he was going to jump up, he started so violently, and I pressed him back.

"She—Why, she's been here all the time—Russ, you haven't double-crossed me?"

"Steele!" I exclaimed. He was certainly out of his head.

"Pure accident, old man."

He appeared to be half stunned, yet an eager, strange, haunting look shone in his eyes. "Fool!" he exclaimed.

"Can't you make the ordeal easier for her?" I asked.

"This'll be hard on Diane. She's got to be told things!"

"Ah!" breathed Steele, sinking back. "Make it easier for her—Russ, you're a damned schemer. You have given me the double-cross. You have and she's going to."

"We're in bad, both of us," I replied thickly. "I've ideas, crazy enough maybe. I'm between the devil and the deep sea, I tell you. I'm about ready to show yellow. All the same, I say, see Miss Sampson and talk to her, even if you can't talk straight."

"All right, Russ," he replied hurriedly. "But, God, man, don't I look a sight! All this dirt and blood!"

"Well, old man, if she takes that bungled mug of yours in her lap, you can be sure you're loved. You needn't jump out of your boots! Brace up now, for I'm going to bring the girls." As I got up to go I heard him groan. I went round behind the stones and found the girls. "Come on," I said. "He's awake now, but a little queer. Feverish. He gets that way sometimes. It won't last long." I led Miss Sampson and Sally back into the shade of our little camp glade.

Steele had gotten worse all in a moment. Also, the fool had pulled the bandage off his head; his wound had begun to bleed anew, and the flies were paying no attention to his weak efforts to brush them away. His head rolled as we reached his side, and his eyes were certainly wild and wonderful and devouring enough. "Who's that?" he demanded.

"Easy there, old man," I replied. "I've brought the girls." Miss Sampson shook like a leaf in the wind.

"So you've come to see me die?" asked Steele in a deep and hollow voice. Miss Sampson gave me a lightning glance of terror.

"He's only off his head," I said. "Soon as we wash and bathe his head, cool his temperature, he'll be all right."

"Oh!" cried Miss Sampson, and dropped to her knees, flinging her gloves aside. She lifted Steele's head into her lap. When I saw her tears falling upon his face I felt worse than a villain. She bent over him for a moment, and one of the tender hands at his cheeks met the flow of fresh blood and did not shrink. "Sally," she said, "bring the scarf out of my coat. There's a veil too. Bring that. Russ, you get me some water—pour some in the pan there."

"Water!" whispered Steele.

She gave him a drink. Sally came with the scarf and veil, and then she backed away to the stone, and sat there. The sight of blood had made her a little pale and weak. Miss Sampson's hands trembled and her tears still fell, but neither interfered with her tender and skillful dressing of that bullet wound.

Steele certainly said a lot of crazy things. "But why'd you come—why're you so good—when you don't love me?"

"Oh, but—I do—love you," whispered Miss Sampson brokenly.

"How do I know?"

"I am here. I tell you."

There was a silence, during which she kept on bathing his head, and he kept on watching her. "Diane!" he broke out suddenly.

"Yes—yes."

"That won't stop the pain in my head."

"Oh, I hope so."

"Kiss me—that will," he whispered. She obeyed as a child might have, and kissed his damp forehead close to the red furrow where the bullet cut.

"Not there," Steele whispered.

Then blindly, as if drawn by a magnet, she bent to his lips. I could not turn away my head, though my instincts were delicate enough. I believe that kiss was the first kiss of love for both Diane Sampson and Vaughn Steele. It was so strange and so long, and somehow beautiful. Steele looked rapt. I could only see the side of Diane's face, and that was white, like snow. After she raised her head she seemed unable, for a moment, to take up her task where it had been broken off, and Steele lay as if he really were dead. Here I got up, and seating myself beside Sally, I put an arm around her. "Sally dear, there are others," I said.

"Oh, Russ—what's to come of it all?" she faltered, and then she broke down and began to cry softly. I would have been only too glad to tell her what hung in the balance, one way or another, had I known. But surely, catastrophe! Then I heard Steele's voice again and its huskiness, its different tone, made me fearful, made me strain my ears when I tried, or thought I tried, not to listen.

"Diane, you know how hard my duty is, don't you?"

"Yes, I know—I think I know."

"You've guessed—about your father?"

"I've seen all along you must clash. But it needn't be so bad. If I can only bring you two together—Ah! please don't speak any more. You're excited now, just not yourself."

"No, listen. We must clash, your father and I. Diane, he's not—"

"Not what he seems! Oh, I know, to my sorrow."

"What do you know?" She seemed drawn by a will stronger than her own. "To my shame I know. He has been greedy, crafty, unscrupulous—dishonest."

"Diane, if he were only that! That wouldn't make my duty torture. That wouldn't ruin your life. Dear, sweet girl, forgive me—your father's—"

"Hush, Vaughn. You're growing excited. It will not do. Please—please—"

"Diane, your father's—chief of this—gang that I came to break up."

"My God, hear him! How dare you—Oh, Vaughn, poor, poor boy, you're out of your mind! Sally, Russ, what shall we do? He's worse. He's saying the most dreadful things! I—I can't bear to hear him!"

Steele heaved a sigh and closed his eyes. I walked away with Sally, led her to and fro in a shady aisle beyond the rocks, and tried to comfort her as best I could. After a while, when we returned to the glade, Miss Sampson had considerable color in her cheeks, and Steele was leaning against the rock, grave and sad. I saw that he had recovered and he had reached the critical point. "Hello, Russ," he said. "Sprung a surprise on me, didn't you? Miss Sampson says I've been a little flighty while she bandaged me up. I hope I wasn't bad. I certainly feel better now. I seem to—to have dreamed."

Miss Sampson flushed at his concluding words. Then silence ensued. I could not think of anything to say and Sally was dumb. "You all seem very strange," said Miss Sampson.

When Steele's face turned gray to his lips I knew the moment had come. "No doubt. We all feel so deeply for you," he said.

"Me? Why?"

"Because the truth must no longer be concealed."

It was her turn to blanch, and her eyes, strained, dark as night, flashed from one of us to the other.

"The truth! Tell it then." She had more courage than any of us.

"Miss Sampson, your father is the leader of this gang of rustlers I have been tracing. Your cousin George Wright, is his right-hand man."

Miss Sampson heard, but she did not believe.

"Tell her, Russ," Steele added huskily, turning away. Wildly she whirled to me. I would have given anything to have been able to lie to her. As it was I could not speak. But she read the truth in my face. And she collapsed as if she had been shot. I caught her and laid her on the grass.

Sally, murmuring and crying, worked over her. I helped. But Steele stood aloof, dark and silent, as if he hoped she would never return to consciousness.

When she did come to, and began to cry, to moan, to talk frantically, Steele staggered away, while Sally and I made futile efforts to calm her. All we could do was to prevent her doing herself violence. Presently, when her fury of emotion subsided, and she began to show a hopeless stricken shame, I left Sally with her and went off a little way myself. How long I remained absent I had no idea, but it was no inconsiderable length of time. Upon my return, to my surprise and relief, Miss Sampson had recovered her composure, or at least, self-control. She stood leaning against the rock where Steele had been, and at this moment, beyond any doubt, she was supremely more beautiful than I had ever seen her. She was white, tragic, wonderful. "Where is Mr. Steele?" she asked. Her tone and her look did not seem at all suggestive of the mood I expected to find her in—one of beseeching agony, of passionate appeal to Steele not to ruin her father.

"I'll find him," I replied turning away.

Steele was readily found and came back with me. He was as unlike himself as she was strange. But when they again faced each other, then they were indeed new to me.

"I want to know—what you must do," she said. Steele told her briefly, and his voice was stern.

"Those—those criminals outside of my own family don't concern me now. But can my father and cousin be taken without bloodshed? I want to know the absolute truth." Steele knew that they could not be, but he could not tell her so. Again she appealed to me. Thus my part in the situation grew harder. It hurt me so that it made me angry, and my anger made me cruelly frank.

"No. It can't be done. Sampson and Wright will be desperately hard to approach, which'll make the chances even. So, if you must know the truth, it'll be your father and cousin to go under, or it'll be Steele or me, or any combination luck breaks—or all of us!"

Her self-control seemed to fly to the four winds. Swift as light she flung herself down before Steele, against his knees, clasped her arms round him. "Good God! Miss Sampson, you mustn't do that!" implored Steele. He tried to break her hold with shaking hands, but he could not.

"Listen! Listen!" she cried, and her voice made Steele, and Sally and me also, still as the rock behind us. "Hear me! Do you think I beg you to let my father go, for his sake? No! No! I have gloried in your Ranger duty. I have loved you because of it. But some awful tragedy threatens here. Listen, Vaughn Steele. Do not you deny me, as I kneel here. I love you. I never loved any other man. But not for my love do I beseech you.

"There is no help here unless you forswear your duty. Forswear it! Do not kill my father—the father of the woman who loves you. Worse and more horrible it would be to let my father kill you! It's I who make this situation unnatural, impossible. You must forswear your duty. I can live no longer if you don't. I pray you—" Her voice had sunk to a whisper, and now it failed. Then she seemed to get into his arms, to wind herself around him, her hair loosened, her face upturned, white and spent, her arms blindly circling his neck. She was all love, all surrender, all supreme appeal, and these, without her beauty, would have made her wonderful. But her beauty! Would not Steele have been less than a man or more than a man had he been impervious to it? She was like some snow-white exquisite flower, broken, and suddenly blighted. She was a woman then in all that made a woman helpless—in all that made her mysterious, sacred, absolutely and unutterably more than any other thing in life. All this time my gaze had been riveted on her only. But when she lifted her white face, tried to lift it, rather, and he drew her up, and then when both white faces met and seemed to blend in something rapt, awesome, tragic as life—then I saw Steele.

I saw a god, a man as beautiful as she was. They might have stood, indeed, they did stand alone in the heart of a desert—alone in the world—alone with their love and their agony. It was a solemn and profound moment for me. I faintly realized how great it must have been for them, yet all the while there hammered at my mind the vital thing at stake. Had they forgotten, while I remembered? It might have been only a moment that he held her. It might have been my own agitation that conjured up such swift and whirling thoughts. But if my mind sometimes played me false my eyes never had. I thought I saw Diane Sampson die in Steele's arms; I could have sworn his heart was breaking; and mine was on the point of breaking, too.

How beautiful they were! How strong, how mercifully strong, yet shaken, he seemed! How tenderly, hopelessly, fatally appealing she was in that hour of her broken life! If I had been Steele I would have forsworn my duty, honor, name, service for her sake. Had I mind enough to divine his torture, his temptation, his narrow escape? I seemed to feel them, at any rate, and while I saw him with a beautiful light on his face, I saw him also ghastly, ashen, with hands that shook as they groped around her, loosing her, only to draw her convulsively back again. It was the saddest sight I had ever seen. Death was nothing to it. Here was the death of happiness. He must wreck the life of the woman who loved him and whom he loved. I was becoming half frantic, almost ready to cry out the uselessness of this scene, almost on the point of pulling them apart, when Sally dragged me away. Her clinging hold then made me feel perhaps a little of what Miss Sampson's must have been to Steele.

How different the feeling when it was mine! I could have thrust them apart, after all my schemes and tricks, to throw them together, in vague, undefined fear of their embrace. Still, when love beat at my own pulses, when Sally's soft hand held me tight and she leaned to me— that was different. I was glad to be led away—glad to have a chance to pull myself together. But was I to have that chance? Sally, who in the stife of emotion had been forgotten, might have to be reckoned with. Deep within me, some motive, some purpose, was being born in travail. I did not know what, but instinctively I feared Sally. I feared her because I loved her. My wits came back to combat my passion. This hazel-eyed girl, soft, fragile creature, might be harder to move than the Ranger. But could she divine a motive scarcely yet formed in my brain? Suddenly I became cool, with craft to conceal.

"Oh, Russ! What's the matter with you?" she queried quickly. "Can't Diane and Steele, you and I ride away from this bloody, bad country? Our own lives, our happiness, come first, do they not?"

"They ought to, I suppose," I muttered, fighting against the insidious sweetness of her. I knew then I must keep my lips shut or betray myself.

"You look so strange. Russ, I wouldn't want you to kiss me with that mouth. Thin, shut lips— smile! Soften and kiss me! Oh, you're so cold, strange! You chill me!"

"Dear child, I'm badly shaken," I said. "Don't expect me to be natural yet. There are things you can't guess. So much depended upon—Oh, never mind! I'll go now. I want to be alone, to think things out. Let me go, Sally."

She held me only the tighter, tried to pull my face around. How intuitively keen women were. She felt my distress, and that growing, stern, and powerful thing I scarcely dared to acknowledge to myself. Strangely, then, I relaxed and faced her. There was no use trying to foil these feminine creatures. Every second I seemed to grow farther from her. The swiftness of this mood of mine was my only hope. I realized I had to get away quickly, and make up my mind after that what I intended to do. It was an earnest, soulful, and loving pair of eyes that I met. What did she read in mine? Her hands left mine to slide to my shoulders, to slip behind my neck, to lock there like steel bands. Here was my ordeal. Was it to be as terrible as Steele's had been? I thought it would be, and I swore by all that was rising grim and cold in me that I would be strong. Sally gave a little cry that cut like a blade in my heart, and then she was close-pressed upon me, her quivering breast beating against mine, her eyes, dark as night now, searching my soul.

She saw more than I knew, and with her convulsive clasp of me confirmed my half-formed fears. Then she kissed me, kisses that had no more of girlhood or coquetry or joy or anything but woman's passion to blind and hold and tame. By their very intensity I sensed the tiger in me. And it was the tiger that made her new and alluring sweetness fail of its intent. I did not return one of her kisses. Just one kiss given back—and I would be lost.

"Oh, Russ, I'm your promised wife!" she whispered at my lips. "Soon, you said! I want it to be soon! To-morrow!" All the subtlety, the intelligence, the cunning, the charm, the love that made up the whole of woman's power, breathed in her pleading. What speech known to the tongue could have given me more torture? She chose the strongest weapon nature afforded her. And had the calamity to consider been mine alone, I would have laughed at it and taken Sally at her word. Then I told her in short, husky sentences what had depended on Steele: that I loved the Ranger Service, but loved him more; that his character, his life, embodied this Service I loved; that I had ruined him; and now I would forestall him, do his work, force the issue myself or die in the attempt.

"Dearest, it's great of you!" she cried. "But the cost! If you kill one of my kin I'll—I'll shrink from you! If you're killed—Oh, the thought is dreadful! You've done your share. Let Steele—some other Ranger finish it. I swear I don't plead for my uncle or my cousin, for their sakes. If they are vile, let them suffer. Russ, it's you I think of! Oh, my pitiful little dreams! I wanted so to surprise you with my beautiful home—the oranges, the mossy trees, the mocking-birds. Now you'll never, never come!"

"But, Sally, there's a chance—a mere chance I can do the job without—"

Then she let go of me. She had given up. I thought she was going to drop, and drew her toward the stone. I cursed the day I ever saw Neal and the service. Where, now, was the arch prettiness, the gay, sweet charm of Sally Langdon? She looked as if she were suffering from a desperate physical injury. And her final breakdown showed how, one way or another, I was lost to her.

As she sank on the stone I had my supreme wrench, and it left me numb, hard, in a cold sweat. "Don't betray me! I'll forestall him! He's planned nothing for to-day," I whispered hoarsely. "Sally—you dearest, gamest little girl in the world! Remember I loved you, even if I couldn't prove it your way. It's for his sake. I'm to blame for their love. Some day my act will look different to you. Good-by!"

Chapter 13

RUSS SITTELL IN ACTION

I ran like one possessed of devils down that rough slope, hurdling the stones and crashing through the brush, with a sound in my ears that was not all the rush of the wind. When I reached a level I kept running; but something dragged at me. I slowed down to a walk. Never in my life had I been victim of such sensation. I must flee from something that was drawing me back. Apparently one side of my mind was unalterably fixed, while the other was a hurrying conglomeration of flashes of thought, reception of sensations. I could not get calm.

By and by, almost involuntarily, with a fleeting look backward as if in expectation of pursuit, I hurried faster on. Action seemed to make my state less oppressive; it eased the weight upon me. But the farther I went on, the harder it was to continue. I was turning my back upon love, happiness, success in life, perhaps on life itself. I was doing that, but my decision had not been absolute. There seemed no use to go on farther until I was absolutely sure of myself. I received a clear warning thought that such work as seemed haunting and driving me could never be carried out in the mood under which I labored. I hung on to that thought. Several times I slowed up, then stopped, only to tramp on again.

At length, as I mounted a low ridge, Linrock lay bright and green before me, not faraway, and the sight was a conclusive check. There were mesquites on the ridge, and I sought the shade beneath them. It was the noon hour, with hot, glary sun and no wind. Here I had to have out my fight. If ever in my varied life of exciting adventure I strove to think, to understand myself, to see through difficulties, I assuredly strove then. I was utterly unlike myself; I could not bring the old self back; I was not the same man I once had been. But I could understand why. It was because of Sally Langdon, the gay and roguish girl who had bewitched me, the girl whom love had made a woman—the kind of woman meant to make life beautiful for me.

I saw her changing through all those weeks, holding many of the old traits and graces, acquiring new character of mind and body, to become what I had just fled from—a woman sweet, fair, loyal, loving, passionate.

Temptation assailed me. To have her to-morrow—my wife! She had said it. Just twenty-four little hours, and she would be mine—the only woman I had ever really coveted, the only one who had ever found the good in me. The thought was alluring. I followed it out, a long, happy stage-ride back to Austin, and then by train to her home where, as she had said, the oranges grew and the trees waved with streamers of gray moss and the mocking-birds made melody. I pictured that home. I wondered that long before I had not associated wealth and luxury with her family. Always I had owned a weakness for plantations, for the agricultural life with its open air and freedom from towns.

I saw myself riding through the cotton and rice and cane, home to the stately old mansion, where long-eared hounds bayed me welcome and a woman looked for me and met me with happy and beautiful smiles. There might—there *would* be children. And something new, strange, confounding with its emotion, came to life deep in my heart. There would be children! Sally their mother; I their father! The kind of life a lonely Ranger always yearned for and never had! I saw it all, felt it keenly, lived its sweetness in an hour of temptation that made me weak physically and my spirit faint and low.

For what had I turned my back on this beautiful, all-satisfying prospect? Was it to arrest and jail a few rustlers? Was it to meet that mocking Sampson face to face and show him my shield and reach for my gun? Was it to kill that hated Wright? Was it to save the people of Linrock from further greed, raids, murder? Was it to please and aid my old captain, Neal of the Rangers? Was it to save the Service to the State?

No—a thousand times no. It was for the sake of Steele. Because he was a wonderful man! Because I had been his undoing! Because I had thrown Diane Sampson into his arms! That had been my great error. This Ranger had always been the wonder and despair of his fellow officers, so magnificent a machine, so sober, temperate, chaste, so unremittingly loyal to the Service, so strangely stern and faithful to his conception of the law, so perfect in his fidelity to duty. He was the model, the inspiration, the pride of all of us. To me, indeed, he represented the Ranger Service. He was the incarnation of that spirit which fighting Texas had developed to oppose wildness and disorder and crime. He would carry through this Linrock case; but even so, if he were not killed, his career would be ruined. He might save the Service, yet at the cost of his happiness. He was not a machine; he was a man. He might be a perfect Ranger; still he was a human being.

The loveliness, the passion, the tragedy of a woman, great as they were, had not power to shake him from his duty. Futile, hopeless, vain her love had been to influence him. But there had flashed over me with subtle, overwhelming suggestion that not futile, not vain was *my* love to save him! Therefore, beyond and above all other claims, and by reason of my wrong to him, his claim came first.

It was then there was something cold and deathlike in my soul; it was then I bade farewell to Sally Langdon. For I knew, whatever happened, of one thing I was sure—I would have to kill either Sampson or Wright. Snecker could be managed; Sampson might be trapped into arrest; but Wright had no sense, no control, no fear. He would snarl like a panther and go for his gun, and he would have to be killed. This, of all consummations, was the one to be calculated upon. And, of course, by Sally's own words, that contingency would put me forever outside the pale for her.

I did not deceive myself; I did not accept the slightest intimation of hope; I gave her up. And then for a time regret, remorse, pain, darkness worked their will with me.

I came out of it all bitter and callous and sore, in the most fitting of moods to undertake a difficult and deadly enterprise. Miss Sampson completely slipped my mind; Sally became a wraith as of some one dead; Steele began to fade. In their places came the bushy-bearded Snecker, the olive-skinned Sampson with his sharp eyes, and dark, evil faced Wright. Their possibilities began to loom up, and with my speculation returned tenfold more thrilling and sinister the old strange zest of the man-hunt.

It was about one o'clock when I strode into Linrock. The streets for the most part were deserted. I went directly to the hall where Morton and Zimmer, with their men, had been left by Steele to guard the prisoners. I found them camping out in the place, restless, somber, anxious. The fact that only about half the original number of prisoners were left struck me as further indication of Morton's summary dealing. But when I questioned him as to the decrease in number, he said bluntly that they had escaped. I did not know whether or not to believe him. But that didn't matter. I tried to get in some more questions, only I found that Morton and Zimmer meant to be heard first. "Where's Steele?" they demanded.

"He's out of town, in a safe place," I replied. "Too bad hurt for action. I'm to rush through with the rest of the deal."

"That's good. We've waited long enough. This gang has been split, an' if we hurry they'll never get together again. Old man Snecker showed up to-day. He's drawin' the outfit in again. Reckon he's waitin' for orders. Sure he's ragin' since Bo was killed. This old fox will be dangerous if he gets goin'."

"Where is he now?" I queried.

"Over at the Hope So. Must be a dozen of the gang there. But he's the only leader left we know of. If we get him, the rustler gang will be broken for good. He's sent word down here for us to let our prisoners go or there'd be a damn bloody fight. We haven't sent our answer yet. Was hopin' Steele would show up. An' now we're sure glad you're back."

"Morton, I'll take the answer," I replied quickly. "Now there're two things. Do you know if Sampson and Wright are at the ranch?"

"They were an hour ago. We had word. Zimmer saw Dick."

"All right. Have you any horses handy?"

"Sure. Those hitched outside belong to us."

"I want you to take a man with you, in a few moments, and ride round the back roads and up to Sampson's house. Get off and wait under the trees till you hear me shoot or yell, then come fast."

Morton's breast heaved; he whistled as he breathed; his neck churned. "God Almighty! So *there* the scent leads! We always wondered—half believed. But no one spoke—no one had any nerve." Morton moistened his lips; his face was livid; his big hands shook. "Russ, you can gamble on me."

"Good. Well, that's all. Come out and get me a horse."

When I had mounted and was half-way to the Hope So, my plan, as far as Snecker was concerned, had been formed. It was to go boldy into the saloon, ask for the rustler, first pretend I had a reply from Morton and then, when I had Snecker's ear, whisper a message supposedly from Sampson. If Snecker was too keen to be decoyed I could at least surprise him off his guard and kill him, then run for my horse. The plan seemed clever to me. I had only one thing to fear, and that was a possibility of the rustlers having seen my part in Steele's defense the other day. That had to be risked. There were always some kind of risks to be faced.

It was scarcely a block and a half to the Hope So. Before I arrived I knew I had been seen. When I dismounted before the door I felt cold, yet there was an exhilaration in the moment. I never stepped more naturally and carelessly into the saloon. It was full of men. There were men behind the bar helping themselves. Evidently Blandy's place had not been filled. Every face near the door was turned toward me; dark, intent, scowling, malignant they were, and made me need my nerve.

"Say, boys, I've a word for Snecker," I called, quite loud. Nobody stirred. I swept my glance over the crowd, but did not see Snecker. "I'm in some hurry," I added.

"Bill ain't here," said a man at the table nearest me. "Air you comin' from Morton?"

"Nit. But I'm not yellin' this message."

The rustler rose, and in a few long strides confronted me.

"Word from Sampson!" I whispered, and the rustler stared. "I'm in his confidence. He's got to see Bill at once. Sampson sends word he's quit—he's done—he's through. The jig is up, and he means to hit the road out of Linrock."

"Bill'll kill him surer 'n hell," muttered the rustler. "But we all said it'd come to thet. An' what'd Wright say?"

"Wright! Why, he's cashed in. Didn't you-all hear? Reckon Sampson shot him."

The rustler cursed his amaze and swung his rigid arm with fist clenched tight. "When did Wright get it?"

"A little while ago. I don't know how long. Anyway, I saw him lyin' dead on the porch. An' say, pard, I've got to rustle. Send Bill up quick as he comes. Tell him Sampson wants to turn over all his stock an' then light out."

I backed to the door, and the last I saw of the rustler he was standing there in a scowling amaze. I had fooled him all right. If only I had the luck to have Snecker come along soon. Mounting, I trotted the horse leisurely up the street. Business and everything else was at a standstill in Linrock these days. The doors of the stores were barricaded. Down side streets, however, I saw a few people, a buckboard, and stray cattle.

When I reached the edge of town I turned aside a little and took a look at the ruins of Steele's adobe house. The walls and debris had all been flattened, scattered about, and if anything of, value had escaped destruction it had disappeared. Steele, however, had left very little that would have been of further use to him. Turning again, I continued on my way up to the ranch. It seemed that, though I was eager rather than backward, my mind seized avidly upon suggestion or attraction, as if to escape the burden of grim pondering. When about half-way across the flat, and perhaps just out of gun-shot sound of Sampson's house, I heard the rapid clatter of hoofs on the hard road. I wheeled, expecting to see Morton and his man, and was ready to be chagrined at their coming openly instead of by the back way. But this was only one man, and it was not Morton. He seemed of big build, and he bestrode a fine bay horse. There evidently was reason for hurry, too. At about one hundred yards, when I recognized Snecker, complete astonishment possessed me.

Well it was I had ample time to get on my guard! In wheeling my horse I booted him so hard that he reared. As I had been warm I had my sombrero over the pommel of the saddle. And when the head of my horse blocked any possible sight of movement of my hand, I pulled my gun and held it concealed under my sombrero. This rustler had bothered me in my calculations. And here he came galloping, alone. Exultation would have been involuntary then but for the sudden shock, and then the cold settling of temper, the breathless suspense. Snecker pulled his huge bay and pounded to halt abreast of me. Luck favored me. Had I ever had anything but luck in these dangerous deals?

Snecker seemed to fume; internally there was a volcano. His wide sombrero and bushy beard hid all of his face except his eyes, which were deepset furnaces. He, too, like his lieutenant, had been carried completely off balance by the strange message apparently from Sampson. It was Sampson's name that had fooled and decoyed these men. "Hey! You're the feller who jest left word fer some one at the Hope So?" he asked.

"Yes," I replied, while with my left hand I patted the neck of my horse, holding him still.

"Sampson wants me bad, eh?"

"Reckon there's only one man who wants you more."

Steadily, I met his piercing gaze. This was a rustler not to be long victim to any ruse. I waited in cold surety.

"You thet cowboy, Russ?" he asked.

"I was—and I'm not!" I replied significantly.

The violent start of this violent outlaw was a rippling jerk of passion. "What'n hell!" he ejaculated.

"Bill, you're easy."

"Who're you?" he uttered hoarsely.

I watched Snecker with hawk-like keenness. "United States deputy marshal. Bill, you're under arrest!"

He roared a mad curse as his hand clapped down to his gun. Then I fired through my sombrero. Snecker's big horse plunged. The rustler fell back, and one of his legs pitched high as he slid off the lunging steed. His other foot caught in the stirrup. This fact terribly frightened the horse. He bolted, dragging the rustler for a dozen jumps. Then Snecker's foot slipped loose. He lay limp and still and shapeless in the road. I did not need to go back to look him over.

But to make assurance doubly sure, I dismounted, and went back to where he lay. My bullet had gone where it had been aimed. As I rode up into Sampson's court-yard and turned in to the porch I heard loud and angry voices. Sampson and Wright were quarrelling again. How my lucky star guided me! I had no plan of action, but my brain was equal to a hundred lightning-swift evolutions. The voices ceased. The men had heard the horse. Both of them came out on the porch. In an instant I was again the lolling impudent cowboy, half under the influence of liquor.

"It's only Russ and he's drunk," said George Wright contemptuously.

"I heard horses trotting off there," replied Sampson. "Maybe the girls are coming. I bet I teach them not to run off again—Hello, Russ."

He looked haggard and thin, but seemed amiable enough. He was in his shirt-sleeves and he had come out with a gun in his hand. This he laid on a table near the wall. He wore no belt. I rode right up to the porch and, greeting them laconically, made a show of a somewhat tangle-footed cowboy dismounting. The moment I got off and straightened up, I asked no more. The game was mine. It was the great hour of my life and I met it as I had never met another. I looked and acted what I pretended to be, though a deep and intense passion, an almost ungovernable suspense, an icy sickening nausea abided with me. All I needed, all I wanted was to get Sampson and Wright together, or failing that, to maneuver into such position that I had any kind of a chance. Sampson's gun on the table made three distinct objects for me to watch and two of them could change position.

"What do you want here?" demanded Wright. He was red, bloated, thick-lipped, all fiery and sweaty from drink, though sober on the moment, and he had the expression of a desperate man in his last stand. It *was* his last stand, though he was ignorant of that.

"Me—Say, Wright, I ain't fired yet," I replied, in slow-rising resentment.

"Well, you're fired now," he replied insolently.

"Who fires me, I'd like to know?" I walked up on the porch and I had a cigarette in one hand, a match in the other. I struck the match.

"I do," said Wright.

I studied him with apparent amusement. It had taken only one glance around for me to divine that Sampson would enjoy any kind of a clash between Wright and me. "Huh! You fired me once before an' it didn't go, Wright. I reckon you don't stack up here as strong as you think."

He was facing the porch, moody, preoccupied, somber, all the time. Only a little of his mind was concerned with me. Manifestly there were strong forces at work. Both men were strained to a last degree, and Wright could be made to break at almost a word. Sampson laughed mockingly at this sally of mine, and that stung Wright. He stopped his pacing and turned his handsome, fiery eyes on me. "Sampson, I won't stand this man's impudence."

"Aw, Wright, cut that talk. I'm not impudent. Sampson knows I'm a good fellow, on the square, and I have you sized up about O.K."

"All the same, Russ, you'd better dig out," said Sampson. "Don't kick up any fuss. We're busy with deals to-day. And I expect visitors."

"Sure. I won't stay around where I ain't wanted," I replied. Then I lit my cigarette and did not move an inch out of my tracks.

Sampson sat in a chair near the door; the table upon which lay his gun stood between him and Wright. This position did not invite me to start anything. But the tension had begun to be felt. Sampson had his sharp gaze on me. "What'd you come for, anyway?" he asked suddenly.

"Well, I had some news I was asked to fetch in."

"Get it out of you then."

"See here now, Mr. Sampson, the fact is I'm a tender-hearted fellow. I hate to hurt people's feelin's. And if I was to spring this news in Mr. Wright's hearin', why, such a sensitive, high-tempered gentleman as he would go plumb off his nut." Unconcealed sarcasm was the dominant note in that speech. Wright flared up, yet he was eagerly curious. Sampson, probably, thought I was only a little worse for drink, and but for the way I rubbed Wright he would not have tolerated me at all.

"What's this news? You needn't be afraid of my feelings," said Wright.

"Ain't so sure of that," I drawled. "It concerns the lady you're sweet on, an' the ranger you ain't sweet on."

Sampson jumped up. "Russ, had Diane gone out to meet Steele?" he asked angrily.

"Sure she had," I replied.

I thought Wright would choke. He was thick-necked anyway, and the gush of blood made him tear at the soft collar of his shirt. Both men were excited now, moving about, beginning to rouse. I awaited my chance, patient, cold, all my feelings shut in the vise of my will.

"How do you know she met Steele?" demanded Sampson.

"I was there. I met Sally at the same time."

"But why should my daughter meet this Ranger?"

"She's in love with him and he's in love with her."

The simple statement might have had the force of a juggernaut. I reveled in Wright's state, but I felt sorry for Sampson. He had not outlived his pride. Then I saw the leaping thought—would this daughter side against him? Would she help to betray him? He seemed to shrivel up, to grow old while I watched him.

Wright, finding his voice, cursed Diane, cursed the Ranger, then Sampson, then me.

"You damned, selfish fool!" cried Sampson, in deep, bitter scorn. "All you think of is yourself. Your loss of the girl! Think once of me—my home—my life!"

Then the connection subtly put out by Sampson apparently dawned upon the other. Somehow, through this girl, her father and cousin were to be betrayed. I got that impression, though I could not tell how true it was. Certainly, Wright's jealousy was his paramount emotion.

Sampson thrust me sidewise off the porch. "Go away," he ordered. He did not look around to see if I came back. Quickly I leaped to my former position. He confronted Wright. He was beyond the table where the gun lay. They were close together. My moment had come. The game was mine—and a ball of fire burst in my brain to race all over me.

"To hell with you!" burst out Wright incoherently. He was frenzied. "I'll have her or nobody else will!"

"You never will," returned Sampson stridently. "So help me God, I'd rather see her Ranger Steele's wife than yours!"

While Wright absorbed that shock Sampson leaned toward him, all of hate and menace in his mien. They had forgotten the half-drunken cowboy. "Wright, you made me what I am," continued Sampson. "I backed you, protected you, finally I went in with you. Now it's ended. I quit you. I'm done!" Their gray, passion-corded faces were still as stones.

"Gentlemen," I called in clear, high, far-reaching voice, the intonation of authority, "you're both done!"

They wheeled to confront me, to see my leveled gun. "Don't move! Not a muscle! Not a finger!" I warned. Sampson read what Wright had not the mind to read. His face turned paler gray, to ashen.

"What d'ye mean?" yelled Wright fiercely, shrilly. It was not in him to obey my command, to see impending death. All quivering and strung, yet with perfect control, I raised my left hand to turn back a lapel of my open vest. The silver shield flashed brightly.

"United States deputy marshal in service of Ranger Steele!"

Wright howled like a dog. With barbarous and insane fury, with sheer, impotent folly, he swept a clawing hand for his gun. My shot broke his action as it cut short his life. Before Wright even tottered, before he loosed the gun, Sampson leaped behind him, clasped him with his left arm, quick as lightning jerked the gun from both clutching fingers and sheath. I shot at Sampson, then again, then a third time. All my bullets sped into the upheld nodding Wright. Sampson had protected himself with the body of the dead man. I had seen red flashes, puffs of smoke, had heard quick reports. Something stung my left arm. Then a blow like wind, light of sound yet shocking in impact, struck me, knocked me flat. The hot rend of lead followed the blow. My heart seemed to explode, yet my mind kept extraordinarily clear and rapid.

I raised myself, felt a post at my shoulder, leaned on it. I heard Sampson work the action of Wright's gun. I heard the hammer click, fall upon empty shells. He had used up all the loads in Wright's gun. I heard him curse as a man cursed at defeat. I waited, cool and sure now, for him to show his head or other vital part from behind his bolster. He tried to lift the dead man, to edge him closer toward the table where the gun lay. But, considering the peril of exposing himself, he found the task beyond him. He bent, peering at me under Wright's arm. Sampson's eyes were the eyes of a man who meant to kill me. There was never any mistaking the strange and terrible light of eyes like those.

More than once I had a chance to aim at them, at the top of Sampson's head, at a strip of his side. But I had only two shells left. I wanted to make sure. Suddenly I remembered Morton and his man. Then I pealed out a cry—hoarse, strange, yet far-reaching. It was answered by a shout. Sampson heard it. It called forth all that was in the man. He flung Wright's body off. But even as it dropped, before Sampson could recover to leap as he surely intended for the gun, I covered him, called piercingly to him. I could kill him there or as he moved. But one chance I gave him.

"Don't jump for the gun! Don't! I'll kill you! I've got two shells left! Sure as God, I'll kill you!"

He stood perhaps ten feet from the table where his gun lay. I saw him calculating chances. He was game. He had the courage that forced me to respect him. I just saw him measure the distance to that gun. He was magnificent. He meant to do it. I would have to kill him.

"Sampson, listen!" I cried, very swiftly. "The game's up! You're done! But think of your daughter! I'll spare your life, I'll give you freedom on one condition. For her sake! I've got you nailed—all the proofs. It was I behind the wall the other night. Blome, Hilliard, Pickens, Bo Snecker, are dead. I killed Bo Snecker on the way up here. There lies Wright. You're alone. And here comes Morton and his men to my aid.

"Give up! Surrender! Consent to demands and I'll spare you. You can go free back to your old country. It's for Diane's sake! Her life, perhaps her happiness, can be saved! Hurry, man! Your answer!"

"Suppose I refuse?" he queried, with a dark and terrible earnestness.

"Then I'll kill you in your tracks! You can't move a hand! Your word or death! Hurry, Sampson! I can't last much longer. But I can kill you before I drop. Be a man! For her sake! Quick! Another second now—By God, I'll kill you!"

"All right, Russ! I give my word," he said, and deliberately walked to the chair and fell into it, just as Morton came running up with his man.

"Put away your gun," I ordered them. "The game's up. Snecker and Wright are dead. Sampson is my prisoner. He has my word he'll be protected. It's for you to draw up papers with him. He'll divide all his property, every last acre, every head of stock as you and Zimmer dictate. He gives up all. Then he's free to leave the country, and he's never to return."

Chapter 14

THROUGH THE VALLEY

Sampson looked strangely at the great bloody blot on my breast and his look made me conscious of a dark hurrying of my mind. Morton came stamping up the steps with blunt queries, with anxious mien. When he saw the front of me he halted, threw wide his arms.

"There come the girls!" suddenly exclaimed Sampson. "Morton, help me drag Wright inside. They mustn't see him."

I was facing down the porch toward the court and corrals. Miss Sampson and Sally had come in sight, were swiftly approaching, evidently alarmed. Steele, no doubt, had remained out at the camp. I was watching them, wondering what they would do and say presently, and then Sampson and Johnson came to carry me indoors. They laid me on the couch in the parlor where the girls used to be so often.

"Russ, you're pretty hard hit," said Sampson, bending over me, with his hands at my breast. The room was bright with sunshine, yet the light seemed to be fading.

"Reckon I am," I replied.

"I'm sorry. If only you could have told me sooner! Wright, damn him! Always I've split over him!"

"But the last time, Sampson."

"Yes, and I came near driving you to kill me, too. Russ, you talked me out of it. For Diane's sake! She'll be in here in a minute. This'll be harder than facing a gun."

"Hard now. But it'll—turn out—O.K."

"Russ, will you do me a favor?" he asked, and he seemed shamefaced.

"Sure."

"Let Diane and Sally think Wright shot you. He's dead. It can't matter. And you're hard hit. The girls are fond of you. If—if you go under—Russ, the old side of my life is coming back. It's *been* coming. It'll be here just about when she enters this room. And by God, I'd change places with you if I could."

"Glad you—said that, Sampson," I replied. "And sure—Wright plugged me. It's our secret. I've a reason, too, not—that—it—matters—much—now."

The light was fading. I could not talk very well. I felt dumb, strange, locked in ice, with dull little prickings of my flesh, with dim rushing sounds in my ears. But my mind was clear. Evidently there was little to be done. Morton came in, looked at me, and went out. I heard the quick, light steps of the girls on the porch, and murmuring voices.

"Where'm I hit?" I whispered.

"Three places. Arm, shoulder, and a bad one in the breast. It got your lung, I'm afraid. But if you don't go quick, you've a chance."

"Sure I've a chance."

"Russ, I'll tell the girls, do what I can for you, then settle with Morton and clear out."

Just then Diane and Sally entered the room. I heard two low cries, so different in tone, and I saw two dim white faces. Sally flew to my side and dropped to her knees. Both hands went to my face, then to my breast. She lifted them, shaking. They were red. White and mute she gazed from them to me. But some woman's intuition kept her from fainting.

"Papa!" cried Diane, wringing her hands.

"Don't give way," he replied. "Both you girls will need your nerve. Russ is badly hurt. There's little hope for him."

Sally moaned and dropped her face against me, clasping me convulsively. I tried to reach a hand out to touch her, but I could not move. I felt her hair against my face. Diane uttered a low heart-rending cry, which both Sampson and I understood.

"Listen, let me tell it quick," he said huskily. "There's been a fight. Russ killed Snecker and Wright. They resisted arrest. It—it was Wright—it was Wright's gun that put Russ down. Russ let me off. In fact, Diane, he saved me. I'm to divide my property—return so far as possible what I've stolen—leave Texas at once and forever. You'll find me back in old Louisiana—if—if you ever want to come home."

As she stood there, realizing her deliverance, with the dark and tragic glory of her eyes passing from her father to me, my own sight shadowed, and I thought if I were dying then, it was not in vain.

"Send—for—Steele," I whispered.

Silently, swiftly, breathlessly they worked over me. I was exquisitely sensitive to touch, to sound, but I could not see anything. By and by all was quiet, and I slipped into a black void. Familiar heavy swift footsteps, the thump of heels of a powerful and striding man, jarred into the blackness that held me, seemed to split it to let me out; and I opened my eyes in a sunlit room to see Sally's face all lined and haggard, to see Miss Sampson fly to the door, and the stalwart Ranger bow his lofty head to enter. However far life had ebbed from me, then it came rushing back, keen-sighted, memorable, with agonizing pain in every nerve. I saw him start, I heard him cry, but I could not speak. He bent over me and I tried to smile. He stood silent, his hand on me, while Diane Sampson told swiftly, brokenly, what had happened.

How she told it! I tried to whisper a protest. To any one on earth except Steele I might have wished to appear a hero. Still, at that moment I had more dread of him than any other feeling. She finished the story with her head on his shoulder, with tears that certainly were in part for me. Once in my life, then, I saw him stunned. But when he recovered it was not Diane that he thought of first, nor of the end of Sampson's power. He turned to me.

"Little hope?" he cried out, with the deep ring in his voice. "No! There's every hope. No bullet hole like that could ever kill this Ranger. Russ!"

I could not answer him. But this time I did achieve a smile. There was no shadow, no pain in his face such as had haunted me in Sally's and Diane's. He could fight death the same as he could fight evil. He vitalized the girls. Diane began to hope; Sally lost her woe. He changed the atmosphere of that room. Something filled it, something like himself, big, virile, strong. The very look of him made me suddenly want to live; and all at once it seemed I felt alive. And that was like taking the deadened ends of nerves to cut them raw and quicken them with fiery current.

From stupor I had leaped to pain, and that tossed me into fever. There were spaces darkened, mercifully shutting me in; there were others of light, where I burned and burned in my heated blood. Sally, like the wraith she had become in my mind, passed in and out; Diane watched and helped in those hours when sight was clear. But always the Ranger was with me. Sometimes I seemed to feel his spirit grappling with mine, drawing me back from the verge. Sometimes, in strange dreams, I saw him there between me and a dark, cold, sinister shape.

The fever passed, and with the first nourishing drink given me I seemed to find my tongue, to gain something.

"Hello, old man," I whispered to Steele.

"Oh, Lord, Russ, to think you would double-cross me the way you did!"

That was his first speech to me after I had appeared to face round from the grave. His good-humored reproach told me more than any other thing how far from his mind was thought of death for me. Then he talked a little to me, cheerfully, with that directness and force characteristic of him always, showing me that the danger was past, and that I would now be rapidly on the mend. I discovered that I cared little whether I was on the mend or not. When I had passed the state of somber unrealities and then the hours of pain and then that first inspiring flush of renewed desire to live, an entirely different mood came over me. But I kept it to myself. I never even asked why, for three days, Sally never entered the room where I lay. I associated this fact, however, with what I had imagined her shrinking from me, her intent and pale face, her singular manner when occasion made it necessary or unavoidable for her to be near me.

No difficulty was there in associating my change of mood with her absence. I brooded. Steele's keen insight betrayed me to him, but all his power and his spirit availed nothing to cheer me. I pretended to be cheerful; I drank and ate anything given me; I was patient and quiet. But I ceased to mend.

Then, one day she came back, and Steele, who was watching me as she entered, quietly got up and without a word took Diane out of the room and left me alone with Sally.

"Russ, I've been sick myself—in bed for three days," she said. "I'm better now. I hope you are. You look so pale. Do you still think, brood about that fight?"

"Yes, I can't forget. I'm afraid it cost me more than life."

Sally was somber, bloomy, thoughtful. "You weren't driven to kill George?" she asked.

"How do you mean?"

"By that awful instinct, that hankering to kill, you once told me these gunmen had."

"No, I can swear it wasn't that. I didn't want to kill him. But he forced me. As I had to go after these two men it was a foregone conclusion about Wright. It was premeditated. I have no excuse."

"Hush—Tell me, if you confronted them, drew on them, then you had a chance to kill my uncle?"

"Yes. I could have done it easily."

"Why, then, didn't you?"

"It was for Diane's sake. I'm afraid I didn't think of you. I had put you out of my mind."

"Well, if a man can be noble at the same time he's terrible, you've been, Russ—I don't know how I feel. I'm sick and I can't think. I see, though, what you saved Diane and Steele. Why, she's touching happiness again, fearfully, yet really. Think of that! God only knows what you did for Steele. If I judged it by his suffering as you lay there about to die it would be beyond words to tell. But, Russ, you're pale and shaky now. Hush! No more talk!"

With all my eyes and mind and heart and soul I watched to see if she shrank from me. She was passive, yet tender as she smoothed my pillow and moved my head. A dark abstraction hung over her, and it was so strange, so foreign to her nature. No sensitiveness on earth could have equaled mine at that moment. And I saw and felt and knew that she did not shrink from me. Thought and feeling escaped me for a while. I dozed. The old shadows floated to and fro.

When I awoke Steele and Diane had just come in. As he bent over me I looked up into his keen gray eyes and there was no mask on my own as I looked up to him.

"Son, the thing that was needed was a change of nurses," he said gently. "I intend to make up some sleep now and leave you in better care."

From that hour I improved. I slept, I lay quietly awake, I partook of nourishing food. I listened and watched, and all the time I gained. But I spoke very little, and though I tried to brighten when Steele was in the room I made only indifferent success of it. Days passed. Sally was almost always with me, yet seldom alone. She was grave where once she had been gay. How I watched her face, praying for that shade to lift! How I listened for a note of the old music in her voice! Sally Langdon had sustained a shock to her soul almost as dangerous as had been the blow at my life. Still I hoped. I had seen other women's deadened and darkened spirits rebound and glow once more. It began to dawn upon me, however, that more than time was imperative if she were ever to become her old self again.

Studying her closer, with less thought of myself and her reaction to my presence, I discovered that she trembled at shadows, seemed like a frightened deer with a step always on its trail, was afraid of the dark. Then I wondered why I had not long before divined one cause of her strangeness. The house where I had killed one of her kin would ever be haunted for her. She had said she was a Southerner and that blood was thick. When I had thought out the matter a little further, I deliberately sat up in bed, scaring the wits out of all my kind nurses.

"Steele, I'll never get well in this house. I want to go home. When can you take me?"

They remonstrated with me and pleaded and scolded, all to little avail. Then they were persuaded to take me seriously, to plan, providing I improved, to start in a few days. We were to ride out of Pecos County together, back along the stage trail to civilization. The look in Sally's eyes decided my measure of improvement. I could have started that very day and have borne up under any pain or distress. Strange to see, too, how Steele and Diane responded to the stimulus of my idea, to the promise of what lay beyond the wild and barren hills!

He told me that day about the headlong flight of every lawless character out of Linrock, the very hour that Snecker and Wright and Sampson were known to have fallen. Steele expressed deep feeling, almost mortification, that the credit of that final coup had gone to him, instead of me. His denial and explanation had been only a few soundless words in the face of a grateful and clamorous populace that tried to reward him, to make him mayor of Linrock. Sampson had made restitution in every case where he had personally gained at the loss of farmer or rancher; and the accumulation of years went far toward returning to Linrock what it had lost in a material way. He had been a poor man when he boarded the stage for Sanderson, on his way out of Texas forever.

Not long afterward I heard Steele talking to Miss Sampson, in a deep and agitated voice. "You must rise above this. When I come upon you alone I see the shadow, the pain in your face. How wonderfully this thing has turned out when it might have ruined you! I expected it to ruin you. Who, but that wild boy in there could have saved us all? Diane, you have had cause for sorrow. But your father is alive and will live it down. Perhaps, back there in Louisiana, the dishonor will never be known. Pecos County is far from your old home. And even in San Antonio and Austin, a man's evil repute means little.

"Then the line between a rustler and a rancher is hard to draw in these wild border days. Rustling is stealing cattle, and I once heard a well-known rancher say that all rich cattlemen had done a little stealing. Your father drifted out here, and like a good many others, he succeeded. It's perhaps just as well not to split hairs, to judge him by the law and morality of a civilized country. Some way or other he drifted in with bad men. Maybe a deal that was honest somehow tied his hands and started him in wrong.

"This matter of land, water, a few stray head of stock had to be decided out of court. I'm sure in his case he never realized where he was drifting. Then one thing led to another, until he was face to face with dealing that took on crooked form. To protect himself he bound men to him. And so the gang developed. Many powerful gangs have developed that way out here. He could not control them. He became involved with them.

"And eventually their dealings became deliberately and boldly dishonest. That meant the inevitable spilling of blood sooner or later, and so he grew into the leader because he was the strongest. Whatever he is to be judged for I think he could have been infinitely worse."

When he ceased speaking I had the same impulse that must have governed Steele—somehow to show Sampson not so black as he was painted, to give him the benefit of a doubt, to arraign him justly in the eyes of Rangers who knew what wild border life was.

"Steele, bring Diane in!" I called. "I've something to tell her." They came quickly, concerned probably at my tone. "I've been hoping for a chance to tell you something, Miss Sampson. That day I came here your father was quarreling with Wright. I had heard them do that before. He hated Wright. The reason came out just before we had the fight. It was my plan to surprise them. I did. I told them you went out to meet Steele—that you two were in love with each other. Wright grew wild. He swore no one would ever have you. Then Sampson said he'd rather have you Steele's wife than Wright's.

"I'll not forget that scene. There was a great deal back of it, long before you ever came out to Linrock. Your father said that he had backed Wright, that the deal had ruined him, made him a rustler. He said he quit; he was done. Now, this is all clear to me, and I want to explain, Miss Sampson. It was Wright who ruined your father. It was Wright who was the rustler. It was Wright who made the gang necessary. But Wright had not the brains or the power to lead men. Because blood is thick, your father became the leader of that gang. At heart he was never a criminal.

"The reason I respected him was because he showed himself a man at the last. He faced me to be shot, and I couldn't do it. As Steele said, you've reason for sorrow. But you must get over it. You mustn't brood. I do not see that you'll be disgraced or dishonored. Of course, that's not the point. The vital thing is whether or not a woman of your high-mindedness had real and lasting cause for shame. Steele says no. I say no."

Then, as Miss Sampson dropped down beside me, her eyes shining and wet, Sally entered the room in time to see her cousin bend to kiss me gratefully with sisterly fervor. Yet it was a woman's kiss, given for its own sake. Sally could not comprehend; it was too sudden, too unheard-of, that Diane Sampson should kiss me, the man she did not love. Sally's white, sad face changed, and in the flaming wave of scarlet that dyed neck and cheek and brow I read with mighty pound of heart that, despite the dark stain between us, she loved me still.

Chapter 15

CONVALESCENCE

Four mornings later we were aboard the stage, riding down the main street, on the way out of Linrock. The whole town turned out to bid us farewell. The cheering, the clamor, the almost passionate fervor of the populace irritated me, and I could not see the incident from their point of view. Never in my life had I been so eager to get out of a place. But then I was morbid, and the whole world hinged on one thing. Morton insisted on giving us an escort as far as Del Rio. It consisted of six cowboys, mounted, with light packs, and they rode ahead of the stage.

We had the huge vehicle to ourselves. A comfortable bed had been rigged up for me by placing boards across from seat to seat, and furnishing it with blankets and pillows. By some squeezing there was still room enough inside for my three companions; but Steele expressed an intention of riding mostly outside, and Miss Sampson's expression betrayed her. I was to be alone with Sally. The prospect thrilled while it saddened me. How different this ride from that first one, with all its promise of adventure and charm!

"It's over!" said Steele thickly. "It's done! I'm glad, for their sakes—glad for ours. We're out of town."

I had been quick to miss the shouts and cheers. And I had been just as quick to see, or to imagine, a subtle change in Sally Langdon's face. We had not traveled a mile before the tension relaxed about her lips, the downcast eyelids lifted, and I saw, beyond any peradventure of doubt, a lighter spirit. Then I relaxed myself, for I had keyed up every nerve to make myself strong for this undertaking. I lay back with closed eyes, weary, aching, in more pain than I wanted them to discover. And I thought and thought.

Miss Sampson had said to me: "Russ, it'll all come right. I can tell you now what you never guessed. For years Sally had been fond of our cousin, George Wright. She hadn't seen him since she was a child. But she remembered. She had an only brother who was the image of George. Sally devotedly loved Arthur. He was killed in the Rebellion. She never got over it. That left her without any family. George and I were her nearest kin.

"How she looked forward to meeting George out here! But he disappointed her right at the start. She hates a drinking man. I think she came to hate George, too. But he always reminded her of Arthur, and she could never get over that. So, naturally, when you killed George she was terribly shocked. There were nights when she was haunted, when I had to stay with her. Vaughn and I have studied her, talked about her, and we think she's gradually recovering. She loved you, too; and Sally doesn't change. Once with her is for always. So let me say to you what you said to me—do not brood. All will yet be well, thank God!"

Those had been words to remember, to make me patient, to lessen my insistent fear. Yet, what did I know of women? Had not Diane Sampson and Sally Langdon amazed and nonplused me many a time, at the very moment when I had calculated to a nicety my conviction of their action, their feeling? It was possible that I had killed Sally's love for me, though I could not believe so; but it was very possible that, still loving me, she might never break down the barrier between us. The beginning of that journey distressed me physically; yet, gradually, as I grew accustomed to the roll of the stage and to occasional jars, I found myself easier in body. Fortunately there had been rain, which settled the dust; and a favorable breeze made riding pleasant, where ordinarily it would have been hot and disagreeable.

We tarried long enough in the little hamlet of Sampson for Steele to get letters from reliable ranchers. He wanted a number of references to verify the Ranger report he had to turn in to Captain Neal. This precaution he took so as to place in Neal's hands all the evidence needed to convince Governor Smith. And now, as Steele returned to us and entered the stage, he spoke of this report. "It's the longest and the best I ever turned in," he said, with a gray flame in his eyes. "I shan't let Russ read it. He's peevish because I want his part put on record. And listen, Diane. There's to be a blank line in this report. Your father's name will never be recorded. Neither the Governor, nor the adjutant-general, nor Captain Neal, nor any one back Austin way will ever know who this mysterious leader of the Pecos gang might have been.

"Even out here very few know. Many supposed, but few knew. I've shut the mouths of those few. That blank line in the report is for a supposed and mysterious leader who vanished. Jack Blome, the reputed leader, and all his lawless associates are dead. Linrock is free and safe now, its future in the hands of roused, determined, and capable men."

We were all silent after Steele ceased talking. I did not believe Diane could have spoken just then. If sorrow and joy could be perfectly blended in one beautiful expression, they were in her face. By and by I dared to say: "And Vaughn Steele, Lone Star Ranger, has seen his last service!"

"Yes," he replied with emotion.

Sally stirred and turned a strange look upon us all. "In that case, then, if I am not mistaken, there were two Lone Star Rangers—and both have seen their last service!" Sally's lips were trembling, the way they trembled when it was impossible to tell whether she was about to laugh or cry. The first hint of her old combative spirit or her old archness! A wave of feeling rushed over me, too much for me in my weakened condition. Dizzy, racked with sudden shooting pains, I closed my eyes; and the happiness I embraced was all the sweeter for the suffering it entailed. Something beat into my ears, into my brain, with the regularity and rapid beat of pulsing blood—not too late! Not too late!

From that moment the ride grew different, even as I improved with leaps and bounds. Sanderson behind us, the long gray barren between Sanderson and the Rio Grande behind us, Del Rio for two days, where I was able to sit up, all behind us—and the eastward trail to Uvalde before us! We were the only passengers on the stage from Del Rio to Uvalde. Perhaps Steele had so managed the journey. Assuredly he had become an individual with whom traveling under the curious gaze of strangers would have been embarrassing. He was most desperately in love. And Diane, all in a few days, while riding these long, tedious miles, ordinarily so fatiguing, had renewed her bloom, had gained what she had lost. She, too, was desperately in love, though she remembered her identity occasionally, and that she was in the company of a badly shot-up young man and a broken-hearted cousin.

Most of the time Diane and Steele rode on top of the stage. When they did ride inside their conduct was not unbecoming; indeed, it was sweet to watch; yet it loosed the fires of jealous rage and longing in me; and certainly had some remarkable effect upon Sally. Gradually she had been losing that strange and somber mood she had acquired, to brighten and change more and more. Perhaps she divined something about Diane and Steele that escaped me. Anyway, all of a sudden she was transformed. "Look here, if you people want to spoon, please get out on top," she said.

If that was not the old Sally Langdon I did not know who it was. Miss Sampson tried to appear offended, and Steele tried to look insulted, but they both failed. They could not have looked anything but happy. Youth and love were too strong for this couple, whom circumstances might well have made grave and thoughtful. They were magnet and steel, powder and spark. Any moment, right before my eyes, I expected them to rush right into each other's arms. And when they refrained, merely substituting clasped hands for a dearer embrace, I closed my eyes and remembered them, as they would live in my memory forever, standing crushed together on the ridge that day, white lips to white lips, embodying all that was beautiful, passionate and tragic.

And I, who had been their undoing, in the end was their salvation. How I hugged that truth to my heart!

It seemed, following Sally's pert remark, that after an interval of decent dignity, Diane and Steele did go out upon the top of the stage. "Russ," whispered Sally, "they're up to something. I heard a few words. I bet you they're going to get married in San Antonio."

"Well, it's about time," I replied.

"But oughtn't they take us into their confidence?"

"Sally, they have forgotten we are upon the earth."

"Oh, I'm so glad they're happy!"

Then there was a long silence. It was better for me to ride lying down, in which position I was at this time. After a mile Sally took my hand and held it without speaking. My heart leaped, but I did not open my eyes or break that spell even with a whisper. "Russ, I must say—tell you—"

She faltered, and still I kept my eyes closed. I did not want to wake up from that dream. "Have I been very—very sad?" she went on.

"Sad and strange, Sally. That was worse than my bullet-holes." She gripped my hand. I felt her hair on my brow, felt her breath on my cheek.

"Russ, I swore—I'd hate you if you—if you—"

"I know. Don't speak of it," I interposed hurriedly.

"But I don't hate you. I—I love you. And I can't give you up!"

"Darling! But, Sally, can you get over it—can you forget?"

"Yes. That horrid black spell had gone with the miles. Little by little, mile after mile, and now it's gone! But I had to come to the point. To go back on my word! To tell you. Russ, you never, *never* had any sense!"

Then I opened my eyes and my arms, too, and we were reunited. It must have been a happy moment, so happy that it numbed me beyond appreciation. "Yes, Sally," I agreed; "but no man ever had such a wonderful girl."

"Russ, I never—took off your ring," she whispered.

"But you hid your hand from my sight," I replied quickly.

"Oh dear Russ, we're crazy—as crazy as those lunatics outside. Let's think a little."

I was very content to have no thought at all, just to see and feel her close to me.

"Russ, will you give up the Ranger Service for me?" she asked.

"Indeed I will."

"And leave this fighting Texas, never to return till the day of guns and Rangers and bad men and even-breaks is past?"

"Yes."

"Will you go with me to my old home? It was beautiful once, Russ, before it was let run to rack and ruin. A thousand acres. An old stone house. Great mossy oaks. A lake and river. There are bear, deer, panther, wild boars in the breaks. You can hunt. And ride! I've horses, Russ, such horses! They could run these scrubby broncos off their legs. Will you come?"

"Come! Sally, I rather think I will. But, dearest, after I'm well again I must work," I said earnestly. "I've got to have a job."

"You're indeed a poor cowboy out of a job! Remember your deceit. Oh, Russ! Well, you'll have work, never fear."

"Sally, is this old home of yours near the one Diane speaks of so much?" I asked.

"Indeed it is. But hers has been kept under cultivation and in repair, while mine has run down. That will be our work, to build it up. So it's settled then?"

"Almost. There are certain—er—formalities—needful in a compact of this kind." She looked inquiringly at me, with a soft flush. "Well, if you are so dense, try to bring back that Sally Langdon who used to torment me. How you broke your promises! How you leaned from your saddle! Kiss me, Sally!"

Later, as we drew close to Uvalde, Sally and I sat in one seat, after the manner of Diane and Vaughn, and we looked out over the west where the sun was setting behind dim and distant mountains. We were fast leaving the wild and barren border. Already it seemed far beyond that broken rugged horizon with its dark line silhouetted against the rosy and golden sky. Already the spell of its wild life and the grim and haunting faces had begun to fade out of my memory. Let newer Rangers, with less to lose, and with the call in their hearts, go on with our work 'till soon that wild border would be safe!

The great Lone Star State must work out its destiny. Some distant day, in the fulness of time, what place the Rangers had in that destiny would be history.

THE LAST OF THE PLAINSMEN

PREFATORY NOTE

Buffalo Jones needs no introduction to American sportsmen, but to these of my readers who are unacquainted with him a few words may not be amiss.

He was born sixty-two years ago on the Illinois prairie, and he has devoted practically all of his life to the pursuit of wild animals. It has been a pursuit which owed its unflagging energy and indomitable purpose to a singular passion, almost an obsession, to capture alive, not to kill. He has caught and broken the will of every well-known wild beast native to western North America. Killing was repulsive to him. He even disliked the sight of a sporting rifle, though for years necessity compelled him to earn his livelihood by supplying the meat of buffalo to the caravans crossing the plains. At last, seeing that the extinction of the noble beasts was inevitable, he smashed his rifle over a wagon wheel and vowed to save the species. For ten years he labored, pursuing, capturing and taming buffalo, for which the West gave him fame, and the name Preserver of the American Bison.

As civilization encroached upon the plains Buffalo Jones ranged slowly westward; and to-day an isolated desert-bound plateau on the north rim of the Grand Canyon of Arizona is his home. There his buffalo browse with the mustang and deer, and are as free as ever they were on the rolling plains.

In the spring of 1907 I was the fortunate companion of the old plainsman on a trip across the desert, and a hunt in that wonderful country of yellow crags, deep canyons and giant pines. I want to tell about it. I want to show the color and beauty of those painted cliffs and the long, brown-matted bluebell-dotted aisles in the grand forests; I want to give a suggestion of the tang of the dry, cool air; and particularly I want to throw a little light upon the life and nature of that strange character and remarkable man, Buffalo Jones.

Happily in remembrance a writer can live over his experiences, and see once more the moonblanched silver mountain peaks against the dark blue sky; hear the lonely sough of the night wind through the pines; feel the dance of wild expectation in the quivering pulse; the stir, the thrill, the joy of hard action in perilous moments; the mystery of man's yearning for the unattainable.

As a boy I read of Boone with a throbbing heart, and the silent moccasined, vengeful Wetzel I loved.

I pored over the deeds of later men—Custer and Carson, those heroes of the plains. And as a man I came to see the wonder, the tragedy of their lives, and to write about them. It has been my destiny—what a happy fulfillment of my dreams of border spirit!—to live for a while in the fast-fading wild environment which produced these great men with the last of the great plainsmen.

ZANE GREY.

CHAPTER 1.

THE ARIZONA DESERT

One afternoon, far out on the sun-baked waste of sage, we made camp near a clump of withered pinyon trees. The cold desert wind came down upon us with the sudden darkness. Even the Mormons, who were finding the trail for us across the drifting sands, forgot to sing and pray at sundown. We huddled round the campfire, a tired and silent little group. When out of the lonely, melancholy night some wandering Navajos stole like shadows to our fire, we hailed their advent with delight. They were good-natured Indians, willing to barter a blanket or bracelet; and one of them, a tall, gaunt fellow, with the bearing of a chief, could speak a little English.

"How," said he, in a deep chest voice.

"Hello, Noddlecoddy," greeted Jim Emmett, the Mormon guide.

"Ugh!" answered the Indian.

"Big paleface—Buffalo Jones—-big chief—buffalo man," introduced Emmett, indicating Jones.

"How." The Navajo spoke with dignity, and extended a friendly hand.

"Jones big white chief—rope buffalo—tie up tight," continued Emmett, making motions with his arm, as if he were whirling a lasso.

"No big—heap small buffalo," said the Indian, holding his hand level with his knee, and smiling broadly.

Jones, erect, rugged, brawny, stood in the full light of the campfire. He had a dark, bronzed, inscrutable face; a stern mouth and square jaw, keen eyes, half-closed from years of searching the wide plains; and deep furrows wrinkling his cheeks. A strange stillness enfolded his feature the tranquility earned from a long life of adventure.

He held up both muscular hands to the Navajo, and spread out his fingers.

"Rope buffalo—heap big buffalo—heap many—one sun."

The Indian straightened up, but kept his friendly smile.

"Me big chief," went on Jones, "me go far north—Land of Little Sticks—Naza! Naza! rope musk-ox; rope White Manitou of Great Slave Naza! Naza!"

"Naza!" replied the Navajo, pointing to the North Star; "no—no."

"Yes me big paleface—me come long way toward setting sun—go cross Big Water—go Buckskin—Siwash—chase cougar."

The cougar, or mountain lion, is a Navajo god and the Navajos hold him in as much fear and reverence as do the Great Slave Indians the musk-ox.

"No kill cougar," continued Jones, as the Indian's bold features hardened. "Run cougar horseback—run long way—dogs chase cougar long time—chase cougar up tree! Me big chief—me climb tree—climb high up—lasso cougar—rope cougar—tie cougar all tight."

The Navajo's solemn face relaxed

136

"White man heap fun. No."

"Yes," cried Jones, extending his great arms. "Me strong; me rope cougar—me tie cougar; ride off wigwam, keep cougar alive."

"No," replied the savage vehemently.

"Yes," protested Jones, nodding earnestly.

"No," answered the Navajo, louder, raising his dark head.

"Yes!" shouted Jones.

"BIG LIE!" the Indian thundered.

Jones joined good-naturedly in the laugh at his expense. The Indian had crudely voiced a skepticism I had heard more delicately hinted in New York, and singularly enough, which had strengthened on our way West, as we met ranchers, prospectors and cowboys. But those few men I had fortunately met, who really knew Jones, more than overbalanced the doubt and ridicule cast upon him. I recalled a scarred old veteran of the plains, who had talked to me in true Western bluntness:

"Say, young feller, I heerd yer couldn't git acrost the Canyon fer the deep snow on the north rim. Wal, ye're lucky. Now, yer hit the trail fer New York, an' keep goin'! Don't ever tackle the desert, 'specially with them Mormons. They've got water on the brain, wusser 'n religion. It's two hundred an' fifty miles from Flagstaff to Jones range, an' only two drinks on the trail. I know this hyar Buffalo Jones. I knowed him way back in the seventies, when he was doin' them ropin' stunts thet made him famous as the preserver of the American bison. I know about that crazy trip of his'n to the Barren Lands, after musk-ox. An' I reckon I kin guess what he'll do over there in the Siwash. He'll rope cougars—sure he will—an' watch 'em jump. Jones would rope the devil, an' tie him down if the lasso didn't burn. Oh! he's hell on ropin' things. An' he's wusser 'n hell on men, an' hosses, an' dogs."

All that my well-meaning friend suggested made me, of course, only the more eager to go with Jones. Where I had once been interested in the old buffalo hunter, I was now fascinated. And now I was with him in the desert and seeing him as he was, a simple, quiet man, who fitted the mountains and the silences, and the long reaches of distance.

"It does seem hard to believe—all this about Jones," remarked Judd, one of Emmett's men.

"How could a man have the strength and the nerve? And isn't it cruel to keep wild animals in captivity? it against God's word?"

Quick as speech could flow, Jones quoted: "And God said, 'Let us make man in our image, and give him dominion over the fish of the sea, the fowls of the air, over all the cattle, and over every creeping thing that creepeth upon the earth'!"

"Dominion—over all the beasts of the field!" repeated Jones, his big voice rolling out. He clenched his huge fists, and spread wide his long arms. "Dominion! That was God's word!" The power and intensity of him could be felt. Then he relaxed, dropped his arms, and once more grew calm. But he had shown a glimpse of the great, strange and absorbing passion of his life. Once he had told me how, when a mere child, he had hazarded limb and neck to capture a fox squirrel, how he had held on to the vicious little animal, though it bit his hand through; how he had never learned to play the games of boyhood; that when the youths of the little Illinois village were at play, he roamed the prairies, or the rolling, wooded hills, or watched a gopher hole. That boy was father of the man: for sixty years an enduring passion for dominion over wild animals had possessed him, and made his life an endless pursuit.

Our guests, the Navajos, departed early, and vanished silently in the gloom of the desert. We settled down again into a quiet that was broken only by the low chant-like song of a praying Mormon. Suddenly the hounds bristled, and old Moze, a surly and aggressive dog, rose and barked at some real or imaginary desert prowler. A sharp command from Jones made Moze crouch down, and the other hounds cowered close together.

"Better tie up the dogs," suggested Jones. "Like as not coyotes run down here from the hills."

The hounds were my especial delight. But Jones regarded them with considerable contempt. When all was said, this was no small wonder, for that quintet of long-eared canines would have tried the patience of a saint. Old Moze was a Missouri hound that Jones had procured in that State of uncertain qualities; and the dog had grown old over coon-trails. He was black and white, grizzled and battlescarred; and if ever a dog had an evil eye, Moze was that dog. He had a way of wagging his tail—an indeterminate, equivocal sort of wag, as if he realized his ugliness and knew he stood little chance of making friends, but was still hopeful and willing. As for me, the first time he manifested this evidence of a good heart under a rough coat, he won me forever.

To tell of Moze's derelictions up to that time would take more space than would a history of the whole trip; but the enumeration of several incidents will at once stamp him as a dog of character, and will establish the fact that even if his progenitors had never taken any blue ribbons, they had at least bequeathed him fighting blood. At Flagstaff we chained him in the yard of a livery stable. Next morning we found him hanging by his chain on the other side of an eight-foot fence. We took him down, expecting to have the sorrowful duty of burying him; but Moze shook himself, wagged his tail and then pitched into the livery stable dog. As a matter of fact, fighting was his forte. He whipped all of the dogs in Flagstaff; and when our blood hounds came on from California, he put three of them hors de combat at once, and subdued the pup with a savage growl. His crowning feat, however, made even the stoical Jones open his mouth in amaze. We had taken Moze to the El Tovar at the Grand Canyon, and finding it impossible to get over to the north rim, we left him with one of Jones's men, called Rust, who was working on the Canyon trail. Rust's instructions were to bring Moze to Flagstaff in two weeks. He brought the dog a little ahead time, and roared his appreciation of the relief it to get the responsibility off his hands. And he related many strange things, most striking of which was how Moze had broken his chain and plunged into the raging Colorado River, and tried to swim it just above the terrible Sockdolager Rapids. Rust and his fellow-workmen watched the dog disappear in the yellow, wrestling, turbulent whirl of waters, and had heard his knell in the booming roar of the falls. Nothing but a fish could live in that current; nothing but a bird could scale those perpendicular marble walls. That night, however, when the men crossed on the tramway, Moze met them with a wag of his tail. He had crossed the river, and he had come back!

To the four reddish-brown, high-framed bloodhounds I had given the names of Don, Tige, Jude and Ranger; and by dint of persuasion, had succeeded in establishing some kind of family relation between them and Moze. This night I tied up the bloodhounds, after bathing and salving their sore feet; and I left Moze free, for he grew fretful and surly under restraint.

The Mormons, prone, dark, blanketed figures, lay on the sand. Jones was crawling into his bed. I walked a little way from the dying fire, and faced the north, where the desert stretched, mysterious and illimitable. How solemn and still it was! I drew in a great breath of the cold air, and thrilled with a nameless sensation. Something was there, away to the northward; it called to me from out of the dark and gloom; I was going to meet it.

I lay down to sleep with the great blue expanse open to my eyes. The stars were very large, and wonderfully bright, yet they seemed so much farther off than I had ever seen them. The wind softly sifted the sand. I hearkened to the tinkle of the cowbells on the hobbled horses. The last thing I remembered was old Moze creeping close to my side, seeking the warmth of my body.

When I awakened, a long, pale line showed out of the dun-colored clouds in the east. It slowly lengthened, and tinged to red. Then the morning broke, and the slopes of snow on the San Francisco peaks behind us glowed a delicate pink. The Mormons were up and doing with the dawn. They were stalwart men, rather silent, and all workers. It was interesting to see them pack for the day's journey. They traveled with wagons and mules, in the most primitive way, which Jones assured me was exactly as their fathers had crossed the plains fifty years before, on the trail to Utah.

All morning we made good time, and as we descended into the desert, the air became warmer, the scrubby cedar growth began to fail, and the bunches of sage were few and far between. I turned often to gaze back at the San Francisco peaks. The snowcapped tips glistened and grew higher, and stood out in startling relief. Some one said they could be seen two hundred miles across the desert, and were a landmark and a fascination to all travelers thitherward.

I never raised my eyes to the north that I did not draw my breath quickly and grow chill with awe and bewilderment with the marvel of the desert. The scaly red ground descended gradually; bare red knolls, like waves, rolled away northward; black buttes reared their flat heads; long ranges of sand flowed between them like streams, and all sloped away to merge into gray, shadowy obscurity, into wild and desolate, dreamy and misty nothingness.

"Do you see those white sand dunes there, more to the left?" asked Emmett. "The Little Colorado runs in there. How far does it look to you?"

"Thirty miles, perhaps," I replied, adding ten miles to my estimate.

"It's seventy-five. We'll get there day after to-morrow. If the snow in the mountains has begun to melt, we'll have a time getting across."

That afternoon, a hot wind blew in my face, carrying fine sand that cut and blinded. It filled my throat, sending me to the water cask till I was ashamed. When I fell into my bed at night, I never turned. The next day was hotter; the wind blew harder; the sand stung sharper.

About noon the following day, the horses whinnied, and the mules roused out of their tardy gait. "They smell water," said Emmett. And despite the heat, and the sand in my nostrils, I smelled it, too. The dogs, poor foot-sore fellows, trotted on ahead down the trail. A few more miles of hot sand and gravel and red stone brought us around a low mesa to the Little Colorado.

It was a wide stream of swiftly running, reddish-muddy water. In the channel, cut by floods, little streams trickled and meandered in all directions. The main part of the river ran in close to the bank we were on. The dogs lolled in the water; the horses and mules tried to run in, but were restrained; the men drank, and bathed their faces. According to my Flagstaff adviser, this was one of the two drinks I would get on the desert, so I availed myself heartily of the opportunity. The water was full of sand, but cold and gratefully thirst-quenching.

The Little Colorado seemed no more to me than a shallow creek; I heard nothing sullen or menacing in its musical flow.

"Doesn't look bad, eh?" queried Emmett, who read my thought. "You'd be surprised to learn how many men and Indians, horses, sheep and wagons are buried under that quicksand."

The secret was out, and I wondered no more. At once the stream and wet bars of sand took on a different color. I removed my boots, and waded out to a little bar. The sand seemed quite firm, but water oozed out around my feet; and when I stepped, the whole bar shook like jelly. I pushed my foot through the crust, and the cold, wet sand took hold, and tried to suck me down.

"How can you ford this stream with horses?" I asked Emmett.

"We must take our chances," replied he. "We'll hitch two teams to one wagon, and run the horses. I've forded here at worse stages than this. Once a team got stuck, and I had to leave it; another time the water was high, and washed me downstream."

Emmett sent his son into the stream on a mule. The rider lashed his mount, and plunging, splashing, crossed at a pace near a gallop. He returned in the same manner, and reported one bad place near the other side.

Jones and I got on the first wagon and tried to coax up the dogs, but they would not come. Emmett had to lash the four horses to start them; and other Mormons riding alongside, yelled at them, and used their whips. The wagon bowled into the water with a tremendous splash. We were wet through before we had gone twenty feet. The plunging horses were lost in yellow spray; the stream rushed through the wheels; the Mormons yelled. I wanted to see, but was lost in a veil of yellow mist. Jones yelled in my ear, but I could not hear what he said. Once the wagon wheels struck a stone or log, almost lurching us overboard. A muddy splash blinded me. I cried out in my excitement, and punched Jones in the back. Next moment, the keen exhilaration of the ride gave way to horror. We seemed to drag, and almost stop. Some one roared: "Horse down!" One instant of painful suspense, in which imagination pictured another tragedy added to the record of this deceitful river—a moment filled with intense feeling, and sensation of splash, and yell, and fury of action; then the three able horses dragged their comrade out of the quicksand. He regained his feet, and plunged on. Spurred by fear, the horses increased their efforts, and amid clouds of spray, galloped the remaining distance to the other side.

Jones looked disgusted. Like all plainsmen, he hated water. Emmett and his men calmly unhitched. No trace of alarm, or even of excitement showed in their bronzed faces.

"We made that fine and easy," remarked Emmett.

So I sat down and wondered what Jones and Emmett, and these men would consider really hazardous. I began to have a feeling that I would find out; that experience for me was but in its infancy; that far across the desert the something which had called me would show hard, keen, perilous life. And I began to think of reserve powers of fortitude and endurance.

The other wagons were brought across without mishap; but the dogs did not come with them. Jones called and called. The dogs howled and howled. Finally I waded out over the wet bars and little streams to a point several hundred yards nearer the dogs. Moze was lying down, but the others were whining and howling in a state of great perturbation. I called and called. They answered, and even ran into the water, but did not start across.

"Hyah, Moze! hyah, you Indian!" I yelled, losing my patience. "You've already swum the Big Colorado, and this is only a brook. Come on!"

This appeal evidently touched Moze, for he barked, and plunged in. He made the water fly, and when carried off his feet, breasted the current with energy and power. He made shore almost even with me, and wagged his tail. Not to be outdone, Jude, Tige and Don followed suit, and first one and then another was swept off his feet and carried downstream. They landed below me. This left Ranger, the pup, alone on the other shore. Of all the pitiful yelps ever uttered by a frightened and lonely puppy, his were the most forlorn I had ever heard. Time after time he plunged in, and with many bitter howls of distress, went back. I kept calling, and at last, hoping to make him come by a show of indifference, I started away. This broke his heart. Putting up his head, he let out a long, melancholy wail, which for aught I knew might have been a prayer, and then consigned himself to the yellow current. Ranger swam like a boy learning. He seemed to be afraid to get wet. His forefeet were continually pawing the air in front of his nose. When he struck the swift place, he went downstream like a flash, but still kept swimming valiantly. I tried to follow along the sand-bar, but found it impossible. I encouraged him by yelling. He drifted far below, stranded on an island, crossed it, and plunged in again, to make shore almost out of my sight. And when at last I got to dry sand, there was Ranger, wet and disheveled, but consciously proud and happy.

After lunch we entered upon the seventy-mile stretch from the Little to the Big Colorado.

Imagination had pictured the desert for me as a vast, sandy plain, flat and monotonous. Reality showed me desolate mountains gleaming bare in the sun, long lines of red bluffs, white sand dunes, and hills of blue clay, areas of level ground—in all, a many-hued, boundless world in itself, wonderful and beautiful, fading all around into the purple haze of deceiving distance.

Thin, clear, sweet, dry, the desert air carried a languor, a dreaminess, tidings of far-off things, and an enthralling promise. The fragrance of flowers, the beauty and grace of women, the sweetness of music, the mystery of life—all seemed to float on that promise. It was the air breathed by the lotus-eaters, when they dreamed, and wandered no more.

Beyond the Little Colorado, we began to climb again. The sand was thick; the horses labored; the drivers shielded their faces. The dogs began to limp and lag. Ranger had to be taken into a wagon; and then, one by one, all of the other dogs except Moze. He refused to ride, and trotted along with his head down.

Far to the front the pink cliffs, the ragged mesas, the dark, volcanic spurs of the Big Colorado stood up and beckoned us onward. But they were a far hundred miles across the shifting sands, and baked day, and ragged rocks. Always in the rear rose the San Francisco peaks, cold and pure, startlingly clear and close in the rare atmosphere.

We camped near another water hole, located in a deep, yellow-colored gorge, crumbling to pieces, a ruin of rock, and silent as the grave. In the bottom of the canyon was a pool of water, covered with green scum. My thirst was effectually quenched by the mere sight of it. I slept poorly, and lay for hours watching the great stars. The silence was painfully oppressive. If Jones had not begun to give a respectable imitation of the exhaust pipe on a steamboat, I should have been compelled to shout aloud, or get up; but this snoring would have dispelled anything. The morning came gray and cheerless. I got up stiff and sore, with a tongue like a rope.

All day long we ran the gauntlet of the hot, flying sand. Night came again, a cold, windy night. I slept well until a mule stepped on my bed, which was conducive to restlessness. At dawn, cold, gray clouds tried to blot out the rosy east. I could hardly get up. My lips were cracked; my tongue swollen to twice its natural size; my eyes smarted and burned. The barrels and kegs of water were exhausted. Holes that had been dug in the dry sand of a dry streambed the night before in the morning yielded a scant supply of muddy alkali water, which went to the horses.

Only twice that day did I rouse to anything resembling enthusiasm. We came to a stretch of country showing the wonderful diversity of the desert land. A long range of beautifully rounded clay stones bordered the trail. So symmetrical were they that I imagined them works of sculptors. Light blue, dark blue, clay blue, marine blue, cobalt blue—every shade of blue was there, but no other color. The other time that I awoke to sensations from without was when we came to the top of a ridge. We had been passing through red-lands. Jones called the place a strong, specific word which really was illustrative of the heat amid those scaling red ridges. We came out where the red changed abruptly to gray. I seemed always to see things first, and I cried out: "Look! here are a red lake and trees!"

"No, lad, not a lake," said old Jim, smiling at me; "that's what haunts the desert traveler. It's only mirage!"

So I awoke to the realization of that illusive thing, the mirage, a beautiful lie, false as stairs of sand. Far northward a clear rippling lake sparkled in the sunshine. Tall, stately trees, with waving green foliage, bordered the water. For a long moment it lay there, smiling in the sun, a thing almost tangible; and then it faded. I felt a sense of actual loss. So real had been the illusion that I could not believe I was not soon to drink and wade and dabble in the cool waters. Disappointment was keen. This is what maddens the prospector or sheep-herder lost in the desert. Was it not a terrible thing to be dying of thirst, to see sparkling water, almost to smell it and then realize suddenly that all was only a lying track of the desert, a lure, a delusion? I ceased to wonder at the Mormons, and their search for water, their talk of water. But I had not realized its true significance. I had not known what water was. I had never appreciated it. So it was my destiny to learn that water is the greatest thing on earth. I hung over a three-foot hole in a dry stream-bed, and watched it ooze and seep through the sand, and fill up—oh, so slowly; and I felt it loosen my parched tongue, and steal through all my dry body with strength and life. Water is said to constitute three fourths of the universe. However that may be, on the desert it is the whole world, and all of life.

Two days passed by, all hot sand and wind and glare. The Mormons sang no more at evening; Jones was silent; the dogs were limp as rags.

At Moncaupie Wash we ran into a sandstorm. The horses turned their backs to it, and bowed their heads patiently. The Mormons covered themselves. I wrapped a blanket round my head and hid behind a sage bush. The wind, carrying the sand, made a strange hollow roar. All was enveloped in a weird yellow opacity. The sand seeped through the sage bush and swept by with a soft, rustling sound, not unlike the wind in the rye. From time to time I raised a corner of my blanket and peeped out. Where my feet had stretched was an enormous mound of sand. I felt the blanket, weighted down, slowly settle over me.

Suddenly as it had come, the sandstorm passed. It left a changed world for us. The trail was covered; the wheels hub-deep in sand; the horses, walking sand dunes. I could not close my teeth without grating harshly on sand.

We journeyed onward, and passed long lines of petrified trees, some a hundred feet in length, lying as they had fallen, thousands of years before. White ants crawled among the ruins. Slowly climbing the sandy trail, we circled a great red bluff with jagged peaks, that had seemed an interminable obstacle. A scant growth of cedar and sage again made its appearance. Here we halted to pass another night. Under a cedar I heard the plaintive, piteous bleat of an animal. I searched, and presently found a little black and white lamb, scarcely able to stand. It came readily to me, and I carried it to the wagon.

"That's a Navajo lamb," said Emmett. "It's lost. There are Navajo Indians close by."

"Away in the desert we heard its cry," quoted one of the Mormons.

Jones and I climbed the red mesa near camp to see the sunset. All the western world was ablaze in golden glory. Shafts of light shot toward the zenith, and bands of paler gold, tinging to rose, circled away from the fiery, sinking globe. Suddenly the sun sank, the gold changed to gray, then to purple, and shadows formed in the deep gorge at our feet. So sudden was the transformation that soon it was night, the solemn, impressive night of the desert. A stillness that seemed too sacred to break clasped the place; it was infinite; it held the bygone ages, and eternity.

More days, and miles, miles, miles! The last day's ride to the Big Colorado was unforgettable. We rode toward the head of a gigantic red cliff pocket, a veritable inferno, immeasurably hot, glaring, awful. It towered higher and higher above us. When we reached a point of this red barrier, we heard the dull rumbling roar of water, and we came out, at length, on a winding trail cut in the face of a blue overhanging the Colorado River. The first sight of most famous and much-heralded wonders of nature is often disappointing; but never can this be said of the blood-hued Rio Colorado. If it had beauty, it was beauty that appalled. So riveted was my gaze that I could hardly turn it across the river, where Emmett proudly pointed out his lonely home—an oasis set down amidst beetling red cliffs. How grateful to the eye was the green of alfalfa and cottonwood! Going round the bluff trail, the wheels had only a foot of room to spare; and the sheer descent into the red, turbid, congested river was terrifying.

I saw the constricted rapids, where the Colorado took its plunge into the box-like head of the Grand Canyon of Arizona; and the deep, reverberating boom of the river, at flood height, was a fearful thing to hear. I could not repress a shudder at the thought of crossing above that rapid.

The bronze walls widened as we proceeded, and we got down presently to a level, where a long wire cable stretched across the river. Under the cable ran a rope. On the other side was an old scow moored to the bank.

"Are we going across in that?" I asked Emmett, pointing to the boat.

"We'll all be on the other side before dark," he replied cheerily.

I felt that I would rather start back alone over the desert than trust myself in such a craft, on such a river. And it was all because I had had experience with bad rivers, and thought I was a judge of dangerous currents. The Colorado slid with a menacing roar out of a giant split in the red wall, and whirled, eddied, bulged on toward its confinement in the iron-ribbed canyon below.

In answer to shots fired, Emmett's man appeared on the other side, and rode down to the ferry landing. Here he got into a skiff, and rowed laboriously upstream for a long distance before he started across, and then swung into the current. He swept down rapidly, and twice the skiff whirled, and completely turned round; but he reached our bank safely. Taking two men aboard he rowed upstream again, close to the shore, and returned to the opposite side in much the same manner in which he had come over.

The three men pushed out the scow, and grasping the rope overhead, began to pull. The big craft ran easily. When the current struck it, the wire cable sagged, the water boiled and surged under it, raising one end, and then the other. Nevertheless, five minutes were all that were required to pull the boat over.

It was a rude, oblong affair, made of heavy planks loosely put together, and it leaked. When Jones suggested that we get the agony over as quickly as possible, I was with him, and we embarked together. Jones said he did not like the looks of the tackle; and when I thought of his by no means small mechanical skill, I had not added a cheerful idea to my consciousness. The horses of the first team had to be dragged upon the scow, and once on, they reared and plunged.

When we started, four men pulled the rope, and Emmett sat in the stern, with the tackle guys in hand. As the current hit us, he let out the guys, which maneuver caused the boat to swing stern downstream. When it pointed obliquely, he made fast the guys again. I saw that this served two purposes: the current struck, slid alongside, and over the stern, which mitigated the danger, and at the same time helped the boat across.

To look at the river was to court terror, but I had to look. It was an infernal thing. It roared in hollow, sullen voice, as a monster growling. It had voice, this river, and one strangely changeful. It moaned as if in pain—it whined, it cried. Then at times it would seem strangely silent. The current as complex and mutable as human life. It boiled, beat and bulged. The bulge itself was an incompressible thing, like a roaring lift of the waters from submarine explosion. Then it would smooth out, and run like oil. It shifted from one channel to another, rushed to the center of the river, then swung close to one shore or the other. Again it swelled near the boat, in great, boiling, hissing eddies.

"Look! See where it breaks through the mountain!" yelled Jones in my ear.

I looked upstream to see the stupendous granite walls separated in a gigantic split that must have been made by a terrible seismic disturbance; and from this gap poured the dark, turgid, mystic flood.

I was in a cold sweat when we touched shore, and I jumped long before the boat was properly moored.

Emmett was wet to the waist where the water had surged over him. As he sat rearranging some tackle I remarked to him that of course he must be a splendid swimmer, or he would not take such risks.

"No, I can't swim a stroke," he replied; "and it wouldn't be any use if I could. Once in there a man's a goner."

"You've had bad accidents here?" I questioned.

"No, not bad. We only drowned two men last year. You see, we had to tow the boat up the river, and row across, as then we hadn't the wire. Just above, on this side, the boat hit a stone, and the current washed over her, taking off the team and two men."

"Didn't you attempt to rescue them?" I asked, after waiting a moment.

"No use. They never came up."

"Isn't the river high now?" I continued, shuddering as I glanced out at the whirling logs and drifts.

"High, and coming up. If I don't get the other teams over to-day I'll wait until she goes down. At this season she rises and lowers every day or so, until June then comes the big flood, and we don't cross for months."

I sat for three hours watching Emmett bring over the rest of his party, which he did without accident, but at the expense of great effort. And all the time in my ears dinned the roar, the boom, the rumble of this singularly rapacious and purposeful river—a river of silt, a red river of dark, sinister meaning, a river with terrible work to perform, a river which never gave up its dead.

CHAPTER 2.

THE RANGE

After a much-needed rest at Emmett's, we bade good-by to him and his hospitable family, and under the guidance of his man once more took to the wind-swept trail. We pursued a southwesterly course now, following the lead of the craggy red wall that stretched on and on for hundreds of miles into Utah. The desert, smoky and hot, fell away to the left, and in the foreground a dark, irregular line marked the Grand Canyon cutting through the plateau.

The wind whipped in from the vast, open expanse, and meeting an obstacle in the red wall, turned north and raced past us. Jones's hat blew off, stood on its rim, and rolled. It kept on rolling, thirty miles an hour, more or less; so fast, at least, that we were a long time catching up to it with a team of horses. Possibly we never would have caught it had not a stone checked its flight. Further manifestation of the power of the desert wind surrounded us on all sides. It had hollowed out huge stones from the cliffs, and tumbled them to the plain below; and then, sweeping sand and gravel low across the desert floor, had cut them deeply, until they rested on slender pedestals, thus sculptoring grotesque and striking monuments to the marvelous persistence of this element of nature.

Late that afternoon, as we reached the height of the plateau, Jones woke up and shouted: "Ha! there's Buckskin!"

Far southward lay a long, black mountain, covered with patches of shining snow. I could follow the zigzag line of the Grand Canyon splitting the desert plateau, and saw it disappear in the haze round the end of the mountain. From this I got my first clear impression of the topography of the country surrounding our objective point. Buckskin mountain ran its blunt end eastward to the Canyon—in fact, formed a hundred miles of the north rim. As it was nine thousand feet high it still held the snow, which had occasioned our lengthy desert ride to get back of the mountain. I could see the long slopes rising out of the desert to meet the timber.

As we bowled merrily down grade I noticed that we were no longer on stony ground, and that a little scant silvery grass had made its appearance. Then little branches of green, with a blue flower, smiled out of the clayish sand.

All of a sudden Jones stood up, and let out a wild Comanche yell. I was more startled by the yell than by the great hand he smashed down on my shoulder, and for the moment I was dazed.

"There! look! look! the buffalo! Hi! Hi! Hi!"

Below us, a few miles on a rising knoll, a big herd of buffalo shone black in the gold of the evening sun. I had not Jones's incentive, but I felt enthusiasm born of the wild and beautiful picture, and added my yell to his. The huge, burly leader of the herd lifted his head, and after regarding us for a few moments calmly went on browsing.

The desert had fringed away into a grand rolling pastureland, walled in by the red cliffs, the slopes of Buckskin, and further isolated by the Canyon. Here was a range of twenty-four hundred square miles without a foot of barb-wire, a pasture fenced in by natural forces, with the splendid feature that the buffalo could browse on the plain in winter, and go up into the cool foothills of Buckskin in summer.

From another ridge we saw a cabin dotting the rolling plain, and in half an hour we reached it. As we climbed down from the wagon a brown and black dog came dashing out of the cabin, and promptly jumped at Moze. His selection showed poor discrimination, for Moze whipped him before I could separate them. Hearing Jones heartily greeting some one, I turned in his direction, only to be distracted by another dog fight. Don had tackled Moze for the seventh time. Memory rankled in Don, and he needed a lot of whipping, some of which he was getting when I rescued him.

Next moment I was shaking hands with Frank and Jim, Jones's ranchmen. At a glance I liked them both. Frank was short and wiry, and had a big, ferocious mustache, the effect of which was softened by his kindly brown eyes. Jim was tall, a little heavier; he had a careless, tidy look; his eyes were searching, and though he appeared a young man, his hair was white.

"I shore am glad to see you all," said Jim, in slow, soft, Southern accent.

"Get down, get down," was Frank's welcome—a typically Western one, for we had already gotten down; "an' come in. You must be worked out. Sure you've come a long way." He was quick of speech, full of nervous energy, and beamed with hospitality.

The cabin was the rudest kind of log affair, with a huge stone fireplace in one end, deer antlers and coyote skins on the wall, saddles and cowboys' traps in a corner, a nice, large, promising cupboard, and a table and chairs. Jim threw wood on a smoldering fire, that soon blazed and crackled cheerily.

I sank down into a chair with a feeling of blessed relief. Ten days of desert ride behind me! Promise of wonderful days before me, with the last of the old plainsmen. No wonder a sweet sense of ease stole over me, or that the fire seemed a live and joyously welcoming thing, or that Jim's deft maneuvers in preparation of supper roused in me a rapt admiration.

"Twenty calves this spring!" cried Jones, punching me in my sore side. "Ten thousand dollars worth of calves!"

He was now altogether a changed man; he looked almost young; his eyes danced, and he rubbed his big hands together while he plied Frank with questions. In strange surroundings—that is, away from his Native Wilds, Jones had been a silent man; it had been almost impossible to get anything out of him. But now I saw that I should come to know the real man. In a very few moments he had talked more than on all the desert trip, and what he said, added to the little I had already learned, put me in possession of some interesting information as to his buffalo.

Some years before he had conceived the idea of hybridizing buffalo with black Galloway cattle; and with the characteristic determination and energy of the man, he at once set about finding a suitable range. This was difficult, and took years of searching. At last the wild north rim of the Grand Canyon, a section unknown except to a few Indians and mustang hunters, was settled upon. Then the gigantic task of transporting the herd of buffalo by rail from Montana to Salt Lake was begun. The two hundred and ninety miles of desert lying between the home of the Mormons and Buckskin Mountain was an obstacle almost insurmountable. The journey was undertaken and found even more trying than had been expected. Buffalo after buffalo died on the way. Then Frank, Jones's right-hand man, put into execution a plan he had been thinking of—

namely, to travel by night. It succeeded. The buffalo rested in the day and traveled by easy stages by night, with the result that the big herd was transported to the ideal range.

Here, in an environment strange to their race, but peculiarly adaptable, they thrived and multiplied. The hybrid of the Galloway cow and buffalo proved a great success. Jones called the new species "Cattalo." The cattalo took the hardiness of the buffalo, and never required artificial food or shelter. He would face the desert storm or blizzard and stand stock still in his tracks until the weather cleared. He became quite domestic, could be easily handled, and grew exceedingly fat on very little provender. The folds of his stomach were so numerous that they digested even the hardest and flintiest of corn. He had fourteen ribs on each side, while domestic cattle had only thirteen; thus he could endure rougher work and longer journeys to water. His fur was so dense and glossy that it equaled that of the unplucked beaver or otter, and was fully as valuable as the buffalo robe. And not to be overlooked by any means was the fact that his meat was delicious.

Jones had to hear every detail of all that had happened since his absence in the East, and he was particularly inquisitive to learn all about the twenty cattalo calves. He called different buffalo by name; and designated the calves by descriptive terms, such as "Whiteface" and "Crosspatch." He almost forgot to eat, and kept Frank too busy to get anything into his own mouth. After supper he calmed down.

"How about your other man—Mr. Wallace, I think you said?" asked Frank.

"We expected to meet him at Grand Canyon Station, and then at Flagstaff. But he didn't show up. Either he backed out or missed us. I'm sorry; for when we get up on Buckskin, among the wild horses and cougars, we'll be likely to need him."

"I reckon you'll need me, as well as Jim," said Frank dryly, with a twinkle in his eye. "The buffs are in good shape an' can get along without me for a while."

"That'll be fine. How about cougar sign on the mountain?"

"Plenty. I've got two spotted near Clark Spring. Comin' over two weeks ago I tracked them in the snow along the trail for miles. We'll ooze over that way, as it's goin' toward the Siwash. The Siwash breaks of the Canyon—there's the place for lions. I met a wild-horse wrangler not long back, an' he was tellin' me about Old Tom an' the colts he'd killed this winter."

Naturally, I here expressed a desire to know more of Old Tom.

"He's the biggest cougar ever known of in these parts. His tracks are bigger than a horse's, an' have been seen on Buckskin for twelve years. This wrangler—his name is Clark—said he'd turned his saddle horse out to graze near camp, an' Old Tom sneaked in an' downed him. The lions over there are sure a bold bunch. Well, why shouldn't they be? No one ever hunted them. You see, the mountain is hard to get at. But now you're here, if it's big cats you want we sure can find them. Only be easy, be easy. You've all the time there is. An' any job on Buckskin will take time. We'll look the calves over, an' you must ride the range to harden up. Then we'll ooze over toward Oak. I expect it'll be boggy, an' I hope the snow melts soon."

"The snow hadn't melted on Greenland point," replied Jones. "We saw that with a glass from the El Tovar. We wanted to cross that way, but Rust said Bright Angel Creek was breast high to a horse, and that creek is the trail."

"There's four feet of snow on Greenland," said Frank. "It was too early to come that way. There's only about three months in the year the Canyon can be crossed at Greenland."

"I want to get in the snow," returned Jones. "This bunch of long-eared canines I brought never smelled a lion track. Hounds can't be trained quick without snow. You've got to see what they're trailing, or you can't break them."

Frank looked dubious. "'Pears to me we'll have trouble gettin' a lion without lion dogs. It takes a long time to break a hound off of deer, once he's chased them. Buckskin is full of deer, wolves, coyotes, and there's the wild horses. We couldn't go a hundred feet without crossin' trails."

"How's the hound you and Jim fetched in las' year? Has he got a good nose? Here he is—I like his head. Come here, Bowser—what's his name?"

"Jim named him Sounder, because he sure has a voice. It's great to hear him on a trail. Sounder has a nose that can't be fooled, an' he'll trail anythin'; but I don't know if he ever got up a lion."

Sounder wagged his bushy tail and looked up affectionately at Frank. He had a fine head, great brown eyes, very long ears and curly brownish-black hair. He was not demonstrative, looked rather askance at Jones, and avoided the other dogs.

"That dog will make a great lion-chaser," said Jones, decisively, after his study of Sounder. "He and Moze will keep us busy, once they learn we want lions."

"I don't believe any dog-trainer could teach them short of six months," replied Frank. "Sounder is no spring chicken; an' that black and dirty white cross between a cayuse an' a barb-wire fence is an old dog. You can't teach old dogs new tricks."

Jones smiled mysteriously, a smile of conscious superiority, but said nothing.

"We'll shore hev a storm to-morrow," said Jim, relinquishing his pipe long enough to speak. He had been silent, and now his meditative gaze was on the west, through the cabin window, where a dull afterglow faded under the heavy laden clouds of night and left the horizon dark.

I was very tired when I lay down, but so full of excitement that sleep did not soon visit my eyelids. The talk about buffalo, wild-horse hunters, lions and dogs, the prospect of hard riding and unusual adventure; the vision of Old Tom that had already begun to haunt me, filled my mind with pictures and fancies. The other fellows dropped off to sleep, and quiet reigned. Suddenly a succession of queer, sharp barks came from the plain, close to the cabin. Coyotes were paying us a call, and judging from the chorus of yelps and howls from our dogs, it was not a welcome visit. Above the medley rose one big, deep, full voice that I knew at once belonged to Sounder. Then all was quiet again. Sleep gradually benumbed my senses. Vague phrases dreamily drifted to and fro in my mind: "Jones's wild range—Old Tom—Sounder—great name—great voice—Sounder! Sounder! Sounder—"

Next morning I could hardly crawl out of my sleeping-bag. My bones ached, my muscles protested excruciatingly, my lips burned and bled, and the cold I had contracted on the desert clung to me. A good brisk walk round the corrals, and then breakfast, made me feel better.

"Of course you can ride?" queried Frank.

My answer was not given from an overwhelming desire to be truthful. Frank frowned a little, as it wondering how a man could have the nerve to start out on a jaunt with Buffalo Jones without being a good horseman. To be unable to stick on the back of a wild mustang, or a cayuse, was an unpardonable sin in Arizona. My frank admission was made relatively, with my mind on what cowboys held as a standard of horsemanship.

The mount Frank trotted out of the corral for me was a pure white, beautiful mustang, nervous, sensitive, quivering. I watched Frank put on the saddle, and when he called me I did not fail to catch a covert twinkle in his merry brown eyes. Looking away toward Buckskin Mountain, which was coincidentally in the direction of home, I said to myself: "This may be where you get on, but most certainly it is where you get off!"

Jones was already riding far beyond the corral, as I could see by a cloud of dust; and I set off after him, with the painful consciousness that I must have looked to Frank and Jim much as Central Park equestrians had often looked to me. Frank shouted after me that he would catch up with us out on the range. I was not in any great hurry to overtake Jones, but evidently my horse's inclinations differed from mine; at any rate, he made the dust fly, and jumped the little sage bushes.

Jones, who had tarried to inspect one of the pools—formed of running water from the corrals—greeted me as I came up with this cheerful observation.

"What in thunder did Frank give you that white nag for? The buffalo hate white horses—anything white. They're liable to stampede off the range, or chase you into the canyon."

I replied grimly that, as it was certain something was going to happen, the particular circumstance might as well come off quickly.

We rode over the rolling plain with a cool, bracing breeze in our faces. The sky was dull and mottled with a beautiful cloud effect that presaged wind. As we trotted along Jones pointed out to me and descanted upon the nutritive value of three different kinds of grass, one of which he called the Buffalo Pea, noteworthy for a beautiful blue blossom. Soon we passed out of sight of the cabin, and could see only the billowy plain, the red tips of the stony wall, and the black-fringed crest of Buckskin. After riding a while we made out some cattle, a few of which were on the range, browsing in the lee of a ridge. No sooner had I marked them than Jones let out another Comanche yell.

"Wolf!" he yelled; and spurring his big bay, he was off like the wind.

A single glance showed me several cows running as if bewildered, and near them a big white wolf pulling down a calf. Another white wolf stood not far off. My horse jumped as if he had been shot; and the realization darted upon me that here was where the certain something began. Spot—the mustang had one black spot in his pure white—snorted like I imagined a blooded horse might, under dire insult. Jones's bay had gotten about a hundred paces the start. I lived to learn that Spot hated to be left behind; moreover, he would not be left behind; he was the swiftest horse on the range, and proud of the distinction. I cast one unmentionable word on the breeze toward the cabin and Frank, then put mind and muscle to the sore task of remaining with Spot. Jones was born on a saddle, and had been taking his meals in a saddle for about sixty-three years, and the bay horse could run. Run is not a felicitous word—he flew. And I was rendered mentally deranged for the moment to see that hundred paces between the bay and Spot materially lessen at every jump. Spot lengthened out, seemed to go down near the ground, and cut the air like a high-geared auto. If I had not heard the fast rhythmic beat of his hoofs, and had not bounced high into the air at every jump, I would have been sure I was riding a bird. I tried to stop him. As well might I have tried to pull in the Lusitania with a thread. Spot was out to overhaul that bay, and in spite of me, he was doing it. The wind rushed into my face and sang in my ears. Jones seemed the nucleus of a sort of haze, and it grew larger and larger. Presently he became clearly defined in my sight; the violent commotion under me subsided; I once more felt the saddle, and then I realized that Spot had been content to stop alongside of Jones, tossing his head and champing his bit.

"Well, by George! I didn't know you were in the stretch," cried my companion. "That was a fine little brush. We must have come several miles. I'd have killed those wolves if I'd brought a gun. The big one that had the calf was a bold brute. He never let go until I was within fifty feet of him. Then I almost rode him down. I don't think the calf was much hurt. But those blood-thirsty devils will return, and like as not get the calf. That's the worst of cattle raising. Now, take the buffalo. Do you suppose those wolves could have gotten a buffalo calf out from under the mother? Never. Neither could a whole band of wolves. Buffalo stick close together, and the little ones do not stray. When danger threatens, the herd closes in and faces it and fights. That is what is grand about the buffalo and what made them once roam the prairies in countless, endless droves."

From the highest elevation in that part of the range we viewed the surrounding ridges, flats and hollows, searching for the buffalo. At length we spied a cloud of dust rising from behind an undulating mound, then big black dots hove in sight.

"Frank has rounded up the herd, and is driving it this way. We'll wait," said Jones.

Though the buffalo appeared to be moving fast, a long time elapsed before they reached the foot of our outlook. They lumbered along in a compact mass, so dense that I could not count them, but I estimated the number at seventy-five. Frank was riding zigzag behind them, swinging his lariat and yelling. When he espied us he reined in his horse and waited. Then the herd slowed down, halted and began browsing.

"Look at the cattalo calves," cried Jones, in ecstatic tones. "See how shy they are, how close they stick to their mothers."

The little dark-brown fellows were plainly frightened. I made several unsuccessful attempts to photograph them, and gave it up when Jones told me not to ride too close and that it would be better to wait till we had them in the corral.

He took my camera and instructed me to go on ahead, in the rear of the herd. I heard the click of the instrument as he snapped a picture, and then suddenly heard him shout in alarm: "Look out! look out! pull your horse!"

Thundering hoof-beats pounding the earth accompanied his words. I saw a big bull, with head down, tail raised, charging my horse. He answered Frank's yell of command with a furious grunt. I was paralyzed at the wonderfully swift action of the shaggy brute, and I sat helpless. Spot wheeled as if he were on a pivot and plunged out of the way with a celerity that was astounding. The buffalo stopped, pawed the ground, and angrily tossed his huge head. Frank rode up to him, yelled, and struck him with the lariat, whereupon he gave another toss of his horns, and then returned to the herd.

"It was that darned white nag," said Jones. "Frank, it was wrong to put an inexperienced man on Spot. For that matter, the horse should never be allowed to go near the buffalo."

"Spot knows the buffs; they'd never get to him," replied Frank. But the usual spirit was absent from his voice, and he glanced at me soberly. I knew I had turned white, for I felt the peculiar cold sensation on my face.

"Now, look at that, will you?" cried Jones. "I don't like the looks of that."

He pointed to the herd. They stopped browsing, and were uneasily shifting to and fro. The bull lifted his head; the others slowly grouped together.

"Storm! Sandstorm!" exclaimed Jones, pointing desert-ward. Dark yellow clouds like smoke were rolling, sweeping, bearing down upon us. They expanded, blossoming out like gigantic roses, and whirled and merged into one another, all the time rolling on and blotting out the light.

"We've got to run. That storm may last two days," yelled Frank to me. "We've had some bad ones lately. Give your horse free rein, and cover your face."

A roar, resembling an approaching storm at sea, came on puffs of wind, as the horses got into their stride. Long streaks of dust whipped up in different places; the silver-white grass bent to the ground; round bunches of sage went rolling before us. The puffs grew longer, steadier, harder. Then a shrieking blast howled on our trail, seeming to swoop down on us with a yellow, blinding pall. I shut my eyes and covered my face with a handkerchief. The sand blew so thick that it filled my gloves, pebbles struck me hard enough to sting through my coat.

Fortunately, Spot kept to an easy swinging lope, which was the most comfortable motion for me. But I began to get numb, and could hardly stick on the saddle. Almost before I had dared to hope, Spot stopped. Uncovering my face, I saw Jim in the doorway of the lee side of the cabin. The yellow, streaky, whistling clouds of sand split on the cabin and passed on, leaving a small, dusty space of light.

"Shore Spot do hate to be beat," yelled Jim, as he helped me off. I stumbled into the cabin and fell upon a buffalo robe and lay there absolutely spent. Jones and Frank came in a few minutes apart, each anathematizing the gritty, powdery sand.

All day the desert storm raged and roared. The dust sifted through the numerous cracks in the cabin burdened our clothes, spoiled our food and blinded our eyes. Wind, snow, sleet and rainstorms are discomforting enough under trying circumstances; but all combined, they are nothing to the choking stinging, blinding sandstorm.

"Shore it'll let up by sundown," averred Jim. And sure enough the roar died away about five o'clock, the wind abated and the sand settled.

Just before supper, a knock sounded heavily o the cabin door. Jim opened it to admit one of Emmett's sons and a very tall man whom none of us knew. He was a sand-man. All that was not sand seemed a space or two of corduroy, a big bone-handled knife, a prominent square jaw and bronze cheek and flashing eyes.

"Get down—get down, an' come in, stranger, said Frank cordially.

"How do you do, sir," said Jones.

"Colonel Jones, I've been on your trail for twelve days," announced the stranger, with a grim smile. The sand streamed off his coat in little white streak. Jones appeared to be casting about in his mind.

"I'm Grant Wallace," continued the newcomer. "I missed you at the El Tovar, at Williams and at Flagstaff, where I was one day behind. Was half a day late at the Little Colorado, saw your train cross Moncaupie Wash, and missed you because of the sandstorm there. Saw you from the other side of the Big Colorado as you rode out from Emmett's along the red wall. And here I am. We've never met till now, which obviously isn't my fault."

The Colonel and I fell upon Wallace's neck. Frank manifested his usual alert excitation, and said: "Well, I guess he won't hang fire on a long cougar chase." And Jim—slow, careful Jim, dropped a plate with the exclamation: "Shore it do beat hell!" The hounds sniffed round Wallace, and welcomed him with vigorous tails.

Supper that night, even if we did grind sand with our teeth, was a joyous occasion. The biscuits were flaky and light; the bacon fragrant and crisp. I produced a jar of blackberry jam, which by subtle cunning I had been able to secrete from the Mormons on that dry desert ride, and it was greeted with acclamations of pleasure. Wallace, divested of his sand guise, beamed with the gratification of a hungry man once more in the presence of friends and food. He made large cavities in Jim's great pot of potato stew, and caused biscuits to vanish in a way that would not have shamed a Hindoo magician. The Grand Canyon he dug in my jar of jam, however, could not have been accomplished by legerdemain.

Talk became animated on dogs, cougars, horses and buffalo. Jones told of our experience out on the range, and concluded with some salient remarks.

"A tame wild animal is the most dangerous of beasts. My old friend, Dick Rock, a great hunter and guide out of Idaho, laughed at my advice, and got killed by one of his three-year-old bulls. I told him they knew him just well enough to kill him, and they did. My friend, A. H. Cole, of Oxford, Nebraska, tried to rope a Weetah that was too tame to be safe, and the bull killed him. Same with General Bull, a member of the Kansas Legislature, and two cowboys who went into a corral to tie up a tame elk at the wrong time. I pleaded with them not to undertake it. They had not studied animals as I had. That tame elk killed all of them. He had to be shot in order to get General Bull off his great antlers. You see, a wild animal must learn to respect a man. The way I used to teach the Yellowstone Park bears to be respectful and safe neighbors was to rope them around the front paw, swing them up on a tree clear of the ground, and whip them with a long pole. It was a dangerous business, and looks cruel, but it is the only way I could find to make the bears good. You see, they eat scraps around the hotels and get so tame they will steal everything but red-hot stoves, and will cuff the life out of those who try to shoo them off. But after a bear mother has had a licking, she not only becomes a good bear for the rest of her life, but she tells all her cubs about it with a good smack of her paw, for emphasis, and teaches them to respect peaceable citizens generation after generation.

"One of the hardest jobs I ever tackled was that of supplying the buffalo for Bronx Park. I rounded up a magnificent 'king' buffalo bull, belligerent enough to fight a battleship. When I rode after him the cowmen said I was as good as killed. I made a lance by driving a nail into the end of a short pole and sharpening it. After he had chased me, I wheeled my broncho, and hurled the lance into his back, ripping a wound as long as my hand. That put the fear of Providence into him and took the fight all out of him. I drove him uphill and down, and across canyons at a dead run for eight miles single handed, and loaded him on a freight car; but he came near getting me once or twice, and only quick broncho work and lance play saved me.

"In the Yellowstone Park all our buffaloes have become docile, excepting the huge bull which led them. The Indians call the buffalo leader the 'Weetah,' the master of the herd. It was sure death to go near this one. So I shipped in another Weetah, hoping that he might whip some of the fight out of old Manitou, the Mighty. They came together head on, like a railway collision, and ripped up over a square mile of landscape, fighting till night came on, and then on into the night.

"I jumped into the field with them, chasing them with my biograph, getting a series of moving pictures of that bullfight which was sure the real thing. It was a ticklish thing to do, though knowing that neither bull dared take his eyes off his adversary for a second, I felt reasonably safe. The old Weetah beat the new champion out that night, but the next morning they were at it again, and the new buffalo finally whipped the old one into submission. Since then his spirit has remained broken, and even a child can approach him safely—but the new Weetah is in turn a holy terror.

"To handle buffalo, elk and bear, you must get into sympathy with their methods of reasoning. No tenderfoot stands any show, even with the tame animals of the Yellowstone."

The old buffalo hunter's lips were no longer locked. One after another he told reminiscences of his eventful life, in a simple manner; yet so vivid and gripping were the unvarnished details that I was spellbound.

"Considering what appears the impossibility of capturing a full-grown buffalo, how did you earn the name of preserver of the American bison?" inquired Wallace.

"It took years to learn how, and ten more to capture the fifty-eight that I was able to keep. I tried every plan under the sun. I roped hundreds, of all sizes and ages. They would not live in captivity. If they could not find an embankment over which to break their necks, they would crush their skulls on stones. Failing any means like that, they would lie down, will themselves to die, and die. Think of a savage wild nature that could will its heart to cease beating! But it's true. Finally I found I could keep only calves under three months of age. But to capture them so young entailed time and patience. For the buffalo fight for their young, and when I say fight, I mean till they drop. I almost always had to go alone, because I could neither coax nor hire any one to undertake it with me. Sometimes I would be weeks getting one calf. One day I captured eight—eight little buffalo calves! Never will I forget that day as long as I live!"

"Tell us about it," I suggested, in a matter of fact, round-the-campfire voice. Had the silent plainsman ever told a complete and full story of his adventures? I doubted it. He was not the man to eulogize himself.

A short silence ensued. The cabin was snug and warm; the ruddy embers glowed; one of Jim's pots steamed musically and fragrantly. The hounds lay curled in the cozy chimney corner.

Jones began to talk again, simply and unaffectedly, of his famous exploit; and as he went on so modestly, passing lightly over features we recognized as wonderful, I allowed the fire of my imagination to fuse for myself all the toil, patience, endurance, skill, herculean strength and marvelous courage and unfathomable passion which he slighted in his narrative.

CHAPTER 3.

THE LAST HERD

Over gray No-Man's-Land stole down the shadows of night. The undulating prairie shaded dark to the western horizon, rimmed with a fading streak of light. Tall figures, silhouetted sharply against the last golden glow of sunset, marked the rounded crest of a grassy knoll.

"Wild hunter!" cried a voice in sullen rage, "buffalo or no, we halt here. Did Adams and I hire to cross the Staked Plains? Two weeks in No-Man's-Land, and now we're facing the sand! We've one keg of water, yet you want to keep on. Why, man, you're crazy! You didn't tell us you wanted buffalo alive. And here you've got us looking death in the eye!"

In the grim silence that ensued the two men unhitched the team from the long, light wagon, while the buffalo hunter staked out his wiry, lithe-limbed racehorses. Soon a fluttering blaze threw a circle of light, which shone on the agitated face of Rude and Adams, and the cold, iron-set visage of their brawny leader.

"It's this way," began Jones, in slow, cool voice; "I engaged you fellows, and you promised to stick by me. We've had no luck. But I've finally found sign—old sign, I'll admit the buffalo I'm looking for—the last herd on the plains. For two years I've been hunting this herd. So have other hunters. Millions of buffalo have been killed and left to rot. Soon this herd will be gone, and then the only buffalo in the world will be those I have given ten years of the hardest work in capturing. This is the last herd, I say, and my last chance to capture a calf or two. Do you imagine I'd quit? You fellows go back if you want, but I keep on."

"We can't go back. We're lost. We'll have to go with you. But, man, thirst is not the only risk we run. This is Comanche country. And if that herd is in here the Indians have it spotted."

"That worries me some," replied the plainsman, "but we'll keep on it."

They slept. The night wind swished the grasses; dark storm clouds blotted out the northern stars; the prairie wolves mourned dismally.

Day broke cold, wan, threatening, under a leaden sky. The hunters traveled thirty miles by noon, and halted in a hollow where a stream flowed in wet season. Cottonwood trees were bursting into green; thickets of prickly thorn, dense and matted, showed bright spring buds.

"What is it?" suddenly whispered Rude.

The plainsman lay in strained posture, his ear against the ground.

"Hide the wagon and horses in the clump of cottonwoods," he ordered, tersely. Springing to his feet, he ran to the top of the knoll above the hollow, where he again placed his ear to the ground.

Jones's practiced ear had detected the quavering rumble of far-away, thundering hoofs. He searched the wide waste of plain with his powerful glass. To the southwest, miles distant, a cloud of dust mushroomed skyward. "Not buffalo," he muttered, "maybe wild horses." He watched and waited. The yellow cloud rolled forward, enlarging, spreading out, and drove before it a darkly indistinct, moving mass. As soon as he had one good look at this he ran back to his comrades.

"Stampede! Wild horses! Indians! Look to your rifles and hide!"

Wordless and pale, the men examined their Sharps, and made ready to follow Jones. He slipped into the thorny brake and, flat on his stomach, wormed his way like a snake far into the thickly interlaced web of branches. Rude and Adams crawled after him. Words were superfluous. Quiet, breathless, with beating hearts, the hunters pressed close to the dry grass. A long, low, steady rumble filled the air, and increased in volume till it became a roar. Moments, endless moments, passed. The roar filled out like a flood slowly released from its confines to sweep down with the sound of doom. The ground began to tremble and quake: the light faded; the smell of dust pervaded the thicket, then a continuous streaming roar, deafening as persistent roll of thunder, pervaded the hiding place. The stampeding horses had split round the hollow. The roar lessened. Swiftly as a departing snow-squall rushing on through the pines, the thunderous thud and tramp of hoofs died away.

The trained horses hidden in the cottonwoods never stirred. "Lie low! lie low!" breathed the plainsman to his companions.

Throb of hoofs again became audible, not loud and madly pounding as those that had passed, but low, muffled, rhythmic. Jones's sharp eye, through a peephole in the thicket, saw a cream-colored mustang bob over the knoll, carrying an Indian. Another and another, then a swiftly following, close-packed throng appeared. Bright red feathers and white gleamed; weapons glinted; gaunt, bronzed savage leaned forward on racy, slender mustangs.

The plainsman shrank closer to the ground. "Apache!" he exclaimed to himself, and gripped his rifle. The band galloped down to the hollow, and slowing up, piled single file over the bank. The leader, a short, squat chief, plunged into the brake not twenty yards from the hidden men. Jones recognized the cream mustang; he knew the somber, sinister, broad face. It belonged to the Red Chief of the Apaches.

"Geronimo!" murmured the plainsman through his teeth.

Well for the Apache that no falcon savage eye discovered aught strange in the little hollow! One look at the sand of the stream bed would have cost him his life. But the Indians crossed the thicket too far up; they cantered up the slope and disappeared. The hoof-beats softened and ceased.

"Gone?" whispered Rude.

"Gone. But wait," whispered Jones. He knew the savage nature, and he knew how to wait. After a long time, he cautiously crawled out of the thicket and searched the surroundings with a plainsman's eye. He climbed the slope and saw the clouds of dust, the near one small, the far one large, which told him all he needed to know.

"Comanches?" queried Adams, with a quaver in his voice. He was new to the plains.

"Likely," said Jones, who thought it best not to tell all he knew. Then he added to himself: "We've no time to lose. There's water back here somewhere. The Indians have spotted the buffalo, and were running the horses away from the water."

The three got under way again, proceeding carefully, so as not to raise the dust, and headed due southwest. Scantier and scantier grew the grass; the hollows were washes of sand; steely gray dunes, like long, flat, ocean swells, ribbed the prairie. The gray day declined. Late into the purple night they traveled, then camped without fire.

In the gray morning Jones climbed a high ride and scanned the southwest. Low dun-colored sandhills waved from him down and down, in slow, deceptive descent. A solitary and remote waste reached out into gray infinitude. A pale lake, gray as the rest of that gray expanse, glimmered in the distance.

"Mirage!" he muttered, focusing his glass, which only magnified all under the dead gray, steely sky. "Water must be somewhere; but can that be it? It's too pale and elusive to be real. No life—a blasted, staked plain! Hello!"

A thin, black, wavering line of wild fowl, moving in beautiful, rapid flight, crossed the line of his vision. "Geese flying north, and low. There's water here," he said. He followed the flock with his glass, saw them circle over the lake, and vanish in the gray sheen.

"It's water." He hurried back to camp. His haggard and worn companions scorned his discovery. Adams siding with Rude, who knew the plains, said: "Mirage! the lure of the desert!" Yet dominated by a force too powerful for them to resist, they followed the buffalo-hunter. All day the gleaming lake beckoned them onward, and seemed to recede. All day the drab clouds scudded before the cold north wind. In the gray twilight, the lake suddenly lay before them, as if it had opened at their feet. The men rejoiced, the horses lifted their noses and sniffed the damp air.

The whinnies of the horses, the clank of harness, and splash of water, the whirl of ducks did not blur out of Jones's keen ear a sound that made him jump. It was the thump of hoofs, in a familiar beat, beat, beat. He saw a shadow moving up a ridge. Soon, outlined black against the yet light sky, a lone buffalo cow stood like a statue. A moment she held toward the lake, studying the danger, then went out of sight over the ridge.

Jones spurred his horse up the ascent, which was rather long and steep, but he mounted the summit in time to see the cow join eight huge, shaggy buffalo. The hunter reined in his horse, and standing high in his stirrups, held his hat at arms' length over his head. So he thrilled to a moment he had sought for two years. The last herd of American bison was near at hand. The cow would not venture far from the main herd; the eight stragglers were the old broken-down bulls that had been expelled, at this season, from the herd by younger and more vigorous bulls. The old monarchs saw the hunter at the same time his eyes were gladdened by sight of them, and lumbered away after the cow, to disappear in the gathering darkness. Frightened buffalo always make straight for their fellows; and this knowledge contented Jones to return to the lake, well satisfied that the herd would not be far away in the morning, within easy striking distance by daylight.

At dark the storm which had threatened for days, broke in a fury of rain, sleet and hail. The hunters stretched a piece of canvas over the wheels of the north side of the wagon, and wet and shivering, crawled under it to their blankets. During the night the storm raged with unabated strength.

Dawn, forbidding and raw, lightened to the whistle of the sleety gusts. Fire was out of the question. Chary of weight, the hunters had carried no wood, and the buffalo chips they used for fuel were lumps of ice. Grumbling, Adams and Rude ate a cold breakfast, while Jones, munching a biscuit, faced the biting blast from the crest of the ridge. The middle of the plain below held a ragged, circular mass, as still as stone. It was the buffalo herd, with every shaggy head to the storm. So they would stand, never budging from their tracks, till the blizzard of sleet was over.

Jones, though eager and impatient, restrained himself, for it was unwise to begin operations in the storm. There was nothing to do but wait. Ill fared the hunters that day. Food had to be eaten uncooked. The long hours dragged by with the little group huddled under icy blankets. When darkness fell, the sleet changed to drizzling rain. This blew over at midnight, and a colder wind, penetrating to the very marrow of the sleepless men, made their condition worse. In the after part of the night, the wolves howled mournfully.

With a gray, misty light appearing in the east, Jones threw off his stiff, ice-incased blanket, and crawled out. A gaunt gray wolf, the color of the day and the sand and the lake, sneaked away, looking back. While moving and threshing about to warm his frozen blood, Jones munched another biscuit. Five men crawled from under the wagon, and made an unfruitful search for the whisky. Fearing it, Jones had thrown the bottle away. The men cursed. The patient horses drooped sadly, and shivered in the lee of the improvised tent. Jones kicked the inch-thick casing of ice from his saddle. Kentuck, his racer, had been spared on the whole trip for this day's work. The thoroughbred was cold, but as Jones threw the saddle over him, he showed that he knew the chase ahead, and was eager to be off. At last, after repeated efforts with his benumbed fingers, Jones got the girths tight. He tied a bunch of soft cords to the saddle and mounted.

"Follow as fast as you can," he called to his surly men. "The buffs will run north against the wind. This is the right direction for us; we'll soon leave the sand. Stick to my trail and come a-humming."

From the ridge he met the red sun, rising bright, and a keen northeasterly wind that lashed like a whip. As he had anticipated, his quarry had moved northward. Kentuck let out into a swinging stride, which in an hour had the loping herd in sight. Every jump now took him upon higher ground, where the sand failed, and the grass grew thicker and began to bend under the wind.

In the teeth of the nipping gale Jones slipped close upon the herd without alarming even a cow. More than a hundred little reddish-black calves leisurely loped in the rear. Kentuck, keen to his work, crept on like a wolf, and the hunter's great fist clenched the coiled lasso. Before him expanded a boundless plain. A situation long cherished and dreamed of had become a reality. Kentuck, fresh and strong, was good for all day. Jones gloated over the little red bulls and heifers, as a miser gloats over gold and jewels. Never before had he caught more than two in one day, and often it had taken days to capture one. This was the last herd, this the last opportunity toward perpetuating a grand race of beasts. And with born instinct he saw ahead the day of his life.

At a touch, Kentuck closed in, and the buffalo, seeing him, stampeded into the heaving roll so well known to the hunter. Racing on the right flank of the herd, Jones selected a tawny heifer and shot the lariat after her. It fell true, but being stiff and kinky from the sleet, failed to tighten, and the quick calf leaped through the loop to freedom.

Undismayed the pursuer quickly recovered his rope. Again he whirled and sent the loop. Again it circled true, and failed to close; again the agile heifer bounded through it. Jones whipped the air with the stubborn rope. To lose a chance like that was worse than boy's work.

The third whirl, running a smaller loop, tightened the coil round the frightened calf just back of its ears. A pull on the bridle brought Kentuck to a halt in his tracks, and the baby buffalo rolled over and over in the grass. Jones bounced from his seat and jerked loose a couple of the soft cords. In a twinkling; his big knee crushed down on the calf, and his big hands bound it helpless.

Kentuck neighed. Jones saw his black ears go up. Danger threatened. For a moment the hunter's blood turned chill, not from fear, for he never felt fear, but because he thought the Indians were returning to ruin his work. His eye swept the plain. Only the gray forms of wolves flitted through the grass, here, there, all about him. Wolves! They were as fatal to his enterprise as savages. A trooping pack of prairie wolves had fallen in with the herd and hung close on the trail, trying to cut a calf away from its mother. The gray brutes boldly trotted to within a few yards of him, and slyly looked at him, with pale, fiery eyes. They had already scented his captive. Precious time flew by; the situation, critical and baffling, had never before been met by him. There lay his little calf tied fast, and to the north ran many others, some of which he must— he would have. To think quickly had meant the solving of many a plainsman's problem. Should he stay with his prize to save it, or leave it to be devoured?

"Ha! you old gray devils!" he yelled, shaking his fist at the wolves. "I know a trick or two." Slipping his hat between the legs of the calf, he fastened it securely. This done, he vaulted on Kentuck, and was off with never a backward glance. Certain it was that the wolves would not touch anything, alive or dead, that bore the scent of a human being.

The bison scoured away a long half-mile in the lead, sailing northward like a cloud-shadow over the plain. Kentuck, mettlesome, over-eager, would have run himself out in short order, but the wary hunter, strong to restrain as well as impel, with the long day in his mind, kept the steed in his easy stride, which, springy and stretching, overhauled the herd in the course of several miles.

A dash, a swirl, a shock, a leap, horse and hunter working in perfect accord, and a fine big calf, bellowing lustily, struggled desperately for freedom under the remorseless knee. The big hands toyed with him; and then, secure in the double knots, the calf lay still, sticking out his tongue and rolling his eyes, with the coat of the hunter tucked under his bonds to keep away the wolves.

The race had but begun; the horse had but warmed to his work; the hunter had but tasted of sweet triumph. Another hopeful of a buffalo mother, negligent in danger, truant from his brothers, stumbled and fell in the enmeshing loop. The hunter's vest, slipped over the calf's neck, served as danger signal to the wolves. Before the lumbering buffalo missed their loss, another red and black baby kicked helplessly on the grass and sent up vain, weak calls, and at last lay still, with the hunter's boot tied to his cords.

Four! Jones counted them aloud, add in his mind, and kept on. Fast, hard work, covering upward of fifteen miles, had begun to tell on herd, horse and man, and all slowed down to the call for strength. The fifth time Jones closed in on his game, he encountered different circumstances such as called forth his cunning.

The herd had opened up; the mothers had fallen back to the rear; the calves hung almost out of sight under the shaggy sides of protectors. To try them out Jones darted close and threw his lasso. It struck a cow. With activity incredible in such a huge beast, she lunged at him. Kentuck, expecting just such a move, wheeled to safety. This duel, ineffectual on both sides, kept up for a while, and all the time, man and herd were jogging rapidly to the north.

Jones could not let well enough alone; he acknowledged this even as he swore he must have five. Emboldened by his marvelous luck, and yielding headlong to the passion within, he threw caution to the winds. A lame old cow with a red calf caught his eye; in he spurred his willing horse and slung his rope. It stung the haunch of the mother. The mad grunt she vented was no quicker than the velocity with which she plunged and reared. Jones had but time to swing his leg over the saddle when the hoofs beat down. Kentuck rolled on the plain, flinging his rider from him. The infuriated buffalo lowered her head for the fatal charge on the horse, when the plainsman, jerking out his heavy Colts, shot her dead in her tracks.

Kentuck got to his feet unhurt, and stood his ground, quivering but ready, showing his steadfast courage. He showed more, for his ears lay back, and his eyes had the gleam of the animal that strikes back.

The calf ran round its mother. Jones lassoed it, and tied it down, being compelled to cut a piece from his lasso, as the cords on the saddle had given out. He left his other boot with baby number five. The still heaving, smoking body of the victim called forth the stern, intrepid hunter's pity for a moment. Spill of blood he had not wanted. But he had not been able to avoid it; and mounting again with close-shut jaw and smoldering eye, he galloped to the north.

Kentuck snorted; the pursuing wolves shied off in the grass; the pale sun began to slant westward. The cold iron stirrups froze and cut the hunter's bootless feet.

When once more he came hounding the buffalo, they were considerably winded. Short-tufted tails, raised stiffly, gave warning. Snorts, like puffs of escaping steam, and deep grunts from cavernous chests evinced anger and impatience that might, at any moment, bring the herd to a defiant stand.

He whizzed the shortened noose over the head of a calf that was laboring painfully to keep up, and had slipped down, when a mighty grunt told him of peril. Never looking to see whence it came, he sprang into the saddle. Fiery Kentuck jumped into action, then hauled up with a shock that almost threw himself and rider. The lasso, fast to the horse, and its loop end round the calf, had caused the sudden check.

A maddened cow bore down on Kentuck. The gallant horse straightened in a jump, but dragging the calf pulled him in a circle, and in another moment he was running round and round the howling, kicking pivot. Then ensued a terrible race, with horse and bison describing a twenty-foot circle. Bang! Bang! The hunter fired two shots, and heard the spats of the bullets. But they only augmented the frenzy of the beast. Faster Kentuck flew, snorting in terror; closer drew the dusty, bouncing pursuer; the calf spun like a top; the lasso strung tighter than wire. Jones strained to loosen the fastening, but in vain. He swore at his carelessness in dropping his knife by the last calf he had tied. He thought of shooting the rope, yet dared not risk the shot. A hollow sound turned him again, with the Colts leveled. Bang! Dust flew from the ground beyond the bison.

The two charges left in the gun were all that stood between him and eternity. With a desperate display of strength Jones threw his weight in a backward pull, and hauled Kentuck up. Then he leaned far back in the saddle, and shoved the Colts out beyond the horse's flank. Down went the broad head, with its black, glistening horns. Bang! She slid forward with a crash, plowing the ground with hoofs and nose—spouted blood, uttered a hoarse cry, kicked and died.

Kentuck, for once completely terrorized, reared and plunged from the cow, dragging the calf. Stern command and iron arm forced him to a standstill. The calf, nearly strangled, recovered when the noose was slipped, and moaned a feeble protest against life and captivity. The remainder of Jones's lasso went to bind number six, and one of his socks went to serve as reminder to the persistent wolves.

"Six! On! On! Kentuck! On!" Weakening, but unconscious of it, with bloody hands and feet, without lasso, and with only one charge in his revolver, hatless, coatless, vestless, bootless, the wild hunter urged on the noble horse. The herd had gained miles in the interval of the fight. Game to the backbone, Kentuck lengthened out to overhaul it, and slowly the rolling gap lessened and lessened. A long hour thumped away, with the rumble growing nearer.

Once again the lagging calves dotted the grassy plain before the hunter. He dashed beside a burly calf, grasped its tail, stopped his horse, and jumped. The calf went down with him, and did not come up. The knotted, blood-stained hands, like claws of steel, bound the hind legs close and fast with a leathern belt, and left between them a torn and bloody sock.

"Seven! On! Old Faithfull! We MUST have another! the last! This is your day."

The blood that flecked the hunter was not all his own.

The sun slanted westwardly toward the purpling horizon; the grassy plain gleamed like a ruffled sea of glass; the gray wolves loped on.

When next the hunter came within sight of the herd, over a wavy ridge, changes in its shape and movement met his gaze. The calves were almost done; they could run no more; their mothers faced the south, and trotted slowly to and fro; the bulls were grunting, herding, piling close. It looked as if the herd meant to stand and fight.

This mattered little to the hunter who had captured seven calves since dawn. The first limping calf he reached tried to elude the grasping hand and failed. Kentuck had been trained to wheel to the right or left, in whichever way his rider leaned; and as Jones bent over and caught an upraised tail, the horse turned to strike the calf with both front hoofs. The calf rolled; the horse plunged down; the rider sped beyond to the dust. Though the calf was tired, he still could bellow, and he filled the air with robust bawls.

Jones all at once saw twenty or more buffalo dash in at him with fast, twinkling, short legs. With the thought of it, he was in the air to the saddle. As the black, round mounds charged from every direction, Kentuck let out with all there was left in him. He leaped and whirled, pitched and swerved, in a roaring, clashing, dusty melee. Beating hoofs threw the turf, flying tails whipped the air, and everywhere were dusky, sharp-pointed heads, tossing low. Kentuck squeezed out unscathed. The mob of bison, bristling, turned to lumber after the main herd. Jones seized his opportunity and rode after them, yelling with all his might. He drove them so hard that soon the little fellows lagged paces behind. Only one or two old cows straggled with the calves.

Then wheeling Kentuck, he cut between the herd and a calf, and rode it down. Bewildered, the tously little bull bellowed in great affright. The hunter seized the stiff tail, and calling to his horse, leaped off. But his strength was far spent and the buffalo, larger than his fellows, threshed about and jerked in terror. Jones threw it again and again. But it struggled up, never once ceasing its loud demands for help. Finally the hunter tripped it up and fell upon it with his knees.

Above the rumble of retreating hoofs, Jones heard the familiar short, quick, jarring pound on the turf. Kentuck neighed his alarm and raced to the right. Bearing down on the hunter, hurtling through the air, was a giant furry mass, instinct with fierce life and power—a buffalo cow robbed of her young.

With his senses almost numb, barely able to pull and raise the Colt, the plainsman willed to live, and to keep his captive. His leveled arm wavered like a leaf in a storm.

Bang! Fire, smoke, a shock, a jarring crash, and silence!

The calf stirred beneath him. He put out a hand to touch a warm, furry coat. The mother had fallen beside him. Lifting a heavy hoof, he laid it over the neck of the calf to serve as additional weight. He lay still and listened. The rumble of the herd died away in the distance.

The evening waned. Still the hunter lay quiet. From time to time the calf struggled and bellowed. Lank, gray wolves appeared on all sides; they prowled about with hungry howls, and shoved black-tipped noses through the grass. The sun sank, and the sky paled to opal blue. A star shone out, then another, and another. Over the prairie slanted the first dark shadow of night.

Suddenly the hunter laid his ear to the ground, and listened. Faint beats, like throbs of a pulsing heart, shuddered from the soft turf. Stronger they grew, till the hunter raised his head. Dark forms approached; voices broke the silence; the creaking of a wagon scared away the wolves.

"This way!" shouted the hunter weakly.

"Ha! here he is. Hurt?" cried Rude, vaulting the wheel.

"Tie up this calf. How many—did you find?" The voice grew fainter.

"Seven—alive, and in good shape, and all your clothes."

But the last words fell on unconscious ears.

CHAPTER 4.

THE TRAIL

"Frank, what'll we do about horses?" asked Jones. "Jim'll want the bay, and of course you'll want to ride Spot. The rest of our nags will only do to pack the outfit."

"I've been thinkin'," replied the foreman. "You sure will need good mounts. Now it happens that a friend of mine is just at this time at House Rock Valley, an outlyin' post of one of the big Utah ranches. He is gettin' in the horses off the range, an' he has some crackin' good ones. Let's ooze over there—it's only thirty miles—an' get some horses from him."

We were all eager to act upon Frank's suggestion. So plans were made for three of us to ride over and select our mounts. Frank and Jim would follow with the pack train, and if all went well, on the following evening we would camp under the shadow of Buckskin.

Early next morning we were on our way. I tried to find a soft place on Old Baldy, one of Frank's pack horses. He was a horse that would not have raised up at the trumpet of doom. Nothing under the sun, Frank said, bothered Old Baldy but the operation of shoeing. We made the distance to the outpost by noon, and found Frank's friend a genial and obliging cowboy, who said we could have all the horses we wanted.

While Jones and Wallace strutted round the big corral, which was full of vicious, dusty, shaggy horses and mustangs, I sat high on the fence. I heard them talking about points and girth and stride, and a lot of terms that I could not understand. Wallace selected a heavy sorrel, and Jones a big bay; very like Jim's. I had observed, way over in the corner of the corral, a bunch of cayuses, and among them a clean-limbed black horse. Edging round on the fence I got a closer view, and then cried out that I had found my horse. I jumped down and caught him, much to my surprise, for the other horses were wild, and had kicked viciously. The black was beautifully built, wide-chested and powerful, but not heavy. His coat glistened like sheeny black satin, and he had a white face and white feet and a long mane.

"I don't know about giving you Satan—that's his name," said the cowboy. "The foreman rides him often. He's the fastest, the best climber, and the best dispositioned horse on the range.

"But I guess I can let you have him," he continued, when he saw my disappointed face.

"By George!" exclaimed Jones. "You've got it on us this time."

"Would you like to trade?" asked Wallace, as his sorrel tried to bite him. "That black looks sort of fierce."

I led my prize out of the corral, up to the little cabin nearby, where I tied him, and proceeded to get acquainted after a fashion of my own. Though not versed in horse-lore, I knew that half the battle was to win his confidence. I smoothed his silky coat, and patted him, and then surreptitiously slipped a lump of sugar from my pocket. This sugar, which I had purloined in Flagstaff, and carried all the way across the desert, was somewhat disreputably soiled, and Satan sniffed at it disdainfully. Evidently he had never smelled or tasted sugar. I pressed it into his mouth. He munched it, and then looked me over with some interest. I handed him another lump. He took it and rubbed his nose against me. Satan was mine!

Frank and Jim came along early in the afternoon. What with packing, changing saddles and shoeing the horses, we were all busy. Old Baldy would not be shod, so we let him off till a more opportune time. By four o'clock we were riding toward the slopes of Buckskin, now only a few miles away, standing up higher and darker.

"What's that for?" inquired Wallace, pointing to a long, rusty, wire-wrapped, double-barreled blunderbuss of a shotgun, stuck in the holster of Jones's saddle.

The Colonel, who had been having a fine time with the impatient and curious hounds, did not vouchsafe any information on that score. But very shortly we were destined to learn the use of this incongruous firearm. I was riding in advance of Wallace, and a little behind Jones. The dogs—excepting Jude, who had been kicked and lamed—were ranging along before their master. Suddenly, right before me, I saw an immense jack-rabbit; and just then Moze and Don caught sight of it. In fact, Moze bumped his blunt nose into the rabbit. When it leaped into scared action, Moze yelped, and Don followed suit. Then they were after it in wild, clamoring pursuit. Jones let out the stentorian blast, now becoming familiar, and spurred after them. He reached over, pulled the shotgun out of the holster and fired both barrels at the jumping dogs.

I expressed my amazement in strong language, and Wallace whistled.

Don came sneaking back with his tail between his legs, and Moze, who had cowered as if stung, circled round ahead of us. Jones finally succeeded in gettin him back.

"Come in hyah! You measly rabbit dogs! What do you mean chasing off that way? We're after lions. Lions! understand?"

Don looked thoroughly convinced of his error, but Moze, being more thick-headed, appeared mystified rather than hurt or frightened.

"What size shot do you use?" I asked.

"Number ten. They don't hurt much at seventy five yards," replied our leader. "I use them as sort of a long arm. You see, the dogs must be made to know what we're after. Ordinary means would never do in a case like this. My idea is to break them of coyotes, wolves and deer, and when we cross a lion trail, let them go. I'll teach them sooner than you'd think. Only we must get where we can see what they're trailing. Then I can tell whether to call then back or not."

The sun was gilding the rim of the desert rampart when we began the ascent of the foothills of Buckskin. A steep trail wound zigzag up the mountain We led our horses, as it was a long, hard climb. From time to time, as I stopped to catch my breath I gazed away across the growing void to the gorgeous Pink Cliffs, far above and beyond the red wall which had seemed so high, and then out toward the desert. The irregular ragged crack in the plain, apparently only a thread of broken ground, was the Grand Canyon. How unutterably remote, wild, grand was that world of red and brown, of purple pall, of vague outline!

Two thousand feet, probably, we mounted to what Frank called Little Buckskin. In the west a copper glow, ridged with lead-colored clouds, marked where the sun had set. The air was very thin and icy cold. At the first clump of pinyon pines, we made dry camp. When I sat down it was as if I had been anchored. Frank solicitously remarked that I looked "sort of beat." Jim built a roaring fire and began getting supper. A snow squall came on the rushing wind. The air grew colder, and though I hugged the fire, I could not get warm. When I had satisfied my hunger, I rolled out my sleeping-bag and crept into it. I stretched my aching limbs and did not move again.

Once I awoke, drowsily feeling the warmth of the fire, and I heard Frank say: "He's asleep, dead to the world!"

"He's all in," said Jones. "Riding's what did it You know how a horse tears a man to pieces."

"Will he be able to stand it?" asked Frank, with as much solicitude as if he were my brother. "When you get out after anythin'—well, you're hell. An' think of the country we're goin' into. I know you've never seen the breaks of the Siwash, but I have, an' it's the worst an' roughest country I ever saw. Breaks after breaks, like the ridges on a washboard, headin' on the south slope of Buckskin, an' runnin' down, side by side, miles an' miles, deeper an' deeper, till they run into that awful hole. It will be a killin' trip on men, horses an' dogs. Now, Mr. Wallace, he's been campin' an' roughin' with the Navajos for months; he's in some kind of shape, but—"

Frank concluded his remark with a doubtful pause.

"I'm some worried, too," replied Jones. "But he would come. He stood the desert well enough; even the Mormons said that."

In the ensuing silence the fire sputtered, the glare fitfully merged into dark shadows under the weird pinyons, and the wind moaned through the short branches.

"Wal," drawled a slow, soft voice, "shore I reckon you're hollerin' too soon. Frank's measly trick puttin' him on Spot showed me. He rode out on Spot, an' he rode in on Spot. Shore he'll stay."

It was not all the warmth of the blankets that glowed over me then. The voices died away dreamily, and my eyelids dropped sleepily tight. Late in the night I sat up suddenly, roused by some unusual disturbance. The fire was dead; the wind swept with a rush through the pinyons. From the black darkness came the staccato chorus of coyotes. Don barked his displeasure; Sounder made the welkin ring, and old Moze growled low and deep, grumbling like muttered thunder. Then all was quiet, and I slept.

Dawn, rosy red, confronted me when I opened my eyes. Breakfast was ready; Frank was packing Old Baldy; Jones talked to his horse as he saddled him; Wallace came stooping his giant figure under the pinyons; the dogs, eager and soft-eyed, sat around Jim and begged. The sun peeped over the Pink Cliffs; the desert still lay asleep, tranced in a purple and golden-streaked mist.

"Come, come!" said Jones, in his big voice. "We're slow; here's the sun."

"Easy, easy," replied Frank, "we've all the time there is."

When Frank threw the saddle over Satan I interrupted him and said I would care for my horse henceforward. Soon we were under way, the horses fresh, the dogs scenting the keen, cold air.

The trail rolled over the ridges of pinyon and scrubby pine. Occasionally we could see the black, ragged crest of Buckskin above us. From one of these ridges I took my last long look back at the desert, and engraved on my mind a picture of the red wall, and the many-hued ocean of sand. The trail, narrow and indistinct, mounted the last slow-rising slope; the pinyons failed, and the scrubby pines became abundant. At length we reached the top, and entered the great arched aisles of Buckskin Forest. The ground was flat as a table. Magnificent pine trees, far apart, with branches high and spreading, gave the eye glad welcome. Some of these monarchs were eight feet thick at the base and two hundred feet high. Here and there one lay, gaunt and prostrate, a victim of the wind. The smell of pitch pine was sweetly overpowering.

"When I went through here two weeks ago, the snow was a foot deep, an' I bogged in places," said Frank. "The sun has been oozin' round here some. I'm afraid Jones won't find any snow on this end of Buckskin."

Thirty miles of winding trail, brown and springy from its thick mat of pine needles, shaded always by the massive, seamy-barked trees, took us over the extremity of Buckskin. Then we faced down into the head of a ravine that ever grew deeper, stonier and rougher. I shifted from side to side, from leg to leg in my saddle, dismounted and hobbled before Satan, mounted again, and rode on. Jones called the dogs and complained to them of the lack of snow. Wallace sat his horse comfortably, taking long pulls at his pipe and long gazes at the shaggy sides of the ravine. Frank, energetic and tireless, kept the pack-horses in the trail. Jim jogged on silently. And so we rode down to Oak Spring.

The spring was pleasantly situated in a grove of oaks and Pinyons, under the shadow of three cliffs. Three ravines opened here into an oval valley. A rude cabin of rough-hewn logs stood near the spring.

"Get down, get down," sang out Frank. "We'll hang up here. Beyond Oak is No-Man's-Land. We take our chances on water after we leave here."

When we had unsaddled, unpacked, and got a fire roaring on the wide stone hearth of the cabin, it was once again night.

"Boys," said Jones after supper, "we're now on the edge of the lion country. Frank saw lion sign in here only two weeks ago; and though the snow is gone, we stand a show of finding tracks in the sand and dust. To-morrow morning, before the sun gets a chance at the bottom of these ravines, we'll be up and doing. We'll each take a dog and search in different directions. Keep the dog in leash, and when he opens up, examine the ground carefully for tracks. If a dog opens on any track that you are sure isn't lion's, punish him. And when a lion-track is found, hold the dog in, wait and signal. We'll use a signal I have tried and found far-reaching and easy to yell. Waa-hoo! That's it. Once yelled it means come. Twice means comes quickly. Three times means come—danger!"

In one corner of the cabin was a platform of poles, covered with straw. I threw the sleeping-bag on this, and was soon stretched out. Misgivings as to my strength worried me before I closed my eyes. Once on my back, I felt I could not rise; my chest was sore; my cough deep and rasping. It seemed I had scarcely closed my eyes when Jones's impatient voice recalled me from sweet oblivion.

"Frank, Frank, it's daylight. Jim—boys!" he called.

I tumbled out in a gray, wan twilight. It was cold enough to make the fire acceptable, but nothing like the morning before on Buckskin.

"Come to the festal board," drawled Jim, almost before I had my boots laced.

"Jones," said Frank, "Jim an' I'll ooze round here to-day. There's lots to do, an' we want to have things hitched right before we strike for the Siwash. We've got to shoe Old Baldy, an' if we can't get him locoed, it'll take all of us to do it."

The light was still gray when Jones led off with Don, Wallace with Sounder and I with Moze. Jones directed us to separate, follow the dry stream beds in the ravines, and remember his instructions given the night before.

166

The ravine to the right, which I entered, was choked with huge stones fallen from the cliff above, and pinyons growing thick; and I wondered apprehensively how a man could evade a wild animal in such a place, much less chase it. Old Moze pulled on his chain and sniffed at coyote and deer tracks. And every time he evinced interest in such, I cut him with a switch, which, to tell the truth, he did not notice. I thought I heard a shout, and holding Moze tight, I waited and listened.

"Waa-hoo—waa-hoo!" floated on the air, rather deadened as if it had come from round the triangular cliff that faced into the valley. Urging and dragging Moze, I ran down the ravine as fast as I could, and soon encountered Wallace coming from the middle ravine. "Jones," he said excitedly, "this way—there's the signal again." We dashed in haste for the mouth of the third ravine, and came suddenly upon Jones, kneeling under a pinyon tree. "Boys, look!" he exclaimed, as he pointed to the ground. There, clearly defined in the dust, was a cat track as big as my spread hand, and the mere sight of it sent a chill up my spine. "There's a lion track for you; made by a female, a two-year-old; but can't say if she passed here last night. Don won't take the trail. Try Moze."

I led Moze to the big, round imprint, and put his nose down into it. The old hound sniffed and sniffed, then lost interest.

"Cold!" ejaculated Jones. "No go. Try Sounder. Come, old boy, you've the nose for it."

He urged the reluctant hound forward. Sounder needed not to be shown the trail; he stuck his nose in it, and stood very quiet for a long moment; then he quivered slightly, raised his nose and sought the next track. Step by step he went slowly, doubtfully. All at once his tail wagged stiffly.

"Look at that!" cried Jones in delight. "He's caught a scent when the others couldn't. Hyah, Moze, get back. Keep Moze and Don back; give him room."

Slowly Sounder paced up the ravine, as carefully as if he were traveling on thin ice. He passed the dusty, open trail to a scaly ground with little bits of grass, and he kept on.

We were electrified to hear him give vent to a deep bugle-blast note of eagerness.

"By George, he's got it, boys!" exclaimed Jones, as he lifted the stubborn, struggling hound off the trail. "I know that bay. It means a lion passed here this morning. And we'll get him up as sure as you're alive. Come, Sounder. Now for the horses."

As we ran pell-mell into the little glade, where Jim sat mending some saddle trapping, Frank rode up the trail with the horses.

"Well, I heard Sounder," he said with his genial smile. "Somethin's comin' off, eh? You'll have to ooze round some to keep up with that hound."

I saddled Satan with fingers that trembled in excitement, and pushed my little Remington automatic into the rifle holster.

"Boys, listen," said our leader. "We're off now in the beginning of a hunt new to you. Remember no shooting, no blood-letting, except in self-defense. Keep as close to me as you can. Listen for the dogs, and when you fall behind or separate, yell out the signal cry. Don't forget this. We're bound to lose each other. Look out for the spikes and branches on the trees. If the dogs split, whoever follows the one that trees the lion must wait there till the rest come up. Off now! Come, Sounder; Moze, you rascal, hyah! Come, Don, come, Puppy, and take your medicine."

Except Moze, the hounds were all trembling and running eagerly to and fro. When Sounder was loosed, he led them in a bee-line to the trail, with us cantering after. Sounder worked exactly as before, only he followed the lion tracks a little farther up the ravine before he bayed. He kept going faster and faster, occasionally letting out one deep, short yelp. The other hounds did not give tongue, but eager, excited, baffled, kept at his heels. The ravine was long, and the wash at the bottom, up which the lion had proceeded, turned and twisted round boulders large as houses, and led through dense growths of some short, rough shrub. Now and then the lion tracks showed plainly in the sand. For five miles or more Sounder led us up the ravine, which began to contract and grow steep. The dry stream bed got to be full of thickets of branchless saplings, about the poplar—tall, straight, size of a man's arm, and growing so close we had to press them aside to let our horses through.

Presently Sounder slowed up and appeared at fault. We found him puzzling over an open, grassy patch, and after nosing it for a little while, he began skirting the edge.

"Cute dog!" declared Jones. "That Sounder will make a lion chaser. Our game has gone up here somewhere."

Sure enough, Sounder directly gave tongue from the side of the ravine. It was climb for us now. Broken shale, rocks of all dimensions, pinyons down and pinyons up made ascending no easy problem. We had to dismount and lead the horses, thus losing ground. Jones forged ahead and reached the top of the ravine first. When Wallace and I got up, breathing heavily, Jones and the hounds were out of sight. But Sounder kept voicing his clear call, giving us our direction. Off we flew, over ground that was still rough, but enjoyable going compared to the ravine slopes. The ridge was sparsely covered with cedar and pinyon, through which, far ahead, we pretty soon spied Jones. Wallace signaled, and our leader answered twice. We caught up with him on the brink of another ravine deeper and craggier than the first, full of dead, gnarled pinyon and splintered rocks.

"This gulch is the largest of the three that head in at Oak Spring," said Jones. "Boys, don't forget your direction. Always keep a feeling where camp is, always sense it every time you turn. The dogs have gone down. That lion is in here somewhere. Maybe he lives down in the high cliffs near the spring and came up here last night for a kill he's buried somewhere. Lions never travel far. Hark! Hark! There's Sounder and the rest of them! They've got the scent; they've all got it! Down, boys, down, and ride!"

With that he crashed into the cedar in a way that showed me how impervious he was to slashing branches, sharp as thorns, and steep descent and peril.

Wallace's big sorrel plunged after him and the rolling stones cracked. Suffering as I was by this time, with cramp in my legs, and torturing pain, I had to choose between holding my horse in or falling off; so I chose the former and accordingly got behind.

Dead cedar and pinyon trees lay everywhere, with their contorted limbs reaching out like the arms of a devil-fish. Stones blocked every opening. Making the bottom of the ravine after what seemed an interminable time, I found the tracks of Jones and Wallace. A long "Waa-hoo!" drew me on; then the mellow bay of a hound floated up the ravine. Satan made up time in the sandy stream bed, but kept me busily dodging overhanging branches. I became aware, after a succession of efforts to keep from being strung on pinyons, that the sand before me was clean and trackless. Hauling Satan up sharply, I waited irresolutely and listened. Then from high up the ravine side wafted down a medley of yelps and barks.

"Waa-hoo, waa-hoo!" ringing down the slope, pealed against the cliff behind me, and sent the wild echoes flying. Satan, of his own accord, headed up the incline. Surprised at this, I gave him free rein. How he did climb! Not long did it take me to discover that he picked out easier going than I had. Once I saw Jones crossing a ledge far above me, and I yelled our signal cry. The answer returned clear and sharp; then its echo cracked under the hollow cliff, and crossing and recrossing the ravine, it died at last far away, like the muffled peal of a bell-buoy. Again I heard the blended yelping of the hounds, and closer at hand. I saw a long, low cliff above, and decided that the hounds were running at the base of it. Another chorus of yelps, quicker, wilder than the others, drew a yell from me. Instinctively I knew the dogs had jumped game of some kind. Satan knew it as well as I, for he quickened his pace and sent the stones clattering behind him.

I gained the base of the yellow cliff, but found no tracks in the dust of ages that had crumbled in its shadow, nor did I hear the dogs. Considering how close they had seemed, this was strange. I halted and listened. Silence reigned supreme. The ragged cracks in the cliff walls could have harbored many a watching lion, and I cast an apprehensive glance into their dark confines. Then I turned my horse to get round the cliff and over the ridge. When I again stopped, all I could hear was the thumping of my heart and the labored panting of Satan. I came to a break in the cliff, a steep place of weathered rock, and I put Satan to it. He went up with a will. From the narrow saddle of the ridge-crest I tried to take my bearings. Below me slanted the green of pinyon, with the bleached treetops standing like spears, and uprising yellow stones. Fancying I heard a gunshot, I leaned a straining ear against the soft breeze. The proof came presently in the unmistakable report of Jones's blunderbuss. It was repeated almost instantly, giving reality to the direction, which was down the slope of what I concluded must be the third ravine. Wondering what was the meaning of the shots, and chagrined because I was out of the race, but calmer in mind, I let Satan stand.

Hardly a moment elapsed before a sharp bark tingled in my ears. It belonged to old Moze. Soon I distinguished a rattling of stones and the sharp, metallic clicks of hoofs striking rocks. Then into a space below me loped a beautiful deer, so large that at first I took it for an elk. Another sharp bark, nearer this time, told the tale of Moze's dereliction. In a few moments he came in sight, running with his tongue out and his head high.

"Hyah, you old gladiator! hyah! hyah!" I yelled and yelled again. Moze passed over the saddle on the trail of the deer, and his short bark floated back to remind me how far he was from a lion dog.

Then I divined the meaning of the shotgun reports. The hounds had crossed a fresher trail than that of the lion, and our leader had discovered it. Despite a keen appreciation of Jones's task, I gave way to amusement, and repeated Wallace's paradoxical formula: "Pet the lions and shoot the hounds."

So I headed down the ravine, looking for a blunt, bold crag, which I had descried from camp. I found it before long, and profiting by past failures to judge of distance, gave my first impression a great stretch, and then decided that I was more than two miles from Oak.

Long after two miles had been covered, and I had begun to associate Jim's biscuits with a certain soft seat near a ruddy fire, I was apparently still the same distance from my landmark crag. Suddenly a slight noise brought me to a halt. I listened intently. Only an indistinct rattling of small rocks disturbed the impressive stillness. It might have been the weathering that goes on constantly, and it might have been an animal. I inclined to the former idea till I saw Satan's ears go up. Jones had told me to watch the ears of my horse, and short as had been my acquaintance with Satan, I had learned that he always discovered things more quickly than I. So I waited patiently.

From time to time a rattling roll of pebbles, almost musical, caught my ear. It came from the base of the wall of yellow cliff that barred the summit of all those ridges. Satan threw up his head and nosed the breeze. The delicate, almost stealthy sounds, the action of my horse, the waiting drove my heart to extra work. The breeze quickened and fanned my cheek, and borne upon it came the faint and far-away bay of a hound. It came again and again, each time nearer. Then on a stronger puff of wind rang the clear, deep, mellow call that had given Sounder his beautiful name. Never it seemed had I heard music so blood-stirring. Sounder was on the trail of something, and he had it headed my way. Satan heard, shot up his long ears, and tried to go ahead; but I restrained and soothed him into quiet.

Long moments I sat there, with the poignant consciousness of the wildness of the scene, of the significant rattling of the stones and of the bell-tongued hound baying incessantly, sending warm joy through my veins, the absorption in sensations new, yielding only to the hunting instinct when Satan snorted and quivered. Again the deep-toned bay rang into the silence with its stirring thrill of life. And a sharp rattling of stones just above brought another snort from Satan.

Across an open space in the pinyons a gray form flashed. I leaped off Satan and knelt to get a better view under the trees. I soon made out another deer passing along the base of the cliff. Mounting again, I rode up to the cliff to wait for Sounder.

A long time I had to wait for the hound. It proved that the atmosphere was as deceiving in regard to sound as to sight. Finally Sounder came running along the wall. I got off to intercept him. The crazy fellow—he had never responded to my overtures of friendship—uttered short, sharp yelps of delight, and actually leaped into my arms. But I could not hold him. He darted upon the trail again and paid no heed to my angry shouts. With a resolve to overhaul him, I jumped on Satan and whirled after the hound.

The black stretched out with such a stride that I was at pains to keep my seat. I dodged the jutting rocks and projecting snags; felt stinging branches in my face and the rush of sweet, dry wind. Under the crumbling walls, over slopes of weathered stone and droppings of shelving rock, round protruding noses of cliff, over and under pinyons Satan thundered. He came out on the top of the ridge, at the narrow back I had called a saddle. Here I caught a glimpse of Sounder far below, going down into the ravine from which I had ascended some time before. I called to him, but I might as well have called to the wind.

Weary to the point of exhaustion, I once more turned Satan toward camp. I lay forward on his neck and let him have his will. Far down the ravine I awoke to strange sounds, and soon recognized the cracking of iron-shod hoofs against stone; then voices. Turning an abrupt bend in the sandy wash, I ran into Jones and Wallace.

"Fall in! Line up in the sad procession!" said Jones. "Tige and the pup are faithful. The rest of the dogs are somewhere between the Grand Canyon and the Utah desert."

I related my adventures, and tried to spare Moze and Sounder as much as conscience would permit.

"Hard luck!" commented Jones. "Just as the hounds jumped the cougar—Oh! they bounced him out of the rocks all right—don't you remember, just under that cliff wall where you and Wallace came up to me? Well, just as they jumped him, they ran right into fresh deer tracks. I saw one of the deer. Now that's too much for any hounds, except those trained for lions. I shot at Moze twice, but couldn't turn him. He has to be hurt, they've all got to be hurt to make them understand."

Wallace told of a wild ride somewhere in Jones's wake, and of sundry knocks and bruises he had sustained, of pieces of corduroy he had left decorating the cedars and of a most humiliating event, where a gaunt and bare pinyon snag had penetrated under his belt and lifted him, mad and kicking, off his horse.

"These Western nags will hang you on a line every chance they get," declared Jones, "and don't you overlook that. Well, there's the cabin. We'd better stay here a few days or a week and break in the dogs and horses, for this day's work was apple pie to what we'll get in the Siwash."

I groaned inwardly, and was remorselessly glad to see Wallace fall off his horse and walk on one leg to the cabin. When I got my saddle off Satan, had given him a drink and hobbled him, I crept into the cabin and dropped like a log. I felt as if every bone in my body was broken and my flesh was raw. I got gleeful gratification from Wallace's complaints, and Jones's remark that he had a stitch in his back. So ended the first chase after cougars.

CHAPTER 5.

OAK SPRING

Moze and Don and Sounder straggled into camp next morning, hungry, footsore and scarred; and as they limped in, Jones met them with characteristic speech: "Well, you decided to come in when you got hungry and tired? Never thought of how you fooled me, did you? Now, the first thing you get is a good licking."

He tied them in a little log pen near the cabin and whipped them soundly. And the next few days, while Wallace and I rested, he took them out separately and deliberately ran them over coyote and deer trails. Sometimes we heard his stentorian yell as a forerunner to the blast from his old shotgun. Then again we heard the shots unheralded by the yell. Wallace and I waxed warm under the collar over this peculiar method of training dogs, and each of us made dire threats. But in justice to their implacable trainer, the dogs never appeared to be hurt; never a spot of blood flecked their glossy coats, nor did they ever come home limping. Sounder grew wise, and Don gave up, but Moze appeared not to change.

"All hands ready to rustle," sang out Frank one morning. "Old Baldy's got to be shod."

This brought us all, except Jones, out of the cabin, to see the object of Frank's anxiety tied to a nearby oak. At first I failed to recognize Old Baldy. Vanished was the slow, sleepy, apathetic manner that had characterized him; his ears lay back on his head; fire flashed from his eyes. When Frank threw down a kit-bag, which emitted a metallic clanking, Old Baldy sat back on his haunches, planted his forefeet deep in the ground and plainly as a horse could speak, said "No!"

"Sometimes he's bad, and sometimes worse," growled Frank.

"Shore he's plumb bad this mornin'," replied Jim.

Frank got the three of us to hold Baldy's head and pull him up, then he ventured to lift a hind foot over his line. Old Baldy straightened out his leg and sent Frank sprawling into the dirt. Twice again Frank patiently tried to hold a hind leg, with the same result; and then he lifted a forefoot. Baldy uttered a very intelligible snort, bit through Wallace's glove, yanked Jim off his feet, and scared me so that I let go his forelock. Then he broke the rope which held him to the tree. There was a plunge, a scattering of men, though Jim still valiantly held on to Baldy's head, and a thrashing of scrub pinyon, where Baldy reached out vigorously with his hind feet. But for Jim, he would have escaped.

"What's all the row?" called Jones from the cabin. Then from the door, taking in the situation, he yelled: "Hold on, Jim! Pull down on the ornery old cayuse!"

He leaped into action with a lasso in each hand, one whirling round his head. The slender rope straightened with a whiz and whipped round Baldy's legs as he kicked viciously. Jones pulled it tight, then fastened it with nimble fingers to the tree.

"Let go! let go! Jim!" he yelled, whirling the other lasso. The loop flashed and fell over Baldy's head and tightened round his neck. Jones threw all the weight of his burly form on the lariat, and Baldy crashed to the ground, rolled, tussled, screamed, and then lay on his back, kicking the air with three free legs. "Hold this," ordered Jones, giving the tight rope to Frank.

Whereupon he grabbed my lasso from the saddle, roped Baldy's two forefeet, and pulled him down on his side. This lasso he fastened to a scrub cedar.

"He's chokin'!" said Frank.

"Likely he is," replied Jones shortly. "It'll do him good." But with his big hands he drew the coil loose and slipped it down over Baldy's nose, where he tightened it again.

"Now, go ahead," he said, taking the rope from Frank.

It had all been done in a twinkling. Baldy lay there groaning and helpless, and when Frank once again took hold of the wicked leg, he was almost passive. When the shoeing operation had been neatly and quickly attended to and Baldy released from his uncomfortable position he struggled to his feet with heavy breaths, shook himself, and looked at his master.

"How'd you like being hog-tied?" queried his conqueror, rubbing Baldy's nose. "Now, after this you'll have some manners."

Old Baldy seemed to understand, for he looked sheepish, and lapsed once more into his listless, lazy unconcern.

"Where's Jim's old cayuse, the pack-horse?" asked our leader.

"Lost. Couldn't find him this morning, an' had a deuce of a time findin' the rest of the bunch. Old Baldy was cute. He hid in a bunch of pinyons an' stood quiet so his bell wouldn't ring. I had to trail him."

"Do the horses stray far when they are hobbled?" inquired Wallace.

"If they keep jumpin' all night they can cover some territory. We're now on the edge of the wild horse country, and our nags know this as well as we. They smell the mustangs, an' would break their necks to get away. Satan and the sorrel were ten miles from camp when I found them this mornin'. An' Jim's cayuse went farther, an' we never will get him. He'll wear his hobbles out, then away with the wild horses. Once with them, he'll never be caught again."

On the sixth day of our stay at Oak we had visitors, whom Frank introduced as the Stewart brothers and Lawson, wild-horse wranglers. They were still, dark men, whose facial expression seldom varied; tall and lithe and wiry as the mustangs they rode. The Stewarts were on their way to Kanab, Utah, to arrange for the sale of a drove of horses they had captured and corraled in a narrow canyon back in the Siwash. Lawson said he was at our service, and was promptly hired to look after our horses.

"Any cougar signs back in the breaks?" asked Jones.

"Wal, there's a cougar on every deer trail," replied the elder Stewart, "An' two for every pinto in the breaks. Old Tom himself downed fifteen colts fer us this spring."

"Fifteen colts! That's wholesale murder. Why don't you kill the butcher?"

"We've tried more'n onct. It's a turrible busted up country, them brakes. No man knows it, an' the cougars do. Old Tom ranges all the ridges and brakes, even up on the slopes of Buckskin; but he lives down there in them holes, an' Lord knows, no dog I ever seen could follow him. We tracked him in the snow, an' had dogs after him, but none could stay with him, except two as never cum back. But we've nothin' agin Old Tom like Jeff Clarke, a hoss rustler, who has a string of pintos corraled north of us. Clarke swears he ain't raised a colt in two years."

"We'll put that old cougar up a tree," exclaimed Jones.

"If you kill him we'll make you all a present of a mustang, an' Clarke, he'll give you two each," replied Stewart. "We'd be gettin' rid of him cheap."

173

"How many wild horses on the mountain now?"

"Hard to tell. Two or three thousand, mebbe. There's almost no ketchin' them, an' they regrowin' all the time We ain't had no luck this spring. The bunch in corral we got last year."

"Seen anythin' of the White Mustang?" inquired Frank. "Ever get a rope near him?"

"No nearer'n we hev fer six years back. He can't be ketched. We seen him an' his band of blacks a few days ago, headin' fer a water-hole down where Nail Canyon runs into Kanab Canyon. He's so cunnin' he'll never water at any of our trap corrals. An' we believe he can go without water fer two weeks, unless mebbe he hes a secret hole we've never trailed him to."

"Would we have any chance to see this White Mustang and his band?" questioned Jones.

"See him? Why, thet'd be easy. Go down Snake Gulch, camp at Singin' Cliffs, go over into Nail Canyon, an' wait. Then send some one slippin' down to the water-hole at Kanab Canyon, an' when the band cums in to drink—which I reckon will be in a few days now—hev them drive the mustangs up. Only be sure to hev them get ahead of the White Mustang, so he'll hev only one way to cum, fer he sure is knowin'. He never makes a mistake. Mebbe you'll get to see him cum by like a white streak. Why, I've heerd thet mustang's hoofs ring like bells on the rocks a mile away. His hoofs are harder'n any iron shoe as was ever made. But even if you don't get to see him, Snake Gulch is worth seein'."

I learned later from Stewart that the White Mustang was a beautiful stallion of the wildest strain of mustang blue blood. He had roamed the long reaches between the Grand Canyon and Buckskin toward its southern slope for years; he had been the most sought-for horse by all the wranglers, and had become so shy and experienced that nothing but a glimpse was ever obtained of him. A singular fact was that he never attached any of his own species to his band, unless they were coal black. He had been known to fight and kill other stallions, but he kept out of the well-wooded and watered country frequented by other bands, and ranged the brakes of the Siwash as far as he could range. The usual method, indeed the only successful way to capture wild horses, was to build corrals round the waterholes. The wranglers lay out night after night watching. When the mustangs came to drink—which was always after dark—the gates would be closed on them. But the trick had never even been tried on the White Mustang, for the simple reason that he never approached one of these traps.

"Boys," said Jones, "seeing we need breaking in, we'll give the White Mustang a little run."

This was most pleasurable news, for the wild horses fascinated me. Besides, I saw from the expression on our leader's face that an uncapturable mustang was an object of interest for him.

Wallace and I had employed the last few warm sunny afternoons in riding up and down the valley, below Oak, where there was a fine, level stretch. Here I wore out my soreness of muscle, and gradually overcame my awkwardness in the saddle. Frank's remedy of maple sugar and red pepper had rid me of my cold, and with the return of strength, and the coming of confidence, full, joyous appreciation of wild environment and life made me unspeakably happy. And I noticed that my companions were in like condition of mind, though self-contained where I was exuberant. Wallace galloped his sorrel and watched the crags; Jones talked more kindly to the dogs; Jim baked biscuits indefatigably, and smoked in contented silence; Frank said always: "We'll ooze along easy like, for we've all the time there is." Which sentiment, whether from reiterated suggestion, or increasing confidence in the practical cowboy, or charm of its free import, gradually won us all.

"Boys," said Jones, as we sat round the campfire, "I see you're getting in shape. Well, I've worn off the wire edge myself. And I have the hounds coming fine. They mind me now, but they're mystified. For the life of them they can't understand what I mean. I don't blame them. Wait till, by good luck, we get a cougar in a tree. When Sounder and Don see that, we've lion dogs, boys! we've lion dogs! But Moze is a stubborn brute. In all my years of animal experience, I've never discovered any other way to make animals obey than by instilling fear and respect into their hearts. I've been fond of buffalo, horses and dogs, but sentiment never ruled me. When animals must obey, they must—that's all, and no mawkishness! But I never trusted a buffalo in my life. If I had I wouldn't be here to-night. You all know how many keepers of tame wild animals get killed. I could tell you dozens of tragedies. And I've often thought, since I got back from New York, of that woman I saw with her troop of African lions. I dream about those lions, and see them leaping over her head. What a grand sight that was! But the public is fooled. I read somewhere that she trained those lions by love. I don't believe it. I saw her use a whip and a steel spear. Moreover, I saw many things that escaped most observers—how she entered the cage, how she maneuvered among them, how she kept a compelling gaze on them! It was an admirable, a great piece of work. Maybe she loves those huge yellow brutes, but her life was in danger every moment while she was in that cage, and she knew it. Some day, one of her pets likely the King of Beasts she pets the most will rise up and kill her. That is as certain as death."

CHAPTER 6.

THE WHITE MUSTANG

For thirty miles down Nail Canyon we marked, in every dusty trail and sandy wash, the small, oval, sharply defined tracks of the White Mustang and his band.

The canyon had been well named. It was long, straight and square sided; its bare walls glared steel-gray in the sun, smooth, glistening surfaces that had been polished by wind and water. No weathered heaps of shale, no crumbled piles of stone obstructed its level floor. And, softly toning its drab austerity, here grew the white sage, waving in the breeze, the Indian Paint Brush, with vivid vermilion flower, and patches of fresh, green grass.

"The White King, as we Arizona wild-hoss wranglers calls this mustang, is mighty pertickler about his feed, an' he ranged along here last night, easy like, browsin' on this white sage," said Stewart. Inflected by our intense interest in the famous mustang, and ruffled slightly by Jones's manifest surprise and contempt that no one had captured him, Stewart had volunteered to guide us. "Never knowed him to run in this way fer water; fact is, never knowed Nail Canyon had a fork. It splits down here, but you'd think it was only a crack in the wall. An' thet cunnin' mustang hes been foolin' us fer years about this water-hole."

The fork of Nail Canyon, which Stewart had decided we were in, had been accidentally discovered by Frank, who, in search of our horses one morning had crossed a ridge, to come suddenly upon the blind, box-like head of the canyon. Stewart knew the lay of the ridges and run of the canyons as well as any man could know a country where, seemingly, every rod was ridged and bisected, and he was of the opinion that we had stumbled upon one of the White Mustang's secret passages, by which he had so often eluded his pursuers.

Hard riding had been the order of the day, but still we covered ten more miles by sundown. The canyon apparently closed in on us, so camp was made for the night. The horses were staked out, and supper made ready while the shadows were dropping; and when darkness settled thick over us, we lay under our blankets.

Morning disclosed the White Mustang's secret passage. It was a narrow cleft, splitting the canyon wall, rough, uneven, tortuous and choked with fallen rocks—no more than a wonderful crack in solid stone, opening into another canyon. Above us the sky seemed a winding, flowing stream of blue. The walls were so close in places that a horse with pack would have been blocked, and a rider had to pull his legs up over the saddle. On the far side, the passage fell very suddenly for several hundred feet to the floor of the other canyon. No hunter could have seen it, or suspected it from that side.

"This is Grand Canyon country, an' nobody knows what he's goin' to find," was Frank's comment.

"Now we're in Nail Canyon proper," said Stewart; "An' I know my bearin's. I can climb out a mile below an' cut across to Kanab Canyon, an' slip up into Nail Canyon agin, ahead of the mustangs, an' drive 'em up. I can't miss 'em, fer Kanab Canyon is impassable down a little ways. The mustangs will hev to run this way. So all you need do is go below the break, where I climb out, an' wait. You're sure goin' to get a look at the White Mustang. But wait. Don't expect him before noon, an' after thet, any time till he comes. Mebbe it'll be a couple of days, so keep a good watch."

Then taking our man Lawson, with blankets and a knapsack of food, Stewart rode off down the canyon.

We were early on the march. As we proceeded the canyon lost its regularity and smoothness; it became crooked as a rail fence, narrower, higher, rugged and broken. Pinnacled cliffs, cracked and leaning, menaced us from above. Mountains of ruined wall had tumbled into fragments.

It seemed that Jones, after much survey of different corners, angles and points in the canyon floor, chose his position with much greater care than appeared necessary for the ultimate success of our venture—which was simply to see the White Mustang, and if good fortune attended us, to snap some photographs of this wild king of horses. It flashed over me that, with his ruling passion strong within him, our leader was laying some kind of trap for that mustang, was indeed bent on his capture.

Wallace, Frank and Jim were stationed at a point below the break where Stewart had evidently gone up and out. How a horse could have climbed that streaky white slide was a mystery. Jones's instructions to the men were to wait until the mustangs were close upon them, and then yell and shout and show themselves.

He took me to a jutting corner of cliff, which hid us from the others, and here he exercised still more care in scrutinizing the lay of the ground. A wash from ten to fifteen feet wide, and as deep, ran through the canyon in a somewhat meandering course. At the corner which consumed so much of his attention, the dry ditch ran along the cliff wall about fifty feet out; between it and the wall was good level ground, on the other side huge rocks and shale made it hummocky, practically impassable for a horse. It was plain the mustangs, on their way up, would choose the inside of the wash; and here in the middle of the passage, just round the jutting corner, Jones tied our horses to good, strong bushes. His next act was significant. He threw out his lasso and, dragging every crook out of it, carefully recoiled it, and hung it loose over the pommel of his saddle.

"The White Mustang may be yours before dark," he said with the smile that came so seldom. "Now I placed our horses there for two reasons. The mustangs won't see them till they're right on them. Then you'll see a sight and have a chance for a great picture. They will halt; the stallion will prance, whistle and snort for a fight, and then they'll see the saddles and be off. We'll hide across the wash, down a little way, and at the right time we'll shout and yell to drive them up."

By piling sagebrush round a stone, we made a hiding-place. Jones was extremely cautious to arrange the bunches in natural positions. "A Rocky Mountain Big Horn is the only four-footed beast," he said, "that has a better eye than a wild horse. A cougar has an eye, too; he's used to lying high up on the cliffs and looking down for his quarry so as to stalk it at night; but even a cougar has to take second to a mustang when it comes to sight."

The hours passed slowly. The sun baked us; the stones were too hot to touch; flies buzzed behind our ears; tarantulas peeped at us from holes. The afternoon slowly waned.

At dark we returned to where we had left Wallace and the cowboys. Frank had solved the problem of water supply, for he had found a little spring trickling from a cliff, which, by skillful management, produced enough drink for the horses. We had packed our water for camp use.

"You take the first watch to-night," said Jones to me after supper. "The mustangs might try to slip by our fire in the night and we must keep a watch or them. Call Wallace when your time's up. Now, fellows, roll in."

When the pink of dawn was shading white, we were at our posts. A long, hot day—interminably long, deadening to the keenest interest—passed, and still no mustangs came. We slept and watched again, in the grateful cool of night, till the third day broke.

The hours passed; the cool breeze changed to hot; the sun blazed over the canyon wall; the stones scorched; the flies buzzed. I fell asleep in the scant shade of the sage bushes and awoke, stifled and moist. The old plainsman, never weary, leaned with his back against a stone and watched, with narrow gaze, the canyon below. The steely walls hurt my eyes; the sky was like hot copper. Though nearly wild with heat and aching bones and muscles and the long hours of wait—wait—wait, I was ashamed to complain, for there sat the old man, still and silent. I routed out a hairy tarantula from under a stone and teased him into a frenzy with my stick, and tried to get up a fight between him and a scallop-backed horned-toad that blinked wonderingly at me. Then I espied a green lizard on a stone. The beautiful reptile was about a foot in length, bright green, dotted with red, and he had diamonds for eyes. Nearby a purple flower blossomed, delicate and pale, with a bee sucking at its golden heart. I observed then that the lizard had his jewel eyes upon the bee; he slipped to the edge of the stone, flicked out a long, red tongue, and tore the insect from its honeyed perch. Here were beauty, life and death; and I had been weary for something to look at, to think about, to distract me from the wearisome wait!

"Listen!" broke in Jones's sharp voice. His neck was stretched, his eyes were closed, his ear was turned to the wind.

With thrilling, reawakened eagerness, I strained my hearing. I caught a faint sound, then lost it.

"Put your ear to the ground," said Jones. I followed his advice, and detected the rhythmic beat of galloping horses.

"The mustangs are coming, sure as you're born!" exclaimed Jones.

"There I see the cloud of dust!" cried he a minute later.

In the first bend of the canyon below, a splintered ruin of rock now lay under a rolling cloud of dust. A white flash appeared, a line of bobbing black objects, and more dust; then with a sharp pounding of hoofs, into clear vision shot a dense black band of mustangs, and well in front swung the White King.

"Look! Look! I never saw the beat of that—never in my born days!" cried Jones. "How they move! yet that white fellow isn't half-stretched out. Get your picture before they pass. You'll never see the beat of that."

With long manes and tails flying, the mustangs came on apace and passed us in a trampling roar, the white stallion in the front. Suddenly a shrill, whistling blast, unlike any sound I had ever heard, made the canyon fairly ring. The white stallion plunged back, and his band closed in behind him. He had seen our saddle horses. Then trembling, whinnying, and with arched neck and high-poised head, bespeaking his mettle, he advanced a few paces, and again whistled his shrill note of defiance. Pure creamy white he was, and built like a racer. He pranced, struck his hoofs hard and cavorted; then, taking sudden fright, he wheeled.

It was then, when the mustangs were pivoting, with the white in the lead, that Jones jumped upon the stone, fired his pistol and roared with all his strength. Taking his cue, I did likewise. The band huddled back again, uncertain and frightened, then broke up the canyon.

Jones jumped the ditch with surprising agility, and I followed close at his heels. When we reached our plunging horses, he shouted: "Mount, and hold this passage. Keep close in by that big stone at the turn so they can't run you down, or stampede you. If they head your way, scare them back."

Satan quivered, and when I mounted, reared and plunged. I had to hold him in hard, for he was eager to run. At the cliff wall I was at some pains to check him. He kept champing his bit and stamping his feet.

From my post I could see the mustangs flying before a cloud of dust. Jones was turning in his horse behind a large rock in the middle of the canyon, where he evidently intended to hide. Presently successive yells and shots from our comrades blended in a roar which the narrow box-canyon augmented and echoed from wall to wall. High the White Mustang reared, and above the roar whistled his snort of furious terror. His band wheeled with him and charged back, their hoofs ringing like hammers on iron.

The crafty old buffalo-hunter had hemmed the mustangs in a circle and had left himself free in the center. It was a wily trick, born of his quick mind and experienced eye.

The stallion, closely crowded by his followers, moved swiftly I saw that he must pass near the stone. Thundering, crashing, the horses came on. Away beyond them I saw Frank and Wallace. Then Jones yelled to me: "Open up! open up!"

I turned Satan into the middle of the narrow passage, screaming at the top of my voice and discharging my revolver rapidly.

But the wild horses thundered on. Jones saw that they would not now be balked, and he spurred his bay directly in their path. The big horse, courageous as his intrepid master, dove forward.

Then followed confusion for me. The pound of hoofs, the snorts, a screaming neigh that was frightful, the mad stampede of the mustangs with a whirling cloud of dust, bewildered and frightened me so that I lost sight of Jones. Danger threatened and passed me almost before I was aware of it. Out of the dust a mass of tossing manes, foam-flecked black horses, wild eyes and lifting hoofs rushed at me. Satan, with a presence of mind that shamed mine, leaped back and hugged the wall. My eyes were blinded by dust; the smell of dust choked me. I felt a strong rush of wind and a mustang grazed my stirrup. Then they had passed, on the wings of the dust-laden breeze.

But not all, for I saw that Jones had, in some inexplicable manner, cut the White Mustang and two of his blacks out of the band. He had turned them back again and was pursuing them. The bay he rode had never before appeared to much advantage, and now, with his long, lean, powerful body in splendid action, imbued with the relentless will of his rider, what a picture he presented! How he did run! With all that, the White Mustang made him look dingy and slow. Nevertheless, it was a critical time in the wild career of that king of horses. He had been penned in a space two hundred by five hundred yards, half of which was separated from him by a wide ditch, a yawning chasm that he had refused, and behind him, always keeping on the inside, wheeled the yelling hunter, who savagely spurred his bay and whirled a deadly lasso. He had been cut off and surrounded; the very nature of the rocks and trails of the canyon threatened to end his freedom or his life. Certain it was he preferred to end the latter, for he risked death from the rocks as he went over them in long leaps.

Jones could have roped either of the two blacks, but he hardly noticed them. Covered with dust and splotches of foam, they took their advantage, turned on the circle toward the passage way and galloped by me out of sight. Again Wallace, Frank and Jim let out strings of yells and volleys. The chase was narrowing down. Trapped, the White Mustang King had no chance. What a grand spirit he showed! Frenzied as I was with excitement, the thought occurred to me that this was an unfair battle, that I ought to stand aside and let him pass. But the blood and lust of primitive instinct held me fast. Jones, keeping back, met his every turn. Yet always with lithe and beautiful stride the stallion kept out of reach of the whirling lariat.

"Close in!" yelled Jones, and his voice, powerful with a note of triumph, bespoke the knell of the king's freedom.

The trap closed in. Back and forth at the upper end the White Mustang worked; then rendered desperate by the closing in, he circled round nearer to me. Fire shone in his wild eyes. The wily Jones was not to be outwitted; he kept in the middle, always on the move, and he yelled to me to open up.

I lost my voice again, and fired my last shot. Then the White Mustang burst into a dash of daring, despairing speed. It was his last magnificent effort. Straight for the wash at the upper end he pointed his racy, spirited head, and his white legs stretched far apart, twinkled and stretched again. Jones galloped to cut him off, and the yells he emitted were demoniacal. It was a long, straight race for the mustang, a short curve for the bay.

That the white stallion gained was as sure as his resolve to elude capture, and he never swerved a foot from his course. Jones might have headed him, but manifestly he wanted to ride with him, as well as to meet him, so in case the lasso went true, a terrible shock might be averted.

Up went Jones's arm as the space shortened, and the lasso ringed his head. Out it shot, lengthened like a yellow, striking snake, and fell just short of the flying white tail.

The White Mustang, fulfilling his purpose in a last heroic display of power, sailed into the air, up and up, and over the wide wash like a white streak. Free! the dust rolled in a cloud from under his hoofs, and he vanished.

Jones's superb horse, crashing down on his haunches, just escaped sliding into the hole.

I awoke to the realization that Satan had carried me, in pursuit of the thrilling chase, all the way across the circle without my knowing it.

Jones calmly wiped the sweat from his face, calmly coiled his lasso, and calmly remarked:

"In trying to capture wild animals a man must never be too sure. Now what I thought my strong point was my weak point—the wash. I made sure no horse could ever jump that hole."

CHAPTER 7.

SNAKE GULCH

Not far from the scene of our adventure with the White Streak as we facetious and appreciatively named the mustang, deep, flat cave indented the canyon wall. By reason of its sandy floor and close proximity to Frank's trickling spring, we decided to camp in it. About dawn Lawson and Stewart straggled in on spent horse and found awaiting them a bright fire, a hot supper and cheery comrades.

"Did yu fellars git to see him?" was the ranger's first question.

"Did we get to see him?" echoed five lusty voice as one. "We did!"

It was after Frank, in his plain, blunt speech had told of our experience, that the long Arizonian gazed fixedly at Jones.

"Did yu acktully tech the hair of thet mustang with a rope?"

In all his days Jones never had a greater complement. By way of reply, he moved his big hand to button of his coat, and, fumbling over it, unwound a string of long, white hairs, then said: "I pulled these out of his tail with my lasso; it missed his left hind hoof about six inches."

There were six of the hairs, pure, glistening white, and over three feet long. Stewart examined then in expressive silence, then passed them along; and when they reached me, they stayed.

The cave, lighted up by a blazing fire, appeared to me a forbidding, uncanny place. Small, peculiar round holes, and dark cracks, suggestive of hidden vermin, gave me a creepy feeling; and although not over-sensitive on the subject of crawling, creeping things, I voiced my disgust.

"Say, I don't like the idea of sleeping in this hole. I'll bet it's full of spiders, snakes and centipedes and other poisonous things."

Whatever there was in my inoffensive declaration to rouse the usually slumbering humor of the Arizonians, and the thinly veiled ridicule of Colonel Jones, and a mixture of both in my once loyal California friend, I am not prepared to state. Maybe it was the dry, sweet, cool air of Nail Canyon; maybe my suggestion awoke ticklish associations that worked themselves off thus; maybe it was the first instance of my committing myself to a breach of camp etiquette. Be that as it may, my innocently expressed sentiment gave rise to bewildering dissertations on entomology, and most remarkable and startling tales from first-hand experience.

"Like as not," began Frank in matter-of-fact tone. "Them's tarantuler holes all right. An' scorpions, centipedes an' rattlers always rustle with tarantulers. But we never mind them—not us fellers! We're used to sleepin' with them. Why, I often wake up in the night to see a big tarantuler on my chest, an' see him wink. Ain't thet so, Jim?"

"Shore as hell," drawled faithful, slow Jim.

"Reminds me how fatal the bite of a centipede is," took up Colonel Jones, complacently. "Once I was sitting in camp with a hunter, who suddenly hissed out: 'Jones, for God's sake don't budge! There's a centipede on your arm!' He pulled his Colt, and shot the blamed centipede off as clean as a whistle. But the bullet hit a steer in the leg; and would you believe it, the bullet carried so much poison that in less than two hours the steer died of blood poisoning. Centipedes are so poisonous they leave a blue trail on flesh just by crawling over it. Look there!"

He bared his arm, and there on the brown-corded flesh was a blue trail of something, that was certain. It might have been made by a centipede.

"This is a likely place for them," put in Wallace, emitting a volume of smoke and gazing round the cave walls with the eye of a connoisseur. "My archaeological pursuits have given me great experience with centipedes, as you may imagine, considering how many old tombs, caves and cliff-dwellings I have explored. This Algonkian rock is about the right stratum for centipedes to dig in. They dig somewhat after the manner of the fluviatile long-tailed decapod crustaceans, of the genera Thoracostraca, the common crawfish, you know. From that, of course, you can imagine, if a centipede can bite rock, what a biter he is."

I began to grow weak, and did not wonder to see Jim's long pipe fall from his lips. Frank looked queer around the gills, so to speak, but the gaunt Stewart never batted an eye.

"I camped here two years ago," he said, "An' the cave was alive with rock-rats, mice, snakes, horned-toads, lizards an' a big Gila monster, besides bugs, scorpions' rattlers, an' as fer tarantulers an' centipedes—say! I couldn't sleep fer the noise they made fightin'."

"I seen the same," concluded Lawson, as nonchalant as a wild-horse wrangler well could be. "An' as fer me, now I allus lays perfickly still when the centipedes an' tarantulers begin to drop from their holes in the roof, same as them holes up there. An' when they light on me, I never move, nor even breathe fer about five minutes. Then they take a notion I'm dead an' crawl off. But sure, if I'd breathed I'd been a goner!"

All of this was playfully intended for the extinction of an unoffending and impressionable tenderfoot.

With an admiring glance at my tormentors, I rolled out my sleeping-bag and crawled into it, vowing I would remain there even if devil-fish, armed with pikes, invaded our cave.

Late in the night I awoke. The bottom of the canyon and the outer floor of our cave lay bathed in white, clear moonlight. A dense, gloomy black shadow veiled the opposite canyon wall. High up the pinnacles and turrets pointed toward a resplendent moon. It was a weird, wonderful scene of beauty entrancing, of breathless, dreaming silence that seemed not of life. Then a hoot-owl lamented dismally, his call fitting the scene and the dead stillness; the echoes resounded from cliff to cliff, strangely mocking and hollow, at last reverberating low and mournful in the distance.

How long I lay there enraptured with the beauty of light and mystery of shade, thrilling at the lonesome lament of the owl, I have no means to tell; but I was awakened from my trance by the touch of something crawling over me. Promptly I raised my head. The cave was as light as day. There, sitting sociably on my sleeping-bag was a great black tarantula, as large as my hand.

For one still moment, notwithstanding my contempt for Lawson's advice, I certainly acted upon it to the letter. If ever I was quiet, and if ever I was cold, the time was then. My companions snored in blissful ignorance of my plight. Slight rustling sounds attracted my wary gaze from the old black sentinel on my knee. I saw other black spiders running to and fro on the silver, sandy floor. A giant, as large as a soft-shell crab, seemed to be meditating an assault upon Jones's ear. Another, grizzled and shiny with age or moonbeams I could not tell which—pushed long, tentative feelers into Wallace's cap. I saw black spots darting over the roof. It was not a dream; the cave was alive with tarantulas!

Not improbably my strong impression that the spider on my knee deliberately winked at me was the result of memory, enlivening imagination. But it sufficed to bring to mind, in one rapid, consoling flash, the irrevocable law of destiny—that the deeds of the wicked return unto them again.

I slipped back into my sleeping-bag, with a keen consciousness of its nature, and carefully pulled the flap in place, which almost hermetically sealed me up.

"Hey! Jones! Wallace! Frank! Jim!" I yelled, from the depths of my safe refuge.

Wondering cries gave me glad assurance that they had awakened from their dreams.

"The cave's alive with tarantulas!" I cried, trying to hide my unholy glee.

"I'll be durned if it ain't!" ejaculated Frank.

"Shore it beats hell!" added Jim, with a shake of his blanket.

"Look out, Jones, there's one on your pillow!" shouted Wallace.

Whack! A sharp blow proclaimed the opening of hostilities.

Memory stamped indelibly every word of that incident; but innate delicacy prevents the repetition of all save the old warrior's concluding remarks: "! ! ! place I was ever in! Tarantulas by the million—centipedes, scorpions, bats! Rattlesnakes, too, I'll swear. Look out, Wallace! there, under your blanket!"

From the shuffling sounds which wafted sweetly into my bed, I gathered that my long friend from California must have gone through motions creditable to a contortionist. An ensuing explosion from Jones proclaimed to the listening world that Wallace had thrown a tarantula upon him. Further fearful language suggested the thought that Colonel Jones had passed on the inquisitive spider to Frank. The reception accorded the unfortunate tarantula, no doubt scared out of its wits, began with a wild yell from Frank and ended in pandemonium.

While the confusion kept up, with whacks and blows and threshing about, with language such as never before had disgraced a group of old campers, I choked with rapture, and reveled in the sweetness of revenge.

When quiet reigned once more in the black and white canyon, only one sleeper lay on the moon-silvered sand of the cave.

At dawn, when I opened sleepy eyes, Frank, Slim, Stewart and Lawson had departed, as pre-arranged, with the outfit, leaving the horses belonging to us and rations for the day. Wallace and I wanted to climb the divide at the break, and go home by way of Snake Gulch, and the Colonel acquiesced with the remark that his sixty-three years had taught him there was much to see in the world. Coming to undertake it, we found the climb—except for a slide of weathered rock—no great task, and we accomplished it in half an hour, with breath to spare and no mishap to horses.

But descending into Snake Gulch, which was only a mile across the sparsely cedared ridge, proved to be tedious labor. By virtue of Satan's patience and skill, I forged ahead; which advantage, however, meant more risk for me because of the stones set in motion above. They rolled and bumped and cut into me, and I sustained many a bruise trying to protect the sinewy slender legs of my horse. The descent ended without serious mishap.

Snake Gulch had a character and sublimity which cast Nail Canyon into the obscurity of forgetfulness. The great contrast lay in the diversity of structure. The rock was bright red, with parapet of yellow, that leaned, heaved, bulged outward. These emblazoned cliff walls, two thousand feet high, were cracked from turret to base; they bowled out at such an angle that we were afraid to ride under them. Mountains of yellow rock hung balanced, ready to tumble down at the first angry breath of the gods. We rode among carved stones, pillars, obelisks and sculptured ruined walls of a fallen Babylon. Slides reaching all the way across and far up the canyon wall obstructed our passage. On every stone silent green lizards sunned themselves, gliding swiftly as we came near to their marble homes.

We came into a region of wind-worn caves, of all sizes and shapes, high and low on the cliffs; but strange to say, only on the north side of the canyon they appeared with dark mouths open and uninviting. One, vast and deep, though far off, menaced us as might the cave of a tawny-maned king of beasts; yet it impelled, fascinated and drew us on.

"It's a long, hard climb," said Wallace to the Colonel, as we dismounted.

"Boys, I'm with you," came the reply. And he was with us all the way, as we clambered over the immense blocks and threaded a passage between them and pulled weary legs up, one after the other. So steep lay the jumble of cliff fragments that we lost sight of the cave long before we got near it. Suddenly we rounded a stone, to halt and gasp at the thing looming before us.

The dark portal of death or hell might have yawned there. A gloomy hole, large enough to admit a church, had been hollowed in the cliff by ages of nature's chiseling.

"Vast sepulcher of Time's past, give up thy dead!" cried Wallace, solemnly.

"Oh! dark Stygian cave forlorn!" quoted I, as feelingly as my friend.

Jones hauled us down from the clouds.

"Now, I wonder what kind of a prehistoric animal holed in here?" said he.

Forever the one absorbing interest! If he realized the sublimity of this place, he did not show it.

The floor of the cave ascended from the very threshold. Stony ridges circled from wall to wall. We climbed till we were two hundred feet from the opening, yet we were not half-way to the dome.

Our horses, browsing in the sage far below, looked like ants. So steep did the ascent become that we desisted; for if one of us had slipped on the smooth incline, the result would have been terrible. Our voices rang clear and hollow from the walls. We were so high that the sky was blotted out by the overhanging square, cornice-like top of the door; and the light was weird, dim, shadowy, opaque. It was a gray tomb.

"Waa-hoo!" yelled Jones with all the power of his wide, leather lungs.

Thousands of devilish voices rushed at us, seemingly on puffs of wind. Mocking, deep echoes bellowed from the ebon shades at the back of the cave, and the walls, taking them up, hurled them on again in fiendish concatenation.

We did not again break the silence of that tomb, where the spirits of ages lay in dusty shrouds; and we crawled down as if we had invaded a sanctuary and invoked the wrath of the gods.

We all proposed names: Montezuma's Amphitheater being the only rival of Jones's selection, Echo cave, which we finally chose.

Mounting our horses again, we made twenty miles of Snake Gulch by noon, when we rested for lunch. All the way up we had played the boy's game of spying for sights, with the honors about even. It was a question if Snake Gulch ever before had such a raking over. Despite its name, however, we discovered no snakes.

From the sandy niche of a cliff where we lunched Wallace espied a tomb, and heralded his discovery with a victorious whoop. Digging in old ruins roused in him much the same spirit that digging in old books roused in me. Before we reached him, he had a big bowie-knife buried deep in the red, sandy floor of the tomb.

This one-time sealed house of the dead had been constructed of small stones, held together by a cement, the nature of which, Wallace explained, had never become clear to civilization. It was red in color and hard as flint, harder than the rocks it glued together. The tomb was half-round in shape, and its floor was a projecting shelf of cliff rock. Wallace unearthed bits of pottery, bone and finely braided rope, all of which, to our great disappointment, crumbled to dust in our fingers. In the case of the rope, Wallace assured us, this was a sign of remarkable antiquity.

In the next mile we traversed, we found dozens of these old cells, all demolished except a few feet of the walls, all despoiled of their one-time possessions. Wallace thought these depredations were due to Indians of our own time. Suddenly we came upon Jones, standing under a cliff, with his neck craned to a desperate angle.

"Now, what's that?" demanded he, pointing upward.

High on the cliff wall appeared a small, round protuberance. It was of the unmistakably red color of the other tombs; and Wallace, more excited than he had been in the cougar chase, said it was a sepulcher, and he believed it had never been opened.

From an elevated point of rock, as high up as I could well climb, I decided both questions with my glass. The tomb resembled nothing so much as a mud-wasp's nest, high on a barn wall. The fact that it had never been broken open quite carried Wallace away with enthusiasm.

"This is no mean discovery, let me tell you that," he declared. "I am familiar with the Aztec, Toltec and Pueblo ruins, and here I find no similarity. Besides, we are out of their latitude. An ancient race of people—very ancient indeed lived in this canyon. How long ago, it is impossible to tell."

"They must have been birds," said the practical Jones. "Now, how'd that tomb ever get there? Look at it, will you?"

As near as we could ascertain, it was three hundred feet from the ground below, five hundred from the rim wall above, and could not possibly have been approached from the top. Moreover, the cliff wall was as smooth as a wall of human make.

"There's another one," called out Jones.

"Yes, and I see another; no doubt there are many of them," replied Wallace. "In my mind, only one thing possible accounts for their position. You observe they appear to be about level with each other. Well, once the Canyon floor ran along that line, and in the ages gone by it has lowered, washed away by the rains."

This conception staggered us, but it was the only one conceivable. No doubt we all thought at the same time of the little rainfall in that arid section of Arizona.

"How many years?" queried Jones.

"Years! What are years?" said Wallace. "Thousands of years, ages have passed since the race who built these tombs lived."

Some persuasion was necessary to drag our scientific friend from the spot, where obviously helpless to do anything else, he stood and gazed longingly at the isolated tombs. The canyon widened as we proceeded; and hundreds of points that invited inspection, such as overhanging shelves of rock, dark fissures, caverns and ruins had to be passed by, for lack of time.

Still, a more interesting and important discovery was to come, and the pleasure and honor of it fell to me. My eyes were sharp and peculiarly farsighted—the Indian sight, Jones assured me; and I kept them searching the walls in such places as my companions overlooked. Presently, under a large, bulging bluff, I saw a dark spot, which took the shape of a figure. This figure, I recollected, had been presented to my sight more than once, and now it stopped me. The hard climb up the slippery stones was fatiguing, but I did not hesitate, for I was determined to know. Once upon the ledge, I let out a yell that quickly set my companions in my direction. The figure I had seen was a dark, red devil, a painted image, rude, unspeakably wild, crudely executed, but painted by the hand of man. The whole surface of the cliff wall bore figures of all shapes—men, mammals, birds and strange devices, some in red paint, mostly in yellow. Some showed the wear of time; others were clear and sharp.

Wallace puffed up to me, but he had wind enough left for another whoop. Jones puffed up also, and seeing the first thing a rude sketch of what might have been a deer or a buffalo, he commented thus: "Darn me if I ever saw an animal like that? Boys, this is a find, sure as you're born. Because not even the Piutes ever spoke of these figures. I doubt if they know they're here. And the cowboys and wranglers, what few ever get by here in a hundred years, never saw these things. Beats anything I ever saw on the Mackenzie, or anywhere else."

The meaning of some devices was as mystical as that of others was clear. Two blood-red figures of men, the larger dragging the smaller by the hair, while he waved aloft a blood-red hatchet or club, left little to conjecture. Here was the old battle of men, as old as life. Another group, two figures of which resembled the foregoing in form and action, battling over a prostrate form rudely feminine in outline, attested to an age when men were as susceptible as they are in modern times, but more forceful and original. An odd yellow Indian waved aloft a red hand, which striking picture suggested the idea that he was an ancient Macbeth, listening to the knocking at the gate. There was a character representing a great chief, before whom many figures lay prostrate, evidently slain or subjugated. Large red paintings, in the shape of bats, occupied prominent positions, and must have represented gods or devils. Armies of marching men told of that blight of nations old or young—war. These, and birds unnamable, and beasts unclassable, with dots and marks and hieroglyphics, recorded the history of a bygone people. Symbols they were of an era that had gone into the dim past, leaving only these marks, {Symbols recording the history of a bygone people.} forever unintelligible; yet while they stood, century after century, ineffaceable, reminders of the glory, the mystery, the sadness of life.

"How could paint of any kind last so long? asked Jones, shaking his head doubtfully.

"That is the unsolvable mystery," returned Wallace. "But the records are there. I am absolutely sure the paintings are at least a thousand years old. I have never seen any tombs or paintings similar to them. Snake Gulch is a find, and I shall some day study its wonders."

Sundown caught us within sight of Oak Spring, and we soon trotted into camp to the welcoming chorus of the hounds. Frank and the others had reached the cabin some hours before. Supper was steaming on the hot coals with a delicious fragrance.

Then came the pleasantest time of the day, after a long chase or jaunt—the silent moments, watching the glowing embers of the fire; the speaking moments when a red-blooded story rang clear and true; the twilight moments, when the wood-smoke smelled sweet.

Jones seemed unusually thoughtful. I had learned that this preoccupation in him meant the stirring of old associations, and I waited silently. By and by Lawson snored mildly in a corner; Jim and Frank crawled into their blankets, and all was still. Wallace smoked his Indian pipe and hunted in firelit dreams.

"Boys," said our leader finally, "somehow the echoes dying away in that cave reminded me of the mourn of the big white wolves in the Barren Lands."

Wallace puffed huge clouds of white smoke, and I waited, knowing that I was to hear at last the story of the Colonel's great adventure in the Northland.

CHAPTER 8.

NAZA! NAZA! NAZA!

It was a waiting day at Fort Chippewayan. The lonesome, far-northern Hudson's Bay Trading Post seldom saw such life. Tepees dotted the banks of the Slave River and lines of blanketed Indians paraded its shores. Near the boat landing a group of chiefs, grotesque in semi-barbaric, semicivilized splendor, but black-browed, austere-eyed, stood in savage dignity with folded arms and high-held heads. Lounging on the grassy bank were white men, traders, trappers and officials of the post.

All eyes were on the distant curve of the river where, as it lost itself in a fine-fringed bend of dark green, white-glinting waves danced and fluttered. A June sky lay blue in the majestic stream; ragged, spear-topped, dense green trees massed down to the water; beyond rose bold, bald-knobbed hills, in remote purple relief.

A long Indian arm stretched south. The waiting eyes discerned a black speck on the green, and watched it grow. A flatboat, with a man standing to the oars, bore down swiftly.

Not a red hand, nor a white one, offered to help the voyager in the difficult landing. The oblong, clumsy, heavily laden boat surged with the current and passed the dock despite the boatman's efforts. He swung his craft in below upon a bar and roped it fast to a tree. The Indians crowded above him on the bank. The boatman raised his powerful form erect, lifted a bronzed face which seemed set in craggy hardness, and cast from narrow eyes a keen, cool glance on those above. The silvery gleam in his fair hair told of years.

Silence, impressive as it was ominous, broke only to the rattle of camping paraphernalia, which the voyager threw to a level, grassy bench on the bank. Evidently this unwelcome visitor had journeyed from afar, and his boat, sunk deep into the water with its load of barrels, boxes and bags, indicated that the journey had only begun. Significant, too, were a couple of long Winchester rifles shining on a tarpaulin.

The cold-faced crowd stirred and parted to permit the passage of a tall, thin, gray personage of official bearing, in a faded military coat.

"Are you the musk-ox hunter?" he asked, in tones that contained no welcome.

The boatman greeted this peremptory interlocutor with a cool laugh—a strange laugh, in which the muscles of his face appeared not to play.

"Yes, I am the man," he said.

"The chiefs of the Chippewayan and Great Slave tribes have been apprised of your coming. They have held council and are here to speak with you."

At a motion from the commandant, the line of chieftains piled down to the level bench and formed a half-circle before the voyager. To a man who had stood before grim Sitting Bull and noble Black Thunder of the Sioux, and faced the falcon-eyed Geronimo, and glanced over the sights of a rifle at gorgeous-feathered, wild, free Comanches, this semi-circle of savages—lords of the north—was a sorry comparison. Bedaubed and betrinketed, slouchy and slovenly, these low-statured chiefs belied in appearance their scorn-bright eyes and lofty mien. They made a sad group.

One who spoke in unintelligible language, rolled out a haughty, sonorous voice over the listening multitude. When he had finished, a half-breed interpreter, in the dress of a white man, spoke at a signal from the commandant.

"He says listen to the great orator of the Chippewayan. He has summoned all the chiefs of the tribes south of Great Slave Lake. He has held council. The cunning of the pale-face, who comes to take the musk-oxen, is well known. Let the pale-face hunter return to his own hunting-grounds; let him turn his face from the north. Never will the chiefs permit the white man to take musk-oxen alive from their country. The Ageter, the Musk-ox, is their god. He gives them food and fur. He will never come back if he is taken away, and the reindeer will follow him. The chiefs and their people would starve. They command the pale-face hunter to go back. They cry Naza! Naza! Naza!"

"Say, for a thousand miles I've heard that word Naza!" returned the hunter, with mingled curiosity and disgust. "At Edmonton Indian runners started ahead of me, and every village I struck the redskins would crowd round me and an old chief would harangue at me, and motion me back, and point north with Naza! Naza! Naza! What does it mean?"

"No white man knows; no Indian will tell," answered the interpreter. "The traders think it means the Great Slave, the North Star, the North Spirit, the North Wind, the North Lights and the musk-ox god."

"Well, say to the chiefs to tell Ageter I have been four moons on the way after some of his little Ageters, and I'm going to keep on after them."

"Hunter, you are most unwise," broke in the commandant, in his officious voice. "The Indians will never permit you to take a musk-ox alive from the north. They worship him, pray to him. It is a wonder you have not been stopped."

"Who'll stop me?"

"The Indians. They will kill you if you do not turn back."

"Faugh! to tell an American plainsman that!" The hunter paused a steady moment, with his eyelids narrowing over slits of blue fire. "There is no law to keep me out, nothing but Indian superstition and Naza! And the greed of the Hudson's Bay people. I am an old fox, not to be fooled by pretty baits. For years the officers of this fur-trading company have tried to keep out explorers. Even Sir John Franklin, an Englishman, could not buy food of them. The policy of the company is to side with the Indians, to keep out traders and trappers. Why? So they can keep on cheating the poor savages out of clothing and food by trading a few trinkets and blankets, a little tobacco and rum for millions of dollars worth of furs. Have I failed to hire man after man, Indian after Indian, not to know why I cannot get a helper? Have I, a plainsman, come a thousand miles alone to be scared by you, or a lot of craven Indians? Have I been dreaming of musk-oxen for forty years, to slink south now, when I begin to feel the north? Not I."

Deliberately every chief, with the sound of a hissing snake, spat in the hunter's face. He stood immovable while they perpetrated the outrage, then calmly wiped his cheeks, and in his strange, cool voice, addressed the interpreter.

"Tell them thus they show their true qualities, to insult in council. Tell them they are not chiefs, but dogs. Tell them they are not even squaws, only poor, miserable starved dogs. Tell them I turn my back on them. Tell them the paleface has fought real chiefs, fierce, bold, like eagles, and he turns his back on dogs. Tell them he is the one who could teach them to raise the musk-oxen and the reindeer, and to keep out the cold and the wolf. But they are blinded. Tell them the hunter goes north."

Through the council of chiefs ran a low mutter, as of gathering thunder.

True to his word, the hunter turned his back on them. As he brushed by, his eye caught a gaunt savage slipping from the boat. At the hunter's stern call, the Indian leaped ashore, and started to run. He had stolen a parcel, and would have succeeded in eluding its owner but for an unforeseen obstacle, as striking as it was unexpected.

A white man of colossal stature had stepped in the thief's passage, and laid two great hands on him. Instantly the parcel flew from the Indian, and he spun in the air to fall into the river with a sounding splash. Yells signaled the surprise and alarm caused by this unexpected incident. The Indian frantically swam to the shore. Whereupon the champion of the stranger in a strange land lifted a bag, which gave forth a musical clink of steel, and throwing it with the camp articles on the grassy bench, he extended a huge, friendly hand.

"My name is Rea," he said, in deep, cavernous tones.

"Mine is Jones," replied the hunter, and right quickly did he grip the proffered hand. He saw in Rea a giant, of whom he was but a stunted shadow. Six and one-half feet Rea stood, with yard-wide shoulders, a hulk of bone and brawn. His ponderous, shaggy head rested on a bull neck. His broad face, with its low forehead, its close-shut mastiff under jaw, its big, opaque eyes, pale and cruel as those of a jaguar, marked him a man of terrible brute force.

"Free-trader!" called the commandant "Better think twice before you join fortunes with the musk-ox hunter."

"To hell with you an' your rantin', dog-eared redskins!" cried Rea. "I've run agin a man of my own kind, a man of my own country, an' I'm goin' with him."

With this he thrust aside some encroaching, gaping Indians so unconcernedly and ungently that they sprawled upon the grass.

Slowly the crowd mounted and once more lined the bank.

Jones realized that by some late-turning stroke of fortune, he had fallen in with one of the few free-traders of the province. These free-traders, from the very nature of their calling, which was to defy the fur company, and to trap and trade on their own account—were a hardy and intrepid class of men. Rea's worth to Jones exceeded that of a dozen ordinary men. He knew the ways of the north, the language of the tribes, the habits of animals, the handling of dogs, the uses of food and fuel. Moreover, it soon appeared that he was a carpenter and blacksmith.

"There's my kit," he said, dumping the contents of his bag. It consisted of a bunch of steel traps, some tools, a broken ax, a box of miscellaneous things such as trappers used, and a few articles of flannel. "Thievin' redskins," he added, in explanation of his poverty. "Not much of an outfit. But I'm the man for you. Besides, I had a pal onct who knew you on the plains, called you 'Buff' Jones. Old Jim Bent he was."

"I recollect Jim," said Jones. "He went down in Custer's last charge. So you were Jim's pal. That'd be a recommendation if you needed one. But the way you chucked the Indian overboard got me."

Rea soon manifested himself as a man of few words and much action. With the planks Jones had on board he heightened the stern and bow of the boat to keep out the beating waves in the rapids; he fashioned a steering-gear and a less awkward set of oars, and shifted the cargo so as to make more room in the craft.

"Buff, we're in for a storm. Set up a tarpaulin an' make a fire. We'll pretend to camp to-night. These Indians won't dream we'd try to run the river after dark, and we'll slip by under cover."

The sun glazed over; clouds moved up from the north; a cold wind swept the tips of the spruces, and rain commenced to drive in gusts. By the time it was dark not an Indian showed himself. They were housed from the storm. Lights twinkled in the teepees and the big log cabins of the trading company. Jones scouted round till pitchy black night, when a freezing, pouring blast sent him back to the protection of the tarpaulin. When he got there he found that Rea had taken it down and awaited him. "Off!" said the free-trader; and with no more noise than a drifting feather the boat swung into the current and glided down till the twinkling fires no longer accentuated the darkness.

By night the river, in common with all swift rivers, had a sullen voice, and murmured its hurry, its restraint, its menace, its meaning. The two boat-men, one at the steering gear, one at the oars, faced the pelting rain and watched the dim, dark line of trees. The craft slid noiselessly onward into the gloom.

And into Jones's ears, above the storm, poured another sound, a steady, muffled rumble, like the roll of giant chariot wheels. It had come to be a familiar roar to him, and the only thing which, in his long life of hazard, had ever sent the cold, prickling, tight shudder over his warm skin. Many times on the Athabasca that rumble had presaged the dangerous and dreaded rapids.

"Hell Bend Rapids!" shouted Rea. "Bad water, but no rocks."

The rumble expanded to a roar, the roar to a boom that charged the air with heaviness, with a dreamy burr. The whole indistinct world appeared to be moving to the lash of wind, to the sound of rain, to the roar of the river. The boat shot down and sailed aloft, met shock on shock, breasted leaping dim white waves, and in a hollow, unearthly blend of watery sounds, rode on and on, buffeted, tossed, pitched into a black chaos that yet gleamed with obscure shrouds of light. Then the convulsive stream shrieked out a last defiance, changed its course abruptly to slow down and drown the sound of rapids in muffling distance. Once more the craft swept on smoothly, to the drive of the wind and the rush of the rain.

By midnight the storm cleared. Murky cloud split to show shining, blue-white stars and a fitful moon, that silvered the crests of the spruces and sometimes hid like a gleaming, black-threaded peak behind the dark branches.

Jones, a plainsman all his days, wonderingly watched the moon-blanched water. He saw it shade and darken under shadowy walls of granite, where it swelled with hollow song and gurgle. He heard again the far-off rumble, faint on the night. High cliff banks appeared, walled out the mellow, light, and the river suddenly narrowed. Yawning holes, whirlpools of a second, opened with a gurgling suck and raced with the boat.

On the craft flew. Far ahead, a long, declining plane of jumping frosted waves played dark and white with the moonbeams. The Slave plunged to his freedom, down his riven, stone-spiked bed, knowing no patient eddy, and white-wreathed his dark shiny rocks in spume and spray.

CHAPTER 9.

THE LAND OF THE MUSK-OX

A far cry it was from bright June at Port Chippewayan to dim October on Great Slave Lake.

Two long, laborious months Rea and Jones threaded the crooked shores of the great inland sea, to halt at the extreme northern end, where a plunging rivulet formed the source of a river. Here they found a stone chimney and fireplace standing among the darkened, decayed ruins of a cabin.

"We mustn't lose no time," said Rea. "I feel the winter in the wind. An' see how dark the days are gettin' on us."

"I'm for hunting musk-oxen," replied Jones.

"Man, we're facin' the northern night; we're in the land of the midnight sun. Soon we'll be shut in for seven months. A cabin we want, an' wood, an' meat."

A forest of stunted spruce trees edged on the lake, and soon its dreary solitudes rang to the strokes of axes. The trees were small and uniform in size. Black stumps protruded, here and there, from the ground, showing work of the steel in time gone by. Jones observed that the living trees were no larger in diameter than the stumps, and questioned Rea in regard to the difference in age.

"Cut twenty-five, mebbe fifty years ago," said the trapper.

"But the living trees are no bigger."

"Trees an' things don't grow fast in the north land."

They erected a fifteen-foot cabin round the stone chimney, roofed it with poles and branches of spruce and a layer of sand. In digging near the fireplace Jones unearthed a rusty file and the head of a whisky keg, upon which was a sunken word in unintelligible letters.

"We've found the place," said Rea. "Frank built a cabin here in 1819. An' in 1833 Captain Back wintered here when he was in search of Captain Ross of the vessel Fury. It was those explorin' parties thet cut the trees. I seen Indian sign out there, made last winter, I reckon; but Indians never cut down no trees."

The hunters completed the cabin, piled cords of firewood outside, stowed away the kegs of dried fish and fruits, the sacks of flour, boxes of crackers, canned meats and vegetables, sugar, salt, coffee, tobacco—all of the cargo; then took the boat apart and carried it up the bank, which labor took them less than a week.

Jones found sleeping in the cabin, despite the fire, uncomfortably cold, because of the wide chinks between the logs. It was hardly better than sleeping under the swaying spruces. When he essayed to stop up the crack, a task by no means easy, considering the lack of material—Rea laughed his short "Ho! Ho!" and stopped him with the word, "Wait." Every morning the green ice extended farther out into the lake; the sun paled dim and dimmer; the nights grew colder. On October 8th the thermometer registered several degrees below zero; it fell a little more next night and continued to fall.

"Ho! Ho!" cried Rea. "She's struck the toboggan, an' presently she'll commence to slide. Come on, Buff, we've work to do."

He caught up a bucket, made for their hole in the ice, rebroke a six-inch layer, the freeze of a few hours, and filling his bucket, returned to the cabin. Jones had no inkling of the trapper's intention, and wonderingly he soused his bucket full of water and followed.

By the time he had reached the cabin, a matter of some thirty or forty good paces, the water no longer splashed from his pail, for a thin film of ice prevented. Rea stood fifteen feet from the cabin, his back to the wind, and threw the water. Some of it froze in the air, most of it froze on the logs. The simple plan of the trapper to incase the cabin with ice was easily divined. All day the men worked, easing only when the cabin resembled a glistening mound. It had not a sharp corner nor a crevice. Inside it was warm and snug, and as light as when the chinks were open.

A slight moderation of the weather brought the snow. Such snow! A blinding white flutter of grey flakes, as large as feathers! All day they rustle softly; all night they swirled, sweeping, seeping brushing against the cabin. "Ho! Ho!" roared Rea. "'Tis good; let her snow, an' the reindeer will migrate. We'll have fresh meat." The sun shone again, but not brightly. A nipping wind came down out of the frigid north and crusted the snows. The third night following the storm, when the hunters lay snug under their blankets, a commotion outside aroused them.

"Indians," said Rea, "come north for reindeer."

Half the night, shouting and yelling, barking dogs, hauling of sleds and cracking of dried-skin tepees murdered sleep for those in the cabin. In the morning the level plain and edge of the forest held an Indian village. Caribou hides, strung on forked poles, constituted tent-like habitations with no distinguishable doors. Fires smoked in the holes in the snow. Not till late in the day did any life manifest itself round the tepees, and then a group of children, poorly clad in ragged pieces of blankets and skins, gaped at Jones. He saw their pinched, brown faces, staring, hungry eyes, naked legs and throats, and noted particularly their dwarfish size. When he spoke they fled precipitously a little way, then turned. He called again, and all ran except one small lad. Jones went into the cabin and came out with a handful of sugar in square lumps.

"Yellow Knife Indians," said Rea. "A starved tribe! We're in for it."

Jones made motions to the lad, but he remained still, as if transfixed, and his black eyes stared wonderingly.

"Molar nasu (white man good)," said Rea.

The lad came out of his trance and looked back at his companions, who edged nearer. Jones ate a lump of sugar, then handed one to the little Indian. He took it gingerly, put it into his mouth and immediately jumped up and down.

"Hoppiesharnpoolie! Hoppiesharnpoolie!" he shouted to his brothers and sisters. They came on the run.

"Think he means sweet salt," interpreted Rea. "Of course these beggars never tasted sugar."

The band of youngsters trooped round Jones, and after tasting the white lumps, shrieked in such delight that the braves and squaws shuffled out of the tepees.

In all his days Jones had never seen such miserable Indians. Dirty blankets hid all their person, except straggling black hair, hungry, wolfish eyes and moccasined feet. They crowded into the path before the cabin door and mumbled and stared and waited. No dignity, no brightness, no suggestion of friendliness marked this peculiar attitude.

"Starved!" exclaimed Rea. "They've come to the lake to invoke the Great Spirit to send the reindeer. Buff, whatever you do, don't feed them. If you do, we'll have them on our hands all winter. It's cruel, but, man, we're in the north!"

Notwithstanding the practical trapper's admonition Jones could not resist the pleading of the children. He could not stand by and see them starve. After ascertaining there was absolutely nothing to eat in the tepees, he invited the little ones into the cabin, and made a great pot of soup, into which he dropped compressed biscuits. The savage children were like wildcats. Jones had to call in Rea to assist him in keeping the famished little aborigines from tearing each other to pieces. When finally they were all fed, they had to be driven out of the cabin.

"That's new to me," said Jones. "Poor little beggars!"

Rea doubtfully shook his shaggy head.

Next day Jones traded with the Yellow Knives. He had a goodly supply of baubles, besides blankets, gloves and boxes of canned goods, which he had brought for such trading. He secured a dozen of the large-boned, white and black Indian dogs, huskies, Rea called them—two long sleds with harness and several pairs of snowshoes. This trade made Jones rub his hands in satisfaction, for during all the long journey north he had failed to barter for such cardinal necessities to the success of his venture.

"Better have doled out the grub to them in rations," grumbled Rea.

Twenty-four hours sufficed to show Jones the wisdom of the trapper's words, for in just that time the crazed, ignorant savages had glutted the generous store of food, which should have lasted them for weeks. The next day they were begging at the cabin door. Rea cursed and threatened them with his fists, but they returned again and again.

Days passed. All the time, in light and dark, the Indians filled the air with dismal chant and doleful incantations to the Great Spirit, and the tum! tum! tum! tum! of tomtoms, a specific feature of their wild prayer for food.

But the white monotony of the rolling land and level lake remained unbroken. The reindeer did not come. The days became shorter, dimmer, darker. The mercury kept on the slide.

Forty degrees below zero did not trouble the Indians. They stamped till they dropped, and sang till their voices vanished, and beat the tomtoms everlastingly. Jones fed the children once each day, against the trapper's advice.

One day, while Rea was absent, a dozen braves succeeded in forcing an entrance, and clamored so fiercely, and threatened so desperately, that Jones was on the point of giving them food when the door opened to admit Rea.

With a glance he saw the situation. He dropped the bucket he carried, threw the door wide open and commenced action. Because of his great bulk he seemed slow, but every blow of his sledge-hammer fist knocked a brave against the wall, or through the door into the snow. When he could reach two savages at once, by way of diversion, he swung their heads together with a crack. They dropped like dead things. Then he handled them as if they were sacks of corn, pitching them out into the snow. In two minutes the cabin was clear. He banged the door and slipped the bar in place.

"Buff, I'm goin' to get mad at these thievin' red, skins some day," he said gruffly. The expanse of his chest heaved slightly, like the slow swell of a calm ocean, but there was no other indication of unusual exertion.

Jones laughed, and again gave thanks for the comradeship of this strange man.

Shortly afterward, he went out for wood, and as usual scanned the expanse of the lake. The sun shone mistier and warmer, and frost feathers floated in the air. Sky and sun and plain and lake—all were gray. Jones fancied he saw a distant moving mass of darker shade than the gray background. He called the trapper.

"Caribou," said Rea instantly. "The vanguard of the migration. Hear the Indians! Hear their cry: "Aton! Aton!" they mean reindeer. The idiots have scared the herd with their infernal racket, an' no meat will they get. The caribou will keep to the ice, an' man or Indian can't stalk them there."

For a few moments his companion surveyed the lake and shore with a plainsman's eye, then dashed within, to reappear with a Winchester in each hand. Through the crowd of bewailing, bemoaning Indians; he sped, to the low, dying bank. The hard crust of snow upheld him. The gray cloud was a thousand yards out upon the lake and moving southeast. If the caribou did not swerve from this course they would pass close to a projecting point of land, a half-mile up the lake. So, keeping a wary eye upon them, the hunter ran swiftly. He had not hunted antelope and buffalo on the plains all his life without learning how to approach moving game. As long as the caribou were in action, they could not tell whether he moved or was motionless. In order to tell if an object was inanimate or not, they must stop to see, of which fact the keen hunter took advantage. Suddenly he saw the gray mass slow down and bunch up. He stopped running, to stand like a stump. When the reindeer moved again, he moved, and when they slackened again, he stopped and became motionless. As they kept to their course, he worked gradually closer and closer. Soon he distinguished gray, bobbing heads. When the leader showed signs of halting in his slow trot the hunter again became a statue. He saw they were easy to deceive; and, daringly confident of success, he encroached on the ice and closed up the gap till not more than two hundred yards separated him from the gray, bobbing, antlered mass.

Jones dropped on one knee. A moment only his eyes lingered admiringly on the wild and beautiful spectacle; then he swept one of the rifles to a level. Old habit made the little beaded sight cover first the stately leader. Bang! The gray monarch leaped straight forward, forehoofs up, antlered head back, to fall dead with a crash. Then for a few moments the Winchester spat a deadly stream of fire, and when emptied was thrown down for the other gun, which in the steady, sure hands of the hunter belched death to the caribou.

The herd rushed on, leaving the white surface of the lake gray with a struggling, kicking, bellowing heap. When Jones reached the caribou he saw several trying to rise on crippled legs. With his knife he killed these, not without some hazard to himself. Most of the fallen ones were already dead, and the others soon lay still. Beautiful gray creatures they were, almost white, with wide-reaching, symmetrical horns.

A medley of yells arose from the shore, and Rea appeared running with two sleds, with the whole tribe of Yellow Knives pouring out of the forest behind him.

"Buff, you're jest what old Jim said you was," thundered Rea, as he surveyed the gray pile. "Here's winter meat, an' I'd not have given a biscuit for all the meat I thought you'd get."

"Thirty shots in less than thirty seconds," said Jones, "An' I'll bet every ball I sent touched hair. How many reindeer?"

"Twenty! twenty! Buff, or I've forgot how to count. I guess mebbe you can't handle them shootin' arms. Ho! here comes the howlin' redskins."

Rea whipped out a bowie knife and began disemboweling the reindeer. He had not proceeded far in his task when the crazed savages were around him. Every one carried a basket or receptacle, which he swung aloft, and they sang, prayed, rejoiced on their knees. Jones turned away from the sickening scenes that convinced him these savages were little better than cannibals. Rea cursed them, and tumbled them over, and threatened them with the big bowie. An altercation ensued, heated on his side, frenzied on theirs. Thinking some treachery might befall his comrade, Jones ran into the thick of the group.

"Share with them, Rea, share with them."

Whereupon the giant hauled out ten smoking carcasses. Bursting into a babel of savage glee and tumbling over one another, the Indians pulled the caribou to the shore.

"Thievin' fools," growled Rea, wiping the sweat from his brow. "Said they'd prevailed on the Great Spirit to send the reindeer. Why, they'd never smelled warm meat but for you. Now, Buff, they'll gorge every hair, hide an' hoof of their share in less than a week. Thet's the last we do for the damned cannibals. Didn't you see them eatin' of the raw innards?—faugh! I'm calculatin' we'll see no more reindeer. It's late for the migration. The big herd has driven southward. But we're lucky, thanks to your prairie trainin'. Come on now with the sleds, or we'll have a pack of wolves to fight."

By loading three reindeer on each sled, the hunters were not long in transporting them to the cabin. "Buff, there ain't much doubt about them keepin' nice and cool," said Rea. "They'll freeze, an' we can skin them when we want."

That night the starved wolf dogs gorged themselves till they could not rise from the snow. Likewise the Yellow Knives feasted. How long the ten reindeer might have served the wasteful tribe, Rea and Jones never found out. The next day two Indians arrived with dog-trains, and their advent was hailed with another feast, and a pow-wow that lasted into the night.

"Guess we're goin' to get rid of our blasted hungry neighbors," said Rea, coming in next morning with the water pail, "An' I'll be durned, Buff, if I don't believe them crazy heathen have been told about you. Them Indians was messengers. Grab your gun, an' let's walk over and see."

The Yellow Knives were breaking camp, and the hunters were at once conscious of the difference in their bearing. Rea addressed several braves, but got no reply. He laid his broad hand on the old wrinkled chief, who repulsed him, and turned his back. With a growl, the trapper spun the Indian round, and spoke as many words of the language as he knew. He got a cold response, which ended in the ragged old chief starting up, stretching a long, dark arm northward, and with eyes fixed in fanatical subjection, shouting: "Naza! Naza! Naza!"

"Heathen!" Rea shook his gun in the faces of the messengers. "It'll go bad with you to come Nazain' any longer on our trail. Come, Buff, clear out before I get mad."

When they were once more in the cabin, Rea told Jones that the messengers had been sent to warn the Yellow Knives not to aid the white hunters in any way. That night the dogs were kept inside, and the men took turns in watching. Morning showed a broad trail southward. And with the going of the Yellow Knives the mercury dropped to fifty, and the long, twilight winter night fell.

So with this agreeable riddance and plenty of meat and fuel to cheer them, the hunters sat down in their snug cabin to wait many months for daylight.

Those few intervals when the wind did not blow were the only times Rea and Jones got out of doors. To the plainsman, new to the north, the dim gray world about him was of exceeding interest. Out of the twilight shone a wan, round, lusterless ring that Rea said was the sun. The silence and desolation were heart-numbing.

"Where are the wolves?" asked Jones of Rea.

"Wolves can't live on snow. They're farther south after caribou, or farther north after musk-ox."

In those few still intervals Jones remained out as long as he dared, with the mercury sinking to -sixty degrees. He turned from the wonder of the unreal, remote sun, to the marvel in the north—Aurora borealis—ever-present, ever-changing, ever-beautiful! and he gazed in rapt attention.

"Polar lights," said Rea, as if he were speaking of biscuits. "You'll freeze. It's gettin' cold."

Cold it became, to the matter of -seventy degrees. Frost covered the walls of the cabin and the roof, except just over the fire. The reindeer were harder than iron. A knife or an ax or a steel-trap burned as if it had been heated in fire, and stuck to the hand. The hunters experienced trouble in breathing; the air hurt their lungs.

The months dragged. Rea grew more silent day by day, and as he sat before the fire his wide shoulders sagged lower and lower. Jones, unaccustomed to the waiting, the restraint, the barrier of the north, worked on guns, sleds, harness, till he felt he would go mad. Then to save his mind he constructed a windmill of caribou hides and pondered over it trying to invent, to put into practical use an idea he had once conceived.

Hour after hour he lay under his blankets unable to sleep, and listened to the north wind. Sometimes Rea mumbled in his slumbers; once his giant form started up, and he muttered a woman's name. Shadows from the fire flickered on the walls, visionary, spectral shadows, cold and gray, fitting the north. At such times he longed with all the power of his soul to be among those scenes far southward, which he called home. For days Rea never spoke a word, only gazed into the fire, ate and slept. Jones, drifting far from his real self, feared the strange mood of the trapper and sought to break it, but without avail. More and more he reproached himself, and singularly on the one fact that, as he did not smoke himself, he had brought only a small store of tobacco. Rea, inordinate and inveterate smoker, had puffed away all the weed in clouds of white, then had relapsed into gloom.

CHAPTER 10.

SUCCESS AND FAILURE

At last the marvel in the north dimmed, the obscure gray shade lifted, the hope in the south brightened, and the mercury climbed reluctantly, with a tyrant's hate to relinquish power.

Spring weather at twenty-five below zero! On April 12th a small band of Indians made their appearance. Of the Dog tribe were they, an offcast of the Great Slaves, according to Rea, and as motley, starring and starved as the Yellow Knives. But they were friendly, which presupposed ignorance of the white hunters, and Rea persuaded the strongest brave to accompany them as guide northward after musk-oxen.

On April 16th, having given the Indians several caribou carcasses, and assuring them that the cabin was protected by white spirits, Rea and Jones, each with sled and train of dogs, started out after their guide, who was similarly equipped, over the glistening snow toward the north. They made sixty miles the first day, and pitched their Indian tepee on the shores of Artillery Lake. Traveling northeast, they covered its white waste of one hundred miles in two days. Then a day due north, over rolling, monotonously snowy plain; devoid of rock, tree or shrub, brought them into a country of the strangest, queerest little spruce trees, very slender, and none of them over fifteen feet in height. A primeval forest of saplings.

"Ditchen Nechila," said the guide.

"Land of Sticks Little," translated Rea.

An occasional reindeer was seen and numerous foxes and hares trotted off into the woods, evincing more curiosity than fear. All were silver white, even the reindeer, at a distance, taking the hue of the north. Once a beautiful creature, unblemished as the snow it trod, ran up a ridge and stood watching the hunters. It resembled a monster dog, only it was inexpressibly more wild looking.

"Ho! Ho! there you are!" cried Rea, reaching for his Winchester. "Polar wolf! Them's the white devils we'll have hell with."

As if the wolf understood, he lifted his white, sharp head and uttered a bark or howl that was like nothing so much as a haunting, unearthly mourn. The animal then merged into the white, as if he were really a spirit of the world whence his cry seemed to come.

In this ancient forest of youthful appearing trees, the hunters cut firewood to the full carrying capacity of the sleds. For five days the Indian guide drove his dogs over the smooth crust, and on the sixth day, about noon, halting in a hollow, he pointed to tracks in the snow and called out: "Ageter! Ageter! Ageter!"

The hunters saw sharply defined hoof-marks, not unlike the tracks of reindeer, except that they were longer. The tepee was set up on the spot and the dogs unharnessed.

The Indian led the way with the dogs, and Rea and Jones followed, slipping over the hard crust without sinking in and traveling swiftly. Soon the guide, pointing, again let out the cry: "Ageter!" at the same moment loosing the dogs.

Some few hundred yards down the hollow, a number of large black animals, not unlike the shaggy, humpy buffalo, lumbered over the snow. Jones echoed Rea's yell, and broke into a run, easily distancing the puffing giant.

The musk-oxen squared round to the dogs, and were soon surrounded by the yelping pack. Jones came up to find six old bulls uttering grunts of rage and shaking ram-like horns at their tormentors. Notwithstanding that for Jones this was the cumulation of years of desire, the crowning moment, the climax and fruition of long-harbored dreams, he halted before the tame and helpless beasts, with joy not unmixed with pain.

"It will be murder!" he exclaimed. "It's like shooting down sheep."

Rea came crashing up behind him and yelled, "Get busy. We need fresh meat, an' I want the skins."

The bulls succumbed to well-directed shots, and the Indian and Rea hurried back to camp with the dogs to fetch the sleds, while Jones examined with warm interest the animals he had wanted to see all his life. He found the largest bull approached within a third of the size of a buffalo. He was of a brownish-black color and very like a large, woolly ram. His head was broad, with sharp, small ears; the horns had wide and flattened bases and lay flat on the head, to run down back of the eyes, then curve forward to a sharp point. Like the bison, the musk ox had short, heavy limbs, covered with very long hair, and small, hard hoofs with hairy tufts inside the curve of bone, which probably served as pads or checks to hold the hoof firm on ice. His legs seemed out of proportion to his body.

Two musk-oxen were loaded on a sled and hauled to camp in one trip. Skinning them was but short work for such expert hands. All the choice cuts of meat were saved. No time was lost in broiling a steak, which they found sweet and juicy, with a flavor of musk that was disagreeable.

"Now, Rea, for the calves," exclaimed Jones, "And then we're homeward bound."

"I hate to tell this redskin," replied Rea. "He'll be like the others. But it ain't likely he'd desert us here. He's far from his base, with nothin' but thet old musket." Rea then commanded the attention of the brave, and began to mangle the Great Slave and Yellow Knife languages. Of this mixture Jones knew but few words. "Ageter nechila," which Rea kept repeating, he knew, however, meant "musk-oxen little."

The guide stared, suddenly appeared to get Rea's meaning, then vigorously shook his head and gazed at Jones in fear and horror. Following this came an action as singular as inexplicable. Slowly rising, he faced the north, lifted his hand, and remained statuesque in his immobility. Then he began deliberately packing his blankets and traps on his sled, which had not been unhitched from the train of dogs.

"Jackoway ditchen hula," he said, and pointed south.

"Jackoway ditchen hula," echoed Rea. "The damned Indian says 'wife sticks none.' He's goin' to quit us. What do you think of thet? His wife's out of wood. Jackoway out of wood, an' here we are two days from the Arctic Ocean. Jones, the damned heathen don't go back!"

The trapper coolly cocked his rifle. The savage, who plainly saw and understood the action, never flinched. He turned his breast to Rea, and there was nothing in his demeanor to suggest his relation to a craven tribe.

"Good heavens, Rea, don't kill him!" exclaimed Jones, knocking up the leveled rifle.

"Why not, I'd like to know?" demanded Rea, as if he were considering the fate of a threatening beast. "I reckon it'd be a bad thing for us to let him go."

"Let him go," said Jones. "We are here on the ground. We have dogs and meat. We'll get our calves and reach the lake as soon as he does, and we might get there before."

"Mebbe we will," growled Rea.

No vacillation attended the Indian's mood. From friendly guide, he had suddenly been transformed into a dark, sullen savage. He refused the musk-ox meat offered by Jones, and he pointed south and looked at the white hunters as if he asked them to go with him. Both men shook their heads in answer. The savage struck his breast a sounding blow and with his index finger pointed at the white of the north, he shouted dramatically: "Naza! Naza! Naza!"

He then leaped upon his sled, lashed his dogs into a run, and without looking back disappeared over a ridge.

The musk-ox hunters sat long silent. Finally Rea shook his shaggy locks and roared. "Ho! Ho! Jackoway out of wood! Jackoway out of wood! Jackoway out of wood!"

On the day following the desertion, Jones found tracks to the north of the camp, making a broad trail in which were numerous little imprints that sent him flying back to get Rea and the dogs. Muskoxen in great numbers had passed in the night, and Jones and Rea had not trailed the herd a mile before they had it in sight. When the dogs burst into full cry, the musk-oxen climbed a high knoll and squared about to give battle.

"Calves! Calves! Calves!" cried Jones.

"Hold back! Hold back! Thet's a big herd, an' they'll show fight."

As good fortune would have it, the herd split up into several sections, and one part, hard pressed by the dogs, ran down the knoll, to be cornered under the lee of a bank. The hunters, seeing this small number, hurried upon them to find three cows and five badly frightened little calves backed against the bank of snow, with small red eyes fastened on the barking, snapping dogs.

To a man of Jones's experience and skill, the capturing of the calves was a ridiculously easy piece of work. The cows tossed their heads, watched the dogs, and forgot their young. The first cast of the lasso settled over the neck of a little fellow. Jones hauled him out over the slippery snow and laughed as he bound the hairy legs. In less time than he had taken to capture one buffalo calf, with half the escort, he had all the little musk-oxen bound fast. Then he signaled this feat by pealing out an Indian yell of victory.

"Buff, we've got 'em," cried Rea; "An' now for the hell of it gettin' 'em home. I'll fetch the sleds. You might as well down thet best cow for me. I can use another skin."

Of all Jones's prizes of captured wild beasts—which numbered nearly every species common to western North America—he took greatest pride in the little musk-oxen. In truth, so great had been his passion to capture some of these rare and inaccessible mammals, that he considered the day's world the fulfillment of his life's purpose. He was happy. Never had he been so delighted as when, the very evening of their captivity, the musk-oxen, evincing no particular fear of him, began to dig with sharp hoofs into the snow for moss. And they found moss, and ate it, which solved Jones's greatest problem. He had hardly dared to think how to feed them, and here they were picking sustenance out of the frozen snow.

"Rea, will you look at that! Rea, will you look at that!" he kept repeating. "See, they're hunting, feed."

And the giant, with his rare smile, watched him play with the calves. They were about two and a half feet high, and resembled long-haired sheep. The ears and horns were undiscernible, and their color considerably lighter than that of the matured beasts.

"No sense of fear of man," said the life-student of animals. "But they shrink from the dogs."

In packing for the journey south, the captives were strapped on the sleds. This circumstance necessitated a sacrifice of meat and wood, which brought grave, doubtful shakes of Rea's great head.

Days of hastening over the icy snow, with short hours for sleep and rest, passed before the hunters awoke to the consciousness that they were lost. The meat they had packed had gone to feed themselves and the dogs. Only a few sticks of wood were left.

"Better kill a calf, an' cook meat while we've got little wood left," suggested Rea.

"Kill one of my calves? I'd starve first!" cried Jones.

The hungry giant said no more.

They headed southwest. All about them glared the grim monotony of the arctics. No rock or bush or tree made a welcome mark upon the hoary plain Wonderland of frost, white marble desert, infinitude of gleaming silences!

Snow began to fall, making the dogs flounder, obliterating the sun by which they traveled. They camped to wait for clearing weather. Biscuits soaked in tea made their meal. At dawn Jones crawled out of the tepee. The snow had ceased. But where were the dogs? He yelled in alarm. Then little mounds of white, scattered here and there became animated, heaved, rocked and rose to dogs. Blankets of snow had been their covering.

Rea had ceased his "Jackoway out of wood," for a reiterated question: "Where are the wolves?"

"Lost," replied Jones in hollow humor.

Near the close of that day, in which they had resumed travel, from the crest of a ridge they descried a long, low, undulating dark line. It proved to be the forest of "Little sticks," where, with grateful assurance of fire and of soon finding their old trail, they made camp.

"We've four biscuits left, an' enough tea for one drink each," said Rea. "I calculate we're two hundred miles from Great Slave Lake. Where are the wolves?"

At that moment the night wind wafted through the forest a long, haunting mourn. The calves shifted uneasily; the dogs raised sharp noses to sniff the air, and Rea, settling back against a tree, cried out: "Ho! Ho!" Again the savage sound, a keen wailing note with the hunger of the northland in it, broke the cold silence. "You'll see a pack of real wolves in a minute," said Rea. Soon a swift pattering of feet down a forest slope brought him to his feet with a curse to reach a brawny hand for his rifle. White streaks crossed the black of the tree trunks; then indistinct forms, the color of snow, swept up, spread out and streaked to and fro. Jones thought the great, gaunt, pure white beasts the spectral wolves of Rea's fancy, for they were silent, and silent wolves must belong to dreams only.

"Ho! Ho!" yelled Rea. "There's green-fire eyes for you, Buff. Hell itself ain't nothin' to these white devils. Get the calves in the tepee, an' stand ready to loose the dogs, for we've got to fight."

201

Raising his rifle he opened fire upon the white foe. A struggling, rustling sound followed the shots. But whether it was the threshing about of wolves dying in agony, or the fighting of the fortunate ones over those shot, could not be ascertained in the confusion.

Following his example Jones also fired rapidly on the other side of the tepee. The same inarticulate, silently rustling wrestle succeeded this volley.

"Wait!" cried Rea. "Be sparin' of cartridges."

The dogs strained at their chains and bravely bayed the wolves. The hunters heaped logs and brush on the fire, which, blazing up, sent a bright light far into the woods. On the outer edge of that circle moved the white, restless, gliding forms.

"They're more afraid of fire than of us," said Jones.

So it proved. When the fire burned and crackled they kept well in the background. The hunters had a long respite from serious anxiety, during which time they collected all the available wood at hand. But at midnight, when this had been mostly consumed, the wolves grew bold again.

"Have you any shots left for the 45-90, besides what's in the magazine?" asked Rea.

"Yes, a good handful."

"Well, get busy."

With careful aim Jones emptied the magazine into the gray, gliding, groping mass. The same rustling, shuffling, almost silent strife ensued.

"Rea, there's something uncanny about those brutes. A silent pack of wolves!"

"Ho! Ho!" rolled the giant's answer through the woods.

For the present the attack appeared to have been effectually checked. The hunters, sparingly adding a little of their fast diminishing pile of fuel to the fire, decided to lie down for much needed rest, but not for sleep. How long they lay there, cramped by the calves, listening for stealthy steps, neither could tell; it might have been moments and it might have been hours. All at once came a rapid rush of pattering feet, succeeded by a chorus of angry barks, then a terrible commingling of savage snarls, growls, snaps and yelps.

"Out!" yelled Rea. "They're on the dogs!"

Jones pushed his cocked rifle ahead of him and straightened up outside the tepee. A wolf, large as a panther and white as the gleaming snow, sprang at him. Even as he discharged his rifle, right against the breast of the beast, he saw its dripping jaws, its wicked green eyes, like spurts of fire and felt its hot breath. It fell at his feet and writhed in the death struggle. Slender bodies of black and white, whirling and tussling together, sent out fiendish uproar. Rea threw a blazing stick of wood among them, which sizzled as it met the furry coats, and brandishing another he ran into the thick of the fight. Unable to stand the proximity of fire, the wolves bolted and loped off into the woods.

"What a huge brute!" exclaimed Jones, dragging the one he had shot into the light. It was a superb animal, thin, supple, strong, with a coat of frosty fur, very long and fine. Rea began at once to skin it, remarking that he hoped to find other pelts in the morning.

Though the wolves remained in the vicinity of camp, none ventured near. The dogs moaned and whined; their restlessness increased as dawn approached, and when the gray light came, Jones founds that some of them had been badly lacerated by the fangs of the wolves. Rea hunted for dead wolves and found not so much as a piece of white fur.

Soon the hunters were speeding southward. Other than a disposition to fight among themselves, the dogs showed no evil effects of the attack. They were lashed to their best speed, for Rea said the white rangers of the north would never quit their trail. All day the men listened for the wild, lonesome, haunting mourn. But it came not.

A wonderful halo of white and gold, that Rea called a sun-dog, hung in the sky all afternoon, and dazzlingly bright over the dazzling world of snow circled and glowed a mocking sun, brother of the desert mirage, beautiful illusion, smiling cold out of the polar blue.

The first pale evening star twinkled in the east when the hunters made camp on the shore of Artilery Lake. At dusk the clear, silent air opened to the sound of a long, haunting mourn.

"Ho! Ho!" called Rea. His hoarse, deep voice rang defiance to the foe.

While he built a fire before the tepee, Jones strode up and down, suddenly to whip out his knife and make for the tame little musk-oxen, now digging the snow. Then he wheeled abruptly and held out the blade to Rea.

"What for?" demanded the giant.

"We've got to eat," said Jones. "And I can't kill one of them. I can't, so you do it."

"Kill one of our calves?" roared Rea. "Not till hell freezes over! I ain't commenced to get hungry. Besides, the wolves are going to eat us, calves and all."

Nothing more was said. They ate their last biscuit. Jones packed the calves away in the tepee, and turned to the dogs. All day they had worried him; something was amiss with them, and even as he went among them a fierce fight broke out. Jones saw it was unusual, for the attacked dogs showed craven fear, and the attacking ones a howling, savage intensity that surprised him. Then one of the vicious brutes rolled his eyes, frothed at the mouth, shuddered and leaped in his harness, vented a hoarse howl and fell back shaking and retching.

"My God! Rea!" cried Jones in horror. "Come here! Look! That dog is dying of rabies! Hydrophobia! The white wolves have hydrophobia!"

"If you ain't right!" exclaimed Rea. "I seen a dog die of thet onct, an' he acted like this. An' thet one ain't all. Look, Buff! look at them green eyes! Didn't I say the white wolves was hell? We'll have to kill every dog we've got."

Jones shot the dog, and soon afterward three more that manifested signs of the disease. It was an awful situation. To kill all the dogs meant simply to sacrifice his life and Rea's; it meant abandoning hope of ever reaching the cabin. Then to risk being bitten by one of the poisoned, maddened brutes, to risk the most horrible of agonizing deaths—that was even worse.

"Rea, we've one chance," cried Jones, with pale face. "Can you hold the dogs, one by one, while muzzle them?"

"Ho! Ho!" replied the giant. Placing his bowie knife between his teeth, with gloved hands he seized and dragged one of the dogs to the campfire. The animal whined and protested, but showed no ill spirit. Jones muzzled his jaws tightly with strong cords. Another and another were tied up, then one which tried to snap at Jones was nearly crushed by the giant's grip. The last, a surly brute, broke out into mad ravings the moment he felt the touch of Jones's hands, and writhing, frothing, he snapped Jones's sleeve. Rea jerked him loose and held him in the air with one arm, while with the other he swung the bowie. They hauled the dead dogs out on the snow, and returning to the fire sat down to await the cry they expected.

Presently, as darkness fastened down tight, it came—the same cry, wild, haunting, mourning. But for hours it was not repeated.

"Better rest some," said Rea; "I'll call you if they come."

Jones dropped to sleep as he touched his blankets. Morning dawned for him, to find the great, dark, shadowy figure of the giant nodding over the fire.

"How's this? Why didn't you call me?" demanded Jones.

"The wolves only fought a little over the dead dogs."

On the instant Jones saw a wolf skulking up the bank. Throwing up his rifle, which he had carried out of the tepee, he took a snap-shot at the beast. It ran off on three legs, to go out of sight over the hank. Jones scrambled up the steep, slippery place, and upon arriving at the ridge, which took several moments of hard work, he looked everywhere for the wolf. In a moment he saw the animal, standing still some hundred or more paces down a hollow. With the quick report of Jones's second shot, the wolf fell and rolled over. The hunter ran to the spot to find the wolf was dead. Taking hold of a front paw, he dragged the animal over the snow to camp. Rea began to skin the animal, when suddenly he exclaimed:

"This fellow's hind foot is gone!"

"That's strange. I saw it hanging by the skin as the wolf ran up the bank. I'll look for it."

By the bloody trail on the snow he returned to the place where the wolf had fallen, and thence back to the spot where its leg had been broken by the bullet. He discovered no sign of the foot.

"Didn't find it, did you?" said Rea.

"No, and it appears odd to me. The snow is so hard the foot could not have sunk."

"Well, the wolf ate his foot, thet's what," returned Rea. "Look at them teeth marks!"

"Is it possible?" Jones stared at the leg Rea held up.

"Yes, it is. These wolves are crazy at times. You've seen thet. An' the smell of blood, an' nothin' else, mind you, in my opinion, made him eat his own' foot. We'll cut him open."

Impossible as the thing seemed to Jones—and he could not but believe further evidence of his own' eyes—it was even stranger to drive a train of mad dogs. Yet that was what Rea and he did, and lashed them, beat them to cover many miles in the long day's journey. Rabies had broken out in several dogs so alarmingly that Jones had to kill them at the end of the run. And hardly had the sound of the shots died when faint and far away, but clear as a bell, bayed on the wind the same haunting mourn of a trailing wolf.

"Ho! Ho! where are the wolves?" cried Rea.

A waiting, watching, sleepless night followed. Again the hunters faced the south. Hour after hour, riding, running, walking, they urged the poor, jaded, poisoned dogs. At dark they reached the head of Artillery Lake. Rea placed the tepee between two huge stones. Then the hungry hunters, tired, grim, silent, desperate, awaited the familiar cry.

It came on the cold wind, the same haunting mourn, dreadful in its significance.

Absence of fire inspirited the wary wolves. Out of the pale gloom gaunt white forms emerged, agile and stealthy, slipping on velvet-padded feet, closer, closer, closer. The dogs wailed in terror.

"Into the tepee!" yelled Rea.

Jones plunged in after his comrade. The despairing howls of the dogs, drowned in more savage, frightful sounds, knelled one tragedy and foreboded a more terrible one. Jones looked out to see a white mass, like leaping waves of a rapid.

"Pump lead into thet!" cried Rea.

Rapidly Jones emptied his rifle into the white fray. The mass split; gaunt wolves leaped high to fall back dead; others wriggled and limped away; others dragged their hind quarters; others darted at the tepee.

"No more cartridges!" yelled Jones.

The giant grabbed the ax, and barred the door of the tepee. Crash! the heavy iron cleaved the skull of the first brute. Crash! it lamed the second. Then Rea stood in the narrow passage between the rocks, waiting with uplifted ax. A shaggy, white demon, snapping his jaws, sprang like a dog. A sodden, thudding blow met him and he slunk away without a cry. Another rabid beast launched his white body at the giant. Like a flash the ax descended. In agony the wolf fell, to spin round and round, running on his hind legs, while his head and shoulders and forelegs remained in the snow. His back was broken.

Jones crouched in the opening of the tepee, knife in hand. He doubted his senses. This was a nightmare. He saw two wolves leap at once. He heard the crash of the ax; he saw one wolf go down and the other slip under the swinging weapon to grasp the giant's hip. Jones's heard the rend of cloth, and then he pounced like a cat, to drive his knife into the body of the beast. Another nimble foe lunged at Rea, to sprawl broken and limp from the iron. It was a silent fight. The giant shut the way to his comrade and the calves; he made no outcry; he needed but one blow for every beast; magnificent, he wielded death and faced it—silent. He brought the white wild dogs of the north down with lightning blows, and when no more sprang to the attack, down on the frigid silence he rolled his cry: "Ho! Ho!"

"Rea! Rea! how is it with you?" called Jones, climbing out.

"A torn coat—no more, my lad."

Three of the poor dogs were dead; the fourth and last gasped at the hunters and died.

The wintry night became a thing of half-conscious past, a dream to the hunters, manifesting its reality only by the stark, stiff bodies of wolves, white in the gray morning.

"If we can eat, we'll make the cabin," said Rea. "But the dogs an' wolves are poison."

"Shall I kill a calf?" asked Jones.

"Ho! Ho! when hell freezes over—if we must!"

Jones found one 45-90 cartridge in all the outfit, and with that in the chamber of his rifle, once more struck south. Spruce trees began to show on the barrens and caribou trails roused hope in the hearts of the hunters.

"Look in the spruces," whispered Jones, dropping the rope of his sled. Among the black trees gray objects moved.

"Caribou!" said Rea. "Hurry! Shoot! Don't miss!"

But Jones waited. He knew the value of the last bullet. He had a hunter's patience. When the caribou came out in an open space, Jones whistled. It was then the rifle grew set and fixed; it was then the red fire belched forth.

At four hundred yards the bullet took some fraction of time to strike. What a long time that was! Then both hunters heard the spiteful spat of the lead. The caribou fell, jumped up, ran down the slope, and fell again to rise no more.

An hour of rest, with fire and meat, changed the world to the hunters; still glistening, it yet had lost its bitter cold its deathlike clutch.

"What's this?" cried Jones.

Moccasin tracks of different sizes, all toeing north, arrested the hunters.

"Pointed north! Wonder what thet means?" Rea plodded on, doubtfully shaking his head.

Night again, clear, cold, silver, starlit, silent night! The hunters rested, listening ever for the haunting mourn. Day again, white, passionless, monotonous, silent day. The hunters traveled on—on—on, ever listening for the haunting mourn.

Another dusk found them within thirty miles of their cabin. Only one more day now.

Rea talked of his furs, of the splendid white furs he could not bring. Jones talked of his little muskoxen calves and joyfully watched them dig for moss in the snow.

Vigilance relaxed that night. Outworn nature rebelled, and both hunters slept.

Rea awoke first, and kicking off the blankets, went out. His terrible roar of rage made Jones fly to his side.

Under the very shadow of the tepee, where the little musk-oxen had been tethered, they lay stretched out pathetically on crimson snow—stiff stone-cold, dead. Moccasin tracks told the story of the tragedy.

Jones leaned against his comrade.

The giant raised his huge fist.

"Jackoway out of wood! Jackoway out of wood!"

Then he choked.

The north wind, blowing through the thin, dark, weird spruce trees, moaned and seemed to sigh, "Naza! Naza! Naza!"

CHAPTER 11.

ON TO THE SIWASH

"Who all was doin' the talkin' last night?" asked Frank next morning, when we were having a late breakfast. "Cause I've a joke on somebody. Jim he talks in his sleep often, an' last night after you did finally get settled down, Jim he up in his sleep an' says: 'Shore he's windy as hell! Shore he's windy as hell'!"

At this cruel exposure of his subjective wanderings, Jim showed extreme humiliation; but Frank's eyes fairly snapped with the fun he got out of telling it. The genial foreman loved a joke. The week's stay at Oak, in which we all became thoroughly acquainted, had presented Jim as always the same quiet character, easy, slow, silent, lovable. In his brother cowboy, however, we had discovered in addition to his fine, frank, friendly spirit, an overwhelming fondness for playing tricks. This boyish mischievousness, distinctly Arizonian, reached its acme whenever it tended in the direction of our serious leader.

Lawson had been dispatched on some mysterious errand about which my curiosity was all in vain. The order of the day was leisurely to get in readiness, and pack for our journey to the Siwash on the morrow. I watered my horse, played with the hounds, knocked about the cliffs, returned to the cabin, and lay down on my bed. Jim's hands were white with flour. He was kneading dough, and had several low, flat pans on the table. Wallace and Jones strolled in, and later Frank, and they all took various positions before the fire. I saw Frank, with the quickness of a sleight-of-hand performer, slip one of the pans of dough on the chair Jones had placed by the table. Jim did not see the action; Jones's and Wallace's backs were turned to Frank, and he did not know I was in the cabin. The conversation continued on the subject of Jones's big bay horse, which, hobbles and all, had gotten ten miles from camp the night before.

"Better count his ribs than his tracks," said Frank, and went on talking as easily and naturally as if he had not been expecting a very entertaining situation.

But no one could ever foretell Colonel Jones's actions. He showed every intention of seating himself in the chair, then walked over to his pack to begin searching for something or other. Wallace, however, promptly took the seat; and what began to be funnier than strange, he did not get up. Not unlikely this circumstance was owing to the fact that several of the rude chairs had soft layers of old blanket tacked on them. Whatever were Frank's internal emotions, he presented a remarkably placid and commonplace exterior; but when Jim began to search for the missing pan of dough, the joker slowly sagged in his chair.

"Shore that beats hell!" said Jim. "I had three pans of dough. Could the pup have taken one?"

Wallace rose to his feet, and the bread pan clattered to the floor, with a clang and a clank, evidently protesting against the indignity it had suffered. But the dough stayed with Wallace, a great white conspicuous splotch on his corduroys. Jim, Frank and Jones all saw it at once.

"Why—Mr. Wal—lace—you set—in the dough!" exclaimed Frank, in a queer, strangled voice. Then he exploded, while Jim fell over the table.

It seemed that those two Arizona rangers, matured men though they were, would die of convulsions. I laughed with them, and so did Wallace, while he brought his one-handled bowie knife into novel use. Buffalo Jones never cracked a smile, though he did remark about the waste of good flour.

Frank's face was a study for a psychologist when Jim actually apologized to Wallace for being so careless with his pans. I did not betray Frank, but I resolved to keep a still closer watch on him. It was partially because of this uneasy sense of his trickiness in the fringe of my mind that I made a discovery. My sleeping-bag rested on a raised platform in one corner, and at a favorable moment I examined the bag. It had not been tampered with, but I noticed a string turning out through a chink between the logs. I found it came from a thick layer of straw under my bed, and had been tied to the end of a flatly coiled lasso. Leaving the thing as it was, I went outside and carelessly chased the hounds round the cabin. The string stretched along the logs to another chink, where it returned into the cabin at a point near where Frank slept. No great power of deduction was necessary to acquaint me with full details of the plot to spoil my slumbers. So I patiently awaited developments.

Lawson rode in near sundown with the carcasses of two beasts of some species hanging over his saddle. It turned out that Jones had planned a surprise for Wallace and me, and it could hardly have been a more enjoyable one, considering the time and place. We knew he had a flock of Persian sheep on the south slope of Buckskin, but had no idea it was within striking distance of Oak. Lawson had that day hunted up the shepherd and his sheep, to return to us with two sixty-pound Persian lambs. We feasted at suppertime on meat which was sweet, juicy, very tender and of as rare a flavor as that of the Rocky Mountain sheep.

My state after supper was one of huge enjoyment and with intense interest I awaited Frank's first spar for an opening. It came presently, in a lull of the conversation.

"Saw a big rattler run under the cabin to-day," he said, as if he were speaking of one of Old Baldy's shoes. "I tried to get a whack at him, but he oozed away too quick."

"Shore I seen him often," put in Jim. Good, old, honest Jim, led away by his trickster comrade! It was very plain. So I was to be frightened by snakes.

"These old canyon beds are ideal dens for rattle snakes," chimed in my scientific California friend. "I have found several dens, but did not molest them as this is a particularly dangerous time of the year to meddle with the reptiles. Quite likely there's a den under the cabin."

While he made this remarkable statement, he had the grace to hide his face in a huge puff of smoke. He, too, was in the plot. I waited for Jones to come out with some ridiculous theory or fact concerning the particular species of snake, but as he did not speak, I concluded they had wisely left him out of the secret. After mentally debating a moment, I decided, as it was a very harmless joke, to help Frank into the fulfillment of his enjoyment.

"Rattlesnakes!" I exclaimed. "Heavens! I'd die if I heard one, let alone seeing it. A big rattler jumped at me one day, and I've never recovered from the shock."

Plainly, Frank was delighted to hear of my antipathy and my unfortunate experience, and he proceeded to expatiate on the viciousness of rattlesnakes, particularly those of Arizona. If I had believed the succeeding stories, emanating from the fertile brains of those three fellows, I should have made certain that Arizona canyons were Brazilian jungles. Frank's parting shot, sent in a mellow, kind voice, was the best point in the whole trick. "Now, I'd be nervous if I had a sleepin' bag like yours, because it's just the place for a rattler to ooze into."

In the confusion and dim light of bedtime I contrived to throw the end of my lasso over the horn of a saddle hanging on the wall, with the intention of augmenting the noise I soon expected to create; and I placed my automatic rifle and .38 S. and W. Special within easy reach of my hand. Then I crawled into my bag and composed myself to listen. Frank soon began to snore, so brazenly, so fictitiously, that I wondered at the man's absorbed intensity in his joke; and I was at great pains to smother in my breast a violent burst of riotous merriment. Jones's snores, however, were real enough, and this made me enjoy the situation all the more; because if he did not show a mild surprise when the catastrophe fell, I would greatly miss my guess. I knew the three wily conspirators were wide-awake. Suddenly I felt a movement in the straw under me and a faint rustling. It was so soft, so sinuous, that if I had not known it was the lasso, I would assuredly have been frightened. I gave a little jump, such as one will make quickly in bed. Then the coil ran out from under the straw. How subtly suggestive of a snake! I made a slight outcry, a big jump, paused a moment for effectiveness in which time Frank forgot to snore—then let out a tremendous yell, grabbed my guns, sent twelve thundering shots through the roof and pulled my lasso.

Crash! the saddle came down, to be followed by sounds not on Frank's programme and certainly not calculated upon by me. But they were all the more effective. I gathered that Lawson, who was not in the secret, and who was a nightmare sort of sleeper anyway, had knocked over Jim's table, with its array of pots and pans and then, unfortunately for Jones had kicked that innocent person in the stomach.

As I lay there in my bag, the very happiest fellow in the wide world, the sound of my mirth was as the buzz of the wings of a fly to the mighty storm. Roar on roar filled the cabin.

When the three hypocrites recovered sufficiently from the startling climax to calm Lawson, who swore the cabin had been attacked by Indians; when Jones stopped roaring long enough to hear it was only a harmless snake that had caused the trouble, we hushed to repose once more—not, however, without hearing some trenchant remarks from the boiling Colonel anent fun and fools, and the indubitable fact that there was not a rattlesnake on Buckskin Mountain.

Long after this explosion had died away, I heard, or rather felt, a mysterious shudder or tremor of the cabin, and I knew that Frank and Jim were shaking with silent laughter. On my own score, I determined to find if Jones, in his strange make-up, had any sense of humor, or interest in life, or feeling, or love that did not center and hinge on four-footed beasts. In view of the rude awakening from what, no doubt, were pleasant dreams of wonderful white and green animals, combining the intelligence of man and strength of brutes—a new species creditable to his genius—I was perhaps unjust in my conviction as to his lack of humor. And as to the other question, whether or not he had any real human feeling for the creatures built in his own image, that was decided very soon and unexpectedly.

The following morning, as soon as Lawson got in with the horses, we packed and started. Rather sorry was I to bid good-by to Oak Spring. Taking the back trail of the Stewarts, we walked the horses all day up a slowly narrowing, ascending canyon. The hounds crossed coyote and deer trails continually, but made no break. Sounder looked up as if to say he associated painful reminiscences with certain kinds of tracks. At the head of the canyon we reached timber at about the time dusk gathered, and we located for the night. Being once again nearly nine thousand feet high, we found the air bitterly cold, making a blazing fire most acceptable.

In the haste to get supper we all took a hand, and some one threw upon our tarpaulin tablecloth a tin cup of butter mixed with carbolic acid—a concoction Jones had used to bathe the sore feet of the dogs. Of course I got hold of this, spread a generous portion on my hot biscuit, placed some red-hot beans on that, and began to eat like a hungry hunter. At first I thought I was only burned. Then I recognized the taste and burn of the acid and knew something was wrong. Picking up the tin, I examined it, smelled the pungent odor and felt a queer numb sense of fear. This lasted only for a moment, as I well knew the use and power of the acid, and had not swallowed enough to hurt me. I was about to make known my mistake in a matter-of-fact way, when it flashed over me the accident could be made to serve a turn.

"Jones!" I cried hoarsely. "What's in this butter?"

"Lord! you haven't eaten any of that. Why, I put carbolic acid in it."

"Oh—oh—oh—I'm poisoned! I ate nearly all of it! Oh—I'm burning up! I'm dying!" With that I began to moan and rock to and fro and hold my stomach.

Consternation preceded shock. But in the excitement of the moment, Wallace—who, though badly scared, retained his wits made for me with a can of condensed milk. He threw me back with no gentle hand, and was squeezing the life out of me to make me open my mouth, when I gave him a jab in his side. I imagined his surprise, as this peculiar reception of his first-aid-to-the-injured made him hold off to take a look at me, and in this interval I contrived to whisper to him: "Joke! Joke! you idiot! I'm only shamming. I want to see if I can scare Jones and get even with Frank. Help me out! Cry! Get tragic!"

From that moment I shall always believe that the stage lost a great tragedian in Wallace. With a magnificent gesture he threw the can of condensed milk at Jones, who was so stunned he did not try to dodge. "Thoughtless man! Murderer! it's too late!" cried Wallace, laying me back across his knees. "It's too late. His teeth are locked. He's far gone. Poor boy! poor boy! Who's to tell his mother?"

I could see from under my hat-brim that the solemn, hollow voice had penetrated the cold exterior of the plainsman. He could not speak; he clasped and unclasped his big hands in helpless fashion. Frank was as white as a sheet. This was simply delightful to me. But the expression of miserable, impotent distress on old Jim's sun-browned face was more than I could stand, and I could no longer keep up the deception. Just as Wallace cried out to Jones to pray—I wished then I had not weakened so soon—I got up and walked to the fire.

"Jim, I'll have another biscuit, please."

His under jaw dropped, then he nervously shoveled biscuits at me. Jones grabbed my hand and cried out with a voice that was new to me: "You can eat? You're better? You'll get over it?"

"Sure. Why, carbolic acid never phases me. I've often used it for rattlesnake bites. I did not tell you, but that rattler at the cabin last night actually bit me, and I used carbolic to cure the poison."

Frank mumbled something about horses, and faded into the gloom. As for Jones, he looked at me rather incredulously, and the absolute, almost childish gladness he manifested because I had been snatched from the grave, made me regret my deceit, and satisfied me forever on one score.

On awakening in the morning I found frost half an inch thick covered my sleeping-bag, whitened the ground, and made the beautiful silver spruce trees silver in hue as well as in name.

We were getting ready for an early start, when two riders, with pack-horses jogging after them, came down the trail from the direction of Oak Spring. They proved to be Jeff Clarke, the wild-horse wrangler mentioned by the Stewarts, and his helper. They were on the way into the breaks for a string of pintos. Clarke was a short, heavily bearded man, of jovial aspect. He said he had met the Stewarts going into Fredonia, and being advised of our destination, had hurried to come up with us. As we did not know, except in a general way, where we were making for, the meeting was a fortunate event.

Our camping site had been close to the divide made by one of the long, wooded ridges sent off by Buckskin Mountain, and soon we were descending again. We rode half a mile down a timbered slope, and then out into a beautiful, flat forest of gigantic pines. Clarke informed us it was a level bench some ten miles long, running out from the slopes of Buckskin to face the Grand Canyon on the south, and the 'breaks of the Siwash on the west. For two hours we rode between the stately lines of trees, and the hoofs of the horses gave forth no sound. A long, silvery grass, sprinkled with smiling bluebells, covered the ground, except close under the pines, where soft red mats invited lounging and rest. We saw numerous deer, great gray mule deer, almost as large as elk. Jones said they had been crossed with elk once, which accounted for their size. I did not see a stump, or a burned tree, or a windfall during the ride.

Clarke led us to the rim of the canyon. Without any preparation—for the giant trees hid the open sky—we rode right out to the edge of the tremendous chasm. At first I did not seem to think; my faculties were benumbed; only the pure sensorial instinct of the savage who sees, but does not feel, made me take note of the abyss. Not one of our party had ever seen the canyon from this side, and not one of us said a word. But Clarke kept talking.

"Wild place this is hyar," he said. "Seldom any one but horse wranglers gits over this far. I've hed a bunch of wild pintos down in a canyon below fer two years. I reckon you can't find no better place fer camp than right hyar. Listen. Do you hear thet rumble? Thet's Thunder Falls. You can only see it from one place, an' thet far off, but thar's brooks you can git at to water the hosses. Fer thet matter, you can ride up the slopes an' git snow. If you can git snow close, it'd be better, fer thet's an all-fired bad trail down fer water."

"Is this the cougar country the Stewarts talked about?" asked Jones.

"Reckon it is. Cougars is as thick in hyar as rabbits in a spring-hole canyon. I'm on the way now to bring up my pintos. The cougars hev cost me hundreds I might say thousands of dollars. I lose hosses all the time; an' damn me, gentlemen, I've never raised a colt. This is the greatest cougar country in the West. Look at those yellow crags! Thar's where the cougars stay. No one ever hunted 'em. It seems to me they can't be hunted. Deer and wild hosses by the thousand browse hyar on the mountain in summer, an' down in the breaks in winter. The cougars live fat. You'll find deer and wild-hoss carcasses all over this country. You'll find lions' dens full of bones. You'll find warm deer left for the coyotes. But whether you'll find the cougars, I can't say. I fetched dogs in hyar, an' tried to ketch Old Tom. I've put them on his trail an' never saw hide nor hair of them again. Jones, it's no easy huntin' hyar."

"Well, I can see that," replied our leader. "I never hunted lions in such a country, and never knew any one who had. We'll have to learn how. We've the time and the dogs, all we need is the stuff in us."

"I hope you fellars git some cougars, an' I believe you will. Whatever you do, kill Old Tom."

"We'll catch him alive. We're not on a hunt to kill cougars," said Jones.

"What!" exclaimed Clarke, looking from Jones to us. His rugged face wore a half-smile.

"Jones ropes cougars, an' ties them up," replied Frank.

"I'm — — if he'll ever rope Old Tom," burst out Clarke, ejecting a huge quid of tobacco. "Why, man alive! it'd be the death of you to git near thet old villain. I never seen him, but I've seen his tracks fer five years. They're larger than any hoss tracks you ever seen. He'll weigh over three hundred, thet old cougar. Hyar, take a look at my man's hoss. Look at his back. See them marks? Wal, Old Tom made them, an' he made them right in camp last fall, when we were down in the canyon."

The mustang to which Clarke called our attention was a sleek cream and white pinto. Upon his side and back were long regular scars, some an inch wide, and bare of hair.

"How on earth did he get rid of the cougar?" asked Jones.

"I don't know. Perhaps he got scared of the dogs. It took thet pinto a year to git well. Old Tom is a real lion. He'll kill a full-grown hoss when he wants, but a yearlin' colt is his especial likin'. You're sure to run acrost his trail, an' you'll never miss it. Wal, if I find any cougar sign down in the canyon, I'll build two fires so as to let you know. Though no hunter, I'm tolerably acquainted with the varmints. The deer an' hosses are rangin' the forest slopes now, an' I think the cougars come up over the rim rock at night an' go back in the mornin'. Anyway, if your dogs can follow the trails, you've got sport, an' more'n sport comin' to you. But take it from me—don't try to rope Old Tom."

After all our disappointments in the beginning of the expedition, our hardship on the desert, our trials with the dogs and horses, it was real pleasure to make permanent camp with wood, water and feed at hand, a soul-stirring, ever-changing picture before us, and the certainty that we were in the wild lairs of the lions—among the Lords of the Crags!

While we were unpacking, every now and then I would straighten up and gaze out beyond. I knew the outlook was magnificent and sublime beyond words, but as yet I had not begun to understand it. The great pine trees, growing to the very edge of the rim, received their full quota of appreciation from me, as did the smooth, flower-decked aisles leading back into the forest.

The location we selected for camp was a large glade, fifty paces or more from the precipice far enough, the cowboys averred, to keep our traps from being sucked down by some of the whirlpool winds, native to the spot. In the center of this glade stood a huge gnarled and blasted old pine, that certainly by virtue of hoary locks and bent shoulders had earned the right to stand aloof from his younger companions. Under this tree we placed all our belongings, and then, as Frank so felicitously expressed it, we were free to "ooze round an' see things."

I believe I had a sort of subconscious, selfish idea that some one would steal the canyon away from me if I did not hurry to make it mine forever; so I sneaked off, and sat under a pine growing on the very rim. At first glance, I saw below me, seemingly miles away, a wild chaos of red and buff mesas rising out of dark purple clefts. Beyond these reared a long, irregular tableland, running south almost to the extent of my vision, which I remembered Clarke had called Powell's

Plateau. I remembered, also, that he had said it was twenty miles distant, was almost that many miles long, was connected to the mainland of Buckskin Mountain by a very narrow wooded dip of land called the Saddle, and that it practically shut us out of a view of the Grand Canyon proper. If that was true, what, then, could be the name of the canyon at my feet? Suddenly, as my gaze wandered from point to point, it was attested by a dark, conical mountain, white-tipped, which rose in the notch of the Saddle. What could it mean? Were there such things as canyon mirages? Then the dim purple of its color told of its great distance from me; and then its familiar shape told I had come into my own again—I had found my old friend once more. For in all that plateau there was only one snow-capped mountain—the San Francisco Peak; and there, a hundred and fifty, perhaps two hundred miles away, far beyond the Grand Canyon, it smiled brightly at me, as it had for days and days across the desert.

Hearing Jones yelling for somebody or everybody, I jumped up to find a procession heading for a point farther down the rim wall, where our leader stood waving his arms. The excitement proved to have been caused by cougar signs at the head of the trail where Clarke had started down.

"They're here, boys, they're here," Jones kept repeating, as he showed us different tracks. "This sign is not so old. Boys, to-morrow we'll get up a lion, sure as you're born. And if we do, and Sounder sees him, then we've got a lion-dog! I'm afraid of Don. He has a fine nose; he can run and fight, but he's been trained to deer, and maybe I can't break him. Moze is still uncertain. If old Jude only hadn't been lamed! She would be the best of the lot. But Sounder is our hope. I'm almost ready to swear by him."

All this was too much for me, so I slipped off again to be alone, and this time headed for the forest. Warm patches of sunlight, like gold, brightened the ground; dark patches of sky, like ocean blue, gleamed between the treetops. Hardly a rustle of wind in the fine-toothed green branches disturbed the quiet. When I got fully out of sight of camp, I started to run as if I were a wild Indian. My running had no aim; just sheer mad joy of the grand old forest, the smell of pine, the wild silence and beauty loosed the spirit in me so it had to run, and I ran with it till the physical being failed.

While resting on a fragrant bed of pine needles, endeavoring to regain control over a truant mind, trying to subdue the encroaching of the natural man on the civilized man, I saw gray objects moving under the trees. I lost them, then saw them, and presently so plainly that, with delight on delight, I counted seventeen deer pass through an open arch of dark green. Rising to my feet, I ran to get round a low mound. They saw me and bounded away with prodigiously long leaps. Bringing their forefeet together, stiff-legged under them, they bounced high, like rubber balls, yet they were graceful.

The forest was so open that I could watch them for a long way; and as I circled with my gaze, a glimpse of something white arrested my attention. A light, grayish animal appeared to be tearing at an old stump. Upon nearer view, I recognized a wolf, and he scented or sighted me at the same moment, and loped off into the shadows of the trees. Approaching the spot where I had marked him I found he had been feeding from the carcass of a horse. The remains had been only partly eaten, and were of an animal of the mustang build that had evidently been recently killed. Frightful lacerations under the throat showed where a lion had taken fatal hold. Deep furrows in the ground proved how the mustang had sunk his hoofs, reared and shaken himself. I traced roughly defined tracks fifty paces to the lee of a little bank, from which I concluded the lion had sprung.

I gave free rein to my imagination and saw the forest dark, silent, peopled by none but its savage denizens, The lion crept like a shadow, crouched noiselessly down, then leaped on his sleeping or browsing prey. The lonely night stillness split to a frantic snort and scream of terror, and the stricken mustang with his mortal enemy upon his back, dashed off with fierce, wild love of life. As he went he felt his foe crawl toward his neck on claws of fire; he saw the tawny body and the gleaming eyes; then the cruel teeth snapped with the sudden bite, and the woodland tragedy ended.

On the spot I conceived an antipathy toward lions. It was born of the frightful spectacle of what had once been a glossy, prancing mustang, of the mute, sickening proof of the survival of the fittest, of the law that levels life.

Upon telling my camp-fellows about my discovery, Jones and Wallace walked out to see it, while Jim told me the wolf I had seen was a "lofer," one of the giant buffalo wolves of Buckskin; and if I would watch the carcass in the mornings and evenings, I would "shore as hell get a plunk at him."

White pine burned in a beautiful, clear blue flame, with no smoke; and in the center of the campfire left a golden heart. But Jones would not have any sitting up, and hustled us off to bed, saying we would be "blamed" glad of it in about fifteen hours. I crawled into my sleeping-bag, made a hood of my Navajo blanket, and peeping from under it, watched the fire and the flickering shadows. The blaze burned down rapidly. Then the stars blinked. Arizona stars would be moons in any other State! How serene, peaceful, august, infinite and wonderfully bright! No breeze stirred the pines. The clear tinkle of the cowbells on the hobbled horses rang from near and distant parts of the forest. The prosaic bell of the meadow and the pasture brook, here, in this environment, jingled out different notes, as clear, sweet, musical as silver bells.

CHAPTER 12.

OLD TOM

At daybreak our leader routed us out. The frost mantled the ground so heavily that it looked like snow, and the rare atmosphere bit like the breath of winter. The forest stood solemn and gray; the canyon lay wrapped in vapory slumber.

Hot biscuits and coffee, with a chop or two of the delicious Persian lamb meat, put a less Spartan tinge on the morning, and gave Wallace and me more strength—we needed not incentive to leave the fire, hustle our saddles on the horses and get in line with our impatient leader. The hounds scampered over the frost, shoving their noses at the tufts of grass and bluebells. Lawson and Jim remained in camp; the rest of us trooped southwest.

A mile or so in that direction, the forest of pine ended abruptly, and a wide belt of low, scrubby old trees, breast high to a horse, fringed the rim of the canyon and appeared to broaden out and grow wavy southward. The edge of the forest was as dark and regular as if a band of woodchoppers had trimmed it. We threaded our way through this thicket, all peering into the bisecting deer trails for cougar tracks in the dust.

"Bring the dogs! Hurry!" suddenly called Jones from a thicket.

We lost no time complying, and found him standing in a trail, with his eyes on the sand. "Take a look, boys. A good-sized male cougar passed here last night. Hyar, Sounder, Don, Moze, come on!"

It was a nervous, excited pack of hounds. Old Jude got to Jones first, and she sang out; then Sounder opened with his ringing bay, and before Jones could mount, a string of yelping dogs sailed straight for the forest.

"Ooze along, boys!" yelled Frank, wheeling Spot.

With the cowboy leading, we strung into the pines, and I found myself behind. Presently even Wallace disappeared. I almost threw the reins at Satan, and yelled for him to go. The result enlightened me. Like an arrow from a bow, the black shot forward. Frank had told me of his speed, that when he found his stride it was like riding a flying feather to be on him. Jones, fearing he would kill me, had cautioned me always to hold him in, which I had done. Satan stretched out with long graceful motions; he did not turn aside for logs, but cleared them with easy and powerful spring, and he swerved only slightly to the trees. This latter, I saw at once, made the danger for me. It became a matter of saving my legs and dodging branches. The imperative need of this came to me with convincing force. I dodged a branch on one tree, only to be caught square in the middle by a snag on another. Crack! If the snag had not broken, Satan would have gone on riderless, and I would have been left hanging, a pathetic and drooping monition to the risks of the hunt. I kept ducking my head, now and then falling flat over the pommel to avoid a limb that would have brushed me off, and hugging the flanks of my horse with my knees. Soon I was at Wallace's heels, and had Jones in sight. Now and then glimpses of Frank's white horse gleamed through the trees.

We began to circle toward the south, to go up and down shallow hollows, to find the pines thinning out; then we shot out of the forest into the scrubby oak. Riding through this brush was the cruelest kind of work, but Satan kept on close to the sorrel. The hollows began to get deeper, and the ridges between them narrower. No longer could we keep a straight course.

On the crest of one of the ridges we found Jones awaiting us. Jude, Tige and Don lay panting at his feet. Plainly the Colonel appeared vexed.

"Listen," he said, when we reined in.

We complied, but did not hear a sound.

"Frank's beyond there some place," continued Jones, "but I can't see him, nor hear the hounds anymore. Don and Tige split again on deer trails. Old Jude hung on the lion track, but I stopped her here. There's something I can't figure. Moze held a beeline southwest, and he yelled seldom. Sounder gradually stopped baying. Maybe Frank can tell us something."

Jones's long drawn-out signal was answered from the direction he expected, and after a little time, Frank's white horse shone out of the gray-green of a ledge a mile away.

This drew my attention to our position. We were on a high ridge out in the open, and I could see fifty miles of the shaggy slopes of Buckskin. Southward the gray, ragged line seemed to stop suddenly, and beyond it purple haze hung over a void I knew to be the canyon. And facing west, I came, at last, to understand perfectly the meaning of the breaks in the Siwash. They were nothing more than ravines that headed up on the slopes and ran down, getting steeper and steeper, though scarcely wider, to break into the canyon. Knife-crested ridges rolled westward, wave on wave, like the billows of a sea. I appreciated that these breaks were, at their sources, little washes easy to jump across, and at their mouths a mile deep and impassable. Huge pine trees shaded these gullies, to give way to the gray growth of stunted oak, which in turn merged into the dark green of pinyon. A wonderful country for deer and lions, it seemed to me, but impassable, all but impossible for a hunter.

Frank soon appeared, brushing through the bending oaks, and Sounder trotted along behind him.

"Where's Moze?" inquired Jones.

"The last I heard of Moze he was out of the brush, goin' across the pinyon flat, right for the canyon. He had a hot trail."

"Well, we're certain of one thing; if it was a deer, he won't come back soon, and if it was a lion, he'll tree it, lose the scent, and come back. We've got to show the hounds a lion in a tree. They'd run a hot trail, bump into a tree, and then be at fault. What was wrong with Sounder?"

"I don't know. He came back to me."

"We can't trust him, or any of them yet. Still, maybe they're doing better than we know."

The outcome of the chase, so favorably started was a disappointment, which we all felt keenly. After some discussion, we turned south, intending to ride down to the rim wall and follow it back to camp. I happened to turn once, perhaps to look again at the far-distant pink cliffs of Utah, or the wave-like dome of Trumbull Mountain, when I saw Moze trailing close behind me. My yell halted the Colonel.

"Well, I'll be darned!" ejaculated he, as Moze hove in sight. "Come hyar, you rascal!"

He was a tired dog, but had no sheepish air about him, such as he had worn when lagging in from deer chases. He wagged his tail, and flopped down to pant and pant, as if to say: "What's wrong with you guys?"

"Boys, for two cents I'd go back and put Jude on that trail. It's just possible that Moze treed a lion. But—well, I expect there's more likelihood of his chasing the lion over the rim; so we may as well keep on. The strange thing is that Sounder wasn't with Moze. There may have been two lions. You see we are up a tree ourselves. I have known lions to run in pairs, and also a mother keep four two-year-olds with her. But such cases are rare. Here, in this country, though, maybe they run round and have parties."

As we left the breaks behind we got out upon a level pinyon flat. A few cedars grew with the pinyons. Deer runways and trails were thick.

"Boys, look at that," said Jones. "This is great lion country, the best I ever saw."

He pointed to the sunken, red, shapeless remain of two horses, and near them a ghastly scattering of bleached bones. "A lion-lair right here on the flat. Those two horses were killed early this spring, and I see no signs of their carcasses having been covered with brush and dirt. I've got to learn lion lore over again, that's certain."

As we paused at the head of a depression, which appeared to be a gap in the rim wall, filled with massed pinyons and splintered piles of yellow stone, caught Sounder going through some interesting moves. He stopped to smell a bush. Then he lifted his head, and electrified me with a great, deep sounding bay.

"Hi! there, listen to that!" yelled Jones "What's Sounder got? Give him room—don't run him down. Easy now, old dog, easy, easy!"

Sounder suddenly broke down a trail. Moze howled, Don barked, and Tige let out his staccato yelp. They ran through the brush here, there, every where. Then all at once old Jude chimed in with her mellow voice, and Jones tumbled off his horse.

"By the Lord Harry! There's something here."

"Here, Colonel, here's the bush Sounder smelt and there's a sandy trail under it," I called.

"There go Don an' Tige down into the break!" cried Frank. "They've got a hot scent!"

Jones stooped over the place I designated, to jerk up with reddening face, and as he flung himself into the saddle roared out: "After Sounder! Old Tom! Old Tom! Old Tom!"

We all heard Sounder, and at the moment of Jones's discovery, Moze got the scent and plunged ahead of us.

"Hi! Hi! Hi! Hi!" yelled the Colonel. Frank sent Spot forward like a white streak. Sounder called to us in irresistible bays, which Moze answered, and then crippled Jude bayed in baffled impotent distress.

The atmosphere was charged with that lion. As if by magic, the excitation communicated itself to all, and men, horses and dogs acted in accord. The ride through the forest had been a jaunt. This was a steeplechase, a mad, heedless, perilous, glorious race. And we had for a pacemaker a cowboy mounted on a tireless mustang.

Always it seemed to me, while the wind rushed, the brush whipped, I saw Frank far ahead, sitting his saddle as if glued there, holding his reins loosely forward. To see him ride so was a beautiful sight. Jones let out his Comanche yell at every dozen jumps and Wallace sent back a thrilling "Waa-hoo-o!" In the excitement I had again checked my horse, and when Jones remembered, and loosed the bridle, how the noble animal responded! The pace he settled into dazed me; I could hardly distinguish the deer trail down which he was thundering. I lost my comrades ahead; the pinyons blurred in my sight; I only faintly heard the hounds. It occurred to me we were making for the breaks, but I did not think of checking Satan. I thought only of flying on faster and faster.

"On! On! old fellow! Stretch out! Never lose this race! We've got to be there at the finish!" I called to Satan, and he seemed to understand and stretched lower, farther, quicker.

The brush pounded my legs and clutched and tore my clothes; the wind whistled; the pinyon branches cut and whipped my face. Once I dodged to the left, as Satan swerved to the right, with the result that I flew out of the saddle, and crashed into a pinyon tree, which marvelously brushed me back into the saddle. The wild yells and deep bays sounded nearer. Satan tripped and plunged down, throwing me as gracefully as an aerial tumbler wings his flight. I alighted in a bush, without feeling of scratch or pain. As Satan recovered and ran past, I did not seek to make him stop, but getting a good grip on the pommel, I vaulted up again. Once more he raced like a wild mustang. And from nearer and nearer in front pealed the alluring sounds of the chase.

Satan was creeping close to Wallace and Jones, with Frank looming white through the occasional pinyons. Then all dropped out of sight, to appear again suddenly. They had reached the first break. Soon I was upon it. Two deer ran out of the ravine, almost brushing my horse in the haste. Satan went down and up in a few giant strides. Only the narrow ridge separated us from another break. It was up and down then for Satan, a work to which he manfully set himself. Occasionally I saw Wallace and Jones, but heard them oftener. All the time the breaks grew deeper, till finally Satan had to zigzag his way down and up. Discouragement fastened on me, when from the summit of the next ridge I saw Frank far down the break, with Jones and Wallace not a quarter of a mile away from him. I sent out a long, exultant yell as Satan crashed into the hard, dry wash in the bottom of the break.

I knew from the way he quickened under me that he intended to overhaul somebody. Perhaps because of the clear going, or because my frenzy had cooled to a thrilling excitement which permitted detail, I saw clearly and distinctly the speeding horsemen down the ravine. I picked out the smooth pieces of ground ahead, and with the slightest touch of the rein on his neck, guided Satan into them. How he ran! The light, quick beats of his hoofs were regular, pounding. Seeing Jones and Wallace sail high into the air, I knew they had jumped a ditch. Thus prepared, I managed to stick on when it yawned before me; and Satan, never slackening, leaped up and up, giving me a new swing.

Dust began to settle in little clouds before me; Frank, far ahead, had turned his mustang up the side of the break; Wallace, within hailing distance, now turned to wave me a hand. The rushing wind fairly sang in my ears; the walls of the break were confused blurs of yellow and green; at every stride Satan seemed to swallow a rod of the white trail.

Jones began to scale the ravine, heading up obliquely far on the side of where Frank had vanished, and as Wallace followed suit, I turned Satan. I caught Wallace at the summit, and we raced together out upon another flat of pinyon. We heard Frank and Jones yelling in a way that caused us to spur our horses frantically. Spot, gleaming white near a clump of green pinyons, was our guiding star. That last quarter of a mile was a ringing run, a ride to remember.

As our mounts crashed back with stiff forelegs and haunches, Wallace and I leaped off and darted into the clump of pinyons, whence issued a hair-raising medley of yells and barks. I saw Jones, then Frank, both waving their arms, then Moze and Sounder running wildly, airlessly about.

"Look there!" rang in my ear, and Jones smashed me on the back with a blow, which at any ordinary time would have laid me flat.

In a low, stubby pinyon tree, scarce twenty feet from us, was a tawny form. An enormous mountain lion, as large as an African lioness, stood planted with huge, round legs on two branches; and he faced us gloomily, neither frightened nor fierce. He watched the running dogs with pale, yellow eyes, waved his massive head and switched a long, black tufted tail.

"It's Old Tom! sure as you're born! It's Old Tom!" yelled Jones. "There's no two lions like that in one country. Hold still now. Jude is here, and she'll see him, she'll show him to the other hounds. Hold still!"

We heard Jude coming at a fast pace for a lame dog, and we saw her presently, running with her nose down for a moment, then up. She entered the clump of trees, and bumped her nose against the pinyon Old Tom was in, and looked up like a dog that knew her business. The series of wild howls she broke into quickly brought Sounder and Moze to her side. They, too, saw the big lion, not fifteen feet over their heads.

We were all yelling and trying to talk at once, in some such state as the dogs.

"Hyar, Moze! Come down out of that!" hoarsely shouted Jones.

Moze had begun to climb the thick, many-branched, low pinyon tree. He paid not the slightest attention to Jones, who screamed and raged at him.

"Cover the lion!" cried he to me. "Don't shoot unless he crouches to jump on me."

The little beaded front-sight wavered slightly as I held my rifle leveled at the grim, snarling face, and out of the corner of my eye, as it were, I saw Jones dash in under the lion and grasp Moze by the hind leg and haul him down. He broke from Jones and leaped again to the first low branch. His master then grasped his collar and carried him to where we stood and held him choking.

"Boys, we can't keep Tom up there. When he jumps, keep out of his way. Maybe we can chase him up a better tree."

Old Tom suddenly left the branches, swinging violently; and hitting the ground like a huge cat on springs, he bounded off, tail up, in a most ludicrous manner. His running, however, did not lack speed, for he quickly outdistanced the bursting hounds.

A stampede for horses succeeded this move. I had difficulty in closing my camera, which I had forgotten until the last moment, and got behind the others. Satan sent the dust flying and the pinyon branches crashing. Hardly had I time to bewail my ill-luck in being left, when I dashed out of a thick growth of trees to come upon my companions, all dismounted on the rim of the Grand Canyon.

"He's gone down! He's gone down!" raged Jones, stamping the ground. "What luck! What miserable luck! But don't quit; spread along the rim, boys, and look for him. Cougars can't fly. There's a break in the rim somewhere."

The rock wall, on which we dizzily stood, dropped straight down for a thousand feet, to meet a long, pinyon-covered slope, which graded a mile to cut off into what must have been the second wall. We were far west of Clarke's trail now, and faced a point above where Kanab Canyon, a red gorge a mile deep, met the great canyon. As I ran along the rim, looking for a fissure or break, my gaze seemed impellingly drawn by the immensity of this thing I could not name, and for which I had as yet no intelligible emotion.

Two "Waa-hoos" in the rear turned me back in double-quick time, and hastening by the horses, I found the three men grouped at the head of a narrow break.

"He went down here. Wallace saw him round the base of that tottering crag."

The break was wedge-shaped, with the sharp end off toward the rim, and it descended so rapidly as to appear almost perpendicular. It was a long, steep slide of small, weathered shale, and a place that no man in his right senses would ever have considered going down. But Jones, designating Frank and me, said in his cool, quick voice:

"You fellows go down. Take Jude and Sounder in leash. If you find his trail below along the wall, yell for us. Meanwhile, Wallace and I will hang over the rim and watch for him."

Going down, in one sense, was much easier than had appeared, for the reason that once started we moved on sliding beds of weathered stone. Each of us now had an avalanche for a steed. Frank forged ahead with a roar, and then seeing danger below, tried to get out of the mass. But the stones were like quicksand; every step he took sunk him in deeper. He grasped the smooth cliff, to find holding impossible. The slide poured over a fall like so much water. He reached and caught a branch of a pinyon, and lifting his feet up, hung on till the treacherous area of moving stones had passed.

While I had been absorbed in his predicament, my avalanche augmented itself by slide on slide, perhaps loosened by his; and before I knew it, I was sailing down with ever-increasing momentum. The sensation was distinctly pleasant, and a certain spirit, before restrained in me, at last ran riot. The slide narrowed at the drop where Frank had jumped, and the stones poured over in a stream. I jumped also, but having a rifle in one hand, failed to hold, and plunged down into the slide again. My feet were held this time, as in a vise. I kept myself upright and waited. Fortunately, the jumble of loose stone slowed and stopped, enabling me to crawl over to one side where there was comparatively good footing. Below us, for fifty yards was a sheet of rough stone, as bare as washed granite well could be. We slid down this in regular schoolboy fashion, and had reached another restricted neck in the fissure, when a sliding crash above warned us that the avalanches had decided to move of their own free will. Only a fraction of a moment had we to find footing along the yellow cliff, when, with a cracking roar, the mass struck the slippery granite. If we had been on that slope, our lives would not have been worth a grain of the dust flying in clouds above us. Huge stones, that had formed the bottom of the slides, shot ahead, and rolling, leaping, whizzed by us with frightful velocity, and the remainder groaned and growled its way down, to thunder over the second fall and die out in a distant rumble.

The hounds had hung back, and were not easily coaxed down to us. From there on, down to the base of the gigantic cliff, we descended with little difficulty.

"We might meet the old gray cat anywheres along here," said Frank.

The wall of yellow limestone had shelves, ledges, fissures and cracks, any one of which might have concealed a lion. On these places I turned dark, uneasy glances. It seemed to me events succeeded one another so rapidly that I had no time to think, to examine, to prepare. We were rushed from one sensation to another.

"Gee! look here," said Frank; "here's his tracks. Did you ever see the like of that?"

Certainly I had never fixed my eyes on such enormous cat-tracks as appeared in the yellow dust at the base of the rim wall. The mere sight of them was sufficient to make a man tremble.

"Hold in the dogs, Frank," I called. "Listen. I think I heard a yell."

From far above came a yell, which, though thinned out by distance, was easily recognized as Jones's. We returned to the opening of the break, and throwing our heads back, looked up the slide to see him coming down.

"Wait for me! Wait for me! I saw the lion go in a cave. Wait for me!"

With the same roar and crack and slide of rocks as had attended our descent, Jones bore down on us. For an old man it was a marvelous performance. He walked on the avalanches as though he wore seven-league boots, and presently, as we began to dodge whizzing bowlders, he stepped down to us, whirling his coiled lasso. His jaw bulged out; a flash made fire in his cold eyes.

"Boys, we've got Old Tom in a corner. I worked along the rim north and looked over every place I could. Now, maybe you won't believe it, but I heard him pant. Yes, sir, he panted like the tired lion he is. Well, presently I saw him lying along the base of the rim wall. His tongue was hanging out. You see, he's a heavy lion, and not used to running long distances. Come on, now. It's not far. Hold in the dogs. You there with the rifle, lead off, and keep your eyes peeled."

Single file, we passed along in the shadow of the great cliff. A wide trail had been worn in the dust.

"A lion run-way," said Jones. "Don't you smell the cat?"

Indeed, the strong odor of cat was very pronounced; and that, without the big fresh tracks, made the skin on my face tighten and chill. As we turned a jutting point in the wall, a number of animals, which I did not recognize, plunged helter-skelter down the canyon slope.

"Rocky Mountain sheep!" exclaimed Jones. "Look! Well, this is a discovery. I never heard of a bighorn in the Canyon."

It was indicative of the strong grip Old Tom had on us that we at once forgot the remarkable fact of coming upon those rare sheep in such a place.

Jones halted us presently before a deep curve described by the rim wall, the extreme end of which terminated across the slope in an impassable projecting corner.

"See across there, boys. See that black hole. Old Tom's in there."

"What's your plan?" queried the cowboy sharply.

"Wait. We'll slip up to get better lay of the land."

We worked our way noiselessly along the rim-wall curve for several hundred yards and came to a halt again, this time with a splendid command of the situation. The trail ended abruptly at the dark cave, so menacingly staring at us, and the corner of the cliff had curled back upon itself. It was a box-trap, with a drop at the end, too great for any beast, a narrow slide of weathered stone running down, and the rim wall trail. Old Tom would plainly be compelled to choose one of these directions if he left his cave.

"Frank, you and I will keep to the wall and stop near that scrub pinyon, this side of the hole. If I rope him, I can use that tree."

Then he turned to me:

"Are you to be depended on here?"

"I? What do you want me to do?" I demanded, and my whole breast seemed to sink in.

"You cut across the head of this slope and take up your position in the slide below the cave, say just by that big stone. From there you can command the cave, our position and your own. Now, if it is necessary to kill this lion to save me or Frank, or, of course, yourself, can you be depended upon to kill him?"

I felt a queer sensation around my heart and a strange tightening of the skin upon my face! What a position for me to be placed in! For one instant I shook like a quivering aspen leaf. Then because of the pride of a man, or perhaps inherited instincts cropping out at this perilous moment, I looked up and answered quietly:

"Yes. I will kill him!"

"Old Tom is cornered, and he'll come out. He can run only two ways: along this trail, or down that slide. I'll take my stand by the scrub pinyon there so I can get a hitch if I rope him. Frank, when I give the word, let the dogs go. Grey, you block the slide. If he makes at us, even if I do get my rope on him, kill him! Most likely he'll jump down hill—then you'll HAVE to kill him! Be quick. Now loose the hounds. Hi! Hi! Hi! Hi!"

I jumped into the narrow slide of weathered stone and looked up. Jones's stentorian yell rose high above the clamor of the hounds. He whirled his lasso.

A huge yellow form shot over the trail and hit the top of the slide with a crash. The lasso streaked out with arrowy swiftness, circled, and snapped viciously close to Old Tom's head. "Kill him! Kill him!" roared Jones. Then the lion leaped, seemingly into the air above me. Instinctively I raised my little automatic rifle. I seemed to hear a million bellowing reports. The tawny body, with its grim, snarling face, blurred in my sight. I heard a roar of sliding stones at my feet. I felt a rush of wind. I caught a confused glimpse of a whirling wheel of fur, rolling down the slide.

Then Jones and Frank were pounding me, and yelling I know not what. From far above came floating down a long "Waa-hoo!" I saw Wallace silhouetted against the blue sky. I felt the hot barrel of my rifle, and shuddered at the bloody stones below me—then, and then only, did I realize, with weakening legs, that Old Tom had jumped at me, and had jumped to his death.

CHAPTER 13.

SINGING CLIFFS

Old Tom had rolled two hundred yards down the canyon, leaving a red trail and bits of fur behind him. When I had clambered down to the steep slide where he had lodged, Sounder and Jude had just decided he was no longer worth biting, and were wagging their tails. Frank was shaking his head, and Jones, standing above the lion, lasso in hand, wore a disconsolate face.

"How I wish I had got the rope on him!"

"I reckon we'd be gatherin' up the pieces of you if you had," said Frank, dryly.

We skinned the old king on the rocky slope of his mighty throne, and then, beginning to feel the effects of severe exertion, we cut across the slope for the foot of the break. Once there, we gazed up in disarray. That break resembled a walk of life—how easy to slip down, how hard to climb! Even Frank, inured as he was to strenuous toil, began to swear and wipe his sweaty brow before we had made one-tenth of the ascent. It was particularly exasperating, not to mention the danger of it, to work a few feet up a slide, and then feel it start to move. We had to climb in single file, which jeopardized the safety of those behind the leader. Sometimes we were all sliding at once, like boys on a pond, with the difference that we were in danger. Frank forged ahead, turning to yell now and then for us to dodge a cracking stone. Faithful old Jude could not get up in some places, so laying aside my rifle, I carried her, and returned for the weapon. It became necessary, presently, to hide behind cliff projections to escape the avalanches started by Frank, and to wait till he had surmounted the break. Jones gave out completely several times, saying the exertion affected his heart. What with my rifle, my camera and Jude, I could offer him no assistance, and was really in need of that myself. When it seemed as if one more step would kill us, we reached the rim, and fell panting with labored chests and dripping skins. We could not speak. Jones had worn a pair of ordinary shoes without thick soles and nails, and it seemed well to speak of them in the past tense. They were split into ribbons and hung on by the laces. His feet were cut and bruised.

On the way back to camp, we encountered Moze and Don coming out of the break where we had started Sounder on the trail. The paws of both hounds were yellow with dust, which proved they had been down under the rim wall. Jones doubted not in the least that they had chased a lion.

Upon examination, this break proved to be one of the two which Clarke used for trails to his wild horse corral in the canyon. According to him, the distance separating them was five miles by the rim wall, and less than half that in a straight line. Therefore, we made for the point of the forest where it ended abruptly in the scrub oak. We got into camp, a fatigued lot of men, horses and dogs. Jones appeared particularly happy, and his first move, after dismounting, was to stretch out the lion skin and measure it.

"Ten feet, three inches and a half!" he sang out.

"Shore it do beat hell!" exclaimed Jim in tones nearer to excitement than any I had ever heard him use.

"Old Tom beats, by two inches, any cougar I ever saw," continued Jones. "He must have weighed more than three hundred. We'll set about curing the hide. Jim, stretch it well on a tree, and we'll take a hand in peeling off the fat."

All of the party worked on the cougar skin that afternoon. The gristle at the base of the neck, where it met the shoulders, was so tough and thick we could not scrape it thin. Jones said this particular spot was so well protected because in fighting, cougars were most likely to bite and claw there. For that matter, the whole skin was tough, tougher than leather; and when it dried, it pulled all the horseshoe nails out of the pine tree upon which we had it stretched.

About time for the sun to set, I strolled along the rim wall to look into the canyon. I was beginning to feel something of its character and had growing impressions. Dark purple smoke veiled the clefts deep down between the mesas. I walked along to where points of cliff ran out like capes and peninsulas, all seamed, cracked, wrinkled, scarred and yellow with age, with shattered, toppling ruins of rocks ready at a touch to go thundering down. I could not resist the temptation to crawl out to the farthest point, even though I shuddered over the yard-wide ridges; and when once seated on a bare promontory, two hundred feet from the regular rim wall, I felt isolated, marooned.

The sun, a liquid red globe, had just touched its under side to the pink cliffs of Utah, and fired a crimson flood of light over the wonderful mountains, plateaus, escarpments, mesas, domes and turrets or the gorge. The rim wall of Powell's Plateau was a thin streak of fire; the timber above like grass of gold; and the long slopes below shaded from bright to dark. Point Sublime, bold and bare, ran out toward the plateau, jealously reaching for the sun. Bass's Tomb peeped over the Saddle. The Temple of Vishnu lay bathed in vapory shading clouds, and the Shinumo Altar shone with rays of glory.

The beginning of the wondrous transformation, the dropping of the day's curtain, was for me a rare and perfect moment. As the golden splendor of sunset sought out a peak or mesa or escarpment, I gave it a name to suit my fancy; and as flushing, fading, its glory changed, sometimes I rechristened it. Jupiter's Chariot, brazen wheeled, stood ready to roll into the clouds. Semiramis's Bed, all gold, shone from a tower of Babylon. Castor and Pollux clasped hands over a Stygian river. The Spur of Doom, a mountain shaft as red as hell, and inaccessible, insurmountable, lured with strange light. Dusk, a bold, black dome, was shrouded by the shadow of a giant mesa. The Star of Bethlehem glittered from the brow of Point Sublime. The Wraith, fleecy, feathered curtain of mist, floated down among the ruins of castles and palaces, like the ghost of a goddess. Vales of Twilight, dim, dark ravines, mystic homes of specters, led into the awful Valley of the Shadow, clothed in purple night.

Suddenly, as the first puff of the night wind fanned my cheek, a strange, sweet, low moaning and sighing came to my ears. I almost thought I was in a dream. But the canyon, now blood-red, was there in overwhelming reality, a profound, solemn, gloomy thing, but real. The wind blew stronger, and then I was to a sad, sweet song, which lulled as the wind lulled. I realized at once that the sound was caused by the wind blowing into the peculiar formations of the cliffs. It changed, softened, shaded, mellowed, but it was always sad. It rose from low, tremulous, sweetly quavering sighs, to a sound like the last woeful, despairing wail of a woman. It was the song of the sea sirens and the music of the waves; it had the soft sough of the night wind in the trees, and the haunting moan of lost spirits.

With reluctance I turned my back to the gorgeously changing spectacle of the canyon and crawled in to the rim wall. At the narrow neck of stone I peered over to look down into misty blue nothingness.

That night Jones told stories of frightened hunters, and assuaged my mortification by saying "buck-fever" was pardonable after the danger had passed, and especially so in my case, because of the great size and fame of Old Tom.

"The worst case of buck-fever I ever saw was on a buffalo hunt I had with a fellow named Williams," went on Jones. "I was one of the scouts leading a wagon-train west on the old Santa Fe trail. This fellow said he was a big hunter, and wanted to kill buffalo, so I took him out. I saw a herd making over the prairie for a hollow where a brook ran, and by hard work, got in ahead of them. I picked out a position just below the edge of the bank, and we lay quiet, waiting. From the direction of the buffalo, I calculated we'd be just about right to get a shot at no very long range. As it was, I suddenly heard thumps on the ground, and cautiously raising my head, saw a huge buffalo bull just over us, not fifteen feet up the bank. I whispered to Williams: 'For God's sake, don't shoot, don't move!' The bull's little fiery eyes snapped, and he reared. I thought we were goners, for when a bull comes down on anything with his forefeet, it's done for. But he slowly settled back, perhaps doubtful. Then, as another buffalo came to the edge of the bank, luckily a little way from us, the bull turned broadside, presenting a splendid target. Then I whispered to Williams: 'Now's your chance. Shoot!' I waited for the shot, but none came. Looking at Williams, I saw he was white and trembling. Big drops of sweat stood out on his brow his teeth chattered, and his hands shook. He had forgotten he carried a rifle."

"That reminds me," said Frank. "They tell a story over at Kanab on a Dutchman named Schmitt. He was very fond of huntin', an' I guess had pretty good success after deer an' small game. One winter he was out in the Pink Cliffs with a Mormon named Shoonover, an' they run into a lammin' big grizzly track, fresh an' wet. They trailed him to a clump of chaparral, an' on goin' clear round it, found no tracks leadin' out. Shoonover said Schmitt commenced to sweat. They went back to the place where the trail led in, an' there they were, great big silver tip tracks, bigger'n hoss-tracks, so fresh thet water was oozin' out of 'em. Schmitt said: 'Zake, you go in und ged him. I hef took sick right now.'"

Happy as we were over the chase of Old Tom, and our prospects for Sounder, Jude and Moze had seen a lion in a tree—we sought our blankets early. I lay watching the bright stars, and listening to the roar of the wind in the pines. At intervals it lulled to a whisper, and then swelled to a roar, and then died away. Far off in the forest a coyote barked once. Time and time again, as I was gradually sinking into slumber, the sudden roar of the wind startled me. I imagined it was the crash of rolling, weathered stone, and I saw again that huge outspread flying lion above me.

I awoke sometime later to find Moze had sought the warmth of my side, and he lay so near my arm that I reached out and covered him with an end of the blanket I used to break the wind. It was very cold and the time must have been very late, for the wind had died down, and I heard not a tinkle from the hobbled horses. The absence of the cowbell music gave me a sense of loneliness, for without it the silence of the great forest was a thing to be felt.

This oppressiveness, however, was broken by a far-distant cry, unlike any sound I had ever heard. Not sure of myself, I freed my ears from the blanketed hood and listened. It came again, a wild cry, that made me think first of a lost child, and then of the mourning wolf of the north. It must have been a long distance off in the forest. An interval of some moments passed, then it pealed out again, nearer this time, and so human that it startled me. Moze raised his head and growled low in his throat and sniffed the keen air.

"Jones, Jones," I called, reaching over to touch the old hunter.

He awoke at once, with the clear-headedness of the light sleeper.

"I heard the cry of some beast," I said, "And it was so weird, so strange. I want to know what it was."

Such a long silence ensued that I began to despair of hearing the cry again, when, with a suddenness which straightened the hair on my head, a wailing shriek, exactly like a despairing woman might give in death agony, split the night silence. It seemed right on us.

"Cougar! Cougar! Cougar!" exclaimed Jones.

"What's up?" queried Frank, awakened by the dogs.

Their howling roused the rest of the party, and no doubt scared the cougar, for his womanish screech was not repeated. Then Jones got up and gatherered his blankets in a roll.

"Where you oozin' for now?" asked Frank, sleepily.

"I think that cougar just came up over the rim on a scouting hunt, and I'm going to go down to the head of the trail and stay there till morning. If he returns that way, I'll put him up a tree."

With this, he unchained Sounder and Don, and stalked off under the trees, looking like an Indian. Once the deep bay of Sounder rang out; Jones's sharp command followed, and then the familiar silence encompassed the forest and was broken no more.

When I awoke all was gray, except toward the canyon, where the little bit of sky I saw through the pines glowed a delicate pink. I crawled out on the instant, got into my boots and coat, and kicked the smoldering fire. Jim heard me, and said:

"Shore you're up early."

"I'm going to see the sunrise from the north rim of the Grand Canon," I said, and knew when I spoke that very few men, out of all the millions of travelers, had ever seen this, probably the most surpassingly beautiful pageant in the world. At most, only a few geologists, scientists, perhaps an artist or two, and horse wranglers, hunters and prospectors have ever reached the rim on the north side; and these men, crossing from Bright Angel or Mystic Spring trails on the south rim, seldom or never get beyond Powell's Plateau.

The frost cracked under my boots like frail ice, and the bluebells peeped wanly from the white. When I reached the head of Clarke's trail it was just daylight; and there, under a pine, I found Jones rolled in his blankets, with Sounder and Moze asleep beside him. I turned without disturbing him, and went along the edge of the forest, but back a little distance from the rim wall.

I saw deer off in the woods, and tarrying, watched them throw up graceful heads, and look and listen. The soft pink glow through the pines deepened to rose, and suddenly I caught a point of red fire. Then I hurried to the place I had named Singing Cliffs, and keeping my eyes fast on the stone beneath me, trawled out to the very farthest point, drew a long, breath, and looked eastward.

The awfulness of sudden death and the glory of heaven stunned me! The thing that had been mystery at twilight, lay clear, pure, open in the rosy hue of dawn. Out of the gates of the morning poured a light which glorified the palaces and pyramids, purged and purified the afternoon's inscrutable clefts, swept away the shadows of the mesas, and bathed that broad, deep world of mighty mountains, stately spars of rock, sculptured cathedrals and alabaster terraces in an artist's dream of color. A pearl from heaven had burst, flinging its heart of fire into this chasm. A stream of opal flowed out of the sun, to touch each peak, mesa, dome, parapet, temple and tower, cliff and cleft into the new-born life of another day.

I sat there for a long time and knew that every second the scene changed, yet I could not tell how. I knew I sat high over a hole of broken, splintered, barren mountains; I knew I could see a hundred miles of the length of it, and eighteen miles of the width of it, and a mile of the depth of it, and the shafts and rays of rose light on a million glancing, many-hued surfaces at once; but that knowledge was no help to me. I repeated a lot of meaningless superlatives to myself, and I found words inadequate and superfluous. The spectacle was too elusive and too great. It was life and death, heaven and hell.

I tried to call up former favorite views of mountain and sea, so as to compare them with this; but the memory pictures refused to come, even with my eyes closed. Then I returned to camp, with unsettled, troubled mind, and was silent, wondering at the strange feeling burning within me.

Jones talked about our visitor of the night before, and said the trail near where he had slept showed only one cougar track, and that led down into the canyon. It had surely been made, he thought, by the beast we had heard. Jones signified his intention of chaining several of the hounds for the next few nights at the head of this trail; so if the cougar came up, they would scent him and let us know. From which it was evident that to chase a lion bound into the canyon and one bound out were two different things.

The day passed lazily, with all of us resting on the warm, fragrant pine-needle beds, or mending a rent in a coat, or working on some camp task impossible of commission on exciting days.

About four o'clock, I took my little rifle and walked off through the woods in the direction of the carcass where I had seen the gray wolf. Thinking it best to make a wide detour, so as to face the wind, I circled till I felt the breeze was favorable to my enterprise, and then cautiously approached the hollow were the dead horse lay. Indian fashion, I slipped from tree to tree, a mode of forest travel not without its fascination and effectiveness, till I reached the height of a knoll beyond which I made sure was my objective point. On peeping out from behind the last pine, I found I had calculated pretty well, for there was the hollow, the big windfall, with its round, starfish-shaped roots exposed to the bright sun, and near that, the carcass. Sure enough, pulling hard at it, was the gray-white wolf I recognized as my "lofer."

But he presented an exceedingly difficult shot. Backing down the ridge, I ran a little way to come up behind another tree, from which I soon shifted to a fallen pine. Over this I peeped, to get a splendid view of the wolf. He had stopped tugging at the horse, and stood with his nose in the air. Surely he could not have scented me, for the wind was strong from him to me; neither could he have heard my soft footfalls on the pine needles; nevertheless, he was suspicious. Loth to spoil the picture he made, I risked a chance, and waited. Besides, though I prided myself on being able to take a fair aim, I had no great hope that I could hit him at such a distance. Presently he returned to his feeding, but not for long. Soon he raised his long, fine-pointed head, and trotted away a few yards, stopped to sniff again, then went back to his gruesome work.

At this juncture, I noiselessly projected my rifle barrel over the log. I had not, however, gotten the sights in line with him, when he trotted away reluctantly, and ascended the knoll on his side of the hollow. I lost him, and had just begun sourly to call myself a mollycoddle hunter, when he reappeared. He halted in an open glade, on the very crest of the knoll, and stood still as a statue wolf, a white, inspiriting target, against a dark green background. I could not stifle a rush of feeling, for I was a lover of the beautiful first, and a hunter secondly; but I steadied down as the front sight moved into the notch through which I saw the black and white of his shoulder.

Spang! How the little Remington sang! I watched closely, ready to send five more missiles after the gray beast. He jumped spasmodically, in a half-curve, high in the air, with loosely hanging head, then dropped in a heap. I yelled like a boy, ran down the hill, up the other side of the hollow, to find him stretched out dead, a small hole in his shoulder where the bullet had entered, a great one where it had come out.

The job I made of skinning him lacked some hundred degrees the perfection of my shot, but I accomplished it, and returned to camp in triumph.

"Shore I knowed you'd plunk him," said Jim very much pleased. "I shot one the other day same way, when he was feedin' off a dead horse. Now thet's a fine skin. Shore you cut through once or twice. But he's only half lofer, the other half in plain coyote. Thet accounts fer his feedin' on dead meat."

My naturalist host and my scientific friend both remarked somewhat grumpily that I seemed to get the best of all the good things. I might have retaliated that I certainly had gotten the worst of all the bad jokes; but, being generously happy over my prize, merely remarked: "If you want fame or wealth or wolves, go out and hunt for them."

Five o'clock supper left a good margin of day, in which my thoughts reverted to the canyon. I watched the purple shadows stealing out of their caverns and rolling up about the base of the mesas. Jones came over to where I stood, and I persuaded him to walk with me along the rim wall. Twilight had stealthily advanced when we reached the Singing Cliffs, and we did not go out upon my promontory, but chose a more comfortable one nearer the wall.

The night breeze had not sprung up yet, so the music of the cliffs was hushed.

"You cannot accept the theory of erosion to account for this chasm?" I asked my companion, referring to a former conversation.

"I can for this part of it. But what stumps me is the mountain range three thousand feet high, crossing the desert and the canyon just above where we crossed the river. How did the river cut through that without the help of a split or earthquake?"

"I'll admit that is a poser to me as well as to you. But I suppose Wallace could explain it as erosion. He claims this whole western country was once under water, except the tips of the Sierra Nevada mountains. There came an uplift of the earth's crust, and the great inland sea began to run out, presumably by way of the Colorado. In so doing it cut out the upper canyon, this gorge eighteen miles wide. Then came a second uplift, giving the river a much greater impetus toward the sea, which cut out the second, or marble canyon. Now as to the mountain range crossing the canyon at right angles. It must have come with the second uplift. If so, did it dam the river back into another inland sea, and then wear down into that red perpendicular gorge we remember so well? Or was there a great break in the fold of granite, which let the river continue on its way?

Or was there, at that particular point, a softer stone, like this limestone here, which erodes easily?"

"You must ask somebody wiser than I."

"Well, let's not perplex our minds with its origin. It is, and that's enough for any mind. Ah! listen! Now you will hear my Singing Cliffs."

From out of the darkening shadows murmurs rose on the softly rising wind. This strange music had a depressing influence; but it did not fill the heart with sorrow, only touched it lightly. And when, with the dying breeze, the song died away, it left the lonely crags lonelier for its death.

The last rosy gleam faded from the tip of Point Sublime; and as if that were a signal, in all the clefts and canyons below, purple, shadowy clouds marshaled their forces and began to sweep upon the battlements, to swing colossal wings into amphitheaters where gods might have warred, slowly to enclose the magical sentinels. Night intervened, and a moving, changing, silent chaos pulsated under the bright stars.

"How infinite all this is! How impossible to understand!" I exclaimed.

"To me it is very simple," replied my comrade. "The world is strange. But this canyon—why, we can see it all! I can't make out why people fuss so over it. I only feel peace. It's only bold and beautiful, serene and silent."

With the words of this quiet old plainsman, my sentimental passion shrank to the true appreciation of the scene. Self passed out to the recurring, soft strains of cliff song. I had been reveling in a species of indulgence, imagining I was a great lover of nature, building poetical illusions over storm-beaten peaks. The truth, told by one who had lived fifty years in the solitudes, among the rugged mountains, under the dark trees, and by the sides of the lonely streams, was the simple interpretation of a spirit in harmony with the bold, the beautiful, the serene, the silent.

He meant the Grand Canyon was only a mood of nature, a bold promise, a beautiful record. He meant that mountains had sifted away in its dust, yet the canyon was young. Man was nothing, so let him be humble. This cataclysm of the earth, this playground of a river was not inscrutable; it was only inevitable—as inevitable as nature herself. Millions of years in the bygone ages it had lain serene under a half moon; it would bask silent under a rayless sun, in the onward edge of time.

It taught simplicity, serenity, peace. The eye that saw only the strife, the war, the decay, the ruin, or only the glory and the tragedy, saw not all the truth. It spoke simply, though its words were grand: "My spirit is the Spirit of Time, of Eternity, of God. Man is little, vain, vaunting. Listen. To-morrow he shall be gone. Peace! Peace!"

CHAPTER 14.

ALL HEROES BUT ONE

As we rode up the slope of Buckskin, the sunrise glinted red-gold through the aisles of frosted pines, giving us a hunter's glad greeting.

With all due respect to, and appreciation of, the breaks of the Siwash, we unanimously decided that if cougars inhabited any other section of canyon country, we preferred it, and were going to find it. We had often speculated on the appearance of the rim wall directly across the neck of the canyon upon which we were located. It showed a long stretch of breaks, fissures, caves, yellow crags, crumbled ruins and clefts green with pinyon pine. As a crow flies, it was only a mile or two straight across from camp, but to reach it, we had to ascend the mountain and head the canyon which deeply indented the slope.

A thousand feet or more above the level bench, the character of the forest changed; the pines grew thicker, and interspersed among them were silver spruces and balsams. Here in the clumps of small trees and underbrush, we began to jump deer, and in a few moments a greater number than I had ever seen in all my hunting experiences loped within range of my eye. I could not look out into the forest where an aisle or lane or glade stretched to any distance, without seeing a big gray deer cross it. Jones said the herds had recently come up from the breaks, where they had wintered. These deer were twice the size of the Eastern species, and as fat as well-fed cattle. They were almost as tame, too. A big herd ran out of one glade, leaving behind several curious does, which watched us intently for a moment, then bounded off with the stiff, springy bounce that so amused me.

Sounder crossed fresh trails one after another; Jude, Tige and Ranger followed him, but hesitated often, barked and whined; Don started off once, to come sneaking back at Jones's stern call. But surly old Moze either would not or could not obey, and away he dashed. Bang! Jones sent a charge of fine shot after him. He yelped, doubled up as if stung, and returned as quickly as he had gone.

"Hyar, you white and black coon dog," said Jones, "get in behind, and stay there."

We turned to the right after a while and got among shallow ravines. Gigantic pines grew on the ridges and in the hollows, and everywhere bluebells shone blue from the white frost. Why the frost did not kill these beautiful flowers was a mystery to me. The horses could not step without crushing them.

Before long, the ravines became so deep that we had to zigzag up and down their sides, and to force our horses through the aspen thickets in the hollows. Once from a ridge I saw a troop of deer, and stopped to watch them. Twenty-seven I counted outright, but there must have been three times that number. I saw the herd break across a glade, and watched them until they were lost in the forest. My companions having disappeared, I pushed on, and while working out of a wide, deep hollow, I noticed the sunny patches fade from the bright slopes, and the golden streaks vanish among the pines. The sky had become overcast, and the forest was darkening. The

"Waa-hoo," I cried out returned in echo only. The wind blew hard in my face, and the pines began to bend and roar. An immense black cloud enveloped Buckskin.

Satan had carried me no farther than the next ridge, when the forest frowned dark as twilight, and on the wind whirled flakes of snow. Over the next hollow, a white pall roared through the trees toward me. Hardly had I time to get the direction of the trail, and its relation to the trees nearby, when the storm enfolded me. Of his own accord Satan stopped in the lee of a bushy spruce. The roar in the pines equaled that of the cave under Niagara, and the bewildering, whirling mass of snow was as difficult to see through as the tumbling, seething waterfall.

I was confronted by the possibility of passing the night there, and calming my fears as best I could, hastily felt for my matches and knife. The prospect of being lost the next day in a white forest was also appalling, but I soon reassured myself that the storm was only a snow squall, and would not last long. Then I gave myself up to the pleasure and beauty of it. I could only faintly discern the dim trees; the limbs of the spruce, which partially protected me, sagged down to my head with their burden; I had but to reach out my hand for a snowball. Both the wind and snow seemed warm. The great flakes were like swan feathers on a summer breeze. There was something joyous in the whirl of snow and roar of wind. While I bent over to shake my holster, the storm passed as suddenly as it had come. When I looked up, there were the pines, like pillars of Parian marble, and a white shadow, a vanishing cloud fled, with receding roar, on the wings of the wind. Fast on this retreat burst the warm, bright sun.

I faced my course, and was delighted to see, through an opening where the ravine cut out of the forest, the red-tipped peaks of the canyon, and the vaulted dome I had named St. Marks. As I started, a new and unexpected after-feature of the storm began to manifest itself. The sun being warm, even to melt the snow, and under the trees a heavy rain fell, and in the glades and hollows a fine mist blew. Exquisite rainbows hung from white-tipped branches and curved over the hollows. Glistening patches of snow fell from the pines, and broke the showers.

In a quarter of an hour, I rode out of the forest to the rim wall on dry ground. Against the green pinyons Frank's white horse stood out conspicuously, and near him browsed the mounts of Jim and Wallace. The boys were not in evidence. Concluding they had gone down over the rim, I dismounted and kicked off my chaps, and taking my rifle and camera, hurried to look the place over.

To my surprise and interest, I found a long section of rim wall in ruins. It lay in a great curve between the two giant capes; and many short, sharp, projecting promontories, like the teeth of a saw, overhung the canyon. The slopes between these points of cliff were covered with a deep growth of pinyon, and in these places descent would be easy. Everywhere in the corrugated wall were rents and rifts; cliffs stood detached like islands near a shore; yellow crags rose out of green clefts; jumble of rocks, and slides of rim wall, broken into blocks, massed under the promontories.

The singular raggedness and wildness of the scene took hold of me, and was not dispelled until the baying of Sounder and Don roused action in me. Apparently the hounds were widely separated. Then I heard Jim's yell. But it ceased when the wind lulled, and I heard it no more. Running back from the point, I began to go down. The way was steep, almost perpendicular; but because of the great stones and the absence of slides, was easy. I took long strides and jumps, and slid over rocks, and swung on pinyon branches, and covered distance like a rolling stone. At the foot of the rim wall, or at a line where it would have reached had it extended regularly, the slope became less pronounced. I could stand up without holding on to a support. The largest pinyons I had seen made a forest that almost stood on end. These trees grew up, down, and out, and twisted in curves, and many were two feet in thickness. During my descent, I halted at intervals to listen, and always heard one of the hounds, sometimes several. But as I descended for a long time, and did not get anywhere or approach the dogs, I began to grow impatient.

A large pinyon, with a dead top, suggested a good outlook, so I climbed it, and saw I could sweep a large section of the slope. It was a strange thing to look down hill, over the tips of green trees. Below, perhaps four hundred yards, was a slide open for a long way; all the rest was green incline, with many dead branches sticking up like spars, and an occasional crag. From this perch I heard the hounds; then followed a yell I thought was Jim's, and after it the bellowing of Wallace's rifle. Then all was silent. The shots had effectually checked the yelping of the hounds. I let out a yell. Another cougar that Jones would not lasso! All at once I heard a familiar sliding of small rocks below me, and I watched the open slope with greedy eyes.

Not a bit surprised was I to see a cougar break out of the green, and go tearing down the slide. In less than six seconds, I had sent six steel-jacketed bullets after him. Puffs of dust rose closer and closer to him as each bullet went nearer the mark and the last showered him with gravel and turned him straight down the canyon slope.

I slid down the dead pinyon and jumped nearly twenty feet to the soft sand below, and after putting a loaded clip in my rifle, began kangaroo leaps down the slope. When I reached the point where the cougar had entered the slide, I called the hounds, but they did not come nor answer me. Notwithstanding my excitement, I appreciated the distance to the bottom of the slope before I reached it. In my haste, I ran upon the verge of a precipice twice as deep as the first rim wall, but one glance down sent me shatteringly backward.

With all the breath I had left I yelled: "Waa-hoo! Waa-hoo!" From the echoes flung at me, I imagined at first that my friends were right on my ears. But no real answer came. The cougar had probably passed along this second rim wall to a break, and had gone down. His trail could easily be taken by any of the hounds. Vexed and anxious, I signaled again and again. Once, long after the echo had gone to sleep in some hollow canyon, I caught a faint "Wa-a-ho-o-o!" But it might have come from the clouds. I did not hear a hound barking above me on the slope; but suddenly, to my amazement, Sounder's deep bay rose from the abyss below. I ran along the rim, called till I was hoarse, leaned over so far that the blood rushed to my head, and then sat down. I concluded this canyon hunting could bear some sustained attention and thought, as well as frenzied action.

Examination of my position showed how impossible it was to arrive at any clear idea of the depth or size, or condition of the canyon slopes from the main rim wall above. The second wall—a stupendous, yellow-faced cliff two thousand feet high—curved to my left round to a point in front of me. The intervening canyon might have been a half mile wide, and it might have been ten miles. I had become disgusted with judging distance. The slope above this second wall facing me ran up far above my head; it fairly towered, and this routed all my former judgments, because I remembered distinctly that from the rim this yellow and green mountain had appeared an insignificant little ridge. But it was when I turned to gaze up behind me that I fully grasped the immensity of the place. This wall and slope were the first two steps down the long stairway of the Grand Canyon, and they towered over me, straight up a half-mile in dizzy height. To think of climbing it took my breath away.

Then again Sounder's bay floated distinctly to me, but it seemed to come from a different point. I turned my ear to the wind, and in the succeeding moments I was more and more baffled. One bay sounded from below and next from far to the right; another from the left. I could not distinguish voice from echo. The acoustic properties of the amphitheater beneath me were too wonderful for my comprehension.

As the bay grew sharper, and correspondingly more significant, I became distracted, and focused a strained vision on the canyon deeps. I looked along the slope to the notch where the wall curved and followed the base line of the yellow cliff. Quite suddenly I saw a very small black object moving with snail-like slowness. Although it seemed impossible for Sounder to be so small, I knew it was he. Having something now to judge distance from, I conceived it to be a mile, without the drop. If I could hear Sounder, he could hear me, so I yelled encouragement. The echoes clapped back at me like so many slaps in the face. I watched the hound until he disappeared among broken heaps of stone, and long after that his bay floated to me.

Having rested, I essayed the discovery of some of my lost companions or the hounds, and began to climb. Before I started, however, I was wise enough to study the rim wall above, to familiarize myself with the break so I would have a landmark. Like horns and spurs of gold the pinnacles loomed up. Massed closely together, they were not unlike an astounding pipe-organ. I had a feeling of my littleness, that I was lost, and should devote every moment and effort to the saving of my life. It did not seem possible I could be hunting. Though I climbed diagonally, and rested often, my heart pumped so hard I could hear it. A yellow crag, with a round head like an old man's cane, appealed to me as near the place where I last heard from Jim, and toward it I labored. Every time I glanced up, the distance seemed the same. A climb which I decided would not take more than fifteen minutes, required an hour.

While resting at the foot of the crag, I heard more baying of hounds, but for my life I could not tell whether the sound came from up or down, and I commenced to feel that I did not much care. Having signaled till I was hoarse, and receiving none but mock answers, I decided that if my companions had not toppled over a cliff, they were wisely withholding their breath.

Another stiff pull up the slope brought me under the rim wall, and there I groaned, because the wall was smooth and shiny, without a break. I plodded slowly along the base, with my rifle ready. Cougar tracks were so numerous I got tired of looking at them, but I did not forget that I might meet a tawny fellow or two among those narrow passes of shattered rock, and under the thick, dark pinyons. Going on in this way, I ran point-blank into a pile of bleached bones before a cave. I had stumbled on the lair of a lion and from the looks of it one like that of Old Tom. I flinched twice before I threw a stone into the dark-mouthed cave. What impressed me as soon as I found I was in no danger of being pawed and clawed round the gloomy spot, was the fact of the bones being there. How did they come on a slope where a man could hardly walk? Only one answer seemed feasible. The lion had made his kill one thousand feet above, had pulled his quarry to the rim and pushed it over. In view of the theory that he might have had to drag his victim from the forest, and that very seldom two lions worked together, the fact of the location of the bones as startling. Skulls of wild horses and deer, antlers and countless bones, all crushed into shapelessness, furnished indubitable proof that the carcasses had fallen from a great height.

Most remarkable of all was the skeleton of a cougar lying across that of a horse. I believed—I could not help but believe that the cougar had fallen with his last victim.

Not many rods beyond the lion den, the rim wall split into towers, crags and pinnacles. I thought I had found my pipe organ, and began to climb toward a narrow opening in the rim. But I lost it. The extraordinarily cut-up condition of the wall made holding to one direction impossible. Soon I realized I was lost in a labyrinth. I tried to find my way down again, but the best I could do was to reach the verge of a cliff, from which I could see the canyon. Then I knew where I was, yet I did not know, so I plodded wearily back. Many a blind cleft did I ascend in the maze of crags. I could hardly crawl along, still I kept at it, for the place was conducive to dire thoughts. A tower of Babel menaced me with tons of loose shale. A tower that leaned more frightfully than the Tower of Pisa threatened to build my tomb. Many a lighthouse-shaped crag sent down little scattering rocks in ominous notice.

After toiling in and out of passageways under the shadows of these strangely formed cliffs, and coming again and again to the same point, a blind pocket, I grew desperate. I named the baffling place Deception Pass, and then ran down a slide. I knew if I could keep my feet I could beat the avalanche. More by good luck than management I outran the roaring stones and landed safely. Then rounding the cliff below, I found myself on a narrow ledge, with a wall to my left, and to the right the tips of pinyon trees level with my feet.

Innocently and wearily I passed round a pillar-like corner of wall, to come face to face with an old lioness and cubs. I heard the mother snarl, and at the same time her ears went back flat, and she crouched. The same fire of yellow eyes, the same grim snarling expression so familiar in my mind since Old Tom had leaped at me, faced me here.

My recent vow of extermination was entirely forgotten and one frantic spring carried me over the ledge.

Crash! I felt the brushing and scratching of branches, and saw a green blur. I went down straddling limbs and hit the ground with a thump. Fortunately, I landed mostly on my feet, in sand, and suffered no serious bruise. But I was stunned, and my right arm was numb for a moment. When I gathered myself together, instead of being grateful the ledge had not been on the face of Point Sublime—from which I would most assuredly have leaped—I was the angriest man ever let loose in the Grand Canyon.

Of course the cougars were far on their way by that time, and were telling neighbors about the brave hunter's leap for life; so I devoted myself to further efforts to find an outlet. The niche I had jumped into opened below, as did most of the breaks, and I worked out of it to the base of the rim wall, and tramped a long, long mile before I reached my own trail leading down. Resting every five steps, I climbed and climbed. My rifle grew to weigh a ton; my feet were lead; the camera strapped to my shoulder was the world. Soon climbing meant trapeze work—long reach of arm, and pull of weight, high step of foot, and spring of body. Where I had slid down with ease, I had to strain and raise myself by sheer muscle. I wore my left glove to tatters and threw it away to put the right one on my left hand. I thought many times I could not make another move; I thought my lungs would burst, but I kept on. When at last I surmounted the rim, I saw Jones, and flopped down beside him, and lay panting, dripping, boiling, with scorched feet, aching limbs and numb chest.

"I've been here two hours," he said, "and I knew things were happening below; but to climb up that slide would kill me. I am not young any more, and a steep climb like this takes a young heart. As it was I had enough work. Look!" He called my attention to his trousers. They had been cut to shreds, and the right trouser leg was missing from the knee down. His shin was bloody. "Moze took a lion along the rim, and I went after him with all my horse could do. I yelled for the boys, but they didn't come. Right here it is easy to go down, but below, where Moze started this lion, it was impossible to get over the rim. The lion lit straight out of the pinyons. I lost ground because of the thick brush and numerous trees. Then Moze doesn't bark often enough. He treed the lion twice. I could tell by the way he opened up and bayed. The rascal coon-dog climbed the trees and chased the lion out. That's what Moze did! I got to an open space and saw him, and was coming up fine when he went down over a hollow which ran into the canyon. My horse tripped and fell, turning clear over with me before he threw me into the brush. I tore my clothes, and got this bruise, but wasn't much hurt. My horse is pretty lame."

I began a recital of my experience, modestly omitting the incident where I bravely faced an old lioness. Upon consulting my watch, I found I had been almost four hours climbing out. At that moment, Frank poked a red face over the rim. He was in shirt sleeves, sweating freely, and wore a frown I had never seen before. He puffed like a porpoise, and at first could hardly speak.

"Where were—you—all?" he panted. "Say! but mebbe this hasn't been a chase! Jim and Wallace an' me went tumblin' down after the dogs, each one lookin' out for his perticilar dog, an' darn me if I don't believe his lion, too. Don took one oozin' down the canyon, with me hot-footin' it after him. An' somewhere he treed thet lion, right below me, in a box canyon, sort of an offshoot of the second rim, an' I couldn't locate him. I blamed near killed myself more'n once. Look at my knuckles! Barked em slidin' about a mile down a smooth wall. I thought once the lion had jumped Don, but soon I heard him barkin' again. All thet time I heard Sounder, an' once I heard the pup. Jim yelled, an' somebody was shootin'. But I couldn't find nobody, or make nobody hear me. Thet canyon is a mighty deceivin' place. You'd never think so till you go down. I wouldn't climb up it again for all the lions in Buckskin. Hello, there comes Jim oozin' up."

Jim appeared just over the rim, and when he got up to us, dusty, torn and fagged out, with Don, Tige and Ranger showing signs of collapse, we all blurted out questions. But Jim took his time.

"Shore thet canyon is one hell of a place," he began finally. "Where was everybody? Tige and the pup went down with me an' treed a cougar. Yes, they did, an' I set under a pinyon holdin' the pup, while Tige kept the cougar treed. I yelled an' yelled. After about an hour or two, Wallace came poundin' down like a giant. It was a sure thing we'd get the cougar; an' Wallace was takin' his picture when the blamed cat jumped. It was embarrassin', because he wasn't polite about how he jumped. We scattered some, an' when Wallace got his gun, the cougar was humpin' down the slope, an' he was goin' so fast an' the pinyons was so thick thet Wallace couldn't get a fair shot, an' missed. Tige an' the pup was so scared by the shots they wouldn't take the trail again. I heard some one shoot about a million times, an' shore thought the cougar was done for. Wallace went plungin' down the slope an' I followed. I couldn't keep up with him—he shore takes long steps— an' I lost him. I'm reckonin' he went over the second wall. Then I made tracks for the top. Boys, the way you can see an' hear things down in thet canyon, an' the way you can't hear an' see things is pretty funny."

"If Wallace went over the second rim wall, will he get back to-day?" we all asked.

"Shore, there's no tellin'."

We waited, lounged, and slept for three hours, and were beginning to worry about our comrade when he hove in sight eastward, along the rim. He walked like a man whose next step would be his last. When he reached us, he fell flat, and lay breathing heavily for a while.

"Somebody once mentioned Israel Putnam's ascent of a hill," he said slowly. "With all respect to history and a patriot, I wish to say Putnam never saw a hill!"

"Ooze for camp," called out Frank.

Five o'clock found us round a bright fire, all casting ravenous eyes at a smoking supper. The smell of the Persian meat would have made a wolf of a vegetarian. I devoured four chops, and could not have been counted in the running. Jim opened a can of maple syrup which he had been saving for a grand occasion, and Frank went him one better with two cans of peaches. How glorious to be hungry—to feel the craving for food, and to be grateful for it, to realize that the best of life lies in the daily needs of existence, and to battle for them!

Nothing could be stronger than the simple enumeration and statement of the facts of Wallace's experience after he left Jim. He chased the cougar, and kept it in sight, until it went over the second rim wall. Here he dropped over a precipice twenty feet high, to alight on a fan-shaped slide which spread toward the bottom. It began to slip and move by jerks, and then started off steadily, with an increasing roar. He rode an avalanche for one thousand feet. The jar loosened bowlders from the walls. When the slide stopped, Wallace extricated his feet and began to dodge the bowlders. He had only time to jump over the large ones or dart to one side out of their way. He dared not run. He had to watch them coming. One huge stone hurtled over his head and smashed a pinyon tree below.

When these had ceased rolling, and he had passed down to the red shale, he heard Sounder baying near, and knew a cougar had been treed or cornered. Hurdling the stones and dead pinyons, Wallace ran a mile down the slope, only to find he had been deceived in the direction. He sheered off to the left. Sounder's illusive bay came up from a deep cleft. Wallace plunged into a pinyon, climbed to the ground, skidded down a solid slide, to come upon an impassable the obstacle in the form of a solid wall of red granite. Sounder appeared and came to him, evidently having given up the chase.

Wallace consumed four hours in making the ascent. In the notch of the curve of the second rim wall, he climbed the slippery steps of a waterfall. At one point, if he had not been six feet five inches tall he would have been compelled to attempt retracing his trail—an impossible task. But his height enabled him to reach a root, by which he pulled himself up. Sounder he lassoed a la Jones, and hauled up. At another spot, which Sounder climbed, he lassoed a pinyon above, and walked up with his feet slipping from under him at every step. The knees of his corduroy trousers were holes, as were the elbows of his coat. The sole of his left boot, which he used most in climbing—was gone, and so was his hat.

CHAPTER 15.

JONES ON COUGARS

The mountain lion, or cougar, of our Rocky Mountain region, is nothing more nor less than the panther. He is a little different in shape, color and size, which vary according to his environment. The panther of the Rockies is usually light, taking the grayish hue of the rocks. He is stockier and heavier of build, and stronger of limb than the Eastern species, which difference comes from climbing mountains and springing down the cliffs after his prey.

In regions accessible to man, or where man is encountered even rarely, the cougar is exceedingly shy, seldom or never venturing from cover during the day. He spends the hours of daylight high on the most rugged cliffs, sleeping and basking in the sunshine, and watching with wonderfully keen sight the valleys below. His hearing equals his sight, and if danger threatens, he always hears it in time to skulk away unseen. At night he steals down the mountain side toward deer or elk he has located during the day. Keeping to the lowest ravines and thickets, he creeps upon his prey. His cunning and ferocity are keener and more savage in proportion to the length of time he has been without food. As he grows hungrier and thinner, his skill and fierce strategy correspondingly increase. A well-fed cougar will creep upon and secure only about one in seven of the deer, elk, antelope or mountain sheep that he stalks. But a starving cougar is another animal. He creeps like a snake, is as sure on the scent as a vulture, makes no more noise than a shadow, and he hides behind a stone or bush that would scarcely conceal a rabbit. Then he springs with terrific force, and intensity of purpose, and seldom fails to reach his victim, and once the claws of a starved lion touch flesh, they never let go.

A cougar seldom pursues his quarry after he has leaped and missed, either from disgust or failure, or knowledge that a second attempt would be futile. The animal making the easiest prey for the cougar is the elk. About every other elk attacked falls a victim. Deer are more fortunate, the ratio being one dead to five leaped at. The antelope, living on the lowlands or upland meadows, escapes nine times out of ten; and the mountain sheep, or bighorn, seldom falls to the onslaught of his enemy.

Once the lion gets a hold with the great forepaw, every movement of the struggling prey sinks the sharp, hooked claws deeper. Then as quickly as is possible, the lion fastens his teeth in the throat of his prey and grips till it is dead. In this way elk have carried lions for many rods. The lion seldom tears the skin of the neck, and never, as is generally supposed, sucks the blood of its victim; but he cuts into the side, just behind the foreshoulder, and eats the liver first. He rolls the skin back as neatly and tightly as a person could do it. When he has gorged himself, he drags the carcass into a ravine or dense thicket, and rakes leaves, sticks or dirt over it to hide it from other animals. Usually he returns to his cache on the second night, and after that the frequency of his visits depends on the supply of fresh prey. In remote regions, unfrequented by man, the lion will guard his cache from coyote and buzzards.

In sex there are about five female lions to one male. This is caused by the jealous and vicious disposition of the male. It is a fact that the old Toms kill every young lion they can catch. Both male and female of the litter suffer alike until after weaning time, and then only the males. In this matter wise animal logic is displayed by the Toms. The domestic cat, to some extent, possesses the same trait. If the litter is destroyed, the mating time is sure to come about regardless of the season. Thus this savage trait of the lions prevents overproduction, and breeds a hardy and intrepid race. If by chance or that cardinal feature of animal life—the survival of the fittest—a young male lion escapes to the weaning time, even after that he is persecuted. Young male lions have been killed and found to have had their flesh beaten until it was a mass of bruises and undoubtedly it had been the work of an old Tom. Moreover, old males and females have been killed, and found to be in the same bruised condition. A feature, and a conclusive one, is the fact that invariably the female is suckling her young at this period, and sustains the bruises in desperately defending her litter.

It is astonishing how cunning, wise and faithful an old lioness is. She seldom leaves her kittens. From the time they are six weeks old she takes them out to train them for the battles of life, and the struggle continues from birth to death. A lion hardly ever dies naturally. As soon as night descends, the lioness stealthily stalks forth, and because of her little ones, takes very short steps. The cubs follow, stepping in their mother's tracks. When she crouches for game, each little lion crouches also, and each one remains perfectly still until she springs, or signals them to come. If she secures the prey, they all gorge themselves. After the feast the mother takes her back trail, stepping in the tracks she made coming down the mountain. And the cubs are very careful to follow suit, and not to leave marks of their trail in the soft snow. No doubt this habit is practiced to keep their deadly enemies in ignorance of their existence. The old Toms and white hunters are their only foes. Indians never kill a lion. This trick of the lions has fooled many a hunter, concerning not only the direction, but particularly the number.

The only successful way to hunt lions is with trained dogs. A good hound can trail them for several hours after the tracks have been made, and on a cloudy or wet day can hold the scent much longer. In snow the hound can trail for three or four days after the track has been made.

When Jones was game warden of the Yellowstone National Park, he had unexampled opportunities to hunt cougars and learn their habits. All the cougars in that region of the Rockies made a rendezvous of the game preserve. Jones soon procured a pack of hounds, but as they had been trained to run deer, foxes and coyotes he had great trouble. They would break on the trail of these animals, and also on elk and antelope just when this was farthest from his wish. He soon realized that to train the hounds was a sore task. When they refused to come back at his call, he stung them with fine shot, and in this manner taught obedience. But obedience was not enough; the hounds must know how to follow and tree a lion. With this in mind, Jones decided to catch a lion alive and give his dogs practical lessons.

A few days after reaching this decision, he discovered the tracks of two lions in the neighborhood of Mt. Everett. The hounds were put on the trail and followed it into an abandoned coal shaft. Jones recognized this as his opportunity, and taking his lasso and an extra rope, he crawled into the hole. Not fifteen feet from the opening sat one of the cougars, snarling and spitting. Jones promptly lassoed it, passed his end of the lasso round a side prop of the shaft, and out to the soldiers who had followed him. Instructing them not to pull till he called, he cautiously began to crawl by the cougar, with the intention of getting farther back and roping its hind leg, so as to prevent disaster when the soldiers pulled it out. He accomplished this, not without some uneasiness in regard to the second lion, and giving the word to his companions, soon had his captive hauled from the shaft and tied so tightly it could not move.

Jones took the cougar and his hounds to an open place in the park, where there were trees, and prepared for a chase. Loosing the lion, he held his hounds back a moment, then let them go. Within one hundred yards the cougar climbed a tree, and the dogs saw the performance. Taking a forked stick, Jones mounted up to the cougar, caught it under the jaw with the stick, and pushed it out. There was a fight, a scramble, and the cougar dashed off to run up another tree. In this manner, he soon trained his hounds to the pink of perfection.

Jones discovered, while in the park, that the cougar is king of all the beasts of North America. Even a grizzly dashed away in great haste when a cougar made his appearance. At the road camp, near Mt. Washburn, during the fall of 1904, the bears, grizzlies and others, were always hanging round the cook tent. There were cougars also, and almost every evening, about dusk, a big fellow would come parading past the tent. The bears would grunt furiously and scamper in every direction. It was easy to tell when a cougar was in the neighborhood, by the peculiar grunts and snorts of the bears, and the sharp, distinct, alarmed yelps of coyotes. A lion would just as lief kill a coyote as any other animal and he would devour it, too. As to the fighting of cougars and grizzlies, that was a mooted question, with the credit on the side of the former.

The story of the doings of cougars, as told in the snow, was intensely fascinating and tragic! How they stalked deer and elk, crept to within springing distance, then crouched flat to leap, was as easy to read as if it had been told in print. The leaps and bounds were beyond belief. The longest leap on a level measured eighteen and one-half feet. Jones trailed a half-grown cougar, which in turn was trailing a big elk. He found where the cougar had struck his game, had clung for many rods, to be dashed off by the low limb of a spruce tree. The imprint of the body of the cougar was a foot deep in the snow; blood and tufts of hair covered the place. But there was no sign of the cougar renewing the chase.

In rare cases cougars would refuse to run, or take to trees. One day Jones followed the hounds, eight in number, to come on a huge Tom holding the whole pack at bay. He walked to and fro, lashing his tail from side to side, and when Jones dashed up, he coolly climbed a tree. Jones shot the cougar, which, in falling, struck one of the hounds, crippling him. This hound would never approach a tree after this incident, believing probably that the cougar had sprung upon him.

Usually the hounds chased their quarry into a tree long before Jones rode up. It was always desirable to kill the animal with the first shot. If the cougar was wounded, and fell or jumped among the dogs, there was sure to be a terrible fight, and the best dogs always received serious injuries, if they were not killed outright. The lion would seize a hound, pull him close, and bite him in the brain.

Jones asserted that a cougar would usually run from a hunter, but that this feature was not to be relied upon. And a wounded cougar was as dangerous as a tiger. In his hunts Jones carried a shotgun, and shells loaded with ball for the cougar, and others loaded with fine shot for the hounds. One day, about ten miles from the camp, the hounds took a trail and ran rapidly, as there were only a few inches of snow. Jones found a large lion had taken refuge in a tree that had fallen against another, and aiming at the shoulder of the beast, he fired both barrels. The cougar made no sign he had been hit. Jones reloaded and fired at the head. The old fellow growled fiercely, turned in the tree and walked down head first, something he would not have been able to do had the tree been upright. The hounds were ready for him, but wisely attacked in the rear. Realizing he had been shooting fine shot at the animal, Jones began a hurried search for a shell loaded with ball. The lion made for him, compelling him to dodge behind trees. Even though the hounds kept nipping the cougar, the persistent fellow still pursued the hunter. At last Jones found the right shell, just as the cougar reached for him. Major, the leader of the hounds, darted bravely in, and grasped the leg of the beast just in the nick of time. This enabled Jones to take aim and fire at close range, which ended the fight. Upon examination, it was discovered the cougar had been half-blinded by the fine shot, which accounted for the ineffectual attempts he had made to catch Jones.

The mountain lion rarely attacks a human being for the purpose of eating. When hungry he will often follow the tracks of people, and under favorable circumstances may ambush them. In the park where game is plentiful, no one has ever known a cougar to follow the trail of a person; but outside the park lions have been known to follow hunters, and particularly stalk little children. The Davis family, living a few miles north of the park, have had children pursued to the very doors of their cabin. And other families relate similar experiences. Jones heard of only one fatality, but he believes that if the children were left alone in the woods, the cougars would creep closer and closer, and when assured there was no danger, would spring to kill.

Jones never heard the cry of a cougar in the National Park, which strange circumstance, considering the great number of the animals there, he believed to be on account of the abundance of game. But he had heard it when a boy in Illinois, and when a man all over the West, and the cry was always the same, weird and wild, like the scream of a terrified woman. He did not understand the significance of the cry, unless it meant hunger, or the wailing mourn of a lioness for her murdered cubs.

The destructiveness of this savage species was murderous. Jones came upon one old Tom's den, where there was a pile of nineteen elk, mostly yearlings. Only five or six had been eaten. Jones hunted this old fellow for months, and found that the lion killed on the average three animals a week. The hounds got him up at length, and chased him to the Yellowstone River, which he swam at a point impassable for man or horse. One of the dogs, a giant bloodhound named Jack, swam the swift channel, kept on after the lion, but never returned. All cougars have their peculiar traits and habits, the same as other creatures, and all old Toms have strongly marked characteristics, but this one was the most destructive cougar Jones ever knew.

During Jones's short sojourn as warden in the park, he captured numerous cougars alive, and killed seventy-two.

CHAPTER 16.

KITTY

It seemed my eyelids had scarcely touched when Jones's exasperating, yet stimulating, yell aroused me. Day was breaking. The moon and stars shone with wan luster. A white, snowy frost silvered the forest. Old Moze had curled close beside me, and now he gazed at me reproachfully and shivered. Lawson came hustling in with the horses. Jim busied himself around the campfire. My fingers nearly froze while I saddled my horse.

At five o'clock we were trotting up the slope of Buckskin, bound for the section of ruined rim wall where we had encountered the convention of cougars. Hoping to save time, we took a short cut, and were soon crossing deep ravines.

The sunrise coloring the purple curtain of cloud over the canyon was too much for me, and I lagged on a high ridge to watch it, thus falling behind my more practical companions. A far-off "Waa-hoo!" brought me to a realization of the day's stern duty and I hurried Satan forward on the trail.

I came suddenly upon our leader, leading his horse through the scrub pinyon on the edge of the canyon, and I knew at once something had happened, for he was closely scrutinizing the ground.

"I declare this beats me all hollow!" began Jones. "We might be hunting rabbits instead of the wildest animals on the continent. We jumped a bunch of lions in this clump of pinyon. There must have been at least four. I thought first we'd run upon an old lioness with cubs, but all the trails were made by full-grown lions. Moze took one north along the rim, same as the other day, but the lion got away quick. Frank saw one lion. Wallace is following Sounder down into the first hollow. Jim has gone over the rim wall after Don. There you are! Four lions playing tag in broad daylight on top of this wall! I'm inclined to believe Clarke didn't exaggerate. But confound the luck! the hounds have split again. They're doing their best, of course, and it's up to us to stay with them. I'm afraid we'll lose some of them. Hello! I hear a signal. That's from Wallace. Waa-hoo! Waa-hoo! There he is, coming out of the hollow."

The tall Californian reached us presently with Sounder beside him. He reported that the hound had chased a lion into an impassable break. We then joined Frank on a jutting crag of the canyon wall.

"Waa-hoo!" yelled Jones. There was no answer except the echo, and it rolled up out of the chasm with strange, hollow mockery.

"Don took a cougar down this slide," said Frank. "I saw the brute, an' Don was makin' him hump. A—ha! There! Listen to thet!"

From the green and yellow depths soared the faint yelp of a hound.

"That's Don! that's Don!" cried Jones. "He's hot on something. Where's Sounder? Hyar, Sounder! By George! there he goes down the slide. Hear him! He's opened up! Hi! Hi! Hi!"

The deep, full mellow bay of the hound came ringing on the clear air.

"Wallace, you go down. Frank and I will climb out on that pointed crag. Grey, you stay here. Then we'll have the slide between us. Listen and watch!"

From my promontory I watched Wallace go down with his gigantic strides, sending the rocks rolling and cracking; and then I saw Jones and Frank crawl out to the end of a crumbling ruin of yellow wall which threatened to go splintering and thundering down into the abyss.

I thought, as I listened to the penetrating voice of the hound, that nowhere on earth could there be a grander scene for wild action, wild life. My position afforded a commanding view over a hundred miles of the noblest and most sublime work of nature. The rim wall where I stood sheered down a thousand feet, to meet a long wooded slope which cut abruptly off into another giant precipice; a second long slope descended, and jumped off into what seemed the grave of the world. Most striking in that vast void were the long, irregular points of rim wall, protruding into the Grand Canyon. From Point Sublime to the Pink Cliffs of Utah there were twelve of these colossal capes, miles apart, some sharp, some round, some blunt, all rugged and bold. The great chasm in the middle was full of purple smoke. It seemed a mighty sepulcher from which misty fumes rolled upward. The turrets, mesas, domes, parapets and escarpments of yellow and red rock gave the appearance of an architectural work of giant hands. The wonderful river of silt, the blood-red, mystic and sullen Rio Colorado, lay hidden except in one place far away, where it glimmered wanly. Thousands of colors were blended before my rapt gaze. Yellow predominated, as the walls and crags lorded it over the lower cliffs and tables; red glared in the sunlight; green softened these two, and then purple and violet, gray, blue and the darker hues shaded away into dim and distinct obscurity.

Excited yells from my companions on the other crag recalled me to the living aspect of the scene. Jones was leaning far down in a niche, at seeming great hazard of life, yelling with all the power of his strong lungs. Frank stood still farther out on a cracked point that made me tremble, and his yell reenforced Jones's. From far below rolled up a chorus of thrilling bays and yelps, and Jim's call, faint, but distinct on that wonderfully thin air, with its unmistakable note of warning.

Then on the slide I saw a lion headed for the rim wall and climbing fast. I added my exultant cry to the medley, and I stretched my arms wide to that illimitable void and gloried in a moment full to the brim of the tingling joy of existence. I did not consider how painful it must have been to the toiling lion. It was only the spell of wild environment, of perilous yellow crags, of thin, dry air, of voice of man and dog, of the stinging expectation of sharp action, of life.

I watched the lion growing bigger and bigger. I saw Don and Sounder run from the pinyon into the open slide, and heard their impetuous burst of wild yelps as they saw their game. Then Jones's clarion yell made me bound for my horse. I reached him, was about to mount, when Moze came trotting toward me. I caught the old gladiator. When he heard the chorus from below, he plunged like a mad bull. With both arms round him I held on. I vowed never to let him get down that slide. He howled and tore, but I held on. My big black horse with ears laid back stood like a rock.

I heard the pattering of little sliding rocks below; stealthy padded footsteps and hard panting breaths, almost like coughs; then the lion passed out of the slide not twenty feet away. He saw us, and sprang into the pinyon scrub with the leap of a scared deer.

Samson himself could no longer have held Moze. Away he darted with his sharp, angry bark. I flung myself upon Satan and rode out to see Jones ahead and Frank flashing through the green on the white horse.

At the end of the pinyon thicket Satan overhauled Jones's bay, and we entered the open forest together. We saw Frank glinting across the dark pines.

"Hi! Hi!" yelled the Colonel.

No need was there to whip or spur those magnificent horses. They were fresh; the course was open, and smooth as a racetrack, and the impelling chorus of the hounds was in full blast. I gave Satan a loose rein, and he stayed neck and neck with the bay. There was not a log, nor a stone, nor a gully. The hollows grew wider and shallower as we raced along, and presently disappeared altogether. The lion was running straight from the canyon, and the certainty that he must sooner or later take to a tree, brought from me a yell of irresistible wild joy.

"Hi! Hi! Hi!" answered Jones.

The whipping wind with its pine-scented fragrance, warm as the breath of summer, was intoxicating as wine. The huge pines, too kingly for close communion with their kind, made wide arches under which the horses stretched out long and low, with supple, springy, powerful strides. Frank's yell rang clear as a bell. We saw him curve to the right, and took his yell as a signal for us to cut across. Then we began to close in on him, and to hear more distinctly the baying of the hounds.

"Hi! Hi! Hi! Hi!" bawled Jones, and his great trumpet voice rolled down the forest glades.

"Hi! Hi! Hi! Hi!" I screeched, in wild recognition of the spirit of the moment.

Fast as they were flying, the bay and the black responded to our cries, and quickened, strained and lengthened under us till the trees sped by in blurs.

There, plainly in sight ahead ran the hounds, Don leading, Sounder next, and Moze not fifty yards, behind a desperately running lion.

There are all-satisfying moments of life. That chase through the open forest, under the stately pines, with the wild, tawny quarry in plain sight, and the glad staccato yelps of the hounds filling my ears and swelling my heart, with the splendid action of my horse carrying me on the wings of the wind, was glorious answer and fullness to the call and hunger of a hunter's blood.

But as such moments must be, they were brief. The lion leaped gracefully into the air, splintering the bark from a pine fifteen feet up, and crouched on a limb. The hounds tore madly round the tree.

"Full-grown female," said Jones calmly, as we dismounted, "and she's ours. We'll call her Kitty."

Kitty was a beautiful creature, long, slender, glossy, with white belly and black-tipped ears and tail. She did not resemble the heavy, grim-faced brute that always hung in the air of my dreams. A low, brooding menacing murmur, that was not a snarl nor a growl, came from her. She watched the dogs with bright, steady eyes, and never so much as looked at us.

The dogs were worth attention, even from us, who certainly did not need to regard them from her personally hostile point of view. Don stood straight up, with his forepaws beating the air; he walked on his hind legs like the trained dog in the circus; he yelped continuously, as if it agonized him to see the lion safe out of his reach. Sounder had lost his identity. Joy had unhinged his mind and had made him a dog of double personality. He had always been unsocial with me, never responding to my attempts to caress him, but now he leaped into my arms and licked my face. He had always hated Jones till that moment, when he raised his paws to his master's breast. And perhaps more remarkable, time and time again he sprang up at Satan's nose, whether to bite him or kiss him, I could not tell. Then old Moze, he of Grand Canyon fame, made the delirious antics of his canine fellows look cheap. There was a small, dead pine that had fallen against a drooping branch of the tree Kitty had taken refuge in, and up this narrow ladder Moze began to climb. He was fifteen feet up, and Kitty had begun to shift uneasily, when Jones saw him.

"Hyar! you wild coon hyar! Git out of that! Come down! Come down!"

But Jones might have been in the bottom of the canyon for all Moze heard or cared. Jones removed his coat, carefully coiled his lasso, and began to go hand and knee up the leaning pine.

"Hyar! dad-blast you, git down!" yelled Jones, and he kicked Moze off. The persistent hound returned, and followed Jones to a height of twenty feet, where again he was thrust off.

"Hold him, one of you!" called Jones.

"Not me," said Frank, "I'm lookin' out for myself."

"Same here," I cried, with a camera in one hand and a rifle in the other. "Let Moze climb if he likes."

Climb he did, to be kicked off again. But he went back. It was a way he had. Jones at last recognized either his own waste of time or Moze's greatness, for he desisted, allowing the hound to keep close after him.

The cougar, becoming uneasy, stood up, reached for another limb, climbed out upon it, and peering down, spat hissingly at Jones. But he kept steadily on with Moze close on his heels. I snapped my camera on them when Kitty was not more than fifteen feet above them. As Jones reached the snag which upheld the leaning tree, she ran out on her branch, and leaped into an adjoining pine. It was a good long jump, and the weight of the animal bent the limb alarmingly.

Jones backed down, and laboriously began to climb the other tree. As there were no branches low down, he had to hug the trunk with arms and legs as a boy climbs. His lasso hampered his progress. When the slow ascent was accomplished up to the first branch, Kitty leaped back into her first perch. Strange to say Jones did not grumble; none of his characteristic impatience manifested itself. I supposed with him all the exasperating waits, vexatious obstacles, were little things preliminary to the real work, to which he had now come. He was calm and deliberate, and slid down the pine, walked back to the leaning tree, and while resting a moment, shook his lasso at Kitty. This action fitted him, somehow; it was so compatible with his grim assurance.

To me, and to Frank, also, for that matter, it was all new and startling, and we were as excited as the dogs. We kept continually moving about, Frank mounted, and I afoot, to get good views of the cougar. When she crouched as if to leap, it was almost impossible to remain under the tree, and we kept moving.

Once more Jones crept up on hands and knees. Moze walked the slanting pine like a rope performer. Kitty began to grow restless. This time she showed both anger and impatience, but did not yet appear frightened. She growled low and deep, opened her mouth and hissed, and swung her tufted tail faster and faster.

"Look out, Jones! look out!" yelled Frank warningly.

Jones, who had reached the trunk of the tree, halted and slipped round it, placing it between him and Kitty. She had advanced on her limb, a few feet above Jones, and threateningly hung over.

Jones backed down a little till she crossed to another branch, then he resumed his former position.

"Watch below," called he.

Hardly any doubt was there as to how we watched. Frank and I were all eyes, except very high and throbbing hearts. When Jones thrashed the lasso at Kitty we both yelled. She ran out on the branch and jumped. This time she fell short of her point, clutched a dead snag, which broke, letting her through a bushy branch from where she hung head downward. For a second she swung free, then reaching toward the tree caught it with front paws, ran down like a squirrel, and leaped off when thirty feet from the ground. The action was as rapid as it was astonishing.

Like a yellow rubber ball she bounded up, and fled with the yelping hounds at her heels. The chase was short. At the end of a hundred yards Moze caught up with her and nipped her. She whirled with savage suddenness, and lunged at Moze, but he cunningly eluded the vicious paws. Then she sought safety in another pine.

Frank, who was as quick as the hounds, almost rode them down in his eagerness. While Jones descended from his perch, I led the two horses down the forest.

This time the cougar was well out on a low spreading branch. Jones conceived the idea of raising the loop of his lasso on a long pole, but as no pole of sufficient length could be found, he tried from the back of his horse. The bay walked forward well enough; when, however, he got under the beast and heard her growl, he reared and almost threw Jones. Frank's horse could not be persuaded to go near the tree. Satan evinced no fear of the cougar, and without flinching carried Jones directly beneath the limb and stood with ears back and forelegs stiff.

"Look at that! look at that!" cried Jones, as the wary cougar pawed the loop aside. Three successive times did Jones have the lasso just ready to drop over her neck, when she flashed a yellow paw and knocked the noose awry. Then she leaped far out over the waiting dogs, struck the ground with a light, sharp thud, and began to run with the speed of a deer. Frank's cowboy training now stood us in good stead. He was off like a shot and turned the cougar from the direction of the canyon. Jones lost not a moment in pursuit, and I, left with Jones's badly frightened bay, got going in time to see the race, but not to assist. For several hundred yards Kitty made the hounds appear slow. Don, being swiftest, gained on her steadily toward the close of the dash, and presently was running under her upraised tail. On the next jump he nipped her. She turned and sent him reeling. Sounder came flying up to bite her flank, and at the same moment fierce old Moze closed in on her. The next instant a struggling mass whirled on the ground. Jones and Frank, yelling like demons, almost rode over it. The cougar broke from her assailants, and dashing away leaped on the first tree. It was a half-dead pine with short snags low down and a big branch extending out over a ravine.

"I think we can hold her now," said Jones. The tree proved to be a most difficult one to climb. Jones made several ineffectual attempts before he reached the first limb, which broke, giving him a hard fall. This calmed me enough to make me take notice of Jones's condition. He was wet with sweat and covered with the black pitch from the pines; his shirt was slit down the arm, and there was blood on his temple and his hand. The next attempt began by placing a good-sized log against the tree, and proved to be the necessary help. Jones got hold of the second limb and pulled himself up.

As he kept on, Kitty crouched low as if to spring upon him. Again Frank and I sent warning calls to him, but he paid no attention to us or to the cougar, and continued to climb. This worried Kitty as much as it did us. She began to move on the snags, stepping from one to the other, every moment snarling at Jones, and then she crawled up. The big branch evidently took her eye. She tried several times to climb up to it, but small snags close together made her distrustful. She walked uneasily out upon two limbs, and as they bent with her weight she hurried back. Twice she did this, each time looking up, showing her desire to leap to the big branch. Her distress became plainly evident; a child could have seen that she feared she would fall. At length, in desperation, she spat at Jones, then ran out and leaped. She all but missed the branch, but succeeded in holding to it and swinging to safety. Then she turned to her tormentor, and gave utterance to most savage sounds. As she did not intimidate her pursuer, she retreated out on the branch, which sloped down at a deep angle, and crouched on a network of small limbs.

When Jones had worked up a little farther, he commanded a splendid position for his operations. Kitty was somewhat below him in a desirable place, yet the branch she was on joined the tree considerably above his head. Jones cast his lasso. It caught on a snag. Throw after throw he made with like result. He recoiled and recast nineteen times, to my count, when Frank made a suggestion.

"Rope those dead snags an' break them off."

This practical idea Jones soon carried out, which left him a clear path. The next fling of the lariat caused the cougar angrily to shake her head. Again Jones sent the noose flying. She pulled it off her back and bit it savagely.

Though very much excited, I tried hard to keep sharp, keen faculties alert so as not to miss a single detail of the thrilling scene. But I must have failed, for all of a sudden I saw how Jones was standing in the tree, something I had not before appreciated. He had one hand hold, which he could not use while recoiling the lasso, and his feet rested upon a precariously frail-appearing, dead snag. He made eleven casts of the lasso, all of which bothered Kitty, but did not catch her. The twelfth caught her front paw. Jones jerked so quickly and hard that he almost lost his balance, and he pulled the noose off. Patiently he recoiled the lasso.

"That's what I want. If I can get her front paw she's ours. My idea is to pull her off the limb, let her hang there, and then lasso her hind legs."

Another cast, the unlucky thirteenth, settled the loop perfectly round her neck. She chewed on the rope with her front teeth and appeared to have difficulty in holding it.

"Easy! Easy! Ooze thet rope! Easy!" yelled the cowboy.

Cautiously Jones took up the slack and slowly tightened the nose, then with a quick jerk, fastened it close round her neck.

We heralded this achievement with yells of triumph that made the forest ring.

Our triumph was short-lived. Jones had hardly moved when the cougar shot straight out into the air. The lasso caught on a branch, hauling her up short, and there she hung in mid-air, writhing, struggling and giving utterance to sounds terribly human. For several seconds she swung, slowly descending, in which frenzied time I, with ruling passion uppermost, endeavored to snap a picture of her.

The unintelligible commands Jones was yelling to Frank and me ceased suddenly with a sharp crack of breaking wood. Then crash! Jones fell out of the tree. The lasso streaked up, ran over the limb, while the cougar dropped pell-mell into the bunch of waiting, howling dogs.

The next few moments it was impossible for me to distinguish what actually transpired. A great flutter of leaves whirled round a swiftly changing ball of brown and black and yellow, from which came a fiendish clamor.

Then I saw Jones plunge down the ravine and bounce here and there in mad efforts to catch the whipping lasso. He was roaring in a way that made all his former yells merely whispers. Starting to run, I tripped on a root, fell prone on my face into the ravine, and rolled over and over until I brought up with a bump against a rock.

What a tableau riveted my gaze! It staggered me so I did not think of my camera. I stood transfixed not fifteen feet from the cougar. She sat on her haunches with body well drawn back by the taut lasso to which Jones held tightly. Don was standing up with her, upheld by the hooked claws in his head. The cougar had her paws outstretched; her mouth open wide, showing long, cruel, white fangs; she was trying to pull the head of the dog to her. Don held back with all his power, and so did Jones. Moze and Sounder were tussling round her body. Suddenly both ears of the dog pulled out, slit into ribbons. Don had never uttered a sound, and once free, he made at her again with open jaws. One blow sent him reeling and stunned. Then began again that wrestling whirl.

"Beat off the dogs! Beat off the dogs!" roared Jones. "She'll kill them! She'll kill them!"

Frank and I seized clubs and ran in upon the confused furry mass, forgetful of peril to ourselves. In the wild contagion of such a savage moment the minds of men revert wholly to primitive instincts. We swung our clubs and yelled; we fought all over the bottom of the ravine, crashing through the bushes, over logs and stones. I actually felt the soft fur of the cougar at one fleeting instant. The dogs had the strength born of insane fighting spirit. At last we pulled them to where Don lay, half-stunned, and with an arm tight round each, I held them while Frank turned to help Jones.

The disheveled Jones, bloody, grim as death, his heavy jaw locked, stood holding to the lasso. The cougar, her sides shaking with short, quick pants, crouched low on the ground with eyes of purple fire.

"For God's sake, get a half-hitch on the saplin'!" called the cowboy.

His quick grasp of the situation averted a tragedy. Jones was nearly exhausted, even as he was beyond thinking for himself or giving up. The cougar sprang, a yellow, frightful flash. Even as she was in the air, Jones took a quick step to one side and dodged as he threw his lasso round the sapling. She missed him, but one alarmingly outstretched paw grazed his shoulder. A twist of Jones's big hand fastened the lasso—and Kitty was a prisoner. While she fought, rolled, twisted, bounded, whirled, writhed with hissing, snarling fury, Jones sat mopping the sweat and blood from his face.

Kitty's efforts were futile; she began to weaken from the choking. Jones took another rope, and tightening a noose around her back paws, which he lassoed as she rolled over, he stretched her out. She began to contract her supple body, gave a savage, convulsive spring, which pulled Jones flat on the ground, then the terrible wrestling started again. The lasso slipped over her back paws. She leaped the whole length of the other lasso. Jones caught it and fastened it more securely; but this precaution proved unnecessary, for she suddenly sank down either exhausted or choked, and gasped with her tongue hanging out. Frank slipped the second noose over her back paws, and Jones did likewise with a third lasso over her right front paw. These lassoes Jones tied to different saplings.

"Now you are a good Kitty," said Jones, kneeling by her. He took a pair of clippers from his hip pocket, and grasping a paw in his powerful fist he calmly clipped the points of the dangerous claws. This done, he called to me to get the collar and chain that were tied to his saddle. I procured them and hurried back. Then the old buffalo hunter loosened the lasso which was round her neck, and as soon as she could move her head, he teased her to bite a club. She broke two good sticks with her sharp teeth, but the third, being solid, did not break. While she was chewing it Jones forced her head back and placed his heavy knee on the club. In a twinkling he had strapped the collar round her neck. The chain he made fast to the sapling. After removing the club from her mouth he placed his knee on her neck, and while her head was in this helpless position he dexterously slipped a loop of thick copper wire over her nose, pushed it back and twisted it tight Following this, all done with speed and precision, he took from his pocket a piece of steel rod, perhaps one-quarter of an inch thick, and five inches long. He pushed this between Kitty's jaws, just back of her great white fangs, and in front of the copper wire. She had been shorn of her sharp weapons; she was muzzled, bound, helpless, an object to pity.

Lastly Jones removed the three lassoes. Kitty slowly gathered her lissom body in a ball and lay panting, with the same brave wildfire in her eyes. Jones stroked her black-tipped ears and ran his hand down her glossy fur. All the time he had kept up a low monotone, talking to her in the strange language he used toward animals. Then he rose to his feet.

"We'll go back to camp now, and get a pack, saddle and horse," he said. "She'll be safe here. We'll rope her again, tie her up, throw her over a pack-saddle, and take her to camp."

To my utter bewilderment the hounds suddenly commenced fighting among themselves. Of all the vicious bloody dog-fights I ever saw that was the worst. I began to belabor them with a club, and Frank sprang to my assistance. Beating had no apparent effect. We broke a dozen sticks, and then Frank grappled with Moze and I with Sounder. Don kept on fighting either one till Jones secured him. Then we all took a rest, panting and weary.

"What's it mean?" I ejaculated, appealing to Jones.

"Jealous, that's all. Jealous over the lion."

We all remained seated, men and hounds, a sweaty, dirty, bloody, ragged group. I discovered I was sorry for Kitty. I forgot all the carcasses of deer and horses, the brutality of this species of cat; and even forgot the grim, snarling yellow devil that had leaped at me. Kitty was beautiful and helpless. How brave she was, too! No sign of fear shone in her wonderful eyes, only hate, defiance, watchfulness.

On the ride back to camp Jones expressed himself thus: "How happy I am that I can keep this lion and the others we are going to capture, for my own. When I was in the Yellowstone Park I did not get to keep one of the many I captured. The military officials took them from me."

When we reached camp Lawson was absent, but fortunately Old Baldy browsed near at hand, and was easily caught. Frank said he would rather take Old Baldy for the cougar than any other horse we had. Leaving me in camp, he and Jones rode off to fetch Kitty.

About five o'clock they came trotting up through the forest with Jim, who had fallen in with them on the way. Old Baldy had remained true to his fame—nothing, not even a cougar bothered him. Kitty, evidently no worse for her experience, was chained to a pine tree about fifty feet from the campfire.

Wallace came riding wearily in, and when he saw the captive, he greeted us with an exultant yell. He got there just in time to see the first special features of Kitty's captivity. The hounds surrounded her, and could not be called off. We had to beat them. Whereupon the six jealous canines fell to fighting among themselves, and fought so savagely as to be deaf to our cries and insensible to blows. They had to be torn apart and chained.

About six o'clock Lawson loped in with the horses. Of course he did not know we had a cougar, and no one seemed interested enough to inform him. Perhaps only Frank and I thought of it; but I saw a merry snap in Frank's eyes, and kept silent. Kitty had hidden behind the pine tree. Lawson, astride Jones' pack horse, a crochety animal, reined in just abreast of the tree, and leisurely threw his leg over the saddle. Kitty leaped out to the extent of her chain, and fairly exploded in a frightful cat-spit.

Lawson had stated some time before that he was afraid of cougars, which was a weakness he need not have divulged in view of what happened. The horse plunged, throwing him ten feet, and snorting in terror, stampeded with the rest of the bunch and disappeared among the pines.

"Why the hell didn't you tell a feller?" reproachfully growled the Arizonian. Frank and Jim held each other upright, and the rest of us gave way to as hearty if not as violent mirth.

We had a gay supper, during which Kitty sat her pine and watched our every movement.

"We'll rest up for a day or two," said Jones "Things have commenced to come our way. If I'm not mistaken we'll bring an old Tom alive into camp. But it would never do for us to get a big Tom in the fix we had Kitty to-day. You see, I wanted to lasso her front paw, pull her off the limb, tie my end of the lasso to the tree, and while she hung I'd go down and rope her hind paws. It all went wrong to-day, and was as tough a job as I ever handled."

Not until late next morning did Lawson corral all the horses. That day we lounged in camp mending broken bridles, saddles, stirrups, lassoes, boots, trousers, leggins, shirts and even broken skins.

During this time I found Kitty a most interesting study. She reminded me of an enormous yellow kitten. She did not appear wild or untamed until approached. Then she slowly sank down, laid back her ears, opened her mouth and hissed and spat, at the same time throwing both paws out viciously. Kitty may have rested, but did not sleep. At times she fought her chain, tugging and straining at it, and trying to bite it through. Everything in reach she clawed, particularly the bark of the tree. Once she tried to hang herself by leaping over a low limb. When any one walked by her she crouched low, evidently imagining herself unseen. If one of us walked toward her, or looked at her, she did not crouch. At other times, noticeably when no one was near, she would roll on her back and extend all four paws in the air. Her actions were beautiful, soft, noiseless, quick and subtle.

The day passed, as all days pass in camp, swiftly and pleasantly, and twilight stole down upon us round the ruddy fire. The wind roared in the pines and lulled to repose; the lonesome, friendly coyote barked; the bells on the hobbled horses jingled sweetly; the great watch stars blinked out of the blue.

The red glow of the burning logs lighted up Jones's calm, cold face. Tranquil, unalterable and peaceful it seemed; yet beneath the peace I thought I saw a suggestion of wild restraint, of mystery, of unslaked life.

Strangely enough, his next words confirmed my last thought.

"For forty years I've had an ambition. It's to get possession of an island in the Pacific, somewhere between Vancouver and Alaska, and then go to Siberia and capture a lot of Russian sables. I'd put them on the island and cross them with our silver foxes. I'm going to try it next year if I can find the time."

The ruling passion and character determine our lives. Jones was sixty-three years old, yet the thing that had ruled and absorbed his mind was still as strong as the longing for freedom in Kitty's wild heart.

Hours after I had crawled into my sleeping-bag, in the silence of night I heard her working to get free. In darkness she was most active, restless, intense. I heard the clink of her chain, the crack of her teeth, the scrape of her claws. How tireless she was. I recalled the wistful light in her eyes that saw, no doubt, far beyond the campfire to the yellow crags, to the great downward slopes, to freedom. I slipped my elbow out of the bag and raised myself. Dark shadows were hovering under the pines. I saw Kitty's eyes gleam like sparks, and I seemed to see in them the hate, the fear, the terror she had of the clanking thing that bound her!

I shivered, perhaps from the cold night wind which moaned through the pines; I saw the stars glittering pale and far off, and under their wan light the still, set face of Jones, and blanketed forms of my other companions.

The last thing I remembered before dropping into dreamless slumber was hearing a bell tinkle in the forest, which I recognized as the one I had placed on Satan.

CHAPTER 17.

CONCLUSION

Kitty was not the only cougar brought into camp alive. The ensuing days were fruitful of cougars and adventure. There were more wild rides to the music of the baying hounds, and more heart-breaking canyon slopes to conquer, and more swinging, tufted tails and snarling savage faces in the pinyons. Once again, I am sorry to relate, I had to glance down the sights of the little Remington, and I saw blood on the stones. Those eventful days sped by all too soon.

When the time for parting came it took no little discussion to decide on the quickest way of getting me to a railroad. I never fully appreciated the inaccessibility of the Siwash until the question arose of finding a way out. To return on our back trail would require two weeks, and to go out by the trail north to Utah meant half as much time over the same kind of desert. Lawson came to our help, however, with the information that an occasional prospector or horse hunter crossed the canyon from the Saddle, where a trail led down to the river.

"I've heard the trail is a bad one," said Lawson, "an' though I never seen it, I reckon it could be found. After we get to the Saddle we'll build two fires on one of the high points an' keep them burnin' well after dark. If Mr. Bass, who lives on the other side, sees the fires he'll come down his trail next mornin' an' meet us at the river. He keeps a boat there. This is takin' a chance, but I reckon it's worth while."

So it was decided that Lawson and Frank would try to get me out by way of the canyon; Wallace intended to go by the Utah route, and Jones was to return at once to his range and his buffalo.

That night round the campfire we talked over the many incidents of the hunt. Jones stated he had never in his life come so near getting his "everlasting" as when the big bay horse tripped on a canyon slope and rolled over him. Notwithstanding the respect with which we regarded his statement we held different opinions. Then, with the unfailing optimism of hunters, we planned another hunt for the next year.

"I'll tell you what," said Jones. "Up in Utah there's a wild region called Pink Cliffs. A few poor sheep-herders try to raise sheep in the valleys. They wouldn't be so poor if it was not for the grizzly and black bears that live on the sheep. We'll go up there, find a place where grass and water can be had, and camp. We'll notify the sheep-herders we are there for business. They'll be only too glad to hustle in with news of a bear, and we can get the hounds on the trail by sun-up. I'll have a dozen hounds then, maybe twenty, and all trained. We'll put every black bear we chase up a tree, and we'll rope and tie him. As to grizzlies—well, I'm not saying so much. They can't climb trees, and they are not afraid of a pack of hounds. If we rounded up a grizzly, got him cornered, and threw a rope on him—there'd be some fun, eh, Jim?"

"Shore there would," Jim replied.

On the strength of this I stored up food for future thought and thus reconciled myself to bidding farewell to the purple canyons and shaggy slopes of Buckskin Mountain.

At five o'clock next morning we were all stirring. Jones yelled at the hounds and untangled Kitty's chain. Jim was already busy with the biscuit dough. Frank shook the frost off the saddles. Wallace was packing. The merry jangle of bells came from the forest, and presently Lawson appeared driving in the horses. I caught my black and saddled him, then realizing we were soon to part I could not resist giving him a hug.

An hour later we all stood at the head of the trail leading down into the chasm. The east gleamed rosy red. Powell's Plateau loomed up in the distance, and under it showed the dark-fringed dip in the rim called the Saddle. Blue mist floated round the mesas and domes.

Lawson led the way down the trail. Frank started Old Baldy with the pack.

"Come," he called, "be oozin' along."

I spoke the last good-by and turned Satan into the narrow trail. When I looked back Jones stood on the rim with the fresh glow of dawn shining on his face. The trail was steep, and claimed my attention and care, but time and time again I gazed back. Jones waved his hand till a huge jutting cliff walled him from view. Then I cast my eyes on the rough descent and the wonderful void beneath me. In my mind lingered a pleasing consciousness of my last sight of the old plainsman. He fitted the scene; he belonged there among the silent pines and the yellow crags.

TO THE LAST MAN

FOREWORD

It was inevitable that in my efforts to write romantic history of the great West I should at length come to the story of a feud. For long I have steered clear of this rock. But at last I have reached it and must go over it, driven by my desire to chronicle the stirring events of pioneer days.

Even to-day it is not possible to travel into the remote corners of the West without seeing the lives of people still affected by a fighting past. How can the truth be told about the pioneering of the West if the struggle, the fight, the blood be left out? It cannot be done. How can a novel be stirring and thrilling, as were those times, unless it be full of sensation? My long labors have been devoted to making stories resemble the times they depict. I have loved the West for its vastness, its contrast, its beauty and color and life, for its wildness and violence, and for the fact that I have seen how it developed great men and women who died unknown and unsung.

In this materialistic age, this hard, practical, swift, greedy age of realism, it seems there is no place for writers of romance, no place for romance itself. For many years all the events leading up to the great war were realistic, and the war itself was horribly realistic, and the aftermath is likewise. Romance is only another name for idealism; and I contend that life without ideals is not worth living. Never in the history of the world were ideals needed so terribly as now. Walter Scott wrote romance; so did Victor Hugo; and likewise Kipling, Hawthorne, Stevenson. It was Stevenson, particularly, who wielded a bludgeon against the realists. People live for the dream in their hearts. And I have yet to know anyone who has not some secret dream, some hope, however dim, some storied wall to look at in the dusk, some painted window leading to the soul. How strange indeed to find that the realists have ideals and dreams! To read them one would think their lives held nothing significant. But they love, they hope, they dream, they sacrifice, they struggle on with that dream in their hearts just the same as others. We all are dreamers, if not in the heavy-lidded wasting of time, then in the meaning of life that makes us work on.

It was Wordsworth who wrote, "The world is too much with us"; and if I could give the secret of my ambition as a novelist in a few words it would be contained in that quotation. My inspiration to write has always come from nature. Character and action are subordinated to setting. In all that I have done I have tried to make people see how the world is too much with them. Getting and spending they lay waste their powers, with never a breath of the free and wonderful life of the open!

So I come back to the main point of this foreword, in which I am trying to tell why and how I came to write the story of a feud notorious in Arizona as the Pleasant Valley War.

Some years ago Mr. Harry Adams, a cattleman of Vermajo Park, New Mexico, told me he had been in the Tonto Basin of Arizona and thought I might find interesting material there concerning this Pleasant Valley War. His version of the war between cattlemen and sheepmen certainly determined me to look over the ground. My old guide, Al Doyle of Flagstaff, had led me over half of Arizona, but never down into that wonderful wild and rugged basin between the

Mogollon Mesa and the Mazatzal Mountains. Doyle had long lived on the frontier and his version of the Pleasant Valley War differed markedly from that of Mr. Adams. I asked other old timers about it, and their remarks further excited my curiosity.

Once down there, Doyle and I found the wildest, most rugged, roughest, and most remarkable country either of us had visited; and the few inhabitants were like the country. I went in ostensibly to hunt bear and lion and turkey, but what I really was hunting for was the story of that Pleasant Valley War. I engaged the services of a bear hunter who had three strapping sons as reserved and strange and aloof as he was. No wheel tracks of any kind had ever come within miles of their cabin. I spent two wonderful months hunting game and reveling in the beauty and grandeur of that Rim Rock country, but I came out knowing no more about the Pleasant Valley War. These Texans and their few neighbors, likewise from Texas, did not talk. But all I saw and felt only inspired me the more. This trip was in the fall of 1918.

The next year I went again with the best horses, outfit, and men the Doyles could provide. And this time I did not ask any questions. But I rode horses—some of them too wild for me— and packed a rifle many a hundred miles, riding sometimes thirty and forty miles a day, and I climbed in and out of the deep canyons, desperately staying at the heels of one of those long-legged Texans. I learned the life of those backwoodsmen, but I did not get the story of the Pleasant Valley War. I had, however, won the friendship of that hardy people.

In 1920 I went back with a still larger outfit, equipped to stay as long as I liked. And this time, without my asking it, different natives of the Tonto came to tell me about the Pleasant Valley War. No two of them agreed on anything concerning it, except that only one of the active participants survived the fighting. Whence comes my title, TO THE LAST MAN. Thus I was swamped in a mass of material out of which I could only flounder to my own conclusion. Some of the stories told me are singularly tempting to a novelist. But, though I believe them myself, I cannot risk their improbability to those who have no idea of the wildness of wild men at a wild time. There really was a terrible and bloody feud, perhaps the most deadly and least known in all the annals of the West. I saw the ground, the cabins, the graves, all so darkly suggestive of what must have happened.

I never learned the truth of the cause of the Pleasant Valley War, or if I did hear it I had no means of recognizing it. All the given causes were plausible and convincing. Strange to state, there is still secrecy and reticence all over the Tonto Basin as to the facts of this feud. Many descendents of those killed are living there now. But no one likes to talk about it. Assuredly many of the incidents told me really occurred, as, for example, the terrible one of the two women, in the face of relentless enemies, saving the bodies of their dead husbands from being devoured by wild hogs. Suffice it to say that this romance is true to my conception of the war, and I base it upon the setting I learned to know and love so well, upon the strange passions of primitive people, and upon my instinctive reaction to the facts and rumors that I gathered.

ZANE GREY.   AVALON, CALIFORNIA,
    April, 1921

CHAPTER I

At the end of a dry, uphill ride over barren country Jean Isbel unpacked to camp at the edge of the cedars where a little rocky canyon green with willow and cottonwood, promised water and grass.

His animals were tired, especially the pack mule that had carried a heavy load; and with slow heave of relief they knelt and rolled in the dust. Jean experienced something of relief himself as he threw off his chaps. He had not been used to hot, dusty, glaring days on the barren lands. Stretching his long length beside a tiny rill of clear water that tinkled over the red stones, he drank thirstily. The water was cool, but it had an acrid taste—an alkali bite that he did not like. Not since he had left Oregon had he tasted clear, sweet, cold water; and he missed it just as he longed for the stately shady forests he had loved. This wild, endless Arizona land bade fair to earn his hatred.

By the time he had leisurely completed his tasks twilight had fallen and coyotes had begun their barking. Jean listened to the yelps and to the moan of the cool wind in the cedars with a sense of satisfaction that these lonely sounds were familiar. This cedar wood burned into a pretty fire and the smell of its smoke was newly pleasant.

"Reckon maybe I'll learn to like Arizona," he mused, half aloud. "But I've a hankerin' for waterfalls an' dark-green forests. Must be the Indian in me.... Anyway, dad needs me bad, an' I reckon I'm here for keeps."

Jean threw some cedar branches on the fire, in the light of which he opened his father's letter, hoping by repeated reading to grasp more of its strange portent. It had been two months in reaching him, coming by traveler, by stage and train, and then by boat, and finally by stage again. Written in lead pencil on a leaf torn from an old ledger, it would have been hard to read even if the writing had been more legible.

"Dad's writin' was always bad, but I never saw it so shaky," said Jean, thinking aloud.

GRASS VALLY, ARIZONA.

Son Jean,—Come home. Here is your home and here your needed. When we left Oregon we all reckoned you would not be long behind. But its years now. I am growing old, son, and you was always my steadiest boy. Not that you ever was so dam steady. Only your wildness seemed more for the woods. You take after mother, and your brothers Bill and Guy take after me. That is the red and white of it. Your part Indian, Jean, and that Indian I reckon I am going to need bad. I am rich in cattle and horses. And my range here is the best I ever seen. Lately we have been losing stock. But that is not all nor so bad. Sheepmen have moved into the Tonto and are grazing down on Grass Vally. Cattlemen and sheepmen can never bide in this country. We have bad times ahead. Reckon I have more reasons to worry and need you, but you must wait to hear that by word of mouth. Whatever your doing, chuck it and rustle for Grass Vally so to make here by spring. I am asking you to take pains to pack in some guns and a lot of shells. And hide them in your outfit. If you meet anyone when your coming down into the Tonto, listen more than you talk. And last, son, dont let anything keep you in Oregon. Reckon you have a sweetheart, and if so fetch her along. With love from your dad,

GASTON ISBEL.

Jean pondered over this letter. Judged by memory of his father, who had always been self-sufficient, it had been a surprise and somewhat of a shock. Weeks of travel and reflection had not helped him to grasp the meaning between the lines.

"Yes, dad's growin' old," mused Jean, feeling a warmth and a sadness stir in him. "He must be 'way over sixty. But he never looked old.... So he's rich now an' losin' stock, an' goin' to be sheeped off his range. Dad could stand a lot of rustlin', but not much from sheepmen."

The softness that stirred in Jean merged into a cold, thoughtful earnestness which had followed every perusal of his father's letter. A dark, full current seemed flowing in his veins, and at times he felt it swell and heat. It troubled him, making him conscious of a deeper, stronger self, opposed to his careless, free, and dreamy nature. No ties had bound him in Oregon, except love for the great, still forests and the thundering rivers; and this love came from his softer side. It had cost him a wrench to leave. And all the way by ship down the coast to San Diego and across the Sierra Madres by stage, and so on to this last overland travel by horseback, he had felt a retreating of the self that was tranquil and happy and a dominating of this unknown somber self, with its menacing possibilities. Yet despite a nameless regret and a loyalty to Oregon, when he lay in his blankets he had to confess a keen interest in his adventurous future, a keen enjoyment of this stark, wild Arizona. It appeared to be a different sky stretching in dark, star-spangled dome over him—closer, vaster, bluer. The strong fragrance of sage and cedar floated over him with the camp-fire smoke, and all seemed drowsily to subdue his thoughts.

At dawn he rolled out of his blankets and, pulling on his boots, began the day with a zest for the work that must bring closer his calling future. White, crackling frost and cold, nipping air were the same keen spurs to action that he had known in the uplands of Oregon, yet they were not wholly the same. He sensed an exhilaration similar to the effect of a strong, sweet wine. His horse and mule had fared well during the night, having been much refreshed by the grass and water of the little canyon. Jean mounted and rode into the cedars with gladness that at last he had put the endless leagues of barren land behind him.

The trail he followed appeared to be seldom traveled. It led, according to the meager information obtainable at the last settlement, directly to what was called the Rim, and from there Grass Valley could be seen down in the Basin. The ascent of the ground was so gradual that only in long, open stretches could it be seen. But the nature of the vegetation showed Jean how he was climbing. Scant, low, scraggy cedars gave place to more numerous, darker, greener, bushier ones, and these to high, full-foliaged, green-berried trees. Sage and grass in the open flats grew more luxuriously. Then came the pinyons, and presently among them the checker-barked junipers. Jean hailed the first pine tree with a hearty slap on the brown, rugged bark. It was a small dwarf pine struggling to live. The next one was larger, and after that came several, and beyond them pines stood up everywhere above the lower trees. Odor of pine needles mingled with the other dry smells that made the wind pleasant to Jean. In an hour from the first line of pines he had ridden beyond the cedars and pinyons into a slowly thickening and deepening forest. Underbrush appeared scarce except in ravines, and the ground in open patches held a bleached grass. Jean's eye roved for sight of squirrels, birds, deer, or any moving creature. It appeared to be a dry, uninhabited forest. About midday Jean halted at a pond of surface water, evidently melted snow, and gave his animals a drink. He saw a few old deer tracks in the mud and several huge bird tracks new to him which he concluded must have been made by wild turkeys.

The trail divided at this pond. Jean had no idea which branch he ought to take. "Reckon it doesn't matter," he muttered, as he was about to remount. His horse was standing with ears up, looking back along the trail. Then Jean heard a clip-clop of trotting hoofs, and presently espied a horseman.

Jean made a pretense of tightening his saddle girths while he peered over his horse at the approaching rider. All men in this country were going to be of exceeding interest to Jean Isbel. This man at a distance rode and looked like all the Arizonians Jean had seen, he had a superb seat in the saddle, and he was long and lean. He wore a huge black sombrero and a soiled red scarf. His vest was open and he was without a coat.

The rider came trotting up and halted several paces from Jean

"Hullo, stranger!" he said, gruffly.

"Howdy yourself!" replied Jean. He felt an instinctive importance in the meeting with the man. Never had sharper eyes flashed over Jean and his outfit. He had a dust-colored, sun-burned face, long, lean, and hard, a huge sandy mustache that hid his mouth, and eyes of piercing light intensity. Not very much hard Western experience had passed by this man, yet he was not old, measured by years. When he dismounted Jean saw he was tall, even for an Arizonian.

"Seen your tracks back a ways," he said, as he slipped the bit to let his horse drink. "Where bound?"

"Reckon I'm lost, all right," replied Jean. "New country for me."

"Shore. I seen thet from your tracks an' your last camp. Wal, where was you headin' for before you got lost?"

The query was deliberately cool, with a dry, crisp ring. Jean felt the lack of friendliness or kindliness in it.

"Grass Valley. My name's Isbel," he replied, shortly.

The rider attended to his drinking horse and presently rebridled him; then with long swing of leg he appeared to step into the saddle.

"Shore I knowed you was Jean Isbel," he said. "Everybody in the Tonto has heerd old Gass Isbel sent fer his boy."

"Well then, why did you ask?" inquired Jean, bluntly.

"Reckon I wanted to see what you'd say."

"So? All right. But I'm not carin' very much for what YOU say."

Their glances locked steadily then and each measured the other by the intangible conflict of spirit.

"Shore thet's natural," replied the rider. His speech was slow, and the motions of his long, brown hands, as he took a cigarette from his vest, kept time with his words. "But seein' you're one of the Isbels, I'll hev my say whether you want it or not. My name's Colter an' I'm one of the sheepmen Gass Isbel's riled with."

"Colter. Glad to meet you," replied Jean. "An' I reckon who riled my father is goin' to rile me."

"Shore. If thet wasn't so you'd not be an Isbel," returned Colter, with a grim little laugh. "It's easy to see you ain't run into any Tonto Basin fellers yet. Wal, I'm goin' to tell you thet your old man gabbed like a woman down at Greaves's store. Bragged aboot you an' how you could fight an' how you could shoot an' how you could track a hoss or a man! Bragged how you'd chase every sheep herder back up on the Rim.... I'm tellin' you because we want you to git our stand right. We're goin' to run sheep down in Grass Valley."

"Ahuh! Well, who's we?" queried Jean, curtly.

"What-at? ... We—I mean the sheepmen rangin' this Rim from Black Butte to the Apache country."

"Colter, I'm a stranger in Arizona," said Jean, slowly. "I know little about ranchers or sheepmen. It's true my father sent for me. It's true, I dare say, that he bragged, for he was given to bluster an' blow. An' he's old now. I can't help it if he bragged about me. But if he has, an' if he's justified in his stand against you sheepmen, I'm goin' to do my best to live up to his brag."

"I get your hunch. Shore we understand each other, an' thet's a powerful help. You take my hunch to your old man," replied Colter, as he turned his horse away toward the left. "Thet trail leadin' south is yours. When you come to the Rim you'll see a bare spot down in the Basin. Thet 'll be Grass Valley."

He rode away out of sight into the woods. Jean leaned against his horse and pondered. It seemed difficult to be just to this Colter, not because of his claims, but because of a subtle hostility that emanated from him. Colter had the hard face, the masked intent, the turn of speech that Jean had come to associate with dishonest men. Even if Jean had not been prejudiced, if he had known nothing of his father's trouble with these sheepmen, and if Colter had met him only to exchange glances and greetings, still Jean would never have had a favorable impression. Colter grated upon him, roused an antagonism seldom felt.

"Heigho!" sighed the young man, "Good-by to huntin' an' fishing'! Dad's given me a man's job."

With that he mounted his horse and started the pack mule into the right-hand trail. Walking and trotting, he traveled all afternoon, toward sunset getting into heavy forest of pine. More than one snow bank showed white through the green, sheltered on the north slopes of shady ravines. And it was upon entering this zone of richer, deeper forestland that Jean sloughed off his gloomy forebodings. These stately pines were not the giant firs of Oregon, but any lover of the woods could be happy under them. Higher still he climbed until the forest spread before and around him like a level park, with thicketed ravines here and there on each side. And presently that deceitful level led to a higher bench upon which the pines towered, and were matched by beautiful trees he took for spruce. Heavily barked, with regular spreading branches, these conifers rose in symmetrical shape to spear the sky with silver plumes. A graceful gray-green moss, waved like veils from the branches. The air was not so dry and it was colder, with a scent and touch of snow. Jean made camp at the first likely site, taking the precaution to unroll his bed some little distance from his fire. Under the softly moaning pines he felt comfortable, having lost the sense of an immeasurable open space falling away from all around him.

The gobbling of wild turkeys awakened Jean, "Chuga-lug, chug-a-lug, chug-a-lug-chug." There was not a great difference between the gobble of a wild turkey and that of a tame one. Jean got up, and taking his rifle went out into the gray obscurity of dawn to try to locate the turkeys. But it was too dark, and finally when daylight came they appeared to be gone. The mule had strayed, and, what with finding it and cooking breakfast and packing, Jean did not make a very early start. On this last lap of his long journey he had slowed down. He was weary of hurrying; the change from weeks in the glaring sun and dust-laden wind to this sweet cool darkly green and brown forest was very welcome; he wanted to linger along the shaded trail. This day he made sure would see him reach the Rim. By and by he lost the trail. It had just worn out from lack of use. Every now and then Jean would cross an old trail, and as he penetrated deeper into the forest every damp or dusty spot showed tracks of turkey, deer, and bear. The amount of bear sign surprised him. Presently his keen nostrils were assailed by a smell of sheep, and soon he rode into a broad sheep, trail. From the tracks Jean calculated that the sheep had passed there the day before.

An unreasonable antipathy seemed born in him. To be sure he had been prepared to dislike sheep, and that was why he was unreasonable. But on the other hand this band of sheep had left a broad bare swath, weedless, grassless, flowerless, in their wake. Where sheep grazed they destroyed. That was what Jean had against them.

An hour later he rode to the crest of a long parklike slope, where new green grass was sprouting and flowers peeped everywhere. The pines appeared far apart; gnarled oak trees showed rugged and gray against the green wall of woods. A white strip of snow gleamed like a moving stream away down in the woods.

Jean heard the musical tinkle of bells and the baa-baa of sheep and the faint, sweet bleating of lambs. As he road toward these sounds a dog ran out from an oak thicket and barked at him. Next Jean smelled a camp fire and soon he caught sight of a curling blue column of smoke, and then a small peaked tent. Beyond the clump of oaks Jean encountered a Mexican lad carrying a carbine. The boy had a swarthy, pleasant face, and to Jean's greeting he replied, "BUENAS DIAS." Jean understood little Spanish, and about all he gathered by his simple queries was that the lad was not alone—and that it was "lambing time."

This latter circumstance grew noisily manifest. The forest seemed shrilly full of incessant baas and plaintive bleats. All about the camp, on the slope, in the glades, and everywhere, were sheep. A few were grazing; many were lying down; most of them were ewes suckling white fleecy little lambs that staggered on their feet. Everywhere Jean saw tiny lambs just born. Their pin-pointed bleats pierced the heavier baa-baa of their mothers.

Jean dismounted and led his horse down toward the camp, where he rather expected to see another and older Mexican, from whom he might get information. The lad walked with him. Down this way the plaintive uproar made by the sheep was not so loud.

"Hello there!" called Jean, cheerfully, as he approached the tent. No answer was forthcoming. Dropping his bridle, he went on, rather slowly, looking for some one to appear. Then a voice from one side startled him.

"Mawnin', stranger."

A girl stepped out from beside a pine. She carried a rifle. Her face flashed richly brown, but she was not Mexican. This fact, and the sudden conviction that she had been watching him, somewhat disconcerted Jean.

"Beg pardon—miss," he floundered. "Didn't expect, to see a—girl.... I'm sort of lost—lookin' for the Rim—an' thought I'd find a sheep herder who'd show me. I can't savvy this boy's lingo."

While he spoke it seemed to him an intentness of expression, a strain relaxed from her face. A faint suggestion of hostility likewise disappeared. Jean was not even sure that he had caught it, but there had been something that now was gone.

"Shore I'll be glad to show y'u," she said.

"Thanks, miss. Reckon I can breathe easy now," he replied,

"It's a long ride from San Diego. Hot an' dusty! I'm pretty tired. An' maybe this woods isn't good medicine to achin' eyes!"

"San Diego! Y'u're from the coast?"

"Yes."

Jean had doffed his sombrero at sight of her and he still held it, rather deferentially, perhaps. It seemed to attract her attention.

"Put on y'ur hat, stranger.... Shore I can't recollect when any man bared his haid to me." She uttered a little laugh in which surprise and frankness mingled with a tint of bitterness.

Jean sat down with his back to a pine, and, laying the sombrero by his side, he looked full at her, conscious of a singular eagerness, as if he wanted to verify by close scrutiny a first hasty impression. If there had been an instinct in his meeting with Colter, there was more in this. The girl half sat, half leaned against a log, with the shiny little carbine across her knees. She had a level, curious gaze upon him, and Jean had never met one just like it. Her eyes were rather a wide oval in shape, clear and steady, with shadows of thought in their amber-brown depths. They seemed to look through Jean, and his gaze dropped first. Then it was he saw her ragged homespun skirt and a few inches of brown, bare ankles, strong and round, and crude worn-out moccasins that failed to hide the shapeliness, of her feet. Suddenly she drew back her stockingless ankles and ill-shod little feet. When Jean lifted his gaze again he found her face half averted and a stain of red in the gold tan of her cheek. That touch of embarrassment somehow removed her from this strong, raw, wild woodland setting. It changed her poise. It detracted from the curious, unabashed, almost bold, look that he had encountered in her eyes.

"Reckon you're from Texas," said Jean, presently.

"Shore am," she drawled. She had a lazy Southern voice, pleasant to hear. "How'd y'u-all guess that?"

"Anybody can tell a Texan. Where I came from there were a good many pioneers an' ranchers from the old Lone Star state. I've worked for several. An', come to think of it, I'd rather hear a Texas girl talk than anybody."

"Did y'u know many Texas girls?" she inquired, turning again to face him.

"Reckon I did—quite a good many."

"Did y'u go with them?"

"Go with them? Reckon you mean keep company. Why, yes, I guess I did—a little," laughed Jean. "Sometimes on a Sunday or a dance once in a blue moon, an' occasionally a ride."

"Shore that accounts," said the girl, wistfully.

"For what?" asked Jean.

"Y'ur bein' a gentleman," she replied, with force. "Oh, I've not forgotten. I had friends when we lived in Texas.... Three years ago. Shore it seems longer. Three miserable years in this damned country!"

Then she bit her lip, evidently to keep back further unwitting utterance to a total stranger. And it was that biting of her lip that drew Jean's attention to her mouth. It held beauty of curve and fullness and color that could not hide a certain sadness and bitterness. Then the whole flashing brown face changed for Jean. He saw that it was young, full of passion and restraint, possessing a power which grew on him. This, with her shame and pathos and the fact that she craved respect, gave a leap to Jean's interest.

"Well, I reckon you flatter me," he said, hoping to put her at her ease again. "I'm only a rough hunter an' fisherman-woodchopper an' horse tracker. Never had all the school I needed—nor near enough company of nice girls like you."

"Am I nice?" she asked, quickly.

"You sure are," he replied, smiling.

"In these rags," she demanded, with a sudden flash of passion that thrilled him. "Look at the holes." She showed rips and worn-out places in the sleeves of her buckskin blouse, through which gleamed a round, brown arm. "I sew when I have anythin' to sew with.... Look at my skirt—a dirty rag. An' I have only one other to my name.... Look!" Again a color tinged her cheeks, most becoming, and giving the lie to her action. But shame could not check her violence now. A dammed-up resentment seemed to have broken out in flood. She lifted the ragged skirt almost to her knees. "No stockings! No Shoes! ... How can a girl be nice when she has no clean, decent woman's clothes to wear?"

"How—how can a girl..." began Jean. "See here, miss, I'm beggin' your pardon for—sort of stirrin' you to forget yourself a little. Reckon I understand. You don't meet many strangers an' I sort of hit you wrong—makin' you feel too much—an' talk too much. Who an' what you are is none of my business. But we met.... An' I reckon somethin' has happened—perhaps more to me than to you.... Now let me put you straight about clothes an' women. Reckon I know most women love nice things to wear an' think because clothes make them look pretty that they're nicer or better. But they're wrong. You're wrong. Maybe it 'd be too much for a girl like you to be happy without clothes. But you can be—you axe just as nice, an'—an' fine—an', for all you know, a good deal more appealin' to some men."

"Stranger, y'u shore must excuse my temper an' the show I made of myself," replied the girl, with composure. "That, to say the least, was not nice. An' I don't want anyone thinkin' better of me than I deserve. My mother died in Texas, an' I've lived out heah in this wild country—a girl alone among rough men. Meetin' y'u to-day makes me see what a hard lot they are—an' what it's done to me."

Jean smothered his curiosity and tried to put out of his mind a growing sense that he pitied her, liked her.

"Are you a sheep herder?" he asked.

"Shore I am now an' then. My father lives back heah in a canyon. He's a sheepman. Lately there's been herders shot at. Just now we're short an' I have to fill in. But I like shepherdin' an' I love the woods, and the Rim Rock an' all the Tonto. If they were all, I'd shore be happy."

"Herders shot at!" exclaimed Jean, thoughtfully. "By whom? An' what for?"

"Trouble brewin' between the cattlemen down in the Basin an' the sheepmen up on the Rim. Dad says there'll shore be hell to pay. I tell him I hope the cattlemen chase him back to Texas."

"Then— Are you on the ranchers' side?" queried Jean, trying to pretend casual interest.

"No. I'll always be on my father's side," she replied, with spirit. "But I'm bound to admit I think the cattlemen have the fair side of the argument."

"How so?"

"Because there's grass everywhere. I see no sense in a sheepman goin' out of his way to surround a cattleman an' sheep off his range. That started the row. Lord knows how it'll end. For most all of them heah are from Texas."

"So I was told," replied Jean. "An' I heard' most all these Texans got run out of Texas. Any truth in that?"

"Shore I reckon there is," she replied, seriously. "But, stranger, it might not be healthy for y'u to, say that anywhere. My dad, for one, was not run out of Texas. Shore I never can see why he came heah. He's accumulated stock, but he's not rich nor so well off as he was back home."

"Are you goin' to stay here always?" queried Jean, suddenly.

"If I do so it 'll be in my grave," she answered, darkly. "But what's the use of thinkin'? People stay places until they drift away. Y'u can never tell.... Well, stranger, this talk is keepin' y'u."

She seemed moody now, and a note of detachment crept into her voice. Jean rose at once and went for his horse. If this girl did not desire to talk further he certainly had no wish to annoy her. His mule had strayed off among the bleating sheep. Jean drove it back and then led his horse up to where the girl stood. She appeared taller and, though not of robust build, she was vigorous and lithe, with something about her that fitted the place. Jean was loath to bid her good-by.

"Which way is the Rim?" he asked, turning to his saddle girths.

"South," she replied, pointing. "It's only a mile or so. I'll walk down with y'u.... Suppose y'u're on the way to Grass Valley?"

"Yes; I've relatives there," he returned. He dreaded her next question, which he suspected would concern his name. But she did not ask. Taking up her rifle she turned away. Jean strode ahead to her side. "Reckon if you walk I won't ride."

So he found himself beside a girl with the free step of a Mountaineer. Her bare, brown head came up nearly to his shoulder. It was a small, pretty head, graceful, well held, and the thick hair on it was a shiny, soft brown. She wore it in a braid, rather untidily and tangled, he thought, and it was tied with a string of buckskin. Altogether her apparel proclaimed poverty.

Jean let the conversation languish for a little. He wanted to think what to say presently, and then he felt a rather vague pleasure in stalking beside her. Her profile was straight cut and exquisite in line. From this side view the soft curve of lips could not be seen.

She made several attempts to start conversation, all of which Jean ignored, manifestly to her growing constraint. Presently Jean, having decided what he wanted to say, suddenly began: "I like this adventure. Do you?"

"Adventure! Meetin' me in the woods?" And she laughed the laugh of youth. "Shore you must be hard up for adventure, stranger."

"Do you like it?" he persisted, and his eyes searched the half-averted face.

"I might like it," she answered, frankly, "if—if my temper had not made a fool of me. I never meet anyone I care to talk to. Why should it not be pleasant to run across some one new—some one strange in this heah wild country?"

"We are as we are," said Jean, simply. "I didn't think you made a fool of yourself. If I thought so, would I want to see you again?"

"Do y'u?" The brown face flashed on him with surprise, with a light he took for gladness. And because he wanted to appear calm and friendly, not too eager, he had to deny himself the thrill of meeting those changing eyes.

"Sure I do. Reckon I'm overbold on such short acquaintance. But I might not have another chance to tell you, so please don't hold it against me."

This declaration over, Jean felt relief and something of exultation. He had been afraid he might not have the courage to make it. She walked on as before, only with her head bowed a little and her eyes downcast. No color but the gold-brown tan and the blue tracery of veins showed in her cheeks. He noticed then a slight swelling quiver of her throat; and he became alive to its graceful contour, and to how full and pulsating it was, how nobly it set into the curve of her shoulder. Here in her quivering throat was the weakness of her, the evidence of her sex, the womanliness that belied the mountaineer stride and the grasp of strong brown hands on a rifle. It had an effect on Jean totally inexplicable to him, both in the strange warmth that stole over him and in the utterance he could not hold back.

"Girl, we're strangers, but what of that? We've met, an' I tell you it means somethin' to me. I've known girls for months an' never felt this way. I don't know who you are an' I don't care. You betrayed a good deal to me. You're not happy. You're lonely. An' if I didn't want to see you again for my own sake I would for yours. Some things you said I'll not forget soon. I've got a sister, an' I know you have no brother. An' I reckon ..."

At this juncture Jean in his earnestness and quite without thought grasped her hand. The contact checked the flow of his speech and suddenly made him aghast at his temerity. But the girl did not make any effort to withdraw it. So Jean, inhaling a deep breath and trying to see through his bewilderment, held on bravely. He imagined he felt a faint, warm, returning pressure. She was young, she was friendless, she was human. By this hand in his Jean felt more than ever the loneliness of her. Then, just as he was about to speak again, she pulled her hand free.

"Heah's the Rim," she said, in her quaint Southern drawl. "An' there's Y'ur Tonto Basin."

Jean had been intent only upon the girl. He had kept step beside her without taking note of what was ahead of him. At her words he looked up expectantly, to be struck mute.

He felt a sheer force, a downward drawing of an immense abyss beneath him. As he looked afar he saw a black basin of timbered country, the darkest and wildest he had ever gazed upon, a hundred miles of blue distance across to an unflung mountain range, hazy purple against the sky. It seemed to be a stupendous gulf surrounded on three sides by bold, undulating lines of peaks, and on his side by a wall so high that he felt lifted aloft on the run of the sky.

"Southeast y'u see the Sierra Anchas," said the girl pointing. "That notch in the range is the pass where sheep are driven to Phoenix an' Maricopa. Those big rough mountains to the south are the Mazatzals. Round to the west is the Four Peaks Range. An' y'u're standin' on the Rim."

Jean could not see at first just what the Rim was, but by shifting his gaze westward he grasped this remarkable phenomenon of nature. For leagues and leagues a colossal red and yellow wall, a rampart, a mountain-faced cliff, seemed to zigzag westward. Grand and bold were the promontories reaching out over the void. They ran toward the westering sun. Sweeping and impressive were the long lines slanting away from them, sloping darkly spotted down to merge into the black timber. Jean had never seen such a wild and rugged manifestation of nature's depths and upheavals. He was held mute.

"Stranger, look down," said the girl.

Jean's sight was educated to judge heights and depths and distances. This wall upon which he stood sheered precipitously down, so far that it made him dizzy to look, and then the craggy broken cliffs merged into red-slided, cedar-greened slopes running down and down into gorges choked with forests, and from which soared up a roar of rushing waters. Slope after slope, ridge beyond ridge, canyon merging into canyon—so the tremendous bowl sunk away to its black, deceiving depths, a wilderness across which travel seemed impossible.

"Wonderful!" exclaimed Jean.

"Indeed it is!" murmured the girl. "Shore that is Arizona. I reckon I love THIS. The heights an' depths—the awfulness of its wilderness!"

"An' you want to leave it?"

"Yes an' no. I don't deny the peace that comes to me heah. But not often do I see the Basin, an' for that matter, one doesn't live on grand scenery."

"Child, even once in a while—this sight would cure any misery, if you only see. I'm glad I came. I'm glad you showed it to me first."

She too seemed under the spell of a vastness and loneliness and beauty and grandeur that could not but strike the heart.

Jean took her hand again. "Girl, say you will meet me here," he said, his voice ringing deep in his ears.

"Shore I will," she replied, softly, and turned to him. It seemed then that Jean saw her face for the first time. She was beautiful as he had never known beauty. Limned against that scene, she gave it life—wild, sweet, young life—the poignant meaning of which haunted yet eluded him. But she belonged there. Her eyes were again searching his, as if for some lost part of herself, unrealized, never known before. Wondering, wistful, hopeful, glad-they were eyes that seemed surprised, to reveal part of her soul.

Then her red lips parted. Their tremulous movement was a magnet to Jean. An invisible and mighty force pulled him down to kiss them. Whatever the spell had been, that rude, unconscious action broke it.

He jerked away, as if he expected to be struck. "Girl—I—I"—he gasped in amaze and sudden-dawning contrition—"I kissed you—but I swear it wasn't intentional—I never thought...."

The anger that Jean anticipated failed to materialize. He stood, breathing hard, with a hand held out in unconscious appeal. By the same magic, perhaps, that had transfigured her a moment past, she was now invested again by the older character.

"Shore I reckon my callin' y'u a gentleman was a little previous," she said, with a rather dry bitterness. "But, stranger, yu're sudden."

264

"You're not insulted?" asked Jean, hurriedly.

"Oh, I've been kissed before. Shore men are all alike."

"They're not," he replied, hotly, with a subtle rush of disillusion, a dulling of enchantment. "Don't you class me with other men who've kissed you. I wasn't myself when I did it an' I'd have gone on my knees to ask your forgiveness.... But now I wouldn't—an' I wouldn't kiss you again, either—even if you—you wanted it."

Jean read in her strange gaze what seemed to him a vague doubt, as if she was questioning him.

"Miss, I take that back," added Jean, shortly. "I'm sorry. I didn't mean to be rude. It was a mean trick for me to kiss you. A girl alone in the woods who's gone out of her way to be kind to me! I don't know why I forgot my manners. An' I ask your pardon."

She looked away then, and presently pointed far out and down into the Basin.

"There's Grass Valley. That long gray spot in the black. It's about fifteen miles. Ride along the Rim that way till y'u cross a trail. Shore y'u can't miss it. Then go down."

"I'm much obliged to you," replied Jean, reluctantly accepting what he regarded as his dismissal. Turning his horse, he put his foot in the stirrup, then, hesitating, he looked across the saddle at the girl. Her abstraction, as she gazed away over the purple depths suggested loneliness and wistfulness. She was not thinking of that scene spread so wondrously before her. It struck Jean she might be pondering a subtle change in his feeling and attitude, something he was conscious of, yet could not define.

"Reckon this is good-by," he said, with hesitation.

"ADIOS, SENOR," she replied, facing him again. She lifted the little carbine to the hollow of her elbow and, half turning, appeared ready to depart.

"Adios means good-by?" he queried.

"Yes, good-by till to-morrow or good-by forever. Take it as y'u like."

"Then you'll meet me here day after to-morrow?" How eagerly he spoke, on impulse, without a consideration of the intangible thing that had changed him!

"Did I say I wouldn't?"

"No. But I reckoned you'd not care to after—" he replied, breaking off in some confusion.

"Shore I'll be glad to meet y'u. Day after to-morrow about mid-afternoon. Right heah. Fetch all the news from Grass Valley."

"All right. Thanks. That'll be—fine," replied Jean, and as he spoke he experienced a buoyant thrill, a pleasant lightness of enthusiasm, such as always stirred boyishly in him at a prospect of adventure. Before it passed he wondered at it and felt unsure of himself. He needed to think.

"Stranger shore I'm not recollectin' that y'u told me who y'u are," she said.

"No, reckon I didn't tell," he returned. "What difference does that make? I said I didn't care who or what you are. Can't you feel the same about me?"

"Shore—I felt that way," she replied, somewhat non-plussed, with the level brown gaze steadily on his face. "But now y'u make me think."

"Let's meet without knowin' any more about each other than we do now."

"Shore. I'd like that. In this big wild Arizona a girl—an' I reckon a man—feels so insignificant. What's a name, anyhow? Still, people an' things have to be distinguished. I'll call y'u 'Stranger' an' be satisfied—if y'u say it's fair for y'u not to tell who y'u are."

"Fair! No, it's not," declared Jean, forced to confession. "My name's Jean—Jean Isbel."

"ISBEL!" she exclaimed, with a violent start. "Shore y'u can't be son of old Gass Isbel.... I've seen both his sons."

"He has three," replied Jean, with relief, now the secret was out. "I'm the youngest. I'm twenty-four. Never been out of Oregon till now. On my way—"

The brown color slowly faded out of her face, leaving her quite pale, with eyes that began to blaze. The suppleness of her seemed to stiffen.

"My name's Ellen Jorth," she burst out, passionately. "Does it mean anythin' to y'u?"

"Never heard it in my life," protested Jean. "Sure I reckoned you belonged to the sheep raisers who 're on the outs with my father. That's why I had to tell you I'm Jean Isbel.... Ellen Jorth. It's strange an' pretty.... Reckon I can be just as good a—a friend to you—"

"No Isbel, can ever be a friend to me," she said, with bitter coldness. Stripped of her ease and her soft wistfulness, she stood before him one instant, entirely another girl, a hostile enemy. Then she wheeled and strode off into the woods.

Jean, in amaze, in consternation, watched her swiftly draw away with her lithe, free step, wanting to follow her, wanting to call to her; but the resentment roused by her suddenly avowed hostility held him mute in his tracks. He watched her disappear, and when the brown-and-green wall of forest swallowed the slender gray form he fought against the insistent desire to follow her, and fought in vain.

CHAPTER II

But Ellen Jorth's moccasined feet did not leave a distinguishable trail on the springy pine needle covering of the ground, and Jean could not find any trace of her.

A little futile searching to and fro cooled his impulse and called pride to his rescue. Returning to his horse, he mounted, rode out behind the pack mule to start it along, and soon felt the relief of decision and action. Clumps of small pines grew thickly in spots on the Rim, making it necessary for him to skirt them; at which times he lost sight of the purple basin. Every time he came back to an opening through which he could see the wild ruggedness and colors and distances, his appreciation of their nature grew on him. Arizona from Yuma to the Little Colorado had been to him an endless waste of wind-scoured, sun-blasted barrenness. This black-forested rock-rimmed land of untrodden ways was a world that in itself would satisfy him. Some instinct in Jean called for a lonely, wild land, into the fastnesses of which he could roam at will and be the other strange self that he had always yearned to be but had never been.

Every few moments there intruded into his flowing consciousness the flashing face of Ellen Jorth, the way she had looked at him, the things she had said. "Reckon I was a fool," he soliloquized, with an acute sense of humiliation. "She never saw how much in earnest I was." And Jean began to remember the circumstances with a vividness that disturbed and perplexed him.

The accident of running across such a girl in that lonely place might be out of the ordinary— but it had happened. Surprise had made him dull. The charm of her appearance, the appeal of her manner, must have drawn him at the very first, but he had not recognized that. Only at her words, "Oh, I've been kissed before," had his feelings been checked in their heedless progress. And the utterance of them had made a difference he now sought to analyze. Some personality in him, some voice, some idea had begun to defend her even before he was conscious that he had arraigned her before the bar of his judgment. Such defense seemed clamoring in him now and he forced himself to listen. He wanted, in his hurt pride, to justify his amazing surrender to a sweet and sentimental impulse.

He realized now that at first glance he should have recognized in her look, her poise, her voice the quality he called thoroughbred. Ragged and stained apparel did not prove her of a common sort. Jean had known a number of fine and wholesome girls of good family; and he remembered his sister. This Ellen Jorth was that kind of a girl irrespective of her present environment. Jean championed her loyally, even after he had gratified his selfish pride.

It was then—contending with an intangible and stealing glamour, unreal and fanciful, like the dream of a forbidden enchantment—that Jean arrived at the part in the little woodland drama where he had kissed Ellen Jorth and had been unrebuked. Why had she not resented his action? Dispelled was the illusion he had been dreamily and nobly constructing. "Oh, I've been kissed before!" The shock to him now exceeded his first dismay. Half bitterly she had spoken, and wholly scornful of herself, or of him, or of all men. For she had said all men were alike. Jean chafed under the smart of that, a taunt every decent man hated. Naturally every happy and healthy young man would want to kiss such red, sweet lips. But if those lips had been for others—never for him! Jean reflected that not since childish games had he kissed a girl—until this brown-faced Ellen Jorth came his way. He wondered at it. Moreover, he wondered at the significance he placed upon it. After all, was it not merely an accident? Why should he remember? Why should he ponder? What was the faint, deep, growing thrill that accompanied some of his thoughts?

Riding along with busy mind, Jean almost crossed a well-beaten trail, leading through a pine thicket and down over the Rim. Jean's pack mule led the way without being driven. And when Jean reached the edge of the bluff one look down was enough to fetch him off his horse. That trail was steep, narrow, clogged with stones, and as full of sharp corners as a crosscut saw. Once on the descent with a packed mule and a spirited horse, Jean had no time for mind wanderings and very little for occasional glimpses out over the cedar tops to the vast blue hollow asleep under a westering sun.

The stones rattled, the dust rose, the cedar twigs snapped, the little avalanches of red earth slid down, the iron-shod hoofs rang on the rocks. This slope had been narrow at the apex in the Rim where the trail led down a crack, and it widened in fan shape as Jean descended. He zigzagged down a thousand feet before the slope benched into dividing ridges. Here the cedars and junipers failed and pines once more hid the sun. Deep ravines were black with brush. From somewhere rose a roar of running water, most pleasant to Jean's ears. Fresh deer and bear tracks covered old ones made in the trail.

Those timbered ridges were but billows of that tremendous slope that now sheered above Jean, ending in a magnificent yellow wall of rock, greened in niches, stained by weather rust, carved and cracked and caverned. As Jean descended farther the hum of bees made melody, the roar of rapid water and the murmur of a rising breeze filled him with the content of the wild. Sheepmen like Colter and wild girls like Ellen Jorth and all that seemed promising or menacing in his father's letter could never change the Indian in Jean. So he thought. Hard upon that conclusion rushed another—one which troubled with its stinging revelation. Surely these influences he had defied were just the ones to bring out in him the Indian he had sensed but had never known. The eventful day had brought new and bitter food for Jean to reflect upon.

The trail landed him in the bowlder-strewn bed of a wide canyon, where the huge trees stretched a canopy of foliage which denied the sunlight, and where a beautiful brook rushed and foamed. Here at last Jean tasted water that rivaled his Oregon springs. "Ah," he cried, "that sure is good!" Dark and shaded and ferny and mossy was this streamway; and everywhere were tracks of game, from the giant spread of a grizzly bear to the tiny, birdlike imprints of a squirrel. Jean heard familiar sounds of deer crackling the dead twigs; and the chatter of squirrels was incessant. This fragrant, cool retreat under the Rim brought back to him the dim recesses of Oregon forests. After all, Jean felt that he would not miss anything that he had loved in the Cascades. But what was the vague sense of all not being well with him—the essence of a faint regret—the insistence of a hovering shadow? And then flashed again, etched more vividly by the repetition in memory, a picture of eyes, of lips—of something he had to forget.

Wild and broken as this rolling Basin floor had appeared from the Rim, the reality of traveling over it made that first impression a deceit of distance. Down here all was on a big, rough, broken scale. Jean did not find even a few rods of level ground. Bowlders as huge as houses obstructed the stream bed; spruce trees eight feet thick tried to lord it over the brawny

Zane Grey Omnibus 3

pines; the ravine was a veritable canyon from which occasional glimpses through the foliage showed the Rim as a lofty red-tipped mountain peak.

Jean's pack mule became frightened at scent of a bear or lion and ran off down the rough trail, imperiling Jean's outfit. It was not an easy task to head him off nor, when that was accomplished, to keep him to a trot. But his fright and succeeding skittishness at least made for fast traveling. Jean calculated that he covered ten miles under the Rim before the character of ground and forest began to change.

The trail had turned southeast. Instead of gorge after gorge, red-walled and choked with forest, there began to be rolling ridges, some high; others were knolls; and a thick cedar growth made up for a falling off of pine. The spruce had long disappeared. Juniper thickets gave way more and more to the beautiful manzanita; and soon on the south slopes appeared cactus and a scrubby live oak. But for the well-broken trail, Jean would have fared ill through this tough brush.

Jean espied several deer, and again a coyote, and what he took to be a small herd of wild horses. No more turkey tracks showed in the dusty patches. He crossed a number of tiny brooklets, and at length came to a place where the trail ended or merged in a rough road that showed evidence of considerable travel. Horses, sheep, and cattle had passed along there that day. This road turned southward, and Jean began to have pleasurable expectations.

The road, like the trail, led down grade, but no longer at such steep angles, and was bordered by cedar and pinyon, jack-pine and juniper, mescal and manzanita. Quite sharply, going around a ridge, the road led Jean's eye down to a small open flat of marshy, or at least grassy, ground. This green oasis in the wilderness of red and timbered ridges marked another change in the character of the Basin. Beyond that the country began to spread out and roll gracefully, its dark-green forest interspersed with grassy parks, until Jean headed into a long, wide gray-green valley surrounded by black-fringed hills. His pulses quickened here. He saw cattle dotting the expanse, and here and there along the edge log cabins and corrals.

As a village, Grass Valley could not boast of much, apparently, in the way of population. Cabins and houses were widely scattered, as if the inhabitants did not care to encroach upon one another. But the one store, built of stone, and stamped also with the characteristic isolation, seemed to Jean to be a rather remarkable edifice. Not exactly like a fort did it strike him, but if it had not been designed for defense it certainly gave that impression, especially from the long, low side with its dark eye-like windows about the height of a man's shoulder. Some rather fine horses were tied to a hitching rail. Otherwise dust and dirt and age and long use stamped this Grass Valley store and its immediate environment.

Jean threw his bridle, and, getting down, mounted the low porch and stepped into the wide open door. A face, gray against the background of gloom inside, passed out of sight just as Jean entered. He knew he had been seen. In front of the long, rather low-ceiled store were four men, all absorbed, apparently, in a game of checkers. Two were playing and two were looking on. One of these, a gaunt-faced man past middle age, casually looked up as Jean entered. But the moment of that casual glance afforded Jean time enough to meet eyes he instinctively distrusted. They masked their penetration. They seemed neither curious nor friendly. They saw him as if he had been merely thin air.

"Good evenin'," said Jean.

After what appeared to Jean a lapse of time sufficient to impress him with a possible deafness of these men, the gaunt-faced one said, "Howdy, Isbel!"

The tone was impersonal, dry, easy, cool, laconic, and yet it could not have been more pregnant with meaning. Jean's sharp sensibilities absorbed much. None of the slouch-sombreroed, long-mustached Texans—for so Jean at once classed them—had ever seen Jean, but they knew him and knew that he was expected in Grass Valley. All but the one who had spoken happened to have their faces in shadow under the wide-brimmed black hats. Motley-garbed, gun-belted, dusty-booted, they gave Jean the same impression of latent force that he had encountered in Colter.

"Will somebody please tell me where to find my father, Gaston Isbel?" inquired Jean, with as civil a tongue as he could command.

Nobody paid the slightest attention. It was the same as if Jean had not spoken. Waiting, half amused, half irritated, Jean shot a rapid glance around the store. The place had felt bare; and Jean, peering back through gloomy space, saw that it did not contain much. Dry goods and sacks littered a long rude counter; long rough shelves divided their length into stacks of canned foods and empty sections; a low shelf back of the counter held a generous burden of cartridge boxes, and next to it stood a rack of rifles. On the counter lay open cases of plug tobacco, the odor of which was second in strength only to that of rum.

Jean's swift-roving eye reverted to the men, three of whom were absorbed in the greasy checkerboard. The fourth man was the one who had spoken and he now deigned to look at Jean. Not much flesh was there stretched over his bony, powerful physiognomy. He stroked a lean chin with a big mobile hand that suggested more of bridle holding than familiarity with a bucksaw and plow handle. It was a lazy hand. The man looked lazy. If he spoke at all it would be with lazy speech, yet Jean had not encountered many men to whom he would have accorded more potency to stir in him the instinct of self-preservation.

"Shore," drawled this gaunt-faced Texan, "old Gass lives aboot a mile down heah." With slow sweep of the big hand he indicated a general direction to the south; then, appearing to forget his questioner, he turned his attention to the game.

Jean muttered his thanks and, striding out, he mounted again, and drove the pack mule down the road. "Reckon I've ran into the wrong folks to-day," he said. "If I remember dad right he was a man to make an' keep friends. Somehow I'll bet there's goin' to be hell." Beyond the store were some rather pretty and comfortable homes, little ranch houses back in the coves of the hills. The road turned west and Jean saw his first sunset in the Tonto Basin. It was a pageant of purple clouds with silver edges, and background of deep rich gold. Presently Jean met a lad driving a cow. "Hello, Johnny!" he said, genially, and with a double purpose. "My name's Jean Isbel. By Golly! I'm lost in Grass Valley. Will you tell me where my dad lives?"

"Yep. Keep right on, an' y'u cain't miss him," replied the lad, with a bright smile. "He's lookin' fer y'u."

"How do you know, boy?" queried Jean, warmed by that smile.

"Aw, I know. It's all over the valley thet y'u'd ride in ter-day. Shore I wus the one thet tole yer dad an' he give me a dollar."

"Was he glad to hear it?" asked Jean, with a queer sensation in his throat.

"Wal, he plumb was."

"An' who told you I was goin' to ride in to-day?"

"I heerd it at the store," replied the lad, with an air of confidence. "Some sheepmen was talkin' to Greaves. He's the storekeeper. I was settin' outside, but I heerd. A Mexican come down off the Rim ter-day an' he fetched the news." Here the lad looked furtively around, then whispered. "An' thet greaser was sent by somebody. I never heerd no more, but them sheepmen looked pretty plumb sour. An' one of them, comin' out, give me a kick, darn him. It shore is the luckedest day fer us cowmen."

"How's that, Johnny?"

"Wal, that's shore a big fight comin' to Grass Valley. My dad says so an' he rides fer yer dad. An' if it comes now y'u'll be heah."

"Ahuh!" laughed Jean. "An' what then, boy?"

The lad turned bright eyes upward. "Aw, now, yu'all cain't come thet on me. Ain't y'u an Injun, Jean Isbel? Ain't y'u a hoss tracker thet rustlers cain't fool? Ain't y'u a plumb dead shot? Ain't y'u wuss'ern a grizzly bear in a rough-an'-tumble? ... Now ain't y'u, shore?"

Jean bade the flattering lad a rather sober good day and rode on his way. Manifestly a reputation somewhat difficult to live up to had preceded his entry into Grass Valley.

Jean's first sight of his future home thrilled him through. It was a big, low, rambling log structure standing well out from a wooded knoll at the edge of the valley. Corrals and barns and sheds lay off at the back. To the fore stretched broad pastures where numberless cattle and horses grazed. At sunset the scene was one of rich color. Prosperity and abundance and peace seemed attendant upon that ranch; lusty voices of burros braying and cows bawling seemed welcoming Jean. A hound bayed. The first cool touch of wind fanned Jean's cheek and brought a fragrance of wood smoke and frying ham.

Horses in the Pasture romped to the fence and whistled at these newcomers. Jean espied a white-faced black horse that gladdened his sight. "Hello, Whiteface! I'll sure straddle you," called Jean. Then up the gentle slope he saw the tall figure of his father—the same as he had seen him thousands of times, bareheaded, shirt sleeved, striding with long step. Jean waved and called to him.

"Hi, You Prodigal!" came the answer. Yes, the voice of his father—and Jean's boyhood memories flashed. He hurried his horse those last few rods. No—dad was not the same. His hair shone gray.

"Here I am, dad," called Jean, and then he was dismounting. A deep, quiet emotion settled over him, stilling the hurry, the eagerness, the pang in his breast.

"Son, I shore am glad to see you," said his father, and wrung his hand. "Wal, wal, the size of you! Shore you've grown, any how you favor your mother."

Jean felt in the iron clasp of hand, in the uplifting of the handsome head, in the strong, fine light of piercing eyes that there was no difference in the spirit of his father. But the old smile could not hide lines and shades strange to Jean.

"Dad, I'm as glad as you," replied Jean, heartily. "It seems long we've been parted, now I see you. Are You well, dad, an' all right?"

"Not complainin', son. I can ride all day same as ever," he said. "Come. Never mind your hosses. They'll be looked after. Come meet the folks.... Wal, wal, you got heah at last."

On the porch of the house a group awaited Jean's coming, rather silently, he thought. Wide-eyed children were there, very shy and watchful. The dark face of his sister corresponded with the image of her in his memory. She appeared taller, more womanly, as she embraced him. "Oh, Jean, Jean, I'm glad you've come!" she cried, and pressed him close. Jean felt in her a woman's anxiety for the present as well as affection for the past. He remembered his aunt Mary, though he had not seen her for years. His half brothers, Bill and Guy, had changed but little except perhaps to grow lean and rangy. Bill resembled his father, though his aspect was jocular rather than serious. Guy was smaller, wiry, and hard as rock, with snapping eyes in a brown, still face, and he had the bow-legs of a cattleman. Both had married in Arizona. Bill's wife, Kate, was a stout, comely little woman, mother of three of the children. The other wife was young, a strapping girl, red headed and freckled, with wonderful lines of pain and strength in her face. Jean remembered, as he looked at her, that some one had written him about the tragedy in her life. When she was only a child the Apaches had murdered all her family. Then next to greet Jean were the little children, all shy, yet all manifestly impressed by the occasion. A warmth and intimacy of forgotten home emotions flooded over Jean. Sweet it was to get home to these relatives who loved him and welcomed him with quiet gladness. But there seemed more. Jean was quick to see the shadow in the eyes of the women in that household and to sense a strange reliance which his presence brought.

"Son, this heah Tonto is a land of milk an' honey," said his father, as Jean gazed spellbound at the bounteous supper.

Jean certainly performed gastronomic feats on this occasion, to the delight of Aunt Mary and the wonder of the children. "Oh, he's starv-ved to death," whispered one of the little boys to his sister. They had begun to warm to this stranger uncle. Jean had no chance to talk, even had he been able to, for the meal-time showed a relaxation of restraint and they all tried to tell him things at once. In the bright lamplight his father looked easier and happier as he beamed upon Jean.

After supper the men went into an adjoining room that appeared most comfortable and attractive. It was long, and the width of the house, with a huge stone fireplace, low ceiling of hewn timbers and walls of the same, small windows with inside shutters of wood, and home-made table and chairs and rugs.

"Wal, Jean, do you recollect them shootin'-irons?" inquired the rancher, pointing above the fireplace. Two guns hung on the spreading deer antlers there. One was a musket Jean's father had used in the war of the rebellion and the other was a long, heavy, muzzle-loading flintlock Kentucky, rifle with which Jean had learned to shoot.

"Reckon I do, dad," replied Jean, and with reverent hands and a rush of memory he took the old gun down.

"Jean, you shore handle thet old arm some clumsy," said Guy Isbel, dryly. And Bill added a remark to the effect that perhaps Jean had been leading a luxurious and tame life back there in Oregon, and then added, "But I reckon he's packin' that six-shooter like a Texan."

"Say, I fetched a gun or two along with me," replied Jean, jocularly. "Reckon I near broke my poor mule's back with the load of shells an' guns. Dad, what was the idea askin' me to pack out an arsenal?"

"Son, shore all shootin' arms an' such are at a premium in the Tonto," replied his father. "An' I was givin' you a hunch to come loaded."

His cool, drawling voice seemed to put a damper upon the pleasantries. Right there Jean sensed the charged atmosphere. His brothers were bursting with utterance about to break forth, and his father suddenly wore a look that recalled to Jean critical times of days long past. But the entrance of the children and the women folk put an end to confidences. Evidently the youngsters were laboring under subdued excitement. They preceded their mother, the smallest boy in the lead. For him this must have been both a dreadful and a wonderful experience, for he seemed to be pushed forward by his sister and brother and mother, and driven by yearnings of his own. "There now, Lee. Say, 'Uncle Jean, what did you fetch us?' The lad hesitated for a shy, frightened look at Jean, and then, gaining something from his scrutiny of his uncle, he toddled forward and bravely delivered the question of tremendous importance.

"What did I fetch you, hey?" cried Jean, in delight, as he took the lad up on his knee. "Wouldn't you like to know? I didn't forget, Lee. I remembered you all. Oh! the job I had packin' your bundle of presents.... Now, Lee, make a guess."

"I dess you fetched a dun," replied Lee.

"A dun!—I'll bet you mean a gun," laughed Jean. "Well, you four-year-old Texas gunman! Make another guess."

That appeared too momentous and entrancing for the other two youngsters, and, adding their shrill and joyous voices to Lee's, they besieged Jean.

"Dad, where's my pack?" cried Jean. "These young Apaches are after my scalp."

"Reckon the boys fetched it onto the porch," replied the rancher.

Guy Isbel opened the door and went out. "By golly! heah's three packs," he called. "Which one do you want, Jean?"

"It's a long, heavy bundle, all tied up," replied Jean.

Guy came staggering in under a burden that brought a whoop from the youngsters and bright gleams to the eyes of the women. Jean lost nothing of this. How glad he was that he had tarried in San Francisco because of a mental picture of this very reception in far-off wild Arizona.

When Guy deposited the bundle on the floor it jarred the room. It gave forth metallic and rattling and crackling sounds.

"Everybody stand back an' give me elbow room," ordered Jean, majestically. "My good folks, I want you all to know this is somethin' that doesn't happen often. The bundle you see here weighed about a hundred pounds when I packed it on my shoulder down Market Street in Frisco. It was stolen from me on shipboard. I got it back in San Diego an' licked the thief. It rode on a burro from San Diego to Yuma an' once I thought the burro was lost for keeps. It came up the Colorado River from Yuma to Ehrenberg an' there went on top of a stage. We got chased by bandits an' once when the horses were gallopin' hard it near rolled off. Then it went on the back of a pack horse an' helped wear him out. An' I reckon it would be somewhere else now if I hadn't fallen in with a freighter goin' north from Phoenix to the Santa Fe Trail. The last lap when it sagged the back of a mule was the riskiest an' full of the narrowest escapes. Twice my mule bucked off his pack an' left my outfit scattered. Worst of all, my precious bundle made the mule top heavy comin' down that place back here where the trail seems to drop off the earth. There I was hard put to keep sight of my pack. Sometimes it was on top an' other times the mule. But it got here at last.... An' now I'll open it."

After this long and impressive harangue, which at least augmented the suspense of the women and worked the children into a frenzy, Jean leisurely untied the many knots round the bundle and unrolled it. He had packed that bundle for just such travel as it had sustained. Three cloth-bound rifles he laid aside, and with them a long, very heavy package tied between two thin wide boards. From this came the metallic clink. "Oo, I know what dem is!" cried Lee, breaking the silence of suspense. Then Jean, tearing open a long flat parcel, spread before the mute, rapt-eyed youngsters such magnificent things, as they had never dreamed of—picture books, mouth-harps, dolls, a toy gun and a toy pistol, a wonderful whistle and a fox horn, and last of all a box of candy. Before these treasures on the floor, too magical to be touched at first, the two little boys and their sister simply knelt. That was a sweet, full moment for Jean; yet even that was clouded by the something which shadowed these innocent children fatefully born in a wild place at a wild time. Next Jean gave to his sister the presents he had brought her—beautiful cloth for a dress, ribbons and a bit of lace, handkerchiefs and buttons and yards of linen, a sewing case and a whole box of spools of thread, a comb and brush and mirror, and lastly a Spanish brooch inlaid with garnets. "There, Ann," said Jean, "I confess I asked a girl friend in Oregon to tell me some things my sister might like." Manifestly there was not much difference in girls. Ann seemed stunned by this munificence, and then awakening, she hugged Jean in a way that took his breath. She was not a child any more, that was certain. Aunt Mary turned knowing eyes upon Jean. "Reckon you couldn't have pleased Ann more. She's engaged, Jean, an' where girls are in that state these things mean a heap.... Ann, you'll be married in that!" And she pointed to the beautiful folds of material that Ann had spread out.

"What's this?" demanded Jean. His sister's blushes were enough to convict her, and they were mightily becoming, too.

"Here, Aunt Mary," went on Jean, "here's yours, an' here's somethin' for each of my new sisters." This distribution left the women as happy and occupied, almost, as the children. It left also another package, the last one in the bundle. Jean laid hold of it and, lifting it, he was about to speak when he sustained a little shock of memory. Quite distinctly he saw two little feet, with bare toes peeping out of worn-out moccasins, and then round, bare, symmetrical ankles that had been scratched by brush. Next he saw Ellen Jorth's passionate face as she looked when she had made the violent action so disconcerting to him. In this happy moment the memory seemed farther off than a few hours. It had crystallized. It annoyed while it drew him. As a result he slowly laid this package aside and did not speak as he had intended to.

"Dad, I reckon I didn't fetch a lot for you an' the boys," continued Jean. "Some knives, some pipes an' tobacco. An' sure the guns."

"Shore, you're a regular Santa Claus, Jean," replied his father. "Wal, wal, look at the kids. An' look at Mary. An' for the land's sake look at Ann! Wal, wal, I'm gettin' old. I'd forgotten the pretty stuff an' gimcracks that mean so much to women. We're out of the world heah. It's just as well you've lived apart from us, Jean, for comin' back this way, with all that stuff, does us a lot of good. I cain't say, son, how obliged I am. My mind has been set on the hard side of life. An' it's shore good to forget—to see the smiles of the women an' the joy of the kids."

At this juncture a tall young man entered the open door. He looked a rider. All about him, even his face, except his eyes, seemed old, but his eyes were young, fine, soft, and dark.

"How do, y'u-all!" he said, evenly.

Ann rose from her knees. Then Jean did not need to be told who this newcomer was.

"Jean, this is my friend, Andrew Colmor."

Jean knew when he met Colmor's grip and the keen flash of his eyes that he was glad Ann had set her heart upon one of their kind. And his second impression was something akin to the one given him in the road by the admiring lad. Colmor's estimate of him must have been a monument built of Ann's eulogies. Jean's heart suffered misgivings. Could he live up to the character that somehow had forestalled his advent in Grass Valley? Surely life was measured differently here in the Tonto Basin.

The children, bundling their treasures to their bosoms, were dragged off to bed in some remote part of the house, from which their laughter and voices came back with happy significance. Jean forthwith had an interested audience. How eagerly these lonely pioneer people listened to news of the outside world! Jean talked until he was hoarse. In their turn his hearers told him much that had never found place in the few and short letters he had received since he had been left in Oregon. Not a word about sheepmen or any hint of rustlers! Jean marked the omission and thought all the more seriously of probabilities because nothing was said. Altogether the evening was a happy reunion of a family of which all living members were there present. Jean grasped that this fact was one of significant satisfaction to his father.

"Shore we're all goin' to live together heah," he declared. "I started this range. I call most of this valley mine. We'll run up a cabin for Ann soon as she says the word. An' you, Jean, where's your girl? I shore told you to fetch her."

"Dad, I didn't have one," replied Jean.

"Wal, I wish you had," returned the rancher. "You'll go courtin' one of these Tonto hussies that I might object to."

"Why, father, there's not a girl in the valley Jean would look twice at," interposed Ann Isbel, with spirit.

Jean laughed the matter aside, but he had an uneasy memory. Aunt Mary averred, after the manner of relatives, that Jean would play havoc among the women of the settlement. And Jean retorted that at least one member of the Isbels; should hold out against folly and fight and love and marriage, the agents which had reduced the family to these few present. "I'll be the last Isbel to go under," he concluded.

"Son, you're talkin' wisdom," said his father. "An' shore that reminds me of the uncle you're named after. Jean Isbel! ... Wal, he was my youngest brother an' shore a fire-eater. Our mother was a French creole from Louisiana, an' Jean must have inherited some of his fightin' nature from her. When the war of the rebellion started Jean an' I enlisted. I was crippled before we ever got to the front. But Jean went through three Years before he was killed. His company had orders to fight to the last man. An' Jean fought an' lived long enough just to be that last man."

At length Jean was left alone with his father.

"Reckon you're used to bunkin' outdoors?" queried the rancher, rather abruptly.

"Most of the time," replied Jean.

"Wal, there's room in the house, but I want you to sleep out. Come get your beddin' an' gun. I'll show you."

They went outside on the porch, where Jean shouldered his roll of tarpaulin and blankets. His rifle, in its saddle sheath, leaned against the door. His father took it up and, half pulling it out, looked at it by the starlight. "Forty-four, eh? Wal, wal, there's shore no better, if a man can hold straight." At the moment a big gray dog trotted up to sniff at Jean. "An' heah's your bunkmate, Shepp. He's part lofer, Jean. His mother was a favorite shepherd dog of mine. His father was a big timber wolf that took us two years to kill. Some bad wolf packs runnin' this Basin."

The night was cold and still, darkly bright under moon and stars; the smell of hay seemed to mingle with that of cedar. Jean followed his father round the house and up a gentle slope of grass to the edge of the cedar line. Here several trees with low-sweeping thick branches formed a dense, impenetrable shade.

"Son, your uncle Jean was scout for Liggett, one of the greatest rebels the South had," said the rancher. "An' you're goin' to be scout for the Isbels of Tonto. Reckon you'll find it 'most as hot as your uncle did.... Spread your bed inside. You can see out, but no one can see you. Reckon there's been some queer happenin's 'round heah lately. If Shepp could talk he'd shore have lots to tell us. Bill an' Guy have been sleepin' out, trailin' strange hoss tracks, an' all that. But shore whoever's been prowlin' around heah was too sharp for them. Some bad, crafty, light-steppin' woodsmen 'round heah, Jean.... Three mawnin's ago, just after daylight, I stepped out the back door an' some one of these sneaks I'm talkin' aboot took a shot at me. Missed my head a quarter of an inch! To-morrow I'll show you the bullet hole in the doorpost. An' some of my gray hairs that 're stickin' in it!"

"Dad!" ejaculated Jean, with a hand outstretched. "That's awful! You frighten me."

"No time to be scared," replied his father, calmly. "They're shore goin' to kill me. That's why I wanted you home.... In there with you, now! Go to sleep. You shore can trust Shepp to wake you if he gets scent or sound.... An' good night, my son. I'm sayin' that I'll rest easy to-night."

Jean mumbled a good night and stood watching his father's shining white head move away under the starlight. Then the tall, dark form vanished, a door closed, and all was still. The dog Shepp licked Jean's hand. Jean felt grateful for that warm touch. For a moment he sat on his roll of bedding, his thought still locked on the shuddering revelation of his father's words, "They're shore goin' to kill me." The shock of inaction passed. Jean pushed his pack in the dark opening and, crawling inside, he unrolled it and made his bed.

When at length he was comfortably settled for the night he breathed a long sigh of relief. What bliss to relax! A throbbing and burning of his muscles seemed to begin with his rest. The cool starlit night, the smell of cedar, the moan of wind, the silence—an were real to his senses. After long weeks of long, arduous travel he was home. The warmth of the welcome still lingered, but it seemed to have been pierced by an icy thrust. What lay before him? The shadow in the eyes of his aunt, in the younger, fresher eyes of his sister—Jean connected that with the meaning of his father's tragic words. Far past was the morning that had been so keen, the breaking of camp in the sunlit forest, the riding down the brown aisles under the pines, the music of bleating lambs that had called him not to pass by. Thought of Ellen Jorth recurred. Had he met her only that morning? She was up there in the forest, asleep under the starlit pines. Who was she? What was her story? That savage fling of her skirt, her bitter speech and passionate flaming face—they haunted Jean. They were crystallizing into simpler memories, growing away from his bewilderment, and therefore at once sweeter and more doubtful. "Maybe she meant differently from what I thought," Jean soliloquized. "Anyway, she was honest." Both shame and thrill possessed him at the recall of an insidious idea—dare he go back and find her and give her the last package of gifts he had brought from the city? What might they mean to poor, ragged, untidy, beautiful Ellen Jorth? The idea grew on Jean. It could not be dispelled. He resisted stubbornly. It was bound to go to its fruition. Deep into his mind had sunk an impression of her need—a material need that brought spirit and pride to abasement. From one picture to another his memory wandered, from one speech and act of hers to another, choosing, selecting, casting aside, until clear and sharp as the stars shone the words, "Oh, I've been kissed before!" That stung him now. By whom? Not by one man, but by several, by many, she had meant. Pshaw! he had only been sympathetic and drawn by a strange girl in the woods. To-morrow he would forget. Work there was for him in Grass Valley. And he reverted uneasily to the remarks of his father until at last sleep claimed him.

A cold nose against his cheek, a low whine, awakened Jean. The big dog Shepp was beside him, keen, wary, intense. The night appeared far advanced toward dawn. Far away a cock crowed; the near-at-hand one answered in clarion voice. "What is it, Shepp?" whispered Jean, and he sat up. The dog smelled or heard something suspicious to his nature, but whether man or animal Jean could not tell.

CHAPTER III

The morning star, large, intensely blue-white, magnificent in its dominance of the clear night sky, hung over the dim, dark valley ramparts. The moon had gone down and all the other stars were wan, pale ghosts.

Presently the strained vacuum of Jean's ears vibrated to a low roar of many hoofs. It came from the open valley, along the slope to the south. Shepp acted as if he wanted the word to run. Jean laid a hand on the dog. "Hold on, Shepp," he whispered. Then hauling on his boots and slipping into his coat Jean took his rifle and stole out into the open. Shepp appeared to be well trained, for it was evident that he had a strong natural tendency to run off and hunt for whatever had roused him. Jean thought it more than likely that the dog scented an animal of some kind. If there were men prowling around the ranch Shepp, might been just as vigilant, but it seemed to Jean that the dog would have shown less eagerness to leave him, or none at all.

In the stillness of the morning it took Jean a moment to locate the direction of the wind, which was very light and coming from the south. In fact that little breeze had borne the low roar of trampling hoofs. Jean circled the ranch house to the right and kept along the slope at the edge of the cedars. It struck him suddenly how well fitted he was for work of this sort. All the work he had ever done, except for his few years in school, had been in the open. All the leisure he had ever been able to obtain had been given to his ruling passion for hunting and fishing. Love of the wild had been born in Jean. At this moment he experienced a grim assurance of what his instinct and his training might accomplish if directed to a stern and daring end. Perhaps his father understood this; perhaps the old Texan had some little reason for his confidence.

Every few paces Jean halted to listen. All objects, of course, were indistinguishable in the dark-gray obscurity, except when he came close upon them. Shepp showed an increasing eagerness to bolt out into the void. When Jean had traveled half a mile from the house he heard a scattered trampling of cattle on the run, and farther out a low strangled bawl of a calf. "Ahuh!" muttered Jean. "Cougar or some varmint pulled down that calf." Then he discharged his rifle in the air and yelled with all his might. It was necessary then to yell again to hold Shepp back.

Thereupon Jean set forth down the valley, and tramped out and across and around, as much to scare away whatever had been after the stock as to look for the wounded calf. More than once he heard cattle moving away ahead of him, but he could not see them. Jean let Shepp go, hoping the dog would strike a trail. But Shepp neither gave tongue nor came back. Dawn began to break, and in the growing light Jean searched around until at last he stumbled over a dead calf, lying in a little bare wash where water ran in wet seasons. Big wolf tracks showed in the soft earth. "Lofers," said Jean, as he knelt and just covered one track with his spread hand. "We had wolves in Oregon, but not as big as these.... Wonder where that half-wolf dog, Shepp, went. Wonder if he can be trusted where wolves are concerned. I'll bet not, if there's a she-wolf runnin' around."

Jean found tracks of two wolves, and he trailed them out of the wash, then lost them in the grass. But, guided by their direction, he went on and climbed a slope to the cedar line, where in the dusty patches he found the tracks again. "Not scared much," he muttered, as he noted the slow trotting tracks. "Well, you old gray lofers, we're goin' to clash." Jean knew from many a futile hunt that wolves were the wariest and most intelligent of wild animals in the quest. From the top of a low foothill he watched the sun rise; and then no longer wondered why his father waxed eloquent over the beauty and location and luxuriance of this grassy valley. But it was large enough to make rich a good many ranchers. Jean tried to restrain any curiosity as to his father's dealings in Grass Valley until the situation had been made clear.

Moreover, Jean wanted to love this wonderful country. He wanted to be free to ride and hunt and roam to his heart's content; and therefore he dreaded hearing his father's claims. But Jean threw off forebodings. Nothing ever turned out so badly as it presaged. He would think the best until certain of the worst. The morning was gloriously bright, and already the frost was glistening wet on the stones. Grass Valley shone like burnished silver dotted with innumerable black spots. Burros were braying their discordant messages to one another; the colts were romping in the fields; stallions were whistling; cows were bawling. A cloud of blue smoke hung low over the ranch house, slowly wafting away on the wind. Far out in the valley a dark group of horsemen were riding toward the village. Jean glanced thoughtfully at them and reflected that he seemed destined to harbor suspicion of all men new and strange to him. Above the distant village stood the darkly green foothills leading up to the craggy slopes, and these ending in the Rim, a red, black-fringed mountain front, beautiful in the morning sunlight, lonely, serene, and mysterious against the level skyline. Mountains, ranges, distances unknown to Jean, always called to him—to come, to seek, to explore, to find, but no wild horizon ever before beckoned to him as this one. And the subtle vague emotion that had gone to sleep with him last night awoke now hauntingly. It took effort to dispel the desire to think, to wonder.

Upon his return to the house, he went around on the valley side, so as to see the place by light of day. His father had built for permanence; and evidently there had been three constructive periods in the history of that long, substantial, picturesque log house. But few nails and little sawed lumber and no glass had been used. Strong and skillful hands, axes and a crosscut saw, had been the prime factors in erecting this habitation of the Isbels.

"Good mawnin', son," called a cheery voice from the porch. "Shore we-all heard you shoot; an' the crack of that forty-four was as welcome as May flowers."

Bill Isbel looked up from a task over a saddle girth and inquired pleasantly if Jean ever slept of nights. Guy Isbel laughed and there was warm regard in the gaze he bent on Jean.

"You old Indian!" he drawled, slowly. "Did you get a bead on anythin'?"

"No. I shot to scare away what I found to be some of your lofers," replied Jean. "I heard them pullin' down a calf. An' I found tracks of two whoppin' big wolves. I found the dead calf, too. Reckon the meat can be saved. Dad, you must lose a lot of stock here."

"Wal, son, you shore hit the nail on the haid," replied the rancher. "What with lions an' bears an' lofers—an' two-footed lofers of another breed—I've lost five thousand dollars in stock this last year."

"Dad! You don't mean it!" exclaimed Jean, in astonishment. To him that sum represented a small fortune.

"I shore do," answered his father.

Jean shook his head as if he could not understand such an enormous loss where there were keen able-bodied men about. "But that's awful, dad. How could it happen? Where were your herders an' cowboys? An' Bill an' Guy?"

Bill Isbel shook a vehement fist at Jean and retorted in earnest, having manifestly been hit in a sore spot. "Where was me an' Guy, huh? Wal, my Oregon brother, we was heah, all year, sleepin' more or less aboot three hours out of every twenty-four—ridin' our boots off—an' we couldn't keep down that loss."

"Jean, you-all have a mighty tumble comin' to you out heah," said Guy, complacently.

"Listen, son," spoke up the rancher. "You want to have some hunches before you figure on our troubles. There's two or three packs of lofers, an' in winter time they are hell to deal with. Lions thick as bees, an' shore bad when the snow's on. Bears will kill a cow now an' then. An' whenever an' old silvertip comes mozyin' across from the Mazatzals he kills stock. I'm in with half a dozen cattlemen. We all work together, an' the whole outfit cain't keep these vermints down. Then two years ago the Hash Knife Gang come into the Tonto."

"Hash Knife Gang? What a pretty name!" replied Jean. "Who're they?"

"Rustlers, son. An' shore the real old Texas brand. The old Lone Star State got too hot for them, an' they followed the trail of a lot of other Texans who needed a healthier climate. Some two hundred Texans around heah, Jean, an' maybe a matter of three hundred inhabitants in the Tonto all told, good an' bad. Reckon it's aboot half an' half."

A cheery call from the kitchen interrupted the conversation of the men.

"You come to breakfast."

During the meal the old rancher talked to Bill and Guy about the day's order of work; and from this Jean gathered an idea of what a big cattle business his father conducted. After breakfast Jean's brothers manifested keen interest in the new rifles. These were unwrapped and cleaned and taken out for testing. The three rifles were forty-four calibre Winchesters, the kind of gun Jean had found most effective. He tried them out first, and the shots he made were satisfactory to him and amazing to the others. Bill had used an old Henry rifle. Guy did not favor any particular rifle. The rancher pinned his faith to the famous old single-shot buffalo gun, mostly called needle gun. "Wal, reckon I'd better stick to mine. Shore you cain't teach an old dog new tricks. But you boys may do well with the forty-fours. Pack 'em on your saddles an' practice when you see a coyote."

Jean found it difficult to convince himself that this interest in guns and marksmanship had any sinister propulsion back of it. His father and brothers had always been this way. Rifles were as important to pioneers as plows, and their skillful use was an achievement every frontiersman tried to attain. Friendly rivalry had always existed among the members of the Isbel family: even Ann Isbel was a good shot. But such proficiency in the use of firearms—and life in the open that was correlative with it—had not dominated them as it had Jean. Bill and Guy Isbel were born cattlemen—chips of the old block. Jean began to hope that his father's letter was an exaggeration, and particularly that the fatalistic speech of last night, "they are goin' to kill me," was just a moody inclination to see the worst side. Still, even as Jean tried to persuade himself of this more hopeful view, he recalled many references to the peculiar reputation of Texans for gun-throwing, for feuds, for never-ending hatreds. In Oregon the Isbels had lived among industrious and peaceful pioneers from all over the States; to be sure, the life had been rough and primitive, and there had been fights on occasions, though no Isbel had ever killed a man. But now they had become fixed in a wilder and sparsely settled country among men of their own breed. Jean was afraid his hopes had only sentiment to foster them. Nevertheless, be forced back a strange, brooding, mental state and resolutely held up the brighter side. Whatever the evil conditions existing in Grass Valley, they could be met with intelligence and courage, with an absolute certainty that it was inevitable they must pass away. Jean refused to consider the old, fatal law that at certain wild times and wild places in the West certain men had to pass away to change evil conditions.

"Wal, Jean, ride around the range with the boys," said the rancher. "Meet some of my neighbors, Jim Blaisdell, in particular. Take a look at the cattle. An' pick out some hosses for yourself."

"I've seen one already," declared Jean, quickly. "A black with white face. I'll take him."

"Shore you know a hoss. To my eye he's my pick. But the boys don't agree. Bill 'specially has degenerated into a fancier of pitchin' hosses. Ann can ride that black. You try him this mawnin'.... An', son, enjoy yourself."

True to his first impression, Jean named the black horse Whiteface and fell in love with him before ever he swung a leg over him. Whiteface appeared spirited, yet gentle. He had been trained instead of being broken. Of hard hits and quirts and spurs he had no experience. He liked to do what his rider wanted him to do.

A hundred or more horses grazed in the grassy meadow, and as Jean rode on among them it was a pleasure to see stallions throw heads and ears up and whistle or snort. Whole troops of colts and two-year-olds raced with flying tails and manes.

Beyond these pastures stretched the range, and Jean saw the gray-green expanse speckled by thousands of cattle. The scene was inspiring. Jean's brothers led him all around, meeting some of the herders and riders employed on the ranch, one of whom was a burly, grizzled man with eyes reddened and narrowed by much riding in wind and sun and dust. His name was Evans and he was father of the lad whom Jean had met near the village. Everts was busily skinning the calf that had been killed by the wolves. "See heah, y'u Jean Isbel," said Everts, "it shore was aboot time y'u come home. We-all heahs y'u hev an eye fer tracks. Wal, mebbe y'u can kill Old Gray, the lofer thet did this job. He's pulled down nine calves as' yearlin's this last two months thet I know of. An' we've not hed the spring round-up."

Grass Valley widened to the southeast. Jean would have been backward about estimating the square miles in it. Yet it was not vast acreage so much as rich pasture that made it such a wonderful range. Several ranches lay along the western slope of this section. Jean was informed that open parks and swales, and little valleys nestling among the foothills, wherever there was water and grass, had been settled by ranchers. Every summer a few new families ventured in.

Blaisdell struck Jean as being a lionlike type of Texan, both in his broad, bold face, his huge head with its upstanding tawny hair like a mane, and in the speech and force that betokened the nature of his heart. He was not as old as Jean's father. He had a rolling voice, with the same drawling intonation characteristic of all Texans, and blue eyes that still held the fire of youth. Quite a marked contrast he presented to the lean, rangy, hard-jawed, intent-eyed men Jean had begun to accept as Texans.

Blaisdell took time for a curious scrutiny and study of Jean, that, frank and kindly as it was, and evidently the adjustment of impressions gotten from hearsay, yet bespoke the attention of one used to judging men for himself, and in this particular case having reasons of his own for so doing.

"Wal, you're like your sister Ann," said Blaisdell. "Which you may take as a compliment, young man. Both of you favor your mother. But you're an Isbel. Back in Texas there are men who never wear a glove on their right hands, an' shore I reckon if one of them met up with you sudden he'd think some graves had opened an' he'd go for his gun."

Blaisdell's laugh pealed out with deep, pleasant roll. Thus he planted in Jean's sensitive mind a significant thought-provoking idea about the past-and-gone Isbels.

His further remarks, likewise, were exceedingly interesting to Jean. The settling of the Tonto Basin by Texans was a subject often in dispute. His own father had been in the first party of adventurous pioneers who had traveled up from the south to cross over the Reno Pass of the Mazatzals into the Basin. "Newcomers from outside get impressions of the Tonto accordin' to the first settlers they meet," declared Blaisdell. "An' shore it's my belief these first impressions never change, just so strong they are! Wal, I've heard my father say there were men in his wagon train that got run out of Texas, but he swore he wasn't one of them. So I reckon that sort of talk held good for twenty years, an' for all the Texans who emigrated, except, of course, such notorious rustlers as Daggs an' men of his ilk. Shore we've got some bad men heah. There's no law. Possession used to mean more than it does now. Daggs an' his Hash Knife Gang have begun to hold forth with a high hand. No small rancher can keep enough stock to pay for his labor."

At the time of which Blaisdell spoke there were not many sheepmen and cattlemen in the Tonto, considering its vast area. But these, on account of the extreme wildness of the broken country, were limited to the comparatively open Grass Valley and its adjacent environs. Naturally, as the inhabitants increased and stock raising grew in proportion the grazing and water rights became matters of extreme importance. Sheepmen ran their flocks up on the Rim in summer time and down into the Basin in winter time. A sheepman could throw a few thousand sheep round a cattleman's ranch and ruin him. The range was free. It was as fair for sheepmen to graze their herds anywhere as it was for cattlemen. This of course did not apply to the few acres of cultivated ground that a rancher could call his own; but very few cattle could have been raised on such limited area. Blaisdell said that the sheepmen were unfair because they could have done just as well, though perhaps at more labor, by keeping to the ridges and leaving the open valley and little flats to the ranchers. Formerly there had been room enough for all; now the grazing ranges were being encroached upon by sheepmen newly come to the Tonto. To Blaisdell's way of thinking the rustler menace was more serious than the sheeping-off of the range, for the simple reason that no cattleman knew exactly who the rustlers were and for the more complex and significant reason that the rustlers did not steal sheep.

"Texas was overstocked with bad men an' fine steers," concluded Blaisdell. "Most of the first an' some of the last have struck the Tonto. The sheepmen have now got distributin' points for wool an' sheep at Maricopa an' Phoenix. They're shore waxin' strong an' bold."

"Ahuh! ... An' what's likely to come of this mess?" queried Jean.

"Ask your dad," replied Blaisdell.

"I will. But I reckon I'd be obliged for your opinion."

"Wal, short an' sweet it's this: Texas cattlemen will never allow the range they stocked to be overrun by sheepmen."

"Who's this man Greaves?" went on Jean. "Never run into anyone like him."

"Greaves is hard to figure. He's a snaky customer in deals. But he seems to be good to the poor people 'round heah. Says he's from Missouri. Ha-ha! He's as much Texan as I am. He rode into the Tonto without even a pack to his name. An' presently he builds his stone house an' freights supplies in from Phoenix. Appears to buy an' sell a good deal of stock. For a while it looked like he was steerin' a middle course between cattlemen an' sheepmen. Both sides made a rendezvous of his store, where he heard the grievances of each. Laterly he's leanin' to the sheepmen. Nobody has accused him of that yet. But it's time some cattleman called his bluff."

"Of course there are honest an' square sheepmen in the Basin?" queried Jean.

"Yes, an' some of them are not unreasonable. But the new fellows that dropped in on us the last few year—they're the ones we're goin' to clash with."

"This—sheepman, Jorth?" went on Jean, in slow hesitation, as if compelled to ask what he would rather not learn.

"Jorth must be the leader of this sheep faction that's harryin' us ranchers. He doesn't make threats or roar around like some of them. But he goes on raisin' an' buyin' more an' more sheep. An' his herders have been grazin' down all around us this winter. Jorth's got to be reckoned with."

"Who is he?"

"Wal, I don't know enough to talk aboot. Your dad never said so, but I think he an' Jorth knew each other in Texas years ago. I never saw Jorth but once. That was in Greaves's barroom. Your dad an' Jorth met that day for the first time in this country. Wal, I've not known men for nothin'. They just stood stiff an' looked at each other. Your dad was aboot to draw. But Jorth made no sign to throw a gun."

Jean saw the growing and weaving and thickening threads of a tangle that had already involved him. And the sudden pang of regret he sustained was not wholly because of sympathies with his own people.

"The other day back up in the woods on the Rim I ran into a sheepman who said his name was Colter. Who is he?

"Colter? Shore he's a new one. What'd he look like?"

Jean described Colter with a readiness that spoke volumes for the vividness of his impressions.

"I don't know him," replied Blaisdell. "But that only goes to prove my contention—any fellow runnin' wild in the woods can say he's a sheepman."

"Colter surprised me by callin' me by my name," continued Jean. "Our little talk wasn't exactly friendly. He said a lot about my bein' sent for to run sheep herders out of the country."

"Shore that's all over," replied Blaisdell, seriously. "You're a marked man already."

"What started such rumor?"

"Shore you cain't prove it by me. But it's not taken as rumor. It's got to the sheepmen as hard as bullets."

"Ahuh! That accunts for Colter's seemin' a little sore under the collar. Well, he said they were goin' to run sheep over Grass Valley, an' for me to take that hunch to my dad."

Blaisdell had his chair tilted back and his heavy boots against a post of the porch. Down he thumped. His neck corded with a sudden rush of blood and his eyes changed to blue fire.

"The hell he did!" he ejaculated, in furious amaze.

Jean gauged the brooding, rankling hurt of this old cattleman by his sudden break from the cool, easy Texan manner. Blaisdell cursed under his breath, swung his arms violently, as if to throw a last doubt or hope aside, and then relapsed to his former state. He laid a brown hand on Jean's knee.

"Two years ago I called the cards," he said, quietly. "It means a Grass Valley war."

Not until late that afternoon did Jean's father broach the subject uppermost in his mind. Then at an opportune moment he drew Jean away into the cedars out of sight.

"Son, I shore hate to make your home-comin' unhappy," he said, with evidence of agitation, "but so help me God I have to do it!"

"Dad, you called me Prodigal, an' I reckon you were right. I've shirked my duty to you. I'm ready now to make up for it," replied Jean, feelingly.

"Wal, wal, shore thats fine-spoken, my boy.... Let's set down heah an' have a long talk. First off, what did Jim Blaisdell tell you?"

Briefly Jean outlined the neighbor rancher's conversation. Then Jean recounted his experience with Colter and concluded with Blaisdell's reception of the sheepman's threat. If Jean expected to see his father rise up like a lion in his wrath he made a huge mistake. This news of Colter and his talk never struck even a spark from Gaston Isbel.

"Wal," he began, thoughtfully, "reckon there are only two points in Jim's talk I need touch on. There's shore goin' to be a Grass Valley war. An' Jim's idea of the cause of it seems to be pretty much the same as that of all the other cattlemen. It 'll go down a black blot on the history page of the Tonto Basin as a war between rival sheepmen an' cattlemen. Same old fight over water an' grass! ... Jean, my son, that is wrong. It 'll not be a war between sheepmen an' cattlemen. But a war of honest ranchers against rustlers maskin' as sheep-raisers! ... Mind you, I don't belittle the trouble between sheepmen an' cattlemen in Arizona. It's real an' it's vital an' it's serious. It 'll take law an' order to straighten out the grazin' question. Some day the government will keep sheep off of cattle ranges.... So get things right in your mind, my son. You can trust your dad to tell the absolute truth. In this fight that 'll wipe out some of the Isbels—maybe all of them—you're on the side of justice an' right. Knowin' that, a man can fight a hundred times harder than he who knows he is a liar an' a thief."

The old rancher wiped his perspiring face and breathed slowly and deeply. Jean sensed in him the rise of a tremendous emotional strain. Wonderingly he watched the keen lined face. More than material worries were at the root of brooding, mounting thoughts in his father's eyes.

"Now next take what Jim said aboot your comin' to chase these sheep-herders out of the valley.... Jean, I started that talk. I had my tricky reasons. I know these greaser sheep-herders an' I know the respect Texans have for a gunman. Some say I bragged. Some say I'm an old fool in his dotage, ravin' aboot a favorite son. But they are people who hate me an' are afraid. True, son, I talked with a purpose, but shore I was mighty cold an' steady when I did it. My feelin' was that you'd do what I'd do if I were thirty years younger. No, I reckoned you'd do more. For I figured on your blood. Jean, you're Indian, an' Texas an' French, an' you've trained yourself in the Oregon woods. When you were only a boy, few marksmen I ever knew could beat you, an' I never saw your equal for eye an' ear, for trackin' a hoss, for all the gifts that make a woodsman.... Wal, rememberin' this an' seein' the trouble ahaid for the Isbels, I just broke out whenever I had a chance. I bragged before men I'd reason to believe would take my words deep. For instance, not long ago I missed some stock, an', happenin' into Greaves's place one Saturday night, I shore talked loud. His barroom was full of men an' some of them were in my black book. Greaves took my talk a little testy. He said. 'Wal, Gass, mebbe you're right aboot some of these cattle thieves livin' among us, but ain't they jest as liable to be some of your friends or relatives as Ted Meeker's or mine or any one around heah?' That was where Greaves an' me fell out. I yelled at him: 'No, by God, they're not! My record heah an' that of my people is open. The least I can say for you, Greaves, an' your crowd, is that your records fade away on dim trails.' Then he said, nasty-like, 'Wal, if you could work out all the dim trails in the Tonto you'd shore be surprised.' An' then I roared. Shore that was the chance I was lookin' for. I swore the trails he hinted of would be tracked to the holes of the rustlers who made them. I told him I had sent for you an' when you got heah these slippery, mysterious thieves, whoever they were, would shore have hell to pay. Greaves said he hoped so, but he was afraid I was partial to my Indian son. Then we had hot words. Blaisdell got between us. When I was leavin' I took a partin' fling at him. 'Greaves, you ought to know the Isbels, considerin' you're from Texas. Maybe you've got reasons for throwin' taunts at my claims for my son Jean. Yes, he's got Indian in him an' that 'll be the worse for the men who will have to meet him. I'm tellin' you, Greaves, Jean Isbel is the black sheep of the family. If you ride down his record you'll find he's shore in line to be another Poggin, or Reddy Kingfisher, or Hardin', or any of the Texas gunmen you ought to remember.... Greaves, there are men rubbin' elbows with you right heah that my Indian son is goin' to track down!'"

Jean bent his head in stunned cognizance of the notoriety with which his father had chosen to affront any and all Tonto Basin men who were under the ban of his suspicion. What a terrible reputation and trust to have saddled upon him! Thrills and strange, heated sensations seemed to rush together inside Jean, forming a hot ball of fire that threatened to explode. A retreating self made feeble protests. He saw his own pale face going away from this older, grimmer man.

"Son, if I could have looked forward to anythin' but blood spillin' I'd never have given you such a name to uphold," continued the rancher. "What I'm goin' to tell you now is my secret. My other sons an' Ann have never heard it. Jim Blaisdell suspects there's somethin' strange, but he doesn't know. I'll shore never tell anyone else but you. An' you must promise to keep my secret now an' after I am gone."

"I promise," said Jean.

"Wal, an' now to get it out," began his father, breathing hard. His face twitched and his hands clenched. "The sheepman heah I have to reckon with is Lee Jorth, a lifelong enemy of mine. We were born in the same town, played together as children, an' fought with each other as boys. We never got along together. An' we both fell in love with the same girl. It was nip an' tuck for a while. Ellen Sutton belonged to one of the old families of the South. She was a beauty, an' much courted, an' I reckon it was hard for her to choose. But I won her an' we became engaged. Then the war broke out. I enlisted with my brother Jean. He advised me to marry Ellen before I left. But I would not. That was the blunder of my life. Soon after our partin' her letters ceased to come. But I didn't distrust her. That was a terrible time an' all was confusion. Then I got crippled an' put in a hospital. An' in aboot a year I was sent back home."

At this juncture Jean refrained from further gaze at his father's face.

"Lee Jorth had gotten out of goin' to war," went on the rancher, in lower, thicker voice. "He'd married my sweetheart, Ellen.... I knew the story long before I got well. He had run after her like a hound after a hare.... An' Ellen married him. Wal, when I was able to get aboot I went to see Jorth an' Ellen. I confronted them. I had to know why she had gone back on me. Lee Jorth hadn't changed any with all his good fortune. He'd made Ellen believe in my dishonor. But, I reckon, lies or no lies, Ellen Sutton was faithless. In my absence he had won her away from me. An' I saw that she loved him as she never had me. I reckon that killed all my generosity. If she'd been imposed upon an' weaned away by his lies an' had regretted me a little I'd have forgiven, perhaps. But she worshiped him. She was his slave. An' I, wal, I learned what hate was.

"The war ruined the Suttons, same as so many Southerners. Lee Jorth went in for raisin' cattle. He'd gotten the Sutton range an' after a few years he began to accumulate stock. In those days every cattleman was a little bit of a thief. Every cattleman drove in an' branded calves he couldn't swear was his. Wal, the Isbels were the strongest cattle raisers in that country. An' I laid a trap for Lee Jorth, caught him in the act of brandin' calves of mine I'd marked, an' I proved him a thief. I made him a rustler. I ruined him. We met once. But Jorth was one Texan not strong on the draw, at least against an Isbel. He left the country. He had friends an' relatives an' they started him at stock raisin' again. But he began to gamble an' he got in with a shady crowd. He went from bad to worse an' then he came back home. When I saw the change in proud, beautiful Ellen Sutton, an' how she still worshiped Jorth, it shore drove me near mad between pity an' hate.... Wal, I reckon in a Texan hate outlives any other feelin'. There came a strange turn of the wheel an' my fortunes changed. Like most young bloods of the day, I drank an' gambled. An' one night I run across Jorth an' a card-sharp friend. He fleeced me. We quarreled. Guns were thrown. I killed my man.... Aboot that period the Texas Rangers had come into existence.... An', son, when I said I never was run out of Texas I wasn't holdin' to strict truth. I rode out on a hoss.

"I went to Oregon. There I married soon, an' there Bill an' Guy were born. Their mother did not live long. An' next I married your mother, Jean. She had some Indian blood, which, for all I could see, made her only the finer. She was a wonderful woman an' gave me the only happiness I ever knew. You remember her, of course, an' those home days in Oregon. I reckon I made another great blunder when I moved to Arizona. But the cattle country had always called me. I had heard of this wild Tonto Basin an' how Texans were settlin' there. An' Jim Blaisdell sent me word to come—that this shore was a garden spot of the West. Wal, it is. An' your mother was gone—

"Three years ago Lee Jorth drifted into the Tonto. An', strange to me, along aboot a year or so after his comin' the Hash Knife Gang rode up from Texas. Jorth went in for raisin' sheep. Along with some other sheepmen he lives up in the Rim canyons. Somewhere back in the wild brakes is the hidin' place of the Hash Knife Gang. Nobody but me, I reckon, associates Colonel Jorth, as he's called, with Daggs an' his gang. Maybe Blaisdell an' a few others have a hunch. But that's no matter. As a sheepman Jorth has a legitimate grievance with the cattlemen. But what could be settled by a square consideration for the good of all an' the future Jorth will never settle. He'll never settle because he is now no longer an honest man. He's in with Daggs. I cain't prove this, son, but I know it. I saw it in Jorth's face when I met him that day with Greaves. I saw more. I shore saw what he is up to. He'd never meet me at an even break. He's dead set on usin' this sheep an' cattle feud to ruin my family an' me, even as I ruined him. But he means more, Jean. This will be a war between Texans, an' a bloody war. There are bad men in this Tonto—some of the worst that didn't get shot in Texas. Jorth will have some of these fellows.... Now, are we goin' to wait to be sheeped off our range an' to be murdered from ambush?"

"No, we are not," replied Jean, quietly.

"Wal, come down to the house," said the rancher, and led the way without speaking until he halted by the door. There he placed his finger on a small hole in the wood at about the height of a man's head. Jean saw it was a bullet hole and that a few gray hairs stuck to its edges. The rancher stepped closer to the door-post, so that his head was within an inch of the wood. Then he looked at Jean with eyes in which there glinted dancing specks of fire, like wild sparks.

"Son, this sneakin' shot at me was made three mawnin's ago. I recollect movin' my haid just when I heard the crack of a rifle. Shore was surprised. But I got inside quick."

Jean scarcely heard the latter part of this speech. He seemed doubled up inwardly, in hot and cold convulsions of changing emotion. A terrible hold upon his consciousness was about to break and let go. The first shot had been fired and he was an Isbel. Indeed, his father had made him ten times an Isbel. Blood was thick. His father did not speak to dull ears. This strife of rising tumult in him seemed the effect of years of calm, of peace in the woods, of dreamy waiting for he knew not what. It was the passionate primitive life in him that had awakened to the call of blood ties.

"That's aboot all, son," concluded the rancher. "You understand now why I feel they're goin' to kill me. I feel it heah." With solemn gesture he placed his broad hand over his heart. "An', Jean, strange whispers come to me at night. It seems like your mother was callin' or tryin' to warn me. I cain't explain these queer whispers. But I know what I know."

"Jorth has his followers. You must have yours," replied Jean, tensely.

"Shore, son, an' I can take my choice of the best men heah," replied the rancher, with pride. "But I'll not do that. I'll lay the deal before them an' let them choose. I reckon it 'll not be a long-winded fight. It 'll be short an bloody, after the way of Texans. I'm lookin' to you, Jean, to see that an Isbel is the last man!"

"My God—dad! is there no other way? Think of my sister Ann—of my brothers' wives—of—of other women! Dad, these damned Texas feuds are cruel, horrible!" burst out Jean, in passionate protest.

"Jean, would it be any easier for our women if we let these men shoot us down in cold blood?"

"Oh no—no, I see, there's no hope of—of.... But, dad, I wasn't thinkin' about myself. I don't care. Once started I'll—I'll be what you bragged I was. Only it's so hard to-to give in."

Jean leaned an arm against the side of the cabin and, bowing his face over it, he surrendered to the irresistible contention within his breast. And as if with a wrench that strange inward hold broke. He let down. He went back. Something that was boyish and hopeful—and in its place slowly rose the dark tide of his inheritance, the savage instinct of self-preservation bequeathed by his Indian mother, and the fierce, feudal blood lust of his Texan father.

Then as he raised himself, gripped by a sickening coldness in his breast, he remembered Ellen Jorth's face as she had gazed dreamily down off the Rim—so soft, so different, with tremulous lips, sad, musing, with far-seeing stare of dark eyes, peering into the unknown, the instinct of life still unlived. With confused vision and nameless pain Jean thought of her.

"Dad, it's hard on—the—the young folks," he said, bitterly. "The sins of the father, you know. An' the other side. How about Jorth? Has he any children?"

What a curious gleam of surprise and conjecture Jean encountered in his father's gaze!

"He has a daughter. Ellen Jorth. Named after her mother. The first time I saw Ellen Jorth I thought she was a ghost of the girl I had loved an' lost. Sight of her was like a blade in my side. But the looks of her an' what she is—they don't gibe. Old as I am, my heart—Bah! Ellen Jorth is a damned hussy!"

Jean Isbel went off alone into the cedars. Surrender and resignation to his father's creed should have ended his perplexity and worry. His instant and burning resolve to be as his father had represented him should have opened his mind to slow cunning, to the craft of the Indian, to the development of hate. But there seemed to be an obstacle. A cloud in the way of vision. A face limned on his memory.

Those damning words of his father's had been a shock—how little or great he could not tell. Was it only a day since he had met Ellen Jorth? What had made all the difference? Suddenly like a breath the fragrance of her hair came back to him. Then the sweet coolness of her lips! Jean trembled. He looked around him as if he were pursued or surrounded by eyes, by instincts, by fears, by incomprehensible things.

"Ahuh! That must be what ails me," he muttered. "The look of her—an' that kiss—they've gone hard me. I should never have stopped to talk. An' I'm to kill her father an' leave her to God knows what."

Something was wrong somewhere. Jean absolutely forgot that within the hour he had pledged his manhood, his life to a feud which could be blotted out only in blood. If he had understood himself he would have realized that the pledge was no more thrilling and unintelligible in its possibilities than this instinct which drew him irresistibly.

"Ellen Jorth! So—my dad calls her a damned hussy! So—that explains the—the way she acted—why she never hit me when I kissed her. An' her words, so easy an' cool-like. Hussy? That means she's bad—bad! Scornful of me—maybe disappointed because my kiss was innocent! It was, I swear. An' all she said: 'Oh, I've been kissed before.'"

Jean grew furious with himself for the spreading of a new sensation in his breast that seemed now to ache. Had he become infatuated, all in a day, with this Ellen Jorth? Was he jealous of the men who had the privilege of her kisses? No! But his reply was hot with shame, with uncertainty. The thing that seemed wrong was outside of himself. A blunder was no crime. To be attracted by a pretty girl in the woods—to yield to an impulse was no disgrace, nor wrong. He had been foolish over a girl before, though not to such a rash extent. Ellen Jorth had stuck in his consciousness, and with her a sense of regret.

Then swiftly rang his father's bitter words, the revealing: "But the looks of her an' what she is—they don't gibe!" In the import of these words hid the meaning of the wrong that troubled him. Broodingly he pondered over them.

"The looks of her. Yes, she was pretty. But it didn't dawn on me at first. I—I was sort of excited. I liked to look at her, but didn't think." And now consciously her face was called up, infinitely sweet and more impelling for the deliberate memory. Flash of brown skin, smooth and clear; level gaze of dark, wide eyes, steady, bold, unseeing; red curved lips, sad and sweet; her strong, clean, fine face rose before Jean, eager and wistful one moment, softened by dreamy musing thought, and the next stormily passionate, full of hate, full of longing, but the more mysterious and beautiful.

"She looks like that, but she's bad," concluded Jean, with bitter finality. "I might have fallen in love with Ellen Jorth if—if she'd been different."

But the conviction forced upon Jean did not dispel the haunting memory of her face nor did it wholly silence the deep and stubborn voice of his consciousness. Later that afternoon he sought a moment with his sister.

"Ann, did you ever meet Ellen Jorth?" he asked.

"Yes, but not lately," replied Ann.

"Well, I met her as I was ridin' along yesterday. She was herdin' sheep," went on Jean, rapidly. "I asked her to show me the way to the Rim. An' she walked with me a mile or so. I can't say the meetin' was not interestin', at least to me.... Will you tell me what you know about her?"

"Sure, Jean," replied his sister, with her dark eyes fixed wonderingly and kindly on his troubled face. "I've heard a great deal, but in this Tonto Basin I don't believe all I hear. What I know I'll tell you. I first met Ellen Jorth two years ago. We didn't know each other's names then. She was the prettiest girl I ever saw. I liked her. She liked me. She seemed unhappy. The next time we met was at a round-up. There were other girls with me and they snubbed her. But I left them and went around with her. That snub cut her to the heart. She was lonely. She had no friends. She talked about herself—how she hated the people, but loved Arizona. She had nothin' fit to wear. I didn't need to be told that she'd been used to better things. Just when it looked as if we were goin' to be friends she told me who she was and asked me my name. I told her. Jean, I couldn't have hurt her more if I'd slapped her face. She turned white. She gasped. And then she ran off. The last time I saw her was about a year ago. I was ridin' a short-cut trail to the ranch where a friend lived. And I met Ellen Jorth ridin' with a man I'd never seen. The trail was overgrown and shady. They were ridin' close and didn't see me right off. The man had his arm round her. She pushed him away. I saw her laugh. Then he got hold of her again and was kissin' her when his horse shied at sight of mine. They rode by me then. Ellen Jorth held her head high and never looked at me."

"Ann, do you think she's a bad girl?" demanded Jean, bluntly.

"Bad? Oh, Jean!" exclaimed Ann, in surprise and embarrassment.

"Dad said she was a damned hussy."

"Jean, dad hates the Jorths."

"Sister, I'm askin' you what you think of Ellen Jorth. Would you be friends with her if you could?"

"Yes."

"Then you don't believe she's bad."

"No. Ellen Jorth is lonely, unhappy. She has no mother. She lives alone among rough men. Such a girl can't keep men from handlin' her and kissin' her. Maybe she's too free. Maybe she's wild. But she's honest, Jean. You can trust a woman to tell. When she rode past me that day her face was white and proud. She was a Jorth and I was an Isbel. She hated herself—she hated me. But no bad girl could look like that. She knows what's said of her all around the valley. But she doesn't care. She'd encourage gossip."

"Thank you, Ann," replied Jean, huskily. "Please keep this—this meetin' of mine with her all to yourself, won't you?"

"Why, Jean, of course I will."

Jean wandered away again, peculiarly grateful to Ann for reviving and upholding something in him that seemed a wavering part of the best of him—a chivalry that had demanded to be killed by judgment of a righteous woman. He was conscious of an uplift, a gladdening of his spirit. Yet the ache remained. More than that, he found himself plunged deeper into conjecture, doubt. Had not the Ellen Jorth incident ended? He denied his father's indictment of her and accepted the faith of his sister. "Reckon that's aboot all, as dad says," he soliloquized. Yet was that all? He paced under the cedars. He watched the sun set. He listened to the coyotes. He lingered there after the call for supper; until out of the tumult of his conflicting emotions and ponderings there evolved the staggering consciousness that he must see Ellen Jorth again.

CHAPTER IV

Ellen Jorth hurried back into the forest, hotly resentful of the accident that had thrown her in contact with an Isbel.

Disgust filled her—disgust that she had been amiable to a member of the hated family that had ruined her father. The surprise of this meeting did not come to her while she was under the spell of stronger feeling. She walked under the trees, swiftly, with head erect, looking straight before her, and every step seemed a relief.

Upon reaching camp, her attention was distracted from herself. Pepe, the Mexican boy, with the two shepherd dogs, was trying to drive sheep into a closer bunch to save the lambs from coyotes. Ellen loved the fleecy, tottering little lambs, and at this season she hated all the prowling beast of the forest. From this time on for weeks the flock would be besieged by wolves, lions, bears, the last of which were often bold and dangerous. The old grizzlies that killed the ewes to eat only the milk-bags were particularly dreaded by Ellen. She was a good shot with a rifle, but had orders from her father to let the bears alone. Fortunately, such sheep-killing bears were but few, and were left to be hunted by men from the ranch. Mexican sheep herders could not be depended upon to protect their flocks from bears. Ellen helped Pepe drive in the stragglers, and she took several shots at coyotes skulking along the edge of the brush. The open glade in the forest was favorable for herding the sheep at night, and the dogs could be depended upon to guard the flock, and in most cases to drive predatory beasts away.

After this task, which brought the time to sunset, Ellen had supper to cook and eat. Darkness came, and a cool night wind set in. Here and there a lamb bleated plaintively. With her work done for the day, Ellen sat before a ruddy camp fire, and found her thoughts again centering around the singular adventure that had befallen her. Disdainfully she strove to think of something else. But there was nothing that could dispel the interest of her meeting with Jean Isbel. Thereupon she impatiently surrendered to it, and recalled every word and action which she could remember. And in the process of this meditation she came to an action of hers, recollection of which brought the blood tingling to her neck and cheeks, so unusually and burningly that she covered them with her hands. "What did he think of me?" she mused, doubtfully. It did not matter what he thought, but she could not help wondering. And when she came to the memory of his kiss she suffered more than the sensation of throbbing scarlet cheeks. Scornfully and bitterly she burst out, "Shore he couldn't have thought much good of me."

The half hour following this reminiscence was far from being pleasant. Proud, passionate, strong-willed Ellen Jorth found herself a victim of conflicting emotions. The event of the day was too close. She could not understand it. Disgust and disdain and scorn could not make this meeting with Jean Isbel as if it had never been. Pride could not efface it from her mind. The more she reflected, the harder she tried to forget, the stronger grew a significance of interest. And when a hint of this dawned upon her consciousness she resented it so forcibly that she lost her temper, scattered the camp fire, and went into the little teepee tent to roll in her blankets.

Thus settled snug and warm for the night, with a shepherd dog curled at the opening of her tent, she shut her eyes and confidently bade sleep end her perplexities. But sleep did not come at her invitation. She found herself wide awake, keenly sensitive to the sputtering of the camp fire, the tinkling of bells on the rams, the bleating of lambs, the sough of wind in the pines, and the hungry sharp bark of coyotes off in the distance. Darkness was no respecter of her pride. The lonesome night with its emphasis of solitude seemed to induce clamoring and strange thoughts, a confusing ensemble of all those that had annoyed her during the daytime. Not for long hours did sheer weariness bring her to slumber.

Ellen awakened late and failed of her usual alacrity. Both Pepe and the shepherd dog appeared to regard her with surprise and solicitude. Ellen's spirit was low this morning; her blood ran sluggishly; she had to fight a mournful tendency to feel sorry for herself. And at first she was not very successful. There seemed to be some kind of pleasure in reveling in melancholy which her common sense told her had no reason for existence. But states of mind persisted in spite of common sense.

"Pepe, when is Antonio comin' back?" she asked.

The boy could not give her a satisfactory answer. Ellen had willingly taken the sheep herder's place for a few days, but now she was impatient to go home. She looked down the green-and-brown aisles of the forest until she was tired. Antonio did not return. Ellen spent the day with the sheep; and in the manifold task of caring for a thousand new-born lambs she forgot herself. This day saw the end of lambing-time for that season. The forest resounded to a babel of baas and bleats. When night came she was glad to go to bed, for what with loss of sleep, and weariness she could scarcely keep her eyes open.

The following morning she awakened early, bright, eager, expectant, full of bounding life, strangely aware of the beauty and sweetness of the scented forest, strangely conscious of some nameless stimulus to her feelings.

Not long was Ellen in associating this new and delightful variety of sensations with the fact that Jean Isbel had set to-day for his ride up to the Rim to see her. Ellen's joyousness fled; her smiles faded. The spring morning lost its magic radiance.

"Shore there's no sense in my lyin' to myself," she soliloquized, thoughtfully. "It's queer of me—feelin' glad aboot him—without knowin'. Lord! I must be lonesome! To be glad of seein' an Isbel, even if he is different!"

Soberly she accepted the astounding reality. Her confidence died with her gayety; her vanity began to suffer. And she caught at her admission that Jean Isbel was different; she resented it in amaze; she ridiculed it; she laughed at her naive confession. She could arrive at no conclusion other than that she was a weak-minded, fluctuating, inexplicable little fool.

But for all that she found her mind had been made up for her, without consent or desire, before her will had been consulted; and that inevitably and unalterably she meant to see Jean Isbel again. Long she battled with this strange decree. One moment she won a victory over, this new curious self, only to lose it the next. And at last out of her conflict there emerged a few convictions that left her with some shreds of pride. She hated all Isbels, she hated any Isbel, and particularly she hated Jean Isbel. She was only curious—intensely curious to see if he would come back, and if he did come what he would do. She wanted only to watch him from some covert. She would not go near him, not let him see her or guess of her presence.

Thus she assuaged her hurt vanity—thus she stifled her miserable doubts.

Long before the sun had begun to slant westward toward the mid-afternoon Jean Isbel had set as a meeting time Ellen directed her steps through the forest to the Rim. She felt ashamed of her eagerness. She had a guilty conscience that no strange thrills could silence. It would be fun to see him, to watch him, to let him wait for her, to fool him.

Like an Indian, she chose the soft pine-needle mats to tread upon, and her light-moccasined feet left no trace. Like an Indian also she made a wide detour, and reached the Rim a quarter of a mile west of the spot where she had talked with Jean Isbel; and here, turning east, she took care to step on the bare stones. This was an adventure, seemingly the first she had ever had in her life. Assuredly she had never before come directly to the Rim without halting to look, to wonder, to worship. This time she scarcely glanced into the blue abyss. All absorbed was she in hiding her tracks. Not one chance in a thousand would she risk. The Jorth pride burned even while the feminine side of her dominated her actions. She had some difficult rocky points to cross, then windfalls to round, and at length reached the covert she desired. A rugged yellow point of the Rim stood somewhat higher than the spot Ellen wanted to watch. A dense thicket of jack pines grew to the very edge. It afforded an ambush that even the Indian eyes Jean Isbel was credited with could never penetrate. Moreover, if by accident she made a noise and excited suspicion, she could retreat unobserved and hide in the huge rocks below the Rim, where a ferret could not locate her.

With her plan decided upon, Ellen had nothing to do but wait, so she repaired to the other side of the pine thicket and to the edge of the Rim where she could watch and listen. She knew that long before she saw Isbel she would hear his horse. It was altogether unlikely that he would come on foot.

"Shore, Ellen Jorth, y'u're a queer girl," she mused. "I reckon I wasn't well acquainted with y'u."

Beneath her yawned a wonderful deep canyon, rugged and rocky with but few pines on the north slope, thick with dark green timber on the south slope. Yellow and gray crags, like turreted castles, stood up out of the sloping forest on the side opposite her. The trees were all sharp, spear pointed. Patches of light green aspens showed strikingly against the dense black. The great slope beneath Ellen was serrated with narrow, deep gorges, almost canyons in themselves. Shadows alternated with clear bright spaces. The mile-wide mouth of the canyon opened upon the Basin, down into a world of wild timbered ranges and ravines, valleys and hills, that rolled and tumbled in dark-green waves to the Sierra Anchas.

But for once Ellen seemed singularly unresponsive to this panorama of wildness and grandeur. Her ears were like those of a listening deer, and her eyes continually reverted to the open places along the Rim. At first, in her excitement, time flew by. Gradually, however, as the sun moved westward, she began to be restless. The soft thud of dropping pine cones, the rustling of squirrels up and down the shaggy-barked spruces, the cracking of weathered bits of rock, these caught her keen ears many times and brought her up erect and thrilling. Finally she heard a sound which resembled that of an unshod hoof on stone. Stealthily then she took her rifle and slipped back through the pine thicket to the spot she had chosen. The little pines were so close together that she had to crawl between their trunks. The ground was covered with a soft bed of pine needles, brown and fragrant. In her hurry she pricked her ungloved hand on a sharp pine cone and drew the blood. She sucked the tiny wound. "Shore I'm wonderin' if that's a bad omen," she muttered, darkly thoughtful. Then she resumed her sinuous approach to the edge of the thicket, and presently reached it.

Ellen lay flat a moment to recover her breath, then raised herself on her elbows. Through an opening in the fringe of buck brush she could plainly see the promontory where she had stood with Jean Isbel, and also the approaches by which he might come. Rather nervously she realized that her covert was hardly more than a hundred feet from the promontory. It was imperative that she be absolutely silent. Her eyes searched the openings along the Rim. The gray form of a deer crossed one of these, and she concluded it had made the sound she had heard. Then she lay down more comfortably and waited. Resolutely she held, as much as possible, to her sensorial perceptions. The meaning of Ellen Jorth lying in ambush just to see an Isbel was a conundrum she refused to ponder in the present. She was doing it, and the physical act had its fascination. Her ears, attuned to all the sounds of the lonely forest, caught them and arranged them according to her knowledge of woodcraft.

A long hour passed by. The sun had slanted to a point halfway between the zenith and the horizon. Suddenly a thought confronted Ellen Jorth: "He's not comin'," she whispered. The instant that idea presented itself she felt a blank sense of loss, a vague regret—something that must have been disappointment. Unprepared for this, she was held by surprise for a moment, and then she was stunned. Her spirit, swift and rebellious, had no time to rise in her defense. She was a lonely, guilty, miserable girl, too weak for pride to uphold, too fluctuating to know her real self. She stretched there, burying her face in the pine needles, digging her fingers into them, wanting nothing so much as that they might hide her. The moment was incomprehensible to Ellen, and utterly intolerable. The sharp pine needles, piercing her wrists and cheeks, and her hot heaving breast, seemed to give her exquisite relief.

The shrill snort of a horse sounded near at hand. With a shock Ellen's body stiffened. Then she quivered a little and her feelings underwent swift change. Cautiously and noiselessly she raised herself upon her elbows and peeped through the opening in the brush. She saw a man tying a horse to a bush somewhat back from the Rim. Drawing a rifle from its saddle sheath he threw it in the hollow of his arm and walked to the edge of the precipice. He gazed away across the Basin and appeared lost in contemplation or thought. Then he turned to look back into the forest, as if he expected some one.

Ellen recognized the lithe figure, the dark face so like an Indian's. It was Isbel. He had come. Somehow his coming seemed wonderful and terrible. Ellen shook as she leaned on her elbows. Jean Isbel, true to his word, in spite of her scorn, had come back to see her. The fact seemed monstrous. He was an enemy of her father. Long had range rumor been bandied from lip to lip—old Gass Isbel had sent for his Indian son to fight the Jorths. Jean Isbel—son of a Texan—unerring shot—peerless tracker—a bad and dangerous man! Then there flashed over Ellen a burning thought—if it were true, if he was an enemy of her father's, if a fight between Jorth and Isbel was inevitable, she ought to kill this Jean Isbel right there in his tracks as he boldly and confidently waited for her. Fool he was to think she would come. Ellen sank down and dropped her head until the strange tremor of her arms ceased. That dark and grim flash of thought retreated. She had not come to murder a man from ambush, but only to watch him, to try to see what he meant, what he thought, to allay a strange curiosity.

After a while she looked again. Isbel was sitting on an upheaved section of the Rim, in a comfortable position from which he could watch the openings in the forest and gaze as well across the west curve of the Basin to the Mazatzals. He had composed himself to wait. He was clad in a buckskin suit, rather new, and it certainly showed off to advantage, compared with the ragged and soiled apparel Ellen remembered. He did not look so large. Ellen was used to the long, lean, rangy Arizonians and Texans. This man was built differently. He had the widest shoulders of any man she had ever seen, and they made him appear rather short. But his lithe, powerful limbs proved he was not short. Whenever he moved the muscles rippled. His hands were clasped round a knee—brown, sinewy hands, very broad, and fitting the thick muscular wrists. His collar was open, and he did not wear a scarf, as did the men Ellen knew. Then her intense curiosity at last brought her steady gaze to Jean Isbel's head and face. He wore a cap, evidently of some thin fur. His hair was straight and short, and in color a dead raven black. His complexion was dark, clear tan, with no trace of red. He did not have the prominent cheek bones nor the high-bridged nose usual with white men who are part Indian. Still he had the Indian look. Ellen caught that in the dark, intent, piercing eyes, in the wide, level, thoughtful brows, in the stern impassiveness of his smooth face. He had a straight, sharp-cut profile.

Ellen whispered to herself: "I saw him right the other day. Only, I'd not admit it.... The finest-lookin' man I ever saw in my life is a damned Isbel! Was that what I come out heah for?"

She lowered herself once more and, folding her arms under her breast, she reclined comfortably on them, and searched out a smaller peephole from which she could spy upon Isbel. And as she watched him the new and perplexing side of her mind waxed busier. Why had he come back? What did he want of her? Acquaintance, friendship, was impossible for them. He had been respectful, deferential toward her, in a way that had strangely pleased, until the surprising moment when he had kissed her. That had only disrupted her rather dreamy pleasure in a situation she had not experienced before. All the men she had met in this wild country were rough and bold; most of them had wanted to marry her, and, failing that, they had persisted in amorous attentions not particularly flattering or honorable. They were a bad lot. And contact with them had dulled some of her sensibilities. But this Jean Isbel had seemed a gentleman. She struggled to be fair, trying to forget her antipathy, as much to understand herself as to give him due credit. True, he had kissed her, crudely and forcibly. But that kiss had not been an insult. Ellen's finer feeling forced her to believe this. She remembered the honest amaze and shame and contrition with which he had faced her, trying awkwardly to explain his bold act. Likewise she recalled the subtle swift change in him at her words, "Oh, I've been kissed before!" She was glad she had said that. Still—was she glad, after all?

She watched him. Every little while he shifted his gaze from the blue gulf beneath him to the forest. When he turned thus the sun shone on his face and she caught the piercing gleam of his dark eyes. She saw, too, that he was listening. Watching and listening for her! Ellen had to still a tumult within her. It made her feel very young, very shy, very strange. All the while she hated him because he manifestly expected her to come. Several times he rose and walked a little way into the woods. The last time he looked at the westering sun and shook his head. His confidence had gone. Then he sat and gazed down into the void. But Ellen knew he did not see anything there. He seemed an image carved in the stone of the Rim, and he gave Ellen a singular impression of loneliness and sadness. Was he thinking of the miserable battle his father had summoned him to lead—of what it would cost—of its useless pain and hatred? Ellen seemed to divine his thoughts. In that moment she softened toward him, and in her soul quivered and stirred an intangible something that was like pain, that was too deep for her understanding. But she felt sorry for an Isbel until the old pride resurged. What if he admired her? She remembered his interest, the wonder and admiration, the growing light in his eyes. And it had not been repugnant to her until he disclosed his name. "What's in a name?" she mused, recalling poetry learned in her girlhood. "'A rose by any other name would smell as sweet'.... He's an Isbel—yet he might be splendid—noble.... Bah! he's not—and I'd hate him anyhow."

All at once Ellen felt cold shivers steal over her. Isbel's piercing gaze was directed straight at her hiding place. Her heart stopped beating. If he discovered her there she felt that she would die of shame. Then she became aware that a blue jay was screeching in a pine above her, and a red squirrel somewhere near was chattering his shrill annoyance. These two denizens of the woods could be depended upon to espy the wariest hunter and make known his presence to their kind. Ellen had a moment of more than dread. This keen-eyed, keen-eared Indian might see right through her brushy covert, might hear the throbbing of her heart. It relieved her immeasurably to see him turn away and take to pacing the promontory, with his head bowed and his hands behind his back. He had stopped looking off into the forest. Presently he wheeled to the west, and by the light upon his face Ellen saw that the time was near sunset. Turkeys were beginning to gobble back on the ridge.

Isbel walked to his horse and appeared to be untying something from the back of his saddle. When he came back Ellen saw that he carried a small package apparently wrapped in paper. With this under his arm he strode off in the direction of Ellen's camp and soon disappeared in the forest.

For a little while Ellen lay there in bewilderment. If she had made conjectures before, they were now multiplied. Where was Jean Isbel going? Ellen sat up suddenly. "Well, shore this heah beats me," she said. "What did he have in that package? What was he goin' to do with it?"

It took no little will power to hold her there when she wanted to steal after him through the woods and find out what he meant. But his reputation influenced even her and she refused to pit her cunning in the forest against his. It would be better to wait until he returned to his horse. Thus decided, she lay back again in her covert and gave her mind over to pondering curiosity. Sooner than she expected she espied Isbel approaching through the forest, empty handed. He had not taken his rifle. Ellen averted her glance a moment and thrilled to see the rifle leaning against a rock. Verily Jean Isbel had been far removed from hostile intent that day. She watched him stride swiftly up to his horse, untie the halter, and mount. Ellen had an impression of his arrowlike straight figure, and sinuous grace and ease. Then he looked back at the promontory, as if to fix a picture of it in his mind, and rode away along the Rim. She watched him out of sight. What ailed her? Something was wrong with her, but she recognized only relief.

When Isbel had been gone long enough to assure Ellen that she might safely venture forth she crawled through the pine thicket to the Rim on the other side of the point. The sun was setting behind the Black Range, shedding a golden glory over the Basin. Westward the zigzag Rim reached like a streamer of fire into the sun. The vast promontories jutted out with blazing beacon lights upon their stone-walled faces. Deep down, the Basin was turning shadowy dark blue, going to sleep for the night.

Ellen bent swift steps toward her camp. Long shafts of gold preceded her through the forest. Then they paled and vanished. The tips of pines and spruces turned gold. A hoarse-voiced old turkey gobbler was booming his chug-a-lug from the highest ground, and the softer chick of hen turkeys answered him. Ellen was almost breathless when she arrived. Two packs and a couple of lop-eared burros attested to the fact of Antonio's return. This was good news for Ellen. She heard the bleat of lambs and tinkle of bells coming nearer and nearer. And she was glad to feel that if Isbel had visited her camp, most probably it was during the absence of the herders.

The instant she glanced into her tent she saw the package Isbel had carried. It lay on her bed. Ellen stared blankly. "The—the impudence of him!" she ejaculated. Then she kicked the package out of the tent. Words and action seemed to liberate a dammed-up hot fury. She kicked the package again, and thought she would kick it into the smoldering camp-fire. But somehow she stopped short of that. She left the thing there on the ground.

Pepe and Antonio hove in sight, driving in the tumbling woolly flock. Ellen did not want them to see the package, so with contempt for herself, and somewhat lessening anger, she kicked it back into the tent. What was in it? She peeped inside the tent, devoured by curiosity. Neat, well wrapped and tied packages like that were not often seen in the Tonto Basin. Ellen decided she would wait until after supper, and at a favorable moment lay it unopened on the fire. What did she care what it contained? Manifestly it was a gift. She argued that she was highly incensed with this insolent Isbel who had the effrontery to approach her with some sort of present.

It developed that the usually cheerful Antonio had returned taciturn and gloomy. All Ellen could get out of him was that the job of sheep herder had taken on hazards inimical to peace-loving Mexicans. He had heard something he would not tell. Ellen helped prepare the supper and she ate in silence. She had her own brooding troubles. Antonio presently told her that her father had said she was not to start back home after dark. After supper the herders repaired to their own tents, leaving Ellen the freedom of her camp-fire. Wherewith she secured the package and brought it forth to burn. Feminine curiosity rankled strong in her breast. Yielding so far as to shake the parcel and press it, and finally tear a comer off the paper, she saw some words written in lead pencil. Bending nearer the blaze, she read, "For my sister Ann." Ellen gazed at the big, bold hand-writing, quite legible and fairly well done. Suddenly she tore the outside wrapper completely off. From printed words on the inside she gathered that the package had come from a store in San Francisco. "Reckon he fetched home a lot of presents for his folks—the kids—and his sister," muttered Ellen. "That was nice of him. Whatever this is he shore meant it for sister Ann.... Ann Isbel. Why, she must be that black-eyed girl I met and liked so well before I knew she was an Isbel.... His sister!"

Whereupon for the second time Ellen deposited the fascinating package in her tent. She could not burn it up just then. She had other emotions besides scorn and hate. And memory of that soft-voiced, kind-hearted, beautiful Isbel girl checked her resentment. "I wonder if he is like his sister," she said, thoughtfully. It appeared to be an unfortunate thought. Jean Isbel certainly resembled his sister. "Too bad they belong to the family that ruined dad."

Ellen went to bed without opening the package or without burning it. And to her annoyance, whatever way she lay she appeared to touch this strange package. There was not much room in the little tent. First she put it at her head beside her rifle, but when she turned over her cheek came in contact with it. Then she felt as if she had been stung. She moved it again, only to touch it presently with her hand. Next she flung it to the bottom of her bed, where it fell upon her feet, and whatever way she moved them she could not escape the pressure of this undesirable and mysterious gift.

By and by she fell asleep, only to dream that the package was a caressing hand stealing about her, feeling for hers, and holding it with soft, strong clasp. When she awoke she had the strangest sensation in her right palm. It was moist, throbbing, hot, and the feel of it on her cheek was strangely thrilling and comforting. She lay awake then. The night was dark and still. Only a low moan of wind in the pines and the faint tinkle of a sheep bell broke the serenity. She felt very small and lonely lying there in the deep forest, and, try how she would, it was impossible to think the same then as she did in the clear light of day. Resentment, pride, anger—these seemed abated now. If the events of the day had not changed her, they had at least brought up softer and kinder memories and emotions than she had known for long. Nothing hurt and saddened her so much as to remember the gay, happy days of her childhood, her sweet mother, her, old home. Then her thought returned to Isbel and his gift. It had been years since anyone had made her a gift. What could this one be? It did not matter. The wonder was that Jean Isbel should bring it to her and that she could be perturbed by its presence. "He meant it for his sister and so he thought well of me," she said, in finality.

Morning brought Ellen further vacillation. At length she rolled the obnoxious package inside her blankets, saying that she would wait until she got home and then consign it cheerfully to the flames. Antonio tied her pack on a burro. She did not have a horse, and therefore had to walk the several miles, to her father's ranch.

She set off at a brisk pace, leading the burro and carrying her rifle. And soon she was deep in the fragrant forest. The morning was clear and cool, with just enough frost to make the sunlit grass sparkle as if with diamonds. Ellen felt fresh, buoyant, singularly full of, life. Her youth would not be denied. It was pulsing, yearning. She hummed an old Southern tune and every step seemed one of pleasure in action, of advance toward some intangible future happiness. All the unknown of life before her called. Her heart beat high in her breast and she walked as one in a dream. Her thoughts were swift-changing, intimate, deep, and vague, not of yesterday or to-day, nor of reality.

The big, gray, white-tailed squirrels crossed ahead of her on the trail, scampered over the piny ground to hop on tree trunks, and there they paused to watch her pass. The vociferous little red squirrels barked and chattered at her. From every thicket sounded the gobble of turkeys. The blue jays squalled in the tree tops. A deer lifted its head from browsing and stood motionless, with long ears erect, watching her go by.

Thus happily and dreamily absorbed, Ellen covered the forest miles and soon reached the trail that led down into the wild brakes of Chevelon Canyon. It was rough going and less conducive to sweet wanderings of mind. Ellen slowly lost them. And then a familiar feeling assailed her, one she never failed to have upon returning to her father's ranch—a reluctance, a bitter dissatisfaction with her home, a loyal struggle against the vague sense that all was not as it should be.

At the head of this canyon in a little, level, grassy meadow stood a rude one-room log shack, with a leaning red-stone chimney on the outside. This was the abode of a strange old man who had long lived there. His name was John Sprague and his occupation was raising burros. No sheep or cattle or horses did he own, not even a dog. Rumor had said Sprague was a prospector, one of the many who had searched that country for the Lost Dutchman gold mine. Sprague knew more about the Basin and Rim than any of the sheepmen or ranchers. From Black Butte to the Cibique and from Chevelon Butte to Reno Pass he knew every trail, canyon, ridge, and spring, and could find his way to them on the darkest night. His fame, however, depended mostly upon the fact that he did nothing but raise burros, and would raise none but black burros with white faces. These burros were the finest bred in ail the Basin and were in great demand. Sprague sold a few every year. He had made a present of one to Ellen, although he hated to part with them. This old man was Ellen's one and only friend.

Upon her trip out to the Rim with the sheep, Uncle John, as Ellen called him, had been away on one of his infrequent visits to Grass Valley. It pleased her now to see a blue column of smoke lazily lifting from the old chimney and to hear the discordant bray of burros. As she entered the clearing Sprague saw her from the door of his shack.

"Hello, Uncle John!" she called.

"Wal, if it ain't Ellen!" he replied, heartily. "When I seen thet white-faced jinny I knowed who was leadin' her. Where you been, girl?"

Sprague was a little, stoop-shouldered old man, with grizzled head and face, and shrewd gray eyes that beamed kindly on her over his ruddy cheeks. Ellen did not like the tobacco stain on his grizzled beard nor the dirty, motley, ragged, ill-smelling garb he wore, but she had ceased her useless attempts to make him more cleanly.

"I've been herdin' sheep," replied Ellen. "And where have y'u been, uncle? I missed y'u on the way over."

"Been packin' in some grub. An' I reckon I stayed longer in Grass Valley than I recollect. But thet was only natural, considerin'—"

"What?" asked Ellen, bluntly, as the old man paused.

Sprague took a black pipe out of his vest pocket and began rimming the bowl with his fingers. The glance he bent on Ellen was thoughtful and earnest, and so kind that she feared it was pity. Ellen suddenly burned for news from the village.

"Wal, come in an' set down, won't you?" he asked.

"No, thanks," replied Ellen, and she took a seat on the chopping block. "Tell me, uncle, what's goin' on down in the Valley?"

"Nothin' much yet—except talk. An' there's a heap of thet."

"Humph! There always was talk," declared Ellen, contemptuously. "A nasty, gossipy, catty hole, that Grass Valley!"

"Ellen, thar's goin' to be war—a bloody war in the ole Tonto Basin," went on Sprague, seriously.

"War! ... Between whom?"

"The Isbels an' their enemies. I reckon most people down thar, an' sure all the cattlemen, air on old Gass's side. Blaisdell, Gordon, Fredericks, Blue—they'll all be in it."

"Who are they goin' to fight?" queried Ellen, sharply.

"Wal, the open talk is thet the sheepmen are forcin' this war. But thar's talk not so open, an' I reckon not very healthy for any man to whisper hyarbouts."

"Uncle John, y'u needn't be afraid to tell me anythin'," said Ellen. "I'd never give y'u away. Y'u've been a good friend to me."

"Reckon I want to be, Ellen," he returned, nodding his shaggy head. "It ain't easy to be fond of you as I am an' keep my mouth shet.... I'd like to know somethin'. Hev you any relatives away from hyar thet you could go to till this fight's over?"

"No. All I have, so far as I know, are right heah."

"How aboot friends?"

"Uncle John, I have none," she said, sadly, with bowed head.

"Wal, wal, I'm sorry. I was hopin' you might git away."

She lifted her face. "Shore y'u don't think I'd run off if my dad got in a fight?" she flashed.

"I hope you will."

"I'm a Jorth," she said, darkly, and dropped her head again.

Sprague nodded gloomily. Evidently he was perplexed and worried, and strongly swayed by affection for her.

"Would you go away with me?" he asked. "We could pack over to the Mazatzals an' live thar till this blows over."

"Thank y'u, Uncle John. Y'u're kind and good. But I'll stay with my father. His troubles are mine."

"Ahuh! ... Wal, I might hev reckoned so.... Ellen, how do you stand on this hyar sheep an' cattle question?"

"I think what's fair for one is fair for another. I don't like sheep as much as I like cattle. But that's not the point. The range is free. Suppose y'u had cattle and I had sheep. I'd feel as free to run my sheep anywhere as y'u were to ran your cattle."

"Right. But what if you throwed your sheep round my range an' sheeped off the grass so my cattle would hev to move or starve?"

"Shore I wouldn't throw my sheep round y'ur range," she declared, stoutly.

"Wal, you've answered half of the question. An' now supposin' a lot of my cattle was stolen by rustlers, but not a single one of your sheep. What 'd you think then?"

"I'd shore think rustlers chose to steal cattle because there was no profit in stealin' sheep."

"Egzactly. But wouldn't you hev a queer idee aboot it?"

"I don't know. Why queer? What 're y'u drivin' at, Uncle John?"

"Wal, wouldn't you git kind of a hunch thet the rustlers was—say a leetle friendly toward the sheepmen?"

Ellen felt a sudden vibrating shock. The blood rushed to her temples. Trembling all over, she rose.

"Uncle John!" she cried.

"Now, girl, you needn't fire up thet way. Set down an' don't—"

"Dare y'u insinuate my father has—"

"Ellen, I ain't insinuatin' nothin'," interrupted the old man. "I'm jest askin' you to think. Thet's all. You're 'most grown into a young woman now. An' you've got sense. Thar's bad times ahead, Ellen. An' I hate to see you mix in them."

"Oh, y'u do make me think," replied Ellen, with smarting tears in her eyes. "Y'u make me unhappy. Oh, I know my dad is not liked in this cattle country. But it's unjust. He happened to go in for sheep raising. I wish he hadn't. It was a mistake. Dad always was a cattleman till we came heah. He made enemies—who—who ruined him. And everywhere misfortune crossed his trail.... But, oh, Uncle John, my dad is an honest man."

"Wal, child, I—I didn't mean to—to make you cry," said the old man, feelingly, and he averted his troubled gaze. "Never mind what I said. I'm an old meddler. I reckon nothin' I could do or say would ever change what's goin' to happen. If only you wasn't a girl! ... Thar I go ag'in. Ellen, face your future an' fight your way. All youngsters hev to do thet. An' it's the right kind of fight thet makes the right kind of man or woman. Only you must be sure to find yourself. An' by thet I mean to find the real, true, honest-to-God best in you an' stick to it an' die fightin' for it. You're a young woman, almost, an' a blamed handsome one. Which means you'll hev more trouble an' a harder fight. This country ain't easy on a woman when once slander has marked her."

"What do I care for the talk down in that Basin?" returned Ellen. "I know they think I'm a hussy. I've let them think it. I've helped them to."

"You're wrong, child," said Sprague, earnestly. "Pride an' temper! You must never let anyone think bad of you, much less help them to."

"I hate everybody down there," cried Ellen, passionately. "I hate them so I'd glory in their thinkin' me bad.... My mother belonged to the best blood in Texas. I am her daughter. I know WHO AND WHAT I AM. That uplifts me whenever I meet the sneaky, sly suspicions of these Basin people. It shows me the difference between them and me. That's what I glory in."

"Ellen, you're a wild, headstrong child," rejoined the old man, in severe tones. "Word has been passed ag'in' your good name—your honor.... An' hevn't you given cause fer thet?"

Ellen felt her face blanch and all her blood rush back to her heart in sickening force. The shock of his words was like a stab from a cold blade. If their meaning and the stem, just light of the old man's glance did not kill her pride and vanity they surely killed her girlishness. She stood mute, staring at him, with her brown, trembling hands stealing up toward her bosom, as if to ward off another and a mortal blow.

"Ellen!" burst out Sprague, hoarsely. "You mistook me. Aw, I didn't mean—what you think, I swear.... Ellen, I'm old an' blunt. I ain't used to wimmen. But I've love for you, child, an' respect, jest the same as if you was my own.... An' I KNOW you're good.... Forgive me.... I meant only hevn't you been, say, sort of—careless?"

"Care-less?" queried Ellen, bitterly and low.

"An' powerful thoughtless an'—an' blind—lettin' men kiss you an' fondle you—when you're really a growed-up woman now?"

"Yes—I have," whispered Ellen.

"Wal, then, why did you let them?

"I—I don't know.... I didn't think. The men never let me alone—never—never! I got tired everlastingly pushin' them away. And sometimes—when they were kind—and I was lonely for something I—I didn't mind if one or another fooled round me. I never thought. It never looked as y'u have made it look.... Then—those few times ridin' the trail to Grass Valley—when people saw me—then I guess I encouraged such attentions.... Oh, I must be—I am a shameless little hussy!"

"Hush thet kind of talk," said the old man, as he took her hand. "Ellen, you're only young an' lonely an' bitter. No mother—no friends—no one but a lot of rough men! It's a wonder you hev kept yourself good. But now your eyes are open, Ellen. They're brave an' beautiful eyes, girl, an' if you stand by the light in them you will come through any trouble. An' you'll be happy. Don't ever forgit that. Life is hard enough, God knows, but it's unfailin' true in the end to the man or woman who finds the best in them an' stands by it."

"Uncle John, y'u talk so—so kindly. Yu make me have hope. There seemed really so little for me to live for—hope for.... But I'll never be a coward again—nor a thoughtless fool. I'll find some good in me—or make some—and never fail it, come what will. I'll remember your words. I'll believe the future holds wonderful things for me.... I'm only eighteen. Shore all my life won't be lived heah. Perhaps this threatened fight over sheep and cattle will blow over.... Somewhere there must be some nice girl to be a friend—a sister to me.... And maybe some man who'd believe, in spite of all they say—that I'm not a hussy."

"Wal, Ellen, you remind me of what I was wantin' to tell you when you just got here.... Yestiddy I heerd you called thet name in a barroom. An' thar was a fellar thar who raised hell. He near killed one man an' made another plumb eat his words. An' he scared thet crowd stiff."

Old John Sprague shook his grizzled head and laughed, beaming upon Ellen as if the memory of what he had seen had warmed his heart.

"Was it—y'u?" asked Ellen, tremulously.

"Me? Aw, I wasn't nowhere. Ellen, this fellar was quick as a cat in his actions an' his words was like lightnin'.'

"Who? she whispered.

"Wal, no one else but a stranger jest come to these parts—an Isbel, too. Jean Isbel."

"Oh!" exclaimed Ellen, faintly.

"In a barroom full of men—almost all of them in sympathy with the sheep crowd—most of them on the Jorth side—this Jean Isbel resented an insult to Ellen Jorth."

"No!" cried Ellen. Something terrible was happening to her mind or her heart.

"Wal, he sure did," replied the old man, "an' it's goin' to be good fer you to hear all about it."

CHAPTER V

Old John Sprague launched into his narrative with evident zest.

"I hung round Greaves' store most of two days. An' I heerd a heap. Some of it was jest plain ole men's gab, but I reckon I got the drift of things concernin' Grass Valley. Yestiddy mornin' I was packin' my burros in Greaves' back yard, takin' my time carryin' out supplies from the store. An' as last when I went in I seen a strange fellar was thar. Strappin' young man—not so young, either—an' he had on buckskin. Hair black as my burros, dark face, sharp eyes—you'd took him fer an Injun. He carried a rifle—one of them new forty-fours—an' also somethin' wrapped in paper thet he seemed partickler careful about. He wore a belt round his middle an' thar was a bowie-knife in it, carried like I've seen scouts an' Injun fighters hev on the frontier in the 'seventies. That looked queer to me, an' I reckon to the rest of the crowd thar. No one overlooked the big six-shooter he packed Texas fashion. Wal, I didn't hev no idee this fellar was an Isbel until I heard Greaves call him thet.

"'Isbel,' said Greaves, 'reckon your money's counterfeit hyar. I cain't sell you anythin'.'

"'Counterfeit? Not much,' spoke up the young fellar, an' he flipped some gold twenties on the bar, where they rung like bells. 'Why not? Ain't this a store? I want a cinch strap.'

"Greaves looked particular sour thet mornin'. I'd been watchin' him fer two days. He hedn't hed much sleep, fer I hed my bed back of the store, an' I heerd men come in the night an' hev long confabs with him. Whatever was in the wind hedn't pleased him none. An' I calkilated thet young Isbel wasn't a sight good fer Greaves' sore eyes, anyway. But he paid no more attention to Isbel. Acted jest as if he hedn't heerd Isbel say he wanted a cinch strap.

"I stayed inside the store then. Thar was a lot of fellars I'd seen, an' some I knowed. Couple of card games goin', an' drinkin', of course. I soon gathered thet the general atmosphere wasn't friendly to Jean Isbel. He seen thet quick enough, but he didn't leave. Between you an' me I sort of took a likin' to him. An' I sure watched him as close as I could, not seemin' to, you know. Reckon they all did the same, only you couldn't see it. It got jest about the same as if Isbel hedn't been in thar, only you knowed it wasn't really the same. Thet was how I got the hunch the crowd was all sheepmen or their friends. The day before I'd heerd a lot of talk about this young Isbel, an' what he'd come to Grass Valley fer, an' what a bad hombre he was. An' when I seen him I was bound to admit he looked his reputation.

"Wal, pretty soon in come two more fellars, an' I knowed both of them. You know them, too, I'm sorry to say. Fer I'm comin' to facts now thet will shake you. The first fellar was your father's Mexican foreman, Lorenzo, and the other was Simm Bruce. I reckon Bruce wasn't drunk, but he'd sure been lookin' on red licker. When he seen Isbel darn me if he didn't swell an' bustle all up like a mad ole turkey gobbler.

"'Greaves,' he said, 'if thet fellar's Jean Isbel I ain't hankerin' fer the company y'u keep.' An' he made no bones of pointin' right at Isbel. Greaves looked up dry an' sour an' he bit out spiteful-like: 'Wal, Simm, we ain't hed a hell of a lot of choice in this heah matter. Thet's Jean Isbel shore enough. Mebbe you can persuade him thet his company an' his custom ain't wanted round heah!'

"Jean Isbel set on the counter an took it all in, but he didn't say nothin'. The way he looked at Bruce was sure enough fer me to see thet thar might be a surprise any minnit. I've looked at a lot of men in my day, an' can sure feel events comin'. Bruce got himself a stiff drink an' then he straddles over the floor in front of Isbel.

"'Air you Jean Isbel, son of ole Gass Isbel?' asked Bruce, sort of lolling back an' givin' a hitch to his belt.

"'Yes sir, you've identified me,' said Isbel, nice an' polite.

"'My name's Bruce. I'm rangin' sheep heahaboots, an' I hev interest in Kurnel Lee Jorth's bizness.'

"'Hod do, Mister Bruce,' replied Isbel, very civil ant cool as you please. Bruce hed an eye fer the crowd thet was now listenin' an' watchin'. He swaggered closer to Isbel.

"'We heerd y'u come into the Tonto Basin to run us sheepmen off the range. How aboot thet?'

"'Wal, you heerd wrong,' said Isbel, quietly. 'I came to work fer my father. Thet work depends on what happens.'

"Bruce began to git redder of face, an' he shook a husky hand in front of Isbel. 'I'll tell y'u this heah, my Nez Perce Isbel—' an' when he sort of choked fer more wind Greaves spoke up, 'Simm, I shore reckon thet Nez Perce handle will stick.' An' the crowd haw-hawed. Then Bruce got goin' ag'in. 'I'll tell y'u this heah, Nez Perce. Thar's been enough happen already to run y'u out of Arizona.'

"'Wal, you don't say! What, fer instance?, asked Isbel, quick an' sarcastic.

"Thet made Bruce bust out puffin' an' spittin': 'Wha-tt, fer instance? Huh! Why, y'u darn half-breed, y'u'll git run out fer makin' up to Ellen Jorth. Thet won't go in this heah country. Not fer any Isbel.'

"'You're a liar,' called Isbel, an' like a big cat he dropped off the counter. I heerd his moccasins pat soft on the floor. An' I bet to myself thet he was as dangerous as he was quick. But his voice an' his looks didn't change even a leetle.

"'I'm not a liar,' yelled Bruce. 'I'll make y'u eat thet. I can prove what I say.... Y'u was seen with Ellen Jorth—up on the Rim—day before yestiddy. Y'u was watched. Y'u was with her. Y'u made up to her. Y'u grabbed her an' kissed her! ... An' I'm heah to say, Nez Perce, thet y'u're a marked man on this range.'

"'Who saw me?' asked Isbel, quiet an' cold. I seen then thet he'd turned white in the face.

"'Yu cain't lie out of it,' hollered Bruce, wavin' his hands. 'We got y'u daid to rights. Lorenzo saw y'u—follered y'u—watched y'u.' Bruce pointed at the grinnin' greaser. 'Lorenzo is Kurnel Jorth's foreman. He seen y'u maulin' of Ellen Jorth. An' when he tells the Kurnel an' Tad Jorth an' Jackson Jorth! ... Haw! Haw! Haw! Why, hell 'd be a cooler place fer yu then this heah Tonto.'

"Greaves an' his gang hed come round, sure tickled clean to thar gizzards at this mess. I noticed, howsomever, thet they was Texans enough to keep back to one side in case this Isbel started any action.... Wal, Isbel took a look at Lorenzo. Then with one swift grab he jerked the little greaser off his feet an' pulled him close. Lorenzo stopped grinnin'. He began to look a leetle sick. But it was plain he hed right on his side.

"'You say you saw me?' demanded Isbel.

"'Si, senor,' replied Lorenzo.

"What did you see?'

"'I see senor an' senorita. I hide by manzanita. I see senorita like grande senor ver mooch. She like senor keese. She—'

"Then Isbel hit the little greaser a back-handed crack in the mouth. Sure it was a crack! Lorenzo went over the counter backward an' landed like a pack load of wood. An' he didn't git up.

"'Mister Bruce,' said Isbel, 'an' you fellars who heerd thet lyin' greaser, I did meet Ellen Jorth. An' I lost my head. I 'I kissed her.... But it was an accident. I meant no insult. I apologized—I tried to explain my crazy action.... Thet was all. The greaser lied. Ellen Jorth was kind enough to show me the trail. We talked a little. Then—I suppose—because she was young an' pretty an' sweet—I lost my head. She was absolutely innocent. Thet damned greaser told a bare-faced lie when he said she liked me. The fact was she despised me. She said so. An' when she learned I was Jean Isbel she turned her back on me an' walked away.'"

At this point of his narrative the old man halted as if to impress Ellen not only with what just had been told, but particularly with what was to follow. The reciting of this tale had evidently given Sprague an unconscious pleasure. He glowed. He seemed to carry the burden of a secret that he yearned to divulge. As for Ellen, she was deadlocked in breathless suspense. All her emotions waited for the end. She begged Sprague to hurry.

"Wal, I wish I could skip the next chapter an' hev only the last to tell," rejoined the old man, and he put a heavy, but solicitous, hand upon hers.... Simm Bruce haw-hawed loud an' loud.... 'Say, Nez Perce,' he calls out, most insolent-like, 'we air too good sheepmen heah to hev the wool pulled over our eyes. We shore know what y'u meant by Ellen Jorth. But y'u wasn't smart when y'u told her y'u was Jean Isbel! ... Haw-haw!'

"Isbel flashed a strange, surprised look from the red-faced Bruce to Greaves and to the other men. I take it he was wonderin' if he'd heerd right or if they'd got the same hunch thet 'd come to him. An' I reckon he determined to make sure.

"'Why wasn't I smart?' he asked.

"'Shore y'u wasn't smart if y'u was aimin' to be one of Ellen Jorth's lovers,' said Bruce, with a leer. 'Fer if y'u hedn't give y'urself away y'u could hev been easy enough.'

"Thar was no mistakin' Bruce's meanin' an' when he got it out some of the men thar laughed. Isbel kept lookin' from one to another of them. Then facin' Greaves, he said, deliberately: 'Greaves, this drunken Bruce is excuse enough fer a show-down. I take it that you are sheepmen, an' you're goin' on Jorth's side of the fence in the matter of this sheep rangin'.'

"'Wal, Nez Perce, I reckon you hit plumb center,' said Greaves, dryly. He spread wide his big hands to the other men, as if to say they'd might as well own the jig was up.

"'All right. You're Jorth's backers. Have any of you a word to say in Ellen Jorth's defense? I tell you the Mexican lied. Believin' me or not doesn't matter. But this vile-mouthed Bruce hinted against thet girl's honor.'

"Ag'in some of the men laughed, but not so noisy, an' there was a nervous shufflin' of feet. Isbel looked sort of queer. His neck had a bulge round his collar. An' his eyes was like black coals of fire. Greaves spread his big hands again, as if to wash them of this part of the dirty argument.

"'When it comes to any wimmen I pass—much less play a hand fer a wildcat like Jorth's gurl,' said Greaves, sort of cold an' thick. 'Bruce shore ought to know her. Accordin' to talk heahaboots an' what HE says, Ellen Jorth has been his gurl fer two years.'

"Then Isbel turned his attention to Bruce an' I fer one begun to shake in my boots.

"'Say thet to me!' he called.

"'Shore she's my gurl, an' thet's why Im a-goin' to hev y'u run off this range.'

"Isbel jumped at Bruce. 'You damned drunken cur! You vile-mouthed liar! ... I may be an Isbel, but by God you cain't slander thet girl to my face! ... Then he moved so quick I couldn't see what he did. But I heerd his fist hit Bruce. It sounded like an ax ag'in' a beef. Bruce fell clear across the room. An' by Jinny when he landed Isbel was thar. As Bruce staggered up, all bloody-faced, bellowin' an' spittin' out teeth Isbel eyed Greaves's crowd an' said: 'If any of y'u make a move it 'll mean gun-play.' Nobody moved, thet's sure. In fact, none of Greaves's outfit was packin' guns, at least in sight. When Bruce got all the way up—he's a tall fellar—why Isbel took a full swing at him an' knocked him back across the room ag'in' the counter. Y'u know when a fellar's hurt by the way he yells. Bruce got thet second smash right on his big red nose.... I never seen any one so quick as Isbel. He vaulted over thet counter jest the second Bruce fell back on it, an' then, with Greaves's gang in front so he could catch any moves of theirs, he jest slugged Bruce right an' left, an' banged his head on the counter. Then as Bruce sunk limp an' slipped down, lookin' like a bloody sack, Isbel let him fall to the floor. Then he vaulted back over the counter. Wipin' the blood off his hands, he throwed his kerchief down in Bruce's face. Bruce wasn't dead or bad hurt. He'd jest been beaten bad. He was moanin' an' slobberin'. Isbel kicked him, not hard, but jest sort of disgustful. Then he faced thet crowd. 'Greaves, thet's what I think of your Simm Bruce. Tell him next time he sees me to run or pull a gun.' An' then Isbel grabbed his rifle an' package off the counter an' went out. He didn't even look back. I seen him nount his horse an' ride away.... Now, girl, what hev you to say?"

Ellen could only say good-by and the word was so low as to be almost inaudible. She ran to her burro. She could not see very clearly through tear-blurred eyes, and her shaking fingers were all thumbs. It seemed she had to rush away—somewhere, anywhere—not to get away from old John Sprague, but from herself—this palpitating, bursting self whose feet stumbled down the trail. All—all seemed ended for her. That interminable story! It had taken so long. And every minute of it she had been helplessly torn asunder by feelings she had never known she possessed. This Ellen Jorth was an unknown creature. She sobbed now as she dragged the burro down the canyon trail. She sat down only to rise. She hurried only to stop. Driven, pursued, barred, she had no way to escape the flaying thoughts, no time or will to repudiate them. The death of her girlhood, the rending aside of a veil of maiden mystery only vaguely instinctively guessed, the barren, sordid truth of her life as seen by her enlightened eyes, the bitter realization of the vileness of men of her clan in contrast to the manliness and chivalry of an enemy, the hard facts of unalterable repute as created by slander and fostered by low minds, all these were forces in a cataclysm that had suddenly caught her heart and whirled her through changes immense and agonizing, to bring her face to face with reality, to force upon her suspicion and doubt of all she had trusted, to warn her of the dark, impending horror of a tragic bloody feud, and lastly to teach her the supreme truth at once so glorious and so terrible—that she could not escape the doom of womanhood.

About noon that day Ellen Jorth arrived at the Knoll, which was the location of her father's ranch. Three canyons met there to form a larger one. The knoll was a symmetrical hill situated at the mouth of the three canyons. It was covered with brush and cedars, with here and there lichened rocks showing above the bleached grass. Below the Knoll was a wide, grassy flat or meadow through which a willow-bordered stream cut its rugged boulder-strewn bed. Water flowed abundantly at this season, and the deep washes leading down from the slopes attested to the fact of cloudbursts and heavy storms. This meadow valley was dotted with horses and cattle, and meandered away between the timbered slopes to lose itself in a green curve. A singular feature of this canyon was that a heavy growth of spruce trees covered the slope facing northwest; and the opposite slope, exposed to the sun and therefore less snowbound in winter, held a sparse growth of yellow pines. The ranch house of Colonel Jorth stood round the rough comer of the largest of the three canyons, and rather well hidden, it did not obtrude its rude and broken-down log cabins, its squalid surroundings, its black mud-holes of corrals upon the beautiful and serene meadow valley.

Ellen Jorth approached her home slowly, with dragging, reluctant steps; and never before in the three unhappy years of her existence there had the ranch seemed so bare, so uncared for, so repugnant to her. As she had seen herself with clarified eyes, so now she saw her home. The cabin that Ellen lived in with her father was a single-room structure with one door and no windows. It was about twenty feet square. The huge, ragged, stone chimney had been built on the outside, with the wide open fireplace set inside the logs. Smoke was rising from the chimney. As Ellen halted at the door and began unpacking her burro she heard the loud, lazy laughter of men. An adjoining log cabin had been built in two sections, with a wide roofed hall or space between them. The door in each cabin faced the other, and there was a tall man standing in one. Ellen recognized Daggs, a neighbor sheepman, who evidently spent more time with her father than at his own home, wherever that was. Ellen had never seen it. She heard this man drawl, "Jorth, heah's your kid come home."

Ellen carried her bed inside the cabin, and unrolled it upon a couch built of boughs in the far corner. She had forgotten Jean Isbel's package, and now it fell out under her sight. Quickly she covered it. A Mexican woman, relative of Antonio, and the only servant about the place, was squatting Indian fashion before the fireplace, stirring a pot of beans. She and Ellen did not get along well together, and few words ever passed between them. Ellen had a canvas curtain stretched upon a wire across a small triangular comer, and this afforded her a little privacy. Her possessions were limited in number. The crude square table she had constructed herself. Upon it was a little old-fashioned walnut-framed mirror, a brush and comb, and a dilapidated ebony cabinet which contained odds and ends the sight of which always brought a smile of derisive self-pity to her lips. Under the table stood an old leather trunk. It had come with her from Texas, and contained clothing and belongings of her mother's. Above the couch on pegs hung her scant wardrobe. A tiny shelf held several worn-out books.

When her father slept indoors, which was seldom except in winter, he occupied a couch in the opposite corner. A rude cupboard had been built against the logs next to the fireplace. It contained supplies and utensils. Toward the center, somewhat closer to the door, stood a crude table and two benches. The cabin was dark and smelled of smoke, of the stale odors of past cooked meals, of the mustiness of dry, rotting timber. Streaks of light showed through the roof where the rough-hewn shingles had split or weathered. A strip of bacon hung upon one side of the cupboard, and upon the other a haunch of venison. Ellen detested the Mexican woman because she was dirty. The inside of the cabin presented the same unkempt appearance usual to it after Ellen had been away for a few days. Whatever Ellen had lost during the retrogression of the Jorths, she had kept her habits of cleanliness, and straightway upon her return she set to work.

The Mexican woman sullenly slouched away to her own quarters outside and Ellen was left to the satisfaction of labor. Her mind was as busy as her hands. As she cleaned and swept and dusted she heard from time to time the voices of men, the clip-clop of shod horses, the bellow of cattle. And a considerable time elapsed before she was disturbed.

A tall shadow darkened the doorway.

"Howdy, little one!" said a lazy, drawling voice. "So y'u-all got home?"

Ellen looked up. A superbly built man leaned against the doorpost. Like most Texans, he was light haired and light eyed. His face was lined and hard. His long, sandy mustache hid his mouth and drooped with a curl. Spurred, booted, belted, packing a heavy gun low down on his hip, he gave Ellen an entirely new impression. Indeed, she was seeing everything strangely.

"Hello, Daggs!" replied Ellen. "Where's my dad?"

"He's playin' cairds with Jackson an' Colter. Shore's playin' bad, too, an' it's gone to his haid."

"Gamblin'?" queried Ellen.

"Mah child, when'd Kurnel Jorth ever play for fun?" said Daggs, with a lazy laugh. "There's a stack of gold on the table. Reckon yo' uncle Jackson will win it. Colter's shore out of luck."

Daggs stepped inside. He was graceful and slow. His long' spurs clinked. He laid a rather compelling hand on Ellen's shoulder.

"Heah, mah gal, give us a kiss," he said.

"Daggs, I'm not your girl," replied Ellen as she slipped out from under his hand.

Then Daggs put his arm round her, not with violence or rudeness, but with an indolent, affectionate assurance, at once bold and self-contained. Ellen, however, had to exert herself to get free of him, and when she had placed the table between them she looked him square in the eyes.

"Daggs, y'u keep your paws off me," she said.

"Aw, now, Ellen, I ain't no bear," he remonstrated. "What's the matter, kid?"

"I'm not a kid. And there's nothin' the matter. Y'u're to keep your hands to yourself, that's all."

He tried to reach her across the table, and his movements were lazy and slow, like his smile. His tone was coaxing.

"Mah dear, shore you set on my knee just the other day, now, didn't you?"

Ellen felt the blood sting her cheeks.

"I was a child," she returned.

"Wal, listen to this heah grown-up young woman. All in a few days! ... Doon't be in a temper, Ellen.... Come, give us a kiss."

She deliberately gazed into his eyes. Like the eyes of an eagle, they were clear and hard, just now warmed by the dalliance of the moment, but there was no light, no intelligence in them to prove he understood her. The instant separated Ellen immeasurably from him and from all of his ilk.

"Daggs, I was a child," she said. "I was lonely—hungry for affection—I was innocent. Then I was careless, too, and thoughtless when I should have known better. But I hardly understood y'u men. I put such thoughts out of my mind. I know now—know what y'u mean—what y'u have made people believe I am."

"Ahuh! Shore I get your hunch," he returned, with a change of tone. "But I asked you to marry me?"

"Yes y'u did. The first day y'u got heah to my dad's house. And y'u asked me to marry y'u after y'u found y'u couldn't have your way with me. To y'u the one didn't mean any more than the other."

"Shore I did more than Simm Bruce an' Colter," he retorted. "They never asked you to marry."

"No, they didn't. And if I could respect them at all I'd do it because they didn't ask me."

"Wal, I'll be dog-goned!" ejaculated Daggs, thoughtfully, as he stroked his long mustache.

"I'll say to them what I've said to y'u," went on Ellen. "I'll tell dad to make y'u let me alone. I wouldn't marry one of y'u—y'u loafers to save my life. I've my suspicions about y'u. Y'u're a bad lot."

Daggs changed subtly. The whole indolent nonchalance of the man vanished in an instant.

"Wal, Miss Jorth, I reckon you mean we're a bad lot of sheepmen?" he queried, in the cool, easy speech of a Texan.

"No," flashed Ellen. "Shore I don't say sheepmen. I say y'u're a BAD LOT."

"Oh, the hell you say!" Daggs spoke as he might have spoken to a man; then turning swiftly on his heel he left her. Outside he encountered Ellen's father. She heard Daggs speak: "Lee, your little wildcat is shore heah. An' take mah hunch. Somebody has been talkin' to her."

"Who has?" asked her father, in his husky voice. Ellen knew at once that he had been drinking.

"Lord only knows," replied Daggs. "But shore it wasn't any friends of ours."

"We cain't stop people's tongues," said Jorth, resignedly

"Wal, I ain't so shore," continued Daggs, with his slow, cool laugh. "Reckon I never yet heard any daid men's tongues wag."

Then the musical tinkle of his spurs sounded fainter. A moment later Ellen's father entered the cabin. His dark, moody face brightened at sight of her. Ellen knew she was the only person in the world left for him to love. And she was sure of his love. Her very presence always made him different. And through the years, the darker their misfortunes, the farther he slipped away from better days, the more she loved him.

"Hello, my Ellen!" he said, and he embraced her. When he had been drinking he never kissed her. "Shore I'm glad you're home. This heah hole is bad enough any time, but when you're gone it's black.... I'm hungry."

Ellen laid food and drink on the table; and for a little while she did not look directly at him. She was concerned about this new searching power of her eyes. In relation to him she vaguely dreaded it.

Lee Jorth had once been a singularly handsome man. He was tall, but did not have the figure of a horseman. His dark hair was streaked with gray, and was white over his ears. His face was sallow and thin, with deep lines. Under his round, prominent, brown eyes, like deadened furnaces, were blue swollen welts. He had a bitter mouth and weak chin, not wholly concealed by gray mustache and pointed beard. He wore a long frock coat and a wide-brimmed sombrero, both black in color, and so old and stained and frayed that along with the fashion of them they betrayed that they had come from Texas with him. Jorth always persisted in wearing a white linen shirt, likewise a relic of his Southern prosperity, and to-day it was ragged and soiled as usual.

Ellen watched her father eat and waited for him to speak. It occured to her strangely that he never asked about the sheep or the new-born lambs. She divined with a subtle new woman's intuition that he cared nothing for his sheep.

"Ellen, what riled Daggs?" inquired her father, presently. "He shore had fire in his eye."

Long ago Ellen had betrayed an indignity she had suffered at the hands of a man. Her father had nearly killed him. Since then she had taken care to keep her troubles to herself. If her father had not been blind and absorbed in his own brooding he would have seen a thousand things sufficient to inflame his Southern pride and temper.

"Daggs asked me to marry him again and I said he belonged to a bad lot," she replied.

Jorth laughed in scorn. "Fool! My God! Ellen, I must have dragged you low—that every damned ru—er—sheepman—who comes along thinks he can marry you."

At the break in his words, the incompleted meaning, Ellen dropped her eyes. Little things once never noted by her were now come to have a fascinating significance.

"Never mind, dad," she replied. "They cain't marry me."

"Daggs said somebody had been talkin' to you. How aboot that?"

"Old John Sprague has just gotten back from Grass Valley," said Ellen. "I stopped in to see him. Shore he told me all the village gossip."

"Anythin' to interest me?" he queried, darkly.

"Yes, dad, I'm afraid a good deal," she said, hesitatingly. Then in accordance with a decision Ellen had made she told him of the rumored war between sheepmen and cattlemen; that old Isbel had Blaisdell, Gordon, Fredericks, Blue and other well-known ranchers on his side; that his son Jean Isbel had come from Oregon with a wonderful reputation as fighter and scout and tracker; that it was no secret how Colonel Lee Jorth was at the head of the sheepmen; that a bloody war was sure to come.

"Hah!" exclaimed Jorth, with a stain of red in his sallow cheek. "Reckon none of that is news to me. I knew all that."

Ellen wondered if he had heard of her meeting with Jean Isbel. If not he would hear as soon as Simm Bruce and Lorenzo came back. She decided to forestall them.

"Dad, I met Jean Isbel. He came into my camp. Asked the way to the Rim. I showed him. We—we talked a little. And shore were gettin' acquainted when—when he told me who he was. Then I left him—hurried back to camp."

"Colter met Isbel down in the woods," replied Jorth, ponderingly. "Said he looked like an Indian—a hard an' slippery customer to reckon with."

"Shore I guess I can indorse what Colter said," returned Ellen, dryly. She could have laughed aloud at her deceit. Still she had not lied.

"How'd this heah young Isbel strike you?" queried her father, suddenly glancing up at her.

Ellen felt the slow, sickening, guilty rise of blood in her face. She was helpless to stop it. But her father evidently never saw it. He was looking at her without seeing her.

"He—he struck me as different from men heah," she stammered.

"Did Sprague tell you aboot this half-Indian Isbel—aboot his reputation?"

"Yes."

"Did he look to you like a real woodsman?"

"Indeed he did. He wore buckskin. He stepped quick and soft. He acted at home in the woods. He had eyes black as night and sharp as lightnin'. They shore saw about all there was to see."

Jorth chewed at his mustache and lost himself in brooding thought.

"Dad, tell me, is there goin' to be a war?" asked Ellen, presently.

What a red, strange, rolling flash blazed in his eyes! His body jerked.

"Shore. You might as well know."

"Between sheepmen and cattlemen?"

"Yes."

"With y'u, dad, at the haid of one faction and Gaston Isbel the other?"

"Daughter, you have it correct, so far as you go."

"Oh! ... Dad, can't this fight be avoided?"

"You forget you're from Texas," he replied.

"Cain't it be helped?" she repeated, stubbornly.

"No!" he declared, with deep, hoarse passion.

"Why not?"

"Wal, we sheepmen are goin' to run sheep anywhere we like on the range. An' cattlemen won't stand for that."

"But, dad, it's so foolish," declared Ellen, earnestly. "Y'u sheepmen do not have to run sheep over the cattle range."

"I reckon we do."

"Dad, that argument doesn't go with me. I know the country. For years to come there will be room for both sheep and cattle without overrunnin'. If some of the range is better in water and grass, then whoever got there first should have it. That shore is only fair. It's common sense, too."

"Ellen, I reckon some cattle people have been prejudicin' you," said Jorth, bitterly.

"Dad!" she cried, hotly.

This had grown to be an ordeal for Jorth. He seemed a victim of contending tides of feeling. Some will or struggle broke within him and the change was manifest. Haggard, shifty-eyed, with wabbling chin, he burst into speech.

"See heah, girl. You listen. There's a clique of ranchers down in the Basin, all those you named, with Isbel at their haid. They have resented sheepmen comin' down into the valley. They want it all to themselves. That's the reason. Shore there's another. All the Isbels are crooked. They're cattle an' horse thieves—have been for years. Gaston Isbel always was a maverick rustler. He's gettin' old now an' rich, so he wants to cover his tracks. He aims to blame this cattle rustlin' an' horse stealin' on to us sheepmen, an' run us out of the country."

Gravely Ellen Jorth studied her father's face, and the newly found truth-seeing power of her eyes did not fail her. In part, perhaps in all, he was telling lies. She shuddered a little, loyally battling against the insidious convictions being brought to fruition. Perhaps in his brooding over his failures and troubles he leaned toward false judgments. Ellen could not attach dishonor to her father's motives or speeches. For long, however, something about him had troubled her, perplexed her. Fearfully she believed she was coming to some revelation, and, despite her keen determination to know, she found herself shrinking.

"Dad, mother told me before she died that the Isbels had ruined you," said Ellen, very low. It hurt her so to see her father cover his face that she could hardly go on. "If they ruined you they ruined all of us. I know what we had once—what we lost again and again—and I see what we are come to now. Mother hated the Isbels. She taught me to hate the very name. But I never knew how they ruined you—or why—or when. And I want to know now."

Then it was not the face of a liar that Jorth disclosed. The present was forgotten. He lived in the past. He even seemed younger 'in the revivifying flash of hate that made his face radiant. The lines burned out. Hate gave him back the spirit of his youth.

"Gaston Isbel an' I were boys together in Weston, Texas," began Jorth, in swift, passionate voice. "We went to school together. We loved the same girl—your mother. When the war broke out she was engaged to Isbel. His family was rich. They influenced her people. But she loved me. When Isbel went to war she married me. He came back an' faced us. God! I'll never forget that. Your mother confessed her unfaithfulness—by Heaven! She taunted him with it. Isbel accused me of winnin' her by lies. But she took the sting out of that.

"Isbel never forgave her an' he hounded me to ruin. He made me out a card-sharp, cheatin' my best friends. I was disgraced. Later he tangled me in the courts—he beat me out of property—an' last by convictin' me of rustlin' cattle he run me out of Texas."

Black and distorted now, Jorth's face was a spectacle to make Ellen sick with a terrible passion of despair and hate. The truth of her father's ruin and her own were enough. What mattered all else? Jorth beat the table with fluttering, nerveless hands that seemed all the more significant for their lack of physical force.

"An' so help me God, it's got to be wiped out in blood!" he hissed.

That was his answer to the wavering and nobility of Ellen. And she in her turn had no answer to make. She crept away into the corner behind the curtain, and there on her couch in the semidarkness she lay with strained heart, and a resurging, unconquerable tumult in her mind. And she lay there from the middle of that afternoon until the next morning.

When she awakened she expected to be unable to rise—she hoped she could not—but life seemed multiplied in her, and inaction was impossible. Something young and sweet and hopeful that had been in her did not greet the sun this morning. In their place was a woman's passion to learn for herself, to watch events, to meet what must come, to survive.

After breakfast, at which she sat alone, she decided to put Isbel's package out of the way, so that it would not be subjecting her to continual annoyance. The moment she picked it up the old curiosity assailed her.

"Shore I'll see what it is, anyway," she muttered, and with swift hands she opened the package. The action disclosed two pairs of fine, soft shoes, of a style she had never seen, and four pairs of stockings, two of strong, serviceable wool, and the others of a finer texture. Ellen looked at them in amaze. Of all things in the world, these would have been the last she expected to see. And, strangely, they were what she wanted and needed most. Naturally, then, Ellen made the mistake of taking them in her hands to feel their softness and warmth.

"Shore! He saw my bare legs! And he brought me these presents he'd intended for his sister.... He was ashamed for me—sorry for me.... And I thought he looked at me bold-like, as I'm used to be looked at heah! Isbel or not, he's shore..."

But Ellen Jorth could not utter aloud the conviction her intelligence tried to force upon her.

"It'd be a pity to burn them," she mused. "I cain't do it. Sometime I might send them to Ann Isbel."

Whereupon she wrapped them up again and hid them in the bottom of the old trunk, and slowly, as she lowered the lid, looking darkly, blankly at the wall, she whispered: "Jean Isbel! ... I hate him!"

Later when Ellen went outdoors she carried her rifle, which was unusual for her, unless she intended to go into the woods.

The morning was sunny and warm. A group of shirt-sleeved men lounged in the hall and before the porch of the double cabin. Her father was pacing up and down, talking forcibly. Ellen heard his hoarse voice. As she approached he ceased talking and his listeners relaxed their attention. Ellen's glance ran over them swiftly—Daggs, with his superb head, like that of a hawk, uncovered to the sun; Colter with his lowered, secretive looks, his sand-gray lean face; Jackson Jorth, her uncle, huge, gaunt, hulking, with white in his black beard and hair, and the fire of a ghoul in his hollow eyes; Tad Jorth, another brother of her father's, younger, red of eye and nose, a weak-chinned drinker of rum. Three other limber-legged Texans lounged there, partners of Daggs, and they were sun-browned, light-haired, blue-eyed men singularly alike in appearance, from their dusty high-heeled boots to their broad black sombreros. They claimed to be sheepmen. All Ellen could be sure of was that Rock Wells spent most of his time there, doing nothing but look for a chance to waylay her; Springer was a gambler; and the third, who answered to the strange name of Queen, was a silent, lazy, watchful-eyed man who never wore a glove on his right hand and who never was seen without a gun within easy reach of that hand.

"Howdy, Ellen. Shore you ain't goin' to say good mawnin' to this heah bad lot?" drawled Daggs, with good-natured sarcasm.

"Why, shore! Good morning, y'u hard-working industrious MANANA sheep raisers," replied Ellen, coolly.

Daggs stared. The others appeared taken back by a greeting so foreign from any to which they were accustomed from her. Jackson Jorth let out a gruff haw-haw. Some of them doffed their sombreros, and Rock Wells managed a lazy, polite good morning. Ellen's father seemed most significantly struck by her greeting, and the least amused.

"Ellen, I'm not likin' your talk," he said, with a frown.

"Dad, when y'u play cards don't y'u call a spade a spade?"

"Why, shore I do."

"Well, I'm calling spades spades."

"Ahuh!" grunted Jorth, furtively dropping his eyes. "Where you goin' with your gun? I'd rather you hung round heah now."

"Reckon I might as well get used to packing my gun all the time," replied Ellen. "Reckon I'll be treated more like a man."

Then the event Ellen had been expecting all morning took place. Simm Bruce and Lorenzo rode around the slope of the Knoll and trotted toward the cabin. Interest in Ellen was relegated to the background.

"Shore they're bustin' with news," declared Daggs.

"They been ridin' some, you bet," remarked another.

"Huh!" exclaimed Jorth. "Bruce shore looks queer to me."

"Red liquor," said Tad Jorth, sententiously. "You-all know the brand Greaves hands out."

"Naw, Simm ain't drunk," said Jackson Jorth. "Look at his bloody shirt."

The cool, indolent interest of the crowd vanished at the red color pointed out by Jackson Jorth. Daggs rose in a single springy motion to his lofty height. The face Bruce turned to Jorth was swollen and bruised, with unhealed cuts. Where his right eye should have been showed a puffed dark purple bulge. His other eye, however, gleamed with hard and sullen light. He stretched a big shaking hand toward Jorth.

"Thet Nez Perce Isbel beat me half to death," he bellowed.

Jorth stared hard at the tragic, almost grotesque figure, at the battered face. But speech failed him. It was Daggs who answered Bruce.

"Wal, Simm, I'll be damned if you don't look it."

"Beat you! What with?" burst out Jorth, explosively.

"I thought he was swingin' an ax, but Greaves swore it was his fists," bawled Bruce, in misery and fury.

"Where was your gun?" queried Jorth, sharply.

"Gun? Hell!" exclaimed Bruce, flinging wide his arms. "Ask Lorenzo. He had a gun. An' he got a biff in the jaw before my turn come. Ask him?"

Attention thus directed to the Mexican showed a heavy discolored swelling upon the side of his olive-skinned face. Lorenzo looked only serious.

"Hah! Speak up," shouted Jorth, impatiently.

"Senor Isbel heet me ver quick," replied Lorenzo, with expressive gesture. "I see thousand stars—then moocho black—all like night."

At that some of Daggs's men lolled back with dry crisp laughter. Daggs's hard face rippled with a smile. But there was no humor in anything for Colonel Jorth.

"Tell us what come off. Quick!" he ordered. "Where did it happen? Why? Who saw it? What did you do?"

Bruce lapsed into a sullen impressiveness. "Wal, I happened in Greaves's store an' run into Jean Isbel. Shore was lookin' fer him. I had my mind made up what to do, but I got to shootin' off my gab instead of my gun. I called him Nez Perce—an' I throwed all thet talk in his face about old Gass Isbel sendin' fer him——an' I told him he'd git run out of the Tonto. Reckon I was jest warmin' up.... But then it all happened. He slugged Lorenzo jest one. An' Lorenzo slid peaceful-like to bed behind the counter. I hadn't time to think of throwin' a gun before he whaled into me. He knocked out two of my teeth. An' I swallered one of them."

Ellen stood in the background behind three of the men and in the shadow. She did not join in the laugh that followed Bruce's remarks. She had known that he would lie. Uncertain yet of her reaction to this, but more bitter and furious as he revealed his utter baseness, she waited for more to be said.

"Wal, I'll be doggoned," drawled Daggs.

"What do you make of this kind of fightin'?" queried Jorth,

"Darn if I know," replied Daggs in perplexity. "Shore an' sartin it's not the way of a Texan. Mebbe this young Isbel really is what old Gass swears he is. Shore Bruce ain't nothin' to give an edge to a real gun fighter. Looks to me like Isbel bluffed Greaves an' his gang an' licked your men without throwin' a gun."

"Maybe Isbel doesn't want the name of drawin' first blood," suggested Jorth.

"That 'd be like Gass," spoke up Rock Wells, quietly. "I onct rode fer Gass in Texas."

"Say, Bruce," said Daggs, "was this heah palaverin' of yours an' Jean Isbel's aboot the old stock dispute? Aboot his father's range an' water? An' partickler aboot, sheep?"

"Wal—I—I yelled a heap," declared Bruce, haltingly, "but I don't recollect all I said—I was riled.... Shore, though it was the same old argyment thet's been fetchin' us closer an' closer to trouble."

Daggs removed his keen hawklike gaze from Bruce. "Wal, Jorth, all I'll say is this. If Bruce is tellin' the truth we ain't got a hell of a lot to fear from this young Isbel. I've known a heap of gun fighters in my day. An' Jean Isbel don't ran true to class. Shore there never was a gunman who'd risk cripplin' his right hand by sluggin' anybody."

"Wal," broke in Bruce, sullenly. "You-all can take it daid straight or not. I don't give a damn. But you've shore got my hunch thet Nez Perce Isbel is liable to handle any of you fellars jest as he did me, an' jest as easy. What's more, he's got Greaves figgered. An' you-all know thet Greaves is as deep in—"

"Shut up that kind of gab," demanded Jorth, stridently. "An' answer me. Was the row in Greaves's barroom aboot sheep?"

"Aw, hell! I said so, didn't I?" shouted Bruce, with a fierce uplift of his distorted face.

Ellen strode out from the shadow of the tall men who had obscured her.

"Bruce, y'u're a liar," she said, bitingly.

The surprise of her sudden appearance seemed to root Bruce to the spot. All but the discolored places on his face turned white. He held his breath a moment, then expelled it hard. His effort to recover from the shock was painfully obvious. He stammered incoherently.

"Shore y'u're more than a liar, too," cried Ellen, facing him with blazing eyes. And the rifle, gripped in both hands, seemed to declare her intent of menace. "That row was not about sheep.... Jean Isbel didn't beat y'u for anythin' about sheep.... Old John Sprague was in Greaves's store. He heard y'u. He saw Jean Isbel beat y'u as y'u deserved.... An' he told ME!"

Ellen saw Bruce shrink in fear of his life; and despite her fury she was filled with disgust that he could imagine she would have his blood on her hands. Then she divined that Bruce saw more in the gathering storm in her father's eyes than he had to fear from her.

"Girl, what the hell are y'u sayin'?" hoarsely called Jorth, in dark amaze.

"Dad, y'u leave this to me," she retorted.

Daggs stepped beside Jorth, significantly on his right side. "Let her alone Lee," he advised, coolly. "She's shore got a hunch on Bruce."

"Simm Bruce, y'u cast a dirty slur on my name," cried Ellen, passionately.

It was then that Daggs grasped Jorth's right arm and held it tight, "Jest what I thought," he said. "Stand still, Lee. Let's see the kid make him showdown."

"That's what jean Isbel beat y'u for," went on Ellen. "For slandering a girl who wasn't there....
Me! Y'u rotten liar!"

"But, Ellen, it wasn't all lies," said Bruce, huskily. "I was half drunk—an' horrible jealous....
You know Lorenzo seen Isbel kissin' you. I can prove thet."

Ellen threw up her head and a scarlet wave of shame and wrath flooded her face.

"Yes," she cried, ringingly. "He saw Jean Isbel kiss me. Once! ... An' it was the only decent
kiss I've had in years. He meant no insult. I didn't know who he was. An' through his kiss I
learned a difference between men.... Y'u made Lorenzo lie. An' if I had a shred of good name left
in Grass Valley you dishonored it.... Y'u made him think I was your girl! Damn y'u! I ought to
kill y'u.... Eat your words now—take them back—or I'll cripple y'u for life!"

Ellen lowered the cocked rifle toward his feet.

"Shore, Ellen, I take back—all I said," gulped Bruce. He gazed at the quivering rifle barrel
and then into the face of Ellen's father. Instinct told him where his real peril lay.

Here the cool and tactful Daggs showed himself master of the situation.

"Heah, listen!" he called. "Ellen, I reckon Bruce was drunk an' out of his haid. He's shore ate
his words. Now, we don't want any cripples in this camp. Let him alone. Your dad got me heah
to lead the Jorths, an' that's my say to you.... Simm, you're shore a low-down lyin' rascal. Keep
away from Ellen after this or I'll bore you myself.... Jorth, it won't be a bad idee for you to forget
you're a Texan till you cool off. Let Bruce stop some Isbel lead. Shore the Jorth-Isbel war is
aboot on, an' I reckon we'd be smart to believe old Gass's talk aboot his Nez Perce son."

CHAPTER VI

From this hour Ellen Jorth bent all of her lately awakened intelligence and will to the only end that seemed to hold possible salvation for her. In the crisis sure to come she did not want to be blind or weak. Dreaming and indolence, habits born in her which were often a comfort to one as lonely as she, would ill fit her for the hard test she divined and dreaded. In the matter of her father's fight she must stand by him whatever the issue or the outcome; in what pertained to her own principles, her womanhood, and her soul she stood absolutely alone.

Therefore, Ellen put dreams aside, and indolence of mind and body behind her. Many tasks she found, and when these were done for a day she kept active in other ways, thus earning the poise and peace of labor.

Jorth rode off every day, sometimes with one or two of the men, often with a larger number. If he spoke of such trips to Ellen it was to give an impression of visiting the ranches of his neighbors or the various sheep camps. Often he did not return the day he left. When he did get back he smelled of rum and appeared heavy from need of sleep. His horses were always dust and sweat covered. During his absences Ellen fell victim to anxious dread until he returned. Daily he grew darker and more haggard of face, more obsessed by some impending fate. Often he stayed up late, haranguing with the men in the dim-lit cabin, where they drank and smoked, but seldom gambled any more. When the men did not gamble something immediate and perturbing was on their minds. Ellen had not yet lowered herself to the deceit and suspicion of eavesdropping, but she realized that there was a climax approaching in which she would deliberately do so.

In those closing May days Ellen learned the significance of many things that previously she had taken as a matter of course. Her father did not run a ranch. There was absolutely no ranching done, and little work. Often Ellen had to chop wood herself. Jorth did not possess a plow. Ellen was bound to confess that the evidence of this lack dumfounded her. Even old John Sprague raised some hay, beets, turnips. Jorth's cattle and horses fared ill during the winter. Ellen remembered how they used to clean up four-inch oak saplings and aspens. Many of them died in the snow. The flocks of sheep, however, were driven down into the Basin in the fall, and across the Reno Pass to Phoenix and Maricopa.

Ellen could not discover a fence post on the ranch, nor a piece of salt for the horses and cattle, nor a wagon, nor any sign of a sheep-shearing outfit. She had never seen any sheep sheared. Ellen could never keep track of the many and different horses running loose and hobbled round the ranch. There were droves of horses in the woods, and some of them wild as deer. According to her long-established understanding, her father and her uncles were keen on horse trading and buying.

Then the many trails leading away from the Jorth ranch—these grew to have a fascination for Ellen; and the time came when she rode out on them to see for herself where they led. The sheep ranch of Daggs, supposed to be only a few miles across the ridges, down in Bear Canyon, never materialized at all for Ellen. This circumstance so interested her that she went up to see her friend Sprague and got him to direct her to Bear Canyon, so that she would be sure not to miss it. And she rode from the narrow, maple-thicketed head of it near the Rim down all its length. She found no ranch, no cabin, not even a corral in Bear Canyon. Sprague said there was only one canyon by that name. Daggs had assured her of the exact location on his place, and so had her father. Had they lied? Were they mistaken in the canyon? There were many canyons, all heading up near the Rim, all running and widening down for miles through the wooded mountain, and vastly different from the deep, short, yellow-walled gorges that cut into the Rim from the Basin side. Ellen investigated the canyons within six or eight miles of her home, both to east and to west. All she discovered was a couple of old log cabins, long deserted. Still, she did not follow out all the trails to their ends. Several of them led far into the deepest, roughest, wildest brakes of gorge and thicket that she had seen. No cattle or sheep had ever been driven over these trails.

This riding around of Ellen's at length got to her father's ears. Ellen expected that a bitter quarrel would ensue, for she certainly would refuse to be confined to the camp; but her father only asked her to limit her riding to the meadow valley, and straightway forgot all about it. In fact, his abstraction one moment, his intense nervousness the next, his harder drinking and fiercer harangues with the men, grew to be distressing for Ellen. They presaged his further deterioration and the ever-present evil of the growing feud.

One day Jorth rode home in the early morning, after an absence of two nights. Ellen heard the clip-clop of, horses long before she saw them.

"Hey, Ellen! Come out heah," called her father.

Ellen left her work and went outside. A stranger had ridden in with her father, a young giant whose sharp-featured face appeared marked by ferret-like eyes and a fine, light, fuzzy beard. He was long, loose jointed, not heavy of build, and he had the largest hands and feet Ellen bad ever seen. Next Ellen espied a black horse they had evidently brought with them. Her father was holding a rope halter. At once the black horse struck Ellen as being a beauty and a thoroughbred.

"Ellen, heah's a horse for you," said Jorth, with something of pride. "I made a trade. Reckon I wanted him myself, but he's too gentle for me an' maybe a little small for my weight."

Delight visited Ellen for the first time in many days. Seldom had she owned a good horse, and never one like this.

"Oh, dad!" she exclaimed, in her gratitude.

"Shore he's yours on one condition," said her father.

"What's that?" asked Ellen, as she laid caressing hands on the restless horse.

"You're not to ride him out of the canyon."

"Agreed.... All daid black, isn't he, except that white face? What's his name, dad?

"I forgot to ask," replied Jorth, as he began unsaddling his own horse. "Slater, what's this heah black's name?"

The lanky giant grinned. "I reckon it was Spades."

"Spades?" ejaculated Ellen, blankly. "What a name! ... Well, I guess it's as good as any. He's shore black."

"Ellen, keep him hobbled when you're not ridin' him," was her father's parting advice as he walked off with the stranger.

Spades was wet and dusty and his satiny skin quivered. He had fine, dark, intelligent eyes that watched Ellen's every move. She knew how her father and his friends dragged and jammed horses through the woods and over the rough trails. It did not take her long to discover that this horse had been a pet. Ellen cleaned his coat and brushed him and fed him. Then she fitted her

318

bridle to suit his head and saddled him. His evident response to her kindness assured her that he was gentle, so she mounted and rode him, to discover he had the easiest gait she had ever experienced. He walked and trotted to suit her will, but when left to choose his own gait he fell into a graceful little pace that was very easy for her. He appeared quite ready to break into a run at her slightest bidding, but Ellen satisfied herself on this first ride with his slower gaits.

"Spades, y'u've shore cut out my burro Jinny," said Ellen, regretfully. "Well, I reckon women are fickle."

Next day she rode up the canyon to show Spades to her friend John Sprague. The old burro breeder was not at home. As his door was open, however, and a fire smoldering, Ellen concluded he would soon return. So she waited. Dismounting, she left Spades free to graze on the new green grass that carpeted the ground. The cabin and little level clearing accentuated the loneliness and wildness of the forest. Ellen always liked it here and had once been in the habit of visiting the old man often. But of late she had stayed away, for the reason that Sprague's talk and his news and his poorly hidden pity depressed her.

Presently she heard hoof beats on the hard, packed trail leading down the canyon in the direction from which she had come. Scarcely likely was it that Sprague should return from this direction. Ellen thought her father had sent one of the herders for her. But when she caught a glimpse of the approaching horseman, down in the aspens, she failed to recognize him. After he had passed one of the openings she heard his horse stop. Probably the man had seen her; at least she could not otherwise account for his stopping. The glimpse she had of him had given her the impression that he was bending over, peering ahead in the trail, looking for tracks. Then she heard the rider come on again, more slowly this time. At length the horse trotted out into the opening, to be hauled up short. Ellen recognized the buckskin-clad figure, the broad shoulders, the dark face of Jean Isbel.

Ellen felt prey to the strangest quaking sensation she had ever suffered. It took violence of her new-born spirit to subdue that feeling.

Isbel rode slowly across the clearing toward her. For Ellen his approach seemed singularly swift—so swift that her surprise, dismay, conjecture, and anger obstructed her will. The outwardly calm and cold Ellen Jorth was a travesty that mocked her—that she felt he would discern.

The moment Isbel drew close enough for Ellen to see his face she experienced a strong, shuddering repetition of her first shock of recognition. He was not the same. The light, the youth was gone. This, however, did not cause her emotion. Was it not a sudden transition of her nature to the dominance of hate? Ellen seemed to feel the shadow of her unknown self standing with her.

Isbel halted his horse. Ellen had been standing near the trunk of a fallen pine and she instinctively backed against it. How her legs trembled! Isbel took off his cap and crushed it nervously in his bare, brown hand.

"Good mornin', Miss Ellen!" he said.

Ellen did not return his greeting, but queried, almost breathlessly, "Did y'u come by our ranch?"

"No. I circled," he replied.

"Jean Isbel! What do y'u want heah?" she demanded.

"Don't you know?" he returned. His eyes were intensely black and piercing. They seemed to search Ellen's very soul. To meet their gaze was an ordeal that only her rousing fury sustained.

Ellen felt on her lips a scornful allusion to his half-breed Indian traits and the reputation that had preceded him. But she could not utter it.

"No," she replied.

"It's hard to call a woman a liar," he returned, bitterly. But you must be—seein' you're a Jorth.

"Liar! Not to y'u, Jean Isbel," she retorted. "I'd not lie to y'u to save my life."

He studied her with keen, sober, moody intent. The dark fire of his eyes thrilled her.

"If that's true, I'm glad," he said.

"Shore it's true. I've no idea why y'u came heah."

Ellen did have a dawning idea that she could not force into oblivion. But if she ever admitted it to her consciousness, she must fail in the contempt and scorn and fearlessness she chose to throw in this man's face.

"Does old Sprague live here?" asked Isbel.

"Yes. I expect him back soon.... Did y'u come to see him?"

"No.... Did Sprague tell you anythin' about the row he saw me in?"

"He—did not," replied Ellen, lying with stiff lips. She who had sworn she could not lie! She felt the hot blood leaving her heart, mounting in a wave. All her conscious will seemed impelled to deceive. What had she to hide from Jean Isbel? And a still, small voice replied that she had to hide the Ellen Jorth who had waited for him that day, who had spied upon him, who had treasured a gift she could not destroy, who had hugged to her miserable heart the fact that he had fought for her name.

"I'm glad of that," Isbel was saying, thoughtfully.

"Did you come heah to see me?" interrupted Ellen. She felt that she could not endure this reiterated suggestion of fineness, of consideration in him. She would betray herself—betray what she did not even realize herself. She must force other footing—and that should be the one of strife between the Jorths and Isbels.

"No—honest, I didn't, Miss Ellen," he rejoined, humbly. "I'll tell you, presently, why I came. But it wasn't to see you.... I don't deny I wanted ... but that's no matter. You didn't meet me that day on the Rim."

"Meet y'u!" she echoed, coldly. "Shore y'u never expected me?"

"Somehow I did," he replied, with those penetrating eyes on her. "I put somethin' in your tent that day. Did you find it?"

"Yes," she replied, with the same casual coldness.

"What did you do with it?"

"I kicked it out, of course," she replied.

She saw him flinch.

"And you never opened it?"

"Certainly not," she retorted, as if forced. "Doon't y'u know anythin' about—about people? ... Shore even if y'u are an Isbel y'u never were born in Texas."

"Thank God I wasn't!" he replied. "I was born in a beautiful country of green meadows and deep forests and white rivers, not in a barren desert where men live dry and hard as the cactus. Where I come from men don't live on hate. They can forgive."

"Forgive! ... Could y'u forgive a Jorth?"

"Yes, I could."

"Shore that's easy to say—with the wrongs all on your side," she declared, bitterly.

"Ellen Jorth, the first wrong was on your side," retorted Jean, his voice fall. "Your father stole my father's sweetheart—by lies, by slander, by dishonor, by makin' terrible love to her in his absence."

"It's a lie," cried Ellen, passionately.

"It is not," he declared, solemnly.

"Jean Isbel, I say y'u lie!"

"No! I say you've been lied to," he thundered.

The tremendous force of his spirit seemed to fling truth at Ellen. It weakened her.

"But—mother loved dad—best."

"Yes, afterward. No wonder, poor woman! ... But it was the action of your father and your mother that ruined all these lives. You've got to know the truth, Ellen Jorth.... All the years of hate have borne their fruit. God Almighty can never save us now. Blood must be spilled. The Jorths and the Isbels can't live on the same earth.... And you've got to know the truth because the worst of this hell falls on you and me."

The hate that he spoke of alone upheld her.

"Never, Jean Isbel!" she cried. "I'll never know truth from y'u.... I'll never share anythin' with y'u—not even hell."

Isbel dismounted and stood before her, still holding his bridle reins. The bay horse champed his bit and tossed his head.

"Why do you hate me so?" he asked. "I just happen to be my father's son. I never harmed you or any of your people. I met you ... fell in love with you in a flash—though I never knew it till after.... Why do you hate me so terribly?"

Ellen felt a heavy, stifling pressure within her breast. "Y'u're an Isbel.... Doon't speak of love to me."

"I didn't intend to. But your—your hate seems unnatural. And we'll probably never meet again.... I can't help it. I love you. Love at first sight! Jean Isbel and Ellen Jorth! Strange, isn't it? ... It was all so strange. My meetin' you so lonely and unhappy, my seein' you so sweet and beautiful, my thinkin' you so good in spite of—"

"Shore it was strange," interrupted Ellen, with scornful laugh. She had found her defense. In hurting him she could hide her own hurt. "Thinking me so good in spite of— Ha-ha! And I said I'd been kissed before!"

"Yes, in spite of everything," he said.

Ellen could not look at him as he loomed over her. She felt a wild tumult in her heart. All that crowded to her lips for utterance was false.

"Yes—kissed before I met you—and since," she said, mockingly. "And I laugh at what y'u call love, Jean Isbel."

"Laugh if you want—but believe it was sweet, honorable—the best in me," he replied, in deep earnestness.

"Bah!" cried Ellen, with all the force of her pain and shame and hate.

"By Heaven, you must be different from what I thought!" exclaimed Isbel, huskily.

"Shore if I wasn't, I'd make myself.... Now, Mister Jean Isbel, get on your horse an' go!"

Something of composure came to Ellen with these words of dismissal, and she glanced up at him with half-veiled eyes. His changed aspect prepared her for some blow.

"That's a pretty black horse."

"Yes," replied Ellen, blankly.

"Do you like him?"

"I—I love him."

"All right, I'll give him to you then. He'll have less work and kinder treatment than if I used him. I've got some pretty hard rides ahead of me."

"Y'u—y'u give—" whispered Ellen, slowly stiffening. "Yes. He's mine," replied Isbel. With that he turned to whistle. Spades threw up his head, snorted, and started forward at a trot. He came faster the closer he got, and if ever Ellen saw the joy of a horse at sight of a beloved master she saw it then. Isbel laid a hand on the animal's neck and caressed him, then, turning back to Ellen, he went on speaking: "I picked him from a lot of fine horses of my father's. We got along well. My sister Ann rode him a good deal.... He was stolen from our pasture day before yesterday. I took his trail and tracked him up here. Never lost his trail till I got to your ranch, where I had to circle till I picked it up again."

"Stolen—pasture—tracked him up heah?" echoed Ellen, without any evidence of emotion whatever. Indeed, she seemed to have been turned to stone.

"Trackin' him was easy. I wish for your sake it 'd been impossible," he said, bluntly.

"For my sake?" she echoed, in precisely the same tone,

Manifestly that tone irritated Isbel beyond control. He misunderstood it. With a hand far from gentle he pushed her bent head back so he could look into her face.

"Yes, for your sake!" he declared, harshly. "Haven't you sense enough to see that? ... What kind of a game do you think you can play with me?"

"Game I ... Game of what?" she asked.

"Why, a—a game of ignorance—innocence—any old game to fool a man who's tryin' to be decent."

This time Ellen mutely looked her dull, blank questioning. And it inflamed Isbel.

"You know your father's a horse thief!" he thundered.

Outwardly Ellen remained the same. She had been prepared for an unknown and a terrible blow. It had fallen. And her face, her body, her hands, locked with the supreme fortitude of pride and sustained by hate, gave no betrayal of the crashing, thundering ruin within her mind and soul. Motionless she leaned there, meeting the piercing fire of Isbel's eyes, seeing in them a righteous and terrible scorn. In one flash the naked truth seemed blazed at her. The faith she had fostered died a sudden death. A thousand perplexing problems were solved in a second of whirling, revealing thought.

"Ellen Jorth, you know your father's in with this Hash Knife Gang of rustlers," thundered Isbel.

"Shore," she replied, with the cool, easy, careless defiance of a Texan.

"You know he's got this Daggs to lead his faction against the Isbels?"

"Shore."

"You know this talk of sheepmen buckin' the cattlemen is all a blind?"

"Shore," reiterated Ellen.

Isbel gazed darkly down upon her. With his anger spent for the moment, he appeared ready to end the interview. But he seemed fascinated by the strange look of her, by the incomprehensible something she emanated. Havoc gleamed in his pale, set face. He shook his dark head and his broad hand went to his breast.

"To think I fell in love with such as you!" he exclaimed, and his other hand swept out in a tragic gesture of helpless pathos and impotence.

The hell Isbel had hinted at now possessed Ellen—body, mind, and soul. Disgraced, scorned by an Isbel! Yet loved by him! In that divination there flamed up a wild, fierce passion to hurt, to rend, to flay, to fling back upon him a stinging agony. Her thought flew upon her like whips. Pride of the Jorths! Pride of the old Texan blue blood! It lay dead at her feet, killed by the scornful words of the last of that family to whom she owed her degradation. Daughter of a horse thief and rustler! Dark and evil and grim set the forces within her, accepting her fate, damning her enemies, true to the blood of the Jorths. The sins of the father must be visited upon the daughter.

"Shore y'u might have had me—that day on the Rim—if y'u hadn't told your name," she said, mockingly, and she gazed into his eyes with all the mystery of a woman's nature.

Isbel's powerful frame shook as with an ague. "Girl, what do you mean?"

"Shore, I'd have been plumb fond of havin' y'u make up to me," she drawled. It possessed her now with irresistible power, this fact of the love he could not help. Some fiendish woman's satisfaction dwelt in her consciousness of her power to kill the noble, the faithful, the good in him.

"Ellen Jorth, you lie!" he burst out, hoarsely.

"Jean, shore I'd been a toy and a rag for these rustlers long enough. I was tired of them.... I wanted a new lover.... And if y'u hadn't give yourself away—"

Isbel moved so swiftly that she did not realize his intention until his hard hand smote her mouth. Instantly she tasted the hot, salty blood from a cut lip.

"Shut up, you hussy!" he ordered, roughly. "Have you no shame? ... My sister Ann spoke well of you. She made excuses—she pitied you."

That for Ellen seemed the culminating blow under which she almost sank. But one moment longer could she maintain this unnatural and terrible poise.

"Jean Isbel—go along with y'u," she said, impatiently. "I'm waiting heah for Simm Bruce!"

At last it was as if she struck his heart. Because of doubt of himself and a stubborn faith in her, his passion and jealousy were not proof against this last stab. Instinctive subtlety inherent in Ellen had prompted the speech that tortured Isbel. How the shock to him rebounded on her! She gasped as he lunged for her, too swift for her to move a hand. One arm crushed round her like a steel band; the other, hard across her breast and neck, forced her head back. Then she tried to wrestle away. But she was utterly powerless. His dark face bent down closer and closer. Suddenly Ellen ceased trying to struggle. She was like a stricken creature paralyzed by the piercing, hypnotic eyes of a snake. Yet in spite of her terror, if he meant death by her, she welcomed it.

"Ellen Jorth, I'm thinkin' yet—you lie!" he said, low and tense between his teeth.

323

"No! No!" she screamed, wildly. Her nerve broke there. She could no longer meet those terrible black eyes. Her passionate denial was not only the last of her shameful deceit; it was the woman of her, repudiating herself and him, and all this sickening, miserable situation.

Isbel took her literally. She had convinced him. And the instant held blank horror for Ellen.

"By God—then I'll have somethin'—of you anyway!" muttered Isbel, thickly.

Ellen saw the blood bulge in his powerful neck. She saw his dark, hard face, strange now, fearful to behold, come lower and lower, till it blurred and obstructed her gaze. She felt the swell and ripple and stretch—then the bind of his muscles, like huge coils of elastic rope. Then with savage rude force his mouth closed on hers. All Ellen's senses reeled, as if she were swooning. She was suffocating. The spasm passed, and a bursting spurt of blood revived her to acute and terrible consciousness. For the endless period of one moment he held her so that her breast seemed crushed. His kisses burned and braised her lips. And then, shifting violently to her neck, they pressed so hard that she choked under them. It was as if a huge bat had fastened upon her throat.

Suddenly the remorseless binding embraces—the hot and savage kisses—fell away from her. Isbel had let go. She saw him throw up his hands, and stagger back a little, all the while with his piercing gaze on her. His face had been dark purple: now it was white.

"No—Ellen Jorth," he panted, "I don't—want any of you—that way." And suddenly he sank on the log and covered his face with his hands. "What I loved in you—was what I thought—you were."

Like a wildcat Ellen sprang upon him, beating him with her fists, tearing at his hair, scratching his face, in a blind fury. Isbel made no move to stop her, and her violence spent itself with her strength. She swayed back from him, shaking so that she could scarcely stand.

"Y'u—damned—Isbel!" she gasped, with hoarse passion. "Y'u insulted me!"

"Insulted you?..." laughed Isbel, in bitter scorn. "It couldn't be done."

"Oh! ... I'll KILL y'u!" she hissed.

Isbel stood up and wiped the red scratches on his face. "Go ahead. There's my gun," he said, pointing to his saddle sheath. "Somebody's got to begin this Jorth-Isbel feud. It'll be a dirty business. I'm sick of it already.... Kill me! ... First blood for Ellen Jorth!"

Suddenly the dark grim tide that had seemed to engulf Ellen's very soul cooled and receded, leaving her without its false strength. She began to sag. She stared at Isbel's gun. "Kill him," whispered the retreating voices of her hate. But she was as powerless as if she were still held in Jean Isbel's giant embrace.

"I—I want to—kill y'u," she whispered, "but I cain't.... Leave me."

"You're no Jorth—the same as I'm no Isbel. We oughtn't be mixed in this deal," he said, somberly. "I'm sorrier for you than I am for myself.... You're a girl.... You once had a good mother—a decent home. And this life you've led here—mean as it's been—is nothin' to what you'll face now. Damn the men that brought you to this! I'm goin' to kill some of them."

With that he mounted and turned away. Ellen called out for him to take his horse. He did not stop nor look back. She called again, but her voice was fainter, and Isbel was now leaving at a trot. Slowly she sagged against the tree, lower and lower. He headed into the trail leading up the canyon. How strange a relief Ellen felt! She watched him ride into the aspens and start up the slope, at last to disappear in the pines. It seemed at the moment that he took with him something which had been hers. A pain in her head dulled the thoughts that wavered to and fro. After he had gone she could not see so well. Her eyes were tired. What had happened to her? There was blood on her hands. Isbel's blood! She shuddered. Was it an omen? Lower she sank against the tree and closed her eyes.

Old John Sprague did not return. Hours dragged by—dark hours for Ellen Jorth lying prostrate beside the tree, hiding the blue sky and golden sunlight from her eyes. At length the lethargy of despair, the black dull misery wore away; and she gradually returned to a condition of coherent thought.

What had she learned? Sight of the black horse grazing near seemed to prompt the trenchant replies. Spades belonged to Jean Isbel. He had been stolen by her father or by one of her father's accomplices. Isbel's vaunted cunning as a tracker had been no idle boast. Her father was a horse thief, a rustler, a sheepman only as a blind, a consort of Daggs, leader of the Hash Knife Gang. Ellen well remembered the ill repute of that gang, way back in Texas, years ago. Her father had gotten in with this famous band of rustlers to serve his own ends—the extermination of the Isbels. It was all very plain now to Ellen.

"Daughter of a horse thief an' rustler!" she muttered.

And her thoughts sped back to the days of her girlhood. Only the very early stage of that time had been happy. In the light of Isbel's revelation the many changes of residence, the sudden moves to unsettled parts of Texas, the periods of poverty and sudden prosperity, all leading to the final journey to this God-forsaken Arizona—these were now seen in their true significance. As far back as she could remember her father had been a crooked man. And her mother had known it. He had dragged her to her ruin. That degradation had killed her. Ellen realized that with poignant sorrow, with a sudden revolt against her father. Had Gaston Isbel truly and dishonestly started her father on his downhill road? Ellen wondered. She hated the Isbels with unutterable and growing hate, yet she had it in her to think, to ponder, to weigh judgments in their behalf. She owed it to something in herself to be fair. But what did it matter who was to blame for the Jorth-Isbel feud? Somehow Ellen was forced to confess that deep in her soul it mattered terribly. To be true to herself—the self that she alone knew—she must have right on her side. If the Jorths were guilty, and she clung to them and their creed, then she would be one of them.

"But I'm not," she mused, aloud. "My name's Jorth, an' I reckon I have bad blood.... But it never came out in me till to-day. I've been honest. I've been good—yes, GOOD, as my mother taught me to be—in spite of all.... Shore my pride made me a fool.... An' now have I any choice to make? I'm a Jorth. I must stick to my father."

All this summing up, however, did not wholly account for the pang in her breast.

What had she done that day? And the answer beat in her ears like a great throbbing hammer-stroke. In an agony of shame, in the throes of hate, she had perjured herself. She had sworn away her honor. She had basely made herself vile. She had struck ruthlessly at the great heart of a man who loved her. Ah! That thrust had rebounded to leave this dreadful pang in her breast. Loved her? Yes, the strange truth, the insupportable truth! She had to contend now, not with her father and her disgrace, not with the baffling presence of Jean Isbel, but with the mysteries of her own soul. Wonder of all wonders was it that such love had been born for her. Shame worse than all other shame was it that she should kill it by a poisoned lie. By what monstrous motive had she done that? To sting Isbel as he had stung her! But that had been base. Never could she have stopped so low except in a moment of tremendous tumult. If she had done sore injury to Isbel what bad she done to herself? How strange, how tenacious had been his faith in her honor! Could she ever forget? She must forget it. But she could never forget the way he had scorned those vile men in Greaves's store—the way he had beaten Bruce for defiling her name—the way he had stubbornly denied her own insinuations. She was a woman now. She had learned something of the complexity of a woman's heart. She could not change nature. And all her passionate being thrilled to the manhood of her defender. But even while she thrilled she acknowledged her hate. It was the contention between the two that caused the pang in her breast. "An' now what's left for me?" murmured Ellen. She did not analyze the significance of what had prompted that query. The most incalculable of the day's disclosures was the wrong she had done herself. "Shore I'm done for, one way or another.... I must stick to Dad.... or kill myself?"

Ellen rode Spades back to the ranch. She rode like the wind. When she swung out of the trail into the open meadow in plain sight of the ranch her appearance created a commotion among the loungers before the cabin. She rode Spades at a full run.

"Who's after you?" yelled her father, as she pulled the black to a halt. Jorth held a rifle. Daggs, Colter, the other Jorths were there, likewise armed, and all watchful, strung with expectancy.

"Shore nobody's after me," replied Ellen. "Cain't I run a horse round heah without being chased?"

Jorth appeared both incensed and relieved.

"Hah! ... What you mean, girl, runnin' like a streak right down on us? You're actin' queer these days, an' you look queer. I'm not likin' it."

"Reckon these are queer times—for the Jorths," replied Ellen, sarcastically.

"Daggs found strange horse tracks crossin' the meadow," said her father. "An' that worried us. Some one's been snoopin' round the ranch. An' when we seen you runnin' so wild we shore thought you was bein' chased."

"No. I was only trying out Spades to see how fast he could run," returned Ellen. "Reckon when we do get chased it'll take some running to catch me."

"Haw! Haw!" roared Daggs. "It shore will, Ellen."

"Girl, it's not only your runnin' an' your looks that's queer," declared Jorth, in dark perplexity. "You talk queer."

"Shore, dad, y'u're not used to hearing spades called spades," said Ellen, as she dismounted.

"Humph!" ejaculated her father, as if convinced of the uselessness of trying to understand a woman. "Say, did you see any strange horse tracks?"

"I reckon I did. And I know who made them."

Jorth stiffened. All the men behind him showed a sudden intensity of suspense.

"Who?" demanded Jorth.

"Shore it was Jean Isbel," replied Ellen, coolly. "He came up heah tracking his black horse."

"Jean—Isbel—trackin'—his—black horse," repeated her father.

"Yes. He's not overrated as a tracker, that's shore."

Blank silence ensued. Ellen cast a slow glance over her father and the others, then she began to loosen the cinches of her saddle. Presently Jorth burst the silence with a curse, and Daggs followed with one of his sardonic laughs.

"Wal, boss, what did I tell you?" he drawled.

Jorth strode to Ellen, and, whirling her around with a strong hand, he held her facing him.

"Did y'u see Isbel?"

"Yes," replied Ellen, just as sharply as her father had asked.

"Did y'u talk to him?"

"Yes."

"What did he want up heah?"

"I told y'u. He was tracking the black horse y'u stole."

Jorth's hand and arm dropped limply. His sallow face turned a livid hue. Amaze merged into discomfiture and that gave place to rage. He raised a hand as if to strike Ellen. And suddenly Daggs's long arm shot out to clutch Jorth's wrist. Wrestling to free himself, Jorth cursed under his breath. "Let go, Daggs," he shouted, stridently. "Am I drunk that you grab me?"

"Wal, y'u ain't drunk, I reckon," replied the rustler, with sarcasm. "But y'u're shore some things I'll reserve for your private ear."

Jorth gained a semblance of composure. But it was evident that he labored under a shock.

"Ellen, did Jean Isbel see this black horse?"

"Yes. He asked me how I got Spades an' I told him."

"Did he say Spades belonged to him?"

"Shore I reckon he, proved it. Y'u can always tell a horse that loves its master."

"Did y'u offer to give Spades back?"

"Yes. But Isbel wouldn't take him."

"Hah! ... An' why not?"

"He said he'd rather I kept him. He was about to engage in a dirty, blood-spilling deal, an' he reckoned he'd not be able to care for a fine horse.... I didn't want Spades. I tried to make Isbel take him. But he rode off.... And that's all there is to that."

"Maybe it's not," replied Jorth, chewing his mustache and eying Ellen with dark, intent gaze. "Y'u've met this Isbel twice."

"It wasn't any fault of mine," retorted Ellen.

"I heah he's sweet on y'u. How aboot that?"

Ellen smarted under the blaze of blood that swept to neck and cheek and temple. But it was only memory which fired this shame. What her father and his crowd might think were matters of supreme indifference. Yet she met his suspicious gaze with truthful blazing eyes.

"I heah talk from Bruce an' Lorenzo," went on her father. "An' Daggs heah—"

"Daggs nothin'!" interrupted that worthy. "Don't fetch me in. I said nothin' an' I think nothin'."

"Yes, Jean Isbel was sweet on me, dad ... but he will never be again," returned Ellen, in low tones. With that she pulled her saddle off Spades and, throwing it over her shoulder, she walked off to her cabin.

Hardly had she gotten indoors when her father entered.

"Ellen, I didn't know that horse belonged to Isbel," he began, in the swift, hoarse, persuasive voice so familiar to Ellen. "I swear I didn't. I bought him—traded with Slater for him.... Honest to God, I never had any idea he was stolen! ... Why, when y'u said 'that horse y'u stole,' I felt as if y'u'd knifed me...."

Ellen sat at the table and listened while her father paced to and fro and, by his restless action and passionate speech, worked himself into a frenzy. He talked incessantly, as if her silence was condemnatory and as if eloquence alone could convince her of his honesty. It seemed that Ellen saw and heard with keener faculties than ever before. He had a terrible thirst for her respect. Not so much for her love, she divined, but that she would not see how he had fallen!

She pitied him with all her heart. She was all he had, as he was all the world to her. And so, as she gave ear to his long, illogical rigmarole of argument and defense, she slowly found that her pity and her love were making vital decisions for her. As of old, in poignant moments, her father lapsed at last into a denunciation of the Isbels and what they had brought him to. His sufferings were real, at least, in Ellen's presence. She was the only link that bound him to long-past happier times. She was her mother over again—the woman who had betrayed another man for him and gone with him to her ruin and death.

"Dad, don't go on so," said Ellen, breaking in upon her father's rant. "I will be true to y'u—as my mother was.... I am a Jorth. Your place is my place—your fight is my fight.... Never speak of the past to me again. If God spares us through this feud we will go away and begin all over again, far off where no one ever heard of a Jorth.... If we're not spared we'll at least have had our whack at these damned Isbels."

CHAPTER VII

During June Jean Isbel did not ride far away from Grass Valley.

Another attempt had been made upon Gaston Isbel's life. Another cowardly shot had been fired from ambush, this time from a pine thicket bordering the trail that led to Blaisdell's ranch. Blaisdell heard this shot, so near his home was it fired. No trace of the hidden foe could be found. The 'ground all around that vicinity bore a carpet of pine needles which showed no trace of footprints. The supposition was that this cowardly attempt had been perpetrated, or certainly instigated, by the Jorths. But there was no proof. And Gaston Isbel had other enemies in the Tonto Basin besides the sheep clan. The old man raged like a lion about this sneaking attack on him. And his friend Blaisdell urged an immediate gathering of their kin and friends. "Let's quit ranchin' till this trouble's settled," he declared. "Let's arm an' ride the trails an' meet these men half-way.... It won't help our side any to wait till you're shot in the back." More than one of Isbel's supporters offered the same advice.

"No; we'll wait till we know for shore," was the stubborn cattleman's reply to all these promptings.

"Know! Wal, hell! Didn't Jean find the black hoss up at Jorth's ranch?" demanded Blaisdell. "What more do we want?"

"Jean couldn't swear Jorth stole the black."

"Wal, by thunder, I can swear to it!" growled Blaisdell. "An' we're losin' cattle all the time. Who's stealin' 'em?"

"We've always lost cattle ever since we started ranchin' heah."

"Gas, I reckon yu want Jorth to start this fight in the open."

"It'll start soon enough," was Isbel's gloomy reply.

Jean had not failed altogether in his tracking of lost or stolen cattle. Circumstances had been against him, and there was something baffling about this rustling. The summer storms set in early, and it had been his luck to have heavy rains wash out fresh tracks that he might have followed. The range was large and cattle were everywhere. Sometimes a loss was not discovered for weeks. Gaston Isbel's sons were now the only men left to ride the range. Two of his riders had quit because of the threatened war, and Isbel had let another go. So that Jean did not often learn that cattle had been stolen until their tracks were old. Added to that was the fact that this Grass Valley country was covered with horse tracks and cattle tracks. The rustlers, whoever they were, had long been at the game, and now that there was reason for them to show their cunning they did it.

Early in July the hot weather came. Down on the red ridges of the Tonto it was hot desert. The nights were cool, the early mornings were pleasant, but the day was something to endure. When the white cumulus clouds rolled up out of the southwest, growing larger and thicker and darker, here and there coalescing into a black thundercloud, Jean welcomed them. He liked to see the gray streamers of rain hanging down from a canopy of black, and the roar of rain on the trees as it approached like a trampling army was always welcome. The grassy flats, the red ridges, the rocky slopes, the thickets of manzanita and scrub oak and cactus were dusty, glaring, throat-parching places under the hot summer sun. Jean longed for the cool heights of the Rim, the shady pines, the dark sweet verdure under the silver spruces, the tinkle and murmur of the clear rills. He often had another longing, too, which he bitterly stifled.

Jean's ally, the keen-nosed shepherd clog, had disappeared one day, and had never returned. Among men at the ranch there was a difference of opinion as to what had happened to Shepp. The old rancher thought he had been poisoned or shot; Bill and Guy Isbel believed he had been stolen by sheep herders, who were always stealing dogs; and Jean inclined to the conviction that Shepp had gone off with the timber wolves. The fact was that Shepp did not return, and Jean missed him.

One morning at dawn Jean heard the cattle bellowing and trampling out in the valley; and upon hurrying to a vantage point he was amazed to see upward of five hundred steers chasing a lone wolf. Jean's father had seen such a spectacle as this, but it was a new one for Jean. The wolf was a big gray and black fellow, rangy and powerful, and until he got the steers all behind him he was rather hard put to it to keep out of their way. Probably he had dogged the herd, trying to sneak in and pull down a yearling, and finally the steers had charged him. Jean kept along the edge of the valley in the hope they would chase him within range of a rifle. But the wary wolf saw Jean and sheered off, gradually drawing away from his pursuers.

Jean returned to the house for his breakfast, and then set off across the valley. His father owned one small flock of sheep that had not yet been driven up on the Rim, where all the sheep in the country were run during the hot, dry summer down on the Tonto. Young Evarts and a Mexican boy named Bernardino had charge of this flock. The regular Mexican herder, a man of experience, had given up his job; and these boys were not equal to the task of risking the sheep up in the enemies' stronghold.

This flock was known to be grazing in a side draw, well up from Grass Valley, where the brush afforded some protection from the sun, and there was good water and a little feed. Before Jean reached his destination he heard a shot. It was not a rifle shot, which fact caused Jean a little concern. Evarts and Bernardino had rifles, but, to his knowledge, no small arms. Jean rode up on one of the black-brushed conical hills that rose on the south side of Grass Valley, and from there he took a sharp survey of the country. At first he made out only cattle, and bare meadowland, and the low encircling ridges and hills. But presently up toward the head of the valley he descried a bunch of horsemen riding toward the village. He could not tell their number. That dark moving mass seemed to Jean to be instinct with life, mystery, menace. Who were they? It was too far for him to recognize horses, let alone riders. They were moving fast, too.

Jean watched them out of sight, then turned his horse downhill again, and rode on his quest. A number of horsemen like that was a very unusual sight around Grass Valley at any time. What then did it portend now? Jean experienced a little shock of uneasy dread that was a new sensation for him. Brooding over this he proceeded on his way, at length to turn into the draw where the camp of the sheep-herders was located. Upon coming in sight of it he heard a hoarse shout. Young Evarts appeared running frantically out of the brush. Jean urged his horse into a run and soon covered the distance between them. Evarts appeared beside himself with terror.

"Boy! what's the matter?" queried Jean, as he dismounted, rifle in hand, peering quickly from Evarts's white face to the camp, and all around.

"Ber-nardino! Ber-nardino!" gasped the boy, wringing his hands and pointing.

Jean ran the few remaining rods to the sheep camp. He saw the little teepee, a burned-out fire, a half-finished meal—and then the Mexican lad lying prone on the ground, dead, with a bullet hole in his ghastly face. Near him lay an old six-shooter.

"Whose gun is that?" demanded Jean, as he picked it up.

"Ber-nardino's," replied Evarts, huskily. "He—he jest got it—the other day."

"Did he shoot himself accidentally?"

"Oh no! No! He didn't do it—atall."

"Who did, then?"

"The men—they rode up—a gang-they did it," panted Evarts.

"Did you know who they were?"

"No. I couldn't tell. I saw them comin' an' I was skeered. Bernardino had gone fer water. I run an' hid in the brush. I wanted to yell, but they come too close.... Then I heerd them talkin'. Bernardino come back. They 'peared friendly-like. Thet made me raise up, to look. An' I couldn't see good. I heerd one of them ask Bernardino to let him see his gun. An' Bernardino handed it over. He looked at the gun an' haw-hawed, an' flipped it up in the air, an' when it fell back in his hand it—it went off bang! ... An' Bernardino dropped.... I hid down close. I was skeered stiff. I heerd them talk more, but not what they said. Then they rode away.... An' I hid there till I seen y'u comin'."

"Have you got a horse?" queried Jean, sharply.

"No. But I can ride one of Bernardino's burros."

"Get one. Hurry over to Blaisdell. Tell him to send word to Blue and Gordon and Fredericks to ride like the devil to my father's ranch. Hurry now!"

Young Evarts ran off without reply. Jean stood looking down at the limp and pathetic figure of the Mexican boy. "By Heaven!" he exclaimed, grimly "the Jorth-Isbel war is on! ... Deliberate, cold-blooded murder! I'll gamble Daggs did this job. He's been given the leadership. He's started it.... Bernardino, greaser or not, you were a faithful lad, and you won't go long unavenged."

Jean had no time to spare. Tearing a tarpaulin out of the teepee he covered the lad with it and then ran for, his horse. Mounting, he galloped down the draw, over the little red ridges, out into the valley, where he put his horse to a run.

Action changed the sickening horror that sight of Bernardino had engendered. Jean even felt a strange, grim relief. The long, dragging days of waiting were over. Jorth's gang had taken the initiative. Blood had begun to flow. And it would continue to flow now till the last man of one faction stood over the dead body of the last man of the other. Would it be a Jorth or an Isbel? "My instinct was right," he muttered, aloud. "That bunch of horses gave me a queer feelin'." Jean gazed all around the grassy, cattle-dotted valley he was crossing so swiftly, and toward the village, but he did not see any sign of the dark group of riders. They had gone on to Greaves's store, there, no doubt, to drink and to add more enemies of the Isbels to their gang. Suddenly across Jean's mind flashed a thought of Ellen Jorth. "What 'll become of her? ... What 'll become of all the women? My sister? ... The little ones?"

No one was in sight around the ranch. Never had it appeared more peaceful and pastoral to Jean. The grazing cattle and horses in the foreground, the haystack half eaten away, the cows in the fenced pasture, the column of blue smoke lazily ascending, the cackle of hens, the solid, well-built cabins—all these seemed to repudiate Jean's haste and his darkness of mind. This place was, his father's farm. There was not a cloud in the blue, summer sky.

As Jean galloped up the lane some one saw him from the door, and then Bill and Guy and their gray-headed father came out upon the porch. Jean saw how he' waved the womenfolk back, and then strode out into the lane. Bill and Guy reached his side as Jean pulled his heaving horse to a halt. They all looked at Jean, swiftly and intently, with a little, hard, fiery gleam strangely identical in the eyes of each. Probably before a word was spoken they knew what to expect.

"Wal, you shore was in a hurry," remarked the father.

"What the hell's up?" queried Bill, grimly.

Guy Isbel remained silent and it was he who turned slightly pale. Jean leaped off his horse.

"Bernardino has just been killed—murdered with his own gun."

Gaston Isbel seemed to exhale a long-dammed, bursting breath that let his chest sag. A terrible deadly glint, pale and cold as sunlight on ice, grew slowly to dominate his clear eyes.

"A-huh!" ejaculated Bill Isbel, hoarsely.

Not one of the three men asked who had done the killing. They were silent a moment, motionless, locked in the secret seclusion of their own minds. Then they listened with absorption to Jean's brief story.

"Wal, that lets us in," said his father. "I wish we had more time. Reckon I'd done better to listen to you boys an' have my men close at hand. Jacobs happened to ride over. That makes five of us besides the women."

"Aw, dad, you don't reckon they'll round us up heah?" asked Guy Isbel.

"Boys, I always feared they might," replied the old man. "But I never really believed they'd have the nerve. Shore I ought to have figgered Daggs better. This heah secret bizness an' shootin' at us from ambush looked aboot Jorth's size to me. But I reckon now we'll have to fight without our friends."

"Let them come," said Jean. "I sent for Blaisdell, Blue, Gordon, and Fredericks. Maybe they'll get here in time. But if they don't it needn't worry us much. We can hold out here longer than Jorth's gang can hang around. We'll want plenty of water, wood, and meat in the house."

"Wal, I'll see to that," rejoined his father. "Jean, you go out close by, where you can see all around, an' keep watch."

"Who's goin' to tell the women?" asked Guy Isbel.

The silence that momentarily ensued was an eloquent testimony to the hardest and saddest aspect of this strife between men. The inevitableness of it in no wise detracted from its sheer uselessness. Men from time immemorial had hated, and killed one another, always to the misery and degradation of their women. Old Gaston Isbel showed this tragic realization in his lined face.

"Wal, boys, I'll tell the women," he said. "Shore you needn't worry none aboot them. They'll be game."

Jean rode away to an open knoll a short distance from the house, and here he stationed himself to watch all points. The cedared ridge back of the ranch was the one approach by which Jorth's gang might come close without being detected, but even so, Jean could see them and ride to the house in time to prevent a surprise. The moments dragged by, and at the end of an hour Jean was in hopes that Blaisdell would soon come. These hopes were well founded. Presently he heard a clatter of hoofs on hard ground to the south, and upon wheeling to look he saw the friendly neighbor coming fast along the road, riding a big white horse. Blaisdell carried a rifle in his hand, and the sight of him gave Jean a glow of warmth. He was one of the Texans who would stand by the Isbels to the last man. Jean watched him ride to the house—watched the meeting between him and his lifelong friend. There floated out to Jean old Blaisdell's roar of rage.

Then out on the green of Grass Valley, where a long, swelling plain swept away toward the village, there appeared a moving dark patch. A bunch of horses! Jean's body gave a slight start—the shock of sudden propulsion of blood through all his veins. Those horses bore riders. They were coming straight down the open valley, on the wagon road to Isbel's ranch. No subterfuge nor secrecy nor sneaking in that advance! A hot thrill ran over Jean.

"By Heaven! They mean business!" he muttered. Up to the last moment he had unconsciously hoped Jorth's gang would not come boldly like that. The verifications of all a Texan's inherited instincts left no doubts, no hopes, no illusions—only a grim certainty that this was not conjecture nor probability, but fact. For a moment longer Jean watched the slowly moving dark patch of horsemen against the green background, then he hurried back to the ranch. His father saw him coming—strode out as before.

"Dad—Jorth is comin'," said Jean, huskily. How he hated to be forced to tell his father that! The boyish love of old had flashed up.

"Whar?" demanded the old man, his eagle gaze sweeping the horizon.

"Down the road from Grass Valley. You can't see from here."

"Wal, come in an' let's get ready."

Isbel's house had not been constructed with the idea of repelling an attack from a band of Apaches. The long living room of the main cabin was the one selected for defense and protection. This room had two windows and a door facing the lane, and a door at each end, one of which opened into the kitchen and the other into an adjoining and later-built cabin. The logs of this main cabin were of large size, and the doors and window coverings were heavy, affording safer protection from bullets than the other cabins.

When Jean went in he seemed to see a host of white faces lifted to him. His sister Ann, his two sisters-in-law, the children, all mutely watched him with eyes that would haunt him.

"Wal, Blaisdell, Jean says Jorth an' his precious gang of rustlers are on the way heah," announced the rancher.

"Damn me if it's not a bad day fer Lee Jorth!" declared Blaisdell.

"Clear off that table," ordered Isbel, "an' fetch out all the guns an' shells we got."

Once laid upon the table these presented a formidable arsenal, which consisted of the three new .44 Winchesters that Jean had brought with him from the coast; the enormous buffalo, or so-called "needle" gun, that Gaston Isbel had used for years; a Henry rifle which Blaisdell had brought, and half a dozen six-shooters. Piles and packages of ammunition littered the table.

"Sort out these heah shells," said Isbel. "Everybody wants to get hold of his own."

Jacobs, the neighbor who was present, was a thick-set, bearded man, rather jovial among those lean-jawed Texans. He carried a .44 rifle of an old pattern. "Wal, boys, if I'd knowed we was in fer some fun I'd hev fetched more shells. Only got one magazine full. Mebbe them new .44's will fit my gun."

It was discovered that the ammunition Jean had brought in quantity fitted Jacob's rifle, a fact which afforded peculiar satisfaction to all the men present.

"Wal, shore we're lucky," declared Gaston Isbel.

The women sat apart, in the comer toward the kitchen, and there seemed to be a strange fascination for them in the talk and action of the men. The wife of Jacobs was a little woman, with homely face and very bright eyes. Jean thought she would be a help in that household during the next doubtful hours.

Every moment Jean would go to the window and peer out down the road. His companions evidently relied upon him, for no one else looked out. Now that the suspense of days and weeks was over, these Texans faced the issue with talk and act not noticeably different from those of ordinary moments.

At last Jean espied the dark mass of horsemen out in the valley road. They were close together, walking their mounts, and evidently in earnest conversation. After several ineffectual attempts Jean counted eleven horses, every one of which he was sure bore a rider.

"Dad, look out!" called Jean.

Gaston Isbel strode to the door and stood looking, without a word.

The other men crowded to the windows. Blaisdell cursed under his breath. Jacobs said: "By Golly! Come to pay us a call!" The women sat motionless, with dark, strained eyes. The children ceased their play and looked fearfully to their mother.

When just out of rifle shot of the cabins the band of horsemen halted and lined up in a half circle, all facing the ranch. They were close enough for Jean to see their gestures, but he could not recognize any of their faces. It struck him singularly that not one of them wore a mask.

"Jean, do you know any of them?" asked his father

"No, not yet. They're too far off."

"Dad, I'll get your old telescope," said Guy Isbel, and he ran out toward the adjoining cabin.

Blaisdell shook his big, hoary head and rumbled out of his bull-like neck, "Wal, now you're heah, you sheep fellars, what are you goin' to do aboot it?"

Guy Isbel returned with a yard-long telescope, which he passed to his father. The old man took it with shaking hands and leveled it. Suddenly it was as if he had been transfixed; then he lowered the glass, shaking violently, and his face grew gray with an exceeding bitter wrath.

"Jorth!" he swore, harshly.

Jean had only to look at his father to know that recognition had been like a mortal shock. It passed. Again the rancher leveled the glass.

"Wal, Blaisdell, there's our old Texas friend, Daggs," he drawled, dryly. "An' Greaves, our honest storekeeper of Grass Valley. An' there's Stonewall Jackson Jorth. An' Tad Jorth, with the same old red nose! ... An', say, damn if one of that gang isn't Queen, as bad a gun fighter as Texas ever bred. Shore I thought he'd been killed in the Big Bend country. So I heard.... An' there's Craig, another respectable sheepman of Grass Valley. Haw-haw! An', wal, I don't recognize any more of them."

Jean forthwith took the glass and moved it slowly across the faces of that group of horsemen. "Simm Bruce," he said, instantly. "I see Colter. And, yes, Greaves is there. I've seen the man next to him—face like a ham...."

"Shore that is Craig," interrupted his father.

Jean knew the dark face of Lee Jorth by the resemblance it bore to Ellen's, and the recognition brought a twinge. He thought, too, that he could tell the other Jorths. He asked his father to describe Daggs and then Queen. It was not likely that Jean would fail to know these several men in the future. Then Blaisdell asked for the telescope and, when he got through looking and cursing, he passed it on to others, who, one by one, took a long look, until finally it came back to the old rancher.

"Wal, Daggs is wavin' his hand heah an' there, like a general aboot to send out scouts. Haw-haw! ... An' 'pears to me he's not overlookin' our hosses. Wal, that's natural for a rustler. He'd have to steal a hoss or a steer before goin' into a fight or to dinner or to a funeral."

"It 'll be his funeral if he goes to foolin' 'round them hosses," declared Guy Isbel, peering anxiously out of the door.

"Wal, son, shore it 'll be somebody's funeral," replied his father.

Jean paid but little heed to the conversation. With sharp eyes fixed upon the horsemen, he tried to grasp at their intention. Daggs pointed to the horses in the pasture lot that lay between him and the house. These animals were the best on the range and belonged mostly to Guy Isbel, who was the horse fancier and trader of the family. His horses were his passion.

"Looks like they'd do some horse stealin'," said Jean.

"Lend me that glass," demanded Guy, forcefully. He surveyed the band of men for a long moment, then he handed the glass back to Jean.

"I'm goin' out there after my bosses," he declared.

"No!" exclaimed his father.

"That gang come to steal an' not to fight. Can't you see that? If they meant to fight they'd do it. They're out there arguin' about my hosses."

Guy picked up his rifle. He looked sullenly determined and the gleam in his eye was one of fearlessness.

"Son, I know Daggs," said his father. "An' I know Jorth. They've come to kill us. It 'll be shore death for y'u to go out there."

"I'm goin', anyhow. They can't steal my hosses out from under my eyes. An' they ain't in range."

"Wal, Guy, you ain't goin' alone," spoke up Jacobs, cheerily, as he came forward.

The red-haired young wife of Guy Isbel showed no change of her grave face. She had been reared in a stern school. She knew men in times like these. But Jacobs's wife appealed to him, "Bill, don't risk your life for a horse or two."

Jacobs laughed and answered, "Not much risk," and went out with Guy. To Jean their action seemed foolhardy. He kept a keen eye on them and saw instantly when the band became aware of Guy's and Jacobs's entrance into the pasture. It took only another second then to realize that Daggs and Jorth had deadly intent. Jean saw Daggs slip out of his saddle, rifle in hand. Others of the gang did likewise, until half of them were dismounted.

"Dad, they're goin' to shoot," called out Jean, sharply. "Yell for Guy and Jacobs. Make them come back."

The old man shouted; Bill Isbel yelled; Blaisdell lifted his stentorian voice.

Jean screamed piercingly: "Guy! Run! Run!"

But Guy Isbel and his companion strode on into the pasture, as if they had not heard, as if no menacing horse thieves were within miles. They had covered about a quarter of the distance across the pasture, and were nearing the horses, when Jean saw red flashes and white puffs of smoke burst out from the front of that dark band of rustlers. Then followed the sharp, rattling crack of rifles.

Guy Isbel stopped short, and, dropping his gun, he threw up his arms and fell headlong. Jacobs acted as if he had suddenly encountered an invisible blow. He had been hit. Turning, he began to run and ran fast for a few paces. There were more quick, sharp shots. He let go of his rifle. His running broke. Walking, reeling, staggering, he kept on. A hoarse cry came from him. Then a single rifle shot pealed out. Jean heard the bullet strike. Jacobs fell to his knees, then forward on his face.

Jean Isbel felt himself turned to marble. The suddenness of this tragedy paralyzed him. His gaze remained riveted on those prostrate forms.

A hand clutched his arm—a shaking woman's hand, slim and hard and tense.

"Bill's—killed!" whispered a broken voice. "I was watchin'.... They're both dead!"

The wives of Jacobs and Guy Isbel had slipped up behind Jean and from behind him they had seen the tragedy.

"I asked Bill—not to—go," faltered the Jacobs woman, and, covering her face with her hands, she groped back to the corner of the cabin, where the other women, shaking and white, received her in their arms. Guy Isbel's wife stood at the window, peering over Jean's shoulder. She had the nerve of a man. She had looked out upon death before.

"Yes, they're dead," she said, bitterly. "An' how are we goin' to get their bodies?"

At this Gaston Isbel seemed to rouse from the cold spell that had transfixed him.

"God, this is hell for our women," he cried out, hoarsely. "My son—my son! ... Murdered by the Jorths!" Then he swore a terrible oath.

Jean saw the remainder of the mounted rustlers get off, and then, all of them leading their horses, they began to move around to the left.

"Dad, they're movin' round," said Jean.

"Up to some trick," declared Bill Isbel.

"Bill, you make a hole through the back wall, say aboot the fifth log up," ordered the father. "Shore we've got to look out."

The elder son grasped a tool and, scattering the children, who had been playing near the back corner, he began to work at the point designated. The little children backed away with fixed, wondering, grave eyes. The women moved their chairs, and huddled together as if waiting and listening.

Jean watched the rustlers until they passed out of his sight. They had moved toward the sloping, brushy ground to the north and west of the cabins.

"Let me know when you get a hole in the back wall," said Jean, and he went through the kitchen and cautiously out another door to slip into a low-roofed, shed-like end of the rambling cabin. This small space was used to store winter firewood. The chinks between the walls had not been filled with adobe clay, and he could see out on three sides. The rustlers were going into the juniper brush. They moved out of sight, and presently reappeared without their horses. It looked to Jean as if they intended to attack the cabins. Then they halted at the edge of the brush and held a long consultation. Jean could see them distinctly, though they were too far distant for him to recognize any particular man. One of them, however, stood and moved apart from the closely massed group. Evidently, from his strides and gestures, he was exhorting his listeners. Jean concluded this was either Daggs or Jorth. Whoever it was had a loud, coarse voice, and this and his actions impressed Jean with a suspicion that the man was under the influence of the bottle.

Presently Bill Isbel called Jean in a low voice. "Jean, I got the hole made, but we can't see anyone."

"I see them," Jean replied. "They're havin' a powwow. Looks to me like either Jorth or Daggs is drunk. He's arguin' to charge us, an' the rest of the gang are holdin' back.... Tell dad, an' all of you keep watchin'. I'll let you know when they make a move."

Jorth's gang appeared to be in no hurry to expose their plan of battle. Gradually the group disintegrated a little; some of them sat down; others walked to and fro. Presently two of them went into the brush, probably back to the horses. In a few moments they reappeared, carrying a pack. And when this was deposited on the ground all the rustlers sat down around it. They had brought food and drink. Jean had to utter a grim laugh at their coolness; and he was reminded of many dare-devil deeds known to have been perpetrated by the Hash Knife Gang. Jean was glad of a reprieve. The longer the rustlers put off an attack the more time the allies of the Isbels would have to get here. Rather hazardous, however, would it be now for anyone to attempt to get to the Isbel cabins in the daytime. Night would be more favorable.

Twice Bill Isbel came through the kitchen to whisper to Jean. The strain in the large room, from which the rustlers could not be seen, must have been great. Jean told him all he had seen and what he thought about it. "Eatin' an' drinkin'!" ejaculated Bill. "Well, I'll be—! That 'll jar the old man. He wants to get the fight over.

"Tell him I said it'll be over too quick—for us—unless are mighty careful," replied Jean, sharply.

Bill went back muttering to himself. Then followed a long wait, fraught with suspense, during which Jean watched the rustlers regale themselves. The day was hot and still. And the unnatural silence of the cabin was broken now and then by the gay laughter of the children. The sound shocked and haunted Jean. Playing children! Then another sound, so faint he had to strain to hear it, disturbed and saddened him—his father's slow tread up and down the cabin floor, to and fro, to and fro. What must be in his father's heart this day!

At length the rustlers rose and, with rifles in hand, they moved as one man down the slope. They came several hundred yards closer, until Jean, grimly cocking his rifle, muttered to himself that a few more rods closer would mean the end of several of that gang. They knew the range of a rifle well enough, and once more sheered off at right angles with the cabin. When they got even with the line of corrals they stooped down and were lost to Jean's sight. This fact caused him alarm. They were, of course, crawling up on the cabins. At the end of that line of corrals ran a ditch, the bank of which was high enough to afford cover. Moreover, it ran along in front of the cabins, scarcely a hundred yards, and it was covered with grass and little clumps of brush, from behind which the rustlers could fire into the windows and through the clay chinks without any considerable risk to themselves. As they did not come into sight again, Jean concluded he had discovered their plan. Still, he waited awhile longer, until he saw faint, little clouds of dust rising from behind the far end of the embankment. That discovery made him rush out, and through the kitchen to the large cabin, where his sudden appearance startled the men.

"Get back out of sight!" he ordered, sharply, and with swift steps he reached the door and closed it. "They're behind the bank out there by the corrals. An' they're goin' to crawl down the ditch closer to us.... It looks bad. They'll have grass an' brush to shoot from. We've got to be mighty careful how we peep out."

"Ahuh! All right," replied his father. "You women keep the kids with you in that corner. An' you all better lay down flat."

Blaisdell, Bill Isbel, and the old man crouched at the large window, peeping through cracks in the rough edges of the logs. Jean took his post beside the small window, with his keen eyes vibrating like a compass needle. The movement of a blade of grass, the flight of a grasshopper could not escape his trained sight.

"Look sharp now!" he called to the other men. "I see dust.... They're workin' along almost to that bare spot on the bank.... I saw the tip of a rifle ... a black hat ... more dust. They're spreadin' along behind the bank."

Loud voices, and then thick clouds of yellow dust, coming from behind the highest and brushiest line of the embankment, attested to the truth of Jean's observation, and also to a reckless disregard of danger.

Suddenly Jean caught a glint of moving color through the fringe of brush. Instantly he was strung like a whipcord.

Then a tall, hatless and coatless man stepped up in plain sight. The sun shone on his fair, ruffled hair. Daggs!

"Hey, you — — Isbels!" he bawled, in magnificent derisive boldness. "Come out an' fight!"

Quick as lightning Jean threw up his rifle and fired. He saw tufts of fair hair fly from Daggs's head. He saw the squirt of red blood. Then quick shots from his comrades rang out. They all hit the swaying body of the rustler. But Jean knew with a terrible thrill that his bullet had killed Daggs before the other three struck. Daggs fell forward, his arms and half his body resting over, the embankment. Then the rustlers dragged him back out of sight. Hoarse shouts rose. A cloud of yellow dust drifted away from the spot.

"Daggs!" burst out Gaston Isbel. "Jean, you knocked off the top of his haid. I seen that when I was pullin' trigger. Shore we over heah wasted our shots."

"God! he must have been crazy or drunk—to pop up there—an' brace us that way," said Blaisdell, breathing hard.

"Arizona is bad for Texans," replied Isbel, sardonically. "Shore it's been too peaceful heah. Rustlers have no practice at fightin'. An' I reckon Daggs forgot."

"Daggs made as crazy a move as that of Guy an' Jacobs," spoke up Jean. "They were overbold, an' he was drunk. Let them be a lesson to us."

Jean had smelled whisky upon his entrance to this cabin. Bill was a hard drinker, and his father was not immune. Blaisdell, too, drank heavily upon occasions. Jean made a mental note that he would not permit their chances to become impaired by liquor.

Rifles began to crack, and puffs of smoke rose all along the embankment for the space of a hundred feet. Bullets whistled through the rude window casing and spattered on the heavy door, and one split the clay between the logs before Jean, narrowly missing him. Another volley followed, then another. The rustlers had repeating rifles and they were emptying their magazines. Jean changed his position. The other men profited by his wise move. The volleys had merged into one continuous rattling roar of rifle shots. Then came a sudden cessation of reports, with silence of relief. The cabin was full of dust, mingled with the smoke from the shots of Jean and his companions. Jean heard the stifled breaths of the children. Evidently they were terror-stricken, but they did not cry out. The women uttered no sound.

A loud voice pealed from behind the embankment.

"Come out an' fight! Do you Isbels want to be killed like sheep?"

This sally gained no reply. Jean returned to his post by the window and his comrades followed his example. And they exercised extreme caution when they peeped out.

"Boys, don't shoot till you see one," said Gaston Isbel. "Maybe after a while they'll get careless. But Jorth will never show himself."

The rustlers did not again resort to volleys. One by one, from different angles, they began to shoot, and they were not firing at random. A few bullets came straight in at the windows to pat into the walls; a few others ticked and splintered the edges of the windows; and most of them broke through the clay chinks between the logs. It dawned upon Jean that these dangerous shots were not accident. They were well aimed, and most of them hit low down. The cunning rustlers had some unerring riflemen and they were picking out the vulnerable places all along the front of the cabin. If Jean had not been lying flat he would have been hit twice. Presently he conceived the idea of driving pegs between the logs, high up, and, kneeling on these, he managed to peep out from the upper edge of the window. But this position was awkward and difficult to hold for long.

He heard a bullet hit one of his comrades. Whoever had been struck never uttered a sound. Jean turned to look. Bill Isbel was holding his shoulder, where red splotches appeared on his shirt. He shook his head at Jean, evidently to make light of the wound. The women and children were lying face down and could not see what was happening. Plain is was that Bill did not want them to know. Blaisdell bound up the bloody shoulder with a scarf.

Steady firing from the rustlers went on, at the rate of one shot every few minutes. The Isbels did not return these. Jean did not fire again that afternoon. Toward sunset, when the besiegers appeared to grow restless or careless, Blaisdell fired at something moving behind the brush; and Gaston Isbel's huge buffalo gun boomed out.

"Wal, what 're they goin' to do after dark, an' what 're WE goin' to do?" grumbled Blaisdell.

"Reckon they'll never charge us," said Gaston.

"They might set fire to the cabins," added Bill Isbel. He appeared to be the gloomiest of the Isbel faction. There was something on his mind.

"Wal, the Jorths are bad, but I reckon they'd not burn us alive," replied Blaisdell.

"Hah!" ejaculated Gaston Isbel. "Much you know aboot Lee Jorth. He would skin me alive an' throw red-hot coals on my raw flesh."

So they talked during the hour from sunset to dark. Jean Isbel had little to say. He was revolving possibilities in his mind. Darkness brought a change in the attack of the rustlers. They stationed men at four points around the cabins; and every few minutes one of these outposts would fire. These bullets embedded themselves in the logs, causing but little anxiety to the Isbels.

"Jean, what you make of it?" asked the old rancher.

"Looks to me this way," replied Jean. "They're set for a long fight. They're shootin' just to let us know they're on the watch."

"Ahuh! Wal, what 're you goin' to do aboot it?"

"I'm goin' out there presently."

Gaston Isbel grunted his satisfaction at this intention of Jean's.

All was pitch dark inside the cabin. The women had water and food at hand. Jean kept a sharp lookout from his window while he ate his supper of meat, bread, and milk. At last the children, worn out by the long day, fell asleep. The women whispered a little in their corner.

About nine o'clock Jean signified his intention of going out to reconnoitre.

"Dad, they've got the best of us in the daytime," he said, "but not after dark."

Jean buckled on a belt that carried shells, a bowie knife, and revolver, and with rifle in hand he went out through the kitchen to the yard. The night was darker than usual, as some of the stars were hidden by clouds. He leaned against the log cabin, waiting for his eyes to become perfectly adjusted to the darkness. Like an Indian, Jean could see well at night. He knew every point around cabins and sheds and corrals, every post, log, tree, rock, adjacent to the ranch. After perhaps a quarter of an hour watching, during which time several shots were fired from behind the embankment and one each from the rustlers at the other locations, Jean slipped out on his quest.

He kept in the shadow of the cabin walls, then the line of orchard trees, then a row of currant bushes. Here, crouching low, he halted to look and listen. He was now at the edge of the open ground, with the gently rising slope before him. He could see the dark patches of cedar and juniper trees. On the north side of the cabin a streak of fire flashed in the blackness, and a shot rang out. Jean heard the bullet bit the cabin. Then silence enfolded the lonely ranch and the darkness lay like a black blanket. A low hum of insects pervaded the air. Dull sheets of lightning illumined the dark horizon to the south. Once Jean heard voices, but could not tell from which direction they came. To the west of him then flared out another rifle shot. The bullet whistled down over Jean to thud into the cabin.

Jean made a careful study of the obscure, gray-black open before him and then the background to his rear. So long as he kept the dense shadows behind him he could not be seen. He slipped from behind his covert and, gliding with absolutely noiseless footsteps, he gained the first clump of junipers. Here he waited patiently and motionlessly for another round of shots from the rustlers. After the second shot from the west side Jean sheered off to the right. Patches of brush, clumps of juniper, and isolated cedars covered this slope, affording Jean a perfect means for his purpose, which was to make a detour and come up behind the rustler who was firing from that side. Jean climbed to the top of the ridge, descended the opposite slope, made his turn to the left, and slowly worked up behind the point near where he expected to locate the rustler. Long habit in the open, by day and night, rendered his sense of direction almost as perfect as sight itself. The first flash of fire he saw from this side proved that he had come straight up toward his man. Jean's intention was to crawl up on this one of the Jorth gang and silently kill him with a knife. If the plan worked successfully, Jean meant to work round to the next rustler. Laying aside his rifle, he crawled forward on hands and knees, making no more sound than a cat. His approach was slow. He had to pick his way, be careful not to break twigs nor rattle stones. His buckskin garments made no sound against the brush. Jean located the rustler sitting on the top of the ridge in the center of an open space. He was alone. Jean saw the dull-red end of the cigarette he was smoking. The ground on the ridge top was rocky and not well adapted for Jean's purpose. He had to abandon the idea of crawling up on the rustler. Whereupon, Jean turned back, patiently and slowly, to get his rifle.

Upon securing it he began to retrace his course, this time more slowly than before, as he was hampered by the rifle. But he did not make the slightest sound, and at length he reached the edge of the open ridge top, once more to espy the dark form of the rustler silhouetted against the sky. The distance was not more than fifty yards.

As Jean rose to his knee and carefully lifted his rifle round to avoid the twigs of a juniper he suddenly experienced another emotion besides the one of grim, hard wrath at the Jorths. It was an emotion that sickened him, made him weak internally, a cold, shaking, ungovernable sensation. Suppose this man was Ellen Jorth's father! Jean lowered the rifle. He felt it shake over his knee. He was trembling all over. The astounding discovery that he did not want to kill Ellen's father—that he could not do it—awakened Jean to the despairing nature of his love for her. In this grim moment of indecision, when he knew his Indian subtlety and ability gave him a great advantage over the Jorths, he fully realized his strange, hopeless, and irresistible love for the girl. He made no attempt to deny it any longer. Like the night and the lonely wilderness around him, like the inevitableness of this Jorth-Isbel feud, this love of his was a thing, a fact, a reality. He breathed to his own inward ear, to his soul—he could not kill Ellen Jorth's father. Feud or no feud, Isbel or not, he could not deliberately do it. And why not? There was no answer. Was he not faithless to his father? He had no hope of ever winning Ellen Jorth. He did not want the love of a girl of her character. But he loved her. And his struggle must be against the insidious and mysterious growth of that passion. It swayed him already. It made him a coward. Through his mind and heart swept the memory of Ellen Jorth, her beauty and charm, her boldness and pathos, her shame and her degradation. And the sweetness of her outweighed the boldness. And the mystery of her arrayed itself in unquenchable protest against her acknowledged shame. Jean lifted his face to the heavens, to the pitiless white stars, to the infinite depths of the dark-blue sky. He could sense the fact of his being an atom in the universe of nature. What was he, what was his revengeful father, what were hate and passion and strife in comparison to the nameless something, immense and everlasting, that he sensed in this dark moment?

But the rustlers—Daggs—the Jorths—they had killed his brother Guy—murdered him brutally and ruthlessly. Guy had been a playmate of Jean's—a favorite brother. Bill had been secretive and selfish. Jean had never loved him as he did Guy. Guy lay dead down there on the meadow. This feud had begun to run its bloody course. Jean steeled his nerve. The hot blood crept back along his veins. The dark and masterful tide of revenge waved over him. The keen edge of his mind then cut out sharp and trenchant thoughts. He must kill when and where he could. This man could hardly be Ellen Jorth's father. Jorth would be with the main crowd, directing hostilities. Jean could shoot this rustler guard and his shot would be taken by the gang as the regular one from their comrade. Then swiftly Jean leveled his rifle, covered the dark form, grew cold and set, and pressed the trigger. After the report he rose and wheeled away. He did not look nor listen for the result of his shot. A clammy sweat wet his face, the hollow of his hands, his breast. A horrible, leaden, thick sensation oppressed his heart. Nature had endowed him with Indian gifts, but the exercise of them to this end caused a revolt in his soul.

Nevertheless, it was the Isbel blood that dominated him. The wind blew cool on his face. The burden upon his shoulders seemed to lift. The clamoring whispers grew fainter in his ears. And by the time he had retraced his cautious steps back to the orchard all his physical being was strung to the task at hand. Something had come between his reflective self and this man of action.

Crossing the lane, he took to the west line of sheds, and passed beyond them into the meadow. In the grass he crawled silently away to the right, using the same precaution that had actuated him on the slope, only here he did not pause so often, nor move so slowly. Jean aimed to go far enough to the right to pass the end of the embankment behind which the rustlers had found such efficient cover. This ditch had been made to keep water, during spring thaws and summer storms, from pouring off the slope to flood the corrals.

Jean miscalculated and found he had come upon the embankment somewhat to the left of the end, which fact, however, caused him no uneasiness. He lay there awhile to listen. Again he heard voices. After a time a shot pealed out. He did not see the flash, but he calculated that it had come from the north side of the cabins.

The next quarter of an hour discovered to Jean that the nearest guard was firing from the top of the embankment, perhaps a hundred yards distant, and a second one was performing the same office from a point apparently only a few yards farther on. Two rustlers close together! Jean had not calculated upon that. For a little while he pondered on what was best to do, and at length decided to crawl round behind them, and as close as the situation made advisable.

He found the ditch behind the embankment a favorable path by which to stalk these enemies. It was dry and sandy, with borders of high weeds. The only drawback was that it was almost impossible for him to keep from brushing against the dry, invisible branches of the weeds. To offset this he wormed his way like a snail, inch by inch, taking a long time before he caught sight of the sitting figure of a man, black against the dark-blue sky. This rustler had fired his rifle three times during Jean's slow approach. Jean watched and listened a few moments, then wormed himself closer and closer, until the man was within twenty steps of him.

Jean smelled tobacco smoke, but could see no light of pipe or cigarette, because the fellow's back was turned.

"Say, Ben," said this man to his companion sitting hunched up a few yards distant, "shore it strikes me queer thet Somers ain't shootin' any over thar."

Jean recognized the dry, drawling voice of Greaves, and the shock of it seemed to contract the muscles of his whole thrilling body, like that of a panther about to spring.

CHAPTER VIII

"Was shore thinkin' thet same," said the other man. "An', say, didn't thet last shot sound too sharp fer Somers's forty-five?"

"Come to think of it, I reckon it did," replied Greaves.

"Wal, I'll go around over thar an' see."

The dark form of the rustler slipped out of sight over the embankment.

"Better go slow an' careful," warned Greaves. "An' only go close enough to call Somers.... Mebbe thet damn half-breed Isbel is comin' some Injun on us."

Jean heard the soft swish of footsteps through wet grass. Then all was still. He lay flat, with his cheek on the sand, and he had to look ahead and upward to make out the dark figure of Greaves on the bank. One way or another he meant to kill Greaves, and he had the will power to resist the strongest gust of passion that had ever stormed his breast. If he arose and shot the rustler, that act would defeat his plan of slipping on around upon the other outposts who were firing at the cabins. Jean wanted to call softly to Greaves, "You're right about the half-breed!" and then, as he wheeled aghast, to kill him as he moved. But it suited Jean to risk leaping upon the man. Jean did not waste time in trying to understand the strange, deadly instinct that gripped him at the moment. But he realized then he had chosen the most perilous plan to get rid of Greaves.

Jean drew a long, deep breath and held it. He let go of his rifle. He rose, silently as a lifting shadow. He drew the bowie knife. Then with light, swift bounds he glided up the bank. Greaves must have heard a rustling—a soft, quick pad of moccasin, for he turned with a start. And that instant Jean's left arm darted like a striking snake round Greaves's neck and closed tight and hard. With his right hand free, holding the knife, Jean might have ended the deadly business in just one move. But when his bared arm felt the hot, bulging neck something terrible burst out of the depths of him. To kill this enemy of his father's was not enough! Physical contact had unleashed the savage soul of the Indian. Yet there was more, and as Jean gave the straining body a tremendous jerk backward, he felt the same strange thrill, the dark joy that he had known when his fist had smashed the face of Simm Bruce. Greaves had leered—he had corroborated Bruce's vile insinuation about Ellen Jorth. So it was more than hate that actuated Jean Isbel.

Greaves was heavy and powerful. He whirled himself, feet first, over backward, in a lunge like that of a lassoed steer. But Jean's hold held. They rolled down the bank into the sandy ditch, and Jean landed uppermost, with his body at right angles with that of his adversary.

"Greaves, your hunch was right," hissed Jean. "It's the half-breed.... An' I'm goin' to cut you—first for Ellen Jorth—an' then for Gaston Isbel!"

Jean gazed down into the gleaming eyes. Then his right arm whipped the big blade. It flashed. It fell. Low down, as far as Jean could reach, it entered Greaves's body.

All the heavy, muscular frame of Greaves seemed to contract and burst. His spring was that of an animal in terror and agony. It was so tremendous that it broke Jean's hold. Greaves let out a strangled yell that cleared, swelling wildly, with a hideous mortal note. He wrestled free. The big knife came out. Supple and swift, he got to his, knees. He had his gun out when Jean reached him again. Like a bear Jean enveloped him. Greaves shot, but he could not raise the gun, nor twist it far enough. Then Jean, letting go with his right arm, swung the bowie. Greaves's strength went out in an awful, hoarse cry. His gun boomed again, then dropped from his hand. He swayed. Jean let go. And that enemy of the Isbels sank limply in the ditch. Jean's eyes roved for his rifle and caught the starlit gleam of it. Snatching it up, he leaped over the embankment and ran straight for the cabins. From all around yells of the Jorth faction attested to their excitement and fury.

A fence loomed up gray in the obscurity. Jean vaulted it, darted across the lane into the shadow of the corral, and soon gained the first cabin. Here he leaned to regain his breath. His heart pounded high and seemed too large for his breast. The hot blood beat and surged all over his body. Sweat poured off him. His teeth were clenched tight as a vise, and it took effort on his part to open his mouth so he could breathe more freely and deeply. But these physical sensations were as nothing compared to the tumult of his mind. Then the instinct, the spell, let go its grip and he could think. He had avenged Guy, he had depleted the ranks of the Jorths, he had made good the brag of his father, all of which afforded him satisfaction. But these thoughts were not accountable for all that he felt, especially for the bittersweet sting of the fact that death to the defiler of Ellen Jorth could not efface the doubt, the regret which seemed to grow with the hours.

Groping his way into the woodshed, he entered the kitchen and, calling low, he went on into the main cabin.

"Jean! Jean!" came his father's shaking voice.

"Yes, I'm back," replied Jean.

"Are—you—all right?"

"Yes. I think I've got a bullet crease on my leg. I didn't know I had it till now.... It's bleedin' a little. But it's nothin'."

Jean heard soft steps and some one reached shaking hands for him. They belonged to his sister Ann. She embraced him. Jean felt the heave and throb of her breast.

"Why, Ann, I'm not hurt," he said, and held her close. "Now you lie down an' try to sleep."

In the black darkness of the cabin Jean led her back to the corner and his heart was full. Speech was difficult, because the very touch of Ann's hands had made him divine that the success of his venture in no wise changed the plight of the women.

"Wal, what happened out there?" demanded Blaisdell.

"I got two of them," replied Jean. "That fellow who was shootin' from the ridge west. An' the other was Greaves."

"Hah!" exclaimed his father.

"Shore then it was Greaves yellin'," declared Blaisdell. "By God, I never heard such yells! Whad 'd you do, Jean?"

"I knifed him. You see, I'd planned to slip up on one after another. An' I didn't want to make noise. But I didn't get any farther than Greaves."

"Wal, I reckon that 'll end their shootin' in the dark," muttered Gaston Isbel. "We've got to be on the lookout for somethin' else—fire, most likely."

The old rancher's surmise proved to be partially correct. Jorth's faction ceased the shooting. Nothing further was seen or heard from them. But this silence and apparent break in the siege were harder to bear than deliberate hostility. The long, dark hours dragged by. The men took turns watching and resting, but none of them slept. At last the blackness paled and gray dawn stole out of the east. The sky turned rose over the distant range and daylight came.

The children awoke hungry and noisy, having slept away their fears. The women took advantage of the quiet morning hour to get a hot breakfast.

"Maybe they've gone away," suggested Guy Isbel's wife, peering out of the window. She had done that several times since daybreak. Jean saw her somber gaze search the pasture until it rested upon the dark, prone shape of her dead husband, lying face down in the grass. Her look worried Jean.

"No, Esther, they've not gone yet," replied Jean. "I've seen some of them out there at the edge of the brush."

Blaisdell was optimistic. He said Jean's night work would have its effect and that the Jorth contingent would not renew the siege very determinedly. It turned out, however, that Blaisdell was wrong. Directly after sunrise they began to pour volleys from four sides and from closer range. During the night Jorth's gang had thrown earth banks and constructed log breastworks, from behind which they were now firing. Jean and his comrades could see the flashes of fire and streaks of smoke to such good advantage that they began to return the volleys.

In half an hour the cabin was so full of smoke that Jean could not see the womenfolk in their corner. The fierce attack then abated somewhat, and the firing became more intermittent, and therefore more carefully aimed. A glancing bullet cut a furrow in Blaisdell's hoary head, making a painful, though not serious wound. It was Esther Isbel who stopped the flow of blood and bound Blaisdell's head, a task which she performed skillfully and without a tremor. The old Texan could not sit still during this operation. Sight of the blood on his hands, which he tried to rub off, appeared to inflame him to a great degree.

"Isbel, we got to go out thar," he kept repeating, "an' kill them all."

"No, we're goin' to stay heah," replied Gaston Isbel. "Shore I'm lookin' for Blue an' Fredericks an' Gordon to open up out there. They ought to be heah, an' if they are y'u shore can bet they've got the fight sized up."

Isbel's hopes did not materialize. The shooting continued without any lull until about midday. Then the Jorth faction stopped.

"Wal, now what's up?" queried Isbel. "Boys, hold your fire an' let's wait."

Gradually the smoke wafted out of the windows and doors, until the room was once more clear. And at this juncture Esther Isbel came over to take another gaze out upon the meadows. Jean saw her suddenly start violently, then stiffen, with a trembling hand outstretched.

"Look!" she cried.

"Esther, get back," ordered the old rancher. "Keep away from that window."

"What the hell!" muttered Blaisdell. "She sees somethin', or she's gone dotty."

Esther seemed turned to stone. "Look! The hogs have broken into the pasture! ... They'll eat Guy's body!"

Everyone was frozen with horror at Esther's statement. Jean took a swift survey of the pasture. A bunch of big black hogs had indeed appeared on the scene and were rooting around in the grass not far from where lay the bodies of Guy Isbel and Jacobs. This herd of hogs belonged to the rancher and was allowed to run wild.

"Jane, those hogs—" stammered Esther Isbel, to the wife of Jacobs. "Come! Look! ... Do y'u know anythin' about hogs?"

The woman ran to the window and looked out. She stiffened as had Esther.

"Dad, will those hogs—eat human flesh?" queried Jean, breathlessly.

The old man stared out of the window. Surprise seemed to hold him. A completely unexpected situation had staggered him.

"Jean—can you—can you shoot that far?" he asked, huskily.

"To those hogs? No, it's out of range."

"Then, by God, we've got to stay trapped in heah an' watch an awful sight," ejaculated the old man, completely unnerved. "See that break in the fence! ... Jorth's done that.... To let in the hogs!"

"Aw, Isbel, it's not so bad as all that," remonstrated Blaisdell, wagging his bloody head. "Jorth wouldn't do such a hell-bent trick."

"It's shore done."

"Wal, mebbe the hogs won't find Guy an' Jacobs," returned Blaisdell, weakly. Plain it was that he only hoped for such a contingency and certainly doubted it.

"Look!" cried Esther Isbel, piercingly. "They're workin' straight up the pasture!"

Indeed, to Jean it appeared to be the fatal truth. He looked blankly, feeling a little sick. Ann Isbel came to peer out of the window and she uttered a cry. Jacobs's wife stood mute, as if dazed.

Blaisdell swore a mighty oath. "— — —! Isbel, we cain't stand heah an' watch them hogs eat our people!"

"Wal, we'll have to. What else on earth can we do?"

Esther turned to the men. She was white and cold, except her eyes, which resembled gray flames.

"Somebody can run out there an' bury our dead men," she said.

"Why, child, it'd be shore death. Y'u saw what happened to Guy an' Jacobs.... We've jest got to bear it. Shore nobody needn't look out—an' see."

Jean wondered if it would be possible to keep from watching. The thing had a horrible fascination. The big hogs were rooting and tearing in the grass, some of them lazy, others nimble, and all were gradually working closer and closer to the bodies. The leader, a huge, gaunt boar, that had fared ill all his life in this barren country, was scarcely fifty feet away from where Guy Isbel lay.

"Ann, get me some of your clothes, an' a sunbonnet—quick," said Jean, forced out of his lethargy. "I'll run out there disguised. Maybe I can go through with it."

"No!" ordered his father, positively, and with dark face flaming. "Guy an' Jacobs are dead. We cain't help them now."

"But, dad—" pleaded Jean. He had been wrought to a pitch by Esther's blaze of passion, by the agony in the face of the other woman.

"I tell y'u no!" thundered Gaston Isbel, flinging his arms wide.

"I WILL GO!" cried Esther, her voice ringing.

"You won't go alone!" instantly answered the wife of Jacobs, repeating unconsciously the words her husband had spoken.

"You stay right heah," shouted Gaston Isbel, hoarsely.

"I'm goin'," replied Esther. "You've no hold over me. My husband is dead. No one can stop me. I'm goin' out there to drive those hogs away an' bury him."

"Esther, for Heaven's sake, listen," replied Isbel. "If y'u show yourself outside, Jorth an' his gang will kin y'u."

"They may be mean, but no white men could be so low as that."

Then they pleaded with her to give up her purpose. But in vain! She pushed them back and ran out through the kitchen with Jacobs's wife following her. Jean turned to the window in time to see both women run out into the lane. Jean looked fearfully, and listened for shots. But only a loud, "Haw! Haw!" came from the watchers outside. That coarse laugh relieved the tension in Jean's breast. Possibly the Jorths were not as black as his father painted them. The two women entered an open shed and came forth with a shovel and spade.

"Shore they've got to hurry," burst out Gaston Isbel.

Shifting his gaze, Jean understood the import of his father's speech. The leader of the hogs had no doubt scented the bodies. Suddenly he espied them and broke into a trot.

"Run, Esther, run!" yelled Jean, with all his might.

That urged the women to flight. Jean began to shoot. The hog reached the body of Guy. Jean's shots did not reach nor frighten the beast. All the hogs now had caught a scent and went ambling toward their leader. Esther and her companion passed swiftly out of sight behind a corral. Loud and piercingly, with some awful note, rang out their screams. The hogs appeared frightened. The leader lifted his long snout, looked, and turned away. The others had halted. Then they, too, wheeled and ran off.

All was silent then in the cabin and also outside wherever the Jorth faction lay concealed. All eyes manifestly were fixed upon the brave wives. They spaded up the sod and dug a grave for Guy Isbel. For a shroud Esther wrapped him in her shawl. Then they buried him. Next they hurried to the side of Jacobs, who lay some yards away. They dug a grave for him. Mrs. Jacobs took off her outer skirt to wrap round him. Then the two women labored hard to lift him and lower him. Jacobs was a heavy man. When he had been covered his widow knelt beside his grave. Esther went back to the other. But she remained standing and did not look as if she prayed. Her aspect was tragic—that of a woman who had lost father, mother, sisters, brother, and now her husband, in this bloody Arizona land.

The deed and the demeanor of these wives of the murdered men surely must have shamed Jorth and his followers. They did not fire a shot during the ordeal nor give any sign of their presence.

Inside the cabin all were silent, too. Jean's eyes blurred so that he continually had to wipe them. Old Isbel made no effort to hide his tears. Blaisdell nodded his shaggy head and swallowed hard. The women sat staring into space. The children, in round-eyed dismay, gazed from one to the other of their elders.

"Wal, they're comin' back," declared Isbel, in immense relief. "An' so help me—Jorth let them bury their daid!"

The fact seemed to have been monstrously strange to Gaston Isbel. When the women entered the old man said, brokenly: "I'm shore glad.... An' I reckon I was wrong to oppose you ... an' wrong to say what I did aboot Jorth."

No one had any chance to reply to Isbel, for the Jorth gang, as if to make up for lost time and surcharged feelings of shame, renewed the attack with such a persistent and furious volleying that the defenders did not risk a return shot. They all had to lie flat next to the lowest log in order to keep from being hit. Bullets rained in through the window. And all the clay between the logs low down was shot away. This fusillade lasted for more than an hour, then gradually the fire diminished on one side and then on the other until it became desultory and finally ceased.

"Ahuh! Shore they've shot their bolt," declared Gaston Isbel.

"Wal, I doon't know aboot that," returned Blaisdell, "but they've shot a hell of a lot of shells."

"Listen," suddenly called Jean. "Somebody's yellin'."

"Hey, Isbel!" came in loud, hoarse voice. "Let your women fight for you."

Gaston Isbel sat up with a start and his face turned livid. Jean needed no more to prove that the derisive voice from outside had belonged to Jorth. The old rancher lunged up to his full height and with reckless disregard of life he rushed to the window. "Jorth," he roared, "I dare you to meet me—man to man!"

This elicited no answer. Jean dragged his father away from the window. After that a waiting silence ensued, gradually less fraught with suspense. Blaisdell started conversation by saying he believed the fight was over for that particular time. No one disputed him. Evidently Gaston Isbel was loath to believe it. Jean, however, watching at the back of the kitchen, eventually discovered that the Jorth gang had lifted the siege. Jean saw them congregate at the edge of the brush, somewhat lower down than they had been the day before. A team of mules, drawing a wagon, appeared on the road, and turned toward the slope. Saddled horses were led down out of the junipers. Jean saw bodies, evidently of dead men, lifted into the wagon, to be hauled away toward the village. Seven mounted men, leading four riderless horses, rode out into the valley and followed the wagon.

"Dad, they've gone," declared Jean. "We had the best of this fight.... If only Guy an' Jacobs had listened!"

The old man nodded moodily. He had aged considerably during these two trying days. His hair was grayer. Now that the blaze and glow of the fight had passed he showed a subtle change, a fixed and morbid sadness, a resignation to a fate he had accepted.

The ordinary routine of ranch life did not return for the Isbels. Blaisdell returned home to settle matters there, so that he could devote all his time to this feud. Gaston Isbel sat down to wait for the members of his clan.

The male members of the family kept guard in turn over the ranch that night. And another day dawned. It brought word from Blaisdell that Blue, Fredericks, Gordon, and Colmor were all at his house, on the way to join the Isbels. This news appeared greatly to rejuvenate Gaston Isbel. But his enthusiasm did not last long. Impatient and moody by turns, he paced or moped around the cabin, always looking out, sometimes toward Blaisdell's ranch, but mostly toward Grass Valley.

It struck Jean as singular that neither Esther Isbel nor Mrs. Jacobs suggested a reburial of their husbands. The two bereaved women did not ask for assistance, but repaired to the pasture, and there spent several hours working over the graves. They raised mounds, which they sodded, and then placed stones at the heads and feet. Lastly, they fenced in the graves.

"I reckon I'll hitch up an' drive back home," said Mrs. Jacobs, when she returned to the cabin. "I've much to do an' plan. Probably I'll go to my mother's home. She's old an' will be glad to have me."

"If I had any place to go to I'd sure go," declared Esther Isbel, bitterly.

Gaston Isbel heard this remark. He raised his face from his hands, evidently both nettled and hurt.

"Esther, shore that's not kind," he said.

The red-haired woman—for she did not appear to be a girl any more—halted before his chair and gazed down at him, with a terrible flare of scorn in her gray eyes.

"Gaston Isbel, all I've got to say to you is this," she retorted, with the voice of a man. "Seein' that you an' Lee Jorth hate each other, why couldn't you act like men? ... You damned Texans, with your bloody feuds, draggin' in every relation, every friend to murder each other! That's not the way of Arizona men.... We've all got to suffer—an' we women be ruined for life—because YOU had differences with Jorth. If you were half a man you'd go out an' kill him yourself, an' not leave a lot of widows an' orphaned children!"

Jean himself writhed under the lash of her scorn. Gaston Isbel turned a dead white. He could not answer her. He seemed stricken with merciless truth. Slowly dropping his head, he remained motionless, a pathetic and tragic figure; and he did not stir until the rapid beat of hoofs denoted the approach of horsemen. Blaisdell appeared on his white charger, leading a pack animal. And behind rode a group of men, all heavily armed, and likewise with packs.

"Get down an' come in," was Isbel's greeting. "Bill—you look after their packs. Better leave the hosses saddled."

The booted and spurred riders trooped in, and their demeanor fitted their errand. Jean was acquainted with all of them. Fredericks was a lanky Texan, the color of dust, and he had yellow, clear eyes, like those of a hawk. His mother had been an Isbel. Gordon, too, was related to Jean's family, though distantly. He resembled an industrious miner more than a prosperous cattleman. Blue was the most striking of the visitors, as he was the most noted. A little, shrunken gray-eyed man, with years of cowboy written all over him, he looked the quiet, easy, cool, and deadly Texan he was reputed to be. Blue's Texas record was shady, and was seldom alluded to, as unfavorable comment had turned out to be hazardous. He was the only one of the group who did not carry a rifle. But he packed two guns, a habit not often noted in Texans, and almost never in Arizonians.

Colmor, Ann Isbel's fiance, was the youngest member of the clan, and the one closest to Jean. His meeting with Ann affected Jean powerfully, and brought to a climax an idea that had been developing in Jean's mind. His sister devotedly loved this lean-faced, keen-eyed Arizonian; and it took no great insight to discover that Colmor reciprocated her affection. They were young. They had long life before them. It seemed to Jean a pity that Colmor should be drawn into this war. Jean watched them, as they conversed apart; and he saw Ann's hands creep up to Colmor's breast, and he saw her dark eyes, eloquent, hungry, fearful, lifted with queries her lips did not speak. Jean stepped beside them, and laid an arm over both their shoulders.

"Colmor, for Ann's sake you'd better back out of this Jorth-Isbel fight," he whispered.

Colmor looked insulted. "But, Jean, it's Ann's father," he said. "I'm almost one of the family."

"You're Ann's sweetheart, an', by Heaven, I say you oughtn't to go with us!" whispered Jean.

"Go—with—you," faltered Ann.

"Yes. Dad is goin' straight after Jorth. Can't you tell that? An' there 'll be one hell of a fight."

Ann looked up into Colmor's face with all her soul in her eyes, but she did not speak. Her look was noble. She yearned to guide him right, yet her lips were sealed. And Colmor betrayed the trouble of his soul. The code of men held him bound, and he could not break from it, though he divined in that moment how truly it was wrong.

"Jean, your dad started me in the cattle business," said Colmor, earnestly. "An' I'm doin' well now. An' when I asked him for Ann he said he'd be glad to have me in the family.... Well, when this talk of fight come up, I asked your dad to let me go in on his side. He wouldn't hear of it. But after a while, as the time passed an' he made more enemies, he finally consented. I reckon he needs me now. An' I can't back out, not even for Ann."

"I would if I were you," replied jean, and knew that he lied.

"Jean, I'm gamblin' to come out of the fight," said Colmor, with a smile. He had no morbid fears nor presentiments, such as troubled jean.

"Why, sure—you stand as good a chance as anyone," rejoined Jean. "It wasn't that I was worryin' about so much."

"What was it, then?" asked Ann, steadily.

"If Andrew DOES come through alive he'll have blood on his hands," returned Jean, with passion. "He can't come through without it.... I've begun to feel what it means to have killed my fellow men.... An' I'd rather your husband an' the father of your children never felt that."

Colmor did not take Jean as subtly as Ann did. She shrunk a little. Her dark eyes dilated. But Colmor showed nothing of her spiritual reaction. He was young. He had wild blood. He was loyal to the Isbels.

"Jean, never worry about my conscience," he said, with a keen look. "Nothin' would tickle me any more than to get a shot at every damn one of the Jorths."

That established Colmor's status in regard to the Jorth-Isbel feud. Jean had no more to say. He respected Ann's friend and felt poignant sorrow for Ann.

Gaston Isbel called for meat and drink to be set on the table for his guests. When his wishes had been complied with the women took the children into the adjoining cabin and shut the door.

"Hah! Wal, we can eat an' talk now."

First the newcomers wanted to hear particulars of what had happened. Blaisdell had told all he knew and had seen, but that was not sufficient. They plied Gaston Isbel with questions. Laboriously and ponderously he rehearsed the experiences of the fight at the ranch, according to his impressions. Bill Isbel was exhorted to talk, but he had of late manifested a sullen and taciturn disposition. In spite of Jean's vigilance Bill had continued to imbibe red liquor. Then Jean was called upon to relate all he had seen and done. It had been Jean's intention to keep his mouth shut, first for his own sake and, secondly, because he did not like to talk of his deeds. But when thus appealed to by these somber-faced, intent-eyed men he divined that the more carefully he described the cruelty and baseness of their enemies, and the more vividly he presented his participation in the first fight of the feud the more strongly he would bind these friends to the Isbel cause. So he talked for an hour, beginning with his meeting with Colter up on the Rim and ending with an account of his killing Greaves. His listeners sat through this long narrative with unabated interest and at the close they were leaning forward, breathless and tense.

"Ah! So Greaves got his desserts at last," exclaimed Gordon.

All the men around the table made comments, and the last, from Blue, was the one that struck Jean forcibly.

"Shore thet was a strange an' a hell of a way to kill Greaves. Why'd you do thet, Jean?"

"I told you. I wanted to avoid noise an' I hoped to get more of them."

Blue nodded his lean, eagle-like head and sat thoughtfully, as if not convinced of anything save Jean's prowess. After a moment Blue spoke again.

"Then, goin' back to Jean's tellin' aboot trackin' rustled Cattle, I've got this to say. I've long suspected thet somebody livin' right heah in the valley has been drivin' off cattle an' dealin' with rustlers. An' now I'm shore of it."

This speech did not elicit the amaze from Gaston Isbel that Jean expected it would.

"You mean Greaves or some of his friends?"

"No. They wasn't none of them in the cattle business, like we are. Shore we all knowed Greaves was crooked. But what I'm figgerin' is thet some so-called honest man in our settlement has been makin' crooked deals."

Blue was a man of deeds rather than words, and so much strong speech from him, whom everybody knew to be remarkably reliable and keen, made a profound impression upon most of the Isbel faction. But, to Jean's surprise, his father did not rave. It was Blaisdell who supplied the rage and invective. Bill Isbel, also, was strangely indifferent to this new element in the condition of cattle dealing. Suddenly Jean caught a vague flash of thought, as if he had intercepted the thought of another's mind, and he wondered—could his brother Bill know anything about this crooked work alluded to by Blue? Dismissing the conjecture, Jean listened earnestly.

"An' if it's true it shore makes this difference—we cain't blame all the rustlin' on to Jorth," concluded Blue.

"Wal, it's not true," declared Gaston Isbel, roughly. "Jorth an' his Hash Knife Gang are at the bottom of all the rustlin' in the valley for years back. An' they've got to be wiped out!"

"Isbel, I reckon we'd all feel better if we talk straight," replied Blue, coolly. "I'm heah to stand by the Isbels. An' y'u know what thet means. But I'm not heah to fight Jorth because he may be a rustler. The others may have their own reasons, but mine is this—you once stood by me in Texas when I was needin' friends. Wal, I'm standin' by y'u now. Jorth is your enemy, an' so he is mine."

Gaston Isbel bowed to this ultimatum, scarcely less agitated than when Esther Isbel had denounced him. His rabid and morbid hate of Jorth had eaten into his heart to take possession there, like the parasite that battened upon the life of its victim. Blue's steely voice, his cold, gray eyes, showed the unbiased truth of the man, as well as his fidelity to his creed. Here again, but in a different manner, Gaston Isbel had the fact flung at him that other men must suffer, perhaps die, for his hate. And the very soul of the old rancher apparently rose in Passionate revolt against the blind, headlong, elemental strength of his nature. So it seemed to Jean, who, in love and pity that hourly grew, saw through his father. Was it too late? Alas! Gaston Isbel could never be turned back! Yet something was altering his brooding, fixed mind.

"Wal," said Blaisdell, gruffly, "let's get down to business.... I'm for havin' Blue be foreman of this heah outfit, an' all of us to do as he says."

Gaston Isbel opposed this selection and indeed resented it. He intended to lead the Isbel faction.

"All right, then. Give us a hunch what we're goin' to do," replied Blaisdell.

"We're goin' to ride off on Jorth's trail—an' one way or another—kill him—KILL HIM! ... I reckon that'll end the fight."

What did old Isbel have in his mind? His listeners shook their heads.

"No," asserted Blaisdell. "Killin' Jorth might be the end of your desires, Isbel, but it 'd never end our fight. We'll have gone too far.... If we take Jorth's trail from heah it means we've got to wipe out that rustler gang, or stay to the last man."

"Yes, by God!" exclaimed Fredericks.

"Let's drink to thet!" said Blue. Strangely they turned to this Texas gunman, instinctively recognizing in him the brain and heart, and the past deeds, that fitted him for the leadership of such a clan. Blue had all in life to lose, and nothing to gain. Yet his spirit was such that he could not lean to all the possible gain of the future, and leave a debt unpaid. Then his voice, his look, his influence were those of a fighter. They all drank with him, even Jean, who hated liquor. And this act of drinking seemed the climax of the council. Preparations were at once begun for their departure on Jorth's trail.

Jean took but little time for his own needs. A horse, a blanket, a knapsack of meat and bread, a canteen, and his weapons, with all the ammunition he could pack, made up his outfit. He wore his buckskin suit, leggings, and moccasins. Very soon the cavalcade was ready to depart. Jean tried not to watch Bill Isbel say good-by to his children, but it was impossible not to. Whatever Bill was, as a man, he was father of those children, and he loved them. How strange that the little ones seemed to realize the meaning of this good-by? They were grave, somber-eyed, pale up to the last moment, then they broke down and wept. Did they sense that their father would never come back? Jean caught that dark, fatalistic presentiment. Bill Isbel's convulsed face showed that he also caught it. Jean did not see Bill say good-by to his wife. But he heard her. Old Gaston Isbel forgot to speak to the children, or else could not. He never looked at them. And his good-by to Ann was as if he were only riding to the village for a day. Jean saw woman's love, woman's intuition, woman's grief in her eyes. He could not escape her. "Oh, Jean! oh, brother!" she whispered as she enfolded him. "It's awful! It's wrong! Wrong! Wrong! ... Good-by! ... If killing MUST be—see that y'u kill the Jorths! ... Good-by!"

Even in Ann, gentle and mild, the Isbel blood spoke at the last. Jean gave Ann over to the pale-faced Colmor, who took her in his arms. Then Jean fled out to his horse. This cold-blooded devastation of a home was almost more than he could bear. There was love here. What would be left?

Colmor was the last one to come out to the horses. He did not walk erect, nor as one whose sight was clear. Then, as the silent, tense, grim men mounted their horses, Bill Isbel's eldest child, the boy, appeared in the door. His little form seemed instinct with a force vastly different from grief. His face was the face of an Isbel.

"Daddy—kill 'em all!" he shouted, with a passion all the fiercer for its incongruity to the treble voice.

So the poison had spread from father to son.

CHAPTER IX

Half a mile from the Isbel ranch the cavalcade passed the log cabin of Evarts, father of the boy who had tended sheep with Bernardino.

It suited Gaston Isbel to halt here. No need to call! Evarts and his son appeared so quickly as to convince observers that they had been watching.

"Howdy, Jake!" said Isbel. "I'm wantin' a word with y'u alone."

"Shore, boss, git down an' come in," replied Evarts.

Isbel led him aside, and said something forcible that Jean divined from the very gesture which accompanied it. His father was telling Evarts that he was not to join in the Isbel-Jorth war. Evarts had worked for the Isbels a long time, and his faithfulness, along with something stronger and darker, showed in his rugged face as he stubbornly opposed Isbel. The old man raised his voice: "No, I tell you. An' that settles it."

They returned to the horses, and, before mounting, Isbel, as if he remembered something, directed his somber gaze on young Evarts.

"Son, did you bury Bernardino?"

"Dad an' me went over yestiddy," replied the lad. "I shore was glad the coyotes hadn't been round."

"How aboot the sheep?"

"I left them there. I was goin' to stay, but bein' all alone—I got skeered.... The sheep was doin' fine. Good water an' some grass. An' this ain't time fer varmints to hang round."

"Jake, keep your eye on that flock," returned Isbel. "An' if I shouldn't happen to come back y'u can call them sheep yours.... I'd like your boy to ride up to the village. Not with us, so anybody would see him. But afterward. We'll be at Abel Meeker's."

Again Jean was confronted with an uneasy premonition as to some idea or plan his father had not shared with his followers. When the cavalcade started on again Jean rode to his father's side and asked him why he had wanted the Evarts boy to come to Grass Valley. And the old man replied that, as the boy could run to and fro in the village without danger, he might be useful in reporting what was going on at Greaves's store, where undoubtedly the Jorth gang would hold forth. This appeared reasonable enough, therefore Jean smothered the objection he had meant to make.

The valley road was deserted. When, a mile farther on, the riders passed a group of cabins, just on the outskirts of the village, Jean's quick eye caught sight of curious and evidently frightened people trying to see while they avoided being seen. No doubt the whole settlement was in a state of suspense and terror. Not unlikely this dark, closely grouped band of horsemen appeared to them as Jorth's gang had looked to Jean. It was an orderly, trotting march that manifested neither hurry nor excitement. But any Western eye could have caught the singular aspect of such a group, as if the intent of the riders was a visible thing.

Soon they reached the outskirts of the village. Here their approach bad been watched for or had been already reported. Jean saw men, women, children peeping from behind cabins and from half-opened doors. Farther on Jean espied the dark figures of men, slipping out the back way through orchards and gardens and running north, toward the center of the village. Could these be friends of the Jorth crowd, on the way with warnings of the approach of the Isbels? Jean felt convinced of it. He was learning that his father had not been absolutely correct in his estimation of the way Jorth and his followers were regarded by their neighbors. Not improbably there were really many villagers who, being more interested in sheep raising than in cattle, had an honest leaning toward the Jorths. Some, too, no doubt, had leanings that were dishonest in deed if not in sincerity.

Gaston Isbel led his clan straight down the middle of the wide road of Grass Valley until he reached a point opposite Abel Meeker's cabin. Jean espied the same curiosity from behind Meeker's door and windows as had been shown all along the road. But presently, at Isbel's call, the door opened and a short, swarthy man appeared. He carried a rifle.

"Howdy, Gass!" he said. "What's the good word?"

"Wal, Abel, it's not good, but bad. An' it's shore started," replied Isbel. "I'm askin' y'u to let me have your cabin."

"You're welcome. I'll send the folks 'round to Jim's," returned Meeker. "An' if y'u want me, I'm with y'u, Isbel."

"Thanks, Abel, but I'm not leadin' any more kin an' friends into this heah deal."

"Wal, jest as y'u say. But I'd like damn bad to jine with y'u.... My brother Ted was shot last night."

"Ted! Is he daid?" ejaculated Isbel, blankly.

"We can't find out," replied Meeker. "Jim says thet Jeff Campbell said thet Ted went into Greaves's place last night. Greaves allus was friendly to Ted, but Greaves wasn't thar—"

"No, he shore wasn't," interrupted Isbel, with a dark smile, "an' he never will be there again."

Meeker nodded with slow comprehension and a shade crossed his face.

"Wal, Campbell claimed he'd heerd from some one who was thar. Anyway, the Jorths were drinkin' hard, an' they raised a row with Ted—same old sheep talk an' somebody shot him. Campbell said Ted was thrown out back, an' he was shore he wasn't killed."

"Ahuh! Wal, I'm sorry, Abel, your family had to lose in this. Maybe Ted's not bad hurt. I shore hope so.... An' y'u an' Jim keep out of the fight, anyway."

"All right, Isbel. But I reckon I'll give y'u a hunch. If this heah fight lasts long the whole damn Basin will be in it, on one side or t'other."

"Abe, you're talkin' sense," broke in Blaisdell. "An' that's why we're up heah for quick action."

"I heerd y'u got Daggs," whispered Meeker, as he peered all around.

"Wal, y'u heerd correct," drawled Blaisdell.

Meeker muttered strong words into his beard. "Say, was Daggs in thet Jorth outfit?"

"He WAS. But he walked right into Jean's forty-four.... An' I reckon his carcass would show some more."

"An' whar's Guy Isbel?" demanded Meeker.

"Daid an' buried, Abel," replied Gaston Isbel. "An' now I'd be obliged if y'u 'll hurry your folks away, an' let us have your cabin an' corral. Have yu got any hay for the hosses?"

"Shore. The barn's half full," replied Meeker, as he turned away. "Come on in."

"No. We'll wait till you've gone."

When Meeker had gone, Isbel and his men sat their horses and looked about them and spoke low. Their advent had been expected, and the little town awoke to the imminence of the impending battle. Inside Meeker's house there was the sound of indistinct voices of women and the bustle incident to a hurried vacating.

Across the wide road people were peering out on all sides, some hiding, others walking to and fro, from fence to fence, whispering in little groups. Down the wide road, at the point where it turned, stood Greaves's fort-like stone house. Low, flat, isolated, with its dark, eye-like windows, it presented a forbidding and sinister aspect. Jean distinctly saw the forms of men, some dark, others in shirt sleeves, come to the wide door and look down the road.

"Wal, I reckon only aboot five hundred good hoss steps are separatin' us from that outfit," drawled Blaisdell.

No one replied to his jocularity. Gaston Isbel's eyes narrowed to a slit in his furrowed face and he kept them fastened upon Greaves's store. Blue, likewise, had a somber cast of countenance, not, perhaps, any darker nor grimmer than those of his comrades, but more representative of intense preoccupation of mind. The look of him thrilled Jean, who could sense its deadliness, yet could not grasp any more. Altogether, the manner of the villagers and the watchful pacing to and fro of the Jorth followers and the silent, boding front of Isbel and his men summed up for Jean the menace of the moment that must very soon change to a terrible reality.

At a call from Meeker, who stood at the back of the cabin, Gaston Isbel rode into the yard, followed by the others of his party. "Somebody look after the hosses," ordered Isbel, as he dismounted and took his rifle and pack. "Better leave the saddles on, leastways till we see what's comin' off."

Jean and Bill Isbel led the horses back to the corral. While watering and feeding them, Jean somehow received the impression that Bill was trying to speak, to confide in him, to unburden himself of some load. This peculiarity of Bill's had become marked when he was perfectly sober. Yet he had never spoken or even begun anything unusual. Upon the present occasion, however, Jean believed that his brother might have gotten rid of his emotion, or whatever it was, had they not been interrupted by Colmor.

"Boys, the old man's orders are for us to sneak round on three sides of Greaves's store, keepin' out of gunshot till we find good cover, an' then crawl closer an' to pick off any of Jorth's gang who shows himself."

Bill Isbel strode off without a reply to Colmor.

"Well, I don't think so much of that," said Jean, ponderingly. "Jorth has lots of friends here. Somebody might pick us off."

"I kicked, but the old man shut me up. He's not to be bucked ag'in' now. Struck me as powerful queer. But no wonder."

"Maybe he knows best. Did he say anythin' about what he an' the rest of them are goin' to do?"

"Nope. Blue taxed him with that an' got the same as me. I reckon we'd better try it out, for a while, anyway."

"Looks like he wants us to keep out of the fight," replied Jean, thoughtfully. "Maybe, though ... Dad's no fool. Colmor, you wait here till I get out of sight. I'll go round an' come up as close as advisable behind Greaves's store. You take the right side. An' keep hid."

With that Jean strode off, going around the barn, straight out the orchard lane to the open flat, and then climbing a fence to the north of the village. Presently he reached a line of sheds and corrals, to which he held until he arrived at the road. This point was about a quarter of a mile from Greaves's store, and around the bend. Jean sighted no one. The road, the fields, the yards, the backs of the cabins all looked deserted. A blight had settled down upon the peaceful activities of Grass Valley. Crossing the road, Jean began to circle until he came close to several cabins, around which he made a wide detour. This took him to the edge of the slope, where brush and thickets afforded him a safe passage to a line directly back of Greaves's store. Then he turned toward it. Soon he was again approaching a cabin of that side, and some of its inmates descried him, Their actions attested to their alarm. Jean half expected a shot from this quarter, such were his growing doubts, but he was mistaken. A man, unknown to Jean, closely watched his guarded movements and then waved a hand, as if to signify to Jean that he had nothing to fear. After this act he disappeared. Jean believed that he had been recognized by some one not antagonistic to the Isbels. Therefore he passed the cabin and, coming to a thick scrub-oak tree that offered shelter, he hid there to watch. From this spot he could see the back of Greaves's store, at a distance probably too far for a rifle bullet to reach. Before him, as far as the store, and on each side, extended the village common. In front of the store ran the road. Jean's position was such that he could not command sight of this road down toward Meeker's house, a fact that disturbed him. Not satisfied with this stand, he studied his surroundings in the hope of espying a better. And he discovered what he thought would be a more favorable position, although he could not see much farther down the road. Jean went back around the cabin and, coming out into the open to the right, he got the corner of Greaves's barn between him and the window of the store. Then he boldly hurried into the open, and soon reached an old wagon, from behind which he proposed to watch. He could not see either window or door of the store, but if any of the Jorth contingent came out the back way they would be within reach of his rifle. Jean took the risk of being shot at from either side.

So sharp and roving was his sight that he soon espied Colmor slipping along behind the trees some hundred yards to the left. All his efforts to catch a glimpse of Bill, however, were fruitless. And this appeared strange to Jean, for there were several good places on the right from which Bill could have commanded the front of Greaves's store and the whole west side.

Colmor disappeared among some shrubbery, and Jean seemed left alone to watch a deserted, silent village. Watching and listening, he felt that the time dragged. Yet the shadows cast by the sun showed him that, no matter how tense he felt and how the moments seemed hours, they were really flying.

Suddenly Jean's ears rang with the vibrant shock of a rifle report. He jerked up, strung and thrilling. It came from in front of the store. It was followed by revolver shots, heavy, booming. Three he counted, and the rest were too close together to enumerate. A single hoarse yell pealed out, somehow trenchant and triumphant. Other yells, not so wild and strange, muffled the first one. Then silence clapped down on the store and the open square.

Jean was deadly certain that some of the Jorth clan would show themselves. He strained to still the trembling those sudden shots and that significant yell had caused him. No man appeared. No more sounds caught Jean's ears. The suspense, then, grew unbearable. It was not that he could not wait for an enemy to appear, but that he could not wait to learn what had happened.

Every moment that he stayed there, with hands like steel on his rifle, with eyes of a falcon, but added to a dreadful, dark certainty of disaster. A rifle shot swiftly followed by revolver shots! What could, they mean? Revolver shots of different caliber, surely fired by different men! What could they mean? It was not these shots that accounted for Jean's dread, but the yell which had followed. All his intelligence and all his nerve were not sufficient to fight down the feeling of calamity. And at last, yielding to it, he left his post, and ran like a deer across the open, through the cabin yard, and around the edge of the slope to the road. Here his caution brought him to a halt. Not a living thing crossed his vision. Breaking into a run, he soon reached the back of Meeker's place and entered, to hurry forward to the cabin.

Colmor was there in the yard, breathing hard, his face working, and in front of him crouched several of the men with rifles ready. The road, to Jean's flashing glance, was apparently deserted. Blue sat on the doorstep, lighting a cigarette. Then on the moment Blaisdell strode to the door of the cabin. Jean had never seen him look like that.

"Jean—look—down the road," he said, brokenly, and with big hand shaking he pointed down toward Greaves's store.

Like lightning Jean's glance shot down—down—down—until it stopped to fix upon the prostrate form of a man, lying in the middle of the road. A man of lengthy build, shirt-sleeved arms flung wide, white head in the dust—dead! Jean's recognition was as swift as his sight. His father! They had killed him! The Jorths! It was done. His father's premonition of death had not been false. And then, after these flashing thoughts, came a sense of blankness, momentarily almost oblivion, that gave place to a rending of the heart. That pain Jean had known only at the death of his mother. It passed, this agonizing pang, and its icy pressure yielded to a rushing gust of blood, fiery as hell.

"Who—did it?" whispered Jean.

"Jorth!" replied Blaisdell, huskily. "Son, we couldn't hold your dad back.... We couldn't. He was like a lion.... An' he throwed his life away! Oh, if it hadn't been for that it 'd not be so awful. Shore, we come heah to shoot an' be shot. But not like that.... By God, it was murder—murder!"

Jean's mute lips framed a query easily read.

"Tell him, Blue. I cain't," continued Blaisdell, and he tramped back into the cabin.

"Set down, Jean, an' take things easy," said Blue, calmly. "You know we all reckoned we'd git plugged one way or another in this deal. An' shore it doesn't matter much how a fellar gits it. All thet ought to bother us is to make shore the other outfit bites the dust—same as your dad had to."

Under this man's tranquil presence, all the more quieting because it seemed to be so deadly sure and cool, Jean felt the uplift of his dark spirit, the acceptance of fatality, the mounting control of faculties that must wait. The little gunman seemed to have about his inert presence something that suggested a rattlesnake's inherent knowledge of its destructiveness. Jean sat down and wiped his clammy face.

"Jean, your dad reckoned to square accounts with Jorth, an' save us all," began Blue, puffing out a cloud of smoke. "But he reckoned too late. Mebbe years; ago—or even not long ago—if he'd called Jorth out man to man there'd never been any Jorth-Isbel war. Gaston Isbel's conscience woke too late. That's how I figger it."

"Hurry! Tell me—how it—happen," panted Jean.

"Wal, a little while after y'u left I seen your dad writin' on a leaf he tore out of a book—Meeker's Bible, as yu can see. I thought thet was funny. An' Blaisdell gave me a hunch. Pretty soon along comes young Evarts. The old man calls him out of our hearin' an' talks to him. Then I seen him give the boy somethin', which I afterward figgered was what he wrote on the leaf out of the Bible. Me an' Blaisdell both tried to git out of him what thet meant. But not a word. I kept watchin' an' after a while I seen young Evarts slip out the back way. Mebbe half an hour I seen a bare-legged kid cross, the road an' go into Greaves's store.... Then shore I tumbled to your dad. He'd sent a note to Jorth to come out an' meet him face to face, man to man! ... Shore it was like readin' what your dad had wrote. But I didn't say nothin' to Blaisdell. I jest watched."

Blue drawled these last words, as if he enjoyed remembrance of his keen reasoning. A smile wreathed his thin lips. He drew twice on the cigarette and emitted another cloud of smoke. Quite suddenly then he changed. He made a rapid gesture—the whip of a hand, significant and passionate. And swift words followed:

"Colonel Lee Jorth stalked out of the store—out into the road—mebbe a hundred steps. Then he halted. He wore his long black coat an' his wide black hat, an' he stood like a stone.

"'What the hell!' burst out Blaisdell, comin' out of his trance.

"The rest of us jest looked. I'd forgot your dad, for the minnit. So had all of us. But we remembered soon enough when we seen him stalk out. Everybody had a hunch then. I called him. Blaisdell begged him to come back. All the fellars; had a say. No use! Then I shore cussed him an' told him it was plain as day thet Jorth didn't hit me like an honest man. I can sense such things. I knew Jorth had trick up his sleeve. I've not been a gun fighter fer nothin'.

"Your dad had no rifle. He packed his gun at his hip. He jest stalked down thet road like a giant, goin' faster an' faster, holdin' his head high. It shore was fine to see him. But I was sick. I heerd Blaisdell groan, an' Fredericks thar cussed somethin' fierce.... When your dad halted—I reckon aboot fifty steps from Jorth—then we all went numb. I heerd your dad's voice—then Jorth's. They cut like knives. Y'u could shore heah the hate they hed fer each other."

Blue had become a little husky. His speech had grown gradually to denote his feeling. Underneath his serenity there was a different order of man.

"I reckon both your dad an' Jorth went fer their guns at the same time—an even break. But jest as they drew, some one shot a rifle from the store. Must hev been a forty-five seventy. A big gun! The bullet must have hit your dad low down, aboot the middle. He acted thet way, sinkin' to his knees. An' he was wild in shootin'—so wild thet he must hev missed. Then he wabbled—an' Jorth run in a dozen steps, shootin' fast, till your dad fell over.... Jorth run closer, bent over him, an' then straightened up with an Apache yell, if I ever heerd one.... An' then Jorth backed slow—lookin' all the time—backed to the store, an' went in."

Blue's voice ceased. Jean seemed suddenly released from an impelling magnet that now dropped him to some numb, dizzy depth. Blue's lean face grew hazy. Then Jean bowed his head in his hands, and sat there, while a slight tremor shook all his muscles at once. He grew deathly cold and deathly sick. This paroxysm slowly wore away, and Jean grew conscious of a dull amaze at the apparent deadness of his spirit. Blaisdell placed a huge, kindly hand on his shoulder.

"Brace up, son!" he said, with voice now clear and resonant. "Shore it's what your dad expected—an' what we all must look for.... If yu was goin' to kill Jorth before—think how — — shore y'u're goin' to kill him now."

"Blaisdell's talkin'," put in Blue, and his voice had a cold ring. "Lee Jorth will never see the sun rise ag'in!"

These calls to the primitive in Jean, to the Indian, were not in vain. But even so, when the dark tide rose in him, there was still a haunting consciousness of the cruelty of this singular doom imposed upon him. Strangely Ellen Jorth's face floated back in the depths of his vision, pale, fading, like the face of a spirit floating by.

"Blue," said Blaisdell, "let's get Isbel's body soon as we dare, an' bury it. Reckon we can, right after dark."

"Shore," replied Blue. "But y'u fellars figger thet out. I'm thinkin' hard. I've got somethin' on my mind."

Jean grew fascinated by the looks and speech and action of the little gunman. Blue, indeed, had something on his mind. And it boded ill to the men in that dark square stone house down the road. He paced to and fro in the yard, back and forth on the path to the gate, and then he entered the cabin to stalk up and down, faster and faster, until all at once he halted as if struck, to upfling his right arm in a singular fierce gesture.

"Jean, call the men in," he said, tersely.

They all filed in, sinister and silent, with eager faces turned to the little Texan. His dominance showed markedly.

"Gordon, y'u stand in the door an' keep your eye peeled," went on Blue. "... Now, boys, listen! I've thought it all out. This game of man huntin' is the same to me as cattle raisin' is to y'u. An' my life in Texas all comes back to me, I reckon, in good stead fer us now. I'm goin' to kill Lee Jorth! Him first, an' mebbe his brothers. I had to think of a good many ways before I hit on one I reckon will be shore. It's got to be SHORE. Jorth has got to die! Wal, heah's my plan.... Thet Jorth outfit is drinkin' some, we can gamble on it. They're not goin' to leave thet store. An' of course they'll be expectin' us to start a fight. I reckon they'll look fer some such siege as they held round Isbel's ranch. But we shore ain't goin' to do thet. I'm goin' to surprise thet outfit. There's only one man among them who is dangerous, an' thet's Queen. I know Queen. But he doesn't know me. An' I'm goin' to finish my job before he gets acquainted with me. After thet, all right!"

Blue paused a moment, his eyes narrowing down, his whole face setting in hard cast of intense preoccupation, as if he visualized a scene of extraordinary nature.

"Wal, what's your trick?" demanded Blaisdell.

"Y'u all know Greaves's store," continued Blue. "How them winders have wooden shutters thet keep a light from showin' outside? Wal, I'm gamblin' thet as soon as it's dark Jorth's gang will be celebratin'. They'll be drinkin' an' they'll have a light, an' the winders will be shut. They're not goin' to worry none aboot us. Thet store is like a fort. It won't burn. An' shore they'd never think of us chargin' them in there. Wal, as soon as it's dark, we'll go round behind the lots an' come up jest acrost the road from Greaves's. I reckon we'd better leave Isbel where he lays till this fight's over. Mebbe y'u 'll have more 'n him to bury. We'll crawl behind them bushes in front of Coleman's yard. An' heah's where Jean comes in. He'll take an ax, an' his guns, of course, an' do some of his Injun sneakin' round to the back of Greaves's store.... An', Jean, y'u must do a slick job of this. But I reckon it 'll be easy fer you. Back there it 'll be dark as pitch, fer anyone lookin' out of the store. An' I'm figgerin' y'u can take your time an' crawl right up. Now if y'u don't remember how Greaves's back yard looks I'll tell y'u."

Here Blue dropped on one knee to the floor and with a finger he traced a map of Greaves's barn and fence, the back door and window, and especially a break in the stone foundation which led into a kind of cellar where Greaves stored wood and other things that could be left outdoors.

"Jean, I take particular pains to show y'u where this hole is," said Blue, "because if the gang runs out y'u could duck in there an' hide. An' if they run out into the yard—wal, y'u'd make it a sorry run fer them.... Wal, when y'u've crawled up close to Greaves's back door, an' waited long enough to see an' listen—then you're to run fast an' swing your ax smash ag'in' the winder. Take a quick peep in if y'u want to. It might help. Then jump quick an' take a swing at the door. Y'u 'll be standin' to one side, so if the gang shoots through the door they won't hit y'u. Bang thet door good an' hard.... Wal, now's where I come in. When y'u swing thet ax I'll shore run fer the front of the store. Jorth an' his outfit will be some attentive to thet poundin' of yours on the back door. So I reckon. An' they'll be lookin' thet way. I'll run in—yell—an' throw my guns on Jorth."

"Humph! Is that all?" ejaculated Blaisdell.

"I reckon thet's all an' I'm figgerin' it's a hell of a lot," responded Blue, dryly. "Thet's what Jorth will think."

"Where do we come in?"

"Wal, y'u all can back me up," replied Blue, dubiously. "Y'u see, my plan goes as far as killin' Jorth—an' mebbe his brothers. Mebbe I'll get a crack at Queen. But I'll be shore of Jorth. After thet all depends. Mebbe it 'll be easy fer me to get out. An' if I do y'u fellars will know it an' can fill thet storeroom full of bullets."

"Wal, Blue, with all due respect to y'u, I shore don't like your plan," declared Blaisdell. "Success depends upon too many little things any one of which might go wrong."

"Blaisdell, I reckon I know this heah game better than y'u," replied Blue. "A gun fighter goes by instinct. This trick will work."

"But suppose that front door of Greaves's store is barred," protested Blaisdell.

"It hasn't got any bar," said Blue.

"Y'u're shore?"

"Yes, I reckon," replied Blue.

"Hell, man! Aren't y'u takin' a terrible chance?" queried Blaisdell.

Blue's answer to that was a look that brought the blood to Blaisdell's face. Only then did the rancher really comprehend how the little gunman had taken such desperate chances before, and meant to take them now, not with any hope or assurance of escaping with his life, but to live up to his peculiar code of honor.

"Blaisdell, did y'u ever heah of me in Texas?" he queried, dryly.

"Wal, no, Blue, I cain't swear I did," replied the rancher, apologetically. "An' Isbel was always sort of' mysterious aboot his acquaintance with you."

"My name's not Blue."

"Ahuh! Wal, what is it, then—if I'm safe to ask?" returned Blaisdell, gruffly.

"It's King Fisher," replied Blue.

The shock that stiffened Blaisdell must have been communicated to the others. Jean certainly felt amaze, and some other emotion not fully realized, when he found himself face to face with one of the most notorious characters ever known in Texas—an outlaw long supposed to be dead.

"Men, I reckon I'd kept my secret if I'd any idee of comin' out of this Isbel-Jorth war alive," said Blue. "But I'm goin' to cash. I feel it heah.... Isbel was my friend. He saved me from bein' lynched in Texas. An' so I'm goin' to kill Jorth. Now I'll take it kind of y'u—if any of y'u come out of this alive—to tell who I was an' why I was on the Isbel side. Because this sheep an' cattle war—this talk of Jorth an' the Hash Knife Gang—it makes me, sick. I KNOW there's been crooked work on Isbel's side, too. An' I never want it on record thet I killed Jorth because he was a rustler."

"By God, Blue! it's late in the day for such talk," burst out Blaisdell, in rage and amaze. "But I reckon y'u know what y'u're talkin' aboot.... Wal, I shore don't want to heah it."

At this juncture Bill Isbel quietly entered the cabin, too late to hear any of Blue's statement. Jean was positive of that, for as Blue was speaking those last revealing words Bill's heavy boots had resounded on the gravel path outside. Yet something in Bill's look or in the way Blue averted his lean face or in the entrance of Bill at that particular moment, or all these together, seemed to Jean to add further mystery to the long secret causes leading up to the Jorth-Isbel war. Did Bill know what Blue knew? Jean had an inkling that he did. And on the moment, so perplexing and bitter, Jean gazed out the door, down the deserted road to where his dead father lay, white-haired and ghastly in the sunlight.

"Blue, you could have kept that to yourself, as well as your real name," interposed Jean, with bitterness. "It's too late now for either to do any good.... But I appreciate your friendship for dad, an' I'm ready to help carry out your plan."

That decision of Jean's appeared to put an end to protest or argument from Blaisdell or any of the others. Blue's fleeting dark smile was one of satisfaction. Then upon most of this group of men seemed to settle a grim restraint. They went out and walked and watched; they came in again, restless and somber. Jean thought that he must have bent his gaze a thousand times down the road to the tragic figure of his father. That sight roused all emotions in his breast, and the one that stirred there most was pity. The pity of it! Gaston Isbel lying face down in the dust of the village street! Patches of blood showed on the back of his vest and one white-sleeved shoulder. He had been shot through. Every time Jean saw this blood he had to stifle a gathering of wild, savage impulses.

Meanwhile the afternoon hours dragged by and the village remained as if its inhabitants had abandoned it. Not even a dog showed on the side road. Jorth and some of his men came out in front of the store and sat on the steps, in close convening groups. Every move they, made seemed significant of their confidence and importance. About sunset they went back into the store, closing door and window shutters. Then Blaisdell called the Isbel faction to have food and drink. Jean felt no hunger. And Blue, who had kept apart from the others, showed no desire to eat. Neither did he smoke, though early in the day he had never been without a cigarette between his lips.

Twilight fell and darkness came. Not a light showed anywhere in the blackness.

"Wal, I reckon it's aboot time," said Blue, and he led the way out of the cabin to the back of the lot. Jean strode behind him, carrying his rifle and an ax. Silently the other men followed. Blue turned to the left and led through the field until he came within sight of a dark line of trees.

"Thet's where the road turns off," he said to Jean. "An' heah's the back of Coleman's place.... Wal, Jean, good luck!"

Jean felt the grip of a steel-like hand, and in the darkness he caught the gleam of Blue's eyes. Jean had no response in words for the laconic Blue, but he wrung the hard, thin hand and hurried away in the darkness.

Once alone, his part of the business at hand rushed him into eager thrilling action. This was the sort of work he was fitted to do. In this instance it was important, but it seemed to him that Blue had coolly taken the perilous part. And this cowboy with gray in his thin hair was in reality the great King Fisher! Jean marveled at the fact. And he shivered all over for Jorth. In ten minutes—fifteen, more or less, Jorth would lie gasping bloody froth and sinking down. Something in the dark, lonely, silent, oppressive summer night told Jean this. He strode on swiftly. Crossing the road at a run, he kept on over the ground he had traversed during the afternoon, and in a few moments he stood breathing hard at the edge of the common behind Greaves's store.

A pin point of light penetrated the blackness. It made Jean's heart leap. The Jorth contingent were burning the big lamp that hung in the center of Greaves's store. Jean listened. Loud voices and coarse laughter sounded discord on the melancholy silence of the night. What Blue had called his instinct had surely guided him aright. Death of Gaston Isbel was being celebrated by revel.

In a few moments Jean had regained his breath. Then all his faculties set intensely to the action at hand. He seemed to magnify his hearing and his sight. His movements made no sound. He gained the wagon, where he crouched a moment.

The ground seemed a pale, obscure medium, hardly more real than the gloom above it. Through this gloom of night, which looked thick like a cloud, but was really clear, shone the thin, bright point of light, accentuating the black square that was Greaves's store. Above this stood a gray line of tree foliage, and then the intensely dark-blue sky studded with white, cold stars.

A hound bayed lonesomely somewhere in the distance. Voices of men sounded more distinctly, some deep and low, others loud, unguarded, with the vacant note of thoughtlessness.

Jean gathered all his forces, until sense of sight and hearing were in exquisite accord with the suppleness and lightness of his movements. He glided on about ten short, swift steps before he halted. That was as far as his piercing eyes could penetrate. If there had been a guard stationed outside the store Jean would have seen him before being seen. He saw the fence, reached it, entered the yard, glided in the dense shadow of the barn until the black square began to loom gray—the color of stone at night. Jean peered through the obscurity. No dark figure of a man showed against that gray wall—only a black patch, which must be the hole in the foundation mentioned. A ray of light now streaked out from the little black window. To the right showed the wide, black door.

Farther on Jean glided silently. Then he halted. There was no guard outside. Jean heard the clink of a cap, the lazy drawl of a Texan, and then a strong, harsh voice—Jorth's. It strung Jean's whole being tight and vibrating. Inside he was on fire while cold thrills rippled over his skin. It took tremendous effort of will to hold himself back another instant to listen, to look, to feel, to make sure. And that instant charged him with a mighty current of hot blood, straining, throbbing, damming.

When Jean leaped this current burst. In a few swift bounds he gained his point halfway between door and window. He leaned his rifle against the stone wall. Then he swung the ax. Crash! The window shutter split and rattled to the floor inside. The silence then broke with a hoarse, "What's thet?"

With all his might Jean swung the heavy ax on the door. Smash! The lower half caved in and banged to the floor. Bright light flared out the hole.

"Look out!" yelled a man, in loud alarm. "They're batterin' the back door!"

Jean swung again, high on the splintered door. Crash! Pieces flew inside.

"They've got axes," hoarsely shouted another voice. "Shove the counter ag'in' the door."

"No!" thundered a voice of authority that denoted terror as well. "Let them come in. Pull your guns an' take to cover!"

"They ain't comin' in," was the hoarse reply. "They'll shoot in on us from the dark."

"Put out the lamp!" yelled another.

Jean's third heavy swing caved in part of the upper half of the door. Shouts and curses intermingled with the sliding of benches across the floor and the hard shuffle of boots. This confusion seemed to be split and silenced by a piercing yell, of different caliber, of terrible meaning. It stayed Jean's swing—caused him to drop the ax and snatch up his rifle.

"DON'T ANYBODY MOVE!"

Like a steel whip this voice cut the silence. It belonged to Blue. Jean swiftly bent to put his eye to a crack in the door. Most of those visible seemed to have been frozen into unnatural positions. Jorth stood rather in front of his men, hatless and coatless, one arm outstretched, and his dark profile set toward a little man just inside the door. This man was Blue. Jean needed only one flashing look at Blue's face, at his leveled, quivering guns, to understand why he had chosen this trick.

"Who're—-you?" demanded Jorth, in husky pants.

"Reckon I'm Isbel's right-hand man," came the biting reply. "Once tolerable well known in Texas.... KING FISHER!"

The name must have been a guarantee of death. Jorth recognized this outlaw and realized his own fate. In the lamplight his face turned a pale greenish white. His outstretched hand began to quiver down.

Blue's left gun seemed to leap up and flash red and explode. Several heavy reports merged almost as one. Jorth's arm jerked limply, flinging his gun. And his body sagged in the middle. His hands fluttered like crippled wings and found their way to his abdomen. His death-pale face never changed its set look nor position toward Blue. But his gasping utterance was one of horrible mortal fury and terror. Then he began to sway, still with that strange, rigid set of his face toward his slayer, until he fell.

His fall broke the spell. Even Blue, like the gunman he was, had paused to watch Jorth in his last mortal action. Jorth's followers began to draw and shoot. Jean saw Blue's return fire bring down a huge man, who fell across Jorth's body. Then Jean, quick as the thought that actuated him, raised his rifle and shot at the big lamp. It burst in a flare. It crashed to the floor. Darkness followed—a blank, thick, enveloping mantle. Then red flashes of guns emphasized the blackness. Inside the store there broke loose a pandemonium of shots, yells, curses, and thudding boots. Jean shoved his rifle barrel inside the door and, holding it low down, he moved it to and fro while he worked lever and trigger until the magazine was empty. Then, drawing his six-shooter, he emptied that. A roar of rifles from the front of the store told Jean that his comrades had entered the fray. Bullets zipped through the door he had broken. Jean ran swiftly round the corner, taking care to sheer off a little to the left, and when he got clear of the building he saw a line of flashes in the middle of the road. Blaisdell and the others were firing into the door of the store. With nimble fingers Jean reloaded his rifle. Then swiftly he ran across the road and down to get behind his comrades. Their shooting had slackened. Jean saw dark forms coming his way.

"Hello, Blaisdell!" he called, warningly.

"That y'u, Jean?" returned the rancher, looming up. "Wal, we wasn't worried aboot y'u."

"Blue?" queried Jean, sharply.

A little, dark figure shuffled past Jean. "Howdy, Jean!" said Blue, dryly. "Y'u shore did your part. Reckon I'll need to be tied up, but I ain't hurt much."

"Colmor's hit," called the voice of Gordon, a few yards distant. "Help me, somebody!"

Jean ran to help Gordon uphold the swaying Colmor. "Are you hurt-bad?" asked Jean, anxiously. The young man's head rolled and hung. He was breathing hard and did not reply. They had almost to carry him.

"Come on, men!" called Blaisdell, turning back toward the others who were still firing. "We'll let well enough alone.... Fredericks, y'u an' Bill help me find the body of the old man. It's heah somewhere."

Farther on down the road the searchers stumbled over Gaston Isbel. They picked him up and followed Jean and Gordon, who were supporting the wounded Colmor. Jean looked back to see Blue dragging himself along in the rear. It was too dark to see distinctly; nevertheless, Jean got the impression that Blue was more severely wounded than he had claimed to be. The distance to Meeker's cabin was not far, but it took what Jean felt to be a long and anxious time to get there. Colmor apparently rallied somewhat. When this procession entered Meeker's yard, Blue was lagging behind.

"Blue, how air y'u?" called Blaisdell, with concern.

"Wal, I got—my boots—on—anyhow," replied Blue, huskily.

He lurched into the yard and slid down on the grass and stretched out.

"Man! Y'u're hurt bad!" exclaimed Blaisdell. The others halted in their slow march and, as if by tacit, unspoken word, lowered the body of Isbel to the ground. Then Blaisdell knelt beside Blue. Jean left Colmor to Gordon and hurried to peer down into Blue's dim face.

"No, I ain't—hurt," said Blue, in a much weaker voice. "I'm—jest killed! ... It was Queen! ... Y'u all heerd me—Queen was—only bad man in that lot. I knowed it.... I could—hev killed him.... But I was—after Lee Jorth an' his brothers...."

Blue's voice failed there.

"Wal!" ejaculated Blaisdell.

"Shore was funny—Jorth's face—when I said—King Fisher," whispered Blue. "Funnier—when I bored—him through.... But it—was—Queen—"

His whisper died away.

"Blue!" called Blaisdell, sharply. Receiving no answer, he bent lower in the starlight and placed a hand upon the man's breast.

"Wal, he's gone.... I wonder if he really was the old Texas King Fisher. No one would ever believe it.... But if he killed the Jorths, I'll shore believe him."

CHAPTER X

Two weeks of lonely solitude in the forest had worked incalculable change in Ellen Jorth.

Late in June her father and her two uncles had packed and ridden off with Daggs, Colter, and six other men, all heavily armed, some somber with drink, others hard and grim with a foretaste of fight. Ellen had not been given any orders. Her father had forgotten to bid her good-by or had avoided it. Their dark mission was stamped on their faces.

They had gone and, keen as had been Ellen's pang, nevertheless, their departure was a relief. She had heard them bluster and brag so often that she had her doubts of any great Jorth-Isbel war. Barking dogs did not bite. Somebody, perhaps on each side, would be badly wounded, possibly killed, and then the feud would go on as before, mostly talk. Many of her former impressions had faded. Development had been so rapid and continuous in her that she could look back to a day-by-day transformation. At night she had hated the sight of herself and when the dawn came she would rise, singing.

Jorth had left Ellen at home with the Mexican woman and Antonio. Ellen saw them only at meal times, and often not then, for she frequently visited old John Sprague or came home late to do her own cooking.

It was but a short distance up to Sprague's cabin, and since she had stopped riding the black horse, Spades, she walked. Spades was accustomed to having grain, and in the mornings he would come down to the ranch and whistle. Ellen had vowed she would never feed the horse and bade Antonio do it. But one morning Antonio was absent. She fed Spades herself. When she laid a hand on him and when he rubbed his nose against her shoulder she was not quite so sure she hated him. "Why should I?" she queried. "A horse cain't help it if he belongs to—to—" Ellen was not sure of anything except that more and more it grew good to be alone.

A whole day in the lonely forest passed swiftly, yet it left a feeling of long time. She lived by her thoughts. Always the morning was bright, sunny, sweet and fragrant and colorful, and her mood was pensive, wistful, dreamy. And always, just as surely as the hours passed, thought intruded upon her happiness, and thought brought memory, and memory brought shame, and shame brought fight. Sunset after sunset she had dragged herself back to the ranch, sullen and sick and beaten. Yet she never ceased to struggle.

The July storms came, and the forest floor that had been so sear and brown and dry and dusty changed as if by magic. The green grass shot up, the flowers bloomed, and along the canyon beds of lacy ferns swayed in the wind and bent their graceful tips over the amber-colored water. Ellen haunted these cool dells, these pine-shaded, mossy-rocked ravines where the brooks tinkled and the deer came down to drink. She wandered alone. But there grew to be company in the aspens and the music of the little waterfalls. If she could have lived in that solitude always, never returning to the ranch home that reminded her of her name, she could have forgotten and have been happy.

She loved the storms. It was a dry country and she had learned through years to welcome the creamy clouds that rolled from the southwest. They came sailing and clustering and darkening at last to form a great, purple, angry mass that appeared to lodge against the mountain rim and burst into dazzling streaks of lightning and gray palls of rain. Lightning seldom struck near the ranch, but up on the Rim there was never a storm that did not splinter and crash some of the noble pines. During the storm season sheep herders and woodsmen generally did not camp under the pines. Fear of lightning was inborn in the natives, but for Ellen the dazzling white streaks or the tremendous splitting, crackling shock, or the thunderous boom and rumble along the battlements of the Rim had no terrors. A storm eased her breast. Deep in her heart was a hidden gathering storm. And somehow, to be out when the elements were warring, when the earth trembled and the heavens seemed to burst asunder, afforded her strange relief.

The summer days became weeks, and farther and farther they carried Ellen on the wings of solitude and loneliness until she seemed to look back years at the self she had hated. And always, when the dark memory impinged upon peace, she fought and fought until she seemed to be fighting hatred itself. Scorn of scorn and hate of hate! Yet even her battles grew to be dreams. For when the inevitable retrospect brought back Jean Isbel and his love and her cowardly falsehood she would shudder a little and put an unconscious hand to her breast and utterly fail in her fight and drift off down to vague and wistful dreams. The clean and healing forest, with its whispering wind and imperious solitude, had come between Ellen and the meaning of the squalid sheep ranch, with its travesty of home, its tragic owner. And it was coming between her two selves, the one that she had been forced to be and the other that she did not know—the thinker, the dreamer, the romancer, the one who lived in fancy the life she loved.

The summer morning dawned that brought Ellen strange tidings. They must have been created in her sleep, and now were realized in the glorious burst of golden sun, in the sweep of creamy clouds across the blue, in the solemn music of the wind in the pines, in the wild screech of the blue jays and the noble bugle of a stag. These heralded the day as no ordinary day. Something was going to happen to her. She divined it. She felt it. And she trembled. Nothing beautiful, hopeful, wonderful could ever happen to Ellen Jorth. She had been born to disaster, to suffer, to be forgotten, and die alone. Yet all nature about her seemed a magnificent rebuke to her morbidness. The same spirit that came out there with the thick, amber light was in her. She lived, and something in her was stronger than mind.

Ellen went to the door of her cabin, where she flung out her arms, driven to embrace this nameless purport of the morning. And a well-known voice broke in upon her rapture.

"Wal, lass, I like to see you happy an' I hate myself fer comin'. Because I've been to Grass Valley fer two days an' I've got news."

Old John Sprague stood there, with a smile that did not hide a troubled look.

"Oh! Uncle John! You startled me," exclaimed Ellen, shocked back to reality. And slowly she added: "Grass Valley! News?"

She put out an appealing hand, which Sprague quickly took in his own, as if to reassure her.

"Yes, an' not bad so far as you Jorths are concerned," he replied. "The first Jorth-Isbel fight has come off.... Reckon you remember makin' me promise to tell you if I heerd anythin'. Wal, I didn't wait fer you to come up."

"So Ellen heard her voice calmly saying. What was this lying calm when there seemed to be a stone hammer at her heart? The first fight—not so bad for the Jorths! Then it had been bad for the Isbels. A sudden, cold stillness fell upon her senses.

"Let's sit down—outdoors," Sprague was saying. "Nice an' sunny this—mornin'. I declare—I'm out of breath. Not used to walkin'. An' besides, I left Grass Valley, in the night—an' I'm tired. But excoose me from hangin' round thet village last night! There was shore—"

"Who—who was killed?" interrupted Ellen, her voice breaking low and deep.

"Guy Isbel an' Bill Jacobs on the Isbel side, an' Daggs, Craig, an' Greaves on your father's side," stated Sprague, with something of awed haste.

"Ah!" breathed Ellen, and she relaxed to sink back against the cabin wall.

Sprague seated himself on the log beside her, turning to face her, and he seemed burdened with grave and important matters.

"I heerd a good many conflictin' stories," he said, earnestly. "The village folks is all skeered an' there's no believin' their gossip. But I got what happened straight from Jake Evarts. The fight come off day before yestiddy. Your father's gang rode down to Isbel's ranch. Daggs was seen to be wantin' some of the Isbel hosses, so Evarts says. An' Guy Isbel an' Jacobs ran out in the pasture. Daggs an' some others shot them down."

"Killed them—that way?" put in Ellen, sharply.

"So Evarts says. He was on the ridge an' swears he seen it all. They killed Guy an' Jacobs in cold blood. No chance fer their lives—not even to fight! ... Wall, hen they surrounded the Isbel cabin. The fight last all thet day an' all night an' the next day. Evarts says Guy an' Jacobs laid out thar all this time. An' a herd of hogs broke in the pasture an' was eatin' the dead bodies ..."

"My God!" burst out Ellen. "Uncle John, y'u shore cain't mean my father wouldn't stop fightin' long enough to drive the hogs off an' bury those daid men?"

"Evarts says they stopped fightin', all right, but it was to watch the hogs," declared Sprague. "An' then, what d' ye think? The wimminfolks come out—the red-headed one, Guy's wife, an' Jacobs's wife—they drove the hogs away an' buried their husbands right there in the pasture. Evarts says he seen the graves."

"It is the women who can teach these bloody Texans a lesson," declared Ellen, forcibly.

"Wal, Daggs was drunk, an' he got up from behind where the gang was hidin', an' dared the Isbels to come out. They shot him to pieces. An' thet night some one of the Isbels shot Craig, who was alone on guard.... An' last—this here's what I come to tell you—Jean Isbel slipped up in the dark on Greaves an' knifed him."

"Why did y'u want to tell me that particularly?" asked Ellen, slowly.

"Because I reckon the facts in the case are queer—an' because, Ellen, your name was mentioned," announced Sprague, positively.

"My name—mentioned?" echoed Ellen. Her horror and disgust gave way to a quickening process of thought, a mounting astonishment. "By whom?"

"Jean Isbel," replied Sprague, as if the name and the fact were momentous.

Ellen sat still as a stone, her hands between her knees. Slowly she felt the blood recede from her face, prickling her kin down below her neck. That name locked her thought.

"Ellen, it's a mighty queer story—too queer to be a lie," went on Sprague. "Now you listen! Evarts got this from Ted Meeker. An' Ted Meeker heerd it from Greaves, who didn't die till the next day after Jean Isbel knifed him. An' your dad shot Ted fer tellin' what he heerd.... No, Greaves wasn't killed outright. He was cut somethin' turrible—in two places. They wrapped him all up an' next day packed him in a wagon back to Grass Valley. Evarts says Ted Meeker was friendly with Greaves an' went to see him as he was layin' in his room next to the store. Wal, accordin' to Meeker's story, Greaves came to an' talked. He said he was sittin' there in the dark, shootin' occasionally at Isbel's cabin, when he heerd a rustle behind him in the grass. He knowed some one was crawlin' on him. But before he could get his gun around he was jumped by what he thought was a grizzly bear. But it was a man. He shut off Greaves's wind an' dragged him back in the ditch. An' he said: 'Greaves, it's the half-breed. An' he's goin' to cut you—FIRST FOR ELLEN JORTH! an' then for Gaston Isbel!' ... Greaves said Jean ripped him with a bowie knife.... An' thet was all Greaves remembered. He died soon after tellin' this story. He must hev fought awful hard. Thet second cut Isbel gave him went clear through him.... Some of the gang was thar when Greaves talked, an' naturally they wondered why Jean Isbel had said 'first for Ellen Jorth.' ... Somebody remembered thet Greaves had cast a slur on your good name, Ellen. An' then they had Jean Isbel's reason fer sayin' thet to Greaves. It caused a lot of talk. An' when Simm Bruce busted in some of the gang haw-hawed him an' said as how he'd get the third cut from Jean Isbel's bowie. Bruce was half drunk an' he began to cuss an' rave about Jean Isbel bein' in love with his girl.... As bad luck would have it, a couple of more fellars come in an' asked Meeker questions. He jest got to thet part, 'Greaves, it's the half-breed, an' he's goin' to cut you—FIRST FOR ELLEN JORTH,' when in walked your father! ... Then it all had to come out—what Jean Isbel had said an' done—an' why. How Greaves had backed Simm Bruce in slurrin' you!"

Sprague paused to look hard at Ellen.

"Oh! Then—what did dad do?" whispered Ellen.

"He said, 'By God! half-breed or not, there's one Isbel who's a man!' An' he killed Bruce on the spot an' gave Meeker a nasty wound. Somebody grabbed him before he could shoot Meeker again. They threw Meeker out an' he crawled to a neighbor's house, where he was when Evarts seen him."

Ellen felt Sprague's rough but kindly hand shaking her. "An' now what do you think of Jean Isbel?" he queried.

A great, unsurmountable wall seemed to obstruct Ellen's thought. It seemed gray in color. It moved toward her. It was inside her brain.

"I tell you, Ellen Jorth," declared the old man, "thet Jean Isbel loves you-loves you turribly—an' he believes you're good."

"Oh no—he doesn't!" faltered Ellen.

"Wal, he jest does."

"Oh, Uncle John, he cain't believe that!" she cried.

"Of course he can. He does. You are good—good as gold, Ellen, an' he knows it.... What a queer deal it all is! Poor devil! To love you thet turribly an' hev to fight your people! Ellen, your dad had it correct. Isbel or not, he's a man.... An' I say what a shame you two are divided by hate. Hate thet you hed nothin' to do with." Sprague patted her head and rose to go. "Mebbe thet fight will end the trouble. I reckon it will. Don't cross bridges till you come to them, Ellen.... I must hurry back now. I didn't take time to unpack my burros. Come up soon.... An', say, Ellen, don't think hard any more of thet Jean Isbel."

Sprague strode away, and Ellen neither heard nor saw him go. She sat perfectly motionless, yet had a strange sensation of being lifted by invisible and mighty power. It was like movement felt in a dream. She was being impelled upward when her body seemed immovable as stone.

When her blood beat down this deadlock of an her physical being and rushed on and on through her veins it gave her an irresistible impulse to fly, to sail through space, to ran and run and ran.

And on the moment the black horse, Spades, coming from the meadow, whinnied at sight of her. Ellen leaped up and ran swiftly, but her feet seemed to be stumbling. She hugged the horse and buried her hot face in his mane and clung to him. Then just as violently she rushed for her saddle and bridle and carried the heavy weight as easily as if it had been an empty sack. Throwing them upon him, she buckled and strapped with strong, eager hands. It never occurred to her that she was not dressed to ride. Up she flung herself. And the horse, sensing her spirit, plunged into strong, free gait down the canyon trail.

The ride, the action, the thrill, the sensations of violence were not all she needed. Solitude, the empty aisles of the forest, the far miles of lonely wilderness—were these the added all? Spades took a swinging, rhythmic lope up the winding trail. The wind fanned her hot face. The sting of whipping aspen branches was pleasant. A deep rumble of thunder shook the sultry air. Up beyond the green slope of the canyon massed the creamy clouds, shading darker and darker. Spades loped on the levels, leaped the washes, trotted over the rocky ground, and took to a walk up the long slope. Ellen dropped the reins over the pommel. Her hands could not stay set on anything. They pressed her breast and flew out to caress the white aspens and to tear at the maple leaves, and gather the lavender juniper berries, and came back again to her heart. Her heart that was going to burst or break! As it had swelled, so now it labored. It could not keep pace with her needs. All that was physical, all that was living in her had to be unleashed.

Spades gained the level forest. How the great, brown-green pines seemed to bend their lofty branches over her, protectively, understandingly. Patches of azure-blue sky flashed between the trees. The great white clouds sailed along with her, and shafts of golden sunlight, flecked with gleams of falling pine needles, shone down through the canopy overhead. Away in front of her, up the slow heave of forest land, boomed the heavy thunderbolts along the battlements of the Rim.

Was she riding to escape from herself? For no gait suited her until Spades was running hard and fast through the glades. Then the pressure of dry wind, the thick odor of pine, the flashes of brown and green and gold and blue, the soft, rhythmic thuds of hoofs, the feel of the powerful horse under her, the whip of spruce branches on her muscles contracting and expanding in hard action—all these sensations seemed to quell for the time the mounting cataclysm in her heart.

The oak swales, the maple thickets, the aspen groves, the pine-shaded aisles, and the miles of silver spruce all sped by her, as if she had ridden the wind; and through the forest ahead shone the vast open of the Basin, gloomed by purple and silver cloud, shadowed by gray storm, and in the west brightened by golden sky.

Straight to the Rim she had ridden, and to the point where she had watched Jean Isbel that unforgetable day. She rode to the promontory behind the pine thicket and beheld a scene which stayed her restless hands upon her heaving breast.

The world of sky and cloud and earthly abyss seemed one of storm-sundered grandeur. The air was sultry and still, and smelled of the peculiar burnt-wood odor caused by lightning striking trees. A few heavy drops of rain were pattering down from the thin, gray edge of clouds overhead. To the east hung the storm—a black cloud lodged against the Rim, from which long, misty veils of rain streamed down into the gulf. The roar of rain sounded like the steady roar of the rapids of a river. Then a blue-white, piercingly bright, ragged streak of lightning shot down out of the black cloud. It struck with a splitting report that shocked the very wall of rock under Ellen. Then the heavens seemed to burst open with thundering crash and close with mighty thundering boom. Long roar and longer rumble rolled away to the eastward. The rain poured down in roaring cataracts.

The south held a panorama of purple-shrouded range and canyon, canyon and range, on across the rolling leagues to the dim, lofty peaks, all canopied over with angry, dusky, low-drifting clouds, horizon-wide, smoky, and sulphurous. And as Ellen watched, hands pressed to her breast, feeling incalculable relief in sight of this tempest and gulf that resembled her soul, the sun burst out from behind the long bank of purple cloud in the west and flooded the world there with golden lightning.

"It is for me!" cried Ellen. "My mind—my heart—my very soul.... Oh, I know! I know now! ... I love him—love him—love him!"

She cried it out to the elements. "Oh, I love Jean Isbel—an' my heart will burst or break!"

The might of her passion was like the blaze of the sun. Before it all else retreated, diminished. The suddenness of the truth dimmed her sight. But she saw clearly enough to crawl into the pine thicket, through the clutching, dry twigs, over the mats of fragrant needles to the covert where she had once spied upon Jean Isbel. And here she lay face down for a while, hands clutching the needles, breast pressed hard upon the ground, stricken and spent. But vitality was exceeding strong in her. It passed, that weakness of realization, and she awakened to the consciousness of love.

But in the beginning it was not consciousness of the man. It was new, sensorial life, elemental, primitive, a liberation of a million inherited instincts, quivering and physical, over which Ellen had no more control than she had over the glory of the sun. If she thought at all it was of her need to be hidden, like an animal, low down near the earth, covered by green thicket, lost in the wildness of nature. She went to nature, unconsciously seeking a mother. And love was a birth from the depths of her, like a rushing spring of pure water, long underground, and at last propelled to the surface by a convulsion.

Ellen gradually lost her tense rigidity and relaxed. Her body softened. She rolled over until her face caught the lacy, golden shadows cast by sun and bough. Scattered drops of rain pattered around her. The air was hot, and its odor was that of dry pine and spruce fragrance penetrated by brimstone from the lightning. The nest where she lay was warm and sweet. No eye save that of nature saw her in her abandonment. An ineffable and exquisite smile wreathed her lips, dreamy, sad, sensuous, the supremity of unconscious happiness. Over her dark and eloquent eyes, as Ellen gazed upward, spread a luminous film, a veil. She was looking intensely, yet she did not see. The wilderness enveloped her with its secretive, elemental sheaths of rock, of tree, of cloud, of sunlight. Through her thrilling skin poured the multiple and nameless sensations of the living organism stirred to supreme sensitiveness. She could not lie still, but all her movements were gentle, involuntary. The slow reaching out of her hand, to grasp at nothing visible, was similar to the lazy stretching of her limbs, to the heave of her breast, to the ripple of muscle.

Ellen knew not what she felt. To live that sublime hour was beyond thought. Such happiness was like the first dawn of the world to the sight of man. It had to do with bygone ages. Her heart, her blood, her flesh, her very bones were filled with instincts and emotions common to the race before intellect developed, when the savage lived only with his sensorial perceptions. Of all happiness, joy, bliss, rapture to which man was heir, that of intense and exquisite preoccupation of the senses, unhindered and unburdened by thought, was the greatest. Ellen felt that which life meant with its inscrutable design. Love was only the realization of her mission on the earth.

The dark storm cloud with its white, ragged ropes of lightning and down-streaming gray veils of rain, the purple gulf rolling like a colored sea to the dim mountains, the glorious golden light of the sun—these had enchanted her eyes with her beauty of the universe. They had burst the windows of her blindness. When she crawled into the green-brown covert it was to escape too great perception. She needed to be encompassed by close, tangible things. And there her body paid the tribute to the realization of life. Shock, convulsion, pain, relaxation, and then unutterable and insupportable sensing of her environment and the heart! In one way she was a wild animal alone in the woods, forced into the mating that meant reproduction of its kind. In another she was an infinitely higher being shot through and through with the most resistless and mysterious transport that life could give to flesh.

And when that spell slackened its hold there wedged into her mind a consciousness of the man she loved—Jean Isbel. Then emotion and thought strove for mastery over her. It was not herself or love that she loved, but a living man. Suddenly he existed so clearly for her that she could see him, hear him, almost feel him. Her whole soul, her very life cried out to him for protection, for salvation, for love, for fulfillment. No denial, no doubt marred the white blaze of her realization. From the instant that she had looked up into Jean Isbel's dark face she had loved him. Only she had not known. She bowed now, and bent, and humbly quivered under the mastery of something beyond her ken. Thought clung to the beginnings of her romance—to the three times she had seen him. Every look, every word, every act of his returned to her now in the light of the truth. Love at first sight! He had sworn it, bitterly, eloquently, scornful of her doubts. And now a blind, sweet, shuddering ecstasy swayed her. How weak and frail seemed her body— too small, too slight for this monstrous and terrible engine of fire and lightning and fury and glory—her heart! It must burst or break. Relentlessly memory pursued Ellen, and her thoughts whirled and emotion conquered her. At last she quivered up to her knees as if lashed to action. It seemed that first kiss of Isbel's, cool and gentle and timid, was on her lips. And her eyes closed and hot tears welled from under her lids. Her groping hands found only the dead twigs and the pine boughs of the trees. Had she reached out to clasp him? Then hard and violent on her mouth and cheek and neck burned those other kisses of Isbel's, and with the flashing, stinging memory came the truth that now she would have bartered her soul for them. Utterly she surrendered to the resistlessness of this love. Her loss of mother and friends, her wandering from one wild place to another, her lonely life among bold and rough men, had developed her for violent love. It overthrew all pride, it engendered humility, it killed hate. Ellen wiped the tears from her eyes, and as she knelt there she swept to her breast a fragrant spreading bough of pine needles. "I'll go to him," she whispered. "I'll tell him of—of my—my love. I'll tell him to take me away—away to the end of the world—away from heah—before it's too late!"

It was a solemn, beautiful moment. But the last spoken words lingered hauntingly. "Too late?" she whispered.

And suddenly it seemed that death itself shuddered in her soul. Too late! It was too late. She had killed his love. That Jorth blood in her—that poisonous hate—had chosen the only way to strike this noble Isbel to the heart. Basely, with an abandonment of womanhood, she had mockingly perjured her soul with a vile lie. She writhed, she shook under the whip of this inconceivable fact. Lost! Lost! She wailed her misery. She might as well be what she had made Jean Isbel think she was. If she had been shamed before, she was now abased, degraded, lost in her own sight. And if she would have given her soul for his kisses, she now would have killed herself to earn back his respect. Jean Isbel had given her at sight the deference that she had unconsciously craved, and the love that would have been her salvation. What a horrible mistake she had made of her life! Not her mother's blood, but her father's—the Jorth blood—had been her ruin.

Again Ellen fell upon the soft pine-needle mat, face down, and she groveled and burrowed there, in an agony that could not bear the sense of light. All she had suffered was as nothing to this. To have awakened to a splendid and uplifting love for a man whom she had imagined she hated, who had fought for her name and had killed in revenge for the dishonor she had avowed— to have lost his love and what was infinitely more precious to her now in her ignominy—his faith in her purity—this broke her heart.

CHAPTER XI

When Ellen, utterly spent in body and mind, reached home that day a melancholy, sultry twilight was falling. Fitful flares of sheet lightning swept across the dark horizon to the east. The cabins were deserted. Antonio and the Mexican woman were gone. The circumstances made Ellen wonder, but she was too tired and too sunken in spirit to think long about it or to care. She fed and watered her horse and left him in the corral. Then, supperless and without removing her clothes, she threw herself upon the bed, and at once sank into heavy slumber.

Sometime during the night she awoke. Coyotes were yelping, and from that sound she concluded it was near dawn. Her body ached; her mind seemed dull. Drowsily she was sinking into slumber again when she heard the rapid clip-clop of trotting horses. Startled, she raised her head to listen. The men were coming back. Relief and dread seemed to clear her stupor.

The trotting horses stopped across the lane from her cabin, evidently at the corral where she had left Spades. She heard him whistle.

From the sound of hoofs she judged the number of horses to be six or eight. Low voices of men mingled with thuds and cracking of straps and flopping of saddles on the ground. After that the heavy tread of boots sounded on the porch of the cabin opposite. A door creaked on its hinges. Next a slow footstep, accompanied by clinking of spurs, approached Ellen's door, and a heavy hand banged upon it. She knew this person could not be her father.

"Hullo, Ellen!"

She recognized the voice as belonging to Colter. Somehow its tone, or something about it, sent a little shiver clown her spine. It acted like a revivifying current. Ellen lost her dragging lethargy.

"Hey, Ellen, are y'u there?" added Colter, louder voice.

"Yes. Of course I'm heah," she replied. "What do y'u want?"

"Wal—I'm shore glad y'u're home," he replied. "Antonio's gone with his squaw. An' I was some worried aboot y'u."

"Who's with y'u, Colter?" queried Ellen, sitting up.

"Rock Wells an' Springer. Tad Jorth was with us, but we had to leave him over heah in a cabin."

"What's the matter with him?"

"Wal, he's hurt tolerable bad," was the slow reply.

Ellen heard Colter's spurs jangle, as if he had uneasily shifted his feet.

"Where's dad an' Uncle Jackson?" asked Ellen.

A silence pregnant enough to augment Ellen's dread finally broke to Colter's voice, somehow different. "Shore they're back on the trail. An' we're to meet them where we left Tad."

"Are yu goin' away again?"

"I reckon.... An', Ellen, y'u're goin' with us."

"I am not," she retorted.

"Wal, y'u are, if I have to pack y'u," he replied, forcibly. "It's not safe heah any more. That damned half-breed Isbel with his gang are on our trail."

That name seemed like a red-hot blade at Ellen's leaden heart. She wanted to fling a hundred queries on Colter, but she could not utter one.

"Ellen, we've got to hit the trail an' hide," continued Colter, anxiously. "Y'u mustn't stay heah alone. Suppose them Isbels would trap y'u! ... They'd tear your clothes off an' rope y'u to a tree. Ellen, shore y'u're goin'.... Y'u heah me!"

"Yes—I'll go," she replied, as if forced.

"Wal—that's good," he said, quickly. "An' rustle tolerable lively. We've got to pack."

The slow jangle of Colter's spurs and his slow steps moved away out of Ellen's hearing. Throwing off the blankets, she put her feet to the floor and sat there a moment staring at the blank nothingness of the cabin interior in the obscure gray of dawn. Cold, gray, dreary, obscure—like her life, her future! And she was compelled to do what was hateful to her. As a Jorth she must take to the unfrequented trails and hide like a rabbit in the thickets. But the interest of the moment, a premonition of events to be, quickened her into action.

Ellen unbarred the door to let in the light. Day was breaking with an intense, clear, steely light in the east through which the morning star still shone white. A ruddy flare betokened the advent of the sun. Ellen unbraided her tangled hair and brushed and combed it. A queer, still pang came to her at sight of pine needles tangled in her brown locks. Then she washed her hands and face. Breakfast was a matter of considerable work and she was hungry.

The sun rose and changed the gray world of forest. For the first time in her life Ellen hated the golden brightness, the wonderful blue of sky, the scream of the eagle and the screech of the jay; and the squirrels she had always loved to feed were neglected that morning.

Colter came in. Either Ellen had never before looked attentively at him or else he had changed. Her scrutiny of his lean, hard features accorded him more Texan attributes than formerly. His gray eyes were as light, as clear, as fierce as those of an eagle. And the sand gray of his face, the long, drooping, fair mustache hid the secrets of his mind, but not its strength. The instant Ellen met his gaze she sensed a power in him that she instinctively opposed. Colter had not been so bold nor so rude as Daggs, but he was the same kind of man, perhaps the more dangerous for his secretiveness, his cool, waiting inscrutableness.

"'Mawnin', Ellen!" he drawled. "Y'u shore look good for sore eyes."

"Don't pay me compliments, Colter," replied Ellen. "An' your eyes are not sore."

"Wal, I'm shore sore from fightin' an' ridin' an' layin' out," he said, bluntly.

"Tell me—what's happened," returned Ellen.

"Girl, it's a tolerable long story," replied Colter. "An' we've no time now. Wait till we get to camp."

"Am I to pack my belongin's or leave them heah?" asked Ellen.

"Reckon y'u'd better leave—them heah."

"But if we did not come back—"

"Wal, I reckon it's not likely we'll come—soon," he said, rather evasively.

"Colter, I'll not go off into the woods with just the clothes I have on my back."

"Ellen, we shore got to pack all the grab we can. This shore ain't goin' to be a visit to neighbors. We're shy pack hosses. But y'u make up a bundle of belongin's y'u care for, an' the things y'u'll need bad. We'll throw it on somewhere."

Colter stalked away across the lane, and Ellen found herself dubiously staring at his tall figure. Was it the situation that struck her with a foreboding perplexity or was her intuition steeling her against this man? Ellen could not decide. But she had to go with him. Her prejudice was unreasonable at this portentous moment. And she could not yet feel that she was solely responsible to herself.

When it came to making a small bundle of her belongings she was in a quandary. She discarded this and put in that, and then reversed the order. Next in preciousness to her mother's things were the long-hidden gifts of Jean Isbel. She could part with neither.

While she was selecting and packing this bundle Colter again entered and, without speaking, began to rummage in the corner where her father kept his possessions. This irritated Ellen.

"What do y'u want there?" she demanded.

"Wal, I reckon your dad wants his papers—an' the gold he left heah—an' a change of clothes. Now doesn't he?" returned Colter, coolly.

"Of course. But I supposed y'u would have me pack them."

Colter vouchsafed no reply to this, but deliberately went on rummaging, with little regard for how he scattered things. Ellen turned her back on him. At length, when he left, she went to her father's corner and found that, as far as she was able to see, Colter had taken neither papers nor clothes, but only the gold. Perhaps, however, she had been mistaken, for she had not observed Colter's departure closely enough to know whether or not he carried a package. She missed only the gold. Her father's papers, old and musty, were scattered about, and these she gathered up to slip in her own bundle.

Colter, or one of the men, had saddled Spades, and he was now tied to the corral fence, champing his bit and pounding the sand. Ellen wrapped bread and meat inside her coat, and after tying this behind her saddle she was ready to go. But evidently she would have to wait, and, preferring to remain outdoors, she stayed by her horse. Presently, while watching the men pack, she noticed that Springer wore a bandage round his head under the brim of his sombrero. His motions were slow and lacked energy. Shuddering at the sight, Ellen refused to conjecture. All too soon she would learn what had happened, and all too soon, perhaps, she herself would be in the midst of another fight. She watched the men. They were making a hurried slipshod job of packing food supplies from both cabins. More than once she caught Colter's gray gleam of gaze on her, and she did not like it.

"I'll ride up an' say good-by to Sprague," she called to Colter.

"Shore y'u won't do nothin' of the kind," he called back.

There was authority in his tone that angered Ellen, and something else which inhibited her anger. What was there about Colter with which she must reckon? The other two Texans laughed aloud, to be suddenly silenced by Colter's harsh and lowered curses. Ellen walked out of hearing and sat upon a log, where she remained until Colter hailed her.

"Get up an' ride," he called.

Ellen complied with this order and, riding up behind the three mounted men, she soon found herself leaving what for years had been her home. Not once did she look back. She hoped she would never see the squalid, bare pretension of a ranch again.

Colter and the other riders drove the pack horses across the meadow, off of the trails, and up the slope into the forest. Not very long did it take Ellen to see that Colter's object was to hide their tracks. He zigzagged through the forest, avoiding the bare spots of dust, the dry, sun-baked flats of clay where water lay in spring, and he chose the grassy, open glades, the long, pine-needle matted aisles. Ellen rode at their heels and it pleased her to watch for their tracks. Colter manifestly had been long practiced in this game of hiding his trail, and he showed the skill of a rustler. But Ellen was not convinced that he could ever elude a real woodsman. Not improbably, however, Colter was only aiming to leave a trail difficult to follow and which would allow him and his confederates ample time to forge ahead of pursuers. Ellen could not accept a certainty of pursuit. Yet Colter must have expected it, and Springer and Wells also, for they had a dark, sinister, furtive demeanor that strangely contrasted with the cool, easy manner habitual to them.

They were not seeking the level routes of the forest land, that was sure. They rode straight across the thick-timbered ridge down into another canyon, up out of that, and across rough, rocky bluffs, and down again. These riders headed a little to the northwest and every mile brought them into wilder, more rugged country, until Ellen, losing count of canyons and ridges, had no idea where she was. No stop was made at noon to rest the laboring, sweating pack animals.

Under circumstances where pleasure might have been possible Ellen would have reveled in this hard ride into a wonderful forest ever thickening and darkening. But the wild beauty of glade and the spruce slopes and the deep, bronze-walled canyons left her cold. She saw and felt, but had no thrill, except now and then a thrill of alarm when Spades slid to his haunches down some steep, damp, piny declivity.

All the woodland, up and down, appeared to be richer greener as they traveled farther west. Grass grew thick and heavy. Water ran in all ravines. The rocks were bronze and copper and russet, and some had green patches of lichen.

Ellen felt the sun now on her left cheek and knew that the day was waning and that Colter was swinging farther to the northwest. She had never before ridden through such heavy forest and down and up such wild canyons. Toward sunset the deepest and ruggedest canyon halted their advance. Colter rode to the right, searching for a place to get down through a spruce thicket that stood on end. Presently he dismounted and the others followed suit. Ellen found she could not lead Spades because he slid down upon her heels, so she looped the end of her reins over the pommel and left him free. She herself managed to descend by holding to branches and sliding all the way down that slope. She heard the horses cracking the brush, snorting and heaving. One pack slipped and had to be removed from the horse, and rolled down. At the bottom of this deep, green-walled notch roared a stream of water. Shadowed, cool, mossy, damp, this narrow gulch seemed the wildest place Ellen had ever seen. She could just see the sunset-flushed, gold-tipped spruces far above her. The men repacked the horse that had slipped his burden, and once more resumed their progress ahead, now turning up this canyon. There was no horse trail, but deer and bear trails were numerous. The sun sank and the sky darkened, but still the men rode on; and the farther they traveled the wilder grew the aspect of the canyon.

At length Colter broke a way through a heavy thicket of willows and entered a side canyon, the mouth of which Ellen had not even descried. It turned and widened, and at length opened out into a round pocket, apparently inclosed, and as lonely and isolated a place as even pursued rustlers could desire. Hidden by jutting wall and thicket of spruce were two old log cabins joined together by roof and attic floor, the same as the double cabin at the Jorth ranch.

Ellen smelled wood smoke, and presently, on going round the cabins, saw a bright fire. One man stood beside it gazing at Colter's party, which evidently he had heard approaching.

"Hullo, Queen!" said Colter. "How's Tad?"

"He's holdin' on fine," replied Queen, bending over the fire, where he turned pieces of meat.

"Where's father?" suddenly asked Ellen, addressing Colter.

As if he had not heard her, he went on wearily loosening a pack.

Queen looked at her. The light of the fire only partially shone on his face. Ellen could not see its expression. But from the fact that Queen did not answer her question she got further intimation of an impending catastrophe. The long, wild ride had helped prepare her for the secrecy and taciturnity of men who had resorted to flight. Perhaps her father had been delayed or was still off on the deadly mission that had obsessed him; or there might, and probably was, darker reason for his absence. Ellen shut her teeth and turned to the needs of her horse. And presently, returning to the fire, she thought of her uncle.

"Queen, is my uncle Tad heah?" she asked.

"Shore. He's in there," replied Queen, pointing at the nearer cabin.

Ellen hurried toward the dark doorway. She could see how the logs of the cabin had moved awry and what a big, dilapidated hovel it was. As she looked in, Colter loomed over her—placed a familiar and somehow masterful hand upon her. Ellen let it rest on her shoulder a moment. Must she forever be repulsing these rude men among whom her lot was cast? Did Colter mean what Daggs had always meant? Ellen felt herself weary, weak in body, and her spent spirit had not rallied. Yet, whatever Colter meant by his familiarity, she could not bear it. So she slipped out from under his hand.

"Uncle Tad, are y'u heah?" she called into the blackness. She heard the mice scamper and rustle and she smelled the musty, old, woody odor of a long-unused cabin.

"Hello, Ellen!" came a voice she recognized as her uncle's, yet it was strange. "Yes. I'm heah—bad luck to me! ... How 're y'u buckin' up, girl?"

"I'm all right, Uncle Tad—only tired an' worried. I—"

"Tad, how's your hurt?" interrupted Colter.

"Reckon I'm easier," replied Jorth, wearily, "but shore I'm in bad shape. I'm still spittin' blood. I keep tellin' Queen that bullet lodged in my lungs-but he says it went through."

"Wal, hang on, Tad!" replied Colter, with a cheerfulness Ellen sensed was really indifferent.

"Oh, what the hell's the use!" exclaimed Jorth. "It's all—up with us—Colter!"

"Wal, shut up, then," tersely returned Colter. "It ain't doin' y'u or us any good to holler."

Tad Jorth did not reply to this. Ellen heard his breathing and it did not seem natural. It rasped a little—came hurriedly—then caught in his throat. Then he spat. Ellen shrunk back against the door. He was breathing through blood.

"Uncle, are y'u in pain?" she asked.

"Yes, Ellen—it burns like hell," he said.

"Oh! I'm sorry.... Isn't there something I can do?"

"I reckon not. Queen did all anybody could do for me—now—unless it's pray."

Colter laughed at this—the slow, easy, drawling laugh of a Texan. But Ellen felt pity for this wounded uncle. She had always hated him. He had been a drunkard, a gambler, a waster of her father's property; and now he was a rustler and a fugitive, lying in pain, perhaps mortally hurt.

"Yes, uncle—I will pray for y'u," she said, softly.

The change in his voice held a note of sadness that she had been quick to catch.

"Ellen, y'u're the only good Jorth—in the whole damned lot," he said. "God! I see it all now.... We've dragged y'u to hell!"

"Yes, Uncle Tad, I've shore been dragged some—but not yet—to hell," she responded, with a break in her voice.

"Y'u will be—Ellen—unless—"

"Aw, shut up that kind of gab, will y'u?" broke in Colter, harshly.

It amazed Ellen that Colter should dominate her uncle, even though he was wounded. Tad Jorth had been the last man to take orders from anyone, much less a rustler of the Hash Knife Gang. This Colter began to loom up in Ellen's estimate as he loomed physically over her, a lofty figure, dark motionless, somehow menacing.

"Ellen, has Colter told y'u yet—aboot—aboot Lee an' Jackson?" inquired the wounded man.

The pitch-black darkness of the cabin seemed to help fortify Ellen to bear further trouble.

"Colter told me dad an' Uncle Jackson would meet us heah," she rejoined, hurriedly.

Jorth could be heard breathing in difficulty, and he coughed and spat again, and seemed to hiss.

"Ellen, he lied to y'u. They'll never meet us—heah!"

"Why not?" whispered Ellen.

"Because—Ellen—" he replied, in husky pants, "your dad an'—uncle Jackson—are daid—an' buried!"

If Ellen suffered a terrible shock it was a blankness, a deadness, and a slow, creeping failure of sense in her knees. They gave way under her and she sank on the grass against the cabin wall. She did not faint nor grow dizzy nor lose her sight, but for a while there was no process of thought in her mind. Suddenly then it was there—the quick, spiritual rending of her heart—followed by a profound emotion of intimate and irretrievable loss—and after that grief and bitter realization.

An hour later Ellen found strength to go to the fire and partake of the food and drink her body sorely needed.

Colter and the men waited on her solicitously, and in silence, now and then stealing furtive glances at her from under the shadow of their black sombreros. The dark night settled down like a blanket. There were no stars. The wind moaned fitfully among the pines, and all about that lonely, hidden recess was in harmony with Ellen's thoughts.

"Girl, y'u're shore game," said Colter, admiringly. "An' I reckon y'u never got it from the Jorths."

"Tad in there—he's game," said Queen, in mild protest.

"Not to my notion," replied Colter. "Any man can be game when he's croakin', with somebody around.... But Lee Jorth an' Jackson—they always was yellow clear to their gizzards. They was born in Louisiana—not Texas.... Shore they're no more Texans than I am. Ellen heah, she must have got another strain in her blood."

To Ellen their words had no meaning. She rose and asked, "Where can I sleep?"

"I'll fetch a light presently an' y'u can make your bed in there by Tad," replied Colter.

"Yes, I'd like that."

"Wal, if y'u reckon y'u can coax him to talk you're shore wrong," declared Colter, with that cold timbre of voice that struck like steel on Ellen's nerves. "I cussed him good an' told him he'd keep his mouth shut. Talkin' makes him cough an' that fetches up the blood.... Besides, I reckon I'm the one to tell y'u how your dad an' uncle got killed. Tad didn't see it done, an' he was bad hurt when it happened. Shore all the fellars left have their idee aboot it. But I've got it straight."

"Colter—tell me now," cried Ellen.

"Wal, all right. Come over heah," he replied, and drew her away from the camp fire, out in the shadow of gloom. "Poor kid! I shore feel bad aboot it." He put a long arm around her waist and drew her against him. Ellen felt it, yet did not offer any resistance. All her faculties seemed absorbed in a morbid and sad anticipation.

"Ellen, y'u shore know I always loved y'u—now don't y 'u?" he asked, with suppressed breath.

"No, Colter. It's news to me—an' not what I want to heah."

"Wal, y'u may as well heah it right now," he said. "It's true. An' what's more—your dad gave y'u to me before he died."

"What! Colter, y'u must be a liar."

"Ellen, I swear I'm not lyin'," he returned, in eager passion. "I was with your dad last an' heard him last. He shore knew I'd loved y'u for years. An' he said he'd rather y'u be left in my care than anybody's."

"My father gave me to y'u in marriage!" ejaculated Ellen, in bewilderment.

Colter's ready assurance did not carry him over this point. It was evident that her words somewhat surprised and disconcerted him for the moment.

"To let me marry a rustler—one of the Hash Knife Gang!" exclaimed Ellen, with weary incredulity.

"Wal, your dad belonged to Daggs's gang, same as I do," replied Colter, recovering his cool ardor.

"No!" cried Ellen.

"Yes, he shore did, for years," declared Colter, positively. "Back in Texas. An' it was your dad that got Daggs to come to Arizona."

Ellen tried to fling herself away. But her strength and her spirit were ebbing, and Colter increased the pressure of his arm. All at once she sank limp. Could she escape her fate? Nothing seemed left to fight with or for.

"All right—don't hold me—so tight," she panted. "Now tell me how dad was killed ... an' who—who—"

Colter bent over so he could peer into her face. In the darkness Ellen just caught the gleam of his eyes. She felt the virile force of the man in the strain of his body as he pressed her close. It all seemed unreal—a hideous dream—the gloom, the moan of the wind, the weird solitude, and this rustler with hand and will like cold steel.

"We'd come back to Greaves's store," Colter began. "An' as Greaves was daid we all got free with his liquor. Shore some of us got drunk. Bruce was drunk, an' Tad in there—he was drunk. Your dad put away more 'n I ever seen him. But shore he wasn't exactly drunk. He got one of them weak an' shaky spells. He cried an' he wanted some of us to get the Isbels to call off the fightin'.... He shore was ready to call it quits. I reckon the killin' of Daggs—an' then the awful way Greaves was cut up by Jean Isbel—took all the fight out of your dad. He said to me, 'Colter, we'll take Ellen an' leave this heah country—an' begin life all over again—where no one knows us.'"

"Oh, did he really say that? ... Did he—really mean it?" murmured Ellen, with a sob.

"I'll swear it by the memory of my daid mother," protested Colter. "Wal, when night come the Isbels rode down on us in the dark an' began to shoot. They smashed in the door—tried to burn us out—an' hollered around for a while. Then they left an' we reckoned there'd be no more trouble that night. All the same we kept watch. I was the soberest one an' I bossed the gang. We had some quarrels aboot the drinkin'. Your dad said if we kept it up it 'd be the end of the Jorths. An' he planned to send word to the Isbels next mawnin' that he was ready for a truce. An' I was to go fix it up with Gaston Isbel. Wal, your dad went to bed in Greaves's room, an' a little while later your uncle Jackson went in there, too. Some of the men laid down in the store an' went to sleep. I kept guard till aboot three in the mawnin'. An' I got so sleepy I couldn't hold my eyes open. So I waked up Wells an' Slater an' set them on guard, one at each end of the store. Then I laid down on the counter to take a nap."

Colter's low voice, the strain and breathlessness of him, the agitation with which he appeared to be laboring, and especially the simple, matter-of-fact detail of his story, carried absolute conviction to Ellen Jorth. Her vague doubt of him had been created by his attitude toward her. Emotion dominated her intelligence. The images, the scenes called up by Colter's words, were as true as the gloom of the wild gulch and the loneliness of the night solitude—as true as the strange fact that she lay passive in the arm of a rustler.

"Wall, after a while I woke up," went on Colter, clearing his throat. "It was gray dawn. All was as still as death.... An' somethin' shore was wrong. Wells an' Slater had got to drinkin' again an' now laid daid drunk or asleep. Anyways, when I kicked them they never moved. Then I heard a moan. It came from the room where your dad an' uncle was. I went in. It was just light enough to see. Your uncle Jackson was layin' on the floor—cut half in two—daid as a door nail.... Your dad lay on the bed. He was alive, breathin' his last.... He says, 'That half-breed Isbel—knifed us—while we slept!' ... The winder shutter was open. I seen where Jean Isbel had come in an' gone out. I seen his moccasin tracks in the dirt outside an' I seen where he'd stepped in Jackson's blood an' tracked it to the winder. Y'u shore can see them bloody tracks yourself, if y'u go back to Greaves's store.... Your dad was goin' fast.... He said, 'Colter—take care of Ellen,' an' I reckon he meant a lot by that. He kept sayin', 'My God! if I'd only seen Gaston Isbel before it was too late!' an' then he raved a little, whisperin' out of his haid.... An' after that he died.... I woke up the men, an' aboot sunup we carried your dad an' uncle out of town an' buried them.... An' them Isbels shot at us while we were buryin' our daid! That's where Tad got his hurt.... Then we hit the trail for Jorth's ranch.... An now, Ellen, that's all my story. Your dad was ready to bury the hatchet with his old enemy. An' that Nez Perce Jean Isbel, like the sneakin' savage he is, murdered your uncle an' your dad.... Cut him horrible—made him suffer tortures of hell—all for Isbel revenge!"

When Colter's husky voice ceased Ellen whispered through lips as cold and still as ice, "Let me go ... leave me—heah—alone!"

"Why, shore! I reckon I understand," replied Colter. "I hated to tell y'u. But y'u had to heah the truth aboot that half-breed.... I'll carry your pack in the cabin an' unroll your blankets."

Releasing her, Colter strode off in the gloom. Like a dead weight, Ellen began to slide until she slipped down full length beside the log. And then she lay in the cool, damp shadow, inert and lifeless so far as outward physical movement was concerned. She saw nothing and felt nothing of the night, the wind, the cold, the falling dew. For the moment or hour she was crushed by despair, and seemed to see herself sinking down and down into a black, bottomless pit, into an abyss where murky tides of blood and furious gusts of passion contended between her body and her soul. Into the stormy blast of hell! In her despair she longed, she ached for death. Born of infidelity, cursed by a taint of evil blood, further cursed by higher instinct for good and happy life, dragged from one lonely and wild and sordid spot to another, never knowing love or peace or joy or home, left to the companionship of violent and vile men, driven by a strange fate to love with unquenchable and insupportable love a' half-breed, a savage, an Isbel, the hereditary enemy of her people, and at last the ruthless murderer of her father—what in the name of God had she left to live for? Revenge! An eye for an eye! A life for a life! But she could not kill Jean Isbel. Woman's love could turn to hate, but not the love of Ellen Jorth. He could drag her by the hair in the dust, beat her, and make her a thing to loathe, and cut her mortally in his savage and implacable thirst for revenge—but with her last gasp she would whisper she loved him and that she had lied to him to kill his faith. It was that—his strange faith in her purity—which had won her love. Of all men, that he should be the one to recognize the truth of her, the womanhood yet unsullied—how strange, how terrible, how overpowering! False, indeed, was she to the Jorths! False as her mother had been to an Isbel! This agony and destruction of her soul was the bitter Dead Sea fruit—the sins of her parents visited upon her.

"I'll end it all," she whispered to the night shadows that hovered over her. No coward was she—no fear of pain or mangled flesh or death or the mysterious hereafter could ever stay her. It would be easy, it would be a last thrill, a transport of self-abasement and supreme self-proof of her love for Jean Isbel to kiss the Rim rock where his feet had trod and then fling herself down into the depths. She was the last Jorth. So the wronged Isbels would be avenged.

"But he would never know—never know—I lied to him!" she wailed to the night wind.

She was lost—lost on earth and to hope of heaven. She had right neither to live nor to die. She was nothing but a little weed along the trail of life, trampled upon, buried in the mud. She was nothing but a single rotten thread in a tangled web of love and hate and revenge. And she had broken.

Lower and lower she seemed to sink. Was there no end to this gulf of despair? If Colter had returned he would have found her a rag and a toy—a creature degraded, fit for his vile embrace. To be thrust deeper into the mire—to be punished fittingly for her betrayal of a man's noble love and her own womanhood—to be made an end of, body, mind, and soul.

But Colter did not return.

The wind mourned, the owls hooted, the leaves rustled, the insects whispered their melancholy night song, the camp-fire flickered and faded. Then the wild forestland seemed to close imponderably over Ellen. All that she wailed in her despair, all that she confessed in her abasement, was true, and hard as life could be—but she belonged to nature. If nature had not failed her, had God failed her? It was there—the lonely land of tree and fern and flower and brook, full of wild birds and beasts, where the mossy rocks could speak and the solitude had ears, where she had always felt herself unutterably a part of creation. Thus a wavering spark of hope quivered through the blackness of her soul and gathered light.

The gloom of the sky, the shifting clouds of dull shade, split asunder to show a glimpse of a radiant star, piercingly white, cold, pure, a steadfast eye of the universe, beyond all understanding and illimitable with its meaning of the past and the present and the future. Ellen watched it until the drifting clouds once more hid it from her strained sight.

What had that star to do with hell? She might be crushed and destroyed by life, but was there not something beyond? Just to be born, just to suffer, just to die—could that be all? Despair did not loose its hold on Ellen, the strife and pang of her breast did not subside. But with the long hours and the strange closing in of the forest around her and the fleeting glimpse of that wonderful star, with a subtle divination of the meaning of her beating heart and throbbing mind, and, lastly, with a voice thundering at her conscience that a man's faith in a woman must not be greater, nobler, than her faith in God and eternity—with these she checked the dark flight of her soul toward destruction.

CHAPTER XII

A chill, gray, somber dawn was breaking when Ellen dragged herself into the cabin and crept under her blankets, there to sleep the sleep of exhaustion.

When she awoke the hour appeared to be late afternoon. Sun and sky shone through the sunken and decayed roof of the old cabin. Her uncle, Tad Jorth, lay upon a blanket bed upheld by a crude couch of boughs. The light fell upon his face, pale, lined, cast in a still mold of suffering. He was not dead, for she heard his respiration.

The floor underneath Ellen's blankets was bare clay. She and Jorth were alone in this cabin. It contained nothing besides their beds and a rank growth of weeds along the decayed lower logs. Half of the cabin had a rude ceiling of rough-hewn boards which formed a kind of loft. This attic extended through to the adjoining cabin, forming the ceiling of the porch-like space between the two structures. There was no partition. A ladder of two aspen saplings, pegged to the logs, and with braces between for steps, led up to the attic.

Ellen smelled wood smoke and the odor of frying meat, and she heard the voices of men. She looked out to see that Slater and Somers had joined their party—an addition that might have strengthened it for defense, but did not lend her own situation anything favorable. Somers had always appeared the one best to avoid.

Colter espied her and called her to "Come an' feed your pale face." His comrades laughed, not loudly, but guardedly, as if noise was something to avoid. Nevertheless, they awoke Tad Jorth, who began to toss and moan on the bed.

Ellen hurried to his side and at once ascertained that he had a high fever and was in a critical condition. Every time he tossed he opened a wound in his right breast, rather high up. For all she could see, nothing had been done for him except the binding of a scarf round his neck and under his arm. This scant bandage had worked loose. Going to the door, she called out:

"Fetch me some water." When Colter brought it, Ellen was rummaging in her pack for some clothing or towel that she could use for bandages.

"Weren't any of y'u decent enough to look after my uncle?" she queried.

"Huh! Wal, what the hell!" rejoined Colter. "We shore did all we could. I reckon y'u think it wasn't a tough job to pack him up the Rim. He was done for then an' I said so."

"I'll do all I can for him," said Ellen.

"Shore. Go ahaid. When I get plugged or knifed by that half-breed I shore hope y'u'll be round to nurse me."

"Y'u seem to be pretty shore of your fate, Colter."

"Shore as hell!" he bit out, darkly. "Somers saw Isbel an' his gang trailin' us to the Jorth ranch."

"Are y'u goin' to stay heah—an' wait for them?"

"Shore I've been quarrelin' with the fellars out there over that very question. I'm for leavin' the country. But Queen, the damn gun fighter, is daid set to kill that cowman, Blue, who swore he was King Fisher, the old Texas outlaw. None but Queen are spoilin' for another fight. All the same they won't leave Tad Jorth heah alone."

Then Colter leaned in at the door and whispered: "Ellen, I cain't boss this outfit. So let's y'u an' me shake 'em. I've got your dad's gold. Let's ride off to-night an' shake this country."

Colter, muttering under his breath, left the door and returned to his comrades. Ellen had received her first intimation of his cowardice; and his mention of her father's gold started a train of thought that persisted in spite of her efforts to put all her mind to attending her uncle. He grew conscious enough to recognize her working over him, and thanked her with a look that touched Ellen deeply. It changed the direction of her mind. His suffering and imminent death, which she was able to alleviate and retard somewhat, worked upon her pity and compassion so that she forgot her own plight. Half the night she was tending him, cooling his fever, holding him quiet. Well she realized that but for her ministrations he would have died. At length he went to sleep.

And Ellen, sitting beside him in the lonely, silent darkness of that late hour, received again the intimation of nature, those vague and nameless stirrings of her innermost being, those whisperings out of the night and the forest and the sky. Something great would not let go of her soul. She pondered.

Attention to the wounded man occupied Ellen; and soon she redoubled her activities in this regard, finding in them something of protection against Colter.

He had waylaid her as she went to a spring for water, and with a lunge like that of a bear he had tried to embrace her. But Ellen had been too quick.

"Wal, are y'u goin' away with me?" he demanded.

"No. I'll stick by my uncle," she replied.

That motive of hers seemed to obstruct his will. Ellen was keen to see that Colter and his comrades were at a last stand and disintegrating under a severe strain. Nerve and courage of the open and the wild they possessed, but only in a limited degree. Colter seemed obsessed by his passion for her, and though Ellen in her stubborn pride did not yet fear him, she realized she ought to. After that incident she watched closely, never leaving her uncle's bedside except when Colter was absent. One or more of the men kept constant lookout somewhere down the canyon.

Day after day passed on the wings of suspense, of watching, of ministering to her uncle, of waiting for some hour that seemed fixed.

Colter was like a hound upon her trail. At every turn he was there to importune her to run off with him, to frighten her with the menace of the Isbels, to beg her to give herself to him. It came to pass that the only relief she had was when she ate with the men or barred the cabin door at night. Not much relief, however, was there in the shut and barred door. With one thrust of his powerful arm Colter could have caved it in. He knew this as well as Ellen. Still she did not have the fear she should have had. There was her rifle beside her, and though she did not allow her mind to run darkly on its possible use, still the fact of its being there at hand somehow strengthened her. Colter was a cat playing with a mouse, but not yet sure of his quarry.

Ellen came to know hours when she was weak—weak physically, mentally, spiritually, morally—when under the sheer weight of this frightful and growing burden of suspense she was not capable of fighting her misery, her abasement, her low ebb of vitality, and at the same time wholly withstanding Colter's advances.

He would come into the cabin and, utterly indifferent to Tad Jorth, he would try to make bold and unrestrained love to Ellen. When he caught her in one of her unresisting moments and was able to hold her in his arms and kiss her he seemed to be beside himself with the wonder of her.

At such moments, if he had any softness or gentleness in him, they expressed themselves in his sooner or later letting her go, when apparently she was about to faint. So it must have become fascinatingly fixed in Colter's mind that at times Ellen repulsed him with scorn and at others could not resist him.

Ellen had escaped two crises in her relation with this man, and as a morbid doubt, like a poisonous fungus, began to strangle her mind, she instinctively divined that there was an approaching and final crisis. No uplift of her spirit came this time—no intimations—no whisperings. How horrible it all was! To long to be good and noble—to realize that she was neither—to sink lower day by day! Must she decay there like one of these rotting logs? Worst of all, then, was the insinuating and ever-growing hopelessness. What was the use? What did it matter? Who would ever think of Ellen Jorth? "O God!" she whispered in her distraction, "is there nothing left—nothing at all?"

A period of several days of less torment to Ellen followed. Her uncle apparently took a turn for the better and Colter let her alone. This last circumstance nonplused Ellen. She was at a loss to understand it unless the Isbel menace now encroached upon Colter so formidably that he had forgotten her for the present.

Then one bright August morning, when she had just begun to relax her eternal vigilance and breathe without oppression, Colter encountered her and, darkly silent and fierce, he grasped her and drew her off her feet. Ellen struggled violently, but the total surprise had deprived her of strength. And that paralyzing weakness assailed her as never before. Without apparent effort Colter carried her, striding rapidly away from the cabins into the border of spruce trees at the foot of the canyon wall.

"Colter—where—oh, where are Y'u takin' me?" she found voice to cry out.

"By God! I don't know," he replied, with strong, vibrant passion. "I was a fool not to carry y'u off long ago. But I waited. I was hopin' y'u'd love me! ... An' now that Isbel gang has corralled us. Somers seen the half-breed up on the rocks. An' Springer seen the rest of them sneakin' around. I run back after my horse an' y'u."

"But Uncle Tad! ... We mustn't leave him alone," cried Ellen.

"We've got to," replied Colter, grimly. "Tad shore won't worry y'u no more—soon as Jean Isbel gets to him."

"Oh, let me stay," implored Ellen. "I will save him."

Colter laughed at the utter absurdity of her appeal and claim. Suddenly he set her down upon her feet. "Stand still," he ordered. Ellen saw his big bay horse, saddled, with pack and blanket, tied there in the shade of a spruce. With swift hands Colter untied him and mounted him, scarcely moving his piercing gaze from Ellen. He reached to grasp her. "Up with y'u! ... Put your foot in the stirrup!" His will, like his powerful arm, was irresistible for Ellen at that moment. She found herself swung up behind him. Then the horse plunged away. What with the hard motion and Colter's iron grasp on her Ellen was in a painful position. Her knees and feet came into violent contact with branches and snags. He galloped the horse, tearing through the dense thicket of willows that served to hide the entrance to the side canyon, and when out in the larger and more open canyon he urged him to a run. Presently when Colter put the horse to a slow rise of ground, thereby bringing him to a walk, it was just in time to save Ellen a serious bruising.

Again the sunlight appeared to shade over. They were in the pines. Suddenly with backward lunge Colter halted the horse. Ellen heard a yell. She recognized Queen's voice.

"Turn back, Colter! Turn back!"

With an oath Colter wheeled his mount. "If I didn't run plump into them," he ejaculated, harshly. And scarcely had the goaded horse gotten a start when a shot rang out. Ellen felt a violent shock, as if her momentum had suddenly met with a check, and then she felt herself wrenched from Colter, from the saddle, and propelled into the air. She alighted on soft ground and thick grass, and was unhurt save for the violent wrench and shaking that had rendered her breathless. Before she could rise Colter was pulling at her, lifting her to her feet. She saw the horse lying with bloody head. Tall pines loomed all around. Another rifle cracked. "Run!" hissed Colter, and he bounded off, dragging her by the hand. Another yell pealed out. "Here we are, Colter!". Again it was Queen's shrill voice. Ellen ran with all her might, her heart in her throat, her sight failing to record more than a blur of passing pines and a blank green wall of spruce. Then she lost her balance, was falling, yet could not fall because of that steel grip on her hand, and was dragged, and finally carried, into a dense shade. She was blinded. The trees whirled and faded. Voices and shots sounded far away. Then something black seemed to be wiped across her feeling.

It turned to gray, to moving blankness, to dim, hazy objects, spectral and tall, like blanketed trees, and when Ellen fully recovered consciousness she was being carried through the forest.

"Wal, little one, that was a close shave for y'u," said Colter's hard voice, growing clearer. "Reckon your keelin' over was natural enough."

He held her lightly in both arms, her head resting above his left elbow. Ellen saw his face as a gray blur, then taking sharper outline, until it stood out distinctly, pale and clammy, with eyes cold and wonderful in their intense flare. As she gazed upward Colter turned his head to look back through the woods, and his motion betrayed a keen, wild vigilance. The veins of his lean, brown neck stood out like whipcords. Two comrades were stalking beside him. Ellen heard their stealthy steps, and she felt Colter sheer from one side or the other. They were proceeding cautiously, fearful of the rear, but not wholly trusting to the fore.

"Reckon we'd better go slow an' look before we leap," said one whose voice Ellen recognized as Springer's.

"Shore. That open slope ain't to my likin', with our Nez Perce friend prowlin' round," drawled Colter, as he set Ellen down on her feet.

Another of the rustlers laughed. "Say, can't he twinkle through the forest? I had four shots at him. Harder to hit than a turkey runnin' crossways."

This facetious speaker was the evil-visaged, sardonic Somers. He carried two rifles and wore two belts of cartridges.

"Ellen, shore y'u ain't so daid white as y'u was," observed Colter, and he chucked her under the chin with familiar hand. "Set down heah. I don't want y'u stoppin' any bullets. An' there's no tellin'."

Ellen was glad to comply with his wish. She had begun to recover wits and strength, yet she still felt shaky. She observed that their position then was on the edge of a well-wooded slope from which she could see the grassy canyon floor below. They were on a level bench, projecting out from the main canyon wall that loomed gray and rugged and pine fringed. Somers and Cotter and Springer gave careful attention to all points of the compass, especially in the direction from which they had come. They evidently anticipated being trailed or circled or headed off, but did not manifest much concern. Somers lit a cigarette; Springer wiped his face with a grimy hand and counted the shells in his belt, which appeared to be half empty. Colter stretched his long neck like a vulture and peered down the slope and through the aisles of the forest up toward the canyon rim.

"Listen!" he said, tersely, and bent his head a little to one side, ear to the slight breeze.

They all listened. Ellen heard the beating of her heart, the rustle of leaves, the tapping of a woodpecker, and faint, remote sounds that she could not name.

"Deer, I reckon," spoke up Somers.

"Ahuh! Wal, I reckon they ain't trailin' us yet," replied Colter. "We gave them a shade better 'n they sent us."

"Short an' sweet!" ejaculated Springer, and he removed his black sombrero to poke a dirty forefinger through a buffet hole in the crown. "Thet's how close I come to cashin'. I was lyin' behind a log, listenin' an' watchin', an' when I stuck my head up a little—zam! Somebody made my bonnet leak."

"Where's Queen?" asked Colter.

"He was with me fust off," replied Somers. "An' then when the shootin' slacked—after I'd plugged thet big, red-faced, white-haired pal of Isbel's—"

"Reckon thet was Blaisdell," interrupted Springer.

"Queen—he got tired layin' low," went on Somers. "He wanted action. I heerd him chewin' to himself, an' when I asked him what was eatin' him he up an' growled he was goin' to quit this Injun fightin'. An' he slipped off in the woods."

"Wal, that's the gun fighter of it," declared Colter, wagging his head, "Ever since that cowman, Blue, braced us an' said he was King Fisher, why Queen has been sulkier an' sulkier. He cain't help it. He'll do the same trick as Blue tried. An' shore he'll get his everlastin'. But he's the Texas breed all right."

"Say, do you reckon Blue really is King Fisher?" queried Somers.

"Naw!" ejaculated Colter, with downward sweep of his hand. "Many a would-be gun slinger has borrowed Fisher's name. But Fisher is daid these many years."

"Ahuh! Wal, mebbe, but don't you fergit it—thet Blue was no would-be," declared Somers. "He was the genuine article."

"I should smile!" affirmed Springer.

The subject irritated Colter, and he dismissed it with another forcible gesture and a counter question.

"How many left in that Isbel outfit?"

"No tellin'. There shore was enough of them," replied Somers. "Anyhow, the woods was full of flyin' bullets.... Springer, did you account for any of them?"

"Nope—not thet I noticed," responded Springer, dryly. "I had my chance at the half-breed.... Reckon I was nervous."

"Was Slater near you when he yelled out?"

"No. He was lyin' beside Somers."

"Wasn't thet a queer way fer a man to act?" broke in Somers. "A bullet hit Slater, cut him down the back as he was lyin' flat. Reckon it wasn't bad. But it hurt him so thet he jumped right up an' staggered around. He made a target big as a tree. An' mebbe them Isbels didn't riddle him!"

"That was when I got my crack at Bill Isbel," declared Colter, with grim satisfaction. "When they shot my horse out from under me I had Ellen to think of an' couldn't get my rifle. Shore had to run, as yu seen. Wal, as I only had my six-shooter, there was nothin' for me to do but lay low an' listen to the sping of lead. Wells was standin' up behind a tree about thirty yards off. He got plugged, an' fallin' over he began to crawl my way, still holdin' to his rifle. I crawled along the log to meet him. But he dropped aboot half-way. I went on an' took his rifle an' belt. When I peeped out from behind a spruce bush then I seen Bill Isbel. He was shootin' fast, an' all of them was shootin' fast. That war, when they had the open shot at Slater.... Wal, I bored Bill Isbel right through his middle. He dropped his rifle an', all bent double, he fooled around in a circle till he flopped over the Rim. I reckon he's layin' right up there somewhere below that daid spruce. I'd shore like to see him."

"I Wal, you'd be as crazy as Queen if you tried thet," declared Somers. "We're not out of the woods yet."

"I reckon not," replied Colter. "An' I've lost my horse. Where'd y'u leave yours?"

"They're down the canyon, below thet willow brake. An' saddled an' none of them tied. Reckon we'll have to look them up before dark."

"Colter, what 're we goin' to do?" demanded Springer.

"Wait heah a while—then cross the canyon an' work round up under the bluff, back to the cabin."

"An' then what?" queried Somers, doubtfully eying Colter.

"We've got to eat—we've got to have blankets," rejoined Colter, testily. "An' I reckon we can hide there an' stand a better show in a fight than runnin' for it in the woods."

"Wal, I'm givin' you a hunch thet it looked like you was runnin' fer it," retorted Somers.

"Yes, an' packin' the girl," added Springer. "Looks funny to me."

Both rustlers eyed Colter with dark and distrustful glances. What he might have replied never transpired, for the reason that his gaze, always shifting around, had suddenly fixed on something.

"Is that a wolf?" he asked, pointing to the Rim.

Both his comrades moved to get in line with his finger. Ellen could not see from her position.

"Shore thet's a big lofer," declared Somers. "Reckon he scented us."

"There he goes along the Rim," observed Colter. "He doesn't act leary. Looks like a good sign to me. Mebbe the Isbels have gone the other way."

"Looks bad to me," rejoined Springer, gloomily.

"An' why?" demanded Colter.

"I seen thet animal. Fust time I reckoned it was a lofer. Second time it was right near them Isbels. An' I'm damned now if I don't believe it's thet half-lofer sheep dog of Gass Isbel's."

"Wal, what if it is?"

"Ha! ... Shore we needn't worry about hidin' out," replied Springer, sententiously. "With thet dog Jean Isbel could trail a grasshopper."

"The hell y'u say!" muttered Colter. Manifestly such a possibility put a different light upon the present situation. The men grew silent and watchful, occupied by brooding thoughts and vigilant surveillance of all points. Somers slipped off into the brush, soon to return, with intent look of importance.

"I heerd somethin'," he whispered, jerking his thumb backward. "Rollin' gravel—crackin' of twigs. No deer! ... Reckon it'd be a good idee for us to slip round acrost this bench."

"Wal, y'u fellars go, an' I'll watch heah," returned Colter.

"Not much," said Somers, while Springer leered knowingly.

Colter became incensed, but he did not give way to it. Pondering a moment, he finally turned to Ellen. "Y'u wait heah till I come back. An' if I don't come in reasonable time y'u slip across the canyon an' through the willows to the cabins. Wait till aboot dark." With that he possessed himself of one of the extra rifles and belts and silently joined his comrades. Together they noiselessly stole into the brush.

Ellen had no other thought than to comply with Colter's wishes. There was her wounded uncle who had been left unattended, and she was anxious to get back to him. Besides, if she had wanted to run off from Colter, where could she go? Alone in the woods, she would get lost and die of starvation. Her lot must be cast with the Jorth faction until the end. That did not seem far away.

Her strained attention and suspense made the moments fly. By and by several shots pealed out far across the side canyon on her right, and they were answered by reports sounding closer to her. The fight was on again. But these shots were not repeated. The flies buzzed, the hot sun beat down and sloped to the west, the soft, warm breeze stirred the aspens, the ravens croaked, the red squirrels and blue jays chattered.

Suddenly a quick, short, yelp electrified Ellen, brought her upright with sharp, listening rigidity. Surely it was not a wolf and hardly could it be a coyote. Again she heard it. The yelp of a sheep dog! She had heard that' often enough to know. And she rose to change her position so she could command a view of the rocky bluff above. Presently she espied what really appeared to be a big timber wolf. But another yelp satisfied her that it really was a dog. She watched him. Soon it became evident that he wanted to get down over the bluff. He ran to and fro, and then out of sight. In a few moments his yelp sounded from lower down, at the base of the bluff, and it was now the cry of an intelligent dog that was trying to call some one to his aid. Ellen grew convinced that the dog was near where Colter had said Bill Isbel had plunged over the declivity. Would the dog yelp that way if the man was dead? Ellen thought not.

No one came, and the continuous yelping of the dog got on Ellen's nerves. It was a call for help. And finally she surrendered to it. Since her natural terror when Colter's horse was shot from under her and she had been dragged away, she had not recovered from fear of the Isbels. But calm consideration now convinced her that she could hardly be in a worse plight in their hands than if she remained in Colter's. So she started out to find the dog.

The wooded bench was level for a few hundred yards, and then it began to heave in rugged, rocky bulges up toward the Rim. It did not appear far to where the dog was barking, but the latter part of the distance proved to be a hard climb over jumbled rocks and through thick brush. Panting and hot, she at length reached the base of the bluff, to find that it was not very high.

The dog espied her before she saw him, for he was coming toward her when she discovered him. Big, shaggy, grayish white and black, with wild, keen face and eyes he assuredly looked the reputation Springer had accorded him. But sagacious, guarded as was his approach, he appeared friendly.

"Hello—doggie!" panted Ellen. "What's—wrong—up heah?"

He yelped, his ears lost their stiffness, his body sank a little, and his bushy tail wagged to and fro. What a gray, clear, intelligent look he gave her! Then he trotted back.

Ellen followed him around a corner of bluff to see the body of a man lying on his back. Fresh earth and gravel lay about him, attesting to his fall from above. He had on neither coat nor hat, and the position of his body and limbs suggested broken bones. As Ellen hurried to his side she saw that the front of his shirt, low down, was a bloody blotch. But he could lift his head; his eyes were open; he was perfectly conscious. Ellen did not recognize the dusty, skinned face, yet the mold of features, the look of the eyes, seemed strangely familiar.

"You're—Jorth's—girl," he said, in faint voice of surprise.

"Yes, I'm Ellen Jorth," she replied. "An' are y'u Bill Isbel?"

"All thet's left of me. But I'm thankin' God somebody come—even a Jorth."

Ellen knelt beside him and examined the wound in his abdomen. A heavy bullet had indeed, as Colter had avowed, torn clear through his middle. Even if he had not sustained other serious injury from the fall over the cliff, that terrible bullet wound meant death very shortly. Ellen shuddered. How inexplicable were men! How cruel, bloody, mindless!

"Isbel, I'm sorry—there's no hope," she said, low voiced. "Y'u've not long to live. I cain't help y'u. God knows I'd do so if I could."

"All over!" he sighed, with his eyes looking beyond her. "I reckon—I'm glad.... But y'u can—do somethin' for or me. Will y'u?"

"Indeed, Yes. Tell me," she replied, lifting his dusty head on her knee. Her hands trembled as she brushed his wet hair back from his clammy brow.

"I've somethin'—on my conscience," he whispered.

The woman, the sensitive in Ellen, understood and pitied him then.

"Yes," she encouraged him.

"I stole cattle—my dad's an' Blaisdell's—an' made deals—with Daggs.... All the crookedness—wasn't on—Jorth's side.... I want—my brother Jean—to know."

"I'll try—to tell him," whispered Ellen, out of her great amaze.

"We were all—a bad lot—except Jean," went on Isbel. "Dad wasn't fair.... God! how he hated Jorth! Jorth, yes, who was—your father.... Wal, they're even now."

"How—so?" faltered Ellen.

"Your father killed dad.... At the last—dad wanted to—save us. He sent word—he'd meet him—face to face—an' let thet end the feud. They met out in the road.... But some one shot dad down—with a rifle—an' then your father finished him."

"An' then, Isbel," added Ellen, with unconscious mocking bitterness, "Your brother murdered my dad!"

"What!" whispered Bill Isbel. "Shore y'u've got—it wrong. I reckon Jean—could have killed—your father.... But he didn't. Queer, we all thought."

"Ah! ... Who did kill my father?" burst out Ellen, and her voice rang like great hammers at her ears.

"It was Blue. He went in the store—alone—faced the whole gang alone. Bluffed them—taunted them—told them he was King Fisher.... Then he killed—your dad—an' Jackson Jorth.... Jean was out—back of the store. We were out—front. There was shootin'. Colmor was hit. Then Blue ran out—bad hurt.... Both of them—died in Meeker's yard."

"An' so Jean Isbel has not killed a Jorth!" said Ellen, in strange, deep voice.

"No," replied Isbel, earnestly. "I reckon this feud—was hardest on Jean. He never lived heah.... An' my sister Ann said—he got sweet on y'u.... Now did he?"

Slow, stinging tears filled Ellen's eyes, and her head sank low and lower.

"Yes—he did," she murmured, tremulously.

"Ahuh! Wal, thet accounts," replied Isbel, wonderingly. "Too bad! ... It might have been.... A man always sees—different when—he's dyin'.... If I had—my life—to live over again! ... My poor kids—deserted in their babyhood—ruined for life! All for nothin'.... May God forgive—"

Then he choked and whispered for water.

Ellen laid his head back and, rising, she took his sombrero and started hurriedly down the slope, making dust fly and rocks roll. Her mind was a seething ferment. Leaping, bounding, sliding down the weathered slope, she gained the bench, to run across that, and so on down into the open canyon to the willow-bordered brook. Here she filled the sombrero with water and started back, forced now to walk slowly and carefully. It was then, with the violence and fury of intense muscular activity denied her, that the tremendous import of Bill Isbel's revelation burst upon her very flesh and blood and transfiguring the very world of golden light and azure sky and speaking forestland that encompassed her.

Not a drop of the precious water did she spill. Not a misstep did she make. Yet so great was the spell upon her that she was not aware she had climbed the steep slope until the dog yelped his welcome. Then with all the flood of her emotion surging and resurging she knelt to allay the parching thirst of this dying enemy whose words had changed frailty to strength, hate to love, and, the gloomy hell of despair to something unutterable. But she had returned too late. Bill Isbel was dead.

CHAPTER XIII

Jean Isbel, holding the wolf-dog Shepp in leash, was on the trail of the most dangerous of Jorth's gang, the gunman Queen. Dark drops of blood on the stones and plain tracks of a rider's sharp-heeled boots behind coverts indicated the trail of a wounded, slow-traveling fugitive. Therefore, Jean Isbel held in the dog and proceeded with the wary eye and watchful caution of an Indian.

Queen, true to his class, and emulating Blue with the same magnificent effrontery and with the same paralyzing suddenness of surprise, had appeared as if by magic at the last night camp of the Isbel faction. Jean had seen him first, in time to leap like a panther into the shadow. But he carried in his shoulder Queen's first bullet of that terrible encounter. Upon Gordon and Fredericks fell the brunt of Queen's fusillade. And they, shot to pieces, staggering and falling, held passionate grip on life long enough to draw and still Queen's guns and send him reeling off into the darkness of the forest.

Unarmed, and hindered by a painful wound, Jean had kept a vigil near camp all that silent and menacing night. Morning disclosed Gordon and Fredericks stark and ghastly beside the burned-out camp-fire, their guns clutched immovably in stiffened hands. Jean buried them as best he could, and when they were under ground with flat stones on their graves he knew himself to be indeed the last of the Isbel clan. And all that was wild and savage in his blood and desperate in his spirit rose to make him more than man and less than human. Then for the third time during these tragic last days the wolf-dog Shepp came to him.

Jean washed the wound Queen had given him and bound it tightly. The keen pang and burn of the lead was a constant and all-powerful reminder of the grim work left for him to do. The whole world was no longer large enough for him and whoever was left of the Jorths. The heritage of blood his father had bequeathed him, the unshakable love for a worthless girl who had so dwarfed and obstructed his will and so bitterly defeated and reviled his poor, romantic, boyish faith, the killing of hostile men, so strange in its after effects, the pursuits and fights, and loss of one by one of his confederates—these had finally engendered in Jean Isbel a wild, unslakable thirst, these had been the cause of his retrogression, these had unalterably and ruthlessly fixed in his darkened mind one fierce passion—to live and die the last man of that Jorth-Isbel feud.

At sunrise Jean left this camp, taking with him only a small knapsack of meat and bread, and with the eager, wild Shepp in leash he set out on Queen's bloody trail.

Black drops of blood on the stones and an irregular trail of footprints proved to Jean that the gunman was hard hit. Here he had fallen, or knelt, or sat down, evidently to bind his wounds. Jean found strips of scarf, red and discarded. And the blood drops failed to show on more rocks. In a deep forest of spruce, under silver-tipped spreading branches, Queen had rested, perhaps slept. Then laboring with dragging steps, not improbably with a lame leg, he had gone on, up out of the dark-green ravine to the open, dry, pine-tipped ridge. Here he had rested, perhaps waited to see if he were pursued. From that point his trail spoke an easy language for Jean's keen eye. The gunman knew he was pursued. He had seen his enemy. Therefore Jean proceeded with a slow caution, never getting within revolver range of ambush, using all his woodcraft to trail this man and yet save himself. Queen traveled slowly, either because he was wounded or else because he tried to ambush his pursuer, and Jean accommodated his pace to that of Queen. From noon of that day they were never far apart, never out of hearing of a rifle shot.

The contrast of the beauty and peace and loneliness of the surroundings to the nature of Queen's flight often obtruded its strange truth into the somber turbulence of Jean's mind, into that fixed columnar idea around which fleeting thoughts hovered and gathered like shadows.

Early frost had touched the heights with its magic wand. And the forest seemed a temple in which man might worship nature and life rather than steal through the dells and under the arched aisles like a beast of prey. The green-and-gold leaves of aspens quivered in the glades; maples in the ravines fluttered their red-and-purple leaves. The needle-matted carpet under the pines vied with the long lanes of silvery grass, alike enticing to the eye of man and beast. Sunny rays of light, flecked with dust and flying insects, slanted down from the overhanging brown-limbed, green-massed foliage. Roar of wind in the distant forest alternated with soft breeze close at hand. Small dove-gray squirrels ran all over the woodland, very curious about Jean and his dog, rustling the twigs, scratching the bark of trees, chattering and barking, frisky, saucy, and bright-eyed. A plaintive twitter of wild canaries came from the region above the treetops—first voices of birds in their pilgrimage toward the south. Pine cones dropped with soft thuds. The blue jays followed these intruders in the forest, screeching their displeasure. Like rain pattered the dropping seeds from the spruces. A woody, earthy, leafy fragrance, damp with the current of life, mingled with a cool, dry, sweet smell of withered grass and rotting pines.

Solitude and lonesomeness, peace and rest, wild life and nature, reigned there. It was a golden-green region, enchanting to the gaze of man. An Indian would have walked there with his spirits.

And even as Jean felt all this elevating beauty and inscrutable spirit his keen eye once more fastened upon the blood-red drops Queen had again left on the gray moss and rock. His wound had reopened. Jean felt the thrill of the scenting panther.

The sun set, twilight gathered, night fell. Jean crawled under a dense, low-spreading spruce, ate some bread and meat, fed the dog, and lay down to rest and sleep. His thoughts burdened him, heavy and black as the mantle of night. A wolf mourned a hungry cry for a mate. Shepp quivered under Jean's hand. That was the call which had lured him from the ranch. The wolf blood in him yearned for the wild. Jean tied the cowhide leash to his wrist. When this dark business was at an end Shepp could be free to join the lonely mate mourning out there in the forest. Then Jean slept.

Dawn broke cold, clear, frosty, with silvered grass sparkling, with a soft, faint rustling of falling aspen leaves. When the sun rose red Jean was again on the trail of Queen. By a frosty-ferned brook, where water tinkled and ran clear as air and cold as ice, Jean quenched his thirst, leaning on a stone that showed drops of blood. Queen, too, had to quench his thirst. What good, what help, Jean wondered, could the cold, sweet, granite water, so dear to woodsmen and wild creatures, do this wounded, hunted rustler? Why did he not wait in the open to fight and face the death he had meted? Where was that splendid and terrible daring of the gunman? Queen's love of life dragged him on and on, hour by hour, through the pine groves and spruce woods, through the oak swales and aspen glades, up and down the rocky gorges, around the windfalls and over the rotting logs.

The time came when Queen tried no more ambush. He gave up trying to trap his pursuer by lying in wait. He gave up trying to conceal his tracks. He grew stronger or, in desperation, increased his energy, so that he redoubled his progress through the wilderness. That, at best, would count only a few miles a day. And he began to circle to the northwest, back toward the deep canyon where Blaisdell and Bill Isbel had reached the end of their trails. Queen had evidently left his comrades, had lone-handed it in his last fight, but was now trying to get back to them. Somewhere in these wild, deep forest brakes the rest of the Jorth faction had found a hiding place. Jean let Queen lead him there.

Ellen Jorth would be with them. Jean had seen her. It had been his shot that killed Colter's horse. And he had withheld further fire because Colter had dragged the girl behind him, protecting his body with hers. Sooner or later Jean would come upon their camp. She would be there. The thought of her dark beauty, wasted in wantonness upon these rustlers, added a deadly rage to the blood lust and righteous wrath of his vengeance. Let her again flaunt her degradation in his face and, by the God she had forsaken, he would kill her, and so end the race of Jorths!

Another night fell, dark and cold, without starlight. The wind moaned in the forest. Shepp was restless. He sniffed the air. There was a step on his trail. Again a mournful, eager, wild, and hungry wolf cry broke the silence. It was deep and low, like that of a baying hound, but infinitely wilder. Shepp strained to get away. During the night, while Jean slept, he managed to chew the cowhide leash apart and run off.

Next day no dog was needed to trail Queen. Fog and low-drifting clouds in the forest and a misty rain had put the rustler off his bearings. He was lost, and showed that he realized it. Strange how a matured man, fighter of a hundred battles, steeped in bloodshed, and on his last stand, should grow panic-stricken upon being lost! So Jean Isbel read the signs of the trail.

Queen circled and wandered through the foggy, dripping forest until he headed down into a canyon. It was one that notched the Rim and led down and down, mile after mile into the Basin. Not soon had Queen discovered his mistake. When he did do so, night overtook him.

The weather cleared before morning. Red and bright the sun burst out of the east to flood that low basin land with light. Jean found that Queen had traveled on and on, hoping, no doubt, to regain what he had lost. But in the darkness he had climbed to the manzanita slopes instead of back up the canyon. And here he had fought the hold of that strange brush of Spanish name until he fell exhausted.

Surely Queen would make his stand and wait somewhere in this devilish thicket for Jean to catch up with him. Many and many a place Jean would have chosen had he been in Queen's place. Many a rock and dense thicket Jean circled or approached with extreme care. Manzanita grew in patches that were impenetrable except for a small animal. The brush was a few feet high, seldom so high that Jean could not look over it, and of a beautiful appearance, having glossy, small leaves, a golden berry, and branches of dark-red color. These branches were tough and unbendable. Every bush, almost, had low branches that were dead, hard as steel, sharp as thorns, as clutching as cactus. Progress was possible only by endless detours to find the half-closed aisles between patches, or else by crashing through with main strength or walking right over the tops. Jean preferred this last method, not because it was the easiest, but for the reason that he could see ahead so much farther. So he literally walked across the tips of the manzanita brush. Often he fell through and had to step up again; many a branch broke with him, letting him down; but for the most part he stepped from fork to fork, on branch after branch, with balance of an Indian and the patience of a man whose purpose was sustaining and immutable.

On that south slope under the Rim the sun beat down hot. There was no breeze to temper the dry air. And before midday Jean was laboring, wet with sweat, parching with thirst, dusty and hot and tiring. It amazed him, the doggedness and tenacity of life shown by this wounded rustler. The time came when under the burning rays of the sun he was compelled to abandon the walk across the tips of the manzanita bushes and take to the winding, open threads that ran between. It would have been poor sight indeed that could not have followed Queen's labyrinthine and broken passage through the brush. Then the time came when Jean espied Queen, far ahead and above, crawling like a black bug along the bright-green slope. Sight then acted upon Jean as upon a hound in the chase. But he governed his actions if he could not govern his instincts. Slowly but surely he followed the dusty, hot trail, and never a patch of blood failed to send a thrill along his veins.

Queen, headed up toward the Rim, finally vanished from sight. Had he fallen? Was he hiding? But the hour disclosed that he was crawling. Jean's keen eye caught the slow moving of the brush and enabled him to keep just so close to the rustler, out of range of the six-shooters he carried. And so all the interminable hours of the hot afternoon that snail-pace flight and pursuit kept on.

Halfway up the Rim the growth of manzanita gave place to open, yellow, rocky slope dotted with cedars. Queen took to a slow-ascending ridge and left his bloody tracks all the way to the top, where in the gathering darkness the weary pursuer lost them.

Another night passed. Daylight was relentless to the rustler. He could not hide his trail. But somehow in a desperate last rally of strength he reached a point on the heavily timbered ridge that Jean recognized as being near the scene of the fight in the canyon. Queen was nearing the rendezvous of the rustlers. Jean crossed tracks of horses, and then more tracks that he was certain had been made days past by his own party. To the left of this ridge must be the deep canyon that had frustrated his efforts to catch up with the rustlers on the day Blaisdell lost his life, and probably Bill Isbel, too. Something warned Jean that he was nearing the end of the trail, and an unaccountable sense of imminent catastrophe seemed foreshadowed by vague dreads and doubts in his gloomy mind. Jean felt the need of rest, of food, of ease from the strain of the last weeks. But his spirit drove him implacably.

Queen's rally of strength ended at the edge of an open, bald ridge that was bare of brush or grass and was surrounded by a line of forest on three sides, and on the fourth by a low bluff which raised its gray head above the pines. Across this dusty open Queen had crawled, leaving unmistakable signs of his condition. Jean took long survey of the circle of trees and of the low, rocky eminence, neither of which he liked. It might be wiser to keep to cover, Jean thought, and work around to where Queen's trail entered the forest again. But he was tired, gloomy, and his eternal vigilance was failing. Nevertheless, he stilled for the thousandth time that bold prompting of his vengeance and, taking to the edge of the forest, he went to considerable pains to circle the open ground. And suddenly sight of a man sitting back against a tree halted Jean.

He stared to make sure his eyes did not deceive him. Many times stumps and snags and rocks had taken on strange resemblance to a standing or crouching man. This was only another suggestive blunder of the mind behind his eyes—what he wanted to see he imagined he saw. Jean glided on from tree to tree until he made sure that this sitting image indeed was that of a man. He sat bolt upright, facing back across the open, hands resting on his knees—and closer scrutiny showed Jean that he held a gun in each hand.

Queen! At the last his nerve had revived. He could not crawl any farther, he could never escape, so with the courage of fatality he chose the open, to face his foe and die. Jean had a thrill of admiration for the rustler. Then he stalked out from under the pines and strode forward with his rifle ready.

A watching man could not have failed to espy Jean. But Queen never made the slightest move. Moreover, his stiff, unnatural position struck Jean so singularly that he halted with a muttered exclamation. He was now about fifty paces from Queen, within range of those small guns. Jean called, sharply, "QUEEN!" Still the figure never relaxed in the slightest.

Jean advanced a few more paces, rifle up, ready to fire the instant Queen lifted a gun. The man's immobility brought the cold sweat to Jean's brow. He stopped to bend the full intense power of his gaze upon this inert figure. Suddenly over Jean flashed its meaning. Queen was dead. He had backed up against the pine, ready to face his foe, and he had died there. Not a shadow of a doubt entered Jean's mind as he started forward again. He knew. After all, Queen's blood would not be on his hands. Gordon and Fredericks in their death throes had given the rustler mortal wounds. Jean kept on, marveling the while. How ghastly thin and hard! Those four days of flight had been hell for Queen.

Jean reached him—looked down with staring eyes. The guns were tied to his hands. Jean started violently as the whole direction of his mind shifted. A lightning glance showed that Queen had been propped against the tree—another showed boot tracks in the dust.

"By Heaven, they've fooled me!" hissed Jean, and quickly as he leaped behind the pine he was not quick enough to escape the cunning rustlers who had waylaid him thus. He felt the shock, the bite and burn of lead before he heard a rifle crack. A bullet had ripped through his left forearm. From behind the tree he saw a puff of white smoke along the face of the bluff—the very spot his keen and gloomy vigilance had descried as one of menace. Then several puffs of white smoke and ringing reports betrayed the ambush of the tricksters. Bullets barked the pine and whistled by. Jean saw a man dart from behind a rock and, leaning over, run for another. Jean's swift shot stopped him midway. He fell, got up, and floundered behind a bush scarcely large enough to conceal him. Into that bush Jean shot again and again. He had no pain in his wounded arm, but the sense of the shock clung in his consciousness, and this, with the tremendous surprise of the deceit, and sudden release of long-dammed overmastering passion, caused him to empty the magazine of his Winchester in a terrible haste to kill the man he had hit.

These were all the loads he had for his rifle. Blood passion had made him blunder. Jean cursed himself, and his hand moved to his belt. His six-shooter was gone. The sheath had been loose. He had tied the gun fast. But the strings had been torn apart. The rustlers were shooting again. Bullets thudded into the pine and whistled by. Bending carefully, Jean reached one of Queen's guns and jerked it from his hand. The weapon was empty. Both of his guns were empty. Jean peeped out again to get the line in which the bullets were coming and, marking a course from his position to the cover of the forest, he ran with all his might. He gained the shelter. Shrill yells behind warned him that he had been seen, that his reason for flight had been guessed. Looking back, he saw two or three men scrambling down the bluff. Then the loud neigh of a frightened horse pealed out.

Jean discarded his useless rifle, and headed down the ridge slope, keeping to the thickest line of pines and sheering around the clumps of spruce. As he ran, his mind whirled with grim thoughts of escape, of his necessity to find the camp where Gordon and Fredericks were buried, there to procure another rifle and ammunition. He felt the wet blood dripping down his arm, yet no pain. The forest was too open for good cover. He dared not run uphill. His only course was ahead, and that soon ended in an abrupt declivity too precipitous to descend. As he halted, panting for breath, he heard the ring of hoofs on stone, then the thudding beat of running horses on soft ground. The rustlers had sighted the direction he had taken. Jean did not waste time to look. Indeed, there was no need, for as he bounded along the cliff to the right a rifle cracked and a bullet whizzed over his head. It lent wings to his feet. Like a deer he sped along, leaping cracks and logs and rocks, his ears filled by the rush of wind, until his quick eye caught sight of thick-growing spruce foliage close to the precipice. He sprang down into the green mass. His weight precipitated him through the upper branches. But lower down his spread arms broke his fall, then retarded it until he caught. A long, swaying limb let him down and down, where he grasped another and a stiffer one that held his weight. Hand over hand he worked toward the trunk of this spruce and, gaining it, he found other branches close together down which he hastened, hold by hold and step by step, until all above him was black, dense foliage, and beneath him the brown, shady slope. Sure of being unseen from above, he glided noiselessly down under the trees, slowly regaining freedom from that constriction of his breast.

Passing on to a gray-lichened cliff, overhanging and gloomy, he paused there to rest and to listen. A faint crack of hoof on stone came to him from above, apparently farther on to the right. Eventually his pursuers would discover that he had taken to the canyon. But for the moment he felt safe. The wound in his forearm drew his attention. The bullet had gone clear through without breaking either bone. His shirt sleeve was soaked with blood. Jean rolled it back and tightly wrapped his scarf around the wound, yet still the dark-red blood oozed out and dripped down into his hand. He became aware of a dull, throbbing pain.

Not much time did Jean waste in arriving at what was best to do. For the time being he had escaped, and whatever had been his peril, it was past. In dense, rugged country like this he could not be caught by rustlers. But he had only a knife left for a weapon, and there was very little meat in the pocket of his coat. Salt and matches he possessed. Therefore the imperative need was for him to find the last camp, where he could get rifle and ammunition, bake bread, and rest up before taking again the trail of the rustlers. He had reason to believe that this canyon was the one where the fight on the Rim, and later, on a bench of woodland below, had taken place.

Thereupon he arose and glided down under the spruces toward the level, grassy open he could see between the trees. And as he proceeded, with the slow step and wary eye of an Indian, his mind was busy.

Queen had in his flight unerringly worked in the direction of this canyon until he became lost in the fog; and upon regaining his bearings he had made a wonderful and heroic effort to surmount the manzanita slope and the Rim and find the rendezvous of his comrades. But he had failed up there on the ridge. In thinking it over Jean arrived at a conclusion that Queen, finding he could go no farther, had waited, guns in hands, for his pursuer. And he had died in this position. Then by strange coincidence his comrades had happened to come across him and, recognizing the situation, they had taken the shells from his guns and propped him up with the idea of luring Jean on. They had arranged a cunning trick and ambush, which had all but snuffed out the last of the Isbels. Colter probably had been at the bottom of this crafty plan. Since the fight at the Isbel ranch, now seemingly far back in the past, this man Colter had loomed up more and more as a stronger and more dangerous antagonist then either Jorth or Daggs. Before that he had been little known to any of the Isbel faction. And it was Colter now who controlled the remnant of the gang and who had Ellen Jorth in his possession.

The canyon wall above Jean, on the right, grew more rugged and loftier, and the one on the left began to show wooded slopes and brakes, and at last a wide expanse with a winding, willow border on the west and a long, low, pine-dotted bench on the east. It took several moments of study for Jean to recognize the rugged bluff above this bench. On up that canyon several miles was the site where Queen had surprised Jean and his comrades at their campfire. Somewhere in this vicinity was the hiding place of the rustlers.

Thereupon Jean proceeded with the utmost stealth, absolutely certain that he would miss no sound, movement, sign, or anything unnatural to the wild peace of the canyon. And his first sense to register something was his keen smell. Sheep! He was amazed to smell sheep. There must be a flock not far away. Then from where he glided along under the trees he saw down to open places in the willow brake and noticed sheep tracks in the dark, muddy bank of the brook. Next he heard faint tinkle of bells, and at length, when he could see farther into the open enlargement of the canyon, his surprised gaze fell upon an immense gray, woolly patch that blotted out acres and acres of grass. Thousands of sheep were grazing there. Jean knew there were several flocks of Jorth's sheep on the mountain in the care of herders, but he had never thought of them being so far west, more than twenty miles from Chevelon Canyon. His roving eyes could not descry any herders or dogs. But he knew there must be dogs close to that immense flock. And, whatever his cunning, he could not hope to elude the scent and sight of shepherd dogs. It would be best to go back the way he had come, wait for darkness, then cross the canyon and climb out, and work around to his objective point. Turning at once, he started to glide back. But almost immediately he was brought stock-still and thrilling by the sound of hoofs.

Horses were coming in the direction he wished to take. They were close. His swift conclusion was that the men who had pursued him up on the Rim had worked down into the canyon. One circling glance showed him that he had no sure covert near at hand. It would not do to risk their passing him there. The border of woodland was narrow and not dense enough for close inspection. He was forced to turn back up the canyon, in the hope of soon finding a hiding place or a break in the wall where he could climb up.

Hugging the base of the wall, he slipped on, passing the point where he had espied the sheep, and gliding on until he was stopped by a bend in the dense line of willows. It sheered to the west there and ran close to the high wall. Jean kept on until he was stooping under a curling border of willow thicket, with branches slim and yellow and masses of green foliage that brushed against the wall. Suddenly he encountered an abrupt corner of rock. He rounded it, to discover that it ran at right angles with the one he had just passed. Peering up through the willows, he ascertained that there was a narrow crack in the main wall of the canyon. It had been concealed by willows low down and leaning spruces above. A wild, hidden retreat! Along the base of the wall there were tracks of small animals. The place was odorous, like all dense thickets, but it was not dry. Water ran through there somewhere. Jean drew easier breath. All sounds except the rustling of birds or mice in the willows had ceased. The brake was pervaded by a dreamy emptiness. Jean decided to steal on a little farther, then wait till he felt he might safely dare go back.

The golden-green gloom suddenly brightened. Light showed ahead, and parting the willows, he looked out into a narrow, winding canyon, with an open, grassy, willow-streaked lane in the center and on each side a thin strip of woodland.

His surprise was short lived. A crashing of horses back of him in the willows gave him a shock. He ran out along the base of the wall, back of the trees. Like the strip of woodland in the main canyon, this one was scant and had but little underbrush. There were young spruces growing with thick branches clear to the grass, and under these he could have concealed himself. But, with a certainty of sheep dogs in the vicinity, he would not think of hiding except as a last resource. These horsemen, whoever they were, were as likely to be sheep herders as not. Jean slackened his pace to look back. He could not see any moving objects, but he still heard horses, though not so close now. Ahead of him this narrow gorge opened out like the neck of a bottle. He would run on to the head of it and find a place to climb to the top.

Hurried and anxious as Jean was, he yet received an impression of singular, wild nature of this side gorge. It was a hidden, pine-fringed crack in the rock-ribbed and canyon-cut tableland. Above him the sky seemed a winding stream of blue. The walls were red and bulged out in spruce-greened shelves. From wall to wall was scarcely a distance of a hundred feet. Jumbles of rock obstructed his close holding to the wall. He had to walk at the edge of the timber. As he progressed, the gorge widened into wilder, ruggeder aspect. Through the trees ahead he saw where the wall circled to meet the cliff on the left, forming an oval depression, the nature of which he could not ascertain. But it appeared to be a small opening surrounded by dense thickets and the overhanging walls. Anxiety augmented to alarm. He might not be able to find a place to scale those rough cliffs. Breathing hard, Jean halted again. The situation was growing critical again. His physical condition was worse. Loss of sleep and rest, lack of food, the long pursuit of Queen, the wound in his arm, and the desperate run for his life—these had weakened him to the extent that if he undertook any strenuous effort he would fail. His cunning weighed all chances.

The shade of wall and foliage above, and another jumble of ruined cliff, hindered his survey of the ground ahead, and he almost stumbled upon a cabin, hidden on three sides, with a small, bare clearing in front. It was an old, ramshackle structure like others he had run across in the canons. Cautiously he approached and peeped around the corner. At first swift glance it had all the appearance of long disuse. But Jean had no time for another look. A clip-clop of trotting horses on hard ground brought the same pell-mell rush of sensations that had driven him to wild flight scarcely an hour past. His body jerked with its instinctive impulse, then quivered with his restraint. To turn back would be risky, to run ahead would be fatal, to hide was his one hope. No covert behind! And the clip-clop of hoofs sounded closer. One moment longer Jean held mastery over his instincts of self-preservation. To keep from running was almost impossible. It was the sheer primitive animal sense to escape. He drove it back and glided along the front of the cabin.

Here he saw that the cabin adjoined another. Reaching the door, he was about to peep in when the thud of hoofs and voices close at hand transfixed him with a grim certainty that he had not an instant to lose. Through the thin, black-streaked line of trees he saw moving red objects. Horses! He must run. Passing the door, his keen nose caught a musty, woody odor and the tail of his eye saw bare dirt floor. This cabin was unused. He halted-gave a quick look back. And the first thing his eye fell upon was a ladder, right inside the door, against the wall. He looked up. It led to a loft that, dark and gloomy, stretched halfway across the cabin. An irresistible impulse drove Jean. Slipping inside, he climbed up the ladder to the loft. It was like night up there. But he crawled on the rough-hewn rafters and, turning with his head toward the opening, he stretched out and lay still.

What seemed an interminable moment ended with a trample of hoofs outside the cabin. It ceased. Jean's vibrating ears caught the jingle of spurs and a thud of boots striking the ground.

"Wal, sweetheart, heah we are home again," drawled a slow, cool, mocking Texas voice.

"Home! I wonder, Colter—did y'u ever have a home—a mother—a sister—much less a sweetheart?" was the reply, bitter and caustic.

Jean's palpitating, hot body suddenly stretched still and cold with intensity of shock. His very bones seemed to quiver and stiffen into ice. During the instant of realization his heart stopped. And a slow, contracting pressure enveloped his breast and moved up to constrict his throat. That woman's voice belonged to Ellen Jorth. The sound of it had lingered in his dreams. He had stumbled upon the rendezvous of the Jorth faction. Hard indeed had been the fates meted out to those of the Isbels and Jorths who had passed to their deaths. But, no ordeal, not even Queen's, could compare with this desperate one Jean must endure. He had loved Ellen Jorth, strangely, wonderfully, and he had scorned repute to believe her good. He had spared her father and her uncle. He had weakened or lost the cause of the Isbels. He loved her now, desperately, deathlessly, knowing from her own lips that she was worthless—loved her the more because he had felt her terrible shame. And to him—the last of the Isbels—had come the cruelest of dooms—to be caught like a crippled rat in a trap; to be compelled to lie helpless, wounded, without a gun; to listen, and perhaps to see Ellen Jorth enact the very truth of her mocking insinuation. His will, his promise, his creed, his blood must hold him to the stem decree that he should be the last man of the Jorth-Isbel war. But could he lie there to hear—to see—when he had a knife and an arm?

CHAPTER XIV

Then followed the leathery flop of saddles to the soft turf and the stamp, of loosened horses.

Jean heard a noise at the cabin door, a rustle, and then a knock of something hard against wood. Silently he moved his head to look down through a crack between the rafters. He saw the glint of a rifle leaning against the sill. Then the doorstep was darkened. Ellen Jorth sat down with a long, tired sigh. She took off her sombrero and the light shone on the rippling, dark-brown hair, hanging in a tangled braid. The curved nape of her neck showed a warm tint of golden tan. She wore a gray blouse, soiled and torn, that clung to her lissome shoulders.

"Colter, what are y'u goin' to do?" she asked, suddenly. Her voice carried something Jean did not remember. It thrilled into the icy fixity of his senses.

"We'll stay heah," was the response, and it was followed by a clinking step of spurred boot.

"Shore I won't stay heah," declared Ellen. "It makes me sick when I think of how Uncle Tad died in there alone—helpless—sufferin'. The place seems haunted."

"Wal, I'll agree that it's tough on y'u. But what the hell CAN we do?"

A long silence ensued which Ellen did not break.

"Somethin' has come off round heah since early mawnin'," declared Colter. "Somers an' Springer haven't got back. An' Antonio's gone.... Now, honest, Ellen, didn't y'u heah rifle shots off somewhere?"

"I reckon I did," she responded, gloomily.

"An' which way?"

"Sounded to me up on the bluff, back pretty far."

"Wal, shore that's my idee. An' it makes me think hard. Y'u know Somers come across the last camp of the Isbels. An' he dug into a grave to find the bodies of Jim Gordon an' another man he didn't know. Queen kept good his brag. He braced that Isbel gang an' killed those fellars. But either him or Jean Isbel went off leavin' bloody tracks. If it was Queen's y'u can bet Isbel was after him. An' if it was Isbel's tracks, why shore Queen would stick to them. Somers an' Springer couldn't follow the trail. They're shore not much good at trackin'. But for days they've been ridin' the woods, hopin' to run across Queen.... Wal now, mebbe they run across Isbel instead. An' if they did an' got away from him they'll be heah sooner or later. If Isbel was too many for them he'd hunt for my trail. I'm gamblin' that either Queen or Jean Isbel is daid. I'm hopin' it's Isbel. Because if he ain't daid he's the last of the Isbels, an' mebbe I'm the last of Jorth's gang.... Shore I'm not hankerin' to meet the half-breed. That's why I say we'll stay heah. This is as good a hidin' place as there is in the country. We've grub. There's water an' grass."

"Me—stay heah with y'u—alone!"

The tone seemed a contradiction to the apparently accepted sense of her words. Jean held his breath. But he could not still the slowly mounting and accelerating faculties within that were involuntarily rising to meet some strange, nameless import. He felt it. He imagined it would be the catastrophe of Ellen Jorth's calm acceptance of Colter's proposition. But down in Jean's miserable heart lived something that would not die. No mere words could kill it. How poignant that moment of her silence! How terribly he realized that if his intelligence and his emotion had believed her betraying words, his soul had not!

But Ellen Jorth did not speak. Her brown head hung thoughtfully. Her supple shoulders sagged a little.

"Ellen, what's happened to y'u?" went on Colter.

"All the misery possible to a woman," she replied, dejectedly.

"Shore I don't mean that way," he continued, persuasively. "I ain't gainsayin' the hard facts of your life. It's been bad. Your dad was no good.... But I mean I can't figger the change in y'u."

"No, I reckon y'u cain't," she said. "Whoever was responsible for your make-up left out a mind—not to say feeling."

Colter drawled a low laugh.

"Wal, have that your own way. But how much longer are yu goin' to be like this heah?"

"Like what?" she rejoined, sharply.

"Wal, this stand-offishness of yours?"

"Colter, I told y'u to let me alone," she said, sullenly.

"Shore. An' y'u did that before. But this time y'u're different.... An' wal, I'm gettin' tired of it."

Here the cool, slow voice of the Texan sounded an inflexibility before absent, a timber that hinted of illimitable power.

Ellen Jorth shrugged her lithe shoulders and, slowly rising, she picked up the little rifle and turned to step into the cabin.

"Colter," she said, "fetch my pack an' my blankets in heah."

"Shore," he returned, with good nature.

Jean saw Ellen Jorth lay the rifle lengthwise in a chink between two logs and then slowly turn, back to the wall. Jean knew her then, yet did not know her. The brown flash of her face seemed that of an older, graver woman. His strained gaze, like his waiting mind, had expected something, he knew not what—a hardened face, a ghost of beauty, a recklessness, a distorted, bitter, lost expression in keeping with her fortunes. But he had reckoned falsely. She did not look like that. There was incalculable change, but the beauty remained, somehow different. Her red lips were parted. Her brooding eyes, looking out straight from under the level, dark brows, seemed sloe black and wonderful with their steady, passionate light.

Jean, in his eager, hungry devouring of the beloved face, did not on the first instant grasp the significance of its expression. He was seeing the features that had haunted him. But quickly he interpreted her expression as the somber, hunted look of a woman who would bear no more. Under the torn blouse her full breast heaved. She held her hands clenched at her sides. She was' listening, waiting for that jangling, slow step. It came, and with the sound she subtly changed. She was a woman hiding her true feelings. She relaxed, and that strong, dark look of fury seemed to fade back into her eyes.

Colter appeared at the door, carrying a roll of blankets and a pack.

"Throw them heah," she said. "I reckon y'u needn't bother coming in."

That angered the man. With one long stride he stepped over the doorsill, down into the cabin, and flung the blankets at her feet and then the pack after it. Whereupon he deliberately sat down in the door, facing her. With one hand he slid off his sombrero, which fell outside, and with the other he reached in his upper vest pocket for the little bag of tobacco that showed there. All the time he looked at her. By the light now unobstructed Jean descried Colter's face; and sight of it then sounded the roll and drum of his passions.

"Wal, Ellen, I reckon we'll have it out right now an' heah," he said, and with tobacco in one hand, paper in the other he began the operations of making a cigarette. However, he scarcely removed his glance from her.

"Yes?" queried Ellen Jorth.

"I'm goin' to have things the way they were before—an' more," he declared. The cigarette paper shook in his fingers.

"What do y'u mean?" she demanded.

"Y'u know what I mean," he retorted. Voice and action were subtly unhinging this man's control over himself.

"Maybe I don't. I reckon y'u'd better talk plain."

The rustler had clear gray-yellow eyes, flawless, like, crystal, and suddenly they danced with little fiery flecks.

"The last time I laid my hand on y'u I got hit for my pains. An' shore that's been ranklin'."

"Colter, y'u'll get hit again if y'u put your hands on me," she said, dark, straight glance on him. A frown wrinkled the level brows.

"Y'u mean that?" he asked, thickly.

"I shore, do."

Manifestly he accepted her assertion. Something of incredulity and bewilderment, that had vied with his resentment, utterly disappeared from his face.

"Heah I've been waitin' for y'u to love me," he declared, with a gesture not without dignified emotion. "Your givin' in without that wasn't so much to me."

And at these words of the rustler's Jean Isbel felt an icy, sickening shudder creep into his soul. He shut his eyes. The end of his dream had been long in coming, but at last it had arrived. A mocking voice, like a hollow wind, echoed through that region—that lonely and ghost-like hall of his heart which had harbored faith.

She burst into speech, louder and sharper, the first words of which Jean's strangely throbbing ears did not distinguish.

"— — you! ... I never gave in to y'u an' I never will."

"But, girl—I kissed y'u—hugged y'u—handled y'u—" he expostulated, and the making of the cigarette ceased.

"Yes, y'u did—y'u brute—when I was so downhearted and weak I couldn't lift my hand," she flashed.

"Ahuh! Y'u mean I couldn't do that now?"

"I should smile I do, Jim Colter!" she replied.

"Wal, mebbe—I'll see—presently," he went on, straining with words. "But I'm shore curious.... Daggs, then—he was nothin' to y'u?"

"No more than y'u," she said, morbidly. "He used to run after me—long ago, it seems..... I was only a girl then—innocent—an' I'd not known any but rough men. I couldn't all the time—every day, every hour—keep him at arm's length. Sometimes before I knew—I didn't care. I was a child. A kiss meant nothing to me. But after I knew—"

Ellen dropped her head in brooding silence.

"Say, do y'u expect me to believe that?" he queried, with a derisive leer.

"Bah! What do I care what y'u believe?" she cried, with lifting head.

"How aboot Simm Brace?"

"That coyote! ... He lied aboot me, Jim Colter. And any man half a man would have known he lied."

"Wal, Simm always bragged aboot y'u bein' his girl," asserted Colter. "An' he wasn't over—particular aboot details of your love-makin'."

Ellen gazed out of the door, over Colter's head, as if the forest out there was a refuge. She evidently sensed more about the man than appeared in his slow talk, in his slouching position. Her lips shut in a firm line, as if to hide their trembling and to still her passionate tongue. Jean, in his absorption, magnified his perceptions. Not yet was Ellen Jorth afraid of this man, but she feared the situation. Jean's heart was at bursting pitch. All within him seemed chaos—a wreck of beliefs and convictions. Nothing was true. He would wake presently out of a nightmare. Yet, as surely as he quivered there, he felt the imminence of a great moment—a lightning flash—a thunderbolt—a balance struck.

Colter attended to the forgotten cigarette. He rolled it, lighted it, all the time with lowered, pondering head, and when he had puffed a cloud of smoke he suddenly looked up with face as hard as flint, eyes as fiery as molten steel.

"Wal, Ellen—how aboot Jean Isbel—our half-breed Nez Perce friend—who was shore seen handlin' y'u familiar?" he drawled.

Ellen Jorth quivered as under a lash, and her brown face turned a dusty scarlet, that slowly receding left her pale.

"Damn y'u, Jim Colter!" she burst out, furiously. "I wish Jean Isbel would jump in that door—or down out of that loft! ... He killed Greaves for defiling my name! ... He'd kill Y'U for your dirty insult.... And I'd like to watch him do it.... Y'u cold-blooded Texan! Y'u thieving rustler! Y'u liar! ... Y'u lied aboot my father's death. And I know why. Y'u stole my father's gold.... An' now y'u want me—y'u expect me to fall into your arms.... My Heaven! cain't y'u tell a decent woman? Was your mother decent? Was your sister decent? ... Bah! I'm appealing to deafness. But y'u'll HEAH this, Jim Colter! ... I'm not what yu think I am! I'm not the—the damned hussy y'u liars have made me out.... I'm a Jorth, alas! I've no home, no relatives, no friends! I've been forced to live my life with rustlers—vile men like y'u an' Daggs an' the rest of your like.... But I've been good! Do y'u heah that? ... I AM good—so help me God, y'u an' all your rottenness cain't make me bad!"

Colter lounged to his tall height and the laxity of the man vanished.

Vanished also was Jean Isbel's suspended icy dread, the cold clogging of his fevered mind—vanished in a white, living, leaping flame.

Silently he drew his knife and lay there watching with the eyes of a wildcat. The instant Colter stepped far enough over toward the edge of the loft Jean meant to bound erect and plunge down upon him. But Jean could wait now. Colter had a gun at his hip. He must never have a chance to draw it.

"Ahuh! So y'u wish Jean Isbel would hop in heah, do y'u?" queried Colter. "Wal, if I had any pity on y'u, that's done for it."

A sweep of his long arm, so swift Ellen had no time to move, brought his hand in clutching contact with her. And the force of it flung her half across the cabin room, leaving the sleeve of her blouse in his grasp. Pantingly she put out that bared arm and her other to ward him off as he took long, slow strides toward her.

Jean rose half to his feet, dragged by almost ungovernable passion to risk all on one leap. But the distance was too great. Colter, blind as he was to all outward things, would hear, would see in time to make Jean's effort futile. Shaking like a leaf, Jean sank back, eye again to the crack between the rafters.

Ellen did not retreat, nor scream, nor move. Every line of her body was instinct with fight, and the magnificent blaze of her eyes would have checked a less callous brute.

Colter's big hand darted between Ellen's arms and fastened in the front of her blouse. He did not try to hold her or draw her close. The unleashed passion of the man required violence. In one savage pull he tore off her blouse, exposing her white, rounded shoulders and heaving bosom, where instantly a wave of red burned upward.

Overcome by the tremendous violence and spirit of the rustler, Ellen sank to her knees, with blanched face and dilating eyes, trying with folded arms and trembling hand to hide her nudity.

At that moment the rapid beat of hoofs on the hard trail outside halted Colter in his tracks.

"Hell!" he exclaimed. "An' who's that?" With a fierce action he flung the remnants of Ellen's blouse in her face and turned to leap out the door.

Jean saw Ellen catch the blouse and try to wrap it around her, while she sagged against the wall and stared at the door. The hoof beats pounded to a solid thumping halt just outside.

"Jim—thar's hell to pay!" rasped out a panting voice.

"Wal, Springer, I reckon I wished y'u'd paid it without spoilin' my deals," retorted Colter, cool and sharp.

"Deals? Ha! Y'u'll be forgettin'—your lady love in a minnit," replied Springer. "When I catch—my breath."

"Where's Somers?" demanded Colter.

"I reckon he's all shot up—if my eyes didn't fool me."

"Where is he?" yelled Colter.

"Jim—he's layin' up in the bushes round thet bluff. I didn't wait to see how he was hurt. But he shore stopped some lead. An' he flopped like a chicken with its—haid cut off."

"Where's Antonio?"

"He run like the greaser he is," declared Springer, disgustedly.

"Ahuh! An' where's Queen?" queried Colter, after a significant pause.

"Dead!"

The silence ensuing was fraught with a suspense that held Jean in cold bonds. He saw the girl below rise from her knees, one hand holding the blouse to her breast, the other extended, and with strange, repressed, almost frantic look she swayed toward the door.

"Wal, talk," ordered Colter, harshly.

"Jim, there ain't a hell of a lot," replied Springer; drawing a deep breath, "but what there is is shore interestin'.... Me an' Somers took Antonio with us. He left his woman with the sheep. An' we rode up the canyon, clumb out on top, an' made a circle back on the ridge. That's the way we've been huntin' fer tracks. Up thar in a bare spot we run plump into Queen sittin' against a tree, right out in the open. Queerest sight y'u ever seen! The damn gunfighter had set down to wait for Isbel, who was trailin' him, as we suspected—-an' he died thar. He wasn't cold when we found him.... Somers was quick to see a trick. So he propped Queen up an' tied the guns to his hands—an', Jim, the queerest thing aboot that deal was this—Queen's guns was empty! Not a shell left! It beat us holler.... We left him thar, an' hid up high on the bluff, mebbe a hundred yards off. The hosses we left back of a thicket. An' we waited thar a long time. But, sure enough, the half-breed come. He was too smart. Too much Injun! He would not cross the open, but went around. An' then he seen Queen. It was great to watch him. After a little he shoved his rifle out an' went right fer Queen. This is when I wanted to shoot. I could have plugged him. But Somers says wait an' make it sure. When Isbel got up to Queen he was sort of half hid by the tree. An' I couldn't wait no longer, so I shot. I hit him, too. We all begun to shoot. Somers showed himself, an' that's when Isbel opened up. He used up a whole magazine on Somers an' then, suddenlike, he quit. It didn't take me long to figger mebbe he was out of shells. When I seen him run I was certain of it. Then we made for the hosses an' rode after Isbel. Pretty soon I seen him runnin' like a deer down the ridge. I yelled an' spurred after him. There is where Antonio quit me. But I kept on. An' I got a shot at Isbel. He ran out of sight. I follered him by spots of blood on the stones an' grass until I couldn't trail him no more. He must have gone down over the cliffs. He couldn't have done nothin' else without me seein' him. I found his rifle, an' here it is to prove what I say. I had to go back to climb down off the Rim, an' I rode fast down the canyon. He's somewhere along that west wall, hidin' in the brush, hard hit if I know anythin' aboot the color of blood."

"Wal! ... that beats me holler, too," ejaculated Colter.

"Jim, what's to be done?" inquired Springer, eagerly. "If we're sharp we can corral that half-breed. He's the last of the Isbels."

"More, pard. He's the last of the Isbel outfit," declared Colter. "If y'u can show me blood in his tracks I'll trail him."

"Y'u can bet I'll show y'u," rejoined the other rustler. "But listen! Wouldn't it be better for us first to see if he crossed the canyon? I reckon he didn't. But let's make sure. An' if he didn't we'll have him somewhar along that west canyon wall. He's not got no gun. He'd never run thet way if he had.... Jim, he's our meat!"

"Shore, he'll have that knife," pondered Colter.

"We needn't worry about thet," said the other, positively. "He's hard hit, I tell y'u. All we got to do is find thet bloody trail again an' stick to it—goin' careful. He's layin' low like a crippled wolf."

"Springer, I want the job of finishin' that half-breed," hissed Colter. "I'd give ten years of my life to stick a gun down his throat an' shoot it off."

"All right. Let's rustle. Mebbe y'u'll not have to give much more 'n ten minnits. Because I tell y'u I can find him. It'd been easy—but, Jim, I reckon I was afraid."

"Leave your hoss for me an' go ahaid," the rustler then said, brusquely. "I've a job in the cabin heah."

"Haw-haw! ... Wal, Jim, I'll rustle a bit down the trail an' wait. No huntin' Jean Isbel alone— not fer me. I've had a queer feelin' about thet knife he used on Greaves. An' I reckon y'u'd oughter let thet Jorth hussy alone long enough to—"

"Springer, I reckon I've got to hawg-tie her—" His voice became indistinguishable, and footfalls attested to a slow moving away of the men.

Jean had listened with ears acutely strung to catch every syllable while his gaze rested upon Ellen who stood beside the door. Every line of her body denoted a listening intensity. Her back was toward Jean, so that he could not see her face. And he did not want to see, but could not help seeing her naked shoulders. She put her head out of the door. Suddenly she drew it in quickly and half turned her face, slowly raising her white arm. This was the left one and bore the marks of Colter's hard fingers.

She gave a little gasp. Her eyes became large and staring. They were bent on the hand that she had removed from a step on the ladder. On hand and wrist showed a bright-red smear of blood.

Jean, with a convulsive leap of his heart, realized that he had left his bloody tracks on the ladder as he had climbed. That moment seemed the supremely terrible one of his life.

Ellen Jorth's face blanched and her eyes darkened and dilated with exceeding amaze and flashing thought to become fixed with horror. That instant was the one in which her reason connected the blood on the ladder with the escape of Jean Isbel.

One moment she leaned there, still as a stone except for her heaving breast, and then her fixed gaze changed to a swift, dark blaze, comprehending, yet inscrutable, as she flashed it up the ladder to the loft. She could see nothing, yet she knew and Jean knew that she knew he was there. A marvelous transformation passed over her features and even over her form. Jean choked with the ache in his throat. Slowly she put the bloody hand behind her while with the other she still held the torn blouse to her breast.

Colter's slouching, musical step sounded outside. And it might have been a strange breath of infinitely vitalizing and passionate life blown into the well-springs of Ellen Jorth's being. Isbel had no name for her then. The spirit of a woman had been to him a thing unknown.

She swayed back from the door against the wall in singular, softened poise, as if all the steel had melted out of her body. And as Colter's tall shadow fell across the threshold Jean Isbel felt himself staring with eyeballs that ached—straining incredulous sight at this woman who in a few seconds had bewildered his senses with her transfiguration. He saw but could not comprehend.

"Jim—I heard—all Springer told y'u," she said. The look of her dumfounded Colter and her voice seemed to shake him visibly.

"Suppose y'u did. What then?" he demanded, harshly, as he halted with one booted foot over the threshold. Malignant and forceful, he eyed her darkly, doubtfully.

"I'm afraid," she whispered.

"What of? Me?"

"No. Of—of Jean Isbel. He might kill y'u and—then where would I be?"

"Wal, I'm damned!" ejaculated the rustler. "What's got into y'u?" He moved to enter, but a sort of fascination bound him.

"Jim, I hated y'u a moment ago," she burst out. "But now—with that Jean Isbel somewhere near—hidin'—watchin' to kill y'u—an' maybe me, too—I—I don't hate y'u any more.... Take me away."

"Girl, have y'u lost your nerve?" he demanded.

"My God! Colter—cain't y'u see?" she implored. "Won't y'u take me away?"

"I shore will—presently," he replied, grimly. "But y'u'll wait till I've shot the lights out of this Isbel."

"No!" she cried. "Take me away now.... An' I'll give in—I'll be what y'u—want.... Y'u can do with me—as y'u like."

Colter's lofty frame leaped as if at the release of bursting blood. With a lunge he cleared the threshold to loom over her.

"Am I out of my haid, or are y'u?" he asked, in low, hoarse voice. His darkly corded face expressed extremest amaze.

"Jim, I mean it," she whispered, edging an inch nearer him, her white face uplifted, her dark eyes unreadable in their eloquence and mystery. "I've no friend but y'u. I'll be—yours.... I'm lost.... What does it matter? If y'u want me—take me NOW—before I kill myself."

"Ellen Jorth, there's somethin' wrong aboot y'u," he responded. "Did y'u tell the truth—when y'u denied ever bein' a sweetheart of Simm Bruce?"

"Yes, I told y'u the truth."

"Ahuh! An' how do y'u account for layin' me out with every dirty name y'u could give tongue to?"

"Oh, it was temper. I wanted to be let alone."

"Temper! Wal, I reckon y'u've got one," he retorted, grimly. "An' I'm not shore y'u're not crazy or lyin'. An hour ago I couldn't touch y'u."

"Y'u may now—if y'u promise to take me away—at once. This place has got on my nerves. I couldn't sleep heah with that Isbel hidin' around. Could y'u?"

"Wal, I reckon I'd not sleep very deep."

"Then let us go."

He shook his lean, eagle-like head in slow, doubtful vehemence, and his piercing gaze studied her distrustfully. Yet all the while there was manifest in his strung frame an almost irrepressible violence, held in abeyance to his will.

"That aboot your bein' so good?" he inquired, with a return of the mocking drawl.

"Never mind what's past," she flashed, with passion dark as his. "I've made my offer."

"Shore there's a lie aboot y'u somewhere," he muttered, thickly.

"Man, could I do more?" she demanded, in scorn.

"No. But it's a lie," he returned. "Y'u'll get me to take y'u away an' then fool me—run off—God knows what. Women are all liars."

Manifestly he could not believe in her strange transformation. Memory of her wild and passionate denunciation of him and his kind must have seared even his calloused soul. But the ruthless nature of him had not weakened nor softened in the least as to his intentions. This weather-vane veering of hers bewildered him, obsessed him with its possibilities. He had the look of a man who was divided between love of her and hate, whose love demanded a return, but whose hate required a proof of her abasement. Not proof of surrender, but proof of her shame! The ignominy of him thirsted for its like. He could grind her beauty under his heel, but he could not soften to this feminine inscrutableness.

And whatever was the truth of Ellen Jorth in this moment, beyond Colter's gloomy and stunted intelligence, beyond even the love of Jean Isbel, it was something that held the balance of mastery. She read Colter's mind. She dropped the torn blouse from her hand and stood there, unashamed, with the wave of her white breast pulsing, eyes black as night and full of hell, her face white, tragic, terrible, yet strangely lovely.

"Take me away," she whispered, stretching one white arm toward him, then the other.

Colter, even as she moved, had leaped with inarticulate cry and radiant face to meet her embrace. But it seemed, just as her left arm flashed up toward his neck, that he saw her bloody hand and wrist. Strange how that checked his ardor—threw up his lean head like that striking bird of prey.

"Blood! What the hell!" he ejaculated, and in one sweep he grasped her. "How'd yu do that? Are y'u cut? ... Hold still."

Ellen could not release her hand.

"I scratched myself," she said.

"Where?... All that blood!" And suddenly he flung her hand back with fierce gesture, and the gleams of his yellow eyes were like the points of leaping flames. They pierced her—read the secret falsity of her. Slowly he stepped backward, guardedly his hand moved to his gun, and his glance circled and swept the interior of the cabin. As if he had the nose of a hound and sight to follow scent, his eyes bent to the dust of the ground before the door. He quivered, grew rigid as stone, and then moved his head with exceeding slowness as if searching through a microscope in the dust—farther to the left—to the foot of the ladder—and up one step—another—a third—all the way up to the loft. Then he whipped out his gun and wheeled to face the girl.

"Ellen, y'u've got your half-breed heah!" he said, with a terrible smile.

She neither moved nor spoke. There was a suggestion of collapse, but it was only a change where the alluring softness of her hardened into a strange, rapt glow. And in it seemed the same mastery that had characterized her former aspect. Herein the treachery of her was revealed. She had known what she meant to do in any case.

Colter, standing at the door, reached a long arm toward the ladder, where he laid his hand on a rung. Taking it away he held it palm outward for her to see the dark splotch of blood.

"See?"

"Yes, I see," she said, ringingly.

Passion wrenched him, transformed him. "All that—aboot leavin' heah—with me—aboot givin' in—was a lie!"

"No, Colter. It was the truth. I'll go—yet—now—if y'u'll spare—HIM!" She whispered the last word and made a slight movement of her hand toward the loft. "Girl!" he exploded, incredulously. "Y'u love this half-breed—this ISBEL! ... Y'u LOVE him!"

"With all my heart! ... Thank God! It has been my glory.... It might have been my salvation.... But now I'll go to hell with y'u—if y'u'll spare him."

"Damn my soul!" rasped out the rustler, as if something of respect was wrung from that sordid deep of him. "Y'u—y'u woman! ... Jorth will turn over in his grave. He'd rise out of his grave if this Isbel got y'u."

"Hurry! Hurry!" implored Ellen. "Springer may come back. I think I heard a call."

"Wal, Ellen Jorth, I'll not spare Isbel—nor y'u," he returned, with dark and meaning leer, as he turned to ascend the ladder.

Jean Isbel, too, had reached the climax of his suspense. Gathering all his muscles in a knot he prepared to leap upon Colter as he mounted the ladder. But, Ellen Jorth screamed piercingly and snatched her rifle from its resting place and, cocking it, she held it forward and low.

"COLTER!"

Her scream and his uttered name stiffened him.

"Y'u will spare Jean Isbel!" she rang out. "Drop that gun-drop it!"

"Shore, Ellen.... Easy now. Remember your temper.... I'll let Isbel off," he panted, huskily, and all his body sank quiveringly to a crouch.

"Drop your gun! Don't turn round.... Colter!—I'LL KILL Y'U!"

But even then he failed to divine the meaning and the spirit of her.

"Aw, now, Ellen," he entreated, in louder, huskier tones, and as if dragged by fatal doubt of her still, he began to turn.

Crash! The rifle emptied its contents in Colter's breast. All his body sprang up. He dropped the gun. Both hands fluttered toward her. And an awful surprise flashed over his face.

"So—help—me—God!" he whispered, with blood thick in his voice. Then darkly, as one groping, he reached for her with shaking hands. "Y'u—y'u white-throated hussy!... I'll ..."

He grasped the quivering rifle barrel. Crash! She shot him again. As he swayed over her and fell she had to leap aside, and his clutching hand tore the rifle from her grasp. Then in convulsion he writhed, to heave on his back, and stretch out—a ghastly spectacle. Ellen backed away from it, her white arms wide, a slow horror blotting out the passion of her face.

Then from without came a shrill call and the sound of rapid footsteps. Ellen leaned against the wall, staring still at Colter. "Hey, Jim—what's the shootin'?" called Springer, breathlessly.

As his form darkened the doorway Jean once again gathered all his muscular force for a tremendous spring.

Springer saw the girl first and he appeared thunderstruck. His jaw dropped. He needed not the white gleam of her person to transfix him. Her eyes did that and they were riveted in unutterable horror upon something on the ground. Thus instinctively directed, Springer espied Colter.

"Y'u—y'u shot him!" he shrieked. "What for—y'u hussy? ... Ellen Jorth, if y'u've killed him, I'll..."

He strode toward where Colter lay.

Then Jean, rising silently, took a step and like a tiger he launched himself into the air, down upon the rustler. Even as he leaped Springer gave a quick, upward look. And he cried out. Jean's moccasined feet struck him squarely and sent him staggering into the wall, where his head hit hard. Jean fell, but bounded up as the half-stunned Springer drew his gun. Then Jean lunged forward with a single sweep of his arm—and looked no more.

Ellen ran swaying out of the door, and, once clear of the threshold, she tottered out on the grass, to sink to her knees. The bright, golden sunlight gleamed upon her white shoulders and arms. Jean had one foot out of the door when he saw her and he whirled back to get her blouse. But Springer had fallen upon it. Snatching up a blanket, Jean ran out.

"Ellen! Ellen! Ellen!" he cried. "It's over!" And reaching her, he tried to wrap her in the blanket.

She wildly clutched his knees. Jean was conscious only of her white, agonized face and the dark eyes with their look of terrible strain.

"Did y'u—did y'u..." she whispered.

"Yes—it's over," he said, gravely. "Ellen, the Isbel-Jorth feud is ended."

"Oh, thank—God!" she cried, in breaking voice. "Jean—y'u are wounded... the blood on the step!"

"My arm. See. It's not bad.... Ellen, let me wrap this round you." Folding the blanket around her shoulders, he held it there and entreated her to get up. But she only clung the closer. She hid her face on his knees. Long shudders rippled over her, shaking the blanket, shaking Jean's hands. Distraught, he did not know what to do. And his own heart was bursting.

"Ellen, you must not kneel—there—that way," he implored.

"Jean! Jean!" she moaned, and clung the tighter.

He tried to lift her up, but she was a dead weight, and with that hold on him seemed anchored at his feet.

"I killed Colter," she gasped. "I HAD to—kill him! ... I offered—to fling myself away...."

"For me!" he cried, poignantly. "Oh, Ellen! Ellen! the world has come to an end! ... Hush! don't keep sayin' that. Of course you killed him. You saved my life. For I'd never have let you go off with him .... Yes, you killed him.... You're a Jorth an' I'm an Isbel ... We've blood on our hands—both of us—I for you an' you for me!"

His voice of entreaty and sadness strengthened her and she raised her white face, loosening her clasp to lean back and look up. Tragic, sweet, despairing, the loveliness of her—the significance of her there on her knees—thrilled him to his soul.

"Blood on my hands!" she whispered. "Yes. It was awful—killing him.... But—all I care for in this world is for your forgiveness—and your faith that saved my soul!"

"Child, there's nothin' to forgive," he responded. "Nothin'... Please, Ellen..."

"I lied to y'u!" she cried. "I lied to y'u!"

"Ellen, listen—darlin'." And the tender epithet brought her head and arms back close-pressed to him. "I know—now," he faltered on. "I found out to-day what I believed. An' I swear to God—by the memory of my dead mother—down in my heart I never, never, never believed what they—what y'u tried to make me believe. NEVER!"

"Jean—I love y'u—love y'u—love y'u!" she breathed with exquisite, passionate sweetness. Her dark eyes burned up into his.

"Ellen, I can't lift you up," he said, in trembling eagerness, signifying his crippled arm. "But I can kneel with you! ..."

CPSIA information can be obtained
at www.ICGtesting.com
Printed in the USA
JSHW041953130420
5046JS00013B/364

9 781492 117674